The Inside Passage

A Novel

The Inside Passage
A Novel

Leftare P. Delis

Published by

Peanut Butter Publishing
226 2nd Ave W
Seattle, WA 98119

ISBN 0-89716-556-X
Library of Congress Catalog Card Number: 94-68382
Printed in the United States of America

35.0094

Cover design by Alice C. Merrill

First printing, September of 1994.

10   9   8   7   6   5   4   3   2   1

Published by

Peanut Butter Publishing
226 2nd Ave W
Seattle, WA 98119
(206) 281-5965

Acknowledgments

The Delis family would like to thank Evelyn Miller for typing the original handwritten manuscript, Wanda Cameron for cheerfully coordinating the early phases of the book's publication, Waverly Fitzgerald for original editing, and Christy Scattarella for final editing. We are also thankful for the assistance and encouragement of Chad Haight, Carolyn Smith, Alice Merrill, Penny Young, David Marty, and Elliott Wolf. Finally, we are grateful to Vikki Leib for drawing the map, Pat Fridell for painting the beautiful cover illustration, and Grant Webb for taking the aerial photograph of Wrangell.

Dedicated to my wife Irene

Prologue

With the innocence of missionaries, apprehensive and expecting the worst, the two schoolteachers stood on the boat deck of the American steamer, waiting for their first view of Wrangell. Since their stop in Ketchikan, their illusions about life in southeastern Alaska had been dissolving. They'd anticipated igloos, sleds and huskies. They'd pictured burly men with scraggly beards, snow that never melted, tundra stretching for miles and tribes of dirty, wandering Eskimos.

"Robert Service was very misleading!" said Lydia Prince, whose picture of Alaska had been formed by reading his poems. "We should have done some research on this place."

Victoria Blaissing murmured in agreement.

Ever since they entered Alaska, the steamer had been proceeding north up a channel lined with countless small islands, which slipped by on either side, lonely and wild. Now the steamer swerved towards the right, rounding a fairly large island, and headed for a sheltered harbor at the northern tip of another island. A strong cold wind soared down from the Stikine River on the mainland to the northeast and hit the ship broadside, hurtling thick sprays of rain onto the boat deck. The womens drew back from the rail.

"I'm glad it's raining," Lydia said. "I don't know why, but I'm glad it's raining."

It wasn't until the steamer was halfway across the channel before they could glimpse the outlines of the rain-drenched town of Wrangell. A clutter of wooden buildings occupied the rising slope of ground behind several docks. A few small crafts, obviously fishing boats, puttered in and out of the mouth of the harbor. They recognized the school immediately due to its imposing shape and structure: a cream-colored stucco building planted halfway up the hill. Scattered here and there, along the slope of the hill and around the harbor, were a number of small wooden frame houses.

As Lydia and Victoria strained their eyes taking in the sight of their new home, the steamer announced its arrival by blowing one short and one long blast from its funnel whistle. Passengers emerged from the depths of the steamer and filed out on the deck.

By the time the steamer had angled into position alongside the dock, it was crowded with people--boys and girls, clean-shaven men, women who talked gaily with one another. Few of them seemed aware of the rain; there were only two or three umbrellas in the crowd. Sea gulls circled the ship and a dog howled mournfully from the hill. Longshoremen stood by with drays to load the supplies which the steamship had brought up from the States. As Lydia and Victoria made their way along the busy dock, they passed several warehouses constructed of corrugated iron and a small, smelly building which appeared to be a shrimp cannery. At the end of the dock, at the corner of Main Street, they found the Wrangell Hotel, a square wooden structure with a corner turret.

It continued to rain steadily for the next three days. The teachers spent most of the time in their hotel room, wondering if it would ever stop. After meeting with the school principal, Mr. Herb Weaver, to discuss their teaching assignments, their main activity was walking down Main Street to eat at Mom's Restaurant, then returning to their room.

Main Street was about two blocks long, dismal and muddy.

As they trudged from the hotel towards the restaurant at the other end of the town, they peered out from under their umbrellas at the fronts of the buildings. Only a few of the stores—Mildred's Dress Shop, Floyd's Curio Shop, Johnson's Sweets and Olson's Merchandise Store—had bothered to dress their fronts, erecting slabs of sidewalk no wider than the width of their premises and providing awnings that gave some relief from the rain. The two bars, the butcher shop, the barber shop, the two liquor stores and a few other diversified business establishments were content to stay as they were, bare and inconsequential.

It wasn't until the rain cleared and they began to search for a house to rent that they began to meet the people. They were surprised to find them so much like themselves, only more so. They were genuinely kind, the sort of kindness that would not chip away with intimate contact. Later when they began to absorb the loneliness and remoteness, the constant rain, the drunkenness and squalor, and the fierce beauty of the land, they also recognized the patience in their eyes and felt the sweetness of their independence.

Book One

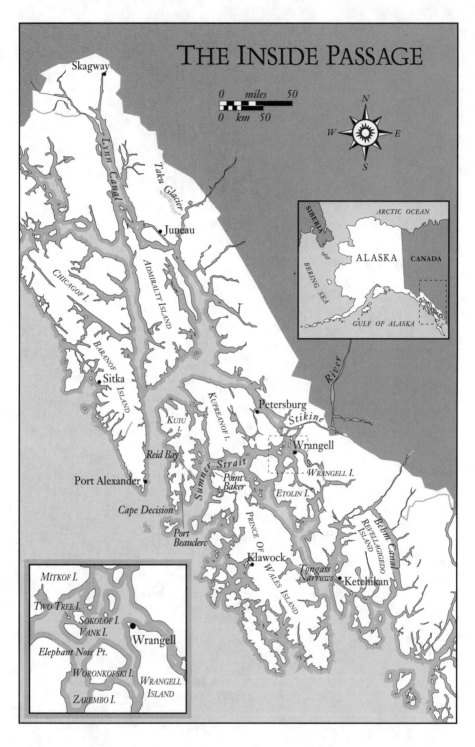

THE INSIDE PASSAGE

Skagway

0   miles   50
0   km   50

N
W   E
S

Lynn Canal

Taku Glacier

Juneau

CHICAGOF I.

ADMIRALTY ISLAND

BARANOF ISLAND

Sitka

KUIU I.

KUPREANOF I.

Reid Bay

Port Alexander

Cape Decision

Port Beauclerc

Petersburg

Stikine

River

Wrangell

Sumner Strait

Point Baker

WRANGELL I.

ETOLIN I.

PRINCE OF WALES ISLAND

Klawock

Tongass Narrows

REVILLAGIGEDO ISLAND

Behm Canal

Ketchikan

SIBERIA

ARCTIC OCEAN

BERING SEA

ALASKA

CANADA

GULF OF ALASKA

MITKOF I.

TWO TREE I.

SOKOLOF I.

VANK I.

Elephant Nose Pt.

WORONKOFSKI I.

ZAREMBO I.

Wrangell

WRANGELL ISLAND

2

Wrangell

1

IT TOOK THREE FULL DAYS, during which the rain persisted, for it to register on the town that the two young ladies, both attractive, both evidently unmarried, had come to stay—at least until the end of the school semester. They had been recruited from San Francisco as relief teachers to fill the vacancies left by Garland Morris and his wife who had skipped town in April, leaving Herb Weaver stranded with two months left before the end of the school year.

The three days passed. The sun came out. May was suddenly lavish and young. The sun cast shafts of light upon the wet land, filled it with sparkle, steam and zest. It was a beautiful day, the 5th of May in 1936, and the winter had been long and hard.

The first day of sunshine, thought Dave Collier glancing out the window of his office. He relayed his thoughts to his patient in the dentist chair, Sam Marcus, one of the few prosperous and respected natives in town. His molars had just been extracted and he bent over the bowl spluttering blood and saliva.

"Yeah," Sam muttered with little enthusiasm.

Dave called his nurse in. "Get rid of everybody in the waiting room! I'm going for a walk!" The determination and aggressiveness in his voice came as a mild shock.

The nurse stared at him with disbelief. "What?" she asked. Dave wondered what had happened to him. The voice that gave the startled order showed authority, as if this was common for him. Beneath the pleasure, he felt a sense of guilt, anticipating the protest of the patients who had waited weeks for appointments. Yet within him something rebelled, demanded an afternoon off, a few hours free after months of steady grind.

"I'm taking the afternoon off!"

The nurse twitched her eyebrows. "Sure, I'll tell everyone in the waiting room." She sighed as she went out.

"OK, Sam, ole boy, you'll be needing falsies, if you don't take care of those choppers," Dave said squirting water into his patient's mouth. By God, he was feeling good. Lightheaded. He'd felt different ever since the two new schoolteachers arrived. "Same as last time?" Sam muttered, agitating the water from one side to the other and blurting it out.

"Yes. And no whiskey for a few hours." Dave patted Sam on the shoulder and escorted him to the door.

He'd watched them for the past three days from this room, one floor above Main Street, as they walked to and fro under their umbrellas, from the hotel to Mom's Restaurant and back again. He'd already made his selection and this surprised him for he wasn't the aggressive type. Forty-two years of bachelorhood testified to that. His friend, Chris, liked the younger, auburn-haired one, though Chris wasn't saying much, which was unlike him.

"You still have that appointment at five with Barbara Bucci," his nurse reminded him. "They don't have a phone so there's no way to cancel it unless you want me to hike out to her house."

He stood before the front window, holding the curtain back with his hand. The force of his guilt was weakening his resolution.

"I'll be back by then," he said. "After you've canceled the other appointments you can take the afternoon off. I can handle Barbara by myself."

Dave stood by the window. He didn't even feel ashamed although his nurse must have guessed his motivation. Across Main Street, a group of natives and whites stood on the sidewalk outside Johnson's Sweets, enjoying the sun. He removed his smock, slipped on his checkered jacket and strode out of the office. As he climbed down the flight of wooden stairs to Main Street, he heard the deep baying blasts of the American steamer's whistle from out in the channel. One short, one long. It was the *North Star*, returning from Juneau. It seemed like just yesterday that it had dropped off the two schoolteachers from the States before continuing north.

A lot of people passed Dave, nodded hello. He saw them as if from a distance. The day was glorious. He swung down the street, toward Mom's Restaurant. Maybe they were there? A cup of coffee would lift him still higher. In anticipation he felt a trembling sweetness in his body.

He wandered into Mom's Restaurant and tried to assume his most professional appearance, the respected and engrossed detachment of a much-needed, overworked man. But when his eyes swept the row of stools to his left, he saw nothing but the familiar sight of fishermen, deck-hands, a store clerk and two elderly women. He felt the people watching him and his self-confidence drowned in a flash of disappointment.

He headed towards the lavatory for he didn't really want anything to eat or drink. He sauntered by the people at the counter and into the back room with its small dance floor, booths and jukebox. The rank odor of the floor oil assailed his nostrils. The clamor from the kitchen was unnerving. He pushed through the dark room and into the lavatory. There he stood before the open blank wall. Water trickled down its surface from a pipe suspended across the top and washed down into the channel below. He felt awkward because he didn't need to go. The door opened and Chris came in.

"Well, God damn, look who's here!"

Dave shifted his body instinctively, embarrassed that he was caught off guard in this situation.

"What are you doing here?" he asked, off-handedly, attempting to assume a natural dignity. "Hasn't that freighter arrived yet?" Chris was waiting for the freighter to deliver the cannery and trap supplies for the fishing season. He quickly zipped up his fly, hoping Chris hadn't noticed his ineffectiveness.

"Be in tomorrow, I hope."

"Seen the girls lately?"

"Did you? God damn, something's got to be done about them."

They meandered back to the counter. Chris Ballard sat down. He was tall and thin, though he didn't seem so tall next to Dave who was six-foot-two. It was hard to tell that Chris was thirty from his appearance. His olive-skinned face was smooth and enigmatic. He had prominent eyes, very dark and fierce, and strong slanting cheek bones that emphasized the determination of his chin and nose. His hair always looked freshly washed, tousled and thick and black as jet.

"I'm starved," Chris said. "I've been out on the channel with the *Verna*. How about you? Hungry?"

The thought of food nauseated Dave. He was as skittish as a patient about to be drilled. "I've been cooped up in that damn office where I feel like a monkey. Let's go for a walk."

"You go, brother Dave. I'm staying here. Who knows," Chris said with a sigh of expectation, "the fair maidens might drop in at any moment now."

Outside, Dave blinked his eyes in the flood of sunlight. He cast his gaze along Main Street. Up by the hotel, a stream of people were pouring out onto the street, passengers from the *North Star* now docked at the Clinton dock. Dave moved off, heading up Main Street, light-footed and expectant, as if something was about to happen.

Tourists passed him, chattering happily, thronging around the totem pole in front of Floyd's Curio Shop. By the time Dave reached the front of the hotel, he felt downright silly. He hadn't seen the girls at all. He lurched into the bar to escape his self-reproach. The bar was jammed with tourists. They were early this year, Dave noticed. Chic-dressed girls, flushed with excitement. Middle-aged women in bright coats. Clean-shaven men in sports jackets. They were all eager and well-dressed, crowding Max, the bartender, for drinks.

Dave edged his way over to the far end of the small bar by the opening that led to the back room. The booths were filled with passengers, except for Holly Dancey and her crowd in their usual booth and the crap game going on in the last booth on the far side. All the passengers were impatient, waiting for their orders. After one quick drink, they were going to see the town. The steamer would be leaving in another hour and this might be their last chance in their entire lives to see Wrangell, Alaska.

"Whiskey and soda," Dave said to Max and was pleased that the bartender bypassed the tourists to wait on him.

He drew a dollar bill from his wallet and laid it on the counter. It was noisy. All around him were tourists with flippant, radiant voices, buying drinks, laughing, drinking, asking questions.

"Do you live here?" It was a young girl, about nineteen, who had suddenly appeared at his elbow. She wanted to find out about Wrangell in one mouthful, at one sitting.

"No," He lied deliberately. "I'm one of the passengers on the ship."

"But I don't think I noticed you on the boat," she protested.

"I was in my stateroom most of the time. Catching up on sleep."

The girl gave a knowing laugh and then returned to a small party of four sitting at one of the round black tables infrequently used except on busy occasions.

"What did I tell you?" one of the men said, "I thought I saw him on the boat."

Noisy. It disturbed the sweet conflict in his heart. The thought that the two schoolteachers lived here in this hotel, might even now be in their room, seemed unreal in the noise of the barroom.

In the rear, some of the passengers were already dancing on the small dance floor. Dave could hear Giff Weeks raving about the crap game. At the side corner booth, where she could see what was happening in both rooms, sat Holly Dancey with her three inseparable friends: Sally, Evelyn and Al, the midget.

"Hi, Dave!" Holly shouted across to him. "What's the matter? Run out of patients?" She didn't wait for an answer. "Come on over."

Dave scuffed over to the open booth.

"Buster likes this," Holly said, nodding towards the hotel owner who was scurrying half-bent across the dance floor bearing a tray of drinks. "It's starting early this year. Money in his pockets. People. Noise." Holly Dancey was forever merry.

"He'll need it," Al, the midget, snickered, as he imitated Holly's mellow bass voice, although his was pitched octaves higher, like a boy's voice before it cracks. "Buster's been dropping plenty in the crap game." The midget's enormous head nodded aft.

"Hey," Holly said, with a flash of amusement in her eyes, "where's your drink?"

"I left it at the bar," Dave said.

"Where's your drink?" Holly asked again, snickering to her friends.

Dave turned and saw Doc Sebannon, the greasy old tramp, sipping on his drink.

"Why, that son of a bitch!" Dave exclaimed.

Holly and her friends burst out laughing.

"The vulture alighted upon the feast," Al purred with delight.

"That old cheese box would steal from his mother," Evelyn added.

Dave went back to the bar and ordered another whiskey and soda. Automatically, without making a fuss, he shunned Doc Sebannon. He'd have one drink and leave for his walk.

"Hello, Mr. Collier," Doc Sebannon said, smiling guilelessly over the rim of his glass. The old Finn never addressed Dave or the regular doctor in town with the title of Doctor. He reserved that honorific for himself. He had been a masseur as a young man in Finland and was still skilled at massaging kinks out of backs and necks. He also made concoctions out of roots and herbs he gathered on the island and sold them as medicines to the fishermen and Indians. His pockets were always bulging with jars of pickled herring which he often bartered for drinks.

Dave ignored him, picked up his drink and spied Violet Lundy, entering the bar like a cat coming in for some easy pickings. Dave watched her thread her way through the crowd, a smile of greeting pasted on her face, her dark eyes already thirsting for whiskey. The jukebox was playing something fast and tricky, "Celery Stalks Along the Highway," and Violet hummed along, out of touch with both the tune and tempo as she nestled between Doc and Dave, standing up, as there were no vacant stools. When someone vacated the stool on the other side of Dave, Violet claimed it, plopping her rump down on the stool, dropping her elbows on the bar, looking sideways and upwards at Dave.

"Hi, Dave. What are you doing?"

Doc Sebannon finished his drink with a sigh of relish, wiped his mouth with the sleeve of his sweat shirt and moved away as if he couldn't stand the smell of her. Violet was a native woman who was married to a white fisherman. Her face was drab except for her lips which were bright with a heavy, greasy lipstick which she kept igniting by running her restless tongue along their curves. Violet was a loner. Not like Holly Dancey and her crowd, who were fun-loving and sociable and paid for their own drinks. Violet was a moocher. She was waiting for the right moment to mooch a drink off Dave. Meanwhile she kept her eyes on him, reminding him of her presence.

Dave generally ignored her as he did Doc. Only now, all at once, he was sorry for her.

"Max," Dave motioned, "a drink for Violet." He tossed a quarter on the bar. Violet said nothing. She looked straight ahead once she got what she wanted. For some reason he was grateful to her for that—he didn't like showiness.

The merriment and the extravagance of the tourists offended him. Their bright clothes and the sound of the cash register clanging, contrasted with the deep throbbing despair that brought him to the bar, hoping for just a glimpse of the girls. He remembered Chris saying: "God damn, something's got to be done about them." Those words boomed down the corridors of his bachelorhood. He felt ripe. He felt that this was the time. After forty-two years, he felt things were going to change.

He left his drink half-finished and went out of the bar into the glare and warmth of the sunshine. Instinctively, he searched the whole of Main Street for the schoolteachers, then turned right and headed back down the street again, walking past Clarence's barber shop, his own apartment house in which he kept his dentist office, Johnny Bugg's bar, the movie theatre. He stopped, looked back, then went on again. He realized he was acting like a child. He hadn't even met her yet, didn't know a thing about her.

He went past Mom's restaurant, past the A&N hall, nodding to people he knew. To his right, a row of flimsy shacks stood on pilings along the edge of the harbor. The tourists milled by in bunches, in pairs, chattering quietly, peering at everything. They were probably heading for Shake's Island to look at the tribal house which had been dedicated the previous summer during a traditional potlatch ceremony.

Dave turned off the main road and onto the sawmill dock. He cut across the splintered planking toward the edge of the dock. He didn't want to see any more tourists. They were always asking questions. Is it true it rains more than it snows in southeastern Alaska? Do the Eskimos, I mean, the Indians, have more privileges than the whites? Where's the Native Institute that's so famous? What do people do besides fish? What do you do for entertainment?

Dave moved past the stretch of slabs and tailings out through the winding heart of the old sawmill, now idle due to a broken head saw. Clean stacks of lumber, two by twelves, four by fours, waited for shipment, stacked along the mill-dock. The mill had been shut down for two weeks. It was always breaking down. There was always talk about building a new one but it never happened.

Dave heard muffled voices and the clank of tools coming from the boiler room. The smell of resin and sawdust hovered in the sun-washed air. He unlatched the latticed gate that separated the mill from the Schnur Salmon Packing cannery. The cannery was closed; the season would not begin for another few weeks. He moved around the main building to the edge of the dock and sat on a cleat in front of the open shed where, during the fishing season, the tins of freshly cooked salmon were packed by hand in cardboard cases.

He sat looking out across the harbor towards the channel, at the sweep of the water with the sun flashing on it in a kind of glory. A stubby-nosed seiner was moving towards Wrangell, crossing the patches of blue-green, dark-blue and purple water, moving into the path of the flashing silver scales and disappearing in the glare. Clouds of peach and of cotton waited against the horizon for the sun to set them on fire and the sky sprawled naked and blue over the islands. The secret of Alaska: the extremes. The good weather and the bad. The independence and loneliness. The remoteness and the beauty.

In the sun, in the spell of quiet, Dave felt the poignancy of the nights of his bachelorhood, empty and wasted, and he was filled with an obsession that they must end. When he first laid eyes on them, then distinguished one from the other, he felt his bachelorhood was thin and brittle, ready to splinter.

To his left, the finger of the breakwater jutted out on an angle from the small peninsula that shaped the south cup of the harbor. Small but adequate, the breakwater caught the incoming swells and storms before they rolled in under the fishing boats tied at the floats on either side. The fishing boats, mostly gill-netters and trollers, lay two and three abreast, tied along the floats in straight lines, noses pointing out towards the channel. Gulls drifted above the boats, spanking white like snowflakes where their flanks touched the sun. Others stood poised on the piling, fluttering their wings nervously in the high ebb tide. The fishermen themselves, that independent species, tinkered about under the masts and guy wires and trolling poles, some shooting the breeze in small groups. Most of them already had their boats ready for the upcoming fishing season; he could see the fresh coats of white and gray and green paints, the bright copper bellies.

Dave rose, fumbled for a cigarette, sat down again. His contentment with his bachelorhood had shattered at the sight of her. She must be thirty, he decided. She looked older than her companion. She wasn't slim, by a long shot, but solid and good to be in bed with. She would fill the long nights of isolation with her warmth.

Dave crushed his cigarette into the dock planking, tossed it over in the water below. He was glad he was here in the late afternoon. To his right, the sun smacking upon the water spread a dazzle of flashes clear across the channel to Elephant Nose, the naturally occurring rock silhouette that looked just like a massive elephant resting its head on the ground marking the northern tip of Woronkofski Island.

It was warm in the sun. He removed his hat and jacket. He liked the small harbor and he liked the quiet. Only the winch aboard *North Star* over at the Clinton Dock dented the silence with its rattling cant. But then Wrangell was generally quiet, except for late at night when the stragglers reeled home from the bars.

Dave got up, put on his hat and coat, sat down again, lit another cigarette. He was suddenly sad. The juice of his excitement mellowed in the light of the sun, the peaceful quiet, the water lapping under him against the piling supporting the dock. He felt incapable of moving, suddenly dreamy and enchanted.

He remembered years ago, going shrimping with Chris in the winter. That was back when Chris' folks still lived in Wrangell and Chris had more time for boating, hunting and fishing. Chris' father, Theodore, owned the shrimp cannery then, working so hard and doing so well that later he sold it and got into the more profitable salmon packing business. Chris was up for the summer from college in the States.

Chris woke him up at four one winter morning, early so he wouldn't lose a day at the office. When they went down to the float where the seiner was moored, the docks were slippery with a thin layer of ice—the harbor water that washed over it had frozen during the cold night. He remembered the smell of coffee as they boarded *The Shrimp*, the roar of the diesel as they growled out of the harbor, past the slanting shadow of the breakwater, into a sulphur-like world of fog, and headed off towards the prawn grounds, around Vank and Sokolof Islands, the seiner purring. It was cold on deck, seining for shrimp. The delicious beauty of the green and rose dawn brought no warmth. Despite the chop of the steel-blue sea, the wind whipping into his eyes, he was reluctant to leave the deck until finally he yielded to the warmth of the galley and breakfast. He was suddenly starved. He was still eating ham and eggs, jelly and toast, coffee and fruit as *The Shrimp* rounded the breakwater and pulled alongside the tall, spidery piling of the shrimp cannery. Happy, exuberant, grateful to Chris for asking him along, Dave returned to his office, with new enthusiasm for his work.

Dave rose, started back through the sawmill. The time had slipped by and it was almost five. Barbara Bucci would be waiting for him in his reception room.

As he went back through the sawmill, he caught a glimpse of the Ballard house, a big white house on the hill. Dave stopped, dropped his cigarette, crushed it with his foot. It seemed strange to him that Chris was content to live in that big, two-story house by himself. His parents had moved down south after his father's accident. Chris stayed in Wrangell. Chris was more Alaskan than anyone. He stayed in Wrangell because there was no other place for him except Wrangell. Even though it meant living alone, waiting from one salmon fishing season to the next, living peacefully and quietly, playing cards, hunting, fishing, drinking.

Dave turned left and headed back towards Main Street. He had his work to keep him busy and his work brought him in contact with most of the one thousand residents of Wrangell. And he had his mother and father living with him in the same apartment. His four older sisters had all married and left Wrangell so he assumed the responsibility for his parents. Only he spent as little time with them as possible, to avoid the silence, the Bible reading, the remorse and bewilderment. He paid their bills but kept to himself, coming and going as he pleased, always eating out and never hearing a word of protest against it. Still, they were there, two old people whose lives had soured leaving them disappointed and bitter, and though it was not much, it did cushion some of his loneliness.

Barbara Bucci was a good patient. Dave injected novocaine in three different places in her gum and worked on her until quarter of six. He was enraptured by his work, drilling deep into a bicuspid, discovering that the nerve was infected and would have to be removed at the next appointment. It wasn't the procedure itself that pleased him, it was being back in the office, where he was alone, so to speak, content and protected, and he worked busily and happily. Barbara couldn't say much since he had her mouth stretched open and when he did change needles she just barely had time to wash out her mouth before he was at it again. Yet throughout the process he was acutely aware of her short tight skirt lying wrinkled above her kneecaps and the silk stockings, the ones she wore at the dances, encasing her sturdy legs. Barbara was married and had three children, yet he was suddenly conscious of her femininity. He wondered what in the hell had come over him.

He worked industriously and Barbara watched him without saying a word. She must have been taken aback by his burst of enthusiasm. He knew that she had a lover, Steve Svenson, a fisherman. The whole town knew about it except her husband, Mitch.

At last he was through.

"Ugh," Barbara said, working her jaw painfully. "You sure tore into me, you big lug."

"I'm going to have to extract the nerve next appointment. It's badly damaged. That will save the tooth for a few years. It will be just like a new one. No feeling at all though."

"Say, what's eating you?" Barbara got up from the chair, straightening her skirt. She was short and plump and had an unexpectedly delightful smile. Most people called her Babs which suited her better than Barbara. Despite a hard life—because of Mitch's aversion to work, they lived in a shack near the native section with no running water and no phone—Babs was always full of cheer. Even her children had that same spark of glowing vitality. It was lacking only in her husband. The contrast was hard to understand other than that Babs thrived in adversity.

"You're just like the rest of them," Babs said teasingly. "Those two new gals in town, eh? They must be something. I haven't laid my eyes on them yet but Mitch saw them in Mom's restaurant. Brother, when Mitch drifts out of his clouds and notices anything, it must be something."

Her words spurred Dave to activity in order to suppress the response in his guts. As Dave cleared the tray, placing the instruments in the sterilizer, a dizzying sweetness flooded his body. It was thrilling to hear Babs speak so forthrightly about the girls, as if they were trophies. He felt a possessive sort of pride.

Babs poked her nose through the curtained window. "I like it here. It's so quiet and peaceful. You sure can see Main Street. What some of the old hens would give for a view like this." Babs giggled. "I bet you spotted those two new schoolteachers before anyone."

"How is Mitch?" Dave asked. He was at a loss without his nurse, who usually took care of scheduling. He searched for the appointment book at her desk in the corner.

"Oh, same as ever. Tired. This is his last day at the sawmill. Working overtime. They did all they could to repair it, but they still can't fix whatever's busted. He comes home barking like an angry dog about how tired he is. You know Mitch."

Dave looked through the crowded appointment book for the next available time. "Maybe there's something wrong with him," he said, just to be saying something. He was very aware of Babs' presence, her breasts and her legs, and this amazed him for he'd never given her a second thought before. Her proximity was like a shadow falling over him, deep and full, and he recoiled within himself.

"Hell, he's always tired. You'd think he was the only one who ever worked. He's always looking for work but never finds any until I find it for him. I got Mitch that job at the sawmill and, brother, it came in handy." Her laugh was nonchalant. "I'm trying to convince him to work the gold mine in Juneau until fishing season," she added with a mischievous glint in her eyes.

"Well," Dave said, filling out the appointment slip and handing it to her, "I can see you at the same time on June second." Babs lingered, holding the piece of paper. Dave slipped out of his white coat. "Care for a drink? You had a rough time."

He went to the cabinet by the front windows and pulled out a quart of Seagrams. It was warm in the room. He raised the center window higher. The sun was crimson. Water from the recent rains lay on the street like pools of chocolate, frosted by the sun with a touch of rose. A few cars and delivery trucks motored by; there weren't many cars in Wrangell since the only road was about seven miles long. It ran out of the town south to the Native Institute which educated native children from all over Alaska.

"God, it's hot," Babs commented. "Not that I'm complaining. Damn, we had a spell of rain." She gulped her drink with two quick swallows, then banged on her breastbone with her free hand. "Water, quick!" she said.

As she gargled, he suddenly began trembling. "Care for another?" he asked. If Steve Svenson was getting into her pants, why couldn't he? This thought so astonished him that he swallowed the next drink in one gulp without tasting it.

"Hey, is it that bad?" Her eyes glowed with devilish amusement. She giggled at Dave and held out her glass for a refill, then drifted into the waiting room. She gawked before the wall mirror, holding back her cheek with her finger. She seemed hesitant about something and sat down on the wicker sofa under the faded portrait of the Taku glacier.

"You know, when we first came to Alaska, I used to miss Mitch so much when he'd be away hunting or working as a deck hand on a fishing boat. But when he came home, he was always the same. Dead tired. I never knew whether he was glad to see me. Or the kids. He seems to think of them as just more mouths to feed."

Dave sat down by Babs and handed her another drink. He couldn't analyze it but he felt close to this woman suddenly.

"He leaves me and the kids and goes away to some logging camp for months, then comes back pretty nearly broke since he gambles away most of the money he earns. Then he has the nerve to get mad when things don't work. I had to plumb the lavatory and connect the oil pipes to the stove when we lived on the float house. You'd think Mitch would do it. We had all the

15

stuff. But he just laid around for three weeks and couldn't get up the gumption to install it. So I did. Hell, the kids were freezing in that back porch with that hole in the crapper."

Dave was too astounded to say anything. He finished off his drink without noticing it.

"Now he's just like a brother to me. Honest, Dave, that's the way I feel about Mitch. I don't expect anything exciting to happen between us anymore. He's a habit, I guess," she said, as though debating with herself, trying to figure out why she tolerated him. "A habit I can't break. He's as exciting as a mule. Comes home, wants his dinner, then plunks his rump in the living room, smokes, listens to the radio and then goes to sleep. Always tired. Never saw a man so tired."

Dave racked his brain to say something. "He'll be coming home soon," he said. "Shouldn't you be fixing his dinner?"

"He's working overtime so they can finish tonight."

"Care for another?"

"What's come over you, Dave? Are you trying to make a pass?"

Before he could answer, as he felt the blood rush to his head, Babs moved closer.

"Listen, Dave, if you've got hot pants . . ." she giggled.

"Hey wait a minute!"

"Oh, shut up. You look just like a scared jack rabbit. If that's what you want. . . ."

He kissed her. He was awkward and hit her teeth with his lip and his body spilled part of the drink in her hand.

"Hold still a minute," she said. She set the drink on the magazine rack. "This is going to be awkward. A wicker sofa isn't the best place to balance the likes of us."

"We can't go in my apartment. My folks . . ."

"Oh, hell, what's wrong with the floor?"

"God damn, Babs, you're swell. You don't have to . . ."

"Listen, this might do you good. You know about Steve and me. Well, I'm crazy about the guy. He's good, Dave. He wants to marry me. But I'll never do that, Dave. You can't spring kids on a guy. Mitch wouldn't give a damn if I divorced him or not. But I couldn't do that to Steve. But that's why I'm not worried about cheating on Mitch. I don't care."

"I'd better lock the door."

"All right, Dave."

Dave practically tip-toed to the door he felt so cautious and stunned. The sun was slanting in through the small side window and fell at the base of the door. A column of dust rose from the worn beige carpet as the line of light disappeared. He was so excited that his back teeth were chattering. The thought of seducing Barbara Bucci was almost like stealing. It had been so long. And he was scared stiff that maybe he'd disappoint her. He wanted more than anything to be good.

Babs had removed two of the cushions off the sofa and laid them on the floor.

"Best in the West," she said with a mischievous giggle.

Dave kissed her and she pulled away.

"Not there, please, Dave. On this side. The other's numb."

As Dave kissed the other side, he thought with excitement, "My life is changing."

2

CLARENCE WICK WAS BUSY. He ran his clippers in brisk, circular motions along the nape of the Indian's neck. Suddenly everyone wanted to be spruced up, clipped and shaved. He had been swamped with customers since early in the morning. They came stampeding into the barber shop in twos and threes. Then, to top it off, the passengers from the *North Star*, evidently unhappy with the ship's barber, had mobbed him while the steamer was in port. He planned to finish the two customers who were waiting, then close the joint. Chuck Alder, the sheriff, was one of those waiting. During the summer, he took tourists on grizzly-hunting expeditions on the mainland and he was recounting the story of one of these trips to Myron Johnson, the owner of the sweet shop.

"What a trip! A fifty thousand dollar yacht, one movie star and his wife, a couple of millionaires and their wives. He-he-he!" Chuck's stories were always punctuated with his high-pitched laugh. "Think there's drinking going on in this town? Aboard that cruiser women drank more than the men. Couldn't get it in their heads that I wouldn't touch the stuff. Thought that everyone up here did. One of the gals kept needling me. Said I wasn't a real sourdough if I didn't drink. The oil man's wife. A real good looker. Big, round, white arms. Built like a smoke house, too." Chuck pulled out a fresh package of cigarettes and began to remove the wrapper. His reddish face was creased in a grin of amused reflection.

"They wanted one grizzly apiece. There were six of them so they wanted six grizzlies. They all had big expensive magnums and were dressed to kill. The minute we got to shore and started out on the trail, they sobered up pretty fast. He-he-he! The movie star and the real estate millionaire were pretty quiet and really pale, walking through all that devil's club and grass as tall as a man's shoulder. The oil man and the gals were all right. The girls were scared but cheerful about it. The oil man, hell, he was a scrapper. Spunky. He walked ahead of me making trail most of the time. The other guys stayed close and behind."

"Next," Clarence said, as he snapped the apron low to the ground so the black patches of hair wouldn't scatter.

Chuck slid into the chair, his genial face still glowing with delight. The Indian stepped outside. Clarence's head jerked to the front window as his eye detected a movement. It was only Red Parker. He slammed the cash register hard. This was about the time, he calculated. They hadn't gone by yet. Unless maybe he missed them but that was unlikely. His eyes hurt from using the poor light in the rear of the shop to cut the hair on the back of a customer's head but he wouldn't turn the chair around because he wanted to keep his eye on the window.

He began working on the sheriff's hair, manipulating the hand clippers carelessly. Each time a shadow of a figure passed the front of the shop he looked up, his heart racing, hoping to catch a glimpse of the girls. Ever since the schoolteachers arrived in Wrangell, Clarence had been in a state of turmoil and high elation. His hands trembled, his neck ached from jerking his head up from his work, and his usual self-possession was rattled.

"He-he-he," Chuck, his head bent forward, continued on with his story, "you ought to have seen their faces when I spotted the first grizzly through the glasses. 'Oh, what a shot!' one of them shouted. 'My God', I said, 'that old she mongrel's a good mile from us. You couldn't hit her with a machine gun.'"

Clarence ignored the sheriff's babble. It was all he could do to contain his jubilation for this was the time when the girls made their nightly trip to the restaurant. The thought was electrifying and he pinched Chuck's skull as he pulled on the clippers.

"Ouch, Clarence! I want a haircut, not a scalping. He-he-he."

The auburn-haired one reminded him of Gwen. Considering how different they were in type, the similarity of the sensation he felt was unbelievable.

"Why don't you turn on your light?" Chuck asked amicably. "The sun's about through."

He recalled the shock of his first sight of her, as the two girls slowed before the puddle of water in front of his shop, tripping gingerly around it. It was as if his scalp had been lifted in a great searing flash of pain, and all at once his monastic existence was thrown into disorder. His peace and his quiet regimen disintegrated.

"Those millionaires let loose when they get out in the open," Myron said with a yawn, conveying the impression that he had only a minimal interest in the sheriff's tale.

"Hey," Clarence said, "the sheriff's passed the orgy stages of his story. We're in the woods now, hunting bear." He felt mean suddenly, for no reason at all. Maybe it was the fact that the sweet shop owner looked so smug, so prosperous. His sharp comment relieved his inner anguish and he cooled quickly, for after all, Myron was a customer.

"He-he-he," Chuck's eyes closed as he savored his memories, "they sure were brave while we were looking for grizzlies. Laughing and tramping about and even complaining a little. But the oil man finally got sore after a few days and went off looking for one by himself. Sure enough, we found him sleeping like a baby, as unconcerned as you please, under a cottonwood, with a grizzly shot clean through the heart lying near him."

Clarence scarcely listened to the sheriff, having developed the habit of paying little attention to his customers while he worked. His excitement was ebbing now that the girls hadn't passed his shop. He was a little angry and peeved. His composure was being ripped to shreds by a restless urge to stop his work and go out searching for them. A glance in the side wall mirror startled him with a glimpse of the pasty whiteness of his face and the glum, taut pain registered on it.

"Anyway, next morning we ran into this grizzly in the thick willows. Big and inquisitive, and he came loping easy towards us to get a better view. The movie star buckled up, froze, and the real estate millionaire froze too. One of the wives screamed. The oil man rushed up before the whole party and laid one neat in his chest. Beautiful fast shot. But the grizzly only bellowed and came rushing at us, mean and crazy with pain, and I raised my gun when I realized the oil man had shot his wad with that single shot. The women were all screaming and the men were like statues. I emptied my thirty-ought-six before it stopped him, ten yards away. He was hard to kill."

"I'll bet he was," Myron agreed halfheartedly. "You can have that kind of vacation."

"Oil man wanted to give me a thousand dollars plus expenses for saving everybody's life but I wouldn't take it. He said his gun jammed on him but we both knew that he folded after the first shot. Couldn't get his nerve up after the grizzly kept right on charging like nothing hit him."

"OK," Clarence said to Chuck. "That's it."

"By God, what's your hurry?" Chuck said grinning, as he eased up out of the chair.

"Heard the boys had quite a crap game last night," Myron said to Chuck as he took his place.

A couple of women tripped past the window and Clarence jerked upright. It was Mrs. Weaver and Mrs. Little. He was aware of his disappointment. He bent to his work with a detached air, glad this was his last customer.

"He-he-he, Chris won four hundred," the sheriff revealed. "He was just having fun, going at it easy-like, but winning most of the money. He seems to win all the time. Guys like Mitch and Red who could use the extra cash never quite get over the hump."

"They play too tight," Myron explained with a worldly air, although he never gambled himself.

A cat meowed in front of the shop and Chuck opened the door to let the animal in. Minnie was a big, wise-looking cat with metallic gray and snow-white fur.

"That God damn cat," Clarence said, "Been away two days now. Probably got herself knocked up again."

Chuck ran his hand tenderly over the crown of the cat's head, between the ears. The room was filled with the sound of the cat's purring. It filled the room with a throbbing delirium as the cat bucked her head deeper into the sheriff's palm.

"This cat's hungry," the sheriff commented.

"The milk I saved for her is probably sour now," Clarence blurted out.

"I hear the two new schoolteachers are looking for a home to rent," the sheriff said, straightening up.

Clarence's breath caught in his chest.

"Do you know of any vacancies?" The sheriff stood in the door.

"Hell, the town's tighter than a drum except for shacks. We ought to have more buildings," Clarence replied. He could barely contain his excitement.

"As sheriff, he gets around," Johnson noted, as the door closed behind the big man. "How's everything, Clarence?" His voice was interested but detached as if he were talking to one of his employees in the sweet shop.

"I bet Chuck did take that grand," Clarence said, referring back to the story of the grizzly hunt.

"Oh, I don't know. Chuck doesn't do it for the money."

"Hell, why not?" Clarence was suddenly resentful. "Those millionaires wouldn't even feel it. I sure would."

Clarence pinned the apron around Myron's neck, surprised to see the ring of stain around Myron's plaid shirt. He buckled the apron and set to work.

Myron had made the polite greeting and wasn't going to say anything more. As long as there were people in the shop there was conversation. Left with only one customer, there was silence. Clarence wondered if it was his fault.

The cat stood meowing at the front of the rear door which led into the lavatory where Clarence kept the cat food in the cooler. Her tail pointed almost straight up and the tip snapped and curled, echoing her hungry clamor. She meowed in short spurts but persistently as if she expected to be obeyed.

"God damn that bitch!" Clarence stammered. He flew to the door. With one hand, he opened the door and with the other hand he grabbed the cat by the neck and threw her in. Rage racked his mind as he stepped into the lavatory and slammed the door behind him. The cat darted into the corner, meowing, her tail twitching. Clarence was so enraged with her that he lunged again for her neck. Minnie shot back behind the bowl of the lavatory.

Clarence castigated himself for taking out his frustration on the poor cat. He paced back and forth in the small room and took a swing at the punching bag which hung in the corner. He worried about what Myron was thinking, sitting in the chair while the barber was in the lavatory taking it out on the cat.

The silence from the other room tormented him, yet he could not make himself go back. He reminded himself that he had asked for this life. He came to Wrangell from the States with the idea of settling down in a world of peace and freedom, getting married, raising a family. But it wasn't enough. Not the nice kid or the big house on the hill. It wasn't what he was hungering for.

He paced back and forth, smacking the palms of his hands with his fists. He should go back to the other room. Myron was waiting for him. Maybe someone else had come in. They were all nice people but he felt their friendliness was false. It began when he divorced Gwen. He knew they couldn't figure that out. Why he left her in the lurch. Gwen loved him. And she was a good mother. It wasn't her fault the second baby was born too soon and died in the incubator. Sure, they were nice, friendly people, but they never invited him anywhere. The only reason they talked to him at all was because he was the only barber in town, and a good one at that. No complaints about his abilities. He got good tips when the catch during fishing season was good.

"Clarence, ole boy, here's a buck for your effort." Silver dollars flashed in the palm of his hand.

"Thanks," he'd say curtly, concealing his contempt in the tight cavern of his chest.

His rage and disgust mounted as he lurched back into the other room. He bit his lip in anguish as he drove the electric clipper hard up Myron's neck. They resented him, really. He was all wrapped up in himself, too glum and sour. He couldn't begin to explain to anyone (except his friend Steve, maybe) that he was only trying to find peace of mind. He wanted a steady simple kind of happiness. And he believed he could only find it alone, separated from others. His thoughts dulled his anger. He worked more carefully. For some reason he wanted to do a good job on Myron. He turned the chair around to take advantage of the fading light from the window and concentrated on Myron's head.

He knew he was lost. After his divorce from Gwen, he had been doing all right, gaining little by little each day towards his goal, minding his own business. The barber shop was doing well and there were some people who did care for him, like Steve, as good a friend as a man could find.

Clarence worked with painstaking slowness, doing a fine, precise job, and feeling better for it. Myron's wife would comment on it. But the fine haircut couldn't cure him. He was falling apart. The shock of seeing that girl had shattered the peace and quiet he had fought for so long to cultivate. He couldn't struggle against it. He had learned that much in this tiny remote fishing town. He had to consent to whatever happened, remain calm and let life slip by without fighting against it. Only he couldn't do that now. Not with that girl in town. Until he had her, his guts, his mind, his whole world would be perched on a precipice, unbalanced, tottering. He would lose his own battle for contentment. He would feel only loss, hunger. He must make her understand all this, make her love him, soothe his restlessness.

Suddenly the shop was empty. Myron was gone. Clarence pulled down the shade. A silver light cut through the window where the shades didn't quite meet. He was alone. Clarence went to the window and peered out, saw natives and whites on the street. It was getting dark but the sky still clung to a bit of sun, a stain of rose that was dissolving in the night like a taillight of an automobile disappearing down a dark road.

He went into the rear room, brought out a quart of milk from the cooler and poured it in a can for the cat. He noticed the punching bag, the only relic of his years in the States, the years he fought at the Y.M.C.A., the Golden Gloves, always shy because of his smallness, afraid of the big guys, yet forcing himself to stand up to them. He debated about punching the bag, but he was too exhausted.

He moved to the other room and sat down in the barber chair. He was still on edge, though with the blinds down the sharpness of it was smoothing out. He was conscious of footsteps and voices outside, the drone of an outboard in the harbor, the scattered patches of hair on the linoleum floor, the smell of soaps, vaseline, hair oils on the shelf and his sad face in the mirror. His face reflected a bitter and unending battle for composure.

He kicked the chair around and faced the south wall. The tiredness ran through his veins, he felt it settling in his body. He would be stiff before he got up and went to the hotel to bathe and change and eat. But the effort required to leave the shop seemed too difficult and he sat there, now happy and at ease. He thought of her beauty. Already before he had even spoken to her, he loved her with all his heart. She brought out his dissatisfaction and restlessness but that was because it had been trapped for so long. He felt wonderful, savoring his privacy, thinking about the schoolteacher, and drifted off to sleep.

"Hey, Clarence, for Christ's sake, are you stone deaf?"

Clarence jerked forward. The door was rattling.

"Who's there?"

"Steve. Let me in."

Clarence rose, stiffly, and unlocked the door.

"What are you doing?" Steve's voice was full of cheer.

"Fell asleep in the chair. I guess I dozed off a little. Say," Clarence remembered, "I thought you were going to have dinner with Babs tonight."

"I am. But only the kids were home when I went by. Mitch is working overtime and Babs hasn't come home from the dentist yet. So I thought I'd take a walk into town and walk her home. Only she's disappeared. The dentist's office is locked. Have you seen her?"

Steve Svenson was a lanky, big-boned Norwegian. His soft, delicate features were almost feminine. His face was long and rosy and weather-stained, with a protruding chin that possessed the faint traces of a cleft. He had kind brown eyes and soft lips that curved in an instant into a friendly smile.

"No, haven't seen her," said Clarence. Suddenly he was almost beside himself with elation. The sight of Steve was invariably uplifting and this moment was no exception. The nap had done him good. He felt fresh and triumphant. If he saw one of the girls now, he would step up to her, introduce himself, make a good impression. "Hey, how about a drink?" Steve asked.

"That's a good idea," Clarence said. "Let's have a beer." He threw off his smock, removed the money from the cash register and locked up the shop. They marched down the street, saying hello to the people they passed. Steve's calm disposition was soothing. Clarence felt a warmth of well-being.

Two of the town's teenage girls ran past them, heading up Main Street, past the hotel and the Clinton dock to the Canadian dock, where two young boys hung over the railing. In a minute the four of them would be lost behind the big warehouse at the other end and could sit and talk and watch the night. He knew the spot well. He knew how the wind felt coming across the channel from the mouth of the Stikine River, the sound of water lapping under the dock, the melancholy in the water, the darkness that always seemed somehow more substantial than his own. It made him feel better as if he'd stepped into a ring, saw a man smaller and lighter than himself in the corner, and beat him up with no mercy because he had no use for weaklings.

The sun still lay behind the islands across the channel in the distance. The water of the channel was flat and waiting. On the land was a hush, filled with a strange urgency as if something was about to happen, some great and wonderful thing, only it never happened. After a while, you realized it was the hush itself, the quiet that filled the town, and the mountains, the straits and coves and streams, the channel itself.

In the hotel bar, Clarence ordered two beers and gazed about happily. Same old crowd, but they seemed friendly and nice all of a sudden. He bought Violet Lundy a drink, before she even got a chance to ask him. He despised the Klootch and her weakness for alcohol but he knew the best way to get her to leave him alone was to give her what she wanted.

"Hey, Max!" Clarence said, spying Holly and her friends in their usual booth and calling out to the bartender. "Set up a round of drinks for Holly and her crowd."

"Say, what's come over you?" Steve asked, perplexed. "I thought you hated drinking. You told me people at bars are hogs at a sty, remember? Wallowing and grunting in their own muck."

"Wait. You haven't seen the new schoolteachers yet."

"Not interested," Steve said and drained half his glass of beer with two swallows. "Babs has got 'em all licked."

"There's one of them, Steve, she's something. I can feel it in my bones. Max!" Clarence cried in jubilation. "Give us two more."

He felt light as air. He sensed eyes watching him, wanted them to be her eyes, wanted her to see him as worldly and entrancing. He dismissed Steve without a second's thought. He knew he was wrong in doing this but he couldn't resist. He floated on nimble toes towards Holly's booth. He knew he wasn't acting normal. It was as if a huge hand were propelling him into a splendid new arena full of excitement and beauty. And he wanted to dance.

"Holly, how about me and you kicking our heels?"

Holly rose, goggle-eyed. Clarence ushered her over to the jukebox and selected the hottest tune: *Bugle Call Rag*.

"Hey, you're nuts!" Holly laughed, pretending to be horrified. Effortlessly, he twirled her about the floor. He was aware that people in the other booths were looking at them dance. He must be doing good since even the crowd gathered about the crap game in the last booth were watching. His feet swam nimbly with the music and he held Holly's big, sturdy body easily in his arms, twirling her about, the sound of trumpet and the wild beat of drums

"Here, barber, you throw 'em."

"You want me to throw the dice?" Clarence twisted uneasily in his chair. "I've never thrown dice in my life. Oh, no," he protested with a shriek in his voice as Giff pressed the dice in his hand, "I couldn't."

"Go ahead. Show these boys how it's done."

Clarence found it hard to speak, as though scissors had snipped his voice. "But I've never thrown them before."

"Then now's the time to start learning," he heard Chris say with a weary sigh.

"Just roll 'em out," Giff said, still pressing the dice into his palms. Clarence closed his hand over them. They were wet and prickly. Without rattling or chanting to them as Giff had done, Clarence let them slide out of his hands onto the table.

"Two sixes," a man cried and a whoop of hands cleared the money from the center of the table.

Clarence stood. "I'm sorry, Giff. I'll pay you back."

"You just save this seat," Giff said with determination. "I'm not through with this bunch yet. I know where there's more money." Giff elbowed his way out of the crowd of onlookers and disappeared. Clarence became panicky. What was he doing, sitting at this table, a total foreigner actually, and after making such a fool of himself? Why the hell did he ever come to the bar? He should have known better. He wanted to leave but Giff had told him to save the seat.

The dice worked their way around, passing from one player to another clockwise. Clarence watched their faces, shining with cruelty and greed, as they drank and peered at the dice and absorbed losses and wins. Money had no value, was tossed about and crumpled and soaked by spilling drinks.

The hotel owner said to Clarence, "It's your turn if you want the dice."

As if in a deep dream, he felt himself reaching into his hip pocket for his billfold, extracted two crisp twenty dollar bills.

"What ya shooting, barber?"

"All of it," he replied, his voice weak and unsteady.

The dice flew out of his hands as if on springs. Eight.

"C'mon, Clarence," someone said. "Let's hurry up!"

He tossed again. Two fives.

A nervous shifting spread about the table. He was conscious of a blare of music, a whirl of voices, feet thumping on the dance floor. More people had come into the bar, evidently. Clarence wiped his hands down on his trouser legs.

"You're delaying the game," the hotel owner said politely.

The dice settled on a pair of fours.

"How much you shooting now?" Chris asked.

He had won!

"Uh, all of it," he said.

The dice had turned, it seemed, and for a good half hour Clarence won steadily. An almost excruciating rapture filled his chest as he watched the silver dollars and greenbacks pile up in front of him. The dice were spinning in a glorious agony of suspense, they were producing a galaxy of sevens and elevens and it was truly a miraculous experience. The pile of money grew.

"All of it," his voice became confident, sounding just like Giff's, and the sweat poured from him and his eyes were moist and he felt invincible.

Steve tapped him on the shoulder. "Good for you," Steve exclaimed. "Say, Clarence," he whispered, "I've got to be going. See you later."

"Stick around, Steve."

But Steve was gone, eager to keep his date with a married woman.

"All of it, boys," Clarence shouted.

Giff bored through the crowd to the table with a stack of fresh bills in his hand. "Say, what the hell's happened?"

"Oh," Clarence smiled, a mixture of joy and pride registering in his voice, as he rose from his chair. "Just having a streak of luck."

"You got close to fifteen hundred in that pile!" Giff exclaimed.

Clarence sat down as though struck in the groin by a foul blow. For a moment he blacked out as he had done a few times while boxing in the ring.

"Get him a drink, someone!" Giff shouted.

A rumble of disgusted voices rang in Clarence's ears. The whiskey was like a whip lashing against his lungs. Clarence rose and stumbled out of the booth.

"What happened to him? Quitting when he's a winner?"

"Lay off!" Giff's voice rose above the noise in the bar and for a moment the tumult subsided. "The guy's sick or something."

Outside, free from the dim and smoke of the bar, the cold air smacked against Clarence and he gulped at the night.

The door opened. "Hey, you forgot something." Giff said with a laugh, handing him a clump of soggy bills. "I'm glad you trimmed them," he said. "There's plenty more to get, too."

Clarence took the wad of money and stuffed it into his front and hip pockets.

"Feel better?"

"Yeah."

"Well, guess I'll get back in."

"I think I'll go up to my room. Feeling kind of weak."

Giff's fleshy face drooped with disappointment, as if Clarence were his protege and had been knocked out in the first round. But Clarence placed more value on the money in his pocket than Giff and the others and he wasn't going back inside to return it to them.

"I really don't like to gamble," Clarence said.

"OK, barber," Giff said and went back into the bar. His big hands pushing open the door looked as a huge as the paws of a bear. Clarence could tell he was angry.

A lot of people were leaving the bar and heading up Main Street towards the theater. It was time for the movie: Gary Cooper in *The Plainsman*. Everyone would be talking about his winnings. He'd be the talk of the town for days.

Clarence stood gloating over his success. Then he saw the schoolteachers emerge from the lobby side of the hotel. They drifted by him as he stood there frozen, his mouth agape.

The bar door swung open and Buster ran out. "Hey, girls, hold on a minute."

The two girls paused in front of the clouded plate glass windows of the bar, not six feet away from Clarence.

"Where are you going?" the hotel owner asked.

"The Weavers invited us to their house for dinner," said the dark-haired one with surprise.

Buster smiled. "Please come in a minute and have a drink before dinner."

The girls hesitated, looked at each other.

"It's on the house," said Buster.

The younger girl shrugged her shoulders. The two girls turned and followed the hotel owner into the noisy barroom.

Clarence's heart slowed, his lungs felt starved for air. She was more beautiful each time he saw her. He was seized by a wild impulse to go back in the bar and show off his gambling prowess for the girls. It would be the perfect introduction. He'd say hello to Buster and Buster would introduce him to the girls, commenting that he, the one and only barber in town, and a good one at that, had just won fifteen hundred dollars shooting craps for a few minutes.

Clarence's memory of the circle of gamblers and his desire to meet the girls melted into a fist which gripped the money in his pocket. Someone might slug him in there. He decided to hold on to the dough until the bank opened in the morning. He strode through the hotel side of the building and up the stairs to his room, going without supper for the first time in months.

3

CHRIS BALLARD WALKED OUT ON THE PORCH and saw the freighter, small in the distance as it swung slowly around Elephant Nose Point, heading towards the harbor, bringing the cannery and trap supplies for the fishing season. It was a single screw old relic of two thousand tons, with a black hull and a white deck structure, still owned and skippered by Marvin Braner, Dad's old friend.

Chris stood on the porch watching the freighter, feeling the warmth and laziness of the afternoon. The clouds seemed to be glued to the sky, not moving. Behind him the large two-storied family house hummed with sound as Mrs. Fremont conducted her semi-weekly cleaning. The house really didn't need cleaning that often, since he was hardly ever there, but he couldn't tell that to Mrs. Fremont.

The whine of the vacuum cleaner and the sound of Mrs. Fremont singing mingled with the laziness of the afternoon. Chris could tell she was in the living room facing the porch. He could visualize her as if he was in the room though he never could be in the same room with Mrs. Fremont while she was busy working because it didn't seem right that a thirty-year-old man should be idle while a woman twice his age earned a few dollars by doing house cleaning for a neighbor. She worked almost at white-heat, actually panting as she scrubbed and mopped, trying to keep her arthritis at bay.

Chris gazed at the clustered town below him, the harbor, the fishing boats tied at the floats. Directly across the road he looked into the unfenced back yard of Gwen Olson's house. Her wash was strung out on guy wires. Raspberry bushes marked the north border. The garden was freshly dug and sprinkled with the first shoots of spring, lettuce sprigs and onion blades, cropping up above the rich wet soil.

He lit a cigarette, watching the sun blink from view as it fell behind the clouds. Streaks of sunlight splayed out across the sky. Deep in the channel, now shaded and gray, the freighter's whistle groaned. Chris' gaze swept past the ship, went beyond to the islands, to the horizon. Two masses of black clouds were moving in from the west, growing larger as they approached the channel. It would be raining before the freighter docked.

The whir of the vacuum cleaner had stopped. It must have been shut off quite a while because he couldn't hear Mrs. Fremont working in the living room. She had mentioned the new schoolteachers when she first arrived in the morning. Something about how the girls were spunky to accept jobs in Alaska in mid-term. He didn't pay too much attention. He remembered seeing them in the bar the night before, after Clarence had quit playing. He had stood back, watched Buster mixing them drinks and chatting with them.

That was all. Only ever since they arrived, he knew there was something going on. When he first saw them eating at Mom's restaurant with the steamer still moored at the Clinton dock, he thought they were tourists. Yet somehow he knew, by the way his appetite disappeared and he couldn't hear what the person next to him was saying, by the way he kept casting shy, thirsty eyes at them as they sat at the other end of the counter, somehow he knew for certain that they were here to stay. For the first time since his folks had gone south he was fidgety and aware of the emptiness of the big house. He was secretly glad that Mrs. Fremont had insisted on tidying up today because, who knew what might happen. But, most significant of all, the last four nights he had had trouble sleeping alone in the double bed.

"Up here the mind and eye are aware of the water, the trees, the islands."

Chris turned and saw Mrs. Fremont, buttoning her sweater. She had come out on the porch and was looking out at the view.

"All through?"

"Yes, Mr. Ballard. Didn't take too long, now did it? And all your fuss about me working so hard."

She gazed past Main Street at the pale motionless bowl of the channel. A troller was approaching the buoy at the mouth of the harbor, rending the stillness with the spat-spat-spat of its gas engine.

"That's Fred Racht, isn't it?" she asked, her eyes on the tiny figure of the man who stood outside his cabin while steering the boat in.

"Couldn't mistake that boat," Chris replied. It was an eyesore compared to the generally well-kept boats in the harbor.

Mrs Fremont breathed deeply. "Beautiful day, isn't it?"

"I think it's going to rain."

She narrowed her eyes and gazed out at the distance. "Yes, those black clouds do look ominous."

"You know you're right," Chris said, "Mind and eye aware . . ."

". . . of the water and the trees and the islands. It's all so beautiful. You can't really forget it, can you? When you go away from Wrangell, it's like a snapshot in the back of your mind."

The telephone shrilled in the hallway.

"Well, good-by, Chris, and take care of yourself." Mrs. Fremont started down the steps as Chris went into the hall.

"Hello," Chris said as he placed the clumsy receiver against his ear and faced the mouthpiece protruding from the wall box.

"Chris," Dave's voice came over the wires. "Sarber's throwing a party tonight."

"Well, so she is," said Chris puzzled, knowing Dave generally didn't care for Miss Sarber's parties. Edna Sarber worked in Olson's Merchandise Store during the day and at the hospital at night. On her infrequent nights off, she liked to have parties which tended to attract the rowdier, less respectable members of Wrangell society.

"They might go there," Dave said. "I told Herb he should bring them up. Show them Wrangell in the rain."

Blood surging, Chris asked, "Dave, are you sure?"

"Yeah, I'll see you there."

Chris hung up. Dave was behaving oddly, he thought. Well, who wasn't? Clarence shooting craps for the first time since he had moved to Wrangell was just as odd as Dave being cheerful.

Chris went upstairs to his room, stretched out on the freshly-made bed, lit a cigarette and stared at the ceiling. A pool of quiet surrounded him, like something substantial and heavy. All of the lethargy and silence of a Wrangell afternoon poured into the room from the open window, into his mind.

He'd noticed her sharp white teeth that curved slightly inward, the sharp yet poised beauty of her white face, the eyebrows accenting her small forehead with a soft, full sweep, the way she sat erect on her stool at Mom's, graceful and at ease. He'd watched her in the wall mirror of the restaurant and, more directly, across the length of the counter. He remembered the first time he saw her. Like a premonition, his throat closed up, choked for air. She was so young, fresh and breathtaking. She was like a blade of light, shining as if she caught the rays of the sun with each movement of her body. For a moment as he sat there unable to keep his eyes off her, he could not bear the fact that they were so separated, had never spoken to one another.

He rose and ran his hand through his rumpled hair. He glanced out the open window. The freighter hadn't moved much since the moment he first saw it. He flicked his cigarette out the window and saw it land across the dirt road at the edge of the grass. Suddenly he found it difficult to be in the house alone. This was a new feeling. The empty house seemed to be telling him things, wanting to be full of the noise and life of a large family.

Maybe it was love this time. Even though he hadn't met her, maybe he was in love with her. Hell, for all he knew, she might even be married, but he knew she wasn't because he had already checked for rings on her left hand. She wore only a green one on her right hand.

Chris wandered down the stairs and out onto the porch. Matt Fleming was wheeling his bicycle down the road, a cigar in his mouth.

"What's the matter, Matt? Did the bike break on you?"

Matt looked up. "Oh, hello Chris. No, just felt like walking." He smacked his lips. Matt looked bad: his skin was dead white, his cheeks hollow, his eyes red-rimmed and burning with sickness.

"How about a glass of water?"

Matt laid his bicycle down and ambled with amazing nimbleness up the porch.

"Can't pedal a bicycle and smoke a cigar both," Matt confessed. "Just gave Danny a piano lesson," he sighed as he must have sighed during the practice lesson. "That boy is a natural born player, if ever I saw one, and he won't practice. Oh, I wish I had his natural abilities when I first started learning the piano."

Chris laughed as he led the way down the hall to the kitchen. "'It's the hard workers that make success, not the gifted'—that's a quote from Theodore Ballard."

Matt drank his water quickly, smacking his lips as though they bothered him. From the cupboard, Chris produced a quart of whiskey, poured himself half of a water glass and sipped it.

"Beautiful day," Matt said, as he filled the glass at the sink by himself. "It's going to rain, though. Clouds moving in from the west." Matt puffed on his cigar, a series of strong, quick draws for the cigar was almost dead now, then a series of deep inhalations, smacking his lips with relish. Matt limited himself to three cigars a day and knew how to derive the maximum enjoyment from each one.

"I told Gwen she better get her wash in," he said. The effort of firing his cigar properly had brought spots of color into his sunken cheeks. This past spring, a doctor in a sanitarium in the States had told Matt that he had only a year to live. He had both TB and stomach cancer. Matt wasn't at all disturbed, or at least so it seemed. He looked sick but it didn't seem to slow him down. He kept going somehow. He didn't ask for sympathy. He seemed to enjoy his life, living alone in a shack out by the graveyard, going swimming whenever the weather permitted, teaching piano to the kids in town, playing gin rummy with the boys down at Johnny Bugg's bar twice a week and playing the organ at the Episcopal church on Sundays. He earned a few extra nickels by digging graves and picking berries in season and selling them to the women in town for making preserves.

"Thanks for the water, Chris." Matt stood before the sink, holding the empty glass under the hot water tap. He wiped it dry with a dishcloth and put it back on the shelf. "Can't be too careful," he smiled. He was like that, conscientious about protecting the health of others. "Say, Chris, now that the weather is warming up, you should come over for a swim. I got Stravinsky's *Firebird Suite* and Ravel's *La Valse* on this last ship." He blushed. "It just about busted me, but, my God, what music! Ravel didn't know how to write a dull note."

Chris watched Matt coast down the hill on his bicycle, turn at the dead end where a string of houses had been built and pedal out of sight, heading left, away from town, towards the graveyard. Chris decided to go down to Main Street.

Gwen Olson was out in her yard, taking down the wash, as he came down the steps. As she removed the big bed sheet, she saw Chris and waved to him. Danny was right beside her.

"It's going to rain," Gwen announced.

"Matt said so," Danny shouted in glee.

"It was a beautiful sight while it lasted," Chris said as the clothes disappeared into the basket. "Especially the pieces facing me."

"The pink one or the beige one?" Gwen asked, referring to her slips.

"I'm color blind," Chris said and headed off down the road, waving at Danny who was still shouting something to him,

Gwen and Jon Olson were nice neighbors. Chris had known Gwen for a long time, before she divorced Clarence even, and she was always full of zest. Like now, as she took down her damp clothes, knowing she would have to rehang them under the porch and in the house. But she wasn't licked. She didn't let a small thing like the weather bother her. Most of the women in Wrangell wouldn't have dreamed of hanging clothes outside because it rained so much. But Gwen did, stringing the clothes out across her back yard in the open, taking a chance, defiant and stubborn even. She strung out her clothes the way she faced life, with purity and spirit, open and unafraid of sudden squalls, of storms, like with Clarence, her first husband. It was obvious she still loved the guy. She wasn't the kind to marry on a whim. Chris had seen her face at the dances at unguarded moments. Jon was usually tired from working in the merchandise store all day and stayed home and took care of Danny. Gwen would go by herself and have a good time. But then she would catch a glimpse of Clarence across the A&N Hall and she would stop having fun all of a sudden. Her face registered a mixture of disbelief and sorrow, as if a dead friend or relative had just pinched her mind. Then she would shake herself free from the mood and resume dancing and laughing with her usual vivacity. Never once did Gwen utter an unkind word against the barber, although the way he asked for a divorce not long after their second child died, the bastard must have deserved it.

Chris came to the bottom of the hill and headed up the main road toward town. Sea gulls were squealing as they circled the edge of the harbor. A seiner left a wide glistening wake in the dark water as it moved past the buoy at the end of the breakwater and into the channel. A fisherman, rowing Indian fashion—standing up, feet straddled across the mid-thwart, pushing the oars instead of pulling them—was heading towards the aeroplane float at the rear of the hotel. Somewhere deep in the harbor, a generator droned faintly.

As Chris passed the A&N Hall, the view of the harbor was cut off by the buildings on the harbor side of Main Street, all built out over the water on pilings. Across the street from Mom's restaurant, in the alley by the shoe shop, he spied Roy Hart's dog, Winchester, a magnificent Siberian husky, black as coal with white markings on his paws and tail, crouched on top of a terrified bitch much too small for him. Winchester was going for all he was worth only the wiry bitch buckled under his weight, slid out from under him and huddled against the wall of the shoe shop. Winchester dashed upon her and nuzzled her out into the alley where there was more room. Chris laughed, moved past the bakery shop and the theater and went into Johnny Bugg's bar.

"Hi Chris," Mitch Bucci called to him from the bar.

"What are you doing here?" Chris asked. "All through at the sawmill?"

"Yeah. Have to wait for a head saw," Mitch snorted. "That'll arrive about the same time the fishing season starts and then there'll be no one around to work in the mill."

Chris stood between the stools as he faced the bar. It was always a little quieter in Johnny Bugg's than at the hotel bar, perhaps because of the gin rummy and pinochle games taking place in the card room in the center of the building. The concentration and wit required by the games suppressed the effects of the beer and whiskey. The bar smelled of rancid tobacco juice and stale beer.

"Pour me a straight one when you get through, Johnny," Chris said to the owner, who was counting a stack of chips that Roy Hart was cashing in.

"Don't hurry him," Roy said, puffing out his chest. It was just like Roy to win and quit playing. Like Clarence the night before. Two of a kind, almost. Only Chris couldn't really place Roy in the same category as Clarence. He had to feign pleasure and friendliness when he was with Roy, though he couldn't stand his smug, self confident airs, which reminded him of his dad and the rivalry and strain of their relationship. Chris was polite to Roy, pretended to enjoy his company, whereas he had hardly anything to do with Clarence except for the necessary trips to his shop for a shave or a haircut. Actually Chris only tolerated Roy because he admired Roy's wife, Bea.

"Twenty-two dollars isn't bad for a few hours," said Roy, chuckling as he settled his bulk on the neighboring stool.

"And Johnny," Chris said, as the bartender poured the whiskey, "get your dice boxes out. I feel hot."

Mitch moved to the stool on the other side of Chris, his eyes alight with interest for Chris didn't shoot for pennies generally.

"For the drink?" Johnny asked, as he placed the two dice boxes on the bar.

"A case of whiskey," said Chris. "I want it for the party at Sarber's tonight."

Johnny's face twisted into a scowl. "Hell, that's pretty steep. You beat me last time, remember, lucky?"

"Last two times," Chris reminded him.

"What are you crying about?" Mitch said to the bar owner. "Look at the percentage in your favor!"

"OK," Johnny conceded and smiled. "God damn, I'm going to take you this time, Chris! I'll whip your ass!"

"If you win," Mitch continued with his analysis of the odds as Johnny picked up four aces on the first flop, "you make a profit of roughly one hundred percent. If Chris wins, you lose forty or fifty percent."

Johnny tossed the last dice and shot a six. Five sixes was the limit and couldn't be beat, only tied. Chris dumped the box three times, scared up only three sixes, and lost the first round.

Johnny shook the dice box with two hands, grinning, sure of himself now. Men came in from the card room to watch this, a more exciting game than gin rummy. They looked curious and a little envious for if Chris lost he would have to pay double the value of a case of whiskey, nearly one hundred dollars.

Johnny, standing behind the bar, rattled the box in his hands like a cocktail shaker, then dipped the box swiftly, releasing five dice which spun out over the shiny black surface of the bar. Four fours. He was hot today. He unloaded the last dice, a deuce. He would roll again, trying to get a four or an ace.

Johnny hit the bar hard as he flipped the box down, imprisoning the lone dice. "Be there, baby," the bartender pleaded. He lifted the box and everyone stared at the all-important bone. Four. Johnny had done it!

It would take five fives or five sixes to win.

Chris didn't even excite the boys by performing the customary shaking. He simply held the box on an angle while the dice spilled out and formed a gentle pattern. Five fives.

Johnny's grin disappeared. "The lucky bastard!" he said, addressing the bystanders huddled around Chris. "One flop and he beats me!"

"You're too confident," Roy told him.

Chris asked, "What are you crying about! That's one horse a piece." He gathered the dice in his hands, plunked them in the box and threw two sixes.

He shoved the sixes aside, picked up the three remaining dice and asked, "How lucky you think you are Johnny? I'll bet you a hundred that I beat you."

Johnny glowered. He was getting riled, judging by the way his eyes were flashing. He wheeled around, banged the "No Sale" key on the register, discovered he didn't have a hundred in it, slammed the drawer shut, reached into his apron, flipped it aside, brought out a thick black billfold and laid five twenties on the bar.

"It's a bet, lucky!"

Chris took a sip of his whiskey, drew out his pocketbook and laid a mess of fives and tens beside the five crisp twenties.

Chris dumped the dice from the box and scored nothing.

"Want to make that a hundred more?" Johnny shouted in glee with a smirk on his face. It was only when Johnny gambled, Chris noticed, that he lost his good nature. When he was tending bar, he was nice and unassuming. He never worried about the hotel bar doing more business than he did or went out of his way to improve the bar's appearance to cash in on the tourist trade. But when he was gambling he was mean and greedy.

"No. I think you got me this time, Johnny," Chris said quietly as he rattled the three dice in the box with one hand. This was his last chance to increase his score. If he didn't make anything more and Johnny beat him, he'd lose the hundred on the bar and would have to pay double for the case of whiskey.

The dice spilled out of the box, clacking as they dribbled across the counter, their upturned faces revealing a pair of fat sixes and an ace. Chris felt a sliver of delight ease into him.

"The lucky bastard! Get the hell away from here!" Johnny said, shoving the money towards Chris.

"Well, aren't you going to try and tie me?" Chris asked though he could scarcely contain an impulse to break out laughing.

Johnny said, "Sure, I'll try. What have I got to lose?"

Johnny flopped three times, coming up with a grand total of three sixes.

Chris scooped up the money and finished his drink in one swallow.

"Have Curly bring a case of Old Forester up to Sarber's tonight in his cab. And buy the boys a round." As he went to the door, he added, "Have one on me, Johnny." He laid a twenty on the bar and left.

Walking down the street, Chris ran into Red Parker, the longshoreman boss, and his wife Shirley, who was a chambermaid at the hotel, each holding onto one of their children.

"Freighter coming in," Red said as he juggled the seven-month baby in his arms.

"Yeah. We'll start unloading in the morning." A drop of rain smacked

Chris on the nose.

"Much freight?"

"I think she's carrying about two hundred tons."

"I better get three gangs," Red said. His name was Rodney and he didn't have a single strand of red hair on his head. But the guys kidded him for so long about his name that his friend, Charlie Zimms, started calling him Red and the nickname stuck. Red was white, Shirley Indian. Both were sober which was unusual. Shirley was carrying a shopping bag in one hand and holding onto their seven-year-old daughter with the other. The girl was looking into in the shop window of Winton's Electric Shop, staring at the aluminum waffle iron with its lid open, exposing the rows of shining teeth.

"What's that, Shirley?" she asked, addressing her mother as if they were sisters. She had probably tucked Shirley into bed plenty of times when Shirley was too drunk to do it herself. Yet today both Red and Shirley looked so respectable, Chris thought, and felt a pang. Shirley wore no make-up, her dark face was quiet and peaceful. Red's eyes were clear, without the glaze they got from drinking wine all the time. His face was smooth-shaven and his breath clean, just a devoted father taking the wife and the kids on a shopping trip.

"That's a waffle iron," Shirley said to the child in her shy deep voice.

"Three gangs should do it," Chris said, peering beyond the street to the channel. "Only Marvin might be in a hurry. Better get four to be sure."

"You're the boss," Red said.

Chris walked quickly up Main Street past the hotel, then cut across and went up the hump of the hill. He paused at the summit of the rise, standing before the new Federal Building, looking out on the channel. Once more the low-slung, plodding freighter rent the air with a mournful blast of short and long notes, announcing its arrival. Drops of rain spattered upon his head in random patterns that had not quite got the feel of the temperature yet, tentative, regrouping and striking again.

Caught up in the anticipation of the pleasures of the rain, of the steady noise drumming upon roofs, of the roar of the small streams that raced down the slopes of the hill to the bay, of the mud clinging to his shoes, of the deeper quality of the silence in the empty streets, Chris moved along, sniffing the odor of the still air, sensing the strain and shift in the voluminous mass of black clouds in the sky.

He headed down to the path that picked up the wooden bridge that ran along the tip of the beach. Unpainted shacks and shoe-shaped houses perched on his right. An old Indian woman with a shawl around her shoulders sat in a rocker on the porch of a sagging clapboard cabin. Chris crossed the line of her unwavering vision and went on. He felt strange and wonderful, as if someone was watching his every move and enjoying the sight. Empty tins and bottles littered the rock-strewn beach to this left. Pools of water from the last rain filled the crevices of the larger rock formations. Boys and girls were playing on the beach amongst the rocks. The rain seemed to charge their actions with urgency and importance. The huge Saint Bernard dog that belonged to Old Man Hobbs was standing motionless by one of the boys near the water line. When the boy tossed a stick out into the bay, the Saint Bernard, barking joyously, splashed into the dark water and returned with the stick.

A wire fence marked the perimeter of the Ballard Cannery. Chris unlatched the gate and hurried down the path in front of the mess hall. The huge, theater-like vault between the fish house and the warehouse was covered with corrugated steel. The rain drummed and crashed on the roof.

Chris walked slowly along the sheds, feeling as he always did when he first came upon the cannery, like a stranger. Every time he entered the office, he expected to see the owner sitting in the swivel chair beside the green metal filing cabinets. He always felt like that. He just couldn't make himself believe it was all his, that he controlled it, gave the orders, sold the merchandise.

He moved past the office to the edge of the awning and stared out across the great widening dock, shaped like a T, now splattered with rain and being washed clean of sea gull droppings. The freighter would arrive in about ten minutes. He would assist with her mooring and then go eat. He was hungry. He'd have a steak and then go up to Sarber's party early. The rain splashed down from the eaves of the sheds, dripping in steady streams into the bay. The water was quiet under the dock, as always in the rain.

He would never feel like he owned the cannery. No matter how well he did, no matter how hard he tried, how many checks he signed, how many decisions he made. He would always feel his Dad's presence, his driving power, his insatiable love for the business. During the lean years, when he couldn't afford to hire a bookkeeper, Theodore sat up nights in the office, working while everyone else slept.

When Chris came back from college, his dad made him second in command at the cannery, but there was always friction, steady and persistent like the silence of the town. Sometimes Chris felt it as outright resentment. He kept out of his dad's way, away from the important canning operation in the fish house. He worked in the warehouse, supervising the packing, gluing and stacking, keeping track of the cases of small and large tins, the different varieties of salmon. It would have been that way forever if the grizzly hadn't changed the picture. There was only one way to do things when Theodore Ballard was in charge: his way.

"Hey there! Anyone on dock?"

The freighter's bow loomed up before the cannery, its mast and side lights lit, and Chris ran across the dock to catch the bow line. The engine ground into reverse as Chris slipped the noose around the cleat. The freighter brought its stern alongside the dock and Chris ran the width of the dock to catch the aft line thrown across by a sailor on the poop deck.

"Thought no one was around," the sailor shouted through the rain at Chris.

Chris ran up the gangway the instant it was brought around and headed forward along the port deck to the pilot house, knowing the skipper would be at the wheel.

"Hello, Chris. You're looking fine, my boy."

"Hello, Marvin. You're right on time."

"This ship's slow as a mule but steady. Saw your folks in Seattle. They're all fine. Theodore looks better."

"That's what Mom told me in her last letter. Do you have the bill of lading on the cargo? We'll begin unloading first thing in the morning. Rod is lining up four gangs."

"Suits me. The quicker, the better. Oh," the skipper produced an envelope from his pea jacket, "here's a letter from your sister."

Chris took the envelope, recognizing Patty's handwriting—tiny, neat and feminine.

"Care for a drink, Chris?"

"Sure, Marvin."

The skipper poured generous portions of whiskey into two water glasses and they toasted. Marvin drained the glass.

"What do you do by yourself all the time up here? Your mom misses you. You should go down and visit, Chris."

Chris set the glass on the chart table. "Some day," he laughed. "What's the news from the States?" He ran his finger along the rim of the glass.

"What you'd expect. There's plenty of talk about the Germans. Papers talking about going to war, but who'd want to fight us after how we showed 'em last time."

"Well, thanks, Marvin. See you tomorrow."

Chris moved away from the cannery, unmindful of the rain. He was so used to it, it didn't bother him; he just pulled up the collar of his wool jacket. He probably should have spent more time with Marvin, maybe had dinner with him. He was Dad's friend. They had gone to school together in Portland at Hill's Military Academy.

But Chris wanted to leave. He couldn't stay cooped up any longer. He needed to get out, breathe fresh air, let the rain soak him. His heart raced with excitement as he strolled down to Mom's restaurant. The idea that he might see the schoolteachers in a few hours was almost tormenting. He'd get to Sarber's early, before the party got wild, and dance with her. He ate his club steak quickly, without tasting it, reading Patty's letter all the while he was eating even though he knew what was in it before he even took it out of the envelope. News about his Dad's health; requests that he come and visit.

After eating, he headed out along the road, passing the A&N Hall and the garage, then stopped. Fanny Sundberg, an umbrella poised over her head, was coming down the path from the hill.

"Hi, Fanny," Chris called out.

Fanny sauntered over to Chris. She was short and statuesque with large, firm breasts. "You're getting soaked," she observed. "Where are you going?"

"Over to Sarber's. She's giving a party."

"Another one? How the hell does that old bag stand the grind?"

"She likes people. Hey, you look glum."

Fanny scowled. "I can't imagine why she lets a bunch of wild hyenas tear her house to shreds."

"Take it easy, baby. You'll blow a fuse," Chris said. He wondered what was bothering her. Maybe something was wrong between her and her husband again.

"You were there the last time I went to one of her parties. Giff was in the lavatory, remember? He couldn't lock the door because Sarber has no lock for it. And Sarber got the whole crowd around the door and opened it. Remember? A beautiful profile shot of Giff Weeks taking a leak."

Chris laughed, recollecting the incident. Later after Fanny had left, Giff opened the door on Miss Sarber herself, squatting on the bowl, her panties stretched between her knees. She waved a drunken acknowledgement at Giff as the crowd roared with laughter.

"It's Alan," Fanny said. "He left me again. He went south on *North Star* yesterday."

"No kidding."

"Yep. We had another fight. Another separation. We come and go like the seasons."

By God, Chris thought, taking a second look at Fanny. I've got a lay. And then he recoiled within himself, felt disturbed, uneasy.

"It's early for the party," she said. "How about getting under the umbrella and walking me around a bit? I feel like a goof walking by myself in the rain with no place to go."

"I'll tell you what," Chris forced the words out against the sudden feeling of revolt in his guts. "Let's go down to the float house and have some coffee."

"What will the neighbors think?" she asked, but she handed Chris the umbrella and stayed beside him as he led the way. They walked in silence, stepping around puddles, slipping in the soft mud in the center of the road where car wheels seldom traveled.

"Anything new?"

"Cut it out, Chris. Let's just walk, huh? No entertainment."

They headed away from town, following the bend of the harbor. Since they had started walking together, turning the corner by the native section, passing Marie's Grocery Store and the obsolete assembly hall, Fanny hadn't said a word.

Now she spoke up, her voice resentful and peeved. "My darling parents are having the Everetts and Johnsons up for a chit-chat and coffee this evening. They're all so contented and secure. Talking about Wrangell—the one topic that never grows stale with them—how they love this quaint little fishing hole, which so reminds Mrs. Johnson of Norway. Those old fogies! They don't know anything but this rotten hole of a town. I can't stand listening to them yapping about the weather, their crocheting, talking about new recipes, blubbering about the neighbors."

Chris shifted the handle of the umbrella to his other hand. Knowing Fanny, he remained silent, listening to the roar of the stream beneath the bridge over which they had just passed. Flimsy houses stood along the harbor's edge on the right, some on logs, others on piling, while the better houses, freshly painted in greens and whites, dressed up with gables and small-paned windows, were set in deep from the road, nestled in the rising slope of land to the left.

"This town destroys you, piece by piece," Fanny said bitterly. "There's nothing here! And yet, you men are lucky. This is what you've dreamed of, isn't it, Chris? I bet when you were in the States you couldn't wait until you came back? Sure, I know your type. You like the independence. You can do whatever you like!" She didn't look at Chris as she spoke.

They approached the opening on the side of the road between Yorgensen's Marine Yard and the old net shed. Down below, resting upon the water on two massive spruce logs, stood the low-squatting, brown-shingled house that Chris had bought from Mitch years ago. He led the way down the slanting, slippery planks to the porch. A seine skiff lay tied to the rail of the porch. The tall totem poles on Shake's Island were visible in the background.

They scuffed their shoes on the mat and Chris opened the door into the kitchen. Fanny went into the living room in the center of the house and busied herself lighting the small oil burner as the house was damp and cold. Chris ignited the stove in the kitchen and prepared the percolator with the necessary amount of water and coffee. The rain drummed on the roof. The float house drifted just a little with the ebb of the tide.

In the cupboard he located a half empty pint of whiskey. He hadn't been in the place for months. He just didn't seem to find any use for it lately.

"Care for a drink, Fanny?" he called out. For some reason he felt bad about what he was doing. He didn't feel the proper glow, he wasn't sure what he wanted. She was here for one thing only, he knew. She was lonely and upset and wanted to be near someone. She had no girlfriends. Most of the girls in town didn't care for Fanny because of her superior airs. Even when people went to the movie and stood in line to buy tickets from Fanny, they scarcely said a word to her other than the customary greeting.

"Hey, you want that drink?"

"All right," Fanny's voice from the other room was glum. "Mix it with water. Just a little."

Chris carried the drinks in, one in each hand, and sat down beside Fanny on the small blue sofa. It was the perfect setting for a seduction with the rain, the warmth, the privacy.

"I'm just not cut out for this town," she muttered and rose, almost spilling her drink. "I can't stand watching everyone act so satisfied. Have you ever noticed that, Chris? Everyone's so content. They don't want to better themselves in any way."

She set her drink down on the small table beside the sofa. "I want to get away from here. But ninety-nine percent of the women up here like it. And why? Some of them let their hair down. They drink and go wild. And the home types—it's so cozy for them in their houses when it rains. They have time to do things, all the little homey things that they never found time to do in the States." Fanny's voice became shrill. "When they come back from the States they tell you, 'Oh yes, it was wonderful down there but I couldn't wait until I got back.'"

"Cool off, Fanny. Come here and sit by me." She had removed her raincoat and her breasts swelled under the fabric of her chartreuse blouse.

"Cut it out, Chris!" she snapped, continuing her pacing. "I should have taken the steamer south instead of Alan. I want to see the tall buildings in the cities and go to the night clubs. I miss shopping in the big department stores. I miss the crowds. I want to have to choose a film from a whole list of shows. This flea house of a theater we have here only shows newsreels and movies that are two years old. We're in a rut, Chris. God damn Alan! Why does he always get to leave when we quarrel?"

"You don't expect him to go live with his dad, do you?"

"Why not? God damn, why can't he go live with the dirty, smelly old undertaker?"

"Listen . . ." Chris began.

"Let's go, Chris. I can't stand being cooped up while it's raining. The only time I feel alive in this hole is when it's raining. I feel like getting out in it."

All at once, as Chris realized his chance of seducing Fanny was vanishing, he definitely wanted her. He rose and put his hands on her waist. "Baby, you look luscious when you pout."

"God damn you, Chris!" She lurched past him, scooped up her raincoat and began to button it.

Chris grabbed Fanny around the shoulders and pulled her down on the sofa. She drove her fist into his throat, gagging him. She ran into the kitchen, grabbed her umbrella and fled from the house. He heard her footsteps running up the planks.

Chris laughed, rubbing his throat, relieved somehow. "I'm out of practice with that dame."

He reached over and picked up her untouched whiskey and drank it. He'd better go on up to Sarber's. Dave would be waiting for him. He knew that the schoolteacher wouldn't be there. He knew that as surely as he knew when he first saw her that she had come to Wrangell to stay.

4

DESPITE HERB WEAVER'S FAULTS, he was pleasant company. Conversation didn't lag when Herb was visiting. Bea Hart was grateful as she half-listened to Herb talking to the new schoolteachers, half-listened to the rain dripping from the eaves and drumming on the roof, a hollow rumbling background for the lively chatter of the people gathered about her dining room table, enjoying a meal of stuffed white goose and roast moose.

"Two more months!" Herb was saying, waving his fork around and forgetting to eat in his enthusiasm. "In two more months, I'll be on my troller fishing off Point Baker. All summer, trolling for those big kings and cohos. My, that's a thrill when you see the old cedar pole bend almost in two from the weight of one of those babies! Sylvia does the steering for me when we run into a school of salmon that are biting. By God, I love to feel the lines rush off on a strike. The kids are all trying to help me pull the big ones in, handing me a gaff, but more often than not they're getting in my way."

"Herb," Sylvia Weaver interjected, "you're making us sound like old salts the way you keep rattling on about that boat of yours. It sounds romantic but try living in a hole the size of a small bathroom with two teenage kids and a husband. You have to cook, wash, eat and sleep in there. The gas engine's right smack in the middle of the foc'sle and the fumes are overpowering." She grinned, for Sylvia enjoyed their summer vacation as much as Herb did. "When it blows, the boat starts jumping and rolling and diving and jerking around like it's gone wild, the pots and dishes bang and clatter, and water seeps up from the bilge . . ."

"We generally duck out before that happens," Herb interrupted, abruptly moving on to a new subject. It was one of the things that made conversation with Herb both difficult and interesting. "Say, we're going to have a dance in town tomorrow night. No special occasion. Everyone is invited, of course—we have no prejudice against the natives. Everyone comes late—an old custom in Wrangell. There'll be parties all over town before it starts, which reminds me, you're invited to our house for a few drinks. Around eleven o'clock everyone starts heading down the hill to the A&N Hall. Matt here plays the piano. Alan Sundberg plays the trumpet, only we won't have Alan with us this time because I heard he went south on the *North Star*. Mitch Bucci plays the violin. . . ."

"That's the only time Mitch combs his hair," said Sylvia with a giggle. "He mats it down over his head and he looks so glum as he fiddles the bow. You'll scream when you see him."

"Now, where was I?" Herb said, forgetting what he had been talking about. "Oh, yes, there's two whales off Point Baker. You see them most all the time when you pass the point. There used to be only one whale there. We called him Old Man Baker. . . ."

"Darling," his wife said, with a wry lift of her eyebrows in the direction of the two girls, "we were talking about the dance this Saturday."

"Oh, sure. We won't have Alan as trumpeter because I heard . . ."

Sylvia interrupted, "Yes, dear, he went south."

Matt broke the moment of awkward silence. "Do either of you girls know how to play an instrument or sing? We're a little short-handed in the orchestra department."

"Matt plays the organ for the Episcopal church," Bea added. "We have a lovely choir." She knew Reverend Rushworth was always looking for new members.

Victoria cleared her throat. "Lydia sang in San Francisco. Maybe . . ." She paused as she intercepted her friend's warning glance across the table.

"Well, I don't mind joining the choir," Lydia said, "but I'm not quite certain, well, I wouldn't care to sing before an audience at a dance."

Matt Fleming smacked his lips after wiping them with a napkin. Bea noted the stains on the cloth. She would separate it from the others later and boil it in water with bleach. Although she liked Matt as much as anyone in Wrangell, his sickness repelled her, made her conscious of her own.

"You're living in the hotel now, aren't you?" Matt asked. "Have you noticed the piano in the library on the first floor? I could come by some afternoon when school is out and we could practice."

"Say," Roy Hart interjected in his hearty voice, as he stood at the head of the table, ready to slice into the roast moose. "There's too much talking going on. No one's eating my wife's cooking."

It was a fairly large gathering, seven in all. From her place at the bottom of the table near the kitchen door, Bea looked up the table, past the Weavers, past Matt, to the two girls sitting one on each side of her husband at the other end of the table. Bea had worked hard all day preparing the dinner. She was so tired she scarcely touched the small portion on her plate.

Bea felt a shiver of joy run up and down her spine. Everyone seemed to be enjoying the meal. Herb and the schoolteachers had already called for second helpings. Roy had gone down early in the morning to Main Street to get the moose and goose from the cold storage locker. But he'd forgotten the wine. Instead of calling Curly and asking him to deliver it in the cab, he went all the way back to town and didn't return until close to five, because he got caught up in a gin rummy game at Johnny Bugg's and his luck was good. Bea had hoped he would help her. She had woken up feeling worse than usual and the extra burden of three more guests had almost made her weep.

The schoolteachers were nice. Bea had invited them and the Weavers as soon as she heard from Sylvia that the girls had arrived. Fresh up from the States, she reflected enviously. They looked so different. They didn't have that air of aloofness, an aura of mystery that she saw in the young women in Wrangell.

The girls were chic and well-tailored. Both wore smart suits. The fragrance of their perfume drifted in the air above the table. Their nails were brilliantly polished, catching the eye as did the bracelets dancing on their wrists. Lydia was very attractive. She wore her auburn hair swept up from the temples and behind her head, exposing her small white ears and slender neck. The other one, Victoria, was older than her friend—about thirty, Bea decided—with a round flushed face and long heavy lids that lay over her large brown eyes, giving her an air of sleepiness.

Yes, she was glad she had invited them over, Bea thought. She knew she had been selfish about it for she wanted desperately to be near someone from the States, just to sit near and watch them and grow envious. Looking over at the girls, she wished that she had invited Chris and Dave too. It would have been more fun for the girls. She was the one that was being selfish. She should have given them an opportunity to meet a few of the eligible bachelors in town.

Herb was talking about Wrangell's first school building, a barn that the first schoolteacher had cleared out herself. Herb talked about the past wistfully, the way most people like to do as if the present were just something that had to be lived in.

Rain. Bea closed her eyes for a moment. She was always conscious of the rain in Wrangell, its persistence. For a moment her whole body rebelled against an attack of dizziness. She rose and moved into the kitchen. Holding on to the sink with both hands, she looked out the rain-washed window. She felt tired, so sick of it all.

Thinking that she must do something to justify her absence, she measured eight tablespoons of coffee into the percolator and returned the can to the gleaming white cupboard with its striped red and white shelf paper. Then she sat down in the chair by the stove, waiting for the coffee to percolate. Through the open door she could hear Herb's voice.

She was trembling. She hadn't felt well since her son's death, three years ago this December. Oh Tom, Tom!" He was so strong and healthy not like his feeble mother. Looking at his strong, square face, she would swell with joy, for he was her flesh, her boy. Big Boy was what she called him when they were alone. She let the grief wash over her. It was unrelenting, like the rain. And ever since Tom's death, she had been failing. It was difficult lately to keep up with the housework, even though there was little to do with only two people in the house.

It wasn't just Tom's death. Hard as that was, it had shattered the facade which hid her weakness. Now the rain and dreariness of life in this small fishing town poured down on her, soaking into her flesh. After eighteen years, she felt unable to bear another minute of it and longed to leave Wrangell forever.

And now into this town came two new girls, fresh from the States. Thank God, they were only committed to a few months until school let out for summer vacation. They would be able to leave before it got under their skins, as it did hers. She wasn't strong enough to fight it and she couldn't ask Roy for help. He had no intention of ever leaving Wrangell. They had arrived in Wrangell when their marriage was young and Tom only two years old and Roy knew immediately that he wanted to stay. Forever. Wrangell suited him, it was what he wanted, needed actually.

Bea frowned, hearing the rain thundering down on the roof of their house. Roy had built it for her after Tom's death, out at the edge of town beyond the power plant. It was one of the few stucco houses in town. He hoped it would lift her spirits but she felt it was an anchor, something to hold her down and keep her pinned to Wrangell. She hated the whole idea, her heart rebelled, but she never said a word to Roy the whole time it was being built.

In the living room Herb was still talking, interrupted occasionally by questions from the schoolteachers. Bea slid the percolator from the hot plates of the range, then sat down by the stove, exhausted. The rain filled the kitchen with its unending beat, both urgent and powerful.

It took being in it year after year to understand the undermining effect of the rain. After a while, it crept into people's bones, poisoned them. It made people fall into hopeless ruts, until they began to fill with rage without being aware of it, taking it out on themselves, their mates, their children. She'd watched the people of Wrangell during a long stretch of rain. The men stayed inside, cooped up playing cards, drinking, restless. The women shopped, not bothering with umbrellas because they couldn't hold groceries and umbrellas both. The children played in it, one of them always coughing. After a while the drinking in Wrangell got worse. Gambling became less of a recreation and more of a necessity. Women screamed at their husbands for losing their summer's savings. Parties grew into knock-down affairs, contests to see who could drink the most or seduce the other fellow's wife. Everyone's morals deteriorated. Deaths, of course, were common whether it rained or not. Men drowned, got killed by bears, died of tuberculosis. Divorces were frequent and sudden, especially when a woman's belly swelled out at the wrong time of the year, after her husband had been away for months fishing or trapping. And the fights. Sometimes at night, in the cabins and shacks along the harbor's edge, she would heard a chair go crashing against a wall, a table overturned, a woman screaming, kids crying. It rained all the time, summer and winter, spring and fall, numbing her veins until she felt soggy.

That's why Bea hadn't been out of the house in weeks. That's why she was frightened lately by the fact that Roy was spending most of his time on Main Street in Johnny Bugg's bar. That's why she wanted to go south for a few months to regain her vitality so she would be able to fight against the apathy brought on by the rain.

Only the rare sunny days made Bea happy. She remembered an extraordinary summer years back when the sun shone for two weeks straight, from four in the morning until eleven at night, splashing the sky with colors, the clear orange and yellows of dawn, the scarlets and magentas of evening. The colors were left in the sky resting on clouds long after the sun had disappeared; the channel rippled with flashes of flame reflected from the clouds. Bea remembered running down to the edge of the channel, bewitched and thrilled, hoping that next summer would contain such a stretch of glorious weather.

By the sound of the dinner things, now only an occasional hesitant tinkle of glass scraping against silverware, Bea realized dinner must be nearly over. She forced herself to rise, took the percolator off the stove and went into the dining room.

In the lamp and ceiling light, the bare plastered walls shone ivory white. She had scrubbed them with soap and water only this week. This morning she had vacuumed the modern French furniture and waxed the Zenith and the breakfront. All in all, the dining room and the living room beyond it were immaculate, the work of an energetic and industrious woman. But she wasn't. She knew it. She was completely inert from the moment she lifted herself out of bed in the morning until that moment at night when she crawled back into it. Only the conditioning of her rigid childhood in Vermont, the years of building a routine based on self-discipline and hard work, kept her going.

Bea set the percolator on the aluminum hot plate and let Roy pour the coffee. Roy was getting fat around the waistline. It came from hanging around the town during the winter months instead of guiding tourists through the dense forests of the Mainland looking for grizzlies. This was the other present she received from Tom's death, although she had been begging Roy to stop for years before. She was scared sick every time he left, endangering his own life to cater to the whims of rich men looking for expensive thrills. Bea adored that little paunch of a belly as she adored everything about her husband.

Bea brought the upside-down cake to the table, then began clearing the dishes. Lydia rose to help and Bea smiled at her gratefully.

"I'll bet you've never seen so much rain before?" Roy asked, addressing Lydia as she stacked the dishes on the table.

"No, I must confess —"

"It rains like the devil up here," said Roy. Bea knew he was addressing her, as well as the girls. "And blows until you think the island's going to sink. But just wait a little while. Wait until you get a taste of Wrangell's freedom. We fish commercially only so many months of the year—the best fishing in the world, too, pleasure instead of work—and then, well, there's nothing else to do but do what you want."

"Say, Roy," Herb interrupted, "that's not true for everyone. I more or less punch a time card...."

"The hunting is terrific, too," Roy went on, ignoring Herb. "And there's trout fishing—I know streams that don't know what a hook feels like...."

Bea led the way into the kitchen.

"The men have it a lot better than we do," she said in a low voice, turning to Lydia. "I do hope you like it up here, despite this infernal rain. With summer almost here, it should start to let up some."

"Everyone up here has been so friendly and nice," the girl replied, "I don't know how to thank you for that wonderful dinner. I won't forget it."

"Some of the fishermen don't have a good season," Herb was saying, contradicting Roy's optimistic picture. "A few bad breaks with their equipment, plus a poor fishing season, and they can't make enough money to pull them through the winter, especially . . . " He stopped abruptly.

"Especially if they spend all their money in the bars!" said Roy indignantly. "Look at me! I'm not the best fisherman in Wrangell and I don't have a particularly large boat, but I can catch enough fish to make it through the winter without having to take another job to make ends meet."

Roy had the table all to himself from then on, rambling on about the pleasures of Wrangell while they sat down to coffee and cake.

"Do you know, I haven't been to the States or seen my parents in eighteen years!" declared Roy. "I'm perfectly content, so why leave?" Roy's gaze moved across from Lydia to Victoria and back again. Bea noticed that Lydia's blue eyes were rapt with attention as she listened to Roy. "I work when I want to, sleep when I want to, go hunting and fishing when I want to. I don't think a man could ask for anything more. I'm independent and I like being independent."

"When I go to the States," Bea interjected—she paused, stabbed by a backlog of despair, recalling the last time she went to the States right after Tom's funeral—"I have to go alone. Roy just won't leave Wrangell."

"Heck, with a woman it's different," Roy announced. "I guess they need a change. I had my fill of the States long ago."

Bea had to check the flood of Roy's enthusiasm before it poisoned the girls. With a twinge of guilt, she proposed a game of poker, which was met with a wave of approval. Bea loved poker. After reading detective novels, poker was her favorite pleasure. Roy became house man and counted out a stack of chips for each of the players and they began playing.

Bea played with glee, concentrating on her cards with death-like tension. Her weariness dissolved, like sugar, in the heat of the game. Luck favored the school principal; he accumulated the bulk of the chips on the table.

About one o'clock in the morning, Herb stopped, shook his head as if to clear it and said, "Oh, I just remembered. I saw Dave today..."

"Of course, you did," Sylvia said with annoyance. "He filled a tooth for you."

"Yes. Well, he wanted me to bring the girls . . ." He glanced down at his watch. "Oh well, it wasn't anything important."

At two o'clock, Lydia and Victoria both yawned at the same time. Bea offered them more coffee, which they accepted and the game went on. At three the girls yawned again.

"Say," Lydia asked, "when do you people go to sleep in Wrangell?"

"Oh, we forgot," Bea said, looking up, dismayed, knowing the game would come to an end. "You're not used to our hours yet."

"We just don't pay much attention to time here," Roy interjected.

As Bea stood on the threshold watching the girls stoop to get into Herb's Studebaker in the steady fall of the rain, the excitement from the card game dimmed in her veins and vanished. She stared dull-eyed at the car as it turned about and lurched forward past the power plant, splashing through the mud. At the edge of her consciousness, she heard the hum of the motor in the power plant across the road. By the light of the lamp post at the edge of the road she could see the puddles in the road and the fall of the rain, glistening dully.

The sweet fresh contact of air revived her to some extent but she felt no better. As Bea closed the door, she heard the flush of the water tank in the lavatory where Roy had gone. She sat down and fingered the imitation pearl necklace at her throat. She wondered if Chris had seen Lydia. But he must have, considering the size of Wrangell.

Whenever she thought of Chris, she remembered her son. They had been good friends, despite the difference in their ages. Chris was almost 10 years older than Tom, yet they appreciated and understood one another. They fed each other's ideals like real friends do. Chris had brought the float house from the Bucci's so he and Tom would have a place to hang out. They used it for storing outboards, tackles and clothes, and as a shelter when they needed to get away. They were both cocky and headstrong, full of wrath and pride, embittered by their conflicts, Tom against his father, Chris against Theodore. Tom and Roy scrapped constantly; there was always friction in the air when they were together. Tom wanted to be on his own at sixteen. He hated school and wanted to quit. Roy, of course, ordered him to remain in school. Roy expected his son to assist on his boat during the fishing season if he wanted to work, but instead Tom pitched fish at the Ballard Cannery. Chris had changed somewhat since those days. He was still a little haughty but he had lost the air of bitterness, since his father had left.

Chris was thirty now. It was time for him to get married. He should go south and find himself a girl. The few available girls in Wrangell had all tried to catch his interest but with little success. They didn't even bother to try anymore. Fanny Regis had a small hold on Chris when she was single. Then like a flash, Alan Sundberg came back from the States and married her so quick, it seemed like it was prearranged. Chris didn't seem to take it very hard. Still there was gossip about Chris and Fanny whenever Alan went south, rumors that Chris went over to the Regis house to visit Fanny and stayed late or that she went down to the float house with him. Chris had been dating Helen Connell last summer but they seemed to drift apart. Chris just couldn't seem to settle down; he liked his independence too much. She wondered if the new schoolteacher was going to change that.

5

I HAVE TO GO, GIFF," CHRIS SAID. They were standing on the bridge in the harbor, looking at the naked flanks of the *Verna* on the gridiron, her starboard listing against the row of creosote piling, her underbelly glowing with a fresh coat of copper paint. Two men in hip boots were slapping on the second coat of paint. "Marvin's freighter should be unloaded by now. If you need me, I'll be there, checking the supplies."

"You ordered plenty of trap wire, I hope," Giff said, thinking he should exert some authority. "Some of those traps out in Sumner are about worn out."

"Plenty," Chris said, matter-of-factly. "We'll start repairing them on Monday."

Giff rubbed his jaw with his fingers as he watched the tall figure move down the bridge and disappear between the shacks in the native section.

Giff's throat rattled and he spat dry. His mouth was parched and burning as it always was before he had his first drink. He decided to go to the bar. It would be open by the time he walked there. He didn't have to return to the gridiron to remove the *Verna* until the tide came in. The *Verna* would be floating and ready then, ready for the season. A small glow of pride welled up in him, spread across his chest and trickled down to his finger tips for the *Verna* was more than just a purse seiner to him. The *Verna* had been built to Theodore's specifications by Yorgensen and named after Theodore's wife. Giff skippered her through all the years with reverence for the *Verna* was a good ship.

The quiet of the morning air was pierced by the harsh, clucking warble of ravens gorging themselves around the mud flats of Shake's Island and under the piling of the houses along the harbor's edge. From where he stood Giff could see the rear of Chris' float house. He spat again, distastefully. The little brat, he'd thought years ago when Chris bought the float house from Mitch Bucci. There wasn't enough room for him in the Ballard home on the hill.

The roof of his mouth ached against his inquisitive demanding tongue. He'd have a good stiff double before he had breakfast. He had to be sure to remember to have breakfast this morning. Lately he'd been forgetting. Generally by noon, food repulsed him.

But Giff didn't move. Instead he crossed the bridge to the opposite rail and let his eye wander out past the breakwater to the expanse of the channel. From this vantage point, the channel seemed almost flat. The water looked striped and painted like a map: black lines enfolding geometrical patterns of crimson, brass, brown and blue-green all the way across to Elephant Nose, massive in green repose.

His thirst grew into a rage. His throat ached for the first sharp swallow of whiskey. It would stimulate his frazzled nerves, settle them down into their proper places. God damn, he should have had an eye opener in his room when he got up.

Giff placed his hands on the sagging board rail. The rain-washed sky was vast, arching over the land in a sweep of blue. For a moment he thought of how it was when he was on the bridge of the *Verna*, cutting across Sumner Strait with the engine wide open in the fever of the season, steering from the controls on the exposed deck, alone in the small square tower of the flying bridge, master of the men below, of himself, of the world. He gazed at the vastness of the sky for hours on end, in a rush of emotion, every nerve in his body vibrating. He viewed the mightiness above him with surprise, and even comradeship. He was glad that he lived under it, that the cathedral dome of the sky was his alone in the summer.

As he walked down the length of the small wooden bridge, his footsteps clattered, disturbing the quiet of the floats below where the fishermen stood bent over tubs after washing their breakfast dishes.

The hotel bar was empty when Giff arrived. He swung his legs over one of the stools and eased onto it.

"What'll it be, Giff?" Max asked cheerfully.

Giff loathed the bartender's bright attitude, his eagerness to get on with the business of getting his customers plastered again.

"Double," Giff mumbled.

It wasn't until later, maybe around noon, when he was plastered, that he could bear being around Max. The familiarity of the place surrounded him— the smells of cigarette smoke and stale beer, the quiet. It was usually quiet in the morning. Giff could enjoy his first few drinks by himself before the stragglers pushed through the door, followed by Holly Dancey and her crowd. By then it was noon and he felt a gnawing in his stomach but he never considered getting something to eat when his belly was full of liquor. The place was warm then and cozy. The noise of the barroom became a full, rich chord, permanent and sustaining, a prelude to the uproar of the night. By then he wasn't thinking of anything but Theodore Ballard, scavenging through his memories of his friend of the past, wading down glass by glass through the passing years, deep into the ash of memory where a man could resurrect a friend. "Beautiful morning," Max chirped, wiping the rim of a beer glass with a fresh towel. He held the glass chest-high, his wrist moving deftly as he twirled the glass through his fingers, while his eyes stared out the front window.

Giff jerked up. He heard voices. Someone had entered the bar without his noticing. God damn, he'd better go eat breakfast and straighten out. He turned his head.

Buster Fountain, the owner of the hotel, was shooting horses at the other end of the bar with Red Parker and Jack Jewell. Buster must have won for he collected double for the drinks and said, "You guys'll never learn, will ya?"

"Hey," Giff called out, "What's going on over at the cannery?"

Red's lips were stained with the red wine he was sipping from his glass. "Hello, Bull," he said. "Old Bull." Red looked cold sober but he was acting screwy.

"Game last night?"

Red nodded with a secret smile and bent down to sip his wine. "Any big winners?"

Red answered the first question. "The freighter'll be unloaded by eight tonight."

Giff wondered what the hell was going on. Was he going crazy or was Red?

Jack filled him in. "Red won six hundred last night. Mostly off me."

Red grinned, so happy with his streak of luck that he couldn't wield his mind and tongue.

Giff laughed. "You can afford it," he said to Jack, who owned two profitable river boats that carried supplies and tourists up the Stikine River. "It's about time someone else got some."

From the lobby they could hear a woman's voice, clear and sparkling, "Can you tell us where we can find Mr. Buster Fountain?"

Two girls came striding into the bar. The auburn-haired one wore a cream-colored jacket and tan slacks, while the other girl wore a loose cardigan which barely concealed the lush curve of her breasts in a tight-fitting sweater beneath.

"Why, good morning Lydia, Victoria," Buster exclaimed. "Did you sleep well last night?"

"Yes, thank you." The one named Lydia shed a bright smile upon Buster who lapped it up, beaming happily. At once the room was charged with their presence, as if the bar had become the set for a movie in the making.

"What can I do for you, girls?" Buster asked, beaming with pleasure, mopping the bar with a towel in a slow circular motion.

"Mr. Fountain . . ."

"Buster, if you don't mind," the hotel owner said. "If you call me Mister, the trade might go elsewhere." Suddenly the bar was still. Giff could hear the towel scratching on the dry spot on the bar, the slow rasp of his own breathing. He downed his drink. It wasn't any of his business what the girls wanted from Buster.

"We've just about given up all hope of finding a house."

"Ah," Buster said. "I thought you were taking one of Guy Eaton's cottages."

"Well, there seems to be some delay. We were wondering if perhaps you might be able to help us."

Buster had stopped mopping and spread his fist out on the crumpled towel, squeezing it as he contemplated his reply. The bastard, Giff thought, unable to repress a stealthy chuckle. Buster was probably trying to figure out how to get one of them into his secret room upstairs. It was the only room with a private bath, besides the bridal suite. Not even Buster's wife knew about its existence.

Buster rubbed his nose with his forefinger, apparently stymied.

Giff heaved himself down from the stool and said to the girls, "There's a pretty nice float house down the road a ways that might be available."

"Heavens!" The brunette exclaimed. "Show us where it is!"

Giff shuddered with anxiety, unaccustomed to the radiant smile flashed upon him. God damn, why the hell did he have to open his big mouth?

"Can we see it today?"

"Well . . ."

"Who's the owner?"

"I'll tell you what," Giff said after a moment of deliberation. "I'll call him up right now. He's at the cannery checking on some supplies." He wished that the girls would stop him. But they were too intent. Giff walked around the bar and whirled the crank on the telephone box. For a moment, Giff convinced himself that Chris would appreciate meeting the girls, even if it meant renting the float house. After all, Chris had no use for it anymore. He waited as Cliff Waverly, the telephone operator, connected him with the cannery.

"Would you care for a drink?" he heard Buster ask the girls.

The door opened from Main Street. A clean-shaven, middle-aged man in a black suit, entered the bar, leading two sleek black Doberman pinschers. Giff recognized Sam Flannery with surprise.

"What brings you to our fair town, Sam?" Buster asked the man who hailed from Port Alexander.

"Is that Giff Weeks?" Sam said, stooping to unfasten the leash buckles from the collars of the dogs.

"Sure is," Giff replied, turning away from the mouthpiece he held in his hand. "Bar business must be bad for you to leave Port Alexander."

"Thought I'd take a little trip before fishing season," Sam replied. "Just came in on the mail boat."

The girls were admiring the two trim, shiny dogs who were behaving well.

Giff heard the voice of Florence Savard, who helped Chris in the office at the cannery at the other end of the wire. "Hello, Florence. May I speak to Chris?" he asked.

Florence hesitated a moment at the other end of the wire, then said, "Chris is out in the yard checking supplies, Giff."

"Well, tell Chris to come down to the hotel bar as soon as he can. I have to talk to him about something important." Giff hung up and went around the bar to the table where the girls had seated themselves.

"Say, I'm Giff Weeks," he said quickly.

"I'm Victoria Blaissing and this is Lydia Prince," said the brunette with the lush figure.

"He's busy, isn't he?" Lydia asked.

"He'll be down in a minute," Giff replied.

He saw the barber pause outside the front of the plate glass window of the bar and peer inside. A moment later, the door opened and the barber stepped in, wearing his white smock. In a rush, he lurched towards the table, spilling out a greeting even before the girls noticed him.

"Hello, Giff," he blurted out, approaching with a hearty, nice-to-see-you-friend smile pasted on his pale face.

What the hell could he do? " Girls, this is Clarence Wick, the only barber in town and a good one at that."

All of a sudden Giff hated Clarence. He hadn't thought much about the crap game the other night but now as he watched Clarence pull up a chair and order a round of beers for the table, his mind filled with a black hatred towards the small, wiry barber. He despised the little bastard. It was like a tidal wave rushing through him, tumultuous, all-engulfing. He quivered with rage as he sat near Clarence.

"Beautiful day, isn't it? Left the shop with two customers in it just to get a little fresh air," Clarence was saying. "Don't have much of a chance to do that cooped up in a shop all day."

Victoria smiled with pleasure. "Thanks for the beer. This is such a friendly town."

"After you get to know it. . . . Well, put it this way, after you stay here six months, you might want to go back to the States." The barber's eyes were fixed on the other girl, the pretty one. The lavatory door slammed shut in the rear room. After inserting some change in the jukebox, Sam snapped his fingers at his two dogs who were resting by one of the booths. They came bounding into the bar before their master.

"Glad to see you, Sam!" Giff waved to him. The strains of *Blue Moon* filled the air.

The two pinschers stood side by side below Sam at the bar, then edged over to the table, their fiery blue-green eyes unblinking. One dog nudged Clarence's arm, then plunked his chin upon Clarence's crossed leg. Lydia stroked the other dog's head but the animal backed away. It waited, nudged Lydia again. The green ring on her finger flashed as she scratched the silky fur that crowned the dog's narrow head but again it backed away. The dog by Clarence's side was behaving in the same querulous manner. It gave a short bark, then trotted around to Victoria. Her fingers fondled the dog's neck fur, but it grew disinterested and loped over to his brother. The two of them approached Lydia, in tandem, each sticking out a right forepaw and running it along her leg. Bending down, Lydia grabbed a paw.

"Hello, fella!" she said with a smile. "Want to shake hands, is that it?" The dogs withdrew their paws, uninterested in the hand shake.

Sam turned from his stool at the bar, eyeing the behavior of his dogs with amusement. "If you give them each a nickel," he said, "they won't bother you." Sam eased down from the stool. "I'm ashamed to confess it, but they're beggars."

Lydia dug into her jacket pocket and held up a quarter and a dime in the palm of her extended hand. "Will this do?" she asked.

"You'll spoil them," Sam replied.

"Here," Clarence said, producing two nickels. "Give 'em these."

Lydia accepted the change. "Where shall I put the money?"

"Just leave the nickels on your palm."

Lydia stretched her upturned hand towards the animals. One dog sniffed, then lapped up one of the nickels in his mouth. He backed against the wall. The other dog stepped forward and scooped the nickel from the girl's palm. Then both of them dashed around behind the bar.

"I've trained them at my bar in Port Alexander," Sam explained. "Now they'll buy themselves a candy bar."

A chorus of barking broke out. Max came running around the bar, with the dogs in hot pursuit, wanting to show the girls how it was done. Holding a Hershey bar high in the air, Max waited until the dog nearest him, staring at the candy with a drooling mouth, had stretched out his tongue with the nickel perched at the tip of the groove. Max picked it off with his thumb and forefinger, wiped it against his uniform and inserted the candy in the dog's mouth.

The two girls giggled.

"Why, that's so cute!" Lydia exclaimed

"I'll be a monkey's uncle," Victoria said.

Sam stuck his fingers in the other dog's mouth and slipped the nickel in his vest pocket. "If you're ever in Port Alexander, drop in and see me," he said. "It's not much of a town—wooden streets, board walks, a few houses—but we like it."

Giff glanced at his watch. What the hell was keeping Chris? He should have told Florence to tell Chris that the teachers were interested in renting the float house. Giff realized that his message had been vague because he wanted to surprise Chris, wanted to see how he would react when he approached the girls for the first time.

Giff's son, Curly, who drove the town's taxi cab, came into the bar just then with his fiance, Diana Johnson, daughter of the owner of the sweet shop.

"Curly," Giff said, "drive over to the Ballard Cannery and tell Chris I want to see him right away."

Curly's eyes were fastened upon Lydia, the presence of his fiance completely forgotten. Giff knew his son hadn't heard a word he said.

"Did you hear what I said, Curly? Go get Chris."

"Aren't you going to introduce us, Pop?"

Giff laughed, then made the introductions. "Now hurry!" he repeated.

Diana sat down by Giff. She was a tall girl with a small body, nearly all legs like a model. She moved with a smooth, swinging action so precise that Giff wondered if Diana practiced her walk before a mirror. She had a long slender neck which she kept exposed by wearing her chestnut-colored hair in a short clipped bob that swept close to her ears. Diana's presence made the gathering settle into a more intimate mood. With her bright smile and sharp voice, she assumed instant command.

"We'd like to have you up for dinner," Diana said after a round of introductions and inquiries about how the girls were enjoying the town and the weather. "We know how hard it is to eat at a restaurant all the time."

"Well . . ." Victoria began, taken aback by the sudden invitation.

"Mom can make the best venison roast," Diana said. "Do you like deer meat?""

"I've never had venison," confessed Victoria. They were still discussing the

The girls wandered into the bedroom which faced the road above, then walked back through the living room into the kitchen which overlooked the harbor that curved behind Shake's Island. From the window they could see old weather-beaten piling jutting up from the gray water, skiffs and trollers moored randomly to floats, and sea gulls circling the harbor, shrieking plaintively.

"Isn't it a dream, Lyddy?"

Lydia seemed hesitant about making a decision. Giff wondered if she was troubled by the way Chris was behaving. What the hell was the matter with the guy? Giff was worried. He wished he hadn't gotten himself messed up with this fool business.

"Would you care for a drink?" Chris asked. "I think there's some whiskey around here."

"No, thanks," said Victoria.

They heard footsteps rumbling down the board planks from the road.

"I hope I'm not intruding?"" It was Herb Weaver. He looked at the girls, "I called at the hotel. They said you were down here considering renting Chris' float house. I just talked to Guy Eaton. He said he'll definitely have a cottage vacant by the end of the week. They're lovely houses and they're situated just above the school building. Ideal when winter comes. That is, if you girls decide to stay for the winter." He paused, looked from one to the other. "You haven't decided on a house yet, have you?" he asked. "Well, no, we haven't, Mr Weaver," said Lydia with uncertainty in her voice. Giff could tell that she was actually considering the float house. It was snug and sturdily built, rising and falling with the flux of the tides, a novelty for girls from the States. Perhaps they would prefer that.

"If you can rent one of Guy's houses you're in luck," observed Chris.

"Yes," Giff added, seeing the value in siding with his boss, "Guy Eaton is a good landlord."

Herb chimed in, "Guy minds his own business, has reasonable rents and he makes it a practice never to enter his tenant's houses unless there's an emergency, something like frozen pipes or water leaks."

"Well, that sounds just fine," Lydia said, after a quick glance at Victoria. "Thanks for helping us in our search," she said, smiling at Giff, then turning to Chris. "We almost had you for our landlord."

"I'll take you up there now, girls," Herb said. "Guy said you should come over to look at the house."

After the principal left with the schoolteachers, Giff and Chris remained on the porch.

"Shall I call Curly to take us back?" Giff asked.

"No."

Chris went into the kitchen, opened a cupboard and found the pint. It was empty. "I think there's a bottle somewhere in the place," he said. "I came down here last night with Fanny and killed this one."

"The bed's not messed up," Giff observed. Chris ignored him, moving into the small lavatory room off the kitchen. He began searching under a pile of boots and slickers, then emerged with a bottle of whiskey.

It was hard for Giff to realize that this boy was his boss. He could never feel like they were on the same plane. Never stir up a spark of interest between them like he could with his father. Theodore was his best friend. He never could speak candidly to Chris. Maybe when he was drunk. Sometimes when he was really plastered and thoughts of Theodore crowded his mind, he spoke to Chris. But it was weak and incoherent and Chris never referred to it the next day. And that was all right. It was OK to leave it that way. It wasn't possible to make a connection with Theodore's son. Not for Giff. There was only one man like Theodore. No one else could hold a candle to Theodore. He had to leave it that way for now. For forever. Never to see Theodore again. He didn't want to see him again, really. Not the way he was now.

Chris ran a knife around the seal of the cap and filled the glasses.

"Here's to a good season," Giff said awkwardly.

Chris said, looking out the window, "You catch fish every year whether the season's good or bad."

"But the town could do with a good season as a whole."

Chris lit a cigarette. "You know, Giff," he said, sipping his drink slowly. "I think she wanted to rent the house."

"Why the hell didn't you give her a sales pitch?" Giff asked.

"I wanted her to decide for herself. Either way it makes no difference to me." He laughed. "I better get back to the cannery." He set his glass down on the wooden drainboard. "It's about time you got the *Verna* off the gridiron."

Giff and Chris parted at the corner by Marie's grocery store, Chris heading down Main Street towards town. Whistling, Giff lumbered through the row of shacks that constituted the native section of Wrangell, although actually there were many native sections in Wrangell, if you wanted to consider most of the houses along the harbor side. At the head of the bridge, Giff climbed down to his skiff which was tied by a bowline around a piling, and rowed over to the *Verna*, floating now above the cross-ties of the gridiron.

"Just about to take her off myself," Clyde, the engineer, said to Giff. Giff ascended the vertical ladder to the bridge above the pilot house and fired up the new Cummings diesel engine. A roaring growl filled the still air and Giff eased the throttle, waiting for the motor to warm.

He waited, as in a dream that lay frozen in his memory. Waited, remembering the night the seiner's engine was warming for her first trial run, after Theodore had christened the thirty-nine foot boat in honor of his wife, Verna, with a formal champagne christening in Yorgensen's Yard. Later with his family aboard, Theodore stepped behind the wheel in the pilot house and assumed command of the *Verna's* maiden trial run. In the bright moonlight, the *Verna's* diesel purred as she warmed. Then with a roar of eagerness, Theodore pulled back on the throttle as the *Verna* surged out into the channel. It had been a wonderful and successful run and a few hours later when Theodore docked the *Verna*, Theodore sent home his wife and two kids while he and Giff strode triumphantly into Johnny Bugg's bar to celebrate the event.

They had drunk steadily until midnight, Giff noting as always how the crowd avoided getting near Theodore. He was always surprised by their diffidence. It seemed to him they should be interested in hearing about how the *Verna* behaved on her trial run or in mixing with a man who had made a powerful figure of himself, who had brought a lot of business to the town. Theodore believed in Wrangell. He had his boats built there instead of in the States. He had risked his own fortune again and again, enlarging his cannery until it had grown into one of the finest in the Southeastern. When automobiles started arriving in the town, Theodore had campaigned in vain for paving Main Street. Very few people sided with Theodore, very few could recognize the importance of such an investment in civic pride. A great majority of the citizens of Wrangell, although they apparently respected Theodore, kept away from him, more from envy than anything else, Giff thought. Because Theodore had the money he sent Chris and Patty to schools in the States to receive a better education than they could at the Wrangell school. And Theodore associated little with most of the folks in town, was almost cold and aloof towards them, but that was because he was always so busy working, improving his business, making more connections in the States to dispose of his canned fish and traveling to Juneau time and time again at his own expense to try to convince the Bureau of Fish and Wildlife Service to extend the salmon fishing season for a few weeks longer. Although he failed, he never grew disheartened and continued his efforts, along with attending to many civic duties in Wrangell. It was because of Theodore's efforts and contributions that they had a new fire truck.

"Verna was certainly happy tonight," Theodore had said, mellowing after the hours of steady drinking in Johnny Bugg's bar. "She's a good wife and I'm proud to have named the boat after her."

"It seemed like she enjoyed the ride," Giff said. He had been aware lately that he usually remained silent until Theodore spoke, then agree with

Theodore wholeheartedly.

Theodore chuckled, "She was as excited as Patty and Chris. Didn't want the boat to turn back." His chuckling swelled into warm laughter and his mustache danced with the motion of his lip. "It was a fine night for a trial run. Plenty of moonlight for visibility."

"You have to be on a boat to see a really fine night," Theodore said. "You have to be away from light and noise—and people. Just the purr of the diesel and the swish of the bow cutting through the still water, the feeling of big things all around you as you stand on the deck soaking in the power and eagerness of the boat, the beauty of the stars . . ."

"Hey," Giff said, laughing, "if I didn't know you better I'd say you were drunk."

"Johnny!" Theodore shouted to the bar owner. "Two more!"

"The *Verna* runs like a dream,'" Giff said. "She has wonderful balance. At first I thought she'd be bottom heavy and list a little to port on account of the fuel tanks . . ."

Theodore interrupted Giff. "Olaf's a good boat builder. It comes naturally for those Norwegians. She ran like a dream, all right. You could scarcely hear her strain to go nine knots."

"Come fishing season she'll make the other seiners in the harbor look sick."

"Wasn't it a glorious night on the channel?" Theodore asked. "I haven't felt that way in years. I should go out more often. On the *Verna* I thought of all the space in the world, all the possibilities. Too often we stay tied down to a home and a job, never noticing the world's complex greatness."

"The skipper of the *Verna* will be a lucky man," Giff said.

"You know who's going to be skipper, don't you?"

"I imagine Pete will. He's been with you the longest and he's one of the best."

"Giff, old boy, get set for a surprise." With that Theodore motioned to Johnny Bugg at the other end of the bar and Johnny approached the two men.

"I want to make a bet with you, Johnny."

The bar that night was packed and Johnny was feeling good.

"Shoot, Theodore. What's the bet?" Johnny pulled out his wallet.

"Giff here is going to be skipper of the *Verna*."

Giff stood up on the foot rail that ran below the stools, jerked up so fast that he sat down again from the effort, unable to believe what he had just heard.

"Yes," Theodore confirmed, turning to Giff. "You're going to skipper the *Verna*."

"Well, what's the bet?" Johnny said somewhat impatiently as customers were clamoring for drinks.

"I'm going to bet you one thousand dollars that Giff will catch more salmon on the *Verna* this coming season than any other seiner in Southeastern."

For a moment Johnny Bugg's face went blank. Even though it seemed that no one was paying any attention to them, the bystanders stopped talking and turned their heads to stare. A circle of quiet lay around them. Johnny was shocked. The bet was fantastically high—just like Theodore—but in that moment of indecision, Johnny must have comprehended the scope of the feat. Hundreds of seiners plied the waters of the Southeastern from Ketchikan to Juneau, from Sitka to Skagway. And there were countless misfortunes that could fall upon any boat during the season: torn nets, ill-timed sets, poor luck, changing tides, engine trouble, collisions, even sinkings.

"Sure, Theodore. Sure, I'll take you up on that bet."

"No money needed for a deposit," Theodore said. "Just your word against mine."

Giff's heart sank and rose for the remainder of the evening like a buoy in a swell.

"I'm thankful for the job as skipper, Theodore. But that bet . . ."

"You'll do it, Giff."

"Hey, Giff," Clyde's voice cut through his dreams. "What are you doing up there on the bridge? Dreaming?"

His engineer's words punctured his thoughts, like someone driving a gaff hook into his memories, snatching them away. Giff grabbed at the spokes of the wheel, glaring at the engineer below but refraining from comment. For a moment Giff had imagined he was at the hotel bar. It was getting bad when he started thinking of Theodore outside of the bar.

Glancing about, Giff threw the *Verna* in gear, eased her off the gridiron, throttled the boat around Shake's Island and came abreast of the float where most of the seiners lay moored. Giff brought the starboard beam alongside the *Happy Day* and shut off the engine.

"Fit as a fiddle," Clyde said.

"Yeah," Giff answered. "Better cast the spare bumper aft." He climbed over the rail of the *Verna*, then across the *Happy Day* and strode up the long narrow float, between the pressing hulls and masts and trolling piles of gill-netters and trollers and seiners. He felt like getting into a crap game. There should be one going by now. He felt lucky as hell all of a sudden. Things had worked out better than he expected this afternoon.

Giff was ahead of the crap game by about a hundred and twenty-five dollars when Chris and Dave strode into the hotel bar. Giff stood up, feeling good because he was winning, because he wasn't drunk, because he had created a new kind of excitement in the town today. He'd go have a drink with Chris and Dave at the bar.

They were both wearing new suits and hats. They looked like tourists.

"Hi Giff!" they both called out, with what seemed like new respect.

"Can I buy you eager beavers a drink with my winnings?" Giff asked. "You know these schoolteachers have given me luck." He counted the wad of crumpled green backs in his hands. "One eighteen ahead."

"I guess you can," Dave said with a smile.

What was wrong with Dave? He never seemed to give a damn for women. God knew, he could have his pick of any woman in the town. Giff wondered where Dave fit in.

The door swished open and Clarence Wick and his friend Steve Svenson entered the bar. They ordered a beer without glancing in their direction, carried the beer with them out into the other room and stood by the huddle of men at the last booth watching the crap game.

"What's this?" Chris asked. "Clarence in the bar for the second time today!" Women are driving him to drink, I guess."

"That son of a bitch!" Giff snarled.

Curly's cab glided to an uncharacteristically smooth stop out in front of the bar, as if it carried fragile glassware. Curly jumped out of the driver's side of the car, made a swift dash around the rear and pulled open the door.

"First time I've ever seen Curly do that for anyone," Dave commented.

Lydia and Victoria stood on the walk as they paid Curly for the fare. The girls went into the hotel and Giff could hear their footsteps ascending the stairs in the hallway.

Chris and Dave could scarcely sit still.

"You sure they won't feel like we're butting in?" Dave asked.

"Hell, I've told you I'm in." Chris patted Giff on the shoulder. "Giff, here, fixed it all up."

Clarence moved into the room, set his half-finished beer on the bar, and strolled through the side door towards the landing.

"You boys better step on it," Giff observed.

"Well, OK," Dave said, with an uncomfortable sigh and followed Chris through the door.

In a moment Chris came rumbling down the stairs three at a time.

"Say, Giff, what's their room number?"

"Second room down from mine," he said. "I think it's one-oh-nine."

Chris disappeared, then reappeared a few moments later, thumping down the stairs again. He ran into the bar and ordered eight bottles of beer. His black eyes were bright as he glanced at Giff with a grin. "Can't go up to their room empty handed. We feel sorry for them, all alone in this big lonely town."

"What's Dave all steamed up about?"

"Believe it or not, Victoria."

Chris gathered the bottles and dashed up the stairs.

Giff ordered a straight shot, changed his mind and had Max mix it with 7-Up. Sometimes he sweetened his drink even though he disliked it that way. Later he would switch back to straight shots or water high to keep his sense of taste working.

Chris was so damned hot all of a sudden, like Theodore in a way. When Johnny Bugg reneged on the thousand dollar bet, Theodore was steaming. He never entered Johnny Bugg's bar again.

Giff remembered the season that year. The fish were elusive during the first runs. The salmon had easy access to the streams because the creek mouths, out of bounds for purse seiners according to the Bureau of Fish and Wildlife Service, were swollen from the heavy rains. However, frantic to do well, Giff drove the *Verna*, without lights, at twilight and before dawn to the mouths of creeks choked with thrashing hordes of salmon and made his sets. Time and again, the *Verna* pulled alongside the unloading platform of the Ballard Cannery with only its nose sticking out above the half-submerged vessel, almost swamped by the load of salmon they carried while other boats arrived mostly empty. So successful was he that other boats started trailing the *Verna* to find out where the fish were running. Giff now had the problem of ducking his followers and seining illegally under the noses of the Fish and Wildlife cutters. He was kept on his guard day and night. And, as he had feared on the *Verna*'s trial run, the *Verna* did list to port, but only when the fuel tanks were half empty. He had to spend the greater part of the week rearranging the tanks and fuel lines on the starboard side so that they would empty, resetting the gauges of the fuel lines with the proper balance. When the second run of the salmon began, all the purse-seiners starting catching fish but Giff had the edge on them with the speed and Theodore favored the *Verna* just a trifle when the boats were lined up off the cannery's docks waiting to be unloaded. The season ended just about when the second run was getting good and Giff for once in his life was grateful. Dazed and relieved, he trudged down to the hotel, killed half a fifth and slept without waking for twenty hours.

The tally sheet of the Ballard Cannery and the other two canneries in Wrangell revealed that the *Verna* had brought in twice as many salmon as any other purse seiner in Wrangell. With this conclusive information, and with information gathered from most of the other canneries in Southeastern, Theodore and Giff marched down one evening to Johnny Bugg's bar to demand payment of the bet.

"Hell, Theodore," Johnny Bugg said with a half hearted guffaw. "I forgot about the bet the day after we made it when I realized how drunk we must have been to make such a fool bet. How could anyone find out whose boat caught the most salmon?"

Theodore opened his briefcase and drew out tally sheets from his cannery and wires from other canneries in Southeastern. "Read these and you'll see how it's done."

Johnny's eyes lost their luster as he glanced at a few of the wires. "Hell, Theodore, you ain't serious?"

"You know very well I am, Johnny. Giff worked his ass off to win this bet and I intend to be paid."

"Now listen, I've had enough of this shit. That bet was crazy and I'm washing my hands of the whole thing."

"Johnny," Theodore's voice was tight but Giff could hear the explosive anger which lay beneath the surface, "if you want more conclusive evidence, I'll go to every town in Southeastern and get notarized tally sheets from the canneries."

Giff held his breath and his heart swelled with joy. Theodore's determination to collect the wager showed his commitment to Giff for he knew that Theodore didn't give one hang for the face value of the bet.

"You're crazy, Theodore. You could never do it. Anyway,"" Johnny Bugg concluded, "I've washed my hands of the whole cock-eyed thing."

"Then I've washed my hands of you and this place, Johnny. You'll never see me in here again."

From that day on neither of them ever set foot in Johnny Bugg's bar. Even with Theodore gone, Giff never even considered it.

The scrape of chairs, the shuffle of feet in the hotel bar, woke Giff from his reverie. The fire siren was shrieking, rising to a crescendo. The siren stopped for a moment, as if panting, then made another long pleading wail. The native section. Before Giff could set down his drink the initial sounds that greeted all the fire warnings in Wrangell had swollen into a clamor. Men dashed towards the door, slipping on their jackets. Footsteps clattered down the stairs of the hotel. The bar noises were gone. The crap game was a thing of the past. Everyone, losers and winners alike, headed towards the fire hall up the street by Sackett's First National Bank.

Chris and Dave lunged out the front door and were gone. Clarence Wick came down the stairs in yellow stockings and slippers and stepped outside for a moment but he showed no sign of going any further. As Giff passed him, he noted the barber's uncertain steps and his yellow stockings and wondered why such a detail seemed significant in the excitement of the moment.

The street was full of men, coming from all directions, ducking out of shops, bars and stores. The women stood with packages in their arms, watching. The rivulets of men formed into a steady swift stream as they poured through the gaping doors of the fire hall. The fire bell was still shrieking. Cliff Waverly, the telephone operator, controlled it from his house on the hill. The new fire truck took off, siren moaning. It sprayed gravel into the air as the tires spun, then grabbed the road and rattled down the center of Main Street towards the native section. Giff jumped onto the rear platform of the second truck, grabbed onto the steel bar before him and found himself between Chris and Dave.

The truck cut the corner of the building too sharply as it turned onto Main Street and almost turned over from the weight of its heavy body. As usual, Curly was driving, gunning the engine for all it was worth. Whoever got to the trucks first got to drive since there were no regular firemen on duty. No matter where Curly was when the fire bell rang, he'd generally get to the fire hall in time to drive one of the trucks. Clang. Clang. Clang. The siren screamed above the bell and the truck thundered down the street bouncing and swaying.

Chris and Dave shouted at each other across the top of Giff's head.

"The nerve of the runt!" Chris was bellowing. He snatched off his new felt hat and stuffed it into his pocket. Chris seldom wore a hat and Giff knew this was the end of the new one. "Coming into their room like that. In his slippers!"

Dave shouted back, "Clarence had no business behaving like that!"

"You're God damn right he didn't!" After all, we were there first!"

Dave's outburst of exultation was twice as loud as Chris' words. "Clarence didn't worry me, Chrissy boy. He might be horning in but his sad little eyes were all over your girl!"

"He looked like a scared rabbit," Chris agreed. Unable to hold still on the swaying platform, he nudged Giff who tightened his hand on the bar, ranting aloud about his son.

"God damn that kid of mine. I'm going to have to talk to him. My arms are about to jerk out of their sockets."

Curly didn't ease up off the accelerator until they had passed the front yard of the sawmill. The truck tore into the narrow opening of the native section and jerked to a stop not ten seconds behind the first engine. The men on the side and the rear platforms sprang off and Chris seized the thin hose that was quickly unwound from the drum.

Smoke was pouring out from the roof of Violet Lundy's house. Probably another fire started by one of Violet's five kids stoking the old pot-bellied stove with too much box wood. It wasn't much of a fire, mostly chimney burn, and Giff quickly located the fog nozzle and Chris clamped it into the spout. Sunday suit and all, Chris was the first to go up the ladder that two men had rigged against the clapboard shack, shouting back to Dave.

"He's still back there—drinking our beer."

"He doesn't drink!" Dave returned with a roar of laughter.

The roof of the sagging shack was a whirl of smoke and Chris disappeared into it.

"That's one thing the girls can't do," Dave said. "They can't keep Chris back from a fire. Now he'll fight the blaze until he's black and soaked."

A gust of wind cleared the smoke a little and they could see Chris, crouched by the chimney with the spray in his hand. His tall thin figure stuck like a spider to the sloping, shingled roof. As usual, he had forgotten to don an oxygen mask or slip on asbestos gloves. As the smoke cleared, another man climbed to the roof with an axe but Chris motioned him back, hating to use the axe unless it was absolutely necessary to spare the house from further damage. With his hands, Chris pulled the rotted and smoldering shingles away from the red-hot pipe of the chimney which stuck out of the ridge of the roof. The fire was deep into the roof and Chris took the axe, hacked a hole in the roof, then directed the spray nozzle inside the cavity. In a moment the fire was extinguished, emitting only white smoke.

Chris came down the ladder, as agile as a spider, flagged down a passing car and herded Dave into it. Giff watched the car turn onto the main road, watched the tail light vanish for it was getting dark. Going back to the hotel, Giff thought, back to start where they left off, before Clarence got the lead.

Giff got a ride back into town on the new fire truck with Curly driving.

"Why the hell do you wanna drive so fast all the time?" he asked his son. "The fire is over. Someday you'll kill someone driving the way you drive."

Curly shrugged off the warning. "Hell with these air brakes, I can stop this buggy quicker than the cab."

The truck turned into the fire hall and Giff jumped down, patting its fender. This was the fire truck purchased with funds Theodore had raised. He headed towards the hotel bar without thinking. It had been a pretty good day. He changed his mind and turned around, heading towards Mom's for a steak.

6

THOUGH IT RAINED AGAIN during the night and for most of the morning, towards late afternoon the sun sent a sliver of light through a rip in the gray clouds. It cast a silvery flare on the oil streaks forming patterns upon the shifting waters in the harbor and touched the islands with a warmth that drew wisps of steam off the wet flanks of the trees. The clouds which regrouped on the western horizon lost their gray luster and shone purple and blue, gold and crimson.

Although it was May, it seemed like October. The air was crisp and mellow and still, with that sweet poignant quality which followed every rain in Wrangell. The harbor was quiet, the docks stretching along the edge of the town were quiet and everywhere there was a sense of the vast emptiness of the land.

Towards evening, long before the dance started at the A&N Hall, a last glimmer of light appeared above the clouds on the western horizon, a light as pale as the halo of an angel. A plane went by, sliding slowly through the clear infinite sky. Almost motionless it flew, a black object through the fantastic tracery of purple, rose, gold and blue.

Later, towards the hour of the dance, Venus appeared in the east, piercing the heavens like a big flailing moth, and a lovely white crescent moon hung close by. Behind the islands, across the channel to the west, a sea of airy blue flooded the horizon until it rose and met the deep blue of the night sky.

———————

Lydia hummed while she danced.

At first Chris liked it. It seemed to bring them closer. She had a nice sense of rhythm and her voice was melodic. But when she kept on humming Chris began to grow uneasy because he was pretty high and he felt like an nincompoop dancing.

"Hey, must you hum all the time?"

She pulled back a little to look survey him as he twirled her about the floor. "My first impression of you was correct."

"What is that?" He was mildly sarcastic.

"You surprise me. Most everyone else likes my humming." Her gaiety and self-assurance dimmed his own.

"But enough's enough."

She fell close into his arms again. Her proximity jarred his sense of rhythm.

"What you think of Alaska so far?" he asked.

She toyed with the question, pursing her lips with casual thoughtfulness. "Oh," she said, "it's what I expected."

They both laughed.

"You have to get used to it," he said trying to quench the enthusiasm in his voice. "It takes time. Finally one morning you wake up and realize where you are." It struck him as odd that he wanted to tell her about Wrangell, wanted her to love it too. "Right now, you and me should be on the skiff out somewhere on the channel . . ."

"Oh, I'd rather be here, thank you," said Lydia, both piqued and intrigued.

They laughed again. They laughed easily together. He was very happy and pretty drunk too.

"I think your dance is absolutely wonderful," she went on. "So informal and gay."

"Right now, there should be a moon."

"Hadn't you noticed? The moon's been out for hours."

He grinned. "Once after a dance I took my skiff out in it the moonlight. It was a fourth of July dance and it was pretty late when I got the notion. I rowed for the exercise even though my skiff had an outboard."

They promenaded about the hall until the musicians began the next number.

"Tell me more," she said. "I like it."

"Do you? Honestly?"

"Honestly."

"You know, you're awfully sure of yourself."

"With you, yes. With you, well, you're like Wrangell."

He laughed. "I knew a long time ago about Wrangell. I knew it from the first. And when I was in the States at school and at college, I knew it all the more."

"Tell me something else that you enjoy doing."

"I enjoy you. You're a knockout."

Lydia smiled. "Music to my ears. Can I hum now?"

"No," said Chris firmly. "You know, once I owned a twenty-two Hornet—that's a small-caliber, high-speed rifle in plain language. I was crazy about that little gun. Shot deer with it. A black bear once too. I used to practice with it up behind the hospital, splitting the forks on the leaves of the tall trees up there. I was good with that gun. But that was because I liked it. It had a nice feel to it . . ." He paused, not knowing how to continue.

"Well, what is this all leading up to? You make me curious!"

"It leads up to this." He looked down at her. She wasn't as tall as she had appeared on the street. "I like the feel of you . . . No, don't say anything. I'm kinda high all of a sudden. Real high. That gun was my world when I was twenty four. Funny to describe it that way. Well, I loaned that gun to a friend of mine once—a few years later—and he took it with him one winter on his boat. I'll even tell you his name. Tom. Tom Hart. A big kid for his age, everybody liked him."

At that moment, Chris felt a tap on his shoulder. He wheeled about to see the smirking face of Clarence Wick.

"Sorry, ole man," the barber said in a croaking voice, as Chris relinquished Lydia to him.

"It's the custom up here," he heard Clarence explain to the girl.

Chris edged off the dance floor and towards the wall, lined with people sitting and empty folding chairs heaped with purses, coats and kerchiefs. The music blasted through the smoky air from the amplifiers on the stage. There was an underlying roar of conversation. It was crowded. Even the balcony which circled the hall in a horseshoe shape was packed, mostly with native women. Almost everyone in Wrangell was there. And drunk. The whole town was on a binge. Chris laughed, feeling high himself, confident, with the bright gleam of a goal ahead of him. He laughed again when he couldn't get anywhere near the punch bowl. Fanny's dad, Tim Regis, was serving the punch as usual. The dance committee always appointed him to this position because of his conviviality.

Waving at Chris, bakery owner Chuck Everett tottered by with Irma Stolte, the librarian. Everyone knew how Irma and Chuck were dead set to be married and then Chuck went to Ketchikan one summer to buy a slicing machine for the bakery and returned with a bride, no slicing machine. Irma said nothing, but married a man 20 years her senior whose complaints about his aching joints made him seem even older.

Irma was playing the piano tonight because Matt Fleming had decided not to come. She left her fur-lined coat draped over the piano stool while she had a dance with Chuck. It was a nice orchestra even without Matt and Alan: saxophone, drums, fiddle and piano when Irma was up there.

Irma Stolte, Chris laughed to himself. Damn, you're feeling good. Once, years ago, Irma had invited Chris up to her house for dinner. Irma's husband had gone south again for another treatment that some highly recommended doctor was giving for arthritis. Chris went, got into an argument with the refined and bookish Irma over some unexpected thing. She got so mad that she called him a prig. He would never forget that. Like a scar. Prig. He knew that she must have wanted a lay. It would have been a good legitimate lay, too, with none the wiser for it. Irma Stolte had made sure she informed all her friends that she had invited Chris up for dinner because she felt sorry for the cannery owner eating out by himself all the time. And she had made certain that Chris would arrive in her house in broad daylight, at five, so that the neighbors would see him come in.

The dinner was surprisingly good, club steak with stuffed baked potatoes and a nice green tossed salad with a gooey, but delicious dressing. Irma was bedecked refreshingly in a soft blue dress with a shy smile softening her normally dour expression. But as the evening wore on, her face took on a nervous, slightly coquettish look, and she told him sincerely what she thought of his drinking and gambling and Bohemian existence. "You make me laugh the way you think you can get away with it," she had said with a fluttery smile.

Chris looked her straight across the table and said—he would never forget it—"Listen, Irma, don't make off as if your B.O don't . . ." Then he had stopped, for she colored and appeared thunderstruck. He was sorry immediately that he had lost his mind for a moment, said such a dirty, horrifying thing.

"My smell has no significance to the gist of this conversation."

"Well, if you don't like the way I live, then you can tell me to leave. Because in a minute I'm going to make a pass at you."

This really shocked Irma. Tears filled her eyes, but she stood firm. "You're nothing but a frightful brute."

He rose from the table and her damp eyes followed his advance toward her.

She laughed, unperturbed. "You make one try and I'll chew your ears off."

He lost his mind again, seemed to tear to pieces in a vow of his defeat, staring at this forthright woman who dared to upset his world with her syrupy accusations.

"You stink," he'd said, picking up his jacket and jamming his arms into the sleeve.

"You're the most insulting brat I've ever had the misfortune to come across," she said, her chin wobbling. "I feel sorry for you."

"I bet you stink sweet." He despised her and wanted to hurt her. He knew he would be sorry later. Irma wasn't really a frustrated woman, and maybe she had invited him over just to be sociable.

At the door, she said, trembling uncontrollably, "One word fully describes you. Prig. And I'm afraid there's nothing that can be done for a prig. Read the Bible, Chris. Tonight. Read it for a week and don't ever dare to approach me again until you do."

Chris didn't read the Bible, although there was a King James version right on the coffee table. Theodore used to read it devotedly on Sunday afternoons, and because of that, Chris hadn't even opened the covers. If the Bible made people like his father and Irma Stolte, then he wanted no part of it.

It wasn't until after Theodore was injured and the family went south that he opened the Bible and discovered he had been wrong.

He had been wrong about so many things. And now there was Lydia. Chris watched the dancers and saw Lydia and Clarence rounding the far turn by the stage. Well, he'd give Clarence this round, then he'd step in. God damn, she was beautiful. She was wearing a soft, seductive dress with puffed sleeves which showed off her small waist. Nice. Very nice. He couldn't get over the way she listened to him, her whole face attentive. It was as if she were thirsty for knowledge, gleaning the most she could from every scrap of information. Chris saw that Dave was dancing with Victoria and then quickly lost sight of them in the shuffle of the crowd. Native couples were dancing swiftly and effortlessly, round and round like dark images on pedestals, doing the Alaskan Hop. Someone slapped him on the shoulder.

"God damn, Chris, this is the best dance I been to in ages," Chuck Everett exclaimed. His pinched square face was peppered with perspiration. "C'mon outside!" He pointed a wavering forefinger to the entrance way. "You can't get to the punch bowl." Chuck pulled out a pint and Chris declined it.

"Put it away," he warned. "Jesus, not here."

Chuck returned it to his pocket.

"You know it's too early to get drunk from a bottle in here."

"I know it. Let's go outside."

They snaked through the jam at the entrance hall. Chris took a swallow from the bottle Chuck handed him and then passed it to Red Parker who had lurched out of the doorway just behind them.

"Whiskey sure helps in the ferment," Red mumbled incoherently. He backed away and wobbled down the street.

Chuck said mischievously, "Just danced with Irma. She wants me to meet her after the dance."

"You God damn liar."

"No, her husband's been away now for three weeks. Maybe she could do with a little."

"You're a God damn liar, Chuck. Why don't you go tell that to your wife?"

"I wanted to but I couldn't find her."

"Say I think you could stand a drink."

"I think so too," Chuck announced, rocking back on his heels and taking another swallow.

"Hey," Chris remembered, "I'm hot on a trail inside. See you later."

Lydia and Clarence were rounding the corner by the stage, doing fairly well for Clarence was nimble on his feet. Chris sprinted through the crowd, tapped Clarence and enjoyed the warm glow which spread through his chest as he did so. Clarence raised no fuss, slinking away quickly as if relieved.

"Now where was I?" asked Chris in the pompous manner of an executive to his secretary.

"Oh, let's see? Something about a gun and a big kid named Tom Hart."

"I'll tell you about that later."

"He was a strange man," Lydia said, nodding her head at the departing Clarence.

"What was the matter?"

"Oh, nothing."

"Well, what made him so strange?" He pulled her a little closer, was startled by the touch of her breasts, pulled away for a second, then gathered her closer again.

Lydia eased back a little. "He was very stiff. Didn't say a word." She laughed a little. "Not like you."

"That's not strange. He was bewitched by your beauty. I'm bewitched. I was bewitched the first moment I laid eyes on you."

She went on talking about Clarence. "He trembled a little. Is he sick? His face is so pale and white. He's so tight."

"I said I was bewitched the first moment I laid eyes on you.'

"What should I say? When was that bewitching moment?"

For the first time he became serious, making his words sound inconsequential though he felt as if he were trying to speak below the surface of water, "I saw you at Mom's restaurant." He made a gourmet slurp with his tongue. "You eat beautifully. Like a hungry bird that's scared of something."

"Chris, you are very, very funny."

"Lydia, I'm crazy about you."

"You fellows in Wrangell aren't as backward as one would expect."

"Is there anything wrong in revealing the true status of one's emotions?"

"Your true status right at this moment isn't true by any means."

"I want to take you out on the channel. Have you ever sung in the open? With only water around you?"

"No, and please don't shout in my face. God, what do you people do up here? Make your own booze?"

"I have. My first date in Wrangell, I rowed a girl out on the channel and sang to her. I made off as if I were singing to myself, but I really was singing to the stars and the water."

"I can't keep up with you. Lead me to the punch bowl for a thirst quencher. It seems to be the fashion here anyway so I don't suppose it will be considered sinful for a schoolteacher to be seen in the proximity of the punch bowl."

"Let's go to Mom's and have a high ball."

"I'd rather not. Please, you're holding me very tight."

"Like I said, you remind me of a twenty-two Hornet I once owned. I like the feel of you . . ." He was aware that he was being crude, corny, but he felt helpless in the grip of his emotions.

The music ended with a crash.

As they moved towards the punch bowl, Lydia asked, "Do they always promenade after every dance?"

"Sure. Old Wrangell custom."

"I think it's so lovely. People walking around. Not like the States where you stay glued to the spot.

"You don't care for the States?"

"I'm neutral about the States. I like it and I don't. I like it when I'm in Wrangell."

"You're the most gorgeous hunk of womanhood that's gracing this glorious A&N dance."

"I repeat, with a slight variation: you men in Wrangell may be deep in the woods but you're not backwards."

As they approached the punch bowl, Chris called out to the postmaster. "Hey, Tim, can you spare a little of that stuff for the fair schoolteacher and me?"

"Well, let's see. First I have to find a ladle."

"No ladle?"

"No, a satisfied customer took it away, saying he was going to frame it. Then there is the question of containers."

"No containers?"

"Someone else walked off with the containers. He felt they were needed so others could properly and enjoyably partake of the soup." Tim loved playing with language, rolling multi-syllabic words around on his tongue, especially when he was partaking of his own concoctions. "Now, see here, young man. Do not insinuate that this center of liquid refreshment is being mismanaged." Tim reached down behind the table and produced two paper cups. "If you can get me a raise, I can further add to your enjoyment by spiking the stuff to the point where a connoisseur's tongue might not be contaminated or misled by the flavor of California orange juice and Hawaiian pineapple . . ."

"It'll do you good to go," Roy Hart said, puffing a cigarette nervously.

"I hate to keep telling you this, darling, but I don't feel like going. You go."

"Without you?"

This option had just occurred to her. "Yes. You go. By yourself. By now, no one will even notice if you arrive alone."

Roy chuckled. "I bet it is a drunken fracas by now."

For a moment Bea could picture the huge hall as if she were there: the crowd, the blaring music, the smoky air, the shuffling feet, the roar by the punch bowl near the entrance way. She didn't understand why she couldn't gather up the energy required to go.

And Roy wanted to go so badly. They hadn't been to a dance in ages. As Bea stared up at her impatient husband, pacing back and forth in the living room as he smoked cigarette after cigarette, she suddenly knew that Roy would go alone. Actually she had known this ever since Roy opened the bottle of cognac after supper. She had taken a few sips to be agreeable, enjoying a sip of the dark liquid, inhaling its strong fragrant perfume.

"I have a terrible headache," she said, moving close to Roy as he sank down into the sofa. "The noise would only make it worse. I hate to be such a bore, darling. I love you so much. I want you to go. You'll have fun."

Roy rose and poured more cognac into the two half-empty glasses. She knew what he was hoping, that he could get her a little drunk and convince her to go. He was restless lately. Maybe she should encourage him to start taking tourists out hunting for bears again.

Roy lit another cigarette. He chain-smoked whenever he was dismayed or perplexed. It didn't worry her since she knew Roy didn't inhale as much as he pretended he did.

"It's eleven thirty," Roy said. "If we call Curly we can be there by twelve. It shouldn't take you long to change."

"You're so sweet, darling." She forced a yawn. "But my head is pounding. I think I just need to go to bed."

As she got up, she realized that the cognac must have affected her. There was a moment of dizziness and then she felt dejected and tired. She plopped down again on the sofa. Roy sat down next to her, putting his arm about her shoulders.

"You're still the most beautiful woman in Wrangell," he said.

From where she sat she could see Tom's portrait staring at her from on top of the mantel. She began to weep for no reason at all.

"Hey, what's the matter?"

"You go, Roy. I'm just a baby. I'll be all right after a good night's sleep."

"But why the tears? For heaven's sake, Bea, have I said something?"

"Roy, bring the cognac here. I didn't finish the glass. Maybe that will help."

A tremendous weakness seized her. She felt it mostly in her veins, in her wrists and joints. She lay back on the sofa and closed her eyes. She was almost getting used to this weary, exhausted state. She lived her life in a sort of dream.

"What is it?" Roy asked, setting the drinks on the end table. "Can't you at least explain it?"

"I love you so much, Roy."

Roy not knowing what to say, sipped his drink and waited.

She'd fallen into such a hopeless rut in this town. There was so little to do. No, that wasn't true, there was plenty to do: the movie on Main Street, the housework, crocheting, friends, but she couldn't seem to find enjoyment in anything. And lately even Roy was different. He was going to town a lot. He hadn't started drinking heavily yet but he was mixing with the wrong crowd at the bar, playing cards all day. It scared Bea.

Only this afternoon, with the roads soggy from the morning rain and Bea wanting Roy to put up a new clothesline for her, he'd risen from the table after lunch and said, "I think I'll go up town and have a beer." He stood there by the table shifting on his feet, looking so uneasy and fidgety that she thought he would explode with restlessness if he remained another minute in the house. "I'll get some groceries and bring back a couple bottles of beer and we'll have 'em for supper." He hadn't mentioned the dance tonight for she hadn't been out of the house for months. No, he was going to wait for the opportune moment, try to coax her into going after the beers.

After he left the house, Bea stayed at the table. She was struck with a wave of love for Roy. Everything he did thrilled her: the way he concentrated on a book, his laziness regarding household chores, his habit of suggesting delightful things at unexpected moments. She realized how lucky she was to have Roy, how much she loved him, how wonderful it was to be able to love someone in that way. After all these years her love for him had only increased.

Yet she wasn't able to get up from the table. She sat there staring at soiled dishes heaped with the remains of the lunch, sensing the warm and irresistible flow of apathy and exhaustion in her veins. She knew that she must go to the States. She hadn't been to the States to see her family since right after Tom's death. She had gone, as usual alone. Nothing she did could persuade Roy to leave Wrangell. Not even if she delivered an ultimatum, if she told him that she was leaving and wouldn't come back. Not come back to him. Or Wrangell.

Roy pushed open the small window in the corner of the room and stared out at the power plant across the road. The noise of the window squeaking open flushed Bea back to the present. She smiled, stretched her legs, the afternoon fantasy of leaving Wrangell still clinging to her mind. She thought of all the years that she had lived with Roy in Wrangell, all the times that she had wanted to burst out in a rage and tell her husband to forget about Wrangell for a few weeks, to extricate himself from the spell the town had cast upon him and come with her on a vacation to the States. But she never did. She had lived with him for so many years and he possessed a remarkable control over her. They both knew it and she could do nothing about it. So she never told him all of her innermost desires and secrets.

Except maybe she could, tonight.

"Want some more cognac, Bea?"

"Yes, Roy. I'm glad you opened the bottle. It was gathering dust. " He sat down beside her on the sofa. "I love you so much, you big goof. Why don't you go to the dance without me? I'll be all right."

She was woozy from the drinks, relaxing under the cognac, her tongue slipping, feeling sorry for herself, revealing a few of her secrets. "Tom's always here, isn't he, Roy?"

"What?"

"Tom is always in the house even though he never stepped foot in it," she said, her voice trailing off. She waved away the drink Roy offered her and glanced out through the bay window to hide her tears. She could see the wet surface of the road gleaming beyond the porch. She heard in the kitchen the drip-drip-drip of the faucet that Roy had planned to fix this week.

"Tom," Bea said and tried to smile. "Tom." She repeated her son's name, speaking the name softly, as if afraid that she might hurt Tom otherwise. She wanted to talk about her son with his father. "Tom was such a big boy. He was too big, Roy. He was too much for himself. He couldn't hold it all in. He had to go like that."

Roy remained still, probably bewildered. He put his hand on her knee.

"I always feel Tom in this house," she whispered, as if she were afraid to hear what she was going to say, as if the words could make her cry even though the tears were always there, ready to spill out. "He's always here."

"You bet, darling," Roy said. He rubbed the flesh of her leg with his warm hand.

"You don't feel him, do you, Roy?"

"No, I don't, Bea. To be truthful . . ."

She was quiet a moment. "I guess that's only natural," she said. "It's different for a mother. I can remember when he was born as clearly as if it happened this morning. Each time I heard him cry I wanted to thrust my breast into his mouth. It was so strange to me. I loved him from the first, so fiercely."

Outside, a car slid around the bend past the power plant, skidding, rear wheels spewing up mud. Bea lowered her head, happy at being able to speak about Tom so freely. "In the hospital, I was in such a turmoil, wanting to run to him whenever he cried, such a hungry baby, the milk rushing to my breasts, and yet I was too weak to get out of bed..."

Bea stopped, realizing that Roy's hand was no longer on her knee. Doggedly she rose and went into the bedroom, beginning to undress. She'd get in bed and Roy could go. For some reason she wanted Roy to go, she wanted him to feel as she did in the house all the time, alone, ineffectual, out of place. She crawled into the far side of the bed, snuggled under the blankets.

"Turn out the lights when you leave, Roy."

"I feel rotten about going, Bea."

"If you will, darling, please send Winchester inside. The dog is such a comfort when you're away, Roy, darling. Oh, I'm so sleepy. . . ."

Sometimes it took Matt Fleming a long stretch of solitude before he could feel pleasure in life stirring within and about him. Sometimes, like today, Matt would wake up in a black mood and grope through the day in an ordeal of despair.

Now he sat hunched up on the front stoop of his cabin, gazing out at the dark waters of the channel. He sat in the open door wondering. Why was he this way? Why did he withdraw like a hermit at times? Why couldn't he just keep moving forwards? There were times, he reflected, when a man has to pause no matter what the consequences and search within himself for the answers. There were times when he was flooded with pure joy after hours spent wading through tides of grief and suffering. It was always then, when he reached a place of quiet resignation, that the secret of fulfillment arrived.

He had always thought of himself as set apart from everything, from other people, even the world about him. He was born that way. He had never married, never really imagined making a go of it. As much as he loved children, Matt was always grateful that none of them were his. He made friends easily with children because he never bossed or lectured them, yet Matt could tolerate children only so long. He was a loner. He came to Alaska with that dream in mind and found what he was seeking in Wrangell. He built his cabin a good ways from town at the outskirts of the road, above the beach so he had easy access to the water when he wanted to go for a swim. Yes, Matt had gone his own way all his life.

Then this spring, Doc Little, worried by his condition, sent him to a sanitorium in the States. The doctor had given Matt eight to ten months. "And that's if you take care of yourself," he told him. "You need plenty of sun and relaxation and proper food." Matt wasn't surprised. His body had told him the same story long before the doctor began his thorough examination. Still it was a kind of relief to know definitely, to know he had that many more months to live.

But he wouldn't leave Wrangell to sit in the sunshine. Why, that was ridiculous. Even going to the States in the first place had been ridiculous, depleting most of the money he had saved for buying records. There were still so many great musical compositions he wanted to study. But then, naturally, he had been curious, too.

Matt was never worried. He took his sickness in stride. Life wasn't any good when it was soft and pliable, when it gave out time unsparingly like a rope that was always slack. No, it was better this way, alone, with the problem of death at the end of the line, giving a dynamic tension to his days. When life was soft, when everything was laid out before him and he had only to choose what he wanted, a man had no reason to die. His death was tasteless. He would die knowing he could have had more. He would die a coward, fighting, tortured by the meaninglessness of things. For Matt, death would be merely the bend before the end of the road. He would make that turn without swerving away. If it wasn't for the fact that he still felt good, better than he was supposed to, he would hope that death would come early, surprise him. But until then, he would swim when he wanted, play the piano until late at night, give piano lessons to the kids in town, dig graves for the undertaker, ride his bicycle and smoke his two cigars a day.

Only today he hadn't smoked any. Today was a black day which had surrounded Matt without warning or mercy. Matt knew he would have to sit for hours on the threshold of his cabin before he could sense the energy of the earth. He would have to look out the window at the darkness and the lamp light on the road by the Hart's house and sing and whistle and savor his precious possessions, his records and piano, before he could feel the bliss and pulse of life again. Soon his broken and discordant singing would begin to stir in his soul, swelling to a harmony greater than any symphony. At last, after hours of disharmony, he felt . . .

But Matt paused, knowing that the moment of rapture had not yet arrived. The pure chorus that he was awaiting in the sky of his being was distant tonight, as remote as the stars in the sky.

He had woken this morning with a pain in his left breast and a black fog numbing his vision and blotting his brain so he couldn't eat, think or feel. Matt had gone for a walk, cutting out back of his cabin, heading towards the back channel through the muskeg. Walking on the muskeg was like stepping on a sponge, since the muskeg was made up of a thin surface layer of plants growing on top of a soggy bog. He had to be careful to avoid stepping in any of the open ponds that dotted its surface. His shoes were soon covered with gluey mud. But he stalked on, determined to burn off the pall that covered his soul.

The wind blew lightly across the muskeg, stirring the low-lying bushes and plants and riffling through the branches of the stunted trees which dotted the lonely landscape. His clothes were damp from brushing up against the dwarfed and crooked Jack pines which grew so slowly that even the small ones which barely came up to his shoulders were probably three or four centuries old. The wind shook branches, lifted leaves, exposing a sea of different shades of green and making the muskeg seem weird and forlorn—like his soul.

Suddenly in the center of the muskeg, Matt stopped, his eye caught by an object in the billowing clouds hanging low over the crest of the hill. A sea gull, its underbelly as white as a gleaming fragment of silver, flapped its wings awkwardly as if it were washing itself, then disappeared. Matt felt a little better at the sight of the sea gull and returned to his cabin.

He couldn't touch any lunch so he played Bach and Handel on the piano. Bach trickled under his fingers, the tonal canon music building cathedrals and forests and grand celestial vistas. Handel raised his hopes only as long as he played Handel, fading the moment his fingers relinquished the keyboard. It was towards evening when the sun had come out for an hour without providing any relief, that Matt realized he would not be able to perform at the piano at the dance that night. It wasn't because he was too weak or afraid that an attack might seize him. No, he couldn't go because his soul wouldn't be there. His spirit would grow even dimmer in the crowd. He might lose himself irrevocably there.

So he sent word to Irma Stolte that she should play for him and stayed at home, singing to himself, hoping to stir an ember of life in his charred being. He waited in the darkness, waited patiently with his eyes on the stars, for he knew if he was patient and calm and sang to himself and listened he would find the spark that would ignite the soul of his being. The moon etched flakes of silver in the heart of the channel; the flakes turned and dripped and threw off quick flashes of light.

Chris tapped Curly's shoulder.

"Enough's enough," he complained.

"Hey, this ain't tag." Curly actually looked belligerent. He kept on holding Lydia.

"You the manager?" Chris said laughing.

"Hell, we just got together."

"Thank you, Curly, old boy."

"I think he was angry at you," Lydia said, moving into Chris' arms. "He certainly is a marvelous dancer."

The first contact with her body stalled him for a moment. She was so soft and yielding. The scent of her perfume made him lightheaded.

"My God," he muttered into her ear, "you jar me."

"Well at last, the first perceptible sign of weakness!" She began to hum, with a mocking smile.

"Stop it," he grinned. "It's coming back. Now, let's see . . ."

"Don't you ever pay attention to the music?" She hummed louder.

"I didn't tell you how I felt when I first laid eyes on you."

"Pray, do tell," Lydia begged, with mock seriousness, and began to hum again.

Chris was beside himself with glee, feeling so very good with this girl, the music and the crowd and the headiness in his mind. Words gushed out effortlessly when he was near her, a million crammed-up words waiting to be spilled out. "Well, it was like my first experience with a grizzly bear . . ."

"Oh, come now," she breathed.

"He was thirty yards away from me. I was crouched in a flat-bottomed skiff in a shallow stream just north of here, off one of the sloughs of the Stikine River. I had gone there to do a little fishing by myself, motored up this stream until the water swallowed and grounded my skiff. Then I just sat back, angling a pole over the side for trout, having a grand time when my eye caught this brown hulking object stalking a windfall at right angle to my vision. Well, when that grizzly and me saw one another I jumped almost clear out of my pants. I never saw anything so huge and, well, magnificent and cool. I jumped up before this beautiful creature, dove frantically for my gun at the bottom of the skiff, banging all over the place, turned, shaking, aimed, got still more scared, eyes swimming out of my sockets . . ."

She was laughing uproariously.

". . . fired, missed, fired again, missed, fired again . . ."

"Missed," she said, laughing.

"Brother, it was a good thing I did miss, considering the condition I was in. If I'd wounded that baby . . ."

"Tell me, Chris, did you jump out of your pants when you saw me?"

"Lydia, I jumped out of something." Chris said earnestly, staring down at her. "I jumped, baby. There something out of the ordinary about that moment, and this one, and the ones coming up."

"You are so, well . . ."

"Sure of myself? We've already covered that. I try not to be but, this time I can't help it because I am sure of myself."

Lydia concentrated on the dancing suddenly, not even humming, which troubled Chris. Hey, take it easy, he told himself. You're pretty high, boy. You'll say something you'll be sorry about later.

Two young native girls wriggled their way through the crowd at the entrance, giggling as they made their way towards the stairway.

"Where did you get it?" one of the girls asked.

"Charlie Zimms came out of the lavatory with it and—I don't know what happened—I just snatched it out of his hand and ran. God, Charlie was pie-eyed."

"You think we should?"

"Sure!" The other girl replied. "We'll make it look like the Fourth!"

They ran up the flight of stairs and over to the edge of the balcony.

"Who's going to throw it?"

"I will!"

With an expert twist of her wrist, the girl threw the roll of toilet paper high over the heads of the dancers below, holding it on to the end until it broke free. It came fluttering down, momentarily entangling the dancers. Before anyone could glance up to see who had thrown it, the two girls were gone.

Gwen Olson thrilled to Dave's schottische. He had a rhythm for the Scandinavian music, almost as if he were a Swede or Norwegian himself. She loved to dance. Jon always stayed home, tired from working in the merchandise store all day. "I'll take care of Danny," he would say, "and you go to the dance with Diana." Gwen wondered what made Jon so good and thoughtful. He never seemed jealous or resentful even though he knew Clarence would probably be at the dances, might even dance with her. He stayed home with Danny with whom he was always gentle and patient, never treating him any differently than he would treat a child of his own, though Danny was Clarence's son. She wanted so much to give Jon a child of his own, to balance the family, to draw them closer together.

Dave scarcely ever spoke when he danced so Gwen never bothered to make conversation with him. It was a relief for she could thrill to the dance as Dave seemed to do, putting her all in it. She stepped in time with Dave, almost on a cloud she was so happy. One, two, three, hop, one, two, three, hop, and her body whirled around, Dave's hands holding her effortlessly, now breaking apart and whirling parallel with one another down the hall while the other couples stepped together with the music, one, two, three, hop, one, two, three, hop. Laughing, Gwen looked up for an instant at Dave's handsome, glowing face and they exchanged quick glances of friendship. As the music brought the dance to a close, the hall rang with the sound of feet in unison: Tat, ta, ta, ta, ta, Tat, Tat.

"Shall we promenade?" Dave asked, taking her arm.

They were strolling around the warm and noisy hall, when Gwen paused for a moment, catching sight of Clarence sitting in one of the folding chairs along the wall between two buxom native women. He was so alone, Gwen thought with a pang, unable to tear her eyes away from him. Lonely. Gwen had never known anyone who could gather so much loneliness about him. It hovered around his sour, white face like a cloud. As she usually did whenever she passed his shop, Gwen waved and smiled cheerfully at him. He needed it, she knew. He counted on it, even though he might not know it. Gwen felt she was the only person in Wrangell who understood Clarence.

His arm in hers, Dave pulled her along and she laughed up at him, a barrier slamming down across the cell in her heart that contained Clarence: his memories, his hard bitter restlessness, her love for him.

If only I can have a child with Jon, she prayed. A child to offset Danny. She hoped that the fact that her period was two weeks overdue meant that her prayers were finally being answered.

Sylvia Weaver frowned. "Herb, will you listen to the music and dance?"

Herb perked up and cocked his ear towards the music, though he couldn't keep in step even when he tried.

"You're a poor dancer at best, darling, and not paying attention isn't helping matters. I must look like a sack of potatoes being dragged around the floor."

With great pains, Herb bestowed all of his powers of concentration on coordinating the music and his steps.

"Lydia and Victoria are certainly making a hit," his wife observed, apparently mollified by his efforts. "The town is in a small upheaval at this very moment. Haven't you noticed?"

"I hope they can teach."

"Victoria certainly has enough experience and Lydia seems to me to be a natural . . ."

"You mean, she's a knockout."

"Chris is pressing for every dance."

"I like them. They're nice girls."

"Herb, as soon as you find the right moment . . ." Sylvia paused deliberately, waiting to be sure Herb had heard her.

"Right moment for what?"

". . . don't forget to ask them about the fall semester."

"Oh, I've already hinted about it when I showed them that cottage from Guy."

"You did! Why didn't you tell me? What did they say?"

"They said nothing. And frankly I don't think they will stay."

"If they like it here, they will. If . . ." she waited, never knowing when her husband's thoughts had drifted away.

"If what?"

"If either one of them falls in love."

Dave was a good dancer and usually liked to dance without talking. He believed in listening to the music in order to follow its rhythm. And he enjoyed the brassy quartet of the orchestra, makeshift as it was, which played at a heated pitch the whole night through, almost as if the amplifier, which was operating without a mishap this evening, might at any moment give out. With Victoria Blaissing in his arms, Dave deliberately kept quiet, though he was tempted to speak to her, to make a complimentary remark.

"I haven't had so much fun in a long time," she said, suddenly.

Dave combed his brain for a reply and found none.

"Mr. Wick is quite an intriguing person," Victoria said into his shoulder. "He doesn't seem to have that, well, dashing air about him."

"You mean he isn't getting stinko?" Dave's voice squeaked out. He realized that making conversation with a young woman was new to him.

She smiled. "No, that's not it. It's on the tip of my tongue but I can't quite come up with the right words."

"Dancing with you, I seem to be having trouble coming up with the right words too," Dave said, with a little laugh which failed miserably.

"Mr. Wick looks so bitter and mysterious. Not like the rest of you Alaskans that I've met," She smiled with satisfaction. "That's what I meant to say."

Dave knew she was digging for information on Clarence, extracting it like a molar. When Dave had cut in on her dance with Clarence, Victoria had let go of the barber reluctantly.

"Well, do you like Alaskans?"

"Very much. It's so new to us, you know. Almost a jolt, if you know what I mean. We expected to see, well, igloos, snow, Eskimos, rough weather and poor school conditions. Heck, the Wrangell school is twice the size of the school where I taught in Berkeley."

"I went to Berkeley once to visit a professor there. It was many years ago. I got my degree at Southern Cal."

"You did? Do you remember the professor's name?"

"Sure. Blackstock. He was crazy about football and I met him at one of the Cal/USC games in Los Angeles. He asked me to stop by Berkeley when I got my D.D. for a little celebration. He hated teaching, hated being cooped up, never tired of listening to my rantings about Alaska.

"Well, why didn't he just up and go?"

Dave gloated, realizing all at once that he had initiated a conversation. "Oh, the usual things," Dave said. "Responsibilities. Family. He had a cute daughter who ate into that slim bank account of his like a busy beaver."

Victoria laughed and Dave felt good.

"Berkeley is a lovely town," she said. "Wonderful in fall when Cal plays football and leaves are falling on the streets."

He'd realized from the first moment when he saw Clarence in the same room with Victoria that she was attracted by him. She was infatuated or something damn close to it. Dave shifted his mind to the music, the words wafting into his mind as he caught the rhythm. He couldn't rave about her flashing eyes. *When it rains, it rains pennies from heaven. Don't you know each cloud contains pennies from heaven.* Dave spun Victoria around recklessly to the music until he felt flushed with exertion and slowed his steps. He was winded already.

"Why so quiet? You're a wonderful dancer."

"It's a darn habit of mine. I can't talk and dance at the same time. It spoils it for me."

"It comes naturally if you're as good as you are."

"Do you compliment all men that way?"

"Only those who merit a compliment."

She looked radiant in an aqua-colored jersey dress with a low V neckline. It contrasted with the good solid stockiness of her body, flushed face and throat. She was wearing shell-rimmed glasses.

"First time I've seen you with glasses," Dave said.

"Oh, I hate to wear the darn things. I wear them mostly at work and when I read. But tonight I had a splitting headache and, with my kind of vision, wearing glasses eases the pain."

She began to talk about the cottage, how they rented it from Guy Eaton, how they almost took Mr. Ballard's "cute" float house, how they planned to fix up the cottage once they moved into it at the end of the next week. It was the regular calisthenics of conversation that any nice sociable woman speaks to any nice sociable man.

Already he knew he wanted to marry her. Victoria's past for some reason didn't concern him. He didn't even care to know about it. The fact that she wore no wedding ring was indication enough that she was available. Since the evening he had seduced Barbara Bucci on the floor of his reception room, Dave had begun to hunger for this girl. The sexual act flicked into his system like the tip end of a whip, arousing him from a long state of dormancy. He wanted more of it. His bachelorhood had been spoiled from that moment. He had lived in the same house with his mother and father for too long. Their disillusionment, their constant bickering about their past, about the present, about their ungrateful children swept away from them to all corners of the States, had begun to fester under Dave's skin. And lately he was beside himself with anxiety about his work, worrying himself with a desire for absolute perfection. He was fussy about germs, despaired when patients disregarded his instructions, nursed an impulse to burst out in a rage at times. At moments, he felt the urge to leave the office and get away by himself, maybe take his 300 Savage and shoot and shoot, maybe head out to Pat's creek and catch some trout. And he was drinking more. He had always been proud of his ability to temper his drinking, unlike the rest. But restraining himself had only made it worse for now he felt like he had lost his self-control entirely. Spending so much time with Chris didn't help either. Chris probably put away a quart a day. And everywhere they went, Chris would pull out a bottle. Up at the house, he'd open a cupboard and produce a quart. Down at the cannery, he had a pint tucked away in one of the drawers of his desk. Lately Dave could hardly wait until the last patient was out of his office to pour himself a stiff one.

The music was slow and dreamy and the girl pressed herself quite close to Dave's body. His mind blanked out for a moment as he became aware of the lush curves of her body, moving with his body in perfect rhythm. But then he remembered that she was much more interested in the barber and he felt the poignancy of all of the nights of his bachelorhood and he was struck with the need to have this woman beside him, to fill the cavity of those nights with her presence.

Gritting his teeth as they began the next number, Dave decided to force himself to talk. "You're not such a bad dancer yourself. In fact I was thinking a moment ago how much I was enjoying the dance with you."

"You're still in rhythm," Victoria said.

"I'm glad that you respect an old tottering bird like me." He stiffened for she was looking at him with sheer amazement.

"Old? Tottering? Say, how old are you?"

"I'm forty two."

"My goodness, I hope I look like you when I'm forty-two."

Dave grew quiet, a hard, defeated quiet, for now he was sure the girl would think of him as an old man. He wished he had kept his mouth shut and just danced.

"Dave," she said, "I scarcely know you at all. But I hope we get to know each other better in the future."

"I hope so, too," said Dave stiffly.

———

Fanny crossed her legs.

"Well, so the big boy finally decided to give itsy-bitsy me a moment of his time."

"You wanna dance or don't you?" Chris asked.

"No, thank you. I prefer to sit and watch."

"God damn you, Fanny, you're the screwiest dame I ever ran across."

Fanny uncrossed her legs, then recrossed them. "Chrissy boy, run off and tend to your schoolteachers."

"What's ailing you? Wanna drink? Your dad is in fine form tonight."

"Funny about him. At home he has a pint a night and it hardly affects him. He reads Thomas Jefferson and loves to listen to me play the piano. But put Mr. Tim Regis in charge of the punch bowl in a crowd like this and he turns into the whole party." Her lips curled.

"Come on, let's dance."

"You can't seem to get it into your thick skull that I hate you. I've always hated you. You're the embodiment of all men in one and I hate you. I hate your money, your face, your smirking love of self."

"Fanny," Chris whispered between clenched teeth. "God, you're going to eat those words. You're going to come begging me for some action before Alan returns from the States."

"And you're going to find yourself resting with your hands crossed on your chest next to that kid you used to chum around with."

Rage overpowered him and he darted away, his pulse in his brain. That bitch, the thought, shaking with anger. That no good bitch! Tom Hart had been a closer friend, despite Chris' being nearly a decade older. Fanny had no right to refer to Tom just as some corpse. Her very words fouled a sacred memory.

A loud argument near the big oil burner interrupted Chris' thoughts. The party was starting to get rough. It was Shirley and Red Parker. Red's face was swimming in tears in the face of Shirley's drunken harangue. It was the first time Chris had ever seen Red cry. He staggered up from his chair and herded his daughter out of the hall.

Shirley came tottering over to Chris, weaving back and forth on her high heels, attempting to assume a dignified composure. Whenever Shirley was sober she was probably as neat and quiet as any woman in Wrangell. She rarely wore lipstick or rouge. But as soon as she started drinking, she started applying makeup and the more she drank the more she applied. During the last hour she had painted her eyebrows a violent jet black and her face was splotched with powder and rouge.

"What a God damn fracas!" she mumbled in her deep bored voice. "That God damn Tim Regis. Won't even give a person a drink!" She went lumbering off towards down the side of the hall. She paused for a moment beside the massive oil stove in the center of the room. It had exploded one cold winter night with a packed house. Ted Savard, the man who sold tickets at the steamship office, and three natives were rushed to the hospital with first and second degree burns.

In the corner of the hall, Chris saw a group of old Indians sitting. Their faces were wrinkled and impassive. The squat old women clutched piles of purses, coats and colorful scarfs. The thin old men sat with their feet close together, clasping babies in their laps. They sat there, not speaking, not minding the people standing in front of them, blocking their view of the dance floor. It reminded Chris of the bingo games every Saturday night at the union hall. The old people had no sap left in them. They rarely left their hovels except for an occasional dance or a bingo game. Their children and their children's children were out painting the town red if they had enough money to buy whiskey but the elders were immune to these wild cravings and lived in a solitude forced upon them by the passage of the years. At the bingo games they hardly uttered a word when one of them won. Watching them, he could imagine that the old men were dreaming of their salad years, of salmon that they smoked and cured, of how their blood ran hot at the sight of a young woman with ebony braids. Now the old folks were resigned, stolid, aloof, as if they possessed a secret which they must guard deep within.

Turning around, Chris bumped into Dave. His friend looked as if he'd just trotted off a basketball court, his face was so ruddy. Dave's right hand fingered a button on his flannel coat.

"How you doing?" Chris asked.

"Oh, so-so," Dave replied weakly. "I feel so stilted."

"Snap out of it, man," Chris said.

Dave stepped aside to let two men go past.

"By God, I feel sick," Hank Connell moaned as he passed through, holding his stomach.

"Why the hell do you have to drink so much?" Roy Hart was scolding him. "You know that stuff is killing you!"

"By God, if a man can't at least drink up here, where in the fucking hell would he be?"

"Hank'll never learn," Dave said to Chris. "You know he's going to die if he keeps on drinking like that with those bleeding ulcers of his."

Chris didn't respond. He was watching Lydia glide by with Herb Weaver.

"How about a drink before you make your next advances?" Dave proposed.

"Suits me. Only I hate to see that lovely gal go on dancing with those other wolves . . ."

"She's in safe hands now. Herb's got her."

Chris and Dave edged up to the rear of the crowd pressing in on the punch bowl.

"Brother," Dave sighed as they waited.

"What's eating you?"

"I'm rusty. I feel like I'm coming out of a cocoon. This is going to shock you. Dave lowered his voice. "I screwed Babs Bucci in my reception room right on the floor."

"Hey, I thought she was Steve's."

"I just got this crazy idea that I should lay her." Dave said with a bitter chuckle. "She was very congenial, receptive, submissive, whatever the hell the word is. It sure floored me. I guess I caught her in the right mood. Or an off one. But something inside of me had to know. Oh, hell, listen to me, will you?"

Chris made a small path through the crowd with his elbows and edged up to the front of the table, Dave behind.

"Was it good?" Chris asked.

"Hey, you guys, quit pushing," complained Chuck Everett. "Mr. Regis is about to go on the air."

"Thank you, my dear Mr. Everett," Tim Regis bowed his head graciously.

"I don't know," Dave said to Chris. "I was so set on giving her a good time. I forgot to think about myself."

Tim stood poised behind the punch bowl, his two hands laced over the rim to signify that he wanted their attention. He cleared his throat, poured a mug of the brew he was serving down his throat, gurgled, swallowed, then addressed the editor of the *Wrangell Star* who stood directly in front of the punch bowl.

"My dear Mr. Cahill," Tim began, "despite your current level of inebriation, you are trying to submerge yourself still further with another serving of this royal fluid, knocked into such a high ratio of compression by yours truly. You hope to create the illusion of escape. Escape with booze. But there is no escape from your conscience, is there? The dread of your life is at last bearing down on you, pummeling you into a frazzle in the rear of your snaky and yellowish skull, exposing the raw naked figment of the coward that you are."

Men were pushing into the crowd to hear Tim razz the editor.

"You son-of-a-bitch," the editor complained. "You're so cockeyed you're lost your glib tongue."

"Lost, he says?" Tim appeared offended. He squirmed all over, then addressed the onlookers. "Have any of you ever heard the illustrious Mr. Cahill deliver a scream so blood-curdling . . . but wait, let's see how the blotched and stigsified editor and chief of the celebrated *Wrangell Star* reacts to the exposé of the blood-curling howl." Tim grabbed the editor by the shoulders. "Coming to you from Wrangell, Alaska, an exclusive on the almost probable death of one, Mr. Mervin Cahill, when attacked by his wife with a butcher knife the preceding evening about six thirty. Well, it seems that the illustrious editor was quite peeved at his wife for locking up the entire supply of whiskey in the house so he threatened to thrash his wife to a pulp for the dastardly deed. He backed her up into the kitchen, blood darkening the whites of his eyes, and against the sideboard the accused wife's hand fell back and curved around the handle of the butcher knife. She glanced at it, saw escape— by God, I knew that word fitted somewhere in the narrative—and rushed at him. Mr. Cahill ran through the kitchen, tripped to the floor over an ottoman and she brought the side of the blade down on his ass. He screamed the scream of a man about to die. I heard it two blocks away while preparing a cocktail for myself before dinner and the hairs on the lower region of my spine stood forth on edge."

"Hell," Chris said, backing away. "We'll never get a drink here. Let's go outside. Bottles are a dime a dozen out there."

Hannah Johnson and Eva Yorgensen sat in folding chairs along the wall, watching the dancers.

"It's such a fine dance. Everyone is happy," said Mrs. Johnson, smiling as she watched her daughter, Diana, dance with her fiance.

Mrs. Yorgensen nodded in agreement. "I'm going to make Olaf dance the Swedish valtz with me tonight if it kills me."

"He makes Diana do such a fine dance," said Mrs. Johnson referring to her future son-in-law, Curly. "They both look so happy."

Mrs. Yorgensen went on, "Olaf was such a man in his younger years. At the dances, he vould tire never. I married him because of how he danced the schottische." They both giggled.

"Everyone is so happy. It makes me mad to sit here idle like an old woman." Myron Johnson never came to the dances.

"Hannah, we are old. All Olaf thinks about now is boats. He's vorking on a blueprint to make someone a fine yacht." She paused, then changed the subject. "You know, I went to Doc Little's office the other afternoon—my back has been ailing me again—but anyvay, vaiting in the reception room who should come in but one of the girls that works for that colored voman, Princess. Very blond and tall, she vas, and sat down by the nurse—there for her weekly check-up, you know. Hannah, I felt sorry for that woman. She was talking to the nurse about sending presents to her two boys down in Seattle living with her mother because one of them has a birthday next month and she said she sends them two presents to keep them from quarreling."

They were silent for a few minutes.

"Isn't that new schoolteacher dancing with Chris beautiful?"

"Chris is so happy," agreed Mrs. Yorgensen, beaming. "Such a fine boy. He's in love. Can't you see how he is?"

———————

Lydia was quiet. No humming. She didn't peek up at him with a face flushed with excitement. So Chris was quiet too. He felt heavy and a little tired for he hadn't danced so much in ages. He held her close and she didn't resist. He laid his cheeks against hers and she didn't pull away. He tried to keep his feet moving nimbly while he savored her nearness. He let himself relax against her, thrilled. Out of the corner of his eye, he could see the glory of her hair, almost strawberry-red, rich, coppery. He could imagine the rest, her blue eyes, the gleaming curve of her teeth, the sharp plane of her cheek bones that seemed so fragile and beautiful.

"This tune is a favorite of mine." She said suddenly, beginning to hum and sing along with the music. *"You go to my head and you linger like a haunting refrain. And I feel you spinning round in my brain, like the bubbles in a glass of champagne."*

"Very nice," he said, automatically.

Lydia was silent again.

"I'm sorry. I shouldn't have said that. Sometimes people spoil a precious moment by making a silly crack." After a moment, he asked, "Is there any particular reason for your interest in the tune?"

"Well, I hope this doesn't disappoint you, but it's one of my father's favorite songs. I'm just a little homesick, I guess. You see, there were three of us girls in the family and Dad was always trying to keep up with us, and all the new fads, the music, as well. He knew all the good orchestras and band leaders. He was even planning to buy a Plymouth convertible only Mom wouldn't let him. Anyway, this was one of his favorite songs and if you memorize the words, you'll find they never leave you, like bubbles in a glass of champagne."

———————

Giff eased down into one of the vacant folding chairs in the corner by the group of natives. By God, it felt good getting off his feet. He'd drunk pretty heavily today. Hell, he drank pretty heavily every day. Giff laughed, as he watched a native not far from him remove one of his new narrow pointed shoes and rub his toes with obvious relief.

The natives loved to dance. They loved the boogie-woogie and the fast swing more than the slower sentimental pieces. They had a way of melting into one another, locking loose and close to one another, then sliding back, flipping out their legs in a swift and easy tempo, holding hands and twirling from the balls of their feet, a vortex of two bodies that began with a bounce and swerve motion that sent then careening around, pushing and kicking the spin faster and faster until they had accelerated their rhythm to twice that of the band. As they spun and flashed through the crowd, it seemed they would collapse from sheer dizziness alone.

The music poured out across the hall, strident yet compelling. For a moment, he wished he was out there, though just as quickly he dismissed the thought. Age and booze and apathy made it impossible. He was hollow and drunk and lost, really lost, in this town that had once belonged to him and Theodore Ballard.

He remembered how it felt to see that stocky figure coming down Main Street looking for Giff, how they would go out to have a few drinks together, maybe talking about an outing to the Mainland or philosophizing about life and the world, the way Theodore liked to do. Theodore talked to him like an equal, sharing his viewpoint which was more expansive than that of any other inhabitant of Wrangell. Theodore's perspective was global; it encompassed the whole universe.

"Have you ever wondered," Theodore would ask, "about the people who are aglow with enthusiasm? It doesn't matter whether they're rich or poor, intellectuals or knotheads. They hardly ever complain. They seem to radiate a warmth that makes the grumblers resentful and apt to bicker about them. Actually, if you study their lives, you'll find that they are hard workers, real devotees of home life and their families. From their own initiative and experience, they have learned what constitutes fulfillment. They find it in the energy of their work, in the peace and bliss of their home, contentment with what they have, watching their children grow, loving their wives. That is the essence of life, Giff, live simply and clean. Enjoy what you have and do not run after what you don't have. True contentment comes from you, your work, your home—nowhere else."

Flushed with his own oratory, Theodore paused and his moustache curled up in a wry smile. "Here I am yapping about the glories of family life and I have a twenty-two year old kid who is as stubborn as a mule and as hard to relate to as a rattlesnake."

He took another sip of his drink. "It's this town. It's Wrangell. Chris is, well, in a sense, he's the epitome of Wrangell. And what makes Wrangell different from the rest of the world? I'll tell you, Giff. The people in it, through sheer boredom, find themselves. They have no alternative. Haven't you ever noticed, Giff, how the people in Wrangell are so unforgettable? Each one is a true individual. And I tell you, it's living on an island that's so remote, the isolation from the rest of the world, the world of factory whistles and highways. It's living at the edge of survival all the time and the rain and beauty and silence that makes the folks in it, the Indians as well as the whites, so real and different, brings out their character so that there's no one else quite like them. People who burn in your memory, that you will never forget. . . ."

That was Theodore's philosophy, Giff reflected, as he watched the gyrations of the dancers on the floor: savor the accomplishments of the past and look for the wonder in the present. But to Giff, the opportunity for wonder was gone, slashed into bloody oblivion by a grizzly bear on a trail between willows on the mainland, just a day's boat ride from Wrangell. It was gone forever, there was little joy left, and time seemed to drag on interminably.

Giff lit a cigarette and extinguished the flame of the match with a flick of his wrist. He noticed Johnny Bugg on the dance floor with his young wife. The bars must be closed. Last winter Johnny had gone south and come back married to this rather homely girl. But she was young and people said she was a good industrious housewife. Giff drew on his cigarette, watching Johnny and his young wife. Giff never spoke to Johnny. Oh, he'd nod his head at Johnny if he happened to meet him on the street or came face to face with him at the dance. Giff kept watching Johnny's young wife, jabbering away for all she was worth about something. Sometimes, like now, he kind of hungered for a woman who would chatter away like Viola used to do. He dropped the cigarette to the floor, crunched it out with his foot. Seeing all the young people on the floor, their flushed, radiant faces, even the old fogeys' wives laughing and having a good time, he wished, just for a moment for Viola, his wife.

It was only a brief moment. Then he reminded himself of how glad he had been to see her go. She was a high strung woman, sophisticated in her way, always in front of a mirror, admiring herself, trying out new ways to wear her hair with special combs and clips, painting her nails. She had married him when he was an up-and-coming baseball star and when his career collapsed, her respect for him began a slow decline. She hated house work, the house was always messy, but then when she did clean up, she was fussy about every little thing, hollering at him because of a dropped cigarette ash, a magazine left on the floor, the way he propped the cushions on the sofa so he could rest his head. She liked sex in the afternoon, liked it when Giff dragged her into the unmade bedroom with the dishes still on the table, the house warm from the oil stove, the town quiet, almost as if it didn't exist. At nights, she complained that she was too tired and it wasn't any use to try because she wouldn't be able to get aroused with him. "Hi, Giff," Chris said, waving from the dance floor.

Giff waved at Chris and the girl in his arms, then felt self-conscious and trudged out the hall where a man could get some air and a gulp of whiskey.

It was near three o'clock and the dance floor was beginning to thin. Dust filled the air. And the time moved slowly, as if wrung out, exhausted. Clarence could see right across the hall without too much interference. But the crowd by the punch bowl was as thick as ever, emitting a roar which competed with the blare of the orchestra which was carrying on without the aid of the amplifier, which had finally conked out with an ear-splitting screech during the last number.

Clarence watched the girl strolling beside Chris as they promenaded about the floor during the interval between numbers. Her breasts lifted beneath the soft fabric of her dress as she took a deep breath of air, after laughing at something Chris had told her. Bitterness filled his mouth.

"You look cold as a clam," Steve said, bouncing off the dance floor. "Cheer up, boy."

Without thinking, Clarence shifted his rump over to the next chair, "Sit down," he said.

"Naw," Steve remained standing. "Going to take Babs for a walk before the dance ends."

"You've got guts," Clarence remarked. "While her husband fiddles . . ."

Steve chuckled. "I've got hot blood for that woman."

Clarence grinned, feeling a little better with Steve nearby. "You sure had hot blood the time I first got to know you."

"I'll never forget that," said Steve, with a roar of laughter. Clarence thought of how they became friends. It was pretty ironic. A nasty remark and he had earned a loyal friend. It seemed the only way Clarence ever got ahead in the world, by playing it dirty.

It was the first time he had ever gotten drunk in Wrangell, the first time he realized that he couldn't drink whiskey like other people could. It made him mean, insulting. He did things he didn't even remember, like tossing Shirley's clothes out of his window into the rain after stripping her. He only heard about it the next day when Buster Fountain blabbed about all the goings-on at the hotel the night before while getting his haircut.

Apparently after two or three drinks, he had gone crazy, told a couple of Klootches that Steve had a dose of clap, a bit of gossip he had picked up in the shop. It spread around town like wildfire. Steve's got a dose of clap. Steve's got a dose of clap. Everyone knew about it and everyone got a kick out of it except for Steve. But Steve didn't do anything about it, even after he found out who had started the rumor, just waited, until one evening when Clarence went down to the harbor to give a haircut and shave to old man Halvord, dying from stomach cancer and unable to leave his boat.

Steve's troller was moored to the same float and when Clarence was done and was striding down the float on his way towards the stairway, Steve was out on the deck of his troller and shouted out to him.

"Hey, barber, hold on a minute."

Clarence pulled up short, surprised. Fishermen from the adjoining trollers and gill-netters stuck their heads from their cabins, for it was dinner time, wondering whose loud voice was shattering the peace of the harbor.

"Sure, Steve. What do you want? A haircut?" Clarence tried to divert him.

"Listen you little runt . . ." Steve was sore. Clarence could see that. He stepped down from the boat to the float, his big hands curling into huge fists. "I'm going to settle a little score with you."

The surprise vanished in Clarence's guts, replaced by a sudden rage. He set down the satchel containing his barber things and began to take stock of the situation, side-stepping and ducking Steve's wild punches.

"You're going to learn to keep your God damn mouth shut!" Steve shouted, flailing out at Clarence with his fists.

Finally, when Steve began to tire, Clarence stepped in quickly, taking advantage of that open, puffing target and gave Steve the licking of his life. He hadn't fought two years in the Golden Gloves for nothing. He left bleeding wounds on Steve's face in two places and a gorgeous shiner under his left eye.

But that was the way they became friends. By fighting. A lot of guys were like that. Beat 'em up and they respected you. Steve had been a real man about it, trooping up to the barber shop about a week later, his face still puffed up, the shiner as blue as paint, and asked where Clarence learned to fight like that.

Clarence gave Steve some pointers on footwork and position and let Steve use the punching bag in the rear of the shop. The friendship grew until the fight was forgotten. Now Clarence realized that without Steve's warm support, living in Wrangell would be unbearable.

The orchestra was mellowing, harmonizing to *Shadows on the Sand.* The few remaining couples on the dance floor moved slowly, as if in a dream.

"Might as well sit down," Steve sighed. "Babs is dancing with Merv Cahill."

Clarence's mind was throbbing with pain. He could feel himself tearing apart, like rotten paper.

"You know," Steve went on, "for a fat old married woman with three kids, that gal hasn't missed a dance all evening. How she loves it! She giggles and twirls and puts a man in the damnedest mood!"

Clarence's right hand folded into a fist. He was enraged now. All evening he had been able somehow to hold back the jabs of anger. But the dance was almost over and the flood of wrath was consuming him, reaching into every nerve. His fingertips had gone numb he was gripping his hand so tightly.

"Look at her," Steve said, nodding towards the nearest couple. He waved and Babs smiled over the editor's shoulder. "She looks fresher than any other woman on the floor. What a dame!" Steve commented.

Clarence watched the beautiful schoolteacher as she moved around the floor, gathered close in the arms of the tall cannery owner.

Steve chuckled. "Haven't had so much fun in a long time. No booze to speak of, either. That dame," he shook his head in tribute, "Babs makes me, well, I never can get over her. She's tough, that baby. When you think what she's gone through with Mitch and she still sticks with him . . ."

Clarence's mind threaded through the babble of Steve's friendly words. He decided he had to try one more time. He would wait for Chris and the girl to circle the floor, then cut in. He got up, poised. But when they approached, he froze. He stood petrified while they flashed before him, tauntingly near, than dancing off in the crowd.

Clarence slumped down into his chair, as he had been doing all evening. Nobody had come around him, except Violet, then Shirley, he recalled reluctantly. He'd turned down the Klootch, but danced with Shirley, only to discover that she was so drunk she was nauseating. He'd dropped her after only one number and slunk back to his chair.

The entire evening filled him with remorse. He might just as well have stayed in his room at the hotel. He hadn't had a drop of whiskey, a startling incongruity in the face of the drunkenness all about him.

He'd danced twice with Lydia. Now his mind picked up and caressed each moment of those dances. He recalled every word, every nuance. His heart floundered under the impact of it. She hummed while he danced with her and he liked her so much for it. Yet he was weak and stiff and couldn't seem to say anything. Her humming was a joy, soothing his stiffness, relaxing him like a warm soft hand, like the way Gwen used to run her hand along the nape of his neck after a long day's work in the shop. During the second dance, Clarence had just begun to say something to the beautiful girl, had just started to throw away his fears and be gay and captivate the girl, when his shoulder winced under a hearty blow. It was Chris, his dark face lit up with a smile, indicating to Clarence that he would finish the dance.

He'd sulked away, wounded, and sat hunched in a corner, the clammy despair whirling inside him, sending out spears of ice through his veins until someone near him said:

"Clarence, you're shivering."

"What?"

"Man, you're shaking!" Steve said. "Snap out of it!"

Clarence rose and wandered down the hall in a daze. "God damn!" he muttered. "God damn!" He headed for the punch bowl.

7

WELL," CHRIS ASKED AS THE STRAINS of *Good Night Sweetheart* lapped across the floor, "what do you think of our quaint little dance?" For some reason he felt he had to ask her this. It seemed very important for him to know, although he couldn't help thinking that she might have been a little put off by the drinking and the wildness and the mingling of whites and Indians.

"Did you say *little* dance?" She peered up at him with amazement. "My goodness, if there were any more people here, the hall, large as it, couldn't have held them. Seriously, Chris, it was wonderful. There seemed to be so much fun in the air, good natural fun, fun that isn't brittle. . . ."

Chris laughed with relief. "Go on, fair lady, pile it on."

She smiled, "There was certainly no lack of fuel." She tossed her head in the direction of the punch bowl as they went out through the door. "Unfortunately, it was a bit difficult to reach. Even Mr. Herb Weaver had a rosy glow from the stuff they served over there."

Lydia looked straight ahead as they passed by a couple kissing in the entrance. A drunken Indian was asleep slumped up against the wall on his feet, head bent to his chest. A bottle was shoved out towards Chris and he declined it, cordially and firmly. Outside, two white boys and two natives were squaring off at one another, one of the native boys muttering something incoherent.

"Hey, break it up," Chuck Alder, the sheriff, said as he positioned himself between the boys.

Chris squirmed a little and felt awkward. Then, in a flash, he realized that he must have made an impression on her since she was willing to go for a walk with him after the dance. Lydia had informed Victoria, who was having coffee with Dave at Mom's, that she was going out with Chris and would see her later in their room at the hotel. Chris wondered suddenly if he would try to kiss her. Hell, why not? He'd wait until they were down the road a ways, maybe go to his float house.

Hand in hand, four women came marching up the center of the road in their stocking feet. They were singing at the top of their lungs. One of them began to rant about something and the singing disappeared in a flurry of giggles.

"See what I mean?" Lydia said. "Moon's gone," she noted and she shivered for it was nippy.

"Say," Chris said, "you know, all I've been doing is talking about myself and Wrangell."

She peered up at him and a serious tone crept into her voice. "As a matter of fact, you did say quite a lot, yet I scarcely know you. It all seemed make-believe. Was most of it true, Chris?"

The change was so abrupt that he glanced aside to make sure she was the same girl.

"I guess so. I was pretty high."

He was suddenly swept with emotion for he was in love with this girl. He watched her draw a deep breath of air. It seemed so nourishing that he could almost feel the cold refreshing draught of air in his own lungs. Her footsteps were almost inaudible beside the crunch of his own shoes on the gravel road. The street was quiet now that they had left the hall behind them. For a curious tense minute, he tried to step as lightly as she was, wanting to be like her. The channel was still and full against the embankment of the shore. From somewhere, deep in the harbor, came the sound water dribbling from a hose into the water.

"I don't know what it is," she said softly, "but I don't believe I've ever felt quite this way before. Time seems . . . Well, up here time doesn't seem to be real. No one *ever* looks at a watch. Do you have a watch, Chris?"

"No. Say, let's skip Wrangell."

"Well," she said, "I could tell you the whole history of my background but somehow this doesn't seem to be the time or place for it. Wrangell has sort of erased a lot of things from my mind. I'm curious about starting school Monday. I'm afraid I might have forgotten how to do it. We really shouldn't have lain around so much. We should have started in teaching right away."

"Maybe you wouldn't have found the cottage."

"And then, well, I'm glad we had the chance to get acquainted. We've met so many nice people. They're all nice. I couldn't find fault with anyone and it makes me wonder . . ."

"About what?"

"Well, how we must compare to them for one thing."

"The States is still written all over you."

"Well, it was a big thing to decide to come up here. If you know what I had to go through, with my mother especially. She wasn't exactly keen about the idea." The girl's voice seemed to hide in her mouth. "If it wasn't for Dad, good ole Dad . . ." She paused, slowing her steps, as if lost in thought. "He's the nicest father anyone could ever hope for. He spoiled all four of us."

"Four?"

"Three daughters and wife. If it hadn't been for Dad, I wouldn't have gone to college, nor to L.A. for the Cal football games with U.S.C and U.C.L.A. Nor up to Wrangell. . . ."

"So you went to Cal? Did you ever go north to the Washington State games?"

"So that's your college?"

"Yes."

"Cal always won that one so there was no need to go."

"Oh, you boosted the morale of the team?" For the first time he felt a twitch of jealousy. "Say, how come you're not engaged or something?"

"If my mother had her way, I would be. In fact I'd be married like my sisters. In fact, that was one of the big reasons I wanted to come up here. It was getting dangerously close, and I wasn't certain. Don . . ."

"Is that his name?" He was holding his breath like he would with a big pot in a poker game at Red's.

"Don Lofton. He used to take me back and forth from Berkeley to San Francisco in his car. After a while, I started making excuses so I could stay in Berkeley. That's how I met Victoria. She was teaching in one of the elementary schools there. I used to stay over at her house. She lived in a little house in a nice residential neighborhood. There was a professor who lived next door, by himself. He used to play his symphony records every night—he loved Mahler and Wagner and Strauss—and he kept his window open for he couldn't be without fresh air and he kept the phonograph turned up high as he was partially deaf. I learned to look forward to those hours at night. . . ." Her voice softened to a husky whisper as she slowed her steps, her eyes on the road. "Really, I don't know why I'm saying all this, but those night's at Vic's were my happiest. It was as if I had been groping, looking for something, flying all around searching for it, and when the professor's music came spilling out into the night air, I could scarcely contain myself I was so happy. I felt as if I were grabbing onto something real and substantial. I loved those hours in Berkeley at Vic's house." She looked up and grinned, ending the conversation. "I got to know quite a few of the great composers as well."

"You'll get a kick out of knowing Matt then." He found her so strange and ethereal. Her voice in the dimness of the road touched the core of his body with a sweetness that was buoyancy itself. His body seemed to float beside her.

"Matt. He plays organ at the Episcopal church. I met him at dinner at the Harts. I thought he was supposed to play the piano tonight?"

"Something went wrong, I guess. He's going to die inside of a year."

"Oh, no!"

"Matt doesn't seem too concerned about it," Chris said. "He'll be out there swimming, the first warm day that comes along. He teaches all the kids in town how to swim, some of the older folk too. If you're out his way, which is a little further along this road by the beach, he usually invites you into his cabin for tea. He has a shelf of tea things reserved for people who drop in."

"What's the matter with him?" Her voice was still tight with concern.

"As near as anyone can figure out, T.B. and cancer both."

"Oh, goodness," the girl cried.

A sound bit into the night, a scraping sound which ended with a resounding clatter. It came from so near that Chris and Lydia both stopped startled, shaken. To their right, was one of the shacks, hovering on piling, that lined the edge of the road along the embankment. In the dim light of the street lamp down the road, the shack was squat and shabby, the roof sagging. A yellow streak of light filtered out of the crack at the base of the door and the one small-paned window in the front glowed with light from behind a shade.

"By God, that sounded like a chair being thrown!" Chris said.

Then a scream pierced the still air and Chris made a dash for the door. It opened before he got to it and a short, husky man stormed out, leaving the door ajar.

"Hey, Swede, what's the matter?"

The man stopped, panting, and Chris saw that his nose was bleeding. "The son-of-a-bitch came home tonight, that's what," he said indignantly. He looked up, saw the crowd of men swarming down the road from the dance hall and took off in the opposite direction.

The sheriff was the first to arrive. "What's happened?" he asked, then stormed into the house without waiting for an answer.

The shack was sectioned off into three tiny, square rooms, with the bedroom-living room facing the road, the kitchen in the middle and the small lavatory in the rear. There were no rugs, no linoleum, just bare wood floors. A woman was lying on the kitchen floor, spread out on her back, a pool of blood around her head. A man stood braced against the wooden sink, his chest rising and falling as he glared at the sprawled woman. A boy of about eight years, wearing a clean flannel nightie, stood in the middle of the room, crying with soft, wet sobs.

"Get the doc," someone shouted. "He's still at the dance."

Chuck bent over the woman. "Nobody touch her!" he ordered. He looked at the man, then knelt down beside the woman again. Although crowded, the shack was neat; only a chair was out of place, sprawled on its side on the floor beside the prostate woman. A thin rank odor of boiled cauliflower and fried fish hung in the air.

When Doc Little hustled in and bent over the fallen woman, Chuck rose and said, "All right, Carl, why don't you tell me what happened?"

The boy began to cry louder and Carl Terjensen scooped him up in his arms, went past Chuck into the front room, stopped when he saw all the people there and juggled the boy in his arms indecisively.

"I don't want to go to bed, Daddy," the boy cried.

Carl carried him back to the kitchen. "I got to put this boy to bed," he said to Chuck.

"All right, everyone, let's clear out, please."

The crowd of people trooped out the front door.

"Well," someone said, "Swede finely got his tit in the wringer."

"I knew he'd get caught sooner or later."

"Jesus, did you get a load of her? She was beaned but good!"

Chris pulled Lydia to one side. He couldn't think of anything to say. Lydia was quiet. The cluster of people stood outside the closed door of the shack, smoking cigarettes, mumbling low now that they were aware of the new schoolteacher in their midst. They all waited to hear what happened, though they all knew. Terjensen was down south and had returned sooner than was expected, probably on a fishing boat from Seattle instead of one of the steamers. Swede Nordstrom was making one of his nightly calls on Margaret Terjensen, that's all.

In a little while, the sheriff came out. "Doc says she's pretty bad. Got to take her to Ketchikan. We need a boat."

Chris said," The *Verna* isn't busy right now. We can take her in that."

"Fine, Chris. We'll have to hurry. Someone go get the ambulance. Her condition is serious."

Chris asked Lydia. "Want to come along? I'll have to find Giff to pilot the boat down."

"Not to Ketchikan," she said quickly.

"Oh, no, just to the harbor. Giff'll take her down."

"Well, maybe I shouldn't, Chris. I'd only be in the way."

"Suit yourself. It won't take long."

"Oh, all right. Maybe I can be some help, change her clothes or something. I once took a course in first aid."

"Swell. C'mon, let's go."

"Hey, Clarence, you look like you just got out of bed."

"Huh?" Clarence shoved his way forward to the punch bowl and motioned to Tim to refill his crumpled paper cup. He ran his hand through his messed-up hair. "Whadda you say?" he asked.

"I said did you just get out of bed?" A roar of laughter pulsated against Clarence's ear drums.

With a sweeping gesture, Tim Regis dribbled some of the punch into the outstretched cup. "It doesn't take long my friend, does it?" he asked, wagging his head. "This stuff is pure tetra ethel . . ."

"Whadda you saying, Tim?" Clarence drained the stuff with slow long gulps, relinquishing the cup from his lips only after the last drop had disappeared. He didn't feel it, his mind boasted, though his face crumpled with grimaces of agony as the strong flavor of the alcohol seared through him.

He had been aware for some time now that he was the center of attraction. No one had seen him in this condition for months. And although there was a certain masochistic pleasure in the role, he was unused to it. There had been some commotion a while back—he recalled hearing a faint and distant scream—which drew most of the crowd away. Now that he was alone with Tim in the sudden quiet of the deserted hall, it took almost all of his will power to keep from lashing out at the smirking bartender. Without the crowd around, Tim was edgy and Clarence had to practically beg him to keep refilling his cup.

"Listen, Clarence, take it easy. By God, you've drunk enough for three people already."

"Chicken shit!" he said, dipping his cup in the bowl.

"Hey, Clarence, keep your claws out of the punch bowl."

A twitch of nervous relief flickered in Tim's face as revelers began to filter back into the hall, jabbering with excitement. Clarence backed away, swallowing his drink, looking about for Chris and the schoolteacher. He'd spotted them leaving together at the end of the dance. By then it was too late, it didn't matter. The alcohol filled him with contempt and frustration. He felt an urge to smash his knuckles into flesh.

He stumbled out the hall. At the corner of the building, he came upon a fisherman, his lips glued to the lips of Vivian, the fiery Indian waitress who worked at Mom's. Clarence pulled the man away from her, jerked him up against the wall and cocked his fist. As the man pivoted into a scared defensive posture, Clarence began to laugh.

"Hey, this is not the way to do it," Clarence mumbled. He wobbled away, defeated. It was her fault that he drank and gambled. She made him do it. He wanted to be like the other bastards, only better than they. Well, he had showed them by winning all that dough during the crap game. It was the old battle, the one he never won, the urge to prove himself better than the other guy.

He lumbered down the road, belching. With each new expulsion from the depths of his belly, his head spun, grew lighter. He stopped, his eyes blinking, examining the two squat ugly totem poles in front of Floyd's Curio Shop. He removed his jackknife from his pocket. Placing it between his teeth, pirate-style, he began to climb, using the indented mouths, feet, ears of the totem pole for footholds. His foot slipped and he came sprawling down. He cursed. A passerby halted, looking down at him and began to laugh.

"Hey, is that you, Clarence?"

"Who the hell you think it is? Beat it!"

"Jesus, are *you* plastered." The passerby was intensely curious. "What are you going to do with that knife?"

"Beat it, brother!"

He began to climb up the totem again but found it impossible, so he started to hack at the mouth of the ferocious looking animal on the base. A trickle of blood ran down the side of his chin from the edge of his lip where the knife had nicked him in the fall. Shavings began to float to the street. God damn, this is all right, he thought.

A thud of footsteps, scrunching in hurry, came dashing towards him.

"He-he-he," he heard Chuck Alder's characteristic laugh. "Not you, too, Clarence!" Chuck reached over and removed the knife firmly and deftly, from the barber's hand. He folded the blade into the guard and dropped it in his pocket.

"You better go home," Chuck said amiably. "He-he-he, can't have you destroying property."

Drunk as he was, Clarence knew better than to disobey the sheriff. Old and scrawny as he was, the bastard was mean and tough.

A black and white bulldog approached Clarence and began to run alongside of him as he swayed down the side of the street, sniffing at his legs. Clarence kicked at him with all his might, catching him square with the toe of his shoe. He laughed as the dog scurried off yipping and squealing in pain.

The street swayed below him as he crossed to the other side. He was dizzy. Blood pounded in his head. He staggered up against the front display window of Winton's Electric Shop and spied the gaping mouth of a waffle iron in the blue interior.

"God damn ugly world," he said and pushed off.

Shirley Parker shuffled past with a hulking, coughing man. Shirley twisted her head over her shoulder to glance at him, but the man grabbed her arm and pulled her up the street.

Arriving at the entrance to the hotel, he tilted his head up to the sky and was amazed at the sight of the black dome hovering over him. It seemed so aloof. He stumbled against the door, wincing at the piercing individuality of all the stars flashing down upon him. He lurched through the protection of the door. The foot of the stairs balked him and he had to hang onto the railing of the banister.

God damn, he would go see her. He'd screw the bitch. She wasn't so hot . . .

The familiar buff-colored wall of the hall reeled before him as he made the turn on the first landing and Clarence steadied himself upright, then wobbled forward. He grew furious at the next turn, by the library, when a figure collided against him, interfering with his progress.

"Watch where you're going!" he shouted. "Well, if it ain't the adenoids himself," he said recognizing Dave Collier.

"Hello, Clarence. A little under the weather, I see," Dave said with a good-natured grin.

"Whadda you know about weather? Beat it, chum! No! Wait!" Clarence squared off,."I'm going to beat the hell out of you."

Laughing, Dave pushed himself by and Clarence fell to the floor, sliding down the wall, from the force of Dave's push.

Dave looked surprised. He stopped to help him get to his feet.

"Beat it, chum. I'll manage."

Dave moved off, glancing once behind him at the struggling figure on the floor before he made the turn and disappeared.

"Oh, God," Clarence moaned suddenly. He sat for a moment with his head in his hands. Then he lurched upright and stumbled down the hall towards his room. He stopped in front of the door to the schoolteachers' room. He turned the knob but it was locked. He fumbled for his own key, which he knew would unlock the door, and opened it. The room was dark. He heard a soft, female voice ask, "Is that you, Lyddy?"

"Is only me, the barber. I want to see you a minute."

"What?" Her voice exploded with fright. "No! You better leave!"

Automatically, Clarence switched on the wall light and wobbled over to the side of the bed where the girl sat petrified. In a daze, he realized it was the wrong girl and a murderous rage filled him. But it vanished quickly in a swamp of despair. The sickness expanded in his body and he belched.

"I'm going to lay you, baby," he muttered and pulled from his wallet three one dollar bills. He slapped them down on the night stand. "I'm gonna take you down the line and you're going to like it."

Clarence dropped onto the bed hands forward, turned around and started to undress.

The girl sat upright, holding the covers to her chest. She seemed unable to move. Her eyes were wide with terror.

"Please," she began. "Please, don't. I'll scream."

But she didn't scream. She wriggled over to the far side of the bed.

"Now Clarence," she said sharply, "is this the way you men in Wrangell treat newcomers? You're behaving rather childishly . . ." She broke off as he threw his coat and vest onto the floor.

He sat down heavily on the bed again and began to untie his shoelaces.

"Clarence!" Her voice was louder and more aggressive. "For heaven's sake, stop this. I'll scream. I'll call for the owner of the hotel and you'll be put in jail."

"The money's on the table," he blurted out as he worked at removing his left shoe. It took both hands to pry it off.

"But I don't want your money. I want you to stop this." She jumped out of the bed—wearing only a silken slip—gathered up his clothes from the floor and flung them into his lap. "Put them back on and leave! Go!"

Clarence got up from the bed, clutching the clothes. He wobbled over to the window, opened it and threw the clothes out.

"Oh, look what you've done," she stammered. She began to cry, huge, choking sobs. "Now how are you going to get out of here?"

"The money is on the table. I got some more in my pocket. You take all you want."

He managed to get his other shoe off and started to pull off his pants.

Victoria ran to the door, opened it and looked out. But there was no one in the hallway. She felt so helpless. She didn't want to scream, have people come pouring in, questions asked. If only Chris and Lyddy would hurry back. If only she had kept Dave talking in the hallway for one more minute, this wouldn't have happened. She glanced about the room for a telephone even though she knew there wasn't one. Her eye fell on a tall, empty vase with a large flaring mouth. She ran to the bureau, took the vase in her hand and turned around.

Clarence was lying on top of the covers on the bed, naked. For a moment, she reeled back, stunned. Then she stumbled over to the bed, realizing that his body seemed familiar. His eyes were closed and he appeared to be fast asleep. She noticed the thin strand of blood on his chin. Her eyes scarcely moved off his pale face yet she was aware of his body—the small chest, the thin, wiry arms, the way he lay sprawled out on his back. Yes, he looked like Lowell, her ex-husband, only Clarence's body was smoother, more virile, stronger looking.

He opened his eyes and mumbled, "All right, I'm ready."

Vic clutched the vase, becoming panicky again, crouching in defense. But a surge of relief overcame her as she realized that he was more asleep then awake. She put the vase back on the bureau. Then the open window caught her eye and her heart fell as she realized that his clothes were somewhere out on the dock below the window. She dressed herself quickly and before she left the room, she threw an extra blanket over Clarence's naked body.

She was making her way down the bare wooden steps, carefully for they creaked and groaned, when she heard Dave Collier call out from the lobby.

"Is that you, Vic?"

She stood, jarred, and watched Dave approach.

"Why, where are you going?" he asked with a quizzical smile. Behind Dave, Vic saw the Indian who was the janitor of the hotel emptying spittoons into a bucket.

"Uh, Dave." She placed her hand on her forehead. "I'm surprised you're still here. My head is acting up again. I'm afraid it's pretty bad. I was looking for some aspirin."

Dave wheeled around and faced the Indian. The dentist was so full of vitality and good health. He was like a big batch of vitamin pills, pure and radiant clear through.

"Snake," Dave asked, "you have any aspirins?"

Snake shook his head no.

"I'll tell you what," Dave said. "I'll go get some from my office."

"Oh, no," she gasped. "That's not necessary. Coffee. Black coffee. That would help, just as well as aspirin."

"Really, it won't be any trouble. My office is only up the street a ways. You

111

go up to your room and I'll be back in a jiffy."

"No, please, Dave," she was frantic. "Thank you. But I don't want to put you to any trouble. Coffee would be better, really."

"Snake," Dave said, a little chagrined, "you have any coffee made?"

The Indian nodded his head, slowly and solemnly. "You bet, Mr. Collier."

"Well, get the lady a cup. Black."

A fever of sickness gripped Clarence's guts. He opened his eyes. He felt like he was choking. There was a revolt going on in his body that began in his stomach and sent blood rushing warm to his cheeks. With great difficulty, he got out of the bed, put on his pants and shoes. He couldn't seem to find his shirt or coat.

The sickness rose to his throat and he belched. He went into the lavatory, his brain pounding. His whole body was wretched with nausea. He sat down on the bowl with his pants on. He dropped his chin in his hands trembling. Without comprehending what he was seeing, his eyes took in the silk hose, hanging on the towel rack.

Suddenly he gasped in uncontrollable agony, and heaved and heaved. There seemed no end. All the while he was conscious of one dull, throbbing worry. Not to get any on the floor. He belched as he ripped off a strip of toilet paper, wiped off the spots on the porcelain and on the floor. He flushed the tank. He stood over the bowl, saliva hanging from his lips, a gritty sour flavor in his mouth, tears in his eyes. He jerked the lever again when the tank filled with water, listening to the whoosh as it emptied out.

He heard the door in the other room open.

"I got you a nice hot cup of coffee," he heard the girl call out, almost gaily. "If you only knew what I had to go through . . ." He came out from the bathroom, cautiously, his eyes narrowed.

"Go away," he muttered and dropped into a chair, closing his eyes.

"Gee, I wish you would take some coffee."

"Coffee? Snake makes coffee downstairs. You want coffee?"

She pulled up the remaining chair in the room. "No, silly. It's for you. Open your eyes. I've brought a cup up for you. It will do you good."

"Coffee. Ugh!"

Victoria skimmed the black coffee with a spoon and placed it near his lips. He swallowed it. "Oh!" he cried, sucking his burnt tongue.

"That's better. I'm sorry it's hot. What happened to you? You've got blood on your chin."

She ladled the coffee out with the spoon and fed him, a sip at a time.

Clarence slurped the coffee, unmindful of the girl, fighting his sickness. He felt like he had to vomit again. He stood up. But the flux passed as he belched once more. He sat back down.

"Open your mouth," she said with a smile. As she spooned the coffee into his mouth, she began to talk quite cheerfully. "You remind me so much of my ex-husband. Your body, your face. He was lean and wiry and strong. He had only one fault."

The coffee was reviving Clarence to some degree. He shouldn't have gone to the punch bowl. He should have known from past experience that he couldn't handle the God damn stuff.

"Lowell couldn't stand living with one person all the time. We wanted to have children so desperately, it would have been so good for us." She paused, patiently waiting for Clarence to open his mouth. "I used to worry about him so much. He'd stay out in the yard, mowing the lawn, planting new seeds, uprooting plants that maybe had just a little spot on them or a few yellow leaves."

Clarence squirmed restlessly, thinking about the other girl. He would have to show her that he was someone to be reckoned with.

Victoria smiled. "Lowell was so fussy and nervous. Always washing and waxing and vacuuming the car. He was busy all the time. When he came in the house, he'd pick up a newspaper or a magazine and read every line in it. I'd try to talk to him about my work, the children and he'd only half-listen. He never seemed to enjoy his food, just picked at it. Then after dinner, he'd be restless, want to see a movie, take a drive, have friends over. He could never relax."

Clarence couldn't figure out why he froze up around Lydia. He had to accost her, tell her all the things he wanted to say. Explain to her that he was crazy about her. He wanted so much to please her, to make her happy. There was so much that he could do to thrill her. He worshipped her. He would give her anything that she wanted. Maybe he should buy her something, a necklace or a ring. That should impress her.

"Well, finally, one Sunday afternoon," Victoria went on, "he just announced that he wanted a divorce. I kept the house. He used to come over to visit about twice a month. He'd mow the lawn for me, bring me candy. I knew he came because he was at a loss and well . . ."

"Did you sleep with him?" Clarence asked, looking up at the girl for the first time since she started plying him with coffee.

"Well," she said, getting up and setting the cup on the bureau. "I guess I shouldn't tell you."

"Then don't."

"Well, I did. I even let him stay overnight. He was bitter and thin. I would make his favorite dinner, roast chicken with okra and lots of seasoning, especially oregano. I got the recipe from a girlfriend of mine who was Greek. I'd like to cook it for you sometime, maybe when we move to the cottage on the hill."

"Where you going to get okra?" He wished the dizziness would leave him.

"If they haven't got canned okra here, I'll order some from the States."

"You really want to cook some for me?"

"Why, of course, I do."

"Because I remind you of your husband?"

"I haven't got a husband," she said smiling and patted him on the hand. "Now I think you better go."

As she helped him up, she said, "You threw your coat and vest out the window. Your shirt, too. Don't forget to go down and get them. Put something on first."

In the hallway, as Clarence stabbed his key into the lock, he heard voices on the landing. He took his time about opening the door because he wanted to see who they were. Although he knew. As his door swung open before him, he saw Chris and Lydia coming around the turn at the far end of the hall. She was clinging to his arm, her face upraised as he whispered something to her. Clarence plunged into his dark room.

––––––––––

The hill seemed to roll under Chris as he walked up it, he felt so good. This was one of the happiest nights of his life. It was too bad about Margaret Terjensen, though. That incident had soured the evening. Lydia wasn't the same afterwards. She had managed to help a little, soothing Margaret when she opened her eyes as they carried her onto the boat. It was pretty obvious that she was hurt bad.

Whistling, Chris climbed the steps to the big frame house. He switched on the light in the hall, then the living room, then went into the kitchen and poured himself a drink. Despite all the drinking he had done tonight, he barely felt it.

As he stood leaning against the sink, nursing his drink, he peered through the open door at the living room. The house was still cluttered with sofas, cushions, crocheted motifs on chair arms, afghans, ottomans, the way his mother had left it. She liked clutter, said it made the place more cheerful.

He switched off all the lights and climbed up to his room. He was aware of an intense happiness. It hurtled upon him with great, almost unbearable, force. He glanced at himself in the mirror. His hair was rumpled and his eyes were wide and strained. Chris smiled at himself. He began to undress slowly, in a trance.

He was aware of how happy he was living in Wrangell. That's why he never left, not even for a short period. He thought of it as staying in practice, like swimming or playing an instrument. Once you stopped, you got rusty. In his case, restless. He wouldn't know what to do with himself in the States.

Sure, he could visit his folks. But seeing Chris, young and healthy would upset his dad terribly. As long as Chris was far away, even though he was living in the house Theodore built and running the cannery Theodore developed, his dad could live in a dream of his youth and capabilities. But Chris' presence would be like a knife, slicing through that dream, releasing the jealousy and hatred which gnawed at his father. As long as everything was going the way Theodore wanted it to go, the entire family obeying his whims to the letter, displaying respect, not questioning his authority, well, everything was all right. There was peace in the family. But change that situation one iota, question one of Theodore's opinions or make a suggestion of how to improve things, and all hell broke loose.

They were both aggressive and there just wasn't enough room for the both of them. Theodore complained that Chris had it too easy and yet it was Theodore who gave it to him, supporting Chris while he attended college so he wouldn't have to work. Then he accused Chris of being spoiled and impulsive. Resentment shadowed their relationship, glaring yet secret, robbing them of the love for which they both yearned.

It was only when Giff was around that Chris ever saw his father mellow. Damn, Giff was the only man in the world who Theodore ever really loved. Giff was the only one who gave Theodore the unquestioning admiration that he craved.

As Chris undressed, he discovered that he was, in contrast to his usual habit, taking great care to fold his clothes neatly and put them on hangers. He began to whistle again.

He was happy in Wrangell. Satisfied. He did as he pleased, lived a good life. He didn't have to fight to get ahead, didn't have to pretend to be someone he wasn't. Life was simple. Hunting in the fall, the intense activity of the fishing season in the summer. Always the card games and dances and the quiet of long, empty days. He loved going out on the channel in a boat by himself, seeing and feeling and being a part of this land. He loved it and yet sometimes he felt enslaved by it.

He hated the constant bickering in the States. Maybe he was prejudiced but it seemed that down there, people squabbled over the smallest things. And they were hostile, suspicious, always figuring someone was out to take away their money. He found it easy to get along with people. All he had to do was be friendly. Kind. Gracious. But in the States, everyone was always trying to better himself, put himself above the others. That wasn't what Chris wanted. He had what he wanted in Wrangell and he wasn't going to take any chances.

He knew his mother and sister missed him. Time was running out. They were getting older. Someday it would be too late. And yet he couldn't go. Although every letter from his Mom contained some polite phrases about how she hoped he would come to visit soon, she never insisted. Verna knew how it was between him and Theodore.

He missed them too. He was lonely sometimes. He remembered Christmas Eve last year when getting drunk at the Regis' Christmas party wasn't enough. There wasn't any real substance to that party for him. Everyone was drunk, the kids were crying, people raising a rumpus. Chris had left, trudged up the hill to the house and up to his bedroom. He remembered lighting a cigarette and crying. He cried until the cigarette had burned down to the flesh of his fingers, never drawing on it, and then he'd stopped, lit a fresh one with trembling fingers and gone to bed. But he couldn't sleep until morning, when he was starting to sober up. He had to lie there all night, alone in the big house on the hill, until he'd sobered up and sleep had come.

But things like that were to be expected. In Wrangell he was free. He felt alive all the time, felt himself, felt the muscles of his legs from walking so much, the chords in his throat from talking and the muscles in his face from laughing from his heart. He was free and independent and he loved the land, the rawness and beauty of it, the fact that it was real and not a dream. Though it seemed more and more like one as time went by. A dream of water and mountains, of boats tied at floats and the growl of a seiner as it thundered out of the harbor leaving behind it a wide, glistening wake. And he loved the people, the wonderful people of Wrangell. . . .

———

Dawn stole east across the sky, spearing the stars one by one, the millions of small and large stars that had glittered alone and in patterns all through the night. In the cold wash of dawn light, all the small stars disappeared leaving only the big ones, separated by vast stretches of space, shining coldly in the light until they too disappeared. The sun rose golden and, behind the sun, the sky was green.

From Matt Fleming's cabin, the view was clear and the air was pure and still. Matt stepped outside for a moment to watch the colors in the sky and the sweep of the placid channel out to Elephant Nose Point.

Matt plunged down the narrow trail from his cabin to the road, suddenly deciding to take a walk along the shore before breakfast. He spied Danny

Olson with a 22 rifle in the crook of his arm, prowling along the edge of the embankment, his gaze trained on the shoreline, perhaps looking for a raven or a gull.

"You're up early," Matt said to the boy and filled his lungs with air for he felt better this morning. He was glad he had skipped the dance the night before.

"I stole out of the house before the folks woke," Danny said. "I took Dad's gun. I'm going to take a few shots and then hurry home with it." Danny sighed. "I have to go to church with Mom."

"Haven't had breakfast then?" said Matt.

"No. This is more fun than breakfast."

"Well, take a few shots and come up to the cabin." Matt smacked his lips, feeling a delicious sense of well being. After breakfast, he would have a cigar. The anticipation changed his mind about the walk.

"Gee thanks, Matt."

Matt pointed a finger along the trail by the trees which led out on the spit of the land to the rocky shore. "Seen a seal out there lately. Might kill yourself one if you're quiet—and lucky."

The boy hurried along the trail with the eager walk of a boy bent upon an important mission.

Ravens ran a thrill of octaves in their throats, a gurgling sound that clattered in the still air, as they hobbled clumsily along the shore, searching between the crevices of rocks for food. The tide was out.

The town is so pure in the morning, Matt thought, as he retraced his steps up the trail to his cabin.

Towards noon, a cold Stikine wind came whipping the clouds from the sky above Wrangell. Some stubborn clouds held on for a while until they were slowly jerked away and torn into pieces. The wind whipped the channel until it lay thrashing wildly. The color of glacier blue was everywhere, a blinding whiteness of blue that shivered in the rush of the wind.

8

"THIS IS YOUR STUDY HOUR," Lydia said to the children. "If you can get all your homework done at this time, you won't have to bother with it at home."

The children were restless at the end of the day so she had decided to make the last hour of the day the study hour. Otherwise, she had not made any changes in the schedule established by her predecessor. Lydia taught all the younger children—thirty-one restless, squirming youngsters in one class-room—while Victoria taught the older children. Now, as the hands of the clock crept towards three o'clock, the small shiftings and whispers of the children fanned across Lydia's mind as she sat at her desk.

It was June already. The term was almost over. After six weeks, she and Vic were just getting used to the work. Since they had moved into the cottage, they had settled into a routine that would soon be over. Idly, she let her pencil drift over a blank piece of paper, scribbling.

The day was hot and quiet and all the tall windows that overlooked the town below were pushed open. All the boys begged for a chance to be window monitor so they could use the tall gaff necessary to open and shut the windows on the top row.

There was a scuffle in the back of the room. Harry Bucci, a sturdy, dark-haired boy who was usually at the heart of any disturbance, was on his feet.

"Sit down, please, Harry," Lydia said crisply. She had met his mother the other night at the Johnson's Sweets and recognized her as one of the women marching down the road in stocking feet after the A&N dance.

The boy slunk back to his chair. He sat right behind the Crawford twins. She still had trouble telling which of the fair-haired boys was Bobby and which was Jimmy. They lived with their parents and younger sister in another one of the Eaton cottages.

"Miss Prince!" Danny Olson waved his hand frantically.

"Yes, Danny."

He came up to whisper in her ear. The boy's face was creased in a rueful frown. He looked so much like Clarence, she thought.

"Yes, Danny," she said to the boy after hearing his plea, "you may go. But after this, you must learn to go during intermissions and recesses."

"Yes, Miss Prince."

Lydia suppressed a smile as the door closed behind him. They were all so full of energy, wanting to try everything, taking on more than they could accomplish, beginning projects they could never finish. They were full of desire to act, to go forward.

Lydia walked across the room to the window, half conscious of the fluttering of papers, the pencils scribbling, the whispers of a group of restless children trying to sit still and concentrate on their studies. At the open window, the fresh air, though still and warm, awoke the odor of chalk and oiled desks behind her.

She looked down on the roof tops of Main Street and out across to the far end of the harbor where the water glowed purple and blue. Although she couldn't see a boat in the harbor, she could hear its faint engine—chut, chut, spatoo. From somewhere behind the building, the sound of a carpenter's hammer punctured the stillness.

Her heart jerked out of its lethargy as she thought of her date with Chris this afternoon. He would meet her at the cottage at three-thirty. They were going to the shore along the north edge of town to shoot ravens. That is, Chris was going to do the shooting!

Nothing was quite the way she expected. Last night Chris had taken her to the movie. Though she had seen the main feature in the States about two years ago, she enjoyed the experience very much. At the ticket window, Chris purchased the tickets from a buxom and sulky girl who glared at him. "Thanks, Fanny," he said with a jaunty air, disregarding her sullen attitude. To the contrary, Jeff Hunt, the manager of the theater beamed at them and thanked them for coming.

They had arrived early and sat downstairs. All the children occupied the front rows, smashing candy wrappers, stamping their feet, shouting to their parents in the balcony or in the back rows and running up and down the one center aisle. As they waited, she noticed that the natives were all filing across towards the right middle section of the chairs, the whites to the left and behind. This struck her as rather odd for usually everyone mixed together. At the dance at the A&N Hall, she'd noticed some of the white girls had danced with the native boys and it was not uncommon to see white men married to native girls and vice versa.

"Well, I see you have racial discrimination after all in this town," she said to Chris.

"Don't be funny," he said. "Just a silly custom at the show." Chris stopped her before she could continue, "Please don't ask why. No one tells them to sit over there."

The lights went out and the newsreel went on. It was old, a good year and a half old, yet Lydia had the strange sensation of reliving the highlights of the past. It was typical of how she experienced time in this town. It was unimportant. Irrelevant. There was a squeal of joy from the children and some of the adults as Mickey Mouse splashed laughing on the screen. The end of the cartoon was greeted with a great howl from the front rows which seemed to indicate complete approbation. This was followed by an old scenic reel about India which lasted for an interminable period amidst a crescendo of squabbling, smashing and stomping from down front. Next were the previews for coming attractions and then a few still slides. One promoted the town's milk delivery service mentioning the quality of milk produced by cows that fed on grass up on the Stikine River. Another announced the arrival of the new summer fashions in suits for men available at Hobson's Merchandise Store. Finally, a slide from the cinema house itself stated that the feature showing tonight would be shown again the following night and asking the audience to **"Please tell your friends."**

The entire theater was in a state of uneasiness by this time. Cigarettes were lit, people coughed and the children were in a small state of pandemonium.

Lydia edged closer to Chris. "Gosh," she yawned, "I'm about to give out."

He laughed. "Have patience, dear lady. This grows on you."

The final and main feature burst onto the screen amidst a roar of applause from the entire audience. The film was old, patched and pock-marked. It recorded the exploits of a keen-eyed cowpuncher portrayed by Richard Dix. The celluloid broke intermittently throughout the performance, followed by groans and stamping feet. Watching the film was somewhat like fitting together a jigsaw puzzle for the film never resumed exactly where it had left off. It might stop right after the hero dispatched a few villains with a few well-aimed blows and then resume with the hero being chased by these same men.

"Is it always like this?" Lydia asked, during a clamoring period of darkness.

Chris said, with a chuckle, "This is the worst. Generally it only breaks once or twice. Maybe the projectionist is pie-eyed tonight. He's not usually so slow and sloppy about fitting the thing together."

When all the bad men were subdued and the hero was galloping away in a trail of dust, the audience rose in a body, for there was no second feature, and filed up the center aisle. It was the custom afterwards for the town to gather at the Johnson's Sweets to play the nickelodeon and talk. Lydia was totally unprepared for the sight of Chris eating ice cream, then topping it off with a cherry coke. She was more familiar with the odors of whiskey and tobacco on his breath.

Yes, she thought, as she stood at the classroom window gazing at the town below, it had been so informal and gay. Later, when most of the folks left, she and Chris remained behind and danced in the small rear room with a few other couples to the music of the nickelodeon.

The savage growl of two dogs fighting somewhere around the school building aroused Lydia from her daydream. She glanced at the wall clock, anxious for the period to end. There were still a few minutes left. She went back to her desk, tidied her things and sat down, crossing her legs and staring at the children without seeing them.

There was so much happening, so much between her and Chris. She could perceive the seriousness of it more and more with each new day. It was June. In a couple of weeks, school would be over and she would have to make some decisions. Should she stay for the fall semester? Remain in Wrangell throughout the long months of summer vacation? What would Vic want to do? If they stayed, it would be impossible to return to San Francisco for a visit—too costly.

Lydia squirmed considering how her mother would respond if she wrote and told her she was planning to stay in Wrangell. Her mother's last letter had made it perfectly clear that Lydia was expected to return at the end of the term, teach at the local elementary school and live at home.

The shuffling sounds of children sliding out of their chairs and gathering up their books and papers in response to the dismissal bell brought Lydia to her feet.

"All right, children, you may go. March out in orderly formation, not like yesterday afternoon."

She let the children out the door, then gathered her own things and went out of the building. She met Vic outside, below the landing.

"Hi, kid," Vic said. "Brother, did I have a rough time today with the Landreth girls . . ." Vic stopped as Herb Weaver came down the steps.

"Hello, girls," he said, with a bright smile. "How did it go, today?"

"Just fine," they replied.

"I'm not through yet," Vic said with a sigh. "I'm keeping the Landreth girls after school. I'd better get back in there."

"Be careful," Herb said to Vic, with a knowing wink. The Landreth girls were as husky and muscular and mean as boys. Herb went off down the hill.

Probably going down to work on his boat, Lydia thought, as she took the path around the building which led up the hill. Sometimes she thought the principal loved his boat more than his wife. In fact, all the men seemed to love their boats. They were always tinkering with engines or painting them. There was always something that needed to be done, something mechanical talk about whenever the men got together.

She climbed up the hill, savoring the effect of the exertion on her lungs and legs. At the cottage, Lydia took a shower and put on her tan gabardine slacks and a russet-colored sweater. She hummed all the while, waiting for Chris. The cottage was such a relief after the hotel. She had gotten tired of the constant music flowing up from the bar, the drunks slobbering in the hallway. She rushed through her make-up; she didn't want to keep Chris waiting. Humming, she brushed up her hair and tied a bandanna over it. She felt revived, free and gay and independent. Being up here alone, away from San Francisco, was doing her good. Against her better judgement, she had become fond of the town and the friendly people in it.

And Chris. Chris was wonderful. So tall and energetic and simple. Her stomach tightened.

She sat down in the small living room and waited. It was odd that Chris was late. He was usually early. The carpet was matted down and dirty. She could see the imprints of muddy soles. It had been raining all the past week and the week before that. Not a steady pouring rain, but a soaking mist that drizzled constantly. Everyone was used to it. The children played out in the muddy roads with no concern. She went to the kitchen and got the carpet sweeper from the broom closet and began sweeping the rug. She liked the four rooms of the cottage, which sat square on the rim of the hill. The walls and ceilings of the living room were painted white. Behind the dark blue davenport, the windows overlooking the channel were draped with a floral print.

Putting the sweeper away, she picked up a dust cloth and began to dust the furniture in the living room. There were some nice pieces: a cherry-finish coffee table with a glass top which sat beside the over-stuffed lounge chair and, in the corner of the room, a mahogany rocker upholstered in a colonial tapestry.

All in all, this was more than she or Vic had expected. The rent was modest and Guy Eaton was a good landlord. He lived with his wife in the cottage just below them. He took pride in his lovely front yard that made the shape of a heart on the hill, ringed by the five white cottages with his own in the center. It was bordered with rocks, lush with lawn, dotted with fir trees and plots of flowers that Mr. Eaton tended with meticulous care.

Chris was a half-hour late when he arrived. He stood before the door, scuffing his shoes, holding a huge shining gun.

"Sorry, I'm late."

"What's that? Looks like a cannon."

"Oh, just a twelve gauge shotgun. I'd have been up sooner," Chris explained, "but I've been chasing all over town trying to locate a gun for you. We'll find one somewhere though," he vowed.

"Me!" she stammered, scared stiff of the ominous-looking thing. "I thought you were going to do the shooting."

"Heck no!" he said. "Let's go."

He lit a cigarette outside while she put the dust cloth away and washed her hands.

"Where to?" she asked, closing the door.

"Main Street. Someone there is sure to have a four ten or near it."

"A what?"

"A lighter gauge shotgun. Twelve gauge might purple your shoulder a little."

They walked down the hill in the hot sun. There was scarcely any humidity in the air. The channel was shimmering in a misty blue haze that reached out to the islands, making them low and colorless.

They crossed Main Street and hiked up the stairs to Dave's dentist office.

"I think Dave's got the right caliber for you," Chris said.

Dave appeared from the dentist room, spruce in his white uniform, his complexion as clear as agate.

"Sorry, Chris," Dave said after hearing what Chris wanted, "but all I have left is that twelve gauge automatic."

"What happened to that four ten? Chris asked.

"I loaned it to Mitch Bucci and he dropped it in a slough."

"Well, thanks anyway, Dave," Chris said and they left.

They hurried down Main Street to the hotel, nodding or saying hello to everyone on the street

"Giff's got a raft of guns. He's sure to have the right one."

An Indian girl was sitting next to Giff at the bar. She had just lit a cigarette for Giff when Chris and Lydia approached them. She held the still burning match in her fingers and faced them with an expression of dumb, gawking curiosity. Both appeared very drunk.

"You'll burn your finger," Giff growled at her. He turned to Chris who had inquired about the gun. "Nope," Giff said. "Smallest I have is a sixteen gauge."

"That's still not right for the frail city lady," Chris laughed.

"Chris, it doesn't matter," Lydia said, slightly vexed. She shivered under the dull and sullen glare of the Indian girl reflected in the wall mirror. "I'd rather watch you do the shooting."

"Heck, no. There's no fun in that," he laughed. "I'll get you a firearm if I have to turn the town inside out."

In front of the hotel, they got into Curly's cab and took off for Roy Hart's house. Curly drove so fast, speeding along the road that followed the contours of the harbor, that it seemed to shrink the size of the town, although it was only about three miles from the hotel to the Hart's home near the south edge of the harbor. Bea opened the door. At once Lydia was caught off guard as she often was when she encountered Bea Hart.

Dark and classic, Bea was the most beautiful woman Lydia had ever seen. As always, she wore a single strand of imitation pearls around her neck. The necklace was typical of her simplicity and charm. She didn't need a lot of fancy clothes or jewelry to attract attention. She didn't put on any airs, yet she had a powerful presence. She was a small woman with an elegant figure and an air of softness that conveyed both sympathy and nurturing. Yet as always, with Bea, Lydia felt uncomfortable, a wave of jealousy that she could not choke back. And Bea's radiance, her softness, her incredible beauty were all the more extraordinary considering that she was at least forty.

Bea called out to Roy who was brushing Winchester on the back porch and when Roy came through the kitchen, Chris explained their mission.

"Sure, I have one, if a twenty gauge will do," Roy said. "It's cleaned and oiled and wouldn't kick a baby."

They thanked Bea and Roy for the gun and went to the door.

"Would you kids like a glass of iced tea?" Bea asked. "It's so warm outside."

"Okay," Chris said. "Plenty of time to do some shooting.'

They drank the iced tea and Roy talked with Chris about the upcoming fishing season and Bea beckoned Lydia to follow her. They went into the bedroom, full of gleaming new furniture, which seemed to be slumbering in the heat. Bea opened a cedar chest and pulled out a comforter she had just finished quilting. It was made of patches of gray and white cloth and bordered in gray.

"It's beautiful," Lydia said. "Wherever do you find time to do it?" At once she was sorry she had said that, for she realized she had never seen Bea out of the house.

"Oh, as Roy would say," Bea said, "that's one thing we have up here. Time. Time on our hands."

Lydia blushed and felt humiliated. She could see that she had grieved Bea in some way. It seemed so easy to do.

The women returned to the living room and Chris stood up and said Curly was waiting outside.

"Oh, goodness," Bea frowned, "we should have invited Curly in for iced tea."

Roy said, "Make Curly a glass and he can return it when he comes around next trip."

Chris handed Curly the glass of tea and he drank it as he drove the cab back to Main Street. "Drop us off at the cannery," Chris said. "We'll start off from there."

The Ballard Cannery was at the other end of town, past the Clinton and Canadian docks. Each packing a shotgun, they walked up dirt road which led past the cannery and the two-story wood bunkhouse where the Filipino workers stayed during the fishing season, heading up towards the north tip of the island. Old frame houses and flimsy clapboard cabins stood on either side of the road. The houses on the left were built on pilings with great spruce logs mounted crosswise under the foundations as protection against the incoming tides.

"Sometimes the tide comes over the porch," Chris said. "At the float house it happened twice in one year. Whole place was flooded a foot high with water. The tide raised the house as far as the length of cable that held the house fast. After the second abnormal tide, we spliced another piece of cable onto it."

"All very interesting," Lydia said. "But what about this gun I'm holding? You don't really expect me to shoot it?"

Chris laughed. "Today you rise and shine—killing ravens."

The road led across a rickety wooden bridge that spanned one of the many streams that emptied in the bay. They stopped for a moment to rest at the bridge and peered off at the group of islands lying west across the shimmering blue haze of the channel.

"It's like a dream," Lydia whispered, noticing for the first time the peace and beauty that lay all around them. Her eyes followed the clear stream of water that flowed below until it fell out of sight over a cluster of rocks. "It soaks into your skin, doesn't it?" she asked.

"It's good country, Lyddy," he said.

Chris leaned the two guns against the bridge railing and lit a cigarette. "You know what my housekeeper told me just the other day? The mind and the eye are constantly aware of the water, the trees, the islands." He paused a moment. "Well," he said, rather abruptly, "we're almost in shooting territory." He picked up the guns. "Here's yours. Just don't be afraid of it."

They crossed the bridge and continued walking along the dirt road. It curved around the side of the tall hill which crowned the northern end of Wrangell Island. To their left, tall trees lined the bluff above the shoreline and a few scattered houses stood in lonely solitude. At the start of the path that led to the beach, Lydia stopped.

"Honestly, Chris, I'm scared to shoot this thing."

Chris took the gun, inserted shells in the magazine and showed her where the safety was. "Place the butt against your shoulder, aim and squeeze the trigger. Nothing to it."

"Uh huh," she said.

Through a gap in the tall spruce and hemlock that fringed the beach, they could see the bay. It looked like a blue dream. The whole land was still. The channel stretched out in a mist of soft blue. The islands in the distance seemed to drift, low and deep, in some ancient heavy green dream. There was not a spark of life, no vivid color in the channel, just an infinity of dreaminess, so warm, so still was the day.

Lydia and Chris jogged down the narrow dirt path which was bordered on either side with thick clusters of wild raspberry and boysenberry bushes. She felt it there too, between the hedges of the narrow trail, the warm dreaminess of the afternoon, the distant humming of solitude wrapped within solitude.

"It's so quiet, Chris."

"It won't be for long." Chris said, pumping a shell into the chamber of his gun.

They came out onto the beach from the path and the mood was there too, on the rocky shore covered with seaweed and wild grass, only this time she felt its power as if she were in the heart of it. The immense space of the channel, the vast stretch of the sky seemed to pounce upon her. The silence, the beauty of the land, which had in it a kind of somber quality, seemed to fill up every nook and corner of the beach. It was like a Beethoven symphony, she thought. Even the water lapping on the shore was hushed. It was so still, with a deep, numbing stillness, almost as if she'd wandered into another person's dream, as if Alaska itself were dreaming.

From the tip of the trees a hundred yards away, where the beach curved out and formed an elbow, a raven, black and shiny as satin, dropped out of a branch and winged low in flight in a straight line towards them. Chris whispered beside her, "Let's see you hit him, it's an easy overhead shot."

She felt a stab of fright in the pit of her belly. She didn't really want to shoot a bird. She remembered once reading a story about a hawk which had been shot by a Japanese farmer. It had turned her against people who shot at birds for pleasure. But it was hard to disappoint Chris. He had gone to so much trouble so that she could participate. She didn't know what to do.

The lone raven flew down from the tree tops in line with the shore. It was a slow, lumbering flight, yet the bird flew straight as an arrow. Lydia shot at it when it was directly overhead. She was so mixed up with fright and guilt that her eyes closed and she swung the barrel skyward without looking. When the eruption died down—in the stillness of the beach it was deafening—Chris was buckled up with laughter. The raven, thank the Lord, was still very much alive, still flying along with its great wings whacking the air. It swerved, dipping, and landed on the edge of the wooden bridge from which the town's refuse truck dumped the garbage into the channel.

"What's so funny?" she asked, dizzy as she lowered the heavy gun, her nostrils prickling with the acrid smell of burnt powder. Then she could no longer suppress her impulse to laugh and crumpled up with laughter beside Chris.

The gunfire stirred the ravens. A flock of them winged out of the trees and came flapping over their heads. Lydia just had time to jerk her head back when Chris lifted his gun against his shoulder and sent off one—two—three—deafening crashes in quick succession. The gunfire shattered the mood. Two large dark objects plummeted in twirling spirals into the water. A horrible ringing grated in her ear drums. She stared at the birds, floating close to shore with their wings outspread and shattered, their heads down. Chris reloaded his gun with fresh shells and frowned.

"I missed on the first shot. Led him too much. They move slow, not like ducks."

She was relieved that Chris didn't bother to retrieve the birds and they jogged side by side over the rocky, grassy edge of the shore towards the trees. Puddles of water lay in the crevices of the rocks and she could see the pools in the distance flashing like upturned mirrors in the sunlight. A small boat chugged by a hundred yards off shore and a native woman with a green handkerchief tied around her head waved at them. Chris waved back.

"Who is she?" Lydia asked.

"Well, let's see," said Chris, pondering the boat's name which was printed in white letters. "That's the *Mary Jane* so I guess that must be Mildred Roosevelt."

"It's nice to know everyone in town, isn't it?"

"Not hard to know everyone in Wrangell."

"I like that, Chris. I like the hellos and good mornings. It's new to me, you know. I've never lived in a small town before."

Yes, she realized, the greetings were important to her. In a way, they woke her up every morning for it was customary to greet everyone you met on the street. Even if you met the same person four or five times, you still exchanged greetings. There was a warmth about it, a bonding that was part of the soul of a small town.

They rounded the bend that jutted down to the shoreline and came to a dent in the trees where a tangle of logs had been washed up along the beach by the tide. The logs were polished bone-white by seawater and sun, with here and there a black charred scar showing where picnickers had camped. Taking her hand, Chris led Lydia behind the logs and they concealed themselves from the ravens perched in the trees. They sat cross-legged on the warm sand behind the blockade of logs, the sun falling hot on their faces. In the small enclosure, the stillness of the land seemed more powerful.

"Why are there so many logs on the beach, Chris? I would think they'd be chopped up and used for firewood."

"They are but we had a pretty stormy winter so we got more logs than usual. Sometimes a scow loaded with logs being tugged to Ketchikan or to our mill gets caught in a bad one and the lashings break or become loose or the tug just abandons the scow and the logs drift to shore. Then there's erosion going on all the time around the islands, with the tide washing away the shoreline and the trees toppling over." Chris reached over and released the safety on Lydia's gun. "Better be still. I want to see you shoot that cannon again." He laughed. "And Roy said it wouldn't kick a baby. How's your shoulder?"

"There's nothing wrong with it," she whispered. "I'm just a fraidy cat."

They sat there for a while in silence. Over the top of the logs, she could see the channel, laying still and creamy. The hazy atmosphere blended with the haziness of the sky and the sun cut through it with a tremendous power that seemed to flatten everything into submissiveness. The islands that loomed low in the distance were bathed in haze.

Chris jerked his head towards a small outcropping of rocks that protruded from the beach about fifty yards away. Behind the jutting white rocks Lydia saw a blur of swift movement. She gasped as she realizing she was seeing a bear, a big black hulk of a bear that stood reared on his hind legs, both front paws clutching a handful of seaweed that he was ripping into shreds with savage swipes of his teeth.

"He likes the taste," Chris whispered, "the salt taste in the seaweed."

Chris got down on his hands and knees and crawled forward towards the rocks. Lydia followed. She was so concerned about duplicating every move that Chris made that she didn't feel afraid. Slowly, Chris rose to his feet. The black bear's head was visible between a small gap in the rocks, his long front claws ripping through the seaweed which filled his frothing mouth. Chris edged forward, his gun poised halfway to his shoulder, and Lydia, scared, decided to stay behind. Chris stole forward, foot by foot. Lydia realized she was taut with fear.

"Chris, Chris," she whispered, "be careful." With a surge of relief she remembered someone telling her recently that bears had poor sight and had to rely almost entirely on their keen sense of smell. Chris was about thirty feet from the rocks. Suddenly, the bear saw him, his red mouth gaping with astonishment. His paws opened, releasing the seaweed, and he scuttled off for the woods. Chris emptied his shotgun at him, taking three separate aims. Each time the gun roared, the rump of the bear would sink, wriggling and sliding across the ground. The frightened bear relieved himself in one long and straight line until the trees enveloped him.

Chris burst out with a peal of laughter.

"What's so funny?"

"Brother! Now there was one scared bear!" said Chris, staring at the long wet track running obliquely across the sand to where the bear had disappeared into the trees.

"The poor thing. You think he'll die? I know you hit him."

"Naw. He'll just have a red-hot behind for a few weeks."

She had to laugh with him now.

"Enjoying yourself?"

"Of course." She looked at his face, taut with laughter. She wanted to say, "It's more than that, Chris, it's what you are, what you make me feel all the time . . ." But her heart bogged down.

"I'm getting hungry," he said. They started back along the beach. "You know, I don't really care for killing ravens. They're scavengers. They help to keep the beach clean."

"Why do you do it then?"

"Oh, I don't know. I don't do it often. Anyway, one or two less doesn't do any harm. Keeps 'em on their toes."

"It was fun, Chris," she said. As they walked back along the road towards town, she thought it was as if the whole afternoon had never happened, as if they had been inside a dream.

9

WHEN CLARENCE CAME INTO the restaurant, Mom was sitting at her desk in front of the plate glass front window separating charge slips.

"Afternoon, Clarence," she said. "You're late today."

"Wasn't hungry," he replied, taking a seat at the counter.

The Indian waitress, Vivian, tripped up to Clarence wiping her hands on a cloth. "Hi, Clarence." She set a glass of water before him, unfolding a menu at the same time.

"Two eggs over. Nothing else. A slice of tomato if he's got any."

"Care for some coffee while you wait?" She folded the menu deftly, dropping it into the prongs behind the napkin stand. She was sharp, Clarence reflected, for a Klootch. Vivian's expression revealed nothing, yet she was sharp in more ways than one.

"No. Give me a glass of that Stikine grass-fed milk."

Clarence ripped a napkin out of the napkin holder and wiped his mouth and forehead. It was raining again, always raining. At least he didn't have to be out in it. It drizzled and stopped, drizzled and stopped. The customers coming into the shop kept making the same old comments. "Remember last year? It rained ninety-two days without letting up." Women had pushed their baby carriages up and down Main Street, leaving the hooded kids outside in the rain while they shopped.

"How's business, Clarence?"

"Same, Mom," he replied but he wasn't sure about that. Ever since the night of the crap game, it seemed to slack off. Men weren't coming in for shaves anymore which made sense since the year was about over. Most everyone was broke, waiting for the fishing season. Yet they still had money to buy drinks at the bars. Vivian was washing glasses at the sink on the other side of the counter, right in front of Clarence. She had a nice build with firm breasts which made a deep V framed by the neckline of her red wool sweater. "I like that sweater," Clarence said. "What's that pinned on it?" It was a pale oval cameo brooch with a carving of a woman's profile in relief.

"You've seen it before," Vi commented.

"It certainly accentuates the positive."

Vi straightened and took a deep breath, her breasts stretching the fabric of the right red wool sweater tight.

"Yes, sir," said Clarence with a smile and stirred in his chair.

Vi wore two diamond rings on her left hand. After her first husband had drowned, she married a white man from Juneau. But she still wore her first husband's engagement ring, even during her second marriage. Vi had loved Art Johansen. She had two kids by him.

The eggs in the oval platter had runny yellow centers. Clarence cursed the cook, probably drunk as usual.

"Vi, tell that son of a bitch I want them over and well done. He should know how to make them by now."

Vi took the platter away, with no resentment, no fuss. Nothing showed on that face of hers but good humor.

"This season better be good," Mom said. "Some of the boys will need it."

Clarence controlled an urge to laugh at Mom's maternal remark. Mom was anything but maternal. Before she married that booze hound, Bud Belmont, Mom had been a free-lance whore, canvassing most of the Southeastern. When her husband spent more time in the bars than he did at sea, she opened the restaurant to support herself. Mom had one fault and it got worse until no one would have her anymore. Her kidneys were shot and the old lady invariably wet the bed at least once or twice before morning.

The eggs, this time, were half burnt. They laid on the platter, thin, dark-brown and as pliable as leather. Clarence ate slowly, dousing the eggs with catsup, and drank his glass of milk.

"Fill her up for me, Vi, please."

"Sure, Clarence." Vi was peppy. She bounced behind the counter instead of walked. She used to pal around with Gwen when Clarence first came to Wrangell. They were wonderful friends. No one would do the things Vi and Gwen did. They went swimming in January in the icy harbor, went trout fishing by themselves in Gwen's father's skiff. Two wonderful, sprightly girls and then they got married. Gwen to Clarence. Vi to Art Johansen. Marriage calmed them down. They both got pregnant right away. They were both happy in their marriages. And then came the report that the tug was broken up in the storm, pieces of it found along the shore, four men missing. The search. The town gathering in a body and going out in an armada of trollers, gill-netters and seiners. Some dragging the straits, others combing the shore along which parts of the tug had washed up. Two weeks went by. Two weeks and then one day they fished out Art Johansen's body.

Clarence never would forget that day as long as he lived. Gwen was in hysterics over her friend's misfortune. "She loved Art so much," she kept saying. "They were so happy together. Now it's all over. Oh, Clarence, her life is over."

They brought Art's body to Wrangell. Vi, who was expecting her second child at the time, came down to the airplane float with the support of her mother and father, to identify what was left of her husband in the coroner's basket.

The girl did not have to nod to Greg Sundberg to confirm the identity of her husband. The coroner knew. The girl's mother and father knew. Everyone in Wrangell knew Art Johansen. Clarence would never forget how Vi looked as she gazed at her dead husband, the agony etched on her tired, puffy face, as Greg solemnly replaced the lid of the wicker basket.

That was Clarence's first taste of death in Alaska. He was to become familiar with it. He would get to know a guy, he would come in his shop day after day and then, one day, he's gone, drowned. No lingering about it. When a guy fell into the icy water, he had about ten minutes to live before he'd be dead from hypothermia.

It was after Art's death that Vi started working with Mom, out of sympathy and necessity, a bond that seemed to tighten with the years. Bud had drowned in the same storm on the same tug.

Clarence drank the rest of his milk and went out on the dismal, drizzling street. He passed the liquor store, the bakery, the theater, the butcher shop, Johnny Bugg's bar, stepping around the puddles. As he approached the barber shop, Roy Hart went gliding past in a hurry.

"Hello, Clarence." There was a kind of condescending smirk in Ray's greeting that caught Clarence unawares, hurting him. He stopped, his hand on the doorknob, puzzled by the man's tone of voice and the expression in his face. He realized that the drizzle had stopped again. In the western sky, the light glowed bronze and silver, refracting off the wet fronts of the business establishments, illuminating display windows, streaking down the street itself. Just like turning a page, the world was suddenly full of a curious light that gilded the shops and stores of Main Street.

Steve was reading the latest issue of *Life* and didn't look up as Clarence came in. Lately Steve had been around more than ever, saying he had nothing else to do until fishing season.

Clarence slipped into his smock and eased into the barber's chair. Often, for diversion, he'd try to coax Steve into working out with him at night when the shop was closed and the shades down. He could use a good round of practice to stay in shape, to sharpen his jabs and build up his wind and limber his sockets in case a need arose to use his fighting skills. But since those few preliminary lessons that Clarence had given Steve years ago, Steve never showed any interest and always declined the use of the punching bag in the rear room. Steve had killed a nine hundred pound bull moose last fall, quartered it and lugged it to the cold storage plant where Butch had ground part of it into hamburger and cut the rest into marked packages, most of it going into the Bucci box, and Steve seemed to think that was all the exercise he needed.

Hank Connell came into the shop and Clarence pushed himself out of the chair. He pinned the apron around Hank's neck and set to work. He was restless. All his life he had been restless. He could never put his finger on what it was that drove him, what he yearned for. But he thought he knew how he had to live to achieve it, a life of quiet and simple routine that he would perfect in the simple quiet of Wrangell. And ever since he'd seen Lydia, his life pattern was crumbling, the life pattern which had meant so much to him that he had wrecked his married life to achieve it. It was as if his whole life had kicked over, flopped on its back and lay wriggling helplessly like a turtle.

"How have you been?" Clarence asked Hank as he plied his razor around Hank's ears.

"Rotten. Been on the wagon since the dance."

"When you go on the wagon," Steve said, "Seagrams loses twenty percent of its business."

"God damn ulcers. You guys don't know how lucky you are. Doc told me it's either get off or go under." Hank gave a scowling grin.

"Don't tell that to Greg," Steve joked. "He's liable to take a bath." The three men laughed, knowing that about the only time Greg Sundberg ever took a bath was when someone in town passed away.

"Greg'll be here long after any of us," Hank said, easing out of the chair.

Hank angled off across the street, walking slowly and stiffly, as if his legs pained him, going past Floyd's Curio Shop and into the small dark hamburger joint operated by his wife and daughter. Hank was a fisherman; he didn't care to own a business. Last year Chris had been going pretty steady with Hank's daughter, Helen. Everyone knew Helen was crazy about Chris but they had drifted apart sometime after the fishing season. Clarence had looked upon the affair with detached amusement. Only now he couldn't help but wonder how his life would be different if Chris had married Helen.

"That son of a bitch is crazy," Steve said, licking his forefinger before he turned a page of the magazine. "Funny isn't it, how a man changes when he stops drinking? Remember Dwight Barnard? It killed him. By God, I was there when it happened. Dwight was playing stud poker at Red's, drinking soda water, and he gets this good hand and suddenly he topples over, kicking and quivering, foaming at the lips. Doc said it was a heart attack. Poor Dwight. By God, he died miserable."

"He should have slacked off easy," Clarence said. "Not all at once."

"Hank's the same way. I'll bet that whole family kills two quarts a day. But Hank's the best damn halibut man in the country. He can sniff the God damn fish."

"At least he doesn't go hog wild when he does drink."

"I'd rather be that way any day," Steve said. "But Hank can't drink at all, considering what booze does to his stomach. If he's got a stomach any more. By God, I've seen Hank cough up blood."

"Steve," Clarence said, taking off his smock, savoring a sudden impulse. "I'm closing up early. What the hell! If anyone wants a haircut, I'll get 'em in the morning."

"Suits me." Steve said.

When they went outside, the glow from the west still hovered in the air, though it was now pale. Clarence locked the door and they headed up the street.

Steve said, "Let's go for a walk. Do you good. It's not good to be cooped up the way you are all the time."

"Naw. We're going to the hotel bar."

"What! Are you crazy, Clarence? After the dance?"

"I'm going to have a plain coke. I'm just going to sit there and watch what happens."

"Clarence, what's ailing you, boy? This is not like you. Forget the sons of bitches."

"We're going to the hotel, Steve. Giff's been too God damn mouthy for me lately."

By the time the two men got to the hotel it was drizzling again. The outlines of the islands across the channel were hidden under the masses of settling clouds.

Steve pushed through the bar door first. There was no bartender behind the counter. The air smelled of soaked wood, crushed cigarette butts, stale beer and whiskey and tobacco juice, the smells that were a familiar to the bar as incense in a church. It was quiet except for the rattling of dice, the shifting of chairs and the sound of hushed voices in the other room where a game was going on.

"Funny thing happened the other night," Steve said, as they settled side by side at the bar. "I dropped in on Babs and God damn if Mitch wasn't there. Kind of embarrassing but that dumb yokel wouldn't know what the score was if somebody told him. He was telling Babs about the job he got lined up on one of Chris' seiners this coming season and Babs was setting up some coffee and sandwiches on the table and invited me to join in."

Clarence scarcely paid any attention to Steve, though he was grateful for his chatter. He was trying to register all the sounds of the almost empty bar, trying to filter out the sounds of the conversation Holly Dancey was making with her friends in the side corner booth, listening for a change in the atmosphere in the crap game in the other room, as if he were expecting trouble. As if now that he was in the bar the place wasn't the same. Giff might follow up on some of the things he'd been bellowing about since the night of the big crap game. Damn, where was the bartender?

"Well," Steve was saying, "while we were eating, little Tony starts climbing out of his crib in the other room and falls to the floor. We all rush into the bedroom and find the poor kid on the floor by the crib, bawling his head off. Mitch examines the baby's head and says, `Hell, you can't hurt him with a sledgehammer' and goes back to the table."

Steve burst out laughing. The sound curdled in Clarence's guts and he wished Steve would stop. In the quiet of the bar it sounded uncouth and Clarence stiffened with tension. Where was Max? Probably shooting craps with the boys in the other room. Well, he'd better not call him. He'd let Steve do it.

Steve chuckled as he lit a cigarette. "Babs brought Tony in to the kitchen and he stopped crying after she gave him a piece of bread. She set him down so that she could finish her coffee and the little mutt sneaks off into the lavatory and brings his little potty to the table. And the little rascal goes up to me and says, `Wanna pee, Mr. Steve? Wanna pee?' He kept offering me his potty and when he saw I wasn't going to pee in it, he thought I guess, that I didn't understand him, so he sets it down on the floor, squats right on it and begins to grunt like he was doing it. By God, we laughed."

Clarence looked around for the bartender.

"Sounds just like the Bucci's," he said, without thinking, although the story did make him feel better. He enjoyed hearing about the inconsequential as well as the important things that went on in Wrangell. No matter what people thought of him as an individual or what circumstances brought them together, in some way, everyone was close. A respect for the dead of Alaska hung invisible in the air. Everyone had to stick together to endure the tragedy and the isolation.

From the corner of his vision, Clarence spotted the white clad bartender pop out from one of the side booths where the crap game was going on and head toward them.

Steve got up from his stool. "Get me a beer, will you, Clarence? I'll be back in a sec." And Steve strode through the other room in the direction of the lavatory door.

Alone. He was suddenly alone and he didn't like it. The whole weight of the place seemed to be bearing down upon him as a moment ago he'd seen those massive gray clouds across the channel bear down on the islands. He sat there on the stool, stiff and cold, and wished Steve was back.

"Sorry to keep you waiting," Max said to Clarence.

From out of nowhere, Violet Lundy sidled up to the bar and plunked down on the stool next to Clarence.

"Hello, darling. Gonna treat me to a beer?" Her low rasping voice had a catch in it, as if the Klootch had a sore throat.

"Hello, Violet," Clarence said. He gave her a half-hearted smile though he despised her. He hated the way she fawned on him in public, although he did sleep with her when loneliness became too much to bear. He despised her and everyone else who haunted bars, despised their infantile weakness for alcohol (although it struck him for a moment that perhaps they didn't come for the alcohol but to escape their own loneliness). Yet as barber in this town, he depended on their good will for his livelihood and so he kept his disapproval and contempt to himself. As for his conduct at the dance, well, that was the first time in years that he had allowed himself to be misled by his inner turmoil and it would be the last, he vowed.

"Hello, Violet," Max said. "Did you see me go?"

"Were you hot?" Violet asked.

"Hot. I'll say I was hot. I threw six passes. God damn, I have no guts. I should have let it ride."

"Max," Clarence said, trying to conceal the irritation in his voice. "Give Violet a drink. And please, Violet, leave me alone. I don't feel so good."

"I hate to see you that way," Violet said huskily and fumbled in her purse for a cigarette.

"Here's a cigarette," Clarence said. "Now go away, will you?" Violet cast him a surprised glance. "Okay," she said, sliding off her stool and ambling away towards the last stool by the front window.

Steve came back and said, "Giff's shooting dice. He looks drunk as hell."

"So what?"

Steve looked at his hands which he placed on the bar. "That old fart is drinking too much."

Clarence acknowledged this comment with a noncommittal humph, but a rash of sweat broke out along his ribs.

"Sometimes," Steve said, "he can be mean as hell when he's been hitting it extra hard."

"I hope to God that bastard does try something," Clarence said. "I hope he comes out here and makes one of those cracks . . ."

"Where's my beer?" Steve asked.

"Max, a plain coke for me and a beer for Steve."

It was quiet again, except for the racket in the other room. Clarence shuddered every time a chair shifted as he imagined Giff's burly figure rising and lunging towards the bar. He kept his ears taut. Holly and her friends were at their usual booth, sipping cocktails and gabbing. They were always gabbing and tittering, and cussing too. By God, those women could cuss, enveloped in a cloud of whiskey and cigarette smoke. Clarence glanced over his right shoulder at the booth. They were not looking at him but had their heads bent close together, apparently discussing some subject that seemed ghastly and taboo.

"Care for another beer, Steve?"

"No. Let's beat it. I don't feel right around here."

"No, Steve, please. You don't seem to understand. If there's going to be any trouble because of that crap game I want to get it over with right now."

Only nothing happened. Clarence and Steve sat at the bar, without speaking. Steve ordered another beer and Clarence a plain coke. Nothing happened. Nothing.

The sensation of inertia returned, this time ten times stronger, draining his strength. For a while he grappled with an impulse to go in the other room himself and have it out with Giff and the other boys. After all, he'd won fair and square. But instead, he dropped off the stool and said, "I think I'll go up to my room."

"All right," Steve sighed with relief. "I'll see you tomorrow."

"You've been swell, Steve."

"Oh, hell, keep your nose clean, for Christ's sake."

Steve left and Clarence went out through the side barroom door to the foot of the stairs. He heard the tinkle of piano keys from the library on the first floor. It must be Matt Fleming, who always played softly in the hotel. In fact, Clarence realized that Matt played softly everywhere, at the dance and at church, and it struck Clarence that the soft music was like Matt himself, remote and serene.

As he reached the landing, he heard a girl's voice spill out, as soft as Matt's music. Clarence stopped, suddenly fearful of continuing. The library room was situated at the corner of the hallway. Its door was always left open by the chambermaid by order of Buster's wife who had decorated the room and took pride in it. Clarence had been inside only a few times but he always looked in as he went by. It was furnished with dark walnut furniture, an old upright piano, an Oriental rug and a breakfront bookcase with locked shelves full of thick classics bound in blue and gold that no one ever read.

With a thump, his heart began to beat again and he moved quietly up the stairs. Matt was sitting on the stool reading the music propped on the rack of the upright piano by the light of the floor lamp that had a wine ruffled shade suspended on a twisted bronze stand. Lydia was standing beside him, singing.

Clarence stepped into the room as if propelled and sat down in the stiff ladder-back chair by the breakfront. The girl glanced sideways at Clarence and smiled at him. He had a reason for intruding, he told himself, and felt a surge of joy because of his secret. He waited. He was glad he had bought the present. As soon as she was through with this number, or as soon as the propitious moment arose, he would present it to her.

He rummaged through his pockets. He had gone into Floyd's Curio Shop looking for a present for her and purchased an Alaskan black diamond ring mounted on four silver prongs. Only now that he had located the felt case in his side coat pocket, he knew that he wouldn't give it to her. He'd known this even while he bought the ring, after he had spent an hour searching through trays of necklaces and brooches, considering Indian-made handbags and earrings fashioned out of colored beads, before deciding on the Alaskan ring.

The girl's voice rose and dimmed with the music. "*Not for just an hour, not for just a day, not for just a year, but always.*"

He wondered why he froze whenever he was around her. When she wasn't around, he was bold, full of things to say. But as soon as he saw her, he was paralyzed.

He glanced at her as she sang along to Matt's music. He was crazy about her, his love was stiff with desire and fulfillment. He wanted so much to please her, to make her happy. He felt there was so much that he could do to thrill her. He clutched the ring case with renewed determination, then released it again as the song came to an end.

"Hello, Clarence," Lydia said. Her voice was cool. She peered at Matt and then, as if she had to create a conversation that involved both of them, she said, "Clarence makes a good audience, don't you think, Mr. Fleming?"

"Sure does," Matt said, smacking his lips as he fumbled with the pages of music before him.

"You sing beautifully," Clarence whispered. She seemed cold. He wondered if Victoria had told her about the scene he made in their room after the dance. She must have, Clarence reasoned, and felt resentful and mortified.

"Do you sing?" Lydia asked, without looking at him. "Would you like to try a duet?"

"Uh, no, I'm afraid I can't sing a note," Clarence said.

She did not press the subject but waited until Matt had selected the next number. The chords fell soft and wistful and Lydia hummed at first, acquainting herself with the pitch of the melody. The drizzle had turned into a sheen of fine rain as it generally did towards evening. And there was a sudden cozy joy in the room, due to the warmth of the light against the growing darkness outside the window, which filled Clarence's heart with comfort.

He must have been wrong, he reflected. She was just taken aback by his entrance. Surely that must be it. Her words were gracious. She was lovely. He sat back, slightly more relaxed, and listened to the music.

"I dream of Jeannie with the light brown hair . . ."

Clarence's eyes devoured her, running down her body, taking in her hair, her face. Each time she turned to face him she smiled and he experienced a cold shuddering explosion of sweat and embarrassment as if he were doing the vocal and it sounded corny. His eyes would meet hers for a brief excruciating instant and then, unable to bear it any longer, he would look away. Her voice flowed in his veins. His eyes wandered picking up small details, stains on the carpet, the girl's white raincoat draped over the wing chair, the umbrella propped up beside it. He noticed the mud clinging to Matt's shoes, the straight lines of the seams on the stockings along the girl's slim calves.

The music stopped and Lydia said, "Let's try *Ave Maria*, Mr. Fleming."

Clarence rose and went to the window and looked out. A light from the hotel lobby glinted on the wet planking of the empty dock below. From this angle, he faced the girl. She began to sing the long, drawn-out notes of *Ave*

Maria. He did not know how long he stood by the window or how long the girl sang, only that it seemed that his happiness would last forever, that there would never be a last chord. But there was.

Chris Ballard strode into the room, went up to the side of the piano, easy-like, familiar, tapped out a cigarette and lighted it.

Clarence shifted back against the window as he faced the cannery owner. "Hello, Chris," he said.

"Hi, Clarence," Chris smiled.

Clarence could hear the faint sound of the rain rubbing on the window, the pounding of the engines in the cold storage plant outside, the girl's voice building to a crescendo of joy within him. Then suddenly his joy dissolved.

The girl turned slowly to face Chris, still holding onto the last note. She nodded her head and smiled and let out her breath.

"I hope I'm not intruding," Chris said. "Vic told me I'd find you here."

"Oh, no, Chris. We're just finishing." She patted Matt's shoulder. "Thank you for accompanying me. It was fun."

"It was a pleasure, ma'am," said Matt.

Lydia turned to Clarence.

"You've taken it all quite well," she said.

He wanted to make a witty and appropriate reply. But his mouth refused to open to disclose any of the things that he yearned to tell her. Instead he mumbled, "You have a lovely voice."

"Thank you, Clarence."

"I'm hungry," Chris said. "I hope you are."

"Ravished," she said laughing and Chris helped her on with her raincoat and they were gone.

Matt ran his fingers along the keyboard, unmindful of Clarence's presence. Clarence felt as if he had been lifted up by a wave and slammed against the shore. He left the room.

The pain took a long time subsiding. He didn't leave his room to go out for the supper. He was caught up in a tide of emotions. He kept reliving the moment, noticing how tall Chris was as he entered the room, hearing the girl's voice again, seeing the smile she bestowed on the cannery owner. The tide surged forward and he thrashed around in it. "I'll show her," he muttered, clenching and unclenching his fists. "I'll show that bitch what a man he really is. She'll learn that Clarence Wick is a man to reckon with, by God."

As the tide slackened, he lay stretched out on his bed, staring at the ceiling, feeling the pool of despair growing around him, pulling him under.

10

CHRIS STEPPED OUT ON DECK as the *Verna* barrelled out of the harbor, rounding the breakwater wall. The waves of wake spread out behind the seiner's stern, making the fishing boats tied to the floats in the harbor pitch and roll and bounce against one another.

"Hey, what's the matter with Giff?" Homer Bray shouted with mild concern as he coiled the spring line aft.

"Giff must feel sprightly today," Chris said and watched the rolling, bucking boats in the harbor disappear behind the breakwater.

"Some of those boys'll raise hell with Giff," Homer said with a yawn as he prepared to go below deck and take a nap in the foc'sle. Homer was a good deckhand. He never complained about hard work, listened to orders dutifully, never offered an opinion and worshipped Giff. Giff had signed him up on the *Verna* for nine seasons in a row. Homer had an owlish face and always seemed to be blinking his bleary eyes, yawning and complaining about being tired. He had an enormous appetite for food and apparently for women, judging by the stories he told of all the women he had seduced. In these tales, Homer was a Lochinvar, absolutely irresistible to the schoolteachers and factory workers of the Midwest.

"Stud Bray, they called me back home," Homer would say, his face all aglow as he recollected the escapades of his youth.

Those escapades were behind him now that he was married. "I only married her because she was thirteen years younger than me. I wanted to be sure I'd be set up proper for my later years," he'd say in explanation.

The deck was suddenly vacant. The morning was warm and soft. The water sparkled with flashes of silver. The forward movement of the seiner created a V of rolling waves.

Chris moved up against the rail, amidship. The low crescent-shaped blur of houses and trees that was Wrangell dimmed from view as the *Verna* headed out the channel towards Sumner Strait. This would probably be their last visit to the fish traps as they had finished most of the repairs already. It was some time yet before fishing season started but it was better to have the repair work done early than wait until the last minute.

Funny, he hated leaving Wrangell lately. Going out to rig the traps just didn't have the same appeal it did before. He would rather meet Lyddy after school, go for a walk, have a shake at the Sweets, go out to the beach. He just couldn't seem to get enough of her.

As he stood on the starboard deck, the wind whipping gently into his face, Chris evoked her image in his imagination. The sensation was delicious. She was more than he had ever hoped for. He could never have dreamed of a girl like Lyddy. Her image rose in him, warming and thrilling him. He pictured the poetry of her features, her nose, her eyebrows, her eyelids, the graceful column of her neck when her hair was brushed up on her head. The pleasure swam in him.

A porpoise caught his eye off the starboard quarter, black and white, with slender fins and a broad tail, leaping gracefully forward above the water, leaving behind a streak of foam. Then Chris spied its mate. The two played together, weaving in and out, describing easy, effortless arcs before the splashing prow of the *Verna*. Chris thrilled to the joy of their flight. They seemed almost motionless, not a muscle twitching in their compact bodies as they hung poised in the air.

Chris breathed in the wind, the purr of the diesel, the water and the islands and wished that Lyddy was with him. He could almost feel her presence, his vision of her was so powerful. For he was crushed with love, he was reckless, rife with love, he was wallowing in love. It was all true and it was part of everything he did. It was this fine sun-washed day, it was being alone on deck, it was catching the movement of the swells pushed into motion by the *Verna*, it was the porpoises.

There were four of them now, slipping through and into the water. For a long time, Chris watched them as they plunged through the water, switching back and forth, playing tag with a clumsy old seiner.

"Say, Chris," the cook beckoned from the galley door. "Giff's just got some hot news over the wireless."

Before Chris entered the deck house he cupped his hands over a cigarette and lit it, wanting to settle down before he approached Giff. He scanned the length of the seiner, fore and aft. Thirty nine feet of wood and steel, regulation size, utilizing every inch for what it was made: purse-seining salmon. The deck house was set forward, almost clear up to the nose, giving the boat a snub-nosed appearance, to create as much space possible on the open deck aft. The deck house ran almost the width of the boat, with only a thin plank of deck on either side for a man to move fore and aft. The galley took up most of the room in the deck house. It was the heart of any seiner, where the crew had coffee while on runs, staying protected from cold and rain. The engine room lay midship, below the galley, and the toilet room was abaft the deck house. It contained a wash basin and hand-pumped toilet bowl, with enough room to fit one man at a time. Sleeping quarters for the five man crew were below deck, forward, bunks tied along the sloping planks of the hull. It was musty and close down there where a man slept with the slap of the waves against the hull tickling his feet. A seiner possessed scant room for comfort. It was built to give a fishing crew as much room as possible on the low open deck for all of the tasks involved in purse-seining salmon: lowering the seine skiff, setting the net, hoisting the full net aboard with the aid of the winch so the salmon could be spilled out, wriggling and thrashing, into the hold.

Chris stepped into the warm galley. It was some time yet before noon but the big oil stove was covered with pots, bubbling and spitting. Carl Terjensen, the cook, was bent over the wooden sink washing fruit. His wife, Margaret, had recovered from the concussion she suffered at his hands but she had taken their son and gone to stay with her sister in the States for a while.

"By God, that looks good Carl," Chris said, looking at the glistening plums, peaches and grapes on the platter. "First fruit of the year, isn't it?"

"Yeah," Carl nodded. "Everything looked so good I bought five pounds of each."

Giff was sitting behind the galley table in the far corner by the port window, a paper and pencil beside him. He was wearing only a T-shirt and poring over a map stretched out on the table in front of him, as if he were reading a story that was not very interesting. It was strange to see Giff reading a chart since he knew the inside passage as well as any man in Southeastern.

"What's up, Giff?" Chris asked.

There was a short silence in the galley as Giff made a notation on the piece of paper.

"Hey, man, pass it around," said Clyde MacDonnell, the machinist mate, to Carl.

Clyde was medium-height and ape-shaped and he generally didn't say much. He stood with his back to the stove, nursing a steaming cup of coffee, his eyes peering over the rim of the mug at the cook and the platter of fruit in his hand. Clyde grabbed at a peach with one of his chubby square hands. It always amazed Chris that he kept his hands absolutely clean without a speck of the grease or oil he'd expect on the hands of a man responsible for tending a 110 Cummings diesel.

"Pretty sweet, huh?" Carl asked.

Clyde bit into the peach and nodded dreamily.

Giff waited as Carl deposited the platter of fruit on the table.

"Well now," Giff said, selecting one of the glossy plums. "Pretty fancy, huh?" Aboard ship, Giff was different than he was on shore. It was almost like night and day. When he stepped aboard the *Verna* to assume command, he went through a metamorphosis. The years slipped away from his corpulent face and he brushed down the band of hair round the naked dome of his head.

His black eyes lost their glazed look and shone pure and bright. His actions were self-conscious, half-sly, half-tolerant, imbued with a knowingness that made everyone else conscious of their actions. His easy assumption of this role derived from his years of experience skippering the *Verna*, the top boat in Wrangell.

At this moment Giff was playing out his role as the skipper by withholding the message he had received over the wireless for as long as he deemed possible, a quirk of his aboard ship when giving commands or responding to queries. It made the men fidgety and tense in his presence. Though they might look relaxed and act informal around Giff, they were always on the alert, not wanting to be caught flat-footed. And all the hands, except for Clyde, respected and imitated Giff. Even Clyde who hated him was never openly defiant. But only aboard ship. In Wrangell, they shunned him. In Wrangell, he was a drunken old fart, pitiful and revolting. Even Clyde showed no hate for Giff ashore. Giff wasn't worth it.

Chris waited with patience and amusement. He knew that Giff was imitating Theodore Ballard and that on the *Verna* where he was indisputably in command, Giff could be that way and get away with it.

"A guy drowned in Sumner," Giff said, without looking up from the chart. "Go give some fruit to Lyle," Giff said to the cook and nodded forward towards the pilot house where Lyle Hobson was standing whale watch. There was a narrow hallway alongside the stove that led into the small cramped pilot house forward. Carl headed down it carrying the platter of fruit.

Giff raised his head high, rubbed his neck, stretched his head and made a small, snorting sigh. "Guy's name is Olerich. From Ketchikan. Ever hear of him?" Giff glanced at Chris with indifference.

"No, never have," Chris said. He reached for a mug above the sink in the storm shelf and poured himself a cup of coffee. He drank it black without sugar.

"Where'd he drown?" Clyde asked, with a solemn and serious air. Chris realized at once that Clyde must have changed since he'd last been aboard the *Verna*, for he too was now imitating Giff. Chris chuckled inwardly. He bet that Clyde already knew the exact location in Sumner where the man drowned. Though Chris owned the boat, Giff was definitely in command. If Chris were to give an order to Giff right now, or even one of the hands, they would feel slighted and resentful.

"Reed's Bay," Giff replied. "The report of his drowning was relayed to us from the cannery. It's a Coast Guard problem but it isn't far off our course and by the time the Coast Guard sends a boat from Ketchikan or Juneau to drag him out there'll be two or three tides gone and that man may never be found."

Giff stretched his bare, hairy arms above his head, snorting. "Of course, it's up to Chris to decide. What do you say, Chris?"

Chris was sure that Giff had already made up his mind.

"Well," Chris said, "The traps are pretty well done anyway. Suit yourself."

"I think we better go," Giff said. "I'll get out the log and put this all down while it's fresh on my mind. The Coast Guard will want to know everything even though they'll have the information."

"Stay where you are," Chris said. "I'll get the log for you."

Chris went forward into the pilot house. The door was closed and Chris laughed, knowing this was because Lyle was a heavy eater. "Can't stand the odor, huh?" Chris asked him.

"I'm so hungry I could eat the ass end off a bear." Lyle said, sinking his teeth into a peach. "What's Carl got for lunch?"

"He's vegetable happy today. Potatoes, string beans and carrots."

"What about meat?"

"There's nothing in the oven. Maybe he's making steak."

"I hope so," Lyle said with good nature.

Lyle was a friendly, easy-going, handsome man of about thirty-two, heavy-set and muscular, with blue eyes, thinning, sandy-colored hair and a complexion much like his personality, clean and rosy. Though his father owned Hobson's Merchandise Store on Main Street, Lyle wouldn't have any part of it. "He loves to be on a boat," Giff always said of Lyle. "He's stronger than any man I've ever known and doesn't complain when the going's tough. I had a lucky hunch to sign him up, as green as he was, when the *Verna* was launched." Giff liked Lyle because Lyle bestowed the same mixture of respect and worship on Giff as Giff did on Theodore. Like Homer, Lyle obeyed Giff's every order with child-like acceptance.

Lyle stood before the wheel, staring straight ahead through the narrow center window of the pilot house, casting a casual yet attentive eye over the expanse of water before the seiner. Chris had always liked Lyle. He wondered why Helen Connell didn't marry such a friendly and good-looking man. Lyle had loved Helen ever since Chris could remember and they had gone together on and off for years. Only something always seemed to crack between them and Helen would go drifting off with some other man, like she did with Chris last year. Lyle always stepped aside like the obedient and courteous admirer that he was, and waited, sometimes for a year, before Helen would decide to go out with him again.

"Pretty rotten about that fisherman drowning," Lyle said to Chris.

"Yeah."

"I wonder how old he was?" Lyle said. "I'll make a guess. I think he's about sixty, you know, like one of those old seedy guys in the harbor."

Chris stood before the control panel, gazing out at the water, and realized that he was killing as much time as he dared before he fetched the log book for Giff. He was playing the same game as Giff. That was it, Chris realized suddenly, why Giff was able to keep the same crew year after year, unlike other seiners. The hands all enjoyed this hide and seek drama they played. Then again, Chris reasoned, there was another good reason to sign on under Giff. The *Verna* was the top boat in Wrangell year after year which was an important consideration when the profit shares were divided at the end of the season.

"Pretty day, isn't it," Lyle said as they approached the pass. "By God, we had a spell of rain though."

Everything was so clear that Elephant Nose looked like it might rear up. Directly across from it stood Two Tree Island, a name which had been more appropriate when it was first named for now there were at least ten trees on the island. Chris stared for a while at the small island, a sour feeling in his stomach. Whenever he saw Two Tree Island, he saw his friend, Tom, and Tom's dead English bulldog and Chris' 22 Hornet lying between them with the snow covering the stock . . .

As the *Verna* moved through the pass, the diesel puttering in a steady monotone, Homer stepped into the pilot house from the galley passageway. HE stood before the window on the other side of Lyle, yawning and blinking his eyes. "Can't sleep today for some reason," he said. "Want me to take over for a while?"

Chris reached under the ceiling atop the bulkhead for the log book and edged back into the galley. His date with Lyddy would be broken, he thought, as he handed Giff the log book. Giff rolled up the chart with fastidious care. By God, Chris reflected, this would be the first day that he hadn't spent with Lyddy since the night of the dance. And tonight they were going to go to the Johnson's to play cards. They were playing a lot lately, mostly penny ante stuff. Lyddy got a big kick out of it, almost like Bea.

The morning slipped by. Chris was surprised at himself for being able to get into the swing of things on the *Verna* so quickly. During the season, he seldom left the cannery. But one summer, his second year back in Wrangell after returning from the States, Chris spent a whole season aboard the *Verna*. He told his father that he thought it would help him understand the perspective of the fishermen. Theodore agreed to the idea wholeheartedly, pleased and yet irritated somehow since the idea had never occurred to him. It was quite a year, with the same crew aboard the *Verna* as now except for the cook. He remembered the hearty, almost joyous reunions with his dad each time the seiner pulled alongside the unloading float at the cannery, then heading out again, becoming familiar with the water passages, the islands, Point Beauclaire, Sumner Strait and even going past Cape Decision once across the stretch of ocean to Port Alexander. Giff had become a hero to Chris, a skipper with a masterful way of running a boat, a droll sense of humor, an uncanny ability to predict where the salmon would be running and an adventuresome spirit. Although there were things Giff did on shore which he couldn't stomach, Chris overlooked that and glorified him for what he was aboard the *Verna*, the finest and smartest ship captain imaginable. Giff was shrewd, cool and efficient and Chris submitted to his orders with absolute trust.

At lunch, the entire crew sat down around the table except for the cook. That was one thing about Carl. He was a fairly good cook, especially when he made his two favorite recipes, baked halibut pudding, heavily creamed and served with shrimp sauce, and a stewed mixture of lamb and cabbage with sour cream that was delicious. But when it came time to eat, Carl left the galley. If they were moving, Carl would relieve whoever was at the wheel. Carl couldn't watch anyone eat. The crew had several long-running jokes about this ranging from "Maybe he can't believe that anyone will eat this stuff" to "The son of a bitch might have poisoned the food and couldn't stand the sight of four dead men at the table."

Homer was the first to come tripping up to the table, after Carl relieved him at the wheel. "Hey, there, looks good, huh?" said Homer, smacking his hands, his whole face crinkling with happiness as he appraised the rib steaks and vegetables. His actions were exact duplicates of Giff's mannerisms. In many ways Homer was like Lyle: easy-going, responsive, a bull for work and not hard to please. Giff used them in his game aboard ship like well-behaved school children. They were no problem nor was the cook. The problem was the machinist mate, Clyde. He was always nursing a grudge against someone and he openly hated Giff.

"Why do you keep Clyde aboard?" Chris had asked Giff once, though it was just to make conversation and none of his business, for the crew was Giff's worry.

"He's the best diesel man in town," Giff said, his voice cool and matter-of-fact. "Otherwise, off he'd go."

Actually Giff needed Clyde to keep him razor sharp at his role as skipper. He made Clyde hate every minute aboard. By constantly coming in as top skipper in Wrangell, Giff tormented Clyde who aspired to be skipper of the *Verna* someday and stuck it out, year after year, determined to break Giff before Giff could break him. The change from the slobbering old drunkard ashore to the efficient skipper aboard ship was at times more than Clyde could bear.

"Some guys are just stupid," Clyde said, shaking his head in disgust as he sliced up the last of his chops before beginning to eat. "Imagine a fisherman drowning while anchored in a cove. It's beyond me."

"We're going straight to Reed's Bay," Giff said, pushing his plate away. His appetite was dainty, unlike his drinking. He nibbled at his chop, took a few bites of vegetables, sipped his cup of coffee and then lit a cigarette. He took a long slow drag, studying the flame as it blackened the paper about the end of the cigarette, and then shook the match out. He picked up the log book beside him, opened it with a brisk, business-like air, planted his elbows on the table and began to read. His voice had an underlying tone of amusement but he read with the reverent high-sounding tones of a priest at high Mass. "Olerich was anchored in a cove in the southwest part of Reed's Bay, in his trolling boat, *Selma O.*, approximately seventy-five yards out from E. L. Tanner's cabin, in six fathoms of water, Tuesday evening, about five thirty." Giff dug a nail between his front tooth and spat out the morsel of food beside him to the floor. "Olerich went ashore to visit Tanner until six thirty, when he departed in his skiff for his trolling boat. He arrived, pulled his skiff aboard and went to the bow of the boat to let out more anchor chain. This was at six fifty-five. After Tanner heard the anchor chain go out, he heard a splash and cries for help. The cries ceased for a moment and were heard a few seconds later when they ceased altogether. During this tine Tanner had called to Olerich to hold on and he would come in his skiff, but the tide was such that Tanner was unable to move his skiff fast enough to save Olerich. On the following day Tanner went to Summit Island and reported the incident to Dewey Sylvester, a fox farmer, who had enough radio to relay the message to the Ballard Cannery in Wrangell."

"Say, that's just about the way it came over the wireless," Lyle said his face shining with astonishment.

"By God, that guy Tanner spared no details," Homer mumbled his mouth full of food. Already he was on his seconds, which was just a good start for Homer.

Giff slammed the log book closed with a loud air of finality and tossed it on the table beside the chart. "We'll be in Reed's Bay sometime late this afternoon if we run steady." Giff paused long enough to make this conjecture seem as though it were the consensus of the crew. He cleared his throat. "Since this is a fairly important mission, we'll break into regular watches. Four on and four off. Homer and I will take the first watch. Clyde and Lyle the next. If we drag him out tonight we might have to go straight to Ketchikan. We'll probably take his boat in too so two men better get some shut eye after chow."

Giff made the mission sound of grave consequence as though this was the first time that any of them had ever embarked on a search for a drowned man. But there was a certain excitement in this departure from routine and the prospect that it might take them to Ketchikan. Chris sat back, drinking his coffee and listening to the men speculate about the drowned man.

"Maybe he committed suicide?" This from Homer, blinking wisely. "You know, because of a personal problem, like he was fed up with his wife."

"I don't think he's married," Lyle started to say. "I'd say he's about sixty."

"Naw, he didn't commit suicide," Clyde said, which was surprising as he scarcely ever spoke with anyone. "Why would he scream for help?"

"He could have swum, I figure," Homer said as he speared himself his fourth chop from the platter in the center of the table.

"Maybe he didn't know how to swim. Lots of fishermen don't, the crazy bastards!" This was from Clyde again, smacking his lips with contempt. Suddenly he rose and went forward to relieve Carl.

No one paid any attention to Clyde. Chris could picture Clyde at the wheel, lighting a cigarette, one chubby paw dangling between the spokes of the wheel, his eye roving ahead of the bow, occasionally gazing out into the distance. For all Clyde's disdain and irritability, he was still a good man to have aboard ship. He helped out where help was needed without being asked and worked as hard and long as anyone. There were no gripes amongst the crew when the shares were distributed at the end of a season.

No sooner had Chris and Lyle gotten up from the table—Homer was knifing into his fifth chop—when a faint tremor stole through the structure of the boat. Giff slid to the port window, his hand on the table, and looked out.

"Well, I'll be darned," Giff said out loud. He jerked his head to one side and pursed his lips in the familiar grimace of his which expressed mild alarm. There was no particular significance to these movements yet the crew watched him as if hypnotized. After some length of time spent in Giff's presence, confined in the small space of the deck house on a seiner, they all began copying his mannerisms. Chris had noticed that around the skipper, the most timid people became confident and expansive simply because Giff was there to be watched and copied.

The boat began to slap steadily under the chop of the changing sea now that they were in Sumner Strait and it became difficult to stand with ease on the waxed linoleum deck. Giff and Chris moved forward into the pilot house where there was just enough standing space to lean against the bulkhead.

"You going to take the wheel?" Clyde asked. His voice had an edge for he was still at the wheel during what was supposed to be Giff and Homer's watch.

The skipper said nothing but rolled the chart in his hand into a tight, cylindrical roll. As skipper, Giff never answered direct questions pertaining to the ship's chores. Probably he considered it an effrontery, especially coming from Clyde, for a query could be construed as an indirect order. So he let the men sweat out the questions until they felt like an idiot for posing them. Sometimes, if Giff was in a benevolent frame of mind, he might give some indication of his response with a kind of sign language or a twist of his facial muscles. But now Giff completely ignored Clyde, not even glancing at him. He slipped the chart and the log book atop the bulkhead, walked around to the open starboard door and stuck his head out.

A black and white tug, riding low in the water and towing a barge loaded with logs, appeared off the starboard quarter in the center of the strait. As the *Verna* came abreast of it, Giff stepped outside for a moment, shading his eyes with his left hand, and waved at the tug. The tremor that had begun with the chop now spread through the craft, a succession of hammering thuds. Clyde pulled the throttle lever back to half speed, somewhat cushioning the boat from the blows of the water, though the empty seiner continued leaping against the rip-tide.

"O.K. mate," Giff said to Clyde, taking over the wheel. Giff shoved the throttle ahead to three quarter speed as the *Verna* moved out of the worst of the chop.

"We'd better get some shut eye before chow," Clyde said to Lyle, who had just entered the pilot house and was staring out the open door.

"I've got a feeling we're in for a blow. Look at that cloud ahead," said Lyle gazing out at the west.

A fat black cloud was ripping into shreds in the otherwise clear sky. The sun was a good distance above it and Chris winced as he glanced out. The sun shining on the wide blue strait had a blinding radiance. This was odd for the morning had been pleasant and warm with the light suffusing the landscape with soft, pastel shades. Now the light glared from the restless back of the water, so that the skipper had to stand back from the wheel under the shade of the ceiling to look out.

"Might be," Clyde said matter-of-factly. Clyde was the bravest man of the crew. Storms didn't phase him a bit. He was nonchalant even while attempting tricky maneuvers that could spell disaster for the boat. Chris remembered one time during a lull in the fishing season when the salmon had seemingly disappeared. They found a narrow, uncharted opening into an island which appeared secretive and compelling. Giff gave the order to go forward, with Clyde at the wheel, and Giff and Homer on the port and starboard bows respectively, sounding depth, using their arms as bumpers to ward off the flanks of the hull from the rocks on either side. They were nervous and excited, shouting commands to Clyde with overly loud voices. Clyde stood at the wheel, capable and indifferent, steering the seiner through the gap at its slowest speed, backing up, inching forward, until they'd sailed through and came out into a beautiful secluded basin in which they dropped anchor and swam. They stayed the night there, enchanted by the beauty and solitude of the lagoon that had seemed to flower out before them, more remarkable because of its mystery. Clyde was the only one who didn't seem impressed. No doubt he was disgruntled because the skipper hadn't run the boat against the rocks and foundered it.

Clyde was always calm and poised, even when making a dangerous crossing because of one of Giff's whims, like the time Giff had a hankering to run over to Port Alexander to see Sam Flannery. They passed the light house at Cape Decision and off towards the west they saw the expanse of the ocean, wide and flat and beckoning, and they were suddenly excited, all except Clyde, about sailing out across its limitless expanse, about going to Port Alexander which was about twenty miles to the northwest, an old remote fishing settlement with one main street lined with old frame saloons and gambling halls, just like in a Western movie. They set out across the open, deadly Pacific Ocean, uneasy without the familiar, protective bulwark of the islands of the Inside Passage. When they reached the finger of rock which created Port Alexander's natural harbor, they were in for a surprise. The salmon were running in hordes and all the trolling boats were full. The one small floating cannery, tied up at the dock was swamped and couldn't process all the fish. Purse seining was restricted there so Giff filled the *Verna* with the salmon, buying it from the fishermen a few cents a pound cheaper than what the local cannery was giving, and they all got drunk that night at Sam Flannery's bar. The next morning, they started back across the ocean with the overloaded *Verna*, her aft deck awash with water, the stubby bow protruding above the water line like the snout of a sea lion. They lumbered across at full speed, although it felt like they were moving no faster than a snail, rocking with the long, sweeping, incoming swells, watching for a sudden storm that would capsize them in their current condition. Finally they spotted the mouth of Cape Decision looming in the distance and as it slowly opened for them and they ducked inside, back in familiar waters, all of the crew had breathed a sigh of relief for they had been in a state of high tension. All except Clyde who had gone below to get some sleep, completely unaffected by the danger of the crossing.

Clyde's true fearlessness emerged whenever the *Verna* was caught in trouble, the many times they ducked out of squalls, those quick-tempered bitter storms that rise within the passages of Southeastern. They would head towards shore, not knowing exactly where they were, unable to make a proper reading on a chart because of the poor visibility, having no idea what lay under the

Verna or ahead, for the spot light on the bridge was inadequate at night during the murky atmosphere of a storm, wondering whether they were going to hit shallow water and be pounded by the waves or if some jutting rock might tear a hole in the planking of the hull. At those times Giff trusted only Clyde at the wheel. Giff poked his head out of one of the side doors in the pilot house, guiding Clyde with called-out instructions, "To the right, Clyde. To the right," he would say, his voice fraught with anxiety. "Now swing her back, easy. There's an opening just ahead. Now! Reverse! Shove her in reverse!" Calmly and slowly, almost as if to spite the skipper's frenzy, Clyde worked the gears and shoved the throttle ahead, the boat shuddering under the strain as the engine revved and carried them back. "Now, try again! Forward! Go slow! To the right!" In all this bedlam, with the waves washing across the boat broadside, Clyde remained matter-of-fact, his gray eyes indifferent, as he steered the craft forward without being able to see a foot ahead, following Giff's shouted directions, "All right, straight ahead! Keep her straight! There! I think we passed the rock! I think, I think, we made it, by God!"

Yes, always at those crucial times, Giff put Clyde at the wheel, knowing that he was most capable man for the job. Yet, though Clyde was radiated confidence and strength in times of stress, Chris couldn't imagine serving under his command. There was no explaining it but Giff despite his overbearing attitude exuded a kind of trustworthiness that made the men feel more at ease than Clyde's calm self-assurance.

After Lyle and Clyde took off for the crew's quarters, Giff shouted for the cook, his face aglow, as if something exciting was about to happen. In the face of the brilliant sun, glaring off the window, Giff put on a pair of dark-lensed, gold-rimmed glasses. He shoved the throttle full speed ahead. Although they had passed the worst of the chop, the *Verna* was having a difficult time adjusting to the swells that swept under it from time to time.

"Get the dishes done quick," said Giff as Homer and Carl entered the pilot house. "We're in for a little blow."

"O.K., skipper."

"That wind is sure to come down on us soon. And when it does," Giff paused, clutching the wheel, seeming to savor the prospect, "it might delay us some on our mission."

"Well, in that case," Carl said, all business, "I'll just have to skip the french fries. I'll make hash with the spareribs."

"You know," Giff said to Chris, after Carl hurried back to his galley, "Carl's sure a whopper in a storm. You haven't seen him in a storm, have you?" Giff laughed. "He stays in the galley and keeps things ship shape. I mean ship shape, too, huh, Homer?"

"That's right," Homer smiled.

"A dish breaks," Giff said, "and Carl picks it up and tosses it overboard. Once the pump tore loose. By God, Carl had one hell of a time plugging it up. What a mess. Water all over the deck. But he managed to mop it up during the storm and the galley was ship shape by the time it was over. You watch him in this one."

The *Verna* began to buck and swerve as it proceeded along Sumner Strait on its way to drag for a drowned fisherman.

11

CHRIS SLUMPED DOWN ON THE PORT DECK, resting his back against the deck house. He could tell it was going to be a hot day. Even though it was only seven o'clock in the morning, the air was warm and still. The *Verna* lay facing south towards the lip of the horseshoe bay, riding anchor against the ebb tide. Chris stared across at the shore at the slanting roof of the trapper's cabin half-hidden by the trees. Smoke wreathed from the cabin's chimney. Chris expected the trapper had probably spotted them already and would come visiting after breakfast.

Chris wished Homer would hurry out of the lavatory. Then, remembering the privacy of the bay, he stood up and relieved himself by urinating over the rail. The stream spattered in the stillness as it struck the water below. Feeling better, Chris lit a cigarette and squatted down. He could hear the clatter Carl made in the galley and Giff's strenuous coughing and hacking below in the foc'sle.

Above the boat's noises, there was the dawn, the freshness of a new morning, the brilliance in the sky above the trees, the sheens of rose and lemon and the aura of gold that glittered in the tree tops ahead of the sun's rise. Mist still clung to the east shore near the mouth of the bay and it looked cool and secret there. A few small purple clouds edged out over the sky above the horseshoe bay and the sun rose, golden and bright. The clouds above it glowed with a wine red brilliance. The water was dark and cold-looking along the shade of shore, but where the sun shone, it was blue and green and silver blue.

The cigarette was heavy and tasteless before breakfast. Chris wished he had a drink, a good slug of whiskey to start the day off. Giff was probably having half a glass full right now.

He stayed looking out over the water as if in a spell, recalling the turbulent passage through the storm the night before, the boat bucking for hours, until they reached the calmer waters of Reed's Bay. It was as if the wind and rain and scudding clouds had washed the world clean to create the purity of this morning.

Homer swung around the deck house, looking bright and fresh. "Say," he said, "what about grappling tackle? How are we going to drag for this guy?" Homer placed his hand around a guy wire and scanned the water about the *Verna*.

"Giff'll think of something, I guess," Chris replied.

Carl rapped on the galley window to indicate that breakfast was ready.

"By God, I'm starved," Homer declared, making a rush around the deck house for the galley door on the starboard side.

The men washed one at a time and came into the galley.

"Well, I see the trapper's in his cabin," Giff said with a sleepy sigh. "As soon as we eat we'll lower the skiff and go ashore and have a chat with the gentleman." Even at this hour, Giff maintained his air of superiority.

They could see the drowned fisherman's troller about twenty yards away out the starboard door which Carl had left open when he'd stepped outside after serving up the meal. It was a low white troller, rather run down, with black lettering on the bow spelling out *Selma O.*, no doubt the name of a relative or sweetheart of the fisherman. It was strange to see the boat riding quietly at anchor in the cove with no one on deck and no smoke spewing from its flue. It seemed that sadness held it there, not the anchor and chain. It was hard to believe anyone could be dead on a day as beautiful as this.

The crew ate almost in silence, slowly clearing the platters of mush and eggs and bacon and toast. Giff and Clyde picked at their mush and eggs with dutiful distaste, knowing that lunch was a long way off. Homer, as usual, surpassed them all. Homer's breakfast appetite was perhaps his keenest, though all meals were highlights in Homer's day. Homer ate as though famished.

"Here comes the trapper now," Giff said, looking out the port window. The man was rowing towards them in a skiff, facing forward as he squatted on the center thwart, pushing his oars slowly. "Well, that'll save us a trip. One of you men better help him aboard. Go catch his line."

Chris rose. "I'll go," he said.

Chris stood on the well deck and caught the line the old man tossed to him and secured it to the cleat.

"Howdy," the trapper said and stepped back to drop his oars against the thwarts. The clatter they made magnified in the stillness, echoing against the trees. The trapper took Chris' hand and swung his leg over the gunwale. "Sure glad to see someone. You the party got my message?"

"Yeah," Chris said. "Had breakfast yet?"

"Something does smell good," the man said and followed Chris into the galley. He was a pear-shaped man, about sixty or sixty-five, very tall and erect. His square white face was freshly shaved and there was a deep scar down the side of his neck. He was so stout around the waistline that his red flannel shirt slid over his belly and his trousers hung stiff from his midsection down so that it appeared he was spindle-legged.

"Howdy, mates," the trapper said. "I'm Everett Tanner. Sure glad to see someone drop in."

"Sit down," Giff said. "Have some breakfast."

Tanner sat down and scooped two eggs onto his plate while Chris got him a mug and poured coffee into it. "Well," Tanner said, bending his head to gaze at the empty troller, "that was a mighty tragic thing to happen to that feller."

"How old was he?" Lyle asked.

"Oh, young feller, twenty five or so."

"Did you see him go under?" Giff inquired.

"Well, not exactly. I know he dropped off his boat cause I heard the anchor chain rattling. Course, the tide's dragged his boat away some now, further north, cause I marked the spot where the boat lay from my cabin when Olerich fell." Tanner paused long enough to stuff one of the eggs and half a piece of buttered toast into his mouth. He chewed and swallowed quickly, like a dog, wolfing the food down without tasting it. Tanner continued, "I heard the splash and his screams but I couldn't see very well across, except for the outline of his boat, on account of the heavy overcast and it was late, six thirty or thereabouts. I heard him splashing and bellowing once more and I yelled to him that I was coming in my skiff but it wasn't no use. He was too far away and couldn't swim, I reckon. Drowned quick as you can say it. I rowed over anyhow to his boat and inspected it. His anchor chain wasn't secured to the forward cleat. I figured he must have dropped overboard while letting out more anchor chain for the rising tide. His foot must have got caught or tangled in it." The trapper slurped the coffee.

"We better get started," Giff said and nodded to the men to get up. "We haven't any tackle with us and so we'll have to make one."

They lowered the *Verna's* seine skiff and rode over to the troller and climbed aboard. Clyde went down into the cabin to inspect the gas engine and get it started. The cabin was long, occupying at least half of the craft, and it was cold and cramped. It smelt of a mixture of oil fumes, fish gear, wet wool and dust. The shelves contained a few supplies, mostly canned food and an open box of crackers. A five gallon barrel of oil occupied the space on one side of the engine, which was in the center of the room, drive shaft and all. There were a few dog-eared comic books scattered over the unmade bunk in the fore-peak of the cabin.

"By God," Clyde said, "what a hole. The bastard sure was dirty."

Outside, on the aft deck, the skipper was bent over on his knees poking around in the tangle of fishing gear in the cockpit, his face furrowed with concentration as he searched for items he could use to rig a dragging tackle. With a hammer, Giff knocked off a long flat board from the narrow gunwale. Then he scooped up a mess of salmon hooks from a small open drawer in the cockpit and proceeded to nail them on the board. On one side of the board, all facing head down, he nailed a row of hooks. Then, flipping the board over, he hammered another row between the hooks on the same side.

"Get me the heaviest lead weights he's got down there," Giff said to Homer. "Where'd Olerich fall approximately?" Giff asked the trapper, looking up from his work.

Tanner pointed his arm diagonally off the port beam. "The boat's drifted a mite northwest. I marked the spot about one hundred fifty yards off shore just beyond where you're anchored now."

"Well, that shouldn't make it too hard," Giff said. He took the four lead weights that Homer fetched from the cockpit, lashed them with a thin line and tied them along the board. He picked up the board and hefted it for weight.

"Well, this ain't much," Giff said, fastening a line around each end of the board, "but it'll have to do."

"By God," Homer squeaked, aghast, gingerly touching one of the gleaming points of the hooks with his fingers, "I hope we snag him in the clothes somewhere."

The engine coughed and wheezed, disturbing the stillness of the day, as Clyde got it started. Exhaust and oil fumes flowed out of the cabin until the engine warmed.

Giff looked around. "Someone better take the skiff back. No use lugging that around with us."

There were so many men standing in the way on the small open stern deck that Chris said he would do it. He stepped off the troller and the skiff teetered slightly with his weight. Lyle unhitched the painter and Chris drove the oars standing up, his legs astraddle of the midships thwart, and slid over to the *Verna*. As he swung on deck and made fast the skiff to the cleat, he heard a splash of water from the troller and knew that the crude tackle had been tossed into the sea and the men had begun to drag for Olerich.

Leave it to Giff, Chris reflected as he watched the troller chugging down the cove, to use a man's own fishing hooks, weights, line and even his own boat to fish him out of the water. They couldn't very well use the *Verna* for her diesel engine wouldn't idle properly at the slow speeds necessary for dragging. They dragged most of the morning with no luck.

Hour after hour the men rode the drowned man's troller back and forth across the area where the trapper indicated that Olerich had drowned, spreading out and widening the search area as they combed the floor of the bay. "I got him," Chris would heard Lyle exclaim. The troller's engine would cough and sputter as it fell to idling speed while Lyle yanked on the line, eventually hauling up an armload of slippery seaweed. Then the engine would cut in again, filling the air with a low chut-chut-chut as they began again. After a while, though they were patrolling not far from the *Verna*, Chris scarcely heard the noise. He sat slouched against the deck house, his shirt off, letting the sun hit his chest.

He gazed out at the water around him. It was everywhere in the Southeastern. Green and purple, shadowed and sparkling. Everywhere there were coves and mysterious little beaches. He knew all the different moods of the water. He had ridden the water in a seiner, a skiff, a cabin cruiser. He remembered the long summer he worked under Giff, the hush he could feel above the sound of the motor, the peace that lay like mist in the straits and channels between the islands.

It was always forever in Southeastern. He never felt that sense of timelessness in the States. In the Southeastern, it was everywhere. He felt it in the woods, while trout-fishing or eagle-hunting, waiting for the elusive prey, catching a glimpse of sunlight green and gold through an opening in the dense trees or watching the moss on the hemlock shivering with the light. He felt it while moving between the islands in a skiff. It seemed to pour down from the ridge line, sweeping down the flank and along the edge of the shore, pressing down on him with a sense of awe. He felt it waiting for the tide between sets, lying on deck in some cove, riding anchor, enjoying the gentle swaying motion as the water played under the keel.

Chris laid on deck in the beautiful sunlit cove, the boat rocking gently in the water that lulled him with its swash and ripple and lap. The magnificent peace which tolled through his being seemed like it was meant for him alone. Alaska was the reason for his existence. His purpose for living was to experience all of it, the peace and the fear, the mystery and the gloom, the storms and the hunting, life and death.

Again Lyle's voice pierced the silence, from somewhere astern of Chris. "Cut her down, Clyde. I've hooked onto something."

Carl stepped out of the galley. "Well, lunch is ready," he announced to Chris. Carl went aft and shouted to the men on the troller. "Hey, you guys, want to eat?" The cook stood there a minute, whiffing the cool fresh breeze blowing southeast. "Sure feels good, that breeze," he said to Chris and disappeared into the galley.

Chris got to his feet as the troller came alongside the *Verna*. He caught the painter Homer tossed to him and looped a half hitch around the cleat.

"No luck, huh?" Chris asked Giff.

"Lots of grass down there," Giff said and headed towards the lavatory.

"He must have drifted quite a ways," the old trapper commented as he lifted his leg over the gunwale. "We certainly combed the spot where he fell in."

In the afternoon, Giff ordered a change of course so they could drag crosswise. At first, Homer, who was taking his turn at the tackle, believed he had snagged onto another clump of grass and did not even shout to Clyde to idle the engine. But the pull on the rope was steady, not like the grass that, once severed from its bed, came up easily. Homer shouted at Clyde to stop the boat.

There had been so many false calls, no one bothered to come help except Chris, who had yet to man the tackle. The idling of the engine made the silence of the cove ominous. Chris waited with subdued anxiety to see what was at the end of the line, which came up effortlessly now that the boat was idle.

It was here, a good hundred yards from shore, that they found Olerich.

The dark hump of the man's back floated to the surface, leaving Chris feeling week. Homer squeaked. His face was drained white and beads of perspiration lathered his forehead. For a moment Chris thought Homer was about to throw up, the sight of the man dangling from the tackle was so unexpected. Homer roped the line and Chris caught it and the man bobbed below him in the water, wearing hip boots rolled down to his knees.

With great exertion the men dragged Olerich over the stern and laid him horizontally across the poop deck. He had a chubby body, now bloated with water, and a smooth, round face. Though his body was not decomposed, gray, high-coned shellfish had fastened themselves upon his exposed flesh, along his hands, face and hair. No one bothered to remove them, although Giff, his face twisting with revulsion, yanked out the hooks which had caught the man about the neck and shoulders.

"We don't need this anymore," Homer said and cast the tackle over board.

"It's a shame," the trapper said.

"Yeah," Giff said, straightening up. "Well, we better shove off." He turned to the trapper. "If the Coast Guard comes here, just tell 'em the Ballard seiner, the *Verna*, from Wrangell, has recovered the body and is taking it and the man's troller to Ketchikan."

"Ballard seiner, the *Verna*," the man mumbled and closed his eyes to memorize the message.

"Say, this guy's engine is plumb shot," Clyde exclaimed irritably, as he came out of the cabin. He glanced down at the body for a moment. "Christ, the guy must have been daffy to ride with it. Needs rings and plugs and a good bore job. It'll strain her to go more than two or three knots an hour."

"In that case," Giff said quickly, "we'll tow her in. Clyde, you and," Giff looked at Chris cautiously—"Chris, you want to ride this baby in?"

"Sure," Chris said, "anything to help."

From his skiff, the trapper waved a final farewell and, fitting his oars into the oarlocks, headed towards shore. Atop the flying bridge, Giff swung the *Verna* around and backed her stern into the bow of the troller where Chris caught the spliced moorage line flung to him by Lyle and secured it to the loggerhead. The two boats connected, they started forward slowly, testing the strength of the tow line. A wind had kicked up towards the late afternoon and no one realized how strong it was until they sailed out of the bay and into Sumner Strait.

The little troller began to jerk and swerve as it followed the wake of the *Verna*, hitting the low swells and white caps without resistance as it strained against the tow line. Sometimes a huge swell would roll under the hull, lifting the bow in a high twisting paroxysm, like a steer lassoed about the neck. Then it would come smashing down, only to jerk forward, pulled by the seiner. The water was greenish-brown under the overcast, silver-gray where the sun was still shining on it. The sky was clogged with great domes of gray-black clouds moving southeastward. Giff was favoring the south shore, as the current was less forceful there, moving now at a steady clip.

"We're making pretty good time," Chris commented after a while.

Clyde was his usual dour self, staring out the window with a contemptuous curl to his lip. "Giff's probably got her opened full speed ahead," Clyde mumbled. "Too fast, I think. This crate ain't used to speed. Liable to tear apart."

"Why don't you start up the motor?" Chris said. "Give it a little cushion."

"Yeah," Clyde said. His voice contained both surprise and offense because Chris had thought of the idea.

The engine made a terrific clatter when it started. Chris squatted down next to Clyde's legs on the pilot house platform, a board that rested just inside the cabin and from which the boat was piloted. Although it wasn't comfortable, it was better than taking the two steps below into the noisy, fume-filled room that contained the engine.

Towards eight o'clock it started to rain, a driving slanting rain that spattered steadily on the cabin. His ears were assailed by the steady thud of the swells slamming into the boat, the rattle of dishes and pots, the creak of planking. An occasional wave washed over the cabin. His nose was clogged with the carbon monoxide and oil fumes leaking up from the engine and his muscles ached. Every now and then Chris would get up to stretch his legs and sometimes he staggered aft along the slippery, bouncing deck and took a glance at Olerich.

It was a dark dungeon of a night. The waves pounded down on them from every side. The wind howled, whipping the water into angry spurts of phosphorescent foam which exploded all around the troller. They could see almost nothing in the pitch-black expanse, no mountains, no shoreline, nothing but the dark water, heaving with its gleaming whitecaps.

"God damn, how that guy lived this long is beyond me," Clyde said as he played with the loose steering wheel in an effort to remain on the trail of the *Verna*'s mast light. "I'll bet he hasn't aligned the steering cable in a month of Sundays. Rudder's loose as my nuts." Clyde stood leaning against the bulkhead. He stared out through the thin square partition of glass, as unaffected about what was happening as if he were playing pinochle in Johnny Bugg's bar in Wrangell.

Actually, their situation was fairly serious. Chris was worried. To make matters worse, the drowned man hadn't been lashed down and he was starting to bounce and roll a little. The aft railing rose only about six inches from the deck and it seemed to Chris that if they hit a good size wave, Olerich would be washed away.

He said to Clyde, "That guy's going to roll off the way we're pitching. He should be tied down."

"Go tie him," Clyde said, disinterested.

Well, kiss my ass, Chris whispered to himself. For a moment it filled him with exasperation. This man worked for him. And then it occurred to Chris that during all the years he had managed the cannery, ever since his father had left Wrangell, this was perhaps the first real order he had ever received. And it grated.

"O.K." Chris said, suppressing his anger.

He stumbled back along the deck, crouched down, holding on to the flimsy starboard rail. Dropping to his knees, he picked up a piece of line from the cockpit and crawled up to the cadaver. The rain pelted down and for a moment Chris paused, staring at Olerich's body. It was surprising how well he could see now that his eyes had grown accustomed to the darkness. But it wasn't so much getting used to the darkness, it was as though the man himself had lighted up so that he could be seen: the round face, the small eyes sunk into cavernous sockets, the black, curly hair. The rain pelted down, soaking the drowned man and Chris wished he had a piece of canvas to cover him. With fierce determination, Chris lifted the body and looped the line around his chest and legs and secured him to the deck.

"Hey, Chris," Clyde was beckoning from the cabin. "Chris . . ."

Chris crawled back along the deck. He was drenched clear through and freezing.

Clyde pointed a chubby paw below to the cabin deck. "Bilge water," he said. "Damn it, she's starting to take on water."

The deck was completely awash with about an inch of dirty, oily water. "By God," Chris exclaimed, "we better start pumping her."

It was queer but now that real trouble had started, which Chris had half-expected all along, his anxiety disappeared. All at once, he was enjoying this strange ride, the black bulging sky, the clouds scudding across it as they had done during the storm last night, the waves thrashing about them.

"Giff better slow her down before he tears all the corking out of the hull," Clyde said, lighting a cigarette with his wind lighter. He clicked it shut. "We'll have to start the bilge pump. Here, you take the wheel."

Clyde braced himself against the bulkhead, tottered down the two steps and started the small one-cylinder auxiliary motor with a cord. The engine sneezed and chugged as it revolved into life and took rhythm, smoking violently. Clyde stayed below hovering over the engine, fussing with the spark and the gas lever until he felt that he was getting the most out of it. The cabin was suffocating, full of exhaust fumes and the racket and stench of the troller's gas engine.

Clyde's eyes were watering as he resumed his place behind the wheel. "Jesus," he exclaimed, "how in hell did that crazy son-of-a-bitch live in this crate?" He rubbed at his eyes. "Hey, I'm hungry. What's he got down there?"

"One box of crackers and some canned food."

"Jesus!" Clyde frowned. "Say, let's flag Giff down and have chow aboard the *Verna*. I could stand a rest and a hot cup of coffee."

"O.K."

Chris stepped outside and then immediately came back into the cabin. Both men stared at each other for it had just occurred to both of them how futile it would be to try to call out to the *Verna*, plowing about twenty yards ahead of them.

"Jesus, we are in a bind." Clyde said.

Chris started laughing. It struck him as funny suddenly, being stranded this way, in a small world of little light and two puttering engines and a corpse.

"Hey, what's that?" Clyde said, peering down between the steps. "Take the wheel."

Beside the bilge pump, next to the stairs, Chris could see a long round piece of metal. Clyde climbed down, stuck his hand under the bottom step and drew forth a long cylindrical tube with a flaring bell at one end. "Well, if this isn't the old boy's fog horn."

Clyde went out on deck and blew into the horn. The sound emitted a rasping squeak, barely making a dent in the howling night. Clyde blew again and again. The horn warmed with each blast and its rasping tone grew smooth, until it was baying mournfully. The *Verna* seemed completely oblivious of them, her mast light unwavering in her course down the strait. Clyde's face was red when he stepped into the cabin, infuriated and out of breath. "You blow for a while, Chris."

Chris decided to go forward around the cabin. That way at least the cabin wouldn't deflect any of the blast. He clung onto the small wood rail that ran about the side of the low cabin and inched forward around the narrow six inch deck until the cabin narrowed to a point and disappeared. He sat astride the bow, bouncing and swerving with it, his legs riding in the water as they dangled over the sides. An occasional wave washed over him. He began to laugh once more. Why the hell had he come up here? Just to prove what a brave man he was? What did it matter if they hailed the *Verna* or not?

He blew into the long tube and was surprised at the horn's deep tones. Surely someone on board the *Verna* would hear. He blew again and again. He blew long and hard until the muscles in his neck began to hurt, taking a deep breath with each effort. A wave washed up against him and sucked the air from his breast. The boat reared up as the tow line stretched against the cleat, shivered, slumped down and lurched forward. Chris fought for balance, almost dropping the horn as he clutched the cleat.

Well, the hell with 'em, Chris decided after delivering a final blast. He started back along the narrow deck, slumped against the cabin, making his way forward by side-stepping his feet inch by inch. He clung onto the rail when the boat pitched and he felt a fresh wave crack over his back. The boat was rolling wildly all of a sudden. Chris found it next to impossible to move. His hands, blue and wet, kept slipping from the rail.

Clyde came out on the deck, bracing himself against the cabin, and extended his arm to Chris. "You've hailed 'em," he shouted. "Giff's turning the boat around."

Chris took Clyde's arm and sidestepped sternwards until his foot touched the open deck. As soon as Giff had swung the *Verna* around, the tow line had slackened and the troller was on her own, which was why she was pitching so badly.

"By God, that's a relief," Chris said.

The *Verna's* low stubby nose swung out of the blackness and approached the troller squarely on her port beam. As she edged upon them, Chris waited for the sea to swing the deck up, then leaped for the *Verna's* deck. Clyde followed. Homer freed the tow line from the cleat and the troller eased away in the darkness, nodding at the end of the line, settled into a trough.

"By God," Homer said, "look what the cat dragged up. You boys ain't having a rough time, are you? Lyle and I are having a wonderful game of gin rummy. Giff's at the wheel."

"You son of a bitch," Clyde said dashing for the galley door, "what's Carl got to eat?"

Inside the warm galley, Homer shook his head with mock pity. "Oh, we ate all that was cooked. T-bone steaks, baked potatoes . . ."

"You guys get those wet clothes off and sit down," Carl said. "I'll have something for you to eat in a minute."

"Hey, Homer," Giff's voice called from the pilot house. "Come here."

"Oh, well, honeymoon's over," Homer smiled. "I was going to tell you all about that Arky schoolteacher that used to keep me doing things for her after school all the time and how I got into her pants in the cloak room one afternoon."

"Homer?" Giff's voice rose.

After Homer replaced him at the wheel, Giff came into the galley, poured himself a cup of coffee and watched the two men take off their clothes by the stove. "How's she going?" he asked.

"You better slow her down. You're tearing the corking out of that tub and she's taking in water."

"Damn. We'll be in this mess all night," Giff said. He looked at Chris, his face impassive. "How you making out? Want Homer or Lyle to relieve you?"

"Nope. Clyde and I are having one helluva time."

"Hey," Clyde commented, sliding behind the table in his shorts, "what about taking a gander at us once in a while?"

"You're doing all right," Giff said. He seemed sore about something. But that was like Giff aboard ship. All business. During fishing season he was always sore, even if the work was being done according to the specifications. It was as if Giff felt that the men resented him for his privilege of running the boat so he acted dissatisfied and grumpy in order for his authority to hold water. Towards the end of a fishing season the men were generally sulky and glad when it was over.

Chris took his shoes off and stuck them under the stove. "Brother, it's wet out there." he said to Carl.

"I'll get you my slickers and hat," Carl said. "And some dry clothes."

Chris and Clyde wolfed down the baked potatoes, garlic bread and steaks. The steaks were almost rare but singed on the outside; they dunked the delicious bread in gravy. They lingered for a while in the warm, well-lighted room over a second cup of coffee.

"Just think," Chris said, "that poor guy is still out there."

Lyle burst out laughing, then sobered quickly. "Gee, he's young. You know, I thought he'd be an old man. Maybe the guy's married, with a kid or two."

"Well," Clyde sighed, uninterested, "we might as well get back if she's still out there."

It was hard to return to the cold and dilapidated troller after the warmth and companionship of the *Verna*. Around midnight it was clear to Chris and Clyde that the inadequate bilge pump wasn't doing much of a job. The cabin deck was awash with at least six inches of water and in the past hour it had risen a good two inches.

"Jesus, either this tub's sprung a leak or the corking's all gone. God damn that Giff!" Clyde growled. "He hasn't slowed down a knot."

"Hey, how about the cockpit?" Chris remarked suddenly. "If she's taking water in here, she must be aft too."

"You better go see, Chris."

Chris staggered outside. He grabbed onto the mast wire and held on to it for dear life. The troller seemed helpless, with water sloshing over the bow and gunwales. Chris suddenly realized that Clyde was afraid of the dead man.

Chris crawled on his hands and knees aft. The wind cut across the boat and nearly ripped off his sou'wester hat. Chris snapped the buckle under his chin, grateful to Carl for lending him his gear. Across the black surface of the sea, the waves came rolling in, weaving and knifing under the hull and slapping it from side to side. Chris knelt down by the cadaver and grabbed onto the edge of the cockpit. He was shocked by the sight of the dark water inside. It was at least half way up, sloshing against the side. Bits of fishing gear were floating in it and the stern was riding low under the weight.

On all fours he scampered back to the cabin in search of a bailing can. His feet sloshed through the bilge water which was up to his ankles. In a corner he located a wash bucket with a good overhead handle, probably used by Olerich to do dishes. He grabbed it and lurched back up the steps, trembling from the chill rising from his feet.

"How bad is it?" Clyde asked at the wheel.

"Half full."

"Jesus H. Christ, start bailing!"

Chris went aft, infuriated with Clyde. He'd have Giff fire the son of a bitch as soon as they got back to Wrangell. He knelt before the cockpit, filled the bucket and lifted it. It was hard to figure out how to dump the water. If he turned right, away from the dead man, he'd wrench his back. If he turned left, he might lose his balance and fall into the cockpit.

Jesus, he thought, gritting his teeth, a little more water couldn't hurt Olerich. He tipped the bucket of water over Olerich's stomach. He scooped up another full bucket and dumped it over the man's stomach. The position was awkward. He had to strain himself to get it up over the belly. The simplest and easiest thing would be to dump the water over the dead man's face as the curve of his swing ran in that direction. Chris paused, panting. This was the first real physical work he'd done in ages. His back muscles were aching already and beginning to stiffen in a knot. By God, he could go for a shot of whiskey. He resumed bailing again, this time over the man's chest. For half an hour he struggled in that position until he gave out. He was so exhausted that the sight of the water splashing over Olerich's face didn't even phase him. He poured tons of water over Olerich's face before he realized what a sap he was. He looked over his shoulder at Clyde standing in the pilot room. Cigarette smoke and gas fumes eddied out of the open slide door. Chris crawled back to the door.

"Clyde, you bail for a while," Chris said. "The bucket's in the cockpit. I'll take over the wheel."

"O.K. Chrissy boy."

"Easy on the Chrissy boy."

Clyde flicked his eyes at Chris in surprise and relinquished the wheel. He got down on his knees and crawled back to the cockpit. Chris lit a cigarette as he watched Clyde slosh his first bucket of water over Olerich's belly.

Chris fought with the loose wheel as he tried to keep the troller lined up with the *Verna*'s mast light. He was impressed with the ease with which Clyde had handled the wheel. The troller would stay directly behind the *Verna*'s stern for a moment, then slide off to port, then come back and slide to starboard like a man riding on water skis behind a motor boat. The ceiling was at least an inch too low for him and so he had to bend his knees to stand behind the wheel. Spray flew against the glass and occasionally a wave whacked into it, drawing a brilliant phosphorescent streak across it. As the boat jounced over the waves his legs grew weak and his concentration slackened. His eyes became fuzzy as they stared out across the night at the bobbing, swaying mast light of the *Verna*.

When the light disappeared he didn't even notice. Numbness was settling into his bones like warm water. The boat reared and tilted, stumbling against the waves, careening over on her beam's ends. The dishes and kettles below were rattling. The water sloshed and slopped on the cabin deck. Chris shook himself too, straightened himself as best he could behind the wheel.

Then he realized he must have dropped off for a minute standing up. He wished that he wore a wrist watch to see what time it was but he knew it must be way past midnight. He strained his eyes through the glass to pick out the light atop the *Verna*. The engine was banging away below him but the momentum it gave off was negligible. The craft seemed to be powerless. Then Chris realized that the *Verna* wasn't anywhere in sight ahead. He let go of the wheel and scrambled out on deck where he could get a better view. He craned his neck from port to starboard.

"Hey, what's happened?" Clyde shouted from the cockpit, sprawled on his knees with the bailing bucket in his hands. "Jesus, what's happened?"

And then Chris realized that the tow line must have snapped for they were drifting to windward and the bow was low and scooping up water. He picked up the fog horn and began to blow into it. Clyde struggled forward. When he saw the sagging bow he rushed into the pilot room and wheeled the troller around until he had her headed down the channel. The fog horn's wail rent the air and Chris felt his lungs would crack.

"No use," Clyde yelled. "Those crazy bastards—not knowing they've broken away from us."

Chris stepped back into the comparative warmth and protection of the pilot platform. He lit a cigarette and leaned against the bulkhead. "Wonder if there's any life preservers aboard," Chris said, with a little laugh.

"Brother, you ain't kidding," Clyde grinned. "I know one guy ain't worried," and Clyde tossed his head aft. Both men laughed. Chris suddenly felt warmer towards Clyde.

"Well, no use standing here," Chris said, tossing his cigarette into the bilge water below the steps. "Might as well do some more bailing."

"Hey, wait, look over there," Clyde said, pointing off the port quarter. "Isn't that the *Verna*'s mast light?"

Chris lunged outside and made out the *Verna*'s port and starboard lights, blue and red, and her white mast light, making an arc towards them.

"They're coming back," Chris said with relief. It was amazing what the sight of the *Verna* did. The ship named after his mother. He felt a wonderful glow in his guts.

Giff was standing forward of the pilot house on the starboard bow clad in seal skins and sou'wester. He was instructing someone at the wheel in the art of navigating a seiner alongside a troller in a sloppy sea. His voice rang with exasperation. The *Verna*'s engine screamed in the night as the boat pulled up much too fast and reversed, her nose bobbing and sloshing in the waves.

Chris inched forward around the cabin and straddled the bow again, his feet dangling over the side. By now it didn't matter. He unbuckled his rain coat so that his arms could have more freedom. The *Verna* swerved close, her stern kicking up a stew as she started to back up. And as the troller floundered, Chris took the tow line and drew it up across him until he had found the broken end. Giff lobbed the *Verna*'s tow line to Chris in a perfect toss and Chris fastened the two securely by making two bowlines and let it go.

"Pretty rough," Giff bellowed. "How are you doing?"

The troller drifted back from the *Verna* and Chris only waved to Giff. The troller jerked as the line caught and the bow hitched up as it began to follow the *Verna*'s wake again.

"Brother, that was some fun," Chris said to Clyde as he ducked into the pilot platform. He was wringing wet down the front as a result of unbuckling his raincoat. Shivering, he wriggled out of the raincoat, then removed the soaked jacket that Carl had loaned him, flapping it to get out some of the water and hanging it on the partition above the steps. But he was so cold he had to put it back on, even though his skin cringed at the touch of the cold wet cloth. He stamped up and down and rubbed his side against the bulkhead to try and generate some heat.

"What I would give for some dry clothes and a slug of whiskey."

"Here, have a dry cigarette." Clyde said, tossing him one.

As Chris struck a match against the bulkhead, the troller's bow lurched down and nearly wrenched crosswise. "Jesus," Chris lamented, "the line's snapped again."

Quickly, Chris scooped up the fog horn and dashed outside, hoping to attract the *Verna* before she got away. With all his might he blew into the horn. It barely seemed to penetrate the howl of the wind and the roar of the waves.

"By God," Clyde shouted, "they're on the ball this time. I guess Giff's got someone on the lookout. They're turning around."

"Well, here goes," Chris said as he prepared to climb forward around the cabin again.

"Hey, you take the wheel," Clyde protested. "You've done enough dirty work."

"Hell, wet as I am, a little more won't hurt," Chris said, starting forward. He snared the wet stringy line in his hands, knotted the two ends together and dropped it away.

"We need cable," he heard Giff's voice shout and then the two boats stretched apart. Chris clung onto the cabin rail until the troller had started ahead. He was so cold when he got back to the cabin that he decided to bail water from the cockpit rather than stand and shiver. The water on the deck below had risen to the level of the first step, sloshing against the planking. Each time the troller tilted, it seemed the weight of the water might push the boat over her side.

For nearly three hours, in the steady rain and cold and darkness, the drowned man was drenched with bucket after bucket of water. Chris and Clyde took turns, spelling each other when they tired. Giff increased the *Verna*'s speed when they entered the Tongass Narrows. Around four thirty in the morning, they arrived in Ketchikan.

Giff went ashore to locate the authorities while Clyde and Chris secured the troller to the float astern of the *Verna*. Together, they hurried into the *Verna*'s galley, puffing and blue. The galley embraced them with a burst of warmth and both men stripped down to their shorts by the roaring oil stove.

"By God, there's nothing like an oil stove for heat."

"Jesus," Clyde said, shivering uncontrollably, "I can't get enough of this."

Homer emerged from the crew quarters carrying an armload of clothes which he distributed, with glowing benevolence, to Clyde and Chris.

"Go on, take 'em, Chris. Try 'em on for size," Homer insisted, pressing into Chris' hands a pair of slippers, faded denim jeans and a dark wool sweater. The jeans yawned around his waist and the legs were four inches too short. The sweater was short and loose around his stomach and tight about the shoulders.

"I feel like a Chinaman," Chris laughed, still shivering.

Carl was frying wieners and making a fresh pot of coffee. He looked sleepy and tired as he stood before the stove, turning the sizzling wiener halves. "Sit down, boys," Carl said. "This will warm you up."

Homer watched Chris and Clyde fall to. "Hell, I ate just a little while ago but I might as well join you."

"By God, Homer," Carl said. "You make life for a cook miserable."

Whereupon Homer, who seemed wide awake, chirped cheerfully. "Just to show you my heart's in the right place, Carl, I won't disappoint you." And Homer proceeded to stash away more than Chris and Clyde together.

"By God, Giff's sure taking a long time finding those authorities," Lyle said, as he came into the galley from the pilot house. "We wired the Coast Guard that we had the body hours ago. At three thirty, we wired them that we'd be in Ketchikan about five. Sure wide awake down here." Lyle's voice contained no ill-feeling whatsoever, but it was low and depressed. Chris realized that Lyle was taking this hard.

The rain drizzled down and Carl cleaned the table and washed the dishes and still Giff hadn't returned. Lyle gave Carl a hand drying the dishes and it occurred to Chris that Homer, who acted genial, was actually selfish and ungracious. He had never seen Homer helping the cook, although everyone else, even Clyde and Giff, pitched in when Carl was overwhelmed.

"Well, I think I'll hit my bunk," Clyde said.

Chris turned on the radio in the galley and sipped his third cup of coffee. The music came out clear as a bell. The clarity was strange for he was used to the land radios in Wrangell. There he had to struggle to hear the program over the static, the whooshing of the ether waves, occasional interruptions of Morse code and incredible smashing sounds which sounded as if someone were crumpling a large sheet of paper in front of the microphone. It was usually not worth the effort except for late at night.

They say that falling in love is wonderful . . .

The coffee was strong and fresh and uplifting. His body, propped up behind the table, was snug and dry, warm and wide awake. The cigarette tasted delicious. The music was low and sad and thrilling. The girl that sang the song had incredible control of her voice. She hit the notes with the correct pitch, savoring the melody. Lyddy swelled into his mind and his well-being soared. For a while he was unaware of anything save the image of the girl. As the song ended, the feeling of comradeship with the crew which he first felt in the troller with Clyde flooded him. He floated in a reverie of good will towards everyone in Wrangell.

There were footsteps and voices outside on the float. Carl opened the door and looked out. "Giff's got someone with him," Carl said. "They're back there looking at the body."

"You better make a pot of coffee," Chris said. "I think they'll need it."

The music poured out, clear and low, a duet.

Two sleepy people, til dawn's early light, too much in love to say goodnight . . .

In a little while the galley door opened. Giff came in with a thin man who was dripping from the rain.

Chris and Homer stood up and Giff said, "This is Mr. Olerich, the boy's father."

"Sit down," Giff said to Mr. Olerich. "Carl, pour us some coffee."

Mr. Olerich sat down behind the table. His brown suit was wrinkled and loose. His face was reddish-colored, lean and leathery where it wasn't covered by his grizzled whiskers. He wore round, steel-rimmed glasses, which were wet and clouded. Though he couldn't possibly see through them, he kept them on. The hot cup of coffee Carl placed before him steamed up under his chin. He bent down and sipped it, without lifting the mug to his lips, and the steam fogged his glasses all the more.

"Say, maybe you're hungry," Giff said. "How about some wieners?"

The man fumbled inside his shirt pocket for a cigarette and made no reply. "Carl, fry up some wieners."

The only noise in the room was the sizzle of wieners, the purr of the fan in the oil stove, the rain and the radio playing a slow ballad. Mr. Olerich sat down next to Homer, Chris was across from them next to Giff. Chris wanted to tell Homer to reach up behind him and shut off the radio but he felt paralyzed.

"Well," Giff said, "I've gotten hold of the Coast Guard. They're going to get the coroner. Sure slow, though," he added.

A restlessness lay about the table. Carl placed the platter of wieners before Giff. Chris twisted in his seat and lit a cigarette off the one he had just finished. Beside Olerich, Homer sat up straight, his face blank and owlish.

"That was my son," the man said suddenly and sighed. His tone was bitter.

"That was too bad," Homer said, blinking his eyes.

"A terrible tragedy," Lyle whispered.

"Where's Clyde?" Giff asked, just to be saying something.

"He went below to his bunk," Chris said.

"Carl," Giff said, "you can go to sleep if you want."

"Oh, I'm not sleepy," Carl said, though it was obvious he was exhausted.

Mr. Olerich seemed nervous. He kept flicking his chin with his thumb nail. Ashes from his cigarette dropped down on his coat and into his coffee. He played with the wiener on the plate before him, then ate half of it, slowly, chewing awkwardly. Chris noticed that he had false teeth. His short bony fingers were square and nicotine stained and the nails were dark with dirt.

Mr. Olerich put down his fork. "Gordon's better off dead," he said slowly and decisively. There was a silence as the impact of his words settled in the room. No one had bothered to turn off the radio, though it had been hushed it seemed by the atmosphere in the galley. In the sudden quiet, the music and the lyrics to the music came through, disturbing and ironical.

I saw those harbor lights, they only told me were parting, those same old harbor lights, that once brought you to me . . .

"Shut that damn thing off!" Giff said with anger.

Homer stretched up behind him and twisted the control dial shut. Now Chris could hear the sound of the rain, soft and steady, filling the room. Occasionally the boat would jounce against its bumpers.

Mr. Olerich bent his head down and slurped his coffee. His cigarette ash grew longer, dangling over his coffee before falling to the side onto the table. He laid his finger on it, squashed it, then rubbed the smear on his clothes.

"He's better off where he is," Olerich said bitterly. He bit his thumb, staring into his cup.

"Oh, come on, Mr. Olerich," Chris said. "You can't mean that."

"Yes, I do," Olerich said, "I'm glad my son's dead. Gordon is better off dead. What did he have to live for? Selma cheats on him every chance she gets. The minute his boat leaves Ketchikan, she's getting drunk, screwing around. Leaves the baby with her aunt." Olerich looked up. "Where is she now?" he asked. "She ain't home. She ain't at her aunt's."

The room was silent. "I wish I were in his shoes. I wish I were dead," Mr. Olerich mumbled. "There's nothing much to live for." He went back to eating his wiener.

It was relief to see the body of Gordon Olerich deposited in the coroner's basket and carted up the float to the hearse. It was relief to the numbed men on the *Verna* to be heading back to Wrangell.

12

ALTHOUGH IT HAD SEEMED like a simple evening at first, it had gone off in an unexpected direction. But that was typical of Wrangell, Dave thought. That was what kept him going when things got too monotonous. He could never predict what would happen next.

Whenever he went down to the Federal Building to collect his mail or Main Street to shop, he ran into people he knew. It was inevitable since Wrangell was so small. They'd start talking, decide to have a shake at the Sweets and before long, someone else would join them, then another. Some of the people would leave and others would take their place. Pretty soon the gathering had a momentum of its own and would sweep them along to some unexpected conclusion.

He'd taken Victoria to the high school basketball game. Chris and Lydia had come along with them. It was a pretty good game, although Juneau's team thrashed Wrangell's, but there was so much cheering each time that Wrangell High scored a bucket that it didn't seem to matter that they lost. This cheerful attitude was no doubt bolstered by all the drinking that had gone on, clandestinely of course, as bottles were shuffled under coats from one group to another, down the stands and up.

Afterwards several groups gathered. Dave and Vic were in a group that tramped down in the drizzle to Mom's where they danced and drank beer. Other groups joined them. The place grew crowded and smoky and noisy. A man drifted from his crowd, planting himself in one booth, then another. Vic danced with other men and Dave danced with other women. It was when he danced with Lydia that he realized for the first time that not everyone was enjoying themselves. Lydia was cold and withdrawn. Her aloofness made her seem even more beautiful than usual.

Vic had told Dave that Lydia was upset because Chris had not notified her about the change in his plans the the night the *Verna* sailed to Reed's Bay and then to Ketchikan. She had been worried during the storms those two nights, her first experience with storms in Wrangell. Not knowing what had happened to Chris made her feel sick and learning that he could have have radioed Wrangell made her furious. So Dave tried to cover for his friend, explaining how Chris was like that, things just slipped his mind when he was the middle of an activity. But it didn't seem to help.

And then, even though it was drizzling, someone announced that Al, the midget, had gotten hold of Beswick's old flat bed truck with a canopy over the side racks and was inviting everyone out to the beach for a picnic. It was crazy, but of course most everyone went. There was a lean-to cabin out at the beach with a large brick fireplace so they could get out of the rain and stay warm. Someone went to wake up Chuck Everett, the baker, to get buns. Someone else went off for the mustard and coffee and someone else fetched the utensils. It wasn't until they got to the picnic grounds that they realized no one had thought of the franks.

By the time the wieners were fetched (Al took the truck back into town and woke up Butch so he could get them out of the cold storage plant,) a great many of the people had decided to go home, hoofing it. Those who still had bottles remained. It was ten after one when Dave had his first hot dog. He decided he might as well stay up for the next two hours or so until the steamer from the south came in.

Throughout the day he had been so wrought up about its arrival that he had scarcely been able to concentrate at work or pay more than superficial attention to Vic. The steamer was bringing up a new, completely modern dental unit, chair and all, that Dave had ordered three weeks ago from Seattle. This unit had everything: a chip blower, an automatic warm air syringe, hot and cold atomizers and hot water at the flick of the finger. No more worrying about the hand pump that always seemed to go dry at the moment when he needed a mouth rinse.

"I'm glad it's Friday," Vic said, munching into a hot dog. "Tomorrow, I'll sleep till noon."

"Having fun?"

"It's been unusual. From a basketball game to dancing . . ." She paused to swallow a mouthful of hot dog. ". . . to a weeny roast by the fire in the rain."

"Well, at least the rain is out there and we're in here."

Vic gave him a quick look of surprise as if she had caught the lack of enthusiasm in his voice. "Uh huh, cozy," she said. She didn't sound like she meant it. He felt she was faking everything tonight.

Dave shifted around to dangle a dog over the coals. In the far corner of the lean-to, he could see Chris and Lydia. The glow from the hot coals dimmed as it reached in their direction but from what Dave could see they must have patched up their quarrel. Lydia was sitting with her back against the wall and Chris was kissing her. It was a long kiss. He wrenched his eyes away, feeling an emptiness in his belly. When he looked back, they were still kissing.

Later, when practically the entire party paired off and no one was inclined to leave the lean-to and search the shore for driftwood with which to revive the expiring coals (they had exhausted the stack of dry hemlock blocks that Matt had left beside the fireplace), Dave suggested walking back to Main Street. It didn't seem right when everyone else was necking to be sitting around watching the coals with Vic and talking. It would take about an hour to walk back to town but it wouldn't be so bad because she had an umbrella.

"See you tomorrow," Dave said, waving at Chris and Lydia who were still in the corner. Chris seemed content and so did she. It made him uncomfortable. People in love always gave off that aroma of abandoned indecency. Their desires were naked, palpable almost. And yet it went beyond that. There was also the sweet courtesy with which they treated everyone, even their friends. And the way their emotions, thoughts and secrets merged, so that they spoke and acted in union.

Dave stifled an oath as he and Vic strode out of the trees and onto the road. It wasn't the sight of Chris and Lydia that frustrated him but his own despair about the routine of his life.

"Steamer should be in by the time we get to Main Street," Dave said. He didn't know why he started the conversation, for all evening he had let Vic make the openings. He was irritated with himself for slipping.

"It's nice walking under the umbrella," Vic said. "I'm almost getting used to it." After a while, she said, "In one week, school will be over." When Dave didn't answer, she went on. "By this time next week it will be summer vacation."

"I'll bet you'll be glad," he said.

"Well, I don't know. We haven't made up our minds yet whether we're going to stay. That is Lyddy hasn't. But I guess after tonight, she probably will want to stay. Brother, there was some mighty powerful necking going on in that corner of the lean-to."

"Yes, there certainly was." In the confined space of the umbrella, her chatter irritated him.

"I've made up my mind. I want to stay for the fall term. Although it will be rough to go through the summer vacation without income. As relief teachers we aren't on the payroll."

"Maybe you could work? There's lots of work during the summer, what with fishing season and all."

"That's what I was telling Lyddy," Vic sighed. "It's harder for her. She keeps getting letters from home."

"Don't you get letters?" At least it was always easy to talk to her.

"Oh sure. But my folks are down in Arizona. They have a little farm down there. They're happy with or without me."

"Sounds like people I'd like to know."

"Mom's so much in love with Dad, she doesn't need anyone else around. Dad's her whole world. We kids always came second. Pop was it, in the house. Her devotion and dependency upon him . . ." She stopped again. "Well, it got to be cloying after a while. As we got older, we felt like we were in the way. There were three of us, two boys and me. When we left home, we just drifted away. I married a man in Berkeley . . ."

Yes, he knew about that. He was interested in this girl. He was in love with her, really. And for a while he had thought that she loved him. They had a standing lunch date each noon. He'd climb up the hill and wait outside the school steps for Vic to come out and they'd go down to Mom's. Usually Lydia would come along with them now that Chris was out almost daily inspecting traps. And they went out most every night too. That's why Wednesday night had been such a blow.

He'd gone up to the cottage and found it dark and deserted. When he questioned Vic the next day at lunch, she said she had gone out with Clarence Wick. She claimed she didn't know Dave was planning to come over even though he was sure he had mentioned it to her.

They were walking rather fast as if both had heavy thoughts and were anxious to drop them by reaching their destination quickly. By the time they got to the cottage they were breathing pretty heavily, though they were both trying to conceal it.

"Would you like to come in for a drink?" Vic asked.

"Oh, all right," Dave said. He looked at his watch, angling his arm so he could read it under the house light. He turned and stared out at the dark channel. "Steamer should be rounding Elephant Nose any time now."

"Well, there it is!" Vic said in surprise, as pinpoints of light appeared in the murky distance. It was so black out on the channel that you couldn't see the islands.

"Hmmm. I think I'll go down. I guess I shouldn't be so anxious or curious—I could just as well see it tomorrow."

"I think I understand," Vic said, folding her umbrella.

Dave kissed her—a quick, impersonal goodnight kiss. And the kiss, as he had expected, was flat. She seemed surprised and certainly wasn't prepared for the swift peck. What had he expected? He was feeling pretty flat himself.

He strode down the hill, not even turning to see her enter the house or wave a final farewell. He scowled as he lunged down the hill.

Vic just didn't seem interested in him. Maybe he was too old or something. He searched his mind for some sign of encouragement. They seemed to have fun lunching together, walking back and forth from school, going to the show, meeting people. She was cheerful and friendly and easy to please but Dave knew that her heart wasn't set on him. A few nights earlier, after the movie, they'd gone for a walk around the road. It was raining and blowing, yet they were nice and snug under the umbrella, muffled in overcoats and gloves. Suddenly she began to talk about her divorced husband and said what a coincidence it was that Clarence looked so much like him. She laughed, trying to make it sound unimportant, but she said that the resemblance was uncanny.

Vic had gone on talking under the umbrella, not looking at him, as if he wasn't there. She was giving Dave a diagnosis of the defects in her marriage, charting the critical stages with precision as they led up to the divorce. Couldn't she understand that he wasn't interested in her past. The past was no good. His folks proved that to him. They were always mumbling about the past, bickering about it, hating it, yet unable to let go of it. Couldn't she understand that for some reason, he didn't want to know about her past.

"He couldn't stand living with one person all the time." She laughed, side-stepped a puddle and Dave brought the umbrella around and over her head. "It was just a matter of time before we separated. I knew it couldn't last."

She quieted, as a couple approached them, then continued after they'd said hello to the Yorgensens.

"Why that man hated to come in the house so much that he would stay out in the yard mowing the lawn and planting new bulbs. He'd even uproot flowers that still had a lot of life in them."

"Vic, really," he'd said at last, "if you don't mind, I don't care to . . ." And he stopped. For she appeared hurt. He had wanted to tell her in his nicest way that her past really didn't matter to him.

"Hi, Dave," Red Parker said, waving at Dave from the edge of the Clinton dock.

"What are you doing here?" Charlie Zimms asked, as he stamped his feet and blew into his hands,

"Got a new dental unit coming in and I want to see that you guys handle it properly."

The steamer's whistle split the darkness and rain of the night with one long and one short blast announcing that it was halfway across the channel. The town's dogs slunk out from under house foundations, steps and porches, to reply with long howls, grief-laden and sustained, one following on the heels of another until the silence and rain drove them back under shelter.

Dave jogged around to the front of the warehouse and stood against the corrugated iron wall facing the harbor. Suddenly his excitement was gone. All day he had been on pins and needles to see the new outfit come in on the steamer. Now he felt drained.

He watched the steamer coming in. The longshoremen stood out on the dock in their boots and slickers that gleamed under the lights. There were a few other people around: old man Clinton himself going with Ted Savard into the ticket office and a few people waiting for passengers. Dave waited under the awning of the warehouse, the thrill of the new unit lost somehow. His mind was insensible to anything but the early morning cold and the rain. He wished that the steamer would hurry so he could go to bed.

A chill crept into his bones and he shivered. It occurred to him that he hadn't been this upset in years. He had been living in a kind of dormancy, half-joyless, half-contented. The last time he had felt this upset was years ago when he sprained his ankle. He was going moose hunting with Chris and a few other men. He had postponed all his appointments for a week. Then he had slipped galloping down the stairs from his apartment, in a hurry to get to the harbor on time to catch the boat. He had almost cried with disgust and self-loathing as he sat on the bottom step nursing the sprained ankle, aware that he would miss the trip.

The grounding rumble of the steamer's engine floated into Dave's ears. He stared at it, vexed with its slow progress. It wasn't like a train, pulling confidently into a station. Instead the steamer took its time, careful of the tricky tide, angling her port beam towards the piling, like a cat creeping along towards its prey.

Funny, he thought, he scarcely ever thought about Clarence although he had known him for years, going to his shop for shaves and haircuts. Now he couldn't stand being around him. Maybe even hated him.

The high white bow of the steamer nosed up to the edge of the dock. The piling grunted as the port beam scraped against it. The stern end of the steamer slid sideways and Dave saw the explosive burst of white water churning aft as the engine sped into reverse to lay the ship flush with the wharf. The small crowd moved forward, waiting for the longshoremen to secure the lines thrown from the fore and aft decks around the cleats on the dock.

There were only a few passengers on the steamer's deck, mostly returning Wrangellites. The onlookers edged closer, thrusting out hands over the ship's railing to clasp the hands of friends and relatives fresh up from the States. They laughed and greeted each other with platitudes ("Just like Wrangell—raining!" "Oh, it's good to be back"). There was a jubilant release of energy in the hush of the night. The passengers were impatient, waiting for the gangway to be strung up in position so they could go home.

Dave watched the small group of passengers on the port deck, most of whom he knew. They filed down the gangway in slow procession followed by luggage-bearing stewards in white coats and black bow ties. As their feet touched the wet solid planking of the dock, Dave could feel the sensation they felt, a moment off-balance between two worlds, a release that was both light and giddy, the departure from the humming luxury vessel to the drab, wet nighttime dock.

He shook hands with Floyd who was one of the passengers and felt no better. He must be crazy, being here at this hour. Things were just not normal any more. For one thing he wasn't seeing much of Chris. Chris never dropped by the office during the day or came to play gin rummy with the boys. He felt the void, especially now that Vic had decided one man wasn't enough for her.

The winch was cranking, hoisting up its first load of cargo from the hold. Dave waited for it to come up, to swing over the side where Red and Charlie would guide the pallet upon the dray. He was about to turn and go home but, on impulse, went over to the longshoremen. Another load swung over the side. It contained a predominance of whiskey, beer and wine although there were a few staples such as soap and canned food.

"By God, I'm glad someone eats and takes a bath once in a while," said Buck Harrington, one of the longshoremen, grabbing the tongue of the next dray and wheeling it off down the dock.

"Come on, Dave," Red said, as the winch brought the next load of cargo creaking down upon them, "give us a hand unloading this tub." Red and Charlie were both sling men. They stood opposite each other, each grabbing a side of the pallet and steadying it over the next dray. "We're short handed tonight," Red said. He was obviously drunk. He struggled to hold himself upright and the breath he blew in Dave's direction stank of sour sherry.

Most of the men didn't show up," Charlie explained. "They're up at Sarber's—throwing a wild party." Charlie was nowhere near as drunk as Red. They were good friends, usually together whether unloading a ship or drinking at the hotel bar.

"Yeah," Red said, "and there's sixty tons of cargo aboard. Fishing season coming up means more stuff ordered. How about it, dentist?"

Dave toyed with the idea. It was so late another hour of sleep didn't matter much, one way or another. He wanted to see the dental unit unloaded and helping the longshoremen would be better than standing around in the rain.

Only two years back, he had longshored regularly during the salmon season when most of the men were out fishing and there was a demand for dock labor. That was before his dental work became more time-consuming and took up most of his evenings. He used to longshore at night after office hours. He had done it primarily for the exercise, and the fun. He liked mingling with a group of men he knew and liked, store clerks, a teacher at the Native Institute, the owner of the hardware shop. He liked using his muscles, working alongside his friends, with no one pushing him if he worked at a decent rate. They'd pile up the cases of salmon on the drays at the canneries, at Ballard Cannery and Schnur's Cannery, then take turns, laughing and joking, steering the dray and pushing it down the long dock towards the freighter. They would smoke or take swigs from someone's bottle while waiting for the crew in the hold of the freighter to stack up the cases. It was a challenge, to be faster than the gang on the freighter. It felt good to take a swig of whiskey and gaze off into the distance, at the pattern of lights formed by the gill-netting boats as they fished for kings around the mouth of the Stikine River and to feel the fresh breeze hitting his nostrils. He remembered the pleasure of opening a just-packed can of salmon with his pocket knife, poking the meat out and eating it warm and juicy before its flavor had been tainted by the tin.

"If you need help," Dave said to Red, "I'm willing to give a hand."

"Great, old boy," Red said. "Since you ain't dressed properly, go over in the warehouse and help Buck unload the drays."

Dave strode across and into the warehouse and began to unload the cases of Seagrams and Old Forester. He worked fast and the dray was unloaded in nothing flat.

"Say, you're hot," Buck said, grinning. "You've still got the old touch."

13

As always in Wrangell, there was the rain, the dark green channel, the islands shrouded by trees and the quiet. Today the sunlight was shining through the rain, striking silver glints on the water. Occasionally the quiet was broken by the sound of a passing boat.

"The rain—does one ever get used to it?" Lyddy asked, turning to Chris. They were standing under the open shed roof of the Ballard Cannery, between the fish house and warehouse.

Chris laughed. "Sure you do."

"There are times, Chris, when I believe there's no place in the world except Wrangell."

"Good, you're turning into a true Alaskan."

"I don't feel like an Alaskan. Although I can tell you're trying to make me one."

"I'm glad," he said. "I want it that way. I want to be the one who makes you a true Alaskan."

"Well, don't worry . . ."

Lyddy gazed out across the wet dock, through the rain, at the shaft of sunlight that fell in the channel. "You'll never know how frightened I was"—she wanted to say terrified, but she didn't want to make him think she was a baby—"when you didn't return to Wrangell those nights. I've never felt so helpless in my entire life."

"I should have radioed the cannery to tell you . . ." He paused, looking back towards the front of the open shed. "Joe's sure taking his time getting those bearings," he said.

"It's cold standing here. Will it take long?"

"Nah. I just want to stay here for a minute so he can tell me what the trouble is. He'll do a better job that way. Once he figures out what's wrong, he'll make a suggestion about how to fix it and I'll say, 'Sure, that's a good idea, Joe,' and then we'll go."

They were planning to go for a walk and she wanted to be on her way. It seemed her whole life was coming down upon her in the open shed with the eaves dripping and the rain spanking against the tin roof.

"Chris, I envy you," she said abruptly.

"Me? Why?"

"Well, you're happy here, aren't you? I mean there is nothing else in all the world for you but this." She waved her hand out across the dock.

"I guess so."

"Don't be modest. I'm serious. You can't seem to understand what this has been like for me. It isn't as if I were prepared." She groped for words. "Wrangell is a tiny island far away from everything I've ever known. And yet I've been happy here. That, and terrified too." There, she'd finally admitted it.

For one of the few times in her life, her confidence had deserted her.

Lydia Prince was just a bundle of terror wrapped around the vision of the man she loved. Despite the fact that she was sure that Chris was all right, that nothing had happened in the storm, the terror would not dissolve.

"Chris," she said, suddenly, "why do you love me? Please tell me the truth." The rain fell and the sunlight pierced through it and the islands sat there wrapped in darkness, waiting.

"Well, now," Chris said, plainly savoring the task of phrasing an answer, "you're probably the most beautiful, bewitching girl I've seen, known or dreamed of."

"No, I don't want that. I want to know the material reason."

"Well, if you must know, I love you simply because I'm crazy about you. I feel I can't get enough of you. When I'm away from you—like those days and nights I was on the *Verna*—I missed you. I felt empty."

"Chris," she said, "I've never met anyone quite like you. You're so much yourself. You don't even own a wrist watch. You don't have a car." She smiled and turned to him. "Are you as rich as everyone else seems to imply?"

"The Ballard fortune is in the neighborhood of two hundred fifty thousand dollars."

The impact of the words exploded in her mind. She was stunned. He was the richest man she had ever dated and yet he was the most natural and unaffected.

"I love you, Chris," she said impulsively. "I love you so very much."

"A gold digger," he scoffed, lifting his eyebrows, though his tone and smile indicated that he understood what she meant and that he was more pleased than ever with himself.

Suddenly she understood everything—his simplicity and his love for Wrangell and the sadness that lay in his heart, that affected everyone in Wrangell. The sadness contained the truth of existence, the necessity of independence, of taking responsibility for one's own pleasure. She saw it now and felt it in the rain under the shed, the sadness that floated from the rain and the islands and the long wet dock that ran out to meet the channel.

"I'll be right back, darling," Chris said, turning, as footfalls sounded at the opposite end of the shed. It was strange, she reflected as she watched Chris duck into the fish house with his mechanic. The whole world was nothing but a hoax, an illusion and yet at the same time, as if to tease you, it was rich and rewarding. Who would have dreamed that this understanding would come to her in Alaska?

Lyddy walked to the edge of the overhang and waited for Chris. Occasionally, the sun burst out from behind the clouds and the rain water running off the eaves would catch the light and glisten like a stream of sparkling stones.

She remembered when she was about eleven, how she became aware of the admiration in her father's eyes when she came into the house. Then she discovered the same admiration in her mother. Lyddy began to realize that it was something about her which created this state of candid admiration. She felt it in the gaze of other people, too, friends and relatives. After a while, she took it for granted. It got to the point where she felt it looking at herself in the bathroom mirror. She felt it with her first brassiere, her first pair of high heels, her first silk stockings, her first pair of pink panties trimmed with lace. Boys flocked about her in high school and she thrilled to it. She would date first one, then another, growing choosy with all the attention, until she had the boy all the girls wanted. Then she wanted more than just a high school kid. She wanted a man with a dark moustache, who would jitterbug, drive a roadster, be slender and six feet one inches tall.

It had been the same way throughout most of her college years until several things happened which suppressed her ebullience. She met Vic, who was cautious and somewhat cynical after her divorce. And she saw how the professor who lived next door existed only in his world of music and teaching. And then Don Lofton seduced her, right in the front seat of his car, as smooth a job of seducing a woman as was ever performed. Her reflection in the gilt-edged mirror of her own self-confidence shattered.

She had slipped. But she knew how it had happened. And this understanding saved her from tumbling further into defeat. She identified the elements: the dance, the frolicking at the beach playground, the insidious pint bottle of whiskey in the glove compartment, sweetened with Coke, Don's urging her: "Go on, Lyddy, have a taste. It'll warm you up." Even though she had been half-drunk, she remembered the details, his hand zipping down his fly, the awkward position and her willingness. She had been willing and even, in her inexperience, helpful, or the seduction could not have succeeded. Her mortification and chagrin afterwards were like a rash on her flesh.

She didn't let Don know of her humiliation. She continued dating him. But there were no more front seat incidents. She scarcely allowed him a kiss. After her period arrived, she began to regain her confidence, though she was much more sober and prudent. Don, poor Don, was so frustrated and distracted and eager for another conquest that he asked her to marry him.

She began to reassess her life. She desired admiration but she didn't want to be inconvenienced by it. She liked to go to a popular movie with Don and then stand in the crowded lobby waiting for the previous picture to end, leaning against the wall, looking bored and sophisticated in elegant clothes. Don would sit on the arm of a chair or stand near her fidgeting, scowling and wondering what the hell this was all about, while the patrons entering the lobby and the ones already in it, cast covetous glances at her. She needed all the adulation that she had become accustomed to, evem if it came from the frank, unguarded stares of strangers.

During that year, Lyddy acquired an abstract, brittle facade. It was if she were wrapped in a little shell that represented the beautiful and correct Miss Lydia Prince. She found this coat of armor rather suitable to her new way of life. After a while, she began to think that this was all there was in life for her—the smugness and the pleasure-instinct and the lilting sense of melancholy which tinged all things. All of this, of course, could not have happened without the knowledge of her beauty and her downfall in Don's car.

Lyddy smiled, thinking of herself as stubborn and self-willed. All the same, she did not want to make any more blunders She had to be sure of herself. She had to be sure of Chris. Of Wrangell. There were some things she knew for certain. That Chris loved her. That she loved him. But somehow this knowledge wasn't enough. Maybe the incident in Don's car had made her wary of everything, even her love for Chris, her whole future.

She was cold standing under the shed. It was raining, steadily as it had been most of the week. When she first woke up and saw the sun out and the sky clear, she thought it wouldn't rain today. But around noon the rain began.

She wondered if this sadness, which had plunged down upon her in the open shed at the cannery, would ever leave. Her entire life was bearing down upon her on an island at the end of the universe. The sadness was mingled with a terrible longing, nameless and as infinite as the silver sunlight and the rain.

The town was desolate. And quiet. Silence flooded the town like fog, streaming in from the ocean. She had never imagined that the world could be so still. Small noises, like hammer-blows or the bark of a dog or the chut-chut-chut of a gas boat drowned in the silence like pebbles tossed in water.

Gray hordes of clouds crawled across Woronkofski Island across the channel. The wind drove the rain clattering onto the tin roof. She wished Chris would hurry up.

Lyddy glanced back at the dark opening leading into the fish house. She could hear the clink of a tool working against metal and the low conversation of Chris and his mechanic exchanging suggestions and facts. They were working on the assembly line, preparing for the approaching fishing season. Chris had taken her through the empty fish house, explaining how the cannery worked. He became quite serious as he described the boats coming in, the salmon being pitched from the holds and streaming up the conveyor belt into the fish bins. There the salmon were segregated and washed. The iron chink machines chopped off the heads and tails and gutted the fish. From there they went to the filler. When the cans emerged from the filler, the women in the line, patched them, weighed them, fed them into the seamer. The sealed silver tins clicked off the line and were stacked by hand in steel trays so they could be rolled into the retorts where the meat was cooked in the tins.

A feeling of something special, of something new and exciting hung in the air, the same feeling one felt before a championship football game or a wedding. Men, and even women, mended nets along the bridge, in front of their houses, on the docks. Men sloshed down the road in hip boots, all business as they moored their boats on gridirons and scraped the slimy, moss-covered hulls and freshened them with dark copper paint. Children ran down to the harbor after school to help paint the deck cabins or to row around the harbor in their fathers' skiffs. They handled the oars expertly, maneuvering the big awkward seine skiffs skillfully in the water, as deft and at home with them as children in the States are with skates and wagons.

The difference was tangible. She could feel it in Chris when he spoke about the operation of the cannery. But what was her part in it? Could she find a place for herself? Could she live here, raise a family here, have her babies at the small hospital with Doc Little assisting? How would she feel watching her children playing in the rain, like the children of Wrangell, who were always outside, dressed lightly, wheeling their bicycles or frolicking in the muddy streets?

Lyddy took a deep breath and stamped her feet. In Wrangell, one didn't have to work for pleasure. It seemed to flow effortlessly. Back in the States, especially when she was at college, pleasure had been something to work at. She felt drained when she came home after a date. But it was different up here. She wasn't sure why. No one seemed to have to try to have fun. Perhaps because the people were not on guard with one another. Except for a few like the sullen girl who sold tickets at the theater. In general, no one adopted a pose. They were simply themselves. And this made the town strong and free.

She toyed with all this in her mind. Only a few days remained before school let out. Well, she had already decided, and she had informed her mother by letter, that she was going to stay in Wrangell for at least a week after the term ended. She wanted to see what Wrangell was like in the summer before making up her mind whether to stay in Wrangell for the fall semester. She had not mentioned Chris.

In fact, besides Vic, the only other person she had talked to about Chris was Bea Hart. For some reason she wanted to tell Bea everything. She felt Bea would steer her straight.

She had liked Bea from the beginning. There was something about Bea, a sort of vulnerability, which touched Lyddy. Even before she had known about the death of Bea's only child, she felt a tenderness towards Bea. She sensed that Bea was unhappy, with her own life, perhaps with her husband, certainly with Alaska itself. She had been terrified that first night Chris was out, even though Bea had reassured her that the men had probably anchored the seiner in some cove in which to escape the storm. "Well," she had said, "now you are one of us. You'll get used to it soon enough if you remain in Wrangell."

Lyddy was grateful that she had walked around the harbor and visited Bea. She had spent the afternoon at the cottage, looking out the window at the channel, at the water as black as ink. There was no sign of the stubby-nosed purse-seiner. As darkness fell, she grew more and more tense, twisting her hands and stamping about the room. Vic was going out with Clarence Wick. This, on top of her anxiety about Chris, bothered Lyddy. Vic seemed delighted by the prospect of her date, going to great pains to get herself ready.

"Darn you, Vic, quit humming," she had snapped once. "It's not as if this is your first date." Her irritation was like an itch that eluded her.

"I like Clarence, Lyddy," Vic had confided, pulling the bobby pins out of her hair. "Clarence is steamed up all the time. Don't you feel it when you're near him? He's always about to explode."

"You can have him," Lyddy said and tripped out of the bedroom. She pulled the living room drape aside and glanced out the window. The channel was a pool of blackness. She could see nothing, no pinpricks of light which would indicate the presence of a boat, only the rain visible under the street lamp pouring down with an intensity that made the night seem urgent.

"See you, darling," Vic had chirped as she strode to the front door, neat and smart, with an umbrella dangling from her wrist.

Lyddy said, "Isn't 'Mr Steamed Up' going to pick you up?"

"Yep. He's coming up in Curly's taxi. First class, that man."

"I thought you had your fill for good of that type?"

"Clarence is different. I know it. He's—well, he's lonely and kind of disgusted with himself. He needs a boost. He's helpless and he needs a good..."

"Oh, don't say anything more," Lyddy snapped. She dropped down onto the sofa and stared at Vic who was brushing bits of lint off her blue coat. In a way, Vic was right. Clarence was rather likeable at first. He was so small and yet so full of destructive frustration. Walking by the shop, Lyddy caught glimpses of Clarence cutting people's hair with the tight glum expression of a man who was bitter about his work and himself. She was also aware of the way he looked at her, especially at the dance when he danced with her, stiff and hard and unable to mutter a word as he held her in his arms. Though she didn't like him, she was naturally pleased that he was infatuated with her. She couldn't figure out why he was going out with Vic.

Headlights cut up the hill through the rain and the cab swept up the hill and stopped below Guy Eaton's place at the foot of the rock-bordered yard.

"Well, so long, honey." Vic had dashed down the gravel path, meeting up with Clarence half-way. They had paused, talking under the umbrella for a moment, then turned and ran head down into Curly's cab.

Being alone in the cottage was unbearable after Vic left. She called the Johnsons and told them that she and Chris wouldn't be coming over since he hadn't returned from his trip. Then she donned her galoshes and raincoat and went for a walk. The town was dark and deserted. The scattered street lights cast reflections on the street, exposing the shallow pools of water that lay along the uneven roads. She felt lost and lonely as she hurried down the hill. The wonderful smell of spruce and hemlock burning in the stoves of the shacks along the harbor's edge nettled her. Everyone in Wrangell was snug and cozy and she was out in the storm, the night howling down upon her, the rain and wind beating into her face.

She felt like an outcast, unwanted by this community in which she didn't belong. She trudged on, listening to the roar of the stream that came down from the hill, pouring under the wooden bridge and out into the harbor. Her head bent, she was barely aware of the houses on either side of the road. Suddenly, without even being aware that she was heading there, she stopped in front of Bea's house. There were lights in all the windows and she felt drawn to knock on the the door. Bea opened it. She was alone, and probably as lonely as Lyddy.

"Good grief, you are venturesome walking around in this mess," Bea exclaimed. "I've got some hot water on the stove. Would you like a cup of tea?"

"Thanks, Bea." She scuffed off her shoes and went into the warm, immaculate kitchen. "I've always loved this kitchen," she said, looking around at the cheerful white surfaces and red-painted trim. "It's so comfortable and homey." She paused, looking down at her dripping coat.

"We generally hang our wet things out on the porch," Bea said. Lyddy went out through the door that Bea opened for her. There was a barrel on the porch and a dog emerged from the opening cut into it, a black dog with thick fur and tail and paws that were marked with white. He looked at Lyddy inquisitively as she removed her raincoat and galoshes.

"So, this is where you live," Lyddy said. "I've always wondered who owned you."

"That's Winchester," Bea called out from the kitchen. "He's great company when Roy's not home."

Inside, Bea removed cups and saucers from the cupboard. "Roy's playing gin rummy at Johnny Bugg's bar," she said with a laugh. Lyddy suddenly realized that it was Bea's laugh that disturbed her. It was a dry brave laugh filled with defeat and submission. "Roy phoned and said he was having a losing streak. He wanted to sit through a few more rounds and see if he could win some of his money back."

In the living room, Lyddy felt on edge. It was the first time she had been alone with Bea and there was an awkwardness, a break in the conversation after they had discussed Chris' absence. Then, as she drank her tea, she realized that Bea was purposely being quiet, that there was no need for constant talk, that two people together could be easy and natural with one another without having to be witty.

"The tea is delicious," Lyddy said, still feeling uncomfortable.

"We drink a lot of tea. It's so refreshing. It gives me a lift."

There was another pause. Bea sat across from Lyddy in the easy chair. She was wearing a crisp polka-dot dress. Despite her liking for Bea, Lyddy didn't know her well enough to introduce another topic of conversation. They sat quietly. Occasionally, Bea stretched her legs out in front of her and leaned back against the chair, as if weary. Then she would straighten up and tip her tea cup to her lips.

Lyddy noticed that Bea's face had changed subtly. Her cheeks sagged a little and she could see the lines of dissatisfaction, tiny but evident, etched alongside her mouth. Bea's lips were still soft and full and her eyes brilliant and dark. But her age was appearing on her face. Lyddy thought of her own mother who had been holding up well, with scarcely a gray hair or wrinkle. Then, during Lyddy's last few months of college, Edna had changed, looked every bit her fifty-three years.

Lyddy sat, drinking her tea mechanically, searching about the room for some subject matter. Her eyes fell upon the photograph on the mantel above the fireplace of a young man she had never seen before.

At first sight, it had startled her. She surmised that it was a photograph of Bea's son, Tom. His face was big and square and his expression sulky, almost as if he had been nursing a grudge when the picture was snapped. Strangely, Tom—if it was Tom—attracted her. His face was suffused with a sort of intensity that made Lyddy wonder what it would have been like to have been alone with him, in a room or in a car, with him watching her with those enormous brown eyes that stared out now across the room.

Casually yet warily, she said, "I don't think I've noticed that photograph before."

"That's Tom," Bea said sharply and quickly. She toyed with the strand of pearls around her neck. "He was grown-up for seventeen. He always wanted to do everything for himself. He worked in the Ballard Cannery during the fishing season and saved his money and bought his own boat." Bea paused, her voice cracking. The room was suddenly full of pain.

As Lyddy sat there, her own anxiety vanished. She'd nearly forgotten the fears which had driven her to knock on Bea's door. She watched Bea as the color returned to her cheeks. Her eyes were full of tears as she spoke about her dead son, deriving nourishment from it. Right then, Lyddy felt what Wrangell women had to put up with, what all women put up with in fishing towns.

"He was our only child," Bea said. " When the news came, when a native boat came in and said they'd spied some wreckage on the south shore of Two Tree Island . . ." Bea paused, then continued. "Of course, no one could tell whose boat it was. Tom was out and was overdue but that was like Tom. He loved the outdoors. He loved it maybe even more than most men." She paused, a tight bitterness in her mouth. "It was Tom's boat. He was returning home in a blinding snow storm . . . You see, he'd ditched school—he was mad about something, I wish I knew what, I've tried to find out, I've asked the teachers, but no one seems to know. He went out on his boat one morning when he should have been in school . . ." Bea's words seemed to be bumping into each other, rubbing up against her guilt and despair. "On top of that—no one can be sure how it happened—the boat was torn up. His engine must have gone out on him and Tom drifted to Two Tree Island." Bea's voice was thick with grief. "Only seven miles more and he would have made it to Wrangell. The boat smashed against the shore and rolled over and filled with water. Tom managed to get ashore, with his dog. When the search party found Tom, there was no evidence of a fire. The few matches he had on him were soaked and it was freezing cold. There were two rocks . . ."

Bea rose and went into the bedroom and returned with two plain rocks which she held out to Lyddy. "He tried to start a fire with these rocks. You can tell by the marks on them. It was snowing all the while and it grew terribly cold, especially towards morning when the snow stopped and the wind blew. That was one of the coldest nights we had that year. And Tom," Bea paused, as she sat down again, staring at the rocks in her hands, "and Tom," she repeated, "he was brave to have done what he did." Bea began crying, trying to speak through her tears, finding it difficult to move her lips and breathe at the same time. "He shot his dog in the head. He had a rifle with him. It was Chris' gun. Tom had borrowed it from Chris just a few weeks before. Then Tom turned the gun on himself."

"Oh, no!" Lyddy gasped.

Bea nodded her head, no longer trying to hold back the tears. "Tom killed himself rather than freeze to death."

After a short pause, Bea said with an anger that seemed incongruous for Lyddy would never have believed that Bea was capable of anger, "Sometimes I hate this place. It will come over me all at once. I forget all the good about it. Have you ever noticed the way most of the people are? They act as if there is never going to be anything else. They are resigned to Wrangell. They couldn't get away even if they wanted to. They're in such a rut they don't realize it. It's deadly to the mind. Most of the people stay in Wrangell because they haven't the money or gumption to move on and try something else."

She looked at Lyddy with a sort of defiant apology in her eyes. "Roy is one of those who can't be budged. Alaska is it for him. He doesn't want to leave Wrangell, no matter how much I beg." Bea cleared her throat quickly as though in a hurry to go on. Lyddy wondered if Bea had ever revealed her feelings about Wrangell to anyone before, especially to a Wrangellite. "It's not all bad. I've loved it up here. There is a freedom here that probably is hard to find elsewhere. But Roy won't leave, even for a short time. He wouldn't even go to Vermont with me after Tom died."

Lyddy sat still, neglecting her tea which had gotten cold. She felt a little better somehow. The sudden candid outburst was good. Perhaps for Bea, too.

She faced Bea and said, "I guess you know about Chris and me. We're serious, Bea. I love Chris." The words rolled off her tongue. As she spoke, she felt exhilarated, sure of her feelings. She loved Chris. It was so good to say it. "And I'm—well, Bea, I'm stymied. I mean there's more to it than meets the eye—"

"Go on," Bea said, "I understand."

"I would have to change my whole life. I'd have to give up all the things I'm used to in the city. I have to accept Wrangell in order to be with Chris."

"That's right," Bea said. "You would have to live in Wrangell. Chris is no different from most of the others. It's something in this country. I feel it—you do when everything is going smoothly. I felt it when Tom was alive. A sort of relief. A sort of answer in the stillness and rain, the feeling of protective walls around you even though there are no walls. I don't know," she went on. "I would like to tell you what it is, but I don't know what it is. But something in Alaska poisons the men into loving it and never wanting to leave."

Lyddy waited, having nothing further to add. Bea said, "I've known Chris since he was a boy. He used to come out this way a lot, packing a gun and shooting at things along the beach. When Tom was fifteen—he was nearly six feet then—Chris took a liking to him. He taught him how to shoot and they'd go out riding together in Chris' motorboat. Chris was Tom's only friend. Tom just didn't find it easy to make friends his own age. He was too quiet, too serious, too big for his age. I certainly appreciated all the time that Chris spent with Tom. He seemed to be the only person who could understand Tom."

"Bea," Lyddy interrupted, "I've enjoyed your company so much." She wanted to leave suddenly. She wanted to get back to town to see if Chris had come in.

Bea smiled. "I guess I've depressed you. It's the rain." They could hear it outside, plunking down like a wall, a protective wall that wrapped in the silence and beauty of Wrangell. "It just never stops. Here it is summer and it's raining. It's not so bad now because it isn't cold. But the rain will slide into winter and winters are long in Wrangell. They never seem to end because the rain scarcely ever stops. The first few winters aren't too bad. I can remember back to the first few years we were here. I was never happier. Making friends, baking and knitting, going to the dances. But winters go on for seven months here and each one is just like the other. Oh, sometimes, there's more snow than rain. Sometimes it's sleet and ice and wind . . ."

A car drove up to the front of the house, sloshing as it made the turn. A door slammed and footsteps came trudging up the front steps to the door.

"That must be Roy," Bea said, rising and going to the door.

Lyddy acted quickly. At the door she uttered a quick greeting to Roy, who stepped into the house peering at Lyddy with a questioning look on his face.

"Will you stop Curly before he leaves?" Lyddy asked.

Surprise still knitting his brow, Roy turned and ran down the walk. He managed to flag down Curly who was ready to take off again, having backed the cab around on the main road.

"You don't have to leave so soon," Bea said.

"It's late, Bea. I've got to be at school early tomorrow to finish checking over some tests." Lyddy thanked Bea for the evening as she donned her rain things on the porch.

"Have you seen Chris in town?" she asked Roy as she went through the living room. He seemed rather peeved that she wasn't noticing him or else that she was leaving in such a rush because he had just arrived.

"No, I haven't," Roy said. "Is he out?" His brow twisted again.

She couldn't stand Roy Hart all of a sudden. "Yes. Well, bye," she said and ran down the steps to the cab.

"Hello, Curly," she said, climbing into the rear seat of the Chevy, glad that she was going back to town. Maybe Chris had come in and was waiting impatiently for her.

14

THEY WERE WALKING ALONG the old dirt road that led to the Back Channel. A heavy wall of tall trees lined the shoreline to their left. In places where there was a gap between the trees, Chris could see the channel, glinting with a silvery sheen across its slate-gray surface. To the right was the muskeg, spotted with dwarfed trees. The dirt road fell and rose before them until it lost itself in the trees at the bottom of the road.

Chris loved the light-hearted spontaneous talk, which wove itself around them like yarn, binding them together. The walk was exhilarating, regardless of the rain, for the rain was light and sparkling with the sunlight which slanted down through it.

Last night he had decided for sure that he wanted to marry Lydia. All at once he knew—it came down on him with the force of a pile driver—that he had to have her. The thought was so strong and so true it made him dizzy. He knew she was his for the asking. He was certain of that. They had been visiting the Weavers and he was so proud of her. He liked looking across at her, at her slender legs elongated by the high heels she wore and the rounded swell of her hips as she sat on the cushion of the sofa next to Sylvia.

She was so easy and comfortable to be with. He felt happy in her presence. He wanted to show off, tell her of all his adventures like the time the outboard ran into a deadhead in one of the sloughs of the Stikine River and twisted the prop. He and Tom Hart had stayed out there for two days, catching a few rainbow trout and killing a young buck, and finally had to row all the way back.

Herb was saying something about the summer, how he couldn't wait until the season started, couldn't wait to get the feel of a king on a hook, yanking and diving and flipping out of the water as he played it in. Lyddy listened intently, never once casting a look at Chris, her slender legs crossed, her hair fluffed out about her shoulders, hands resting in her lap.

By God, he'd thought, she'll make a good wife. He could imagine spending the rest of his life with her. He could imagine going out to visit friends, talking, playing cards and then walking back through the dirt roads to their home. Going home and maybe having a cup of chocolate in the kitchen before bedtime, the oil stove purring and the rain coming down.

"Well," Lyddy said, "this beats everything."

They had arrived at the old L&B Cannery. It had been gutted by fire and now lay rotting in the rain. The grass grew tall around the scattered outbuildings and the machinery lay in the grass rusting. There was no sound but the hushed wet brushing fall of the rain. They stood at the edge of the island. Across the water of the back channel, was the mainland of Canada, with its tall white snow-peaked mountains.

"My goodness," she said, "after all this time I get my first glimpse of snow. Why, there's more snow in California."

"I love you, Lyddy. Are you happy? Wait. Don't answer. Let me tell you how I feel. I am. I'm very happy. O.K., go ahead, are you happy?" Chris asked.

"Yes, I am," she said.

"I can tell you are. I think anyone can tell I am."

"Maybe I can add that I've never felt this way before . . ."

"You couldn't add to my feelings, because I feel better than, well, better than better."

"We could go on like this sounding like a record repeating itself until doom's day."

"There's no doom in my life. That record will always sound good, near it or away. My life right now is loaded with life. Especially since you came to Wrangell."

"I've stumbled into a gushing world of Chris Ballard," she said.

"I'm gushy. Yeah." He laughed too. "But seriously, I want to know everything about you. Your past, how you were raised, what you did when you were growing up . . ."

"Come to think of it, Mr. Ballard," she said, "I scarcely know anything about you or your parents except I know they moved to Seattle after your father's accident. Do you go south much, to visit them?"

"Nah. I just don't feel right in the States."

She was silent, looking out at the mountains.

"What time is it?" he asked.

"Ten to five."

"We're going up to Sarber's. She's giving a potluck dinner."

"Chris, you never warned me! I have to make something to bring and I've got to iron my dress."

"I just remembered it. Sarber called me up this morning and said to bring my girlfriend along." He laughed. "Brother, you're going to be initiated into a real party. Sarber knows how to throw 'em."

They walked through the tall grass, slowly, for there wasn't any path. The grass covered the slight rise that sloped down to the water. Chris felt the drenched wetness about them, noticed the colors, the green in the grass contrasted with the yellow tint of the winter, the gray and silver of the channel. He felt close to her, out here alone together, and he wanted to hold on to it somehow. There had been so many thousands of small moments in his life that had swept by him, events in which he had participated which were lost forever. Every day, every hour he spent with this girl he wanted to preserve. He did not want a moment to go by forsaken.

They stood beside a long, moss-covered retort by an outbuilding that used to be the boiler room and stared out across the edge of Wrangell Island at the mouth of the Stikine River and the Mainland and the snow-covered mountains. Below, just a few yards away, the water murmured against the shore, with a sleepy lapping sound, almost like a small sigh. The wind that rose off the Stikine's back, came running down across the grass, rippling it. An old troller lay on its side, submerged in the shallow water, the hull ripped open, a ghost from the past, waiting for time and water to dissolve it.

"Chris, we shouldn't have come out here. I've got to prepare something for the potluck dinner."

"I've taken care of everything. My housekeeper is going to bake me two raspberry pies and we'll take those up."

"You make me feel helpless—and spoiled."

"Are you sore, darling?"

"Well . . ." She stopped herself.

"Wanna go back?"

"It's lovely here. At the edge of Wrangell. I love the snow and magnificence of those mountains."

"One of my favorite spots. Used to do a lot of necking out here. Which reminds me."

As he turned to her he felt he had never seen anyone so beautiful. Her face was part of the whole scene. They kissed, for the first time that day, and it astonished both of them, so much so that they both smiled self-consciously before continuing with more kisses. They were long insatiable kisses which filled him with yearning, left him feeling weak.

As they walked back, Lyddy along one of the car tracks, he on the sparse tough growth of grass which grew in the center of the road, he felt that he could do so many great and wonderful things for this girl. His whole heart was consumed with the urgency to build, perform, glorify. Along with this urgency, he felt a sense of surrender, to a joy so infinite that it left him rather light-headed. He was awed by his love.

Chris wanted to cling onto this moment forever. There was ecstasy in the clasp of time; a day held and treasured, to be his forever. And now he had someone to share the forever with. Sharing the forever as man and wife. And with children.

He remembered his mother with a bandanna wrapped around her hair working in the kitchen, in the bedrooms, working, working, working, never finding an end of things to do in the big house. She kept it meticulous for Theodore. His mother's face always bore a look of pained resignation, yet she never complained. When Theodore suggested hiring a housekeeper, she protested.

Chris slammed shut the door on this memory. It jammed the machinery of his joy. He was resentful all at once. He was vexed; a vast irritation clouded everything.

"Will you be long?" she asked at the cottage.

"Be back in half an hour."

"I'll try and be ready. What about Vic? She's cooking supper—it was her turn."

"Tell her to stop cooking and come along."

"I'll see."

"Well, goodbye darling."

"Bye for half an hour."

"For half an hour."

Chris went down the path and headed across the hill, past the hospital and then down the road to his house. He whistled as he ran up to his bedroom to change his clothes.

The day was full of different phases, Chris reflected. The cannery, the beginning of the walk, the end of the road where they kissed and felt the peace of the land, the walk back, the getting ready for the party and now, the party.

Somehow he wanted to leave now that he was here in Sarber's dining room eating the stew prepared by Victor, the French fisherman, who lived by himself in his troller in the harbor. It wasn't right somehow, being here with the crowd, drinking and jabbering. As much as he yearned to show her off, Chris really wanted to be alone with Lyddy, maybe go down to the float house where it would take no time at all for the kitchen stove to warm the place. He wouldn't want to go to Lyddy's cottage because Vic might be there. She had declined the invitation to Sarber's party, was probably waiting for Clarence Wick who had been dating her lately. The wind had really come up in the past half hour, howling through the trees behind Sarber's house and lashing rain against the windows. In the float house, Chris imagined, they would make a pot of coffee, keep the stove turned up high, switch on the radio—reception might be good tonight because of the storm.

"Come on, let's dance, Lyddy," Chris said and pushed his plate away.

"But that's a polka and I don't know how to do it your Alaskan way."

"Go ahead, honey," Mona Sarber said from the head of the large table.

"I'll show you," Chris said.

"Please, Chris, I'd rather not," she whispered. She nodded her head at the others who were watching.

"Come on!" Chris yanked her out of her chair quite roughly. He felt ashamed as she went with him without a word into the living room. It didn't seem right to be here with her in this crowd. Mona Sarber and her aged mother, Giff, Holly Dancey, Al the midget, Red Parker and his wife, Shirley, and the others, mostly single men and women or white men married to native women. Actually, it was the riff raff of Wrangell. The boat owners, the whites married to whites, the store people, the old Norwegian and Swedish families, hardly ever showed up for Sarber's parties unless it was an important occasion like a birthday or a shower. Yet Chris had never thought of this crowd in this way before tonight. Coming in, introducing Lyddy to most of them since she didn't know them by name, he could sense her hesitation. She was on guard although she acted friendly and gracious. He even felt himself putting on an act, so false that she must have noticed. He'd have to be careful about this sort of thing in the future. He thought it would be fun to show Lyddy this side of his life. So far he couldn't tell whether it was working out.

The *Beer Barrel Polka* was playing in the living room. Chris spoke up quickly, hoping to conceal his guilt, "Now you put . . ."

"You didn't have to pull me out here," Lyddy said.

"I'm sorry," Chris said, dropping his hands to his sides. "Lyddy, I'm sorry."

"I forgive you," she said with a smile.

"You like the crowd?"

"Of course. They're all nice."

"OK, honey. Now you start with your left foot when the melody begins again. You . . ."

"Chris . . ."

Curly and Sally Hamilton were dancing at the far end of the long room and Curly had his hand firmly curved over Sally's rump.

"By God," Chris grinned, "that kid's drunk as a skunk."

"Hi ya, Chris," Curly waved from the other end. He was holding Sally tight, her brown face pressed up against his white one. Sally didn't seem to enjoy it. She might have if her husband was out of town but Hamp was in the dining room, eating with the rest.

Chris ignored Curly. "All right, honey, now's the time to learn while the floor's practically empty."

"But Chris . . ." she paused. Her eye was still on Curly.

"Forget him. He'll get a punch in the nose before the night's over and that'll settle that."

"Isn't he engaged?"

"Sure. To Diana Johnson."

"Where is she, I wonder?"

"Listen, you wanna dance, or don't you?"

"I'm sorry, Chris."

"All right, baby, this is easy. And it's fun. Hey, Curly," Chris said, "start the record over again."

"This room seems to have been made for a big party," Lyddy said, as they waited. "Miss Sarber doesn't have to worry about anything being broken."

Chris watched Curly stagger across the room towards the phonograph, his light wavy hair tossed over his forehead. The room was certainly a party room. The hardwood floor ran bare across the length of the room. There was one sofa, one chair by the radio-phonograph and a love seat over at the far end underneath the row of windows that looked out on the town. It looked almost like a dance hall in some high class restaurant with a bank of windows affording a view of the outside. There were no knick-knacks, no pictures, no expensive furniture that could be burnt by a cigarette or stained by a spilled drink.

"All right, honey." He stood beside Lyddy and took her hand as the music began again. "I wish Dave was here. He's the one who really knows how to do this stuff."

They were late for the first beat and had to wait until the next bar.

"Why isn't Dave here?"

"Damn, you know, Lyddy."

"No, I don't. Unless you mean Vic."

"Sure. The guy's really hurt. I saw him yesterday. He doesn't try to show it but I think he loves Vic. She's a goof going out with Clarence. He doesn't care for her. . ." He paused, waiting for the right moment in the music. "Here it comes. Now get ready. One, two, three, hop. One, two, three, hop."

Every time you hear that omp pa pa, everybody feels so tra la la—

"Stop!" Chris said, and they waited for a fresh beginning. "It's one two three, spread. One two three, hop. Then twirl around and start the hop all over again. It's easy."

"Uh huh."

"All right, let's go."

They danced the remainder of the record without too much trouble, Lyddy relaxing as she caught on. Towards the end they were beginning to shake shoulders and exaggerate the one-two-three-hop by swinging their bodies from side to side. She laughed as they twirled, hugging long after the music ended.

Sally's husband, Hamp, wandered into the room while Curly was trying to kiss Sally in the far corner of the room. It was ironic, in a way, because everyone knew Sally shacked up with Curly when her husband was out of town but now she looked like the modest good girl repulsing a simple kiss from the drunken Curly. Chris had seen this situation before at parties but he was surprised at the way in which this confrontation unfolded.

"Hey," Hamp said, "what's going on?"

Even from this distance across the room Chris could feel the spite in Curly's attitude. "None of your business, Hamp!"

Hamp stopped short, taken aback. "What's going on?" he inquired again in a perplexed voice, though still good-natured. He was a short slender man of about twenty five, a good three inches shorter than his Indian wife.

Curly was obviously itching for a fight. "Hey, you're not wanted here, Hamp!" Curly sneered, letting go of Sally and stepping forward. Hearing their upraised voices, people came streaming into the room.

Following a half-hearted impulse, after the last stinging retort from Curly, Hamp tossed a listless right at Curly. With astonishing deftness, as if his drunken composure had been a fake, Curly blocked the punch and hauled off with a quick sharp left to Hamp's stomach that stunned both the crowd and Hamp.

Chris could almost feel the driving punch in his own stomach. The blow keeled Hamp over. He sank down on his knees, white and winded, supporting himself with one hand on the floor. Sally knelt beside him and Curly tried to pull her away.

"Let the bastard get up and fight." Curly bellowed. "I haven't got warmed up yet."

Mona sprang upon Curly and bawled him out. "Now listen here! Who do you think you are? Get out! If you can't behave in my house, you'll have to leave." Mona looked injured. Her black eyes were full of bewilderment. She wasn't the type to jump into a fracas and establish order. Generally, if a fight broke out at her parties she'd let the other men quell it. Now she put her hand on Curly's arm. "Apologize to Hamp. I won't have anyone spoil my party."

Curly apologized with obvious reluctance.

Hamp got up groggily, his face pugnacious. "I don't want your God damn apology."

Giff lumbered in between Hamp and Curly, who were facing each other and glaring. "Now see here," he said, staring drunkenly from one to the other, "let's don't start any more trouble." He straightened up and fixed his eye on his son. For a moment he seemed sober. "Sit down and shut up for a while."

"Ok, Giff." Curly said, as if speaking to a stranger.

"Yeah, OK, Giff," Hamp said. Then when Giff lumbered off towards the dining room, Hamp stalked up to Curly, with Sally hanging on to his arm. He jerked himself loose and let fly with a long arching haymaker that ripped into Curly's mouth and knocked him off his feet. Curly fell on his side and lay prone for a moment. Then he pushed himself up, shaking his head and gritting his bloody mouth.

"You son of a bitch," he said to Hamp. Everyone was so stunned that no one stopped Curly from laying into Hamp, landing a few blows into his stomach and a particularly vicious hit to his right eye. Hamp slumped to the floor, groaning, buckled up with pain.

Chris took Lyddy's arm and steered her into the kitchen.

"Does this happen often?" she asked.

"Nah. Damn that Curly. He's rotten sometimes, the little bastard."

"It was his fault, wasn't it? And then that man's wife . . ."

"Forget it, honey. It was just one of those things."

The party never really took off after that. Curly came into the kitchen with Giff. They both had a drink and left. A short while later Sally left with Hamp and so did Holly and Evelyn and their husbands. Hank Connell, who was supposed to be on the wagon, showed up and started drinking. At eleven, Chris and Lyddy said good night to Mona and left the house, walking down the hill in silence, the storm raging upon them.

"You were swell tonight," Chris said, holding his hat down over his head so it wouldn't blow away. "You were so wonderful. I could have eaten you up."

"But why?"

"Just because," he said. They were heading down the hill and that could mean only one thing—they were going to the float house, and she hadn't said a word about it. Suddenly it occurred to Chris that she might be feeling the same way as he had been feeling all night. A violent exultation rose in him. The storm raging down upon them seemed irrelevant. She wanted to go to the float house. The thought of what that meant stunned him.

He could never seem to get enough of her, yet up until now the fact that she was so beautiful and so in love with him had been enough. He was content with that.

The storm raged outside, flailing against the float house and now he knew that she felt the same as he did. Her face was rosy with color, flushed with feeling. He was happy to wait now, sure of himself, of their mutual desire.

"I love you," he said over and over again, kissing her as she sat on his lap in the easy chair. "I love you and I'll always love you." He smiled. "I shouldn't tell you this, but I feel so fortunate to be able to have someone like you to love. Really, I've never been so happy with anything in all my life."

She was warm and she said nothing which was unlike her. Her body, which was stiff against his own when they weren't kissing, grew soft and pliable when they kissed. She moaned slightly when his tongue found her tongue, when his hand rubbed over her breast, her belly.

"You know what?" he asked. He laughed, changed his mind. "I love you, Lyddy."

"I love you too, Chris. I never loved anyone before, Chris. I know that now, have known it for days." They kissed again, then she said, "I know that I couldn't live up here without you."

"I feel the same way, Lyddy. Lately, Wrangell, which before seemed everything, seems trivial and empty without you. I go around in a daze because I'm in love. It's like finding the right niche. There could be no better fit, it is perfect, flawless. There can be no improvement on my love for you."

They were silent for a long while. Chris kissed her eyelids, which were sensitive when closed, her cheeks, which were smooth and so very soft, her lips, soft and full as well and opening to his touch. There had never been a moment in his life quite like this one. There would never be a moment like this again, for either of them. He was certain of that.

15

THAT NIGHT, DURING A LULL IN THE STORM, Leif Halvorson died. Alone in the cabin of his gill-netter, Leif was seized by his nightly paroxysm of coughing, a sound that split the air on the right side of the harbor every evening. In the lamp-lighted hole of his cabin, Leif's face became mottled purple and red with effort as he hacked phlegm into the tin beside his bunk. Every time he thought he might be about to die, Leif made the sign of the cross, believing that this would prevent his death. He was halfway through it, having just brought his fingers to his right shoulder, when his heart gave out and he rolled out of his bunk.

In the nearest troller, Victor was slipping out of his pants, having just come back from Sarber's party, when Leif's hacking ceased. Victor was as familiar with that rattling series of coughs as was Leif himself, having moored beside Leif in the harbor for six years. When the sound ceased, when the night air lay suddenly still except for the moan of the dying wind caressing his boat, Victor stopped and listened intently for the next full minute, his mouth open, his eyes rolling a little, his right hand taut under the loop of the suspender. Then he refastened his suspender and rushed out of the cabin.

Later, towards three in the morning, Victor rowed across the harbor and notified Greg Sundberg that Leif was dead. Greg dressed and drove the old white hearse-and ambulance-wagon out of the blacksmith shop that fronted the road and went sputtering in second gear all the way around to the other side of the harbor. With the aid of a few fisherman they stashed Leif in the rear and Greg drove back alone to his house which was behind the blacksmith shop. Greg wasn't sure yet what price coffin to use. Victor had mentioned that Leif had a savings account in Sackett's Bank. They would have to find out his balance in the morning to determine the cost of the funeral. Before crawling into bed, Greg gulped a straight shot of rum, cussed once or twice and scratched his right knee which had been itching him lately.

Max could tell that his first customer of the morning hadn't gone to bed the night before. Hank Connell was plastered. He staggered into the hotel bar, coat unbuttoned, his hat askew on his head and ordered a drink.

"Listen, Hank, you'd better get some sleep. Go home," Max said. Max was smoking his first cigarette and he wanted to enjoy it. Hank was one of the few men in Wrangell who Max respected and the sight of Hank this morning destroyed all that. He was just like the rest of them, Max decided.

"You'll kill yourself drinking," Max said, looking straight into Hank's eyes. Normally gray, they were a strange violet shade and his face was pale as winter grass. He could scarcely hold himself erect.

"That God damn Sarber threw a party last night," Hank mumbled.

"Go home," Max ordered, not moving to mix the ordered drink.

"I missed the fight but hell . . ."

Greg Sundberg came through the door. Hank wandered off towards the lavatory.

"Morning, Greg," Max said, relieved that Hank was gone. "The usual?" Greg nodded and he mixed up a rum and coke.

Greg mopped his face with his bare hand. "Leif died last night," he muttered. He gulped down his drink and left.

Max lit a fresh cigarette, hating to begin his chores. Leif's death didn't surprise him—everyone had known for months that Leif was on the verge of death—but he thought of the old superstition that deaths came in threes.

Hank staggered to the bar, billfold in hand. "You won't believe this," Hank said, snickering quietly to himself as only a drunk can. Hank pointed an unsteady finger in the direction of the lavatory. "I was taking a leak and I was counting my money and plunk!" Hank reenacted the whole scene with slow gestures of his numbed hands. "In it went!"

"What're you talking about?" Max asked.

"I dropped all my money in the toilet! And a brand new rubber, too!" Hank said with a smirk.

"You're crazy!" Max exclaimed. He realized he wasn't enjoying his second cigarette. This irritated him for he only smoked ten cigarettes a day to coincide with his rush and slack hours respectively. Already two were gone.

"But I tell you, I dropped over eighty dollars in bills, in the toilet."

"Then, why in the hell didn't you take 'em out?" Max roared, infuriated. "A little piss water won't hurt 'em."

Hank was barely able to hold himself up through his arms were fastened over the edge of the bar. "I leaned over to do just that and damn if I didn't press on the lever. Down they went—about eighty dollars."

"Why in the hell did you have to count your money there?" Max asked, shaking his head in disgust.

Suddenly Hank spun around and stumbled out of the bar, his hat tilted back on his head.

Max waited until Hank had reeled out of sight past the front window and then headed back to the toilet room. "I don't believe the son of a bitch," he said, aloud.

A one dollar bill lay on the floor behind the water tank and another one—it looked like a five—was in the bowl itself. Max picked up the dollar bill and pulled out the five from the bowl, wrinkling his face in disgust. He searched for more, but they were gone, flushed down the pipes and into the water below the hotel. He washed both of the bills he had retrieved and laid them on a towel under the bar so that no one would see them. Then he lit a third cigarette. Despite the fact that he was dipping deep into his morning allotment, he knew he was gong to enjoy smoking this one.

———————

Hank Connell rounded the hotel and headed down the dock, bumping against the wall of the cold storage plant on his right. "Must be listing to the starboard," he decided. At the mid-way point, the Clinton dock widened into a sort of landing, where fishing boats unloaded salmon and halibut into the cold storage plant and stocked their holds with ice. Below lay the small boat float, riding low in the bumpy sea. Hank stared at the vertical and crisscrossed pilings which held up the rear of the hotel, trying to determine why this sight was important at this time. He gave up trying to figure it out and wobbled down the steep stairway which led to the small boat float. It was connected by a set of roller bearings to the float below so the stairway could rise and fall as with the tide. Though it wasn't raining, the small float was slick and bobbing under the swells washing through the mouth of the harbor. Only a few skiffs and row-boats were tied to the railings since few fishermen rowed into town this early in the morning. Hank staggered along the slippery float. His head was spinning and he shook it as if to set it on keel.

He looked up at the Clinton dock beside him, the shrimp cannery in the center and the sea gulls circling and squealing over the tall rectangular warehouses fronting the harbor where the American steamship line moored. These familiar sights and the smell of the sea and creosote piling and the dampness of the morning air did little to buoy up Hank's dimming spirits. Buckling twice, and nearly falling over, Hank lurched over onto the small seaplane landing lashed against the city float. For a moment, he wondered what he was doing there. He knew he was looking for something but couldn't remember what. His belly was pierced with pain, as if it contained glass splinters, and he thought for a moment about his ulcers. They must be getting pretty bad if he could feel them as drunk as he was. Deciding to head back home, Hank's foot slipped as he stepped up from the seaplane float to the city float, and he fell into the water. Hank couldn't swim a stroke even though he'd been fishing most all of his life and he was quite a distance down before he began to thrash his arms and legs and strain his head looking for a breath of air. The pressure exploded in his chest, in his brain, in his eardrums. His mouth wrenched open and closed while his throat choked on the gush of water that snuffed out Hank's life.

When he was fifty three dollars in the hole, Chris decided to quit. He blamed his bad luck on his lightheartedness. It was impossible to be happy and win at poker, he reasoned. Winning required seriousness, a determination to beat the other guy. He'd quit after this hand, he decided. He knew he needed sleep if he was going to go out with Lyddy again tonight. After last night, he had felt so good that he didn't want to go home. He walked Lyddy back to the cottage, then joined the poker game that was going on at Red's. He sat down at the table at three-thirty and it was now two in the afternoon.

She was going to cook him a dinner, their first alone at the cottage. He would kiss her, maybe help her set the table, turn on the radio. What would they talk about? But with Lyddy there was always something. Maybe he would tell her about his dad, about the grizzly attack that left his dad crippled. Chris hadn't been on the hunting trip but Giff had related the whole story to him so many times that he could almost see it.

In the small apartment in back of the merchandise store, that Red rented from Jon Olson expressly for gambling, the oil stove sputtered as it shed its heat about the two small rooms. One room was the card room, furnished with seven chairs and a special table with green felt cloth stretched over the edges and a niche at the head for the houseman. In the other room was a single bed, which was usually occupied by someone sleeping, and the table and electric range where Red or Charlie heated cans of chile and made coffee for the boys. Now the place was messy and soiled with mud tracks, cigarette butts and wrappers on the linoleum floor. Everyone was in a daze. They all looked half asleep during the waiting periods, playing their hands tight when they opened or called. Money was scarce now and this changed the men. It exposed a mean streak in them that had been hidden before, hidden by Wrangell. In the States, Chris used to play poker at a cigar joint in Seattle. There the mean streaks were obvious in the hard eyes and foul language of the crafty men who pretended friendship until they saw their opportunity to move in for the kill.

The oil stove exhaled smoke that wafted into his nostrils, a commonplace smell, for all the houses smelled the same, a smell that even though grimy brought a sense of comfort that Chris couldn't recall ever knowing while in Washington State. The dry heavy heat made him sleepy. The familiar sounds pricked at the edges of his torpor: the nervous rattle of chips, Al snoring in the other room, the low serious words that replaced the jokes, the razzing and gossip bantered about during the heavy drinking of the night hours.

Mitch dealt Chris three aces and he perked up, waiting his next turn. He would raise it, he decided. He'd make this last hand a good one. Buster Fountain and Jack Jewell called the opener and Chris clenched his lips to suppress his smile of delight. He liked to win money from these men because they could afford it and because they were really the best players of the lot. He yawned as he raised the pot twenty-five dollars. Buster, looking wide awake, bumped it twenty-five more and Jack called. So did Chris. Chris threw one card away and said, "If I make this, Buster, I'll rip your ass."

Buster stood pat, grinning stupidly, and Jack drew only one.

Maybe the bastard's bluffing, Chris thought as he glanced at Buster and felt his heart racing. The hotel owner could be sneaky at a time like this when everybody else was holding close and waiting for a hand.

Chris buried the card Mitch tossed him. He shuffled his hand one card over the other between his fingers, pretending that he had seen what he drew, and pushed one hundred dollars onto the pot. He could bluff as well as Buster. He knew the odds of filling his hand or drawing an ace were pretty slim.

"Looks like a pot," Charlie commented with an envious glance.

Buster smiled, undismayed. "So you made it, huh, Chrissy boy?"

"I had you beat all the time, hot shot!" Chris said, pretending to recheck his cards as if to make sure that he had read them correctly the first time.

"God damn!" Buster stalled. He scratched his forehead and tipped his hat and rolled his eyes back into his hand.

Chris knew he was going to call. He was just putting on an act.

Buster called and Chris felt a sense of relief.

"Ha!" Jack said, with the same devil-may-care attitude he demonstrated while piloting his river boats, fighting currents and lurching around sandbars, washouts and deadheads. There was no dilly-dallying in the wheel house while he was in command. Orders popped out of Jack's throat as smoothly as if he had rehearsed them ahead of time. "I'll raise you one hundred, Chrissy boy," Jack said.

Chris kept his face still and didn't even glance at his cards or Jack.

"Hey, Red!" Chris called. "Pour me a drink!"

Red winced at the volume in his voice, fearful that the occupants of the apartment above them would complain.

"For Christ's sake, come on!" Jack said in his loud, rasping voice. Chris know at once that Jack had made a powerful hand on his one card draw, possibly an ace flush.

"Hey, where's my drink?" Chris shouted again.

"Jesus Christ!" Chris heard Jack exclaim with disgust as Red got up and poured a drink.

Chris swallowed half of it, then began to pry into his cards with one hand. He saw the three aces and the six of diamonds that he had carried as a diversion. Slowly, he inched into view the corner of the last card. It was the other ace.

"I'll raise you what I've got left," Chris said to Jack. He pushed in a hundred and counted the remainder of his chips. "Forty-one smackers."

"I pass," said Buster, frowning. He showed his hand to the man next to him.

"You're covered!" Jack said. He laid down his hand. "Queens full."

"Aces full," said Chris, flipping his cards out on the table. As he gathered in the money he decided that he'd stay a few more rounds. After all, it would look bad if he quit the game after winning a big pot.

Helen Connell ran into Agnes Fountain inside the shrimp cannery where she had gone to purchase some shrimp for the cafe. Ray was busy weighing a long line of large, restaurant-size tins that had piled up on the roller-conveyor ahead of the scale. There was no sales counter in the small place for most of the shrimp was shipped to the States. The room was warm and musty with the odor of fresh-seined crustaceans. A row of women, mostly natives, stood beside sloping bins piled high with the orange-red shrimp. Some shelled and shucked them by hand while others packed them in tins that were lidded by an old hand-type press.

"How's Buster?" Helen asked.

"Oh, he's playing poker again. They've been at it since last night."

"That must be where Dad is," Helen said. "He hasn't been home." She ate one of the small meaty shrimp while she waited.

Ray came over to them.

"Give me ten pounds of the shelled ones," Helen said and glanced out the window to the harbor below as Ray thrust his hand into a paper bag and began to fill it with shrimp from one of the boxes.

The harbor scene seemed normal, she thought, except for the two boys on the skiff who were rowing rather wildly towards the float, thrashing their oars without coordination. From the shrimp cannery one could see almost half of the harbor, clear across to the Schnur Salmon Packing wharf. As usual, there was a lone fisherman rowing towards town standing up. A white troller skimmed by the man, rocking his skiff, as it chut-chut-chuted out of sight towards the south end of the harbor to its float. From the shrimp cannery, one could see the rear of Main Street, the real waterfront of the town, with its wooden buildings supported by the jumbled patterns of piling that always appeared much too flimsy to support the structures. The two boys directly below banged their skiff against the float and jumped off without bothering to tie it up. One of them was yelling.

"There's a dead man under the piling of the hotel. There's a dead man!"

The voice carried clearly into the shrimp cannery. Helen stood petrified, before the window, unable to move a muscle.

"Looks like Hank Connell," the boy shouted to the first man who reached the float. "He's caught between two pilings, under there."

"Oh, my God, no!" Helen gasped. "Not Dad!"

Chris took a drink straight from the fresh pint bottle while Red counted his chips and exchanged them for greenbacks. Chris stepped out of the apartment house, feeling dizzy. He knew he needed sleep if he was going to see Lyddy. He strode through the slushy alley behind Olson's and heard voices on Main Street. Although he wondered what all the excitement was about, he was so tired he just headed up the hill towards home.

After last night in the float house, he wanted more. Even during he poker game, he had missed Lyddy. He wanted her to share everything he felt. Without her, nothing felt quite real. Even this moment seemed unreal.

And yet he knew that there was something wrong, had felt it even more emphatically each day. It was as if she were butting in. During the poker game he felt resentful because he couldn't stay as long as he wanted. And there were times when Lyddy commented on Alaska when he felt irritated. She would tell him things that he already knew. Love and the prospect of marriage had brought with them a sense of obligation.

As he climbed up the hill in the rain, he sniffed the air which was filled with the teeming smell of grass that grew profusely on the hillside. It was a green smell of luxuriant wildness, of inordinate growth. The houses lay scattered about without any pattern, front porches and back yards angling off in all directions, looking more like houses in the country than in a compact town. The road was lined with mountain ash and hemlock, spruce and cedar, all dripping with the rain which filtered through their foliage.

He thought of Lyddy in the float house last night. She had said, "Oh, Chris, I'm so happy. Really, I've never been so happy in my life. Your float house is a dream. It's a secret, yours and mine. Oh, Chris, hold me tight. I love you so awfully much."

Now Chris walked up the hill alone, thinking about loneliness. He couldn't be sure, looking back, that he had ever felt lonely before. But his past was dark to him, like an unlit room. All he had now was this moment and the memory of a night of love and poker and the soft rain.

He tossed a match to the side of the road as he lit a cigarette. Below in the harbor, a seine boat sped towards the float, the sound of its diesel motor throbbing in the air.

The sun was in view, a molten disc cradled in golden clouds beneath a phosphorescent white sky. A strange, almost blinding light filled the sky and spangled the land, while the rain pelted down fast and white. And then, as if drawn into a vortex, all the clouds in the sky began racing behind the sun. The whole western sky became absolutely clear and blue. The masses of clouds behind the sun and along the ridge of the distant islands were the color of apricots. The land sparkled with radiance and the rain still fell, though not as decisive as before.

Chris walked up the dirt road, up through the familiar nightfall of Wrangell. He had walked up this hill probably ten thousand times. He'd left bars, parties, friends' houses, dim, smoke-filled, card rooms (those were the times he remembered best) and cut up the path by Olson's store and along the trail by the ball park, his weary mind ringing with static, happy if he'd won, mad if he lost, rehashing all the bum plays, marveling at the good ones.

Chris turned the corner and saw his house, set in from the road, with its long unlit porch and flight of wooden steps. He and Patty used to see who could jump from the highest up. Once, after an all-night, all-day poker game, he'd turned the corner and caught his sister on the porch, sneaking a smoke at nineteen.

"Hello, darling," she called out. He wondered what she was thinking about that made her so cheerful, not Wrangell surely, perhaps the States.

"Hi, Patty. What are you doing up so late?"

"Couldn't sleep. Thought I'd take a walk."

"Did you?"

"Yep. Always do what I plan."

"What's your next plan?" It was light talk but he liked being light with her.

As always when they were rather intimate together, she disconcerted him. "Plan to stay the way I am, I guess. Plan to be healthy and satisfied, Chris. Sounds silly, doesn't it?"

"Coming from a woman . . ." He paused and cleared his throat. "You hear, I said a woman? Well, coming from a woman that's the silliest darn thing I ever heard. Women usually talk about clothes and boyfriends."

"So far, clothes and boyfriends just haven't seemed very important to me." Patty was staring at the swings at the other end of the ball park. They were barely visible in the summer darkness. Her voice had a peremptory tone rather astonishing in such a young woman as if she were seeing her whole life ahead of her and commenting on the pattern of it.

"Hey, let's hit the hay."

Pat hadn't taken a single drag on her cigarette since he had come up on the porch. She was probably ashamed about it though Chris was the only one in the family—and probably Wrangell—who knew she smoked for she bummed all her cigarettes from him. "You go on in, Chris. I want to stay out here for a while."

"Goodnight, kid."

"Goodnight, Chris."

And he had gone in the house, dismayed but not knowing where the fault lay. Patty was one dame he never could figure out.

Still puzzled by the significance of this long-past conversation, Chris wandered into the kitchen and poured himself half a glass of whiskey. He took it into the living room and noticed that it was six o'clock. He only had an hour to rest and clean up before going to the cottage for dinner.

The house was dim without the lights on. The sunlight glowed around the edges of the drawn blinds. He sprawled on the carpet before the fireplace, sipping his drink until he finished it. He felt hollow and buttoned his coat for it was cold in the big house. His eyelids were heavy and he closed them and felt quite dizzy as if the wonderful and varied events of the last 24 hours were spinning in his brain. He saw the walk, the party, the girl, the hundreds of poker hands he had studied, discarded.

He wanted to urinate but didn't dare get up. He knew he was going to fall asleep and, if he could resist the urge to go to the lavatory now, the urge would wake him later. This was how he got up in the mornings without an alarm clock. If he needed to be up early, for a fishing trip, he wouldn't urinate before going to bed. The urgency in his groin usually woke him around dawn.

He liked to stretch back on something hard. He liked to feel his bones and flesh resting on hard planks or across the hard floor. It seemed like a break from convention, to stretch out on the floor without any of the preliminary preparations, no brushing teeth, face-washing or putting on pajamas (which he hated anyway). It was more than that. He felt the luxury of nestling between fresh sheets in a soft bed removed him from the rawness and crudeness of life.

Just before he fell asleep, he thought of all the nights he had slept alone in this house. He missed his sister, he realized, and this was a loneliness he had felt many times before.

Clarence Wick stood by the hotel with his friend, Steve, peering off across the channel at the horizon.

"Now listen," Clarence said, "when we come back I want you to beat it as soon as we tie up the boat."

"Sure, Clarence," Steve said. "I'll go over there now."

"Yeah. You should just be lying down or doing nothing. I don't want her to think this is planned. When we get to your boat, act surprised, maybe a little dopey, like you've been asleep."

"I got ya, Clarence. Good lay, huh?"

"Oh, she'll do. She's got high ideas about marriage. I can smell that already." He laughed scornfully. "She sure was scared stiff in the hotel last time. Damn, which reminds me, have you got any oil in your boat? I got to oil those damn springs on my bed. Last time, she was so damn worried about the springs I had to quit." Clarence chuckled. "Like a sap I told her who was rooming on either side of me."

"How can you oil mattress springs?" Steve asked. "By God, how the hell did you get her up there in the first place? She's got guts for a schoolteacher or else she's nuts about you."

"I got her wrapped around my little finger." Clarence said with a frown. "Ain't it a bitch? It's easy to get the ones you don't want."

"What time you think you'll be down there? I'll tidy up the place a bit. I just got some fresh sheets from the laundry."

"Yeah. Jesus, clean it up. I want her to think this is class." He paused. "God damn it , Steve, it doesn't seem to be doing any good. Lydia's still ga ga about Chris. She don't even look in the shop anymore when she walks by."

"Well, Jesus Christ, Clarence, what do you expect?" Steve sounded amazed.

"I thought—well, never mind. You better go. We'll be down there in about an hour. If it rains we'll be down sooner. We'll take Curly's cab."

"Looks like it's going to rain," Steve commented, staring at the black clouds descending on the sunset.

"Then hurry."

"So long, Clarence."

"Be careful," Steve said as he walked away. "This was a bad day in Wrangell."

Clarence nodded at Steve, glanced at his wrist watch and crossed Main Street. It was time to go up the hill to get Vic. Maybe, if he was lucky, she would invite him in and he'd get a chance to see Lydia and talk with her.

Greg Sundberg was sweating and puffing as he returned to the morgue with a new manila rope. He'd broken the old pulley line this afternoon on Leif Halvorson, while trying to move the dead man from the emergency wicker case onto the dressing table. Just as Greg had the corpse hoisted free from the case, the line snapped, dumping Leif on the floor and upsetting the dressing table. This was a problem for Greg since he was small, short-winded and fat. It had taken the greater part of the day to get Leif up on the table. Victor came over in the afternoon to help. Unfortunately, Victor was drunk and was more of a hindrance than a help the whole time they washed and changed Leif, especially when it came to the necktie. Victor was sentimental about this detail and wanted to make the knot his own way. Apparently he had forgotten how to do it and struggled over the tie for nearly an hour while Greg whacked off the crating boards from a plain cedar casket and prepared it for Leif. To add to Greg's grievance, it wasn't an hour after Greg and Victor had driven the hearse down to the old union hall and deposited the casket on the stand before the small stage when the boys found Hank Connell under the hotel.

Greg ate his dinner first before tackling Hank. In the morgue Greg fitted one end of the new rope through the block pulley and hung the block to the eye bolt in the ceiling. He looped the line around under Hank's arms and fastened it with two half hitches. Then he sat down on a box to have a cigarette.

The room was lit only by a small uncovered light bulb suspended by a cord from the center of the ceiling. It cast great shadows in the corners which were full of cobwebs, stacks of caskets (still in their shipping crates) and piles of loose boards. The corpse table, a couple of four by twelve boards bridged across two saw horses, lay underneath the light.

Squashing out his cigarette, Greg got up and placed his feet below the tackle block. As he began to pull on the rope, Hank's head emerged from the wicker basket into which his body had been placed after it was removed from the piling. The pulley screeched each time Greg yanked on the line.

Grunting with the effort, Greg struggled with the tall hefty cadaver and heaved it over onto the slab of boards. Hank's long arms kept falling over the sides and this seemed to infuriate Greg. After straightening the body, he had to pick up the dangling arms and drape them back over the man's stomach.

Just when he got the body arranged to his liking, Hank's daughter, Helen, tiptoed into the room at the back of the blacksmith shop which Greg used as a morgue. She was clutching an armload of clothes.

"What's that for?" Greg asked.

"We decided he should wear this suit," she said. "He always liked this one." It was a new-looking blue serge suit with gray pinstripes that Greg couldn't recall ever seeing Hank wear. She went away without glancing at the body on the table.

16

THIS IS FUN," VIC SAID, unbuttoning her coat collar for the wind wasn't cold. She was thrilled by the boat ride.

They were sitting on the troller's aft deck, knees bent, staring at the greenish-white and black wake flowing away from the boat's stern. The steady puttering of the boat's engine filled the night air, filled the silence that seemed to brood like a forest just beyond the engine's racket. The night air was invigorating and Vic was glad she'd changed into slacks and put a scarf over her head when Clarence suggested the boat ride out in the channel. She wondered why he seemed so disgruntled.

Wrangell lay off their stern, disappearing into the darkness, except for a smattering of dock lights and a few isolated street lamps on the hill. The rain clouds had all retreated when the sun set. The night sky above was studded with multitudes of tiny scintillating stars that gave the sky depth and sweep.

"You're awfully quiet tonight," Vic ventured, not knowing how to approach this tense, perplexing man.

"Feel kind of tired tonight. Had a pretty rough day."

"I noticed your shop was quite full this afternoon when I walked by."

"That way all day. Natives getting all sheiked up for some party they're throwing tonight."

"Death doesn't stop anything in Wrangell," Vic said, lamely. She was at a loss for conversation and yet she felt compelled to talk, to let Clarence know she appreciated the idea of the boat ride. There was so little one could do in Wrangell, she was beginning to realize. Especially with Clarence. He seemed to have no friends other than the man in the cabin piloting the boat. Either no one invited Clarence anywhere, or if they did, he declined the invitations. And there was no place one could go unless one had friends. Clarence had no car—they'd gone to the movies practically each night they'd dated. Of five shows they'd attended, she'd already seen three of them in the States and the other two were terrible. He wouldn't take her to the bars, not that she minded that, but at least he could have proposed going and she could have refused. He wouldn't even take her to Mom's to drink beer and dance a little like most of the other couples did. He was so tense, so ready to explode. It was more out of sympathy and against all her good judgment that Victoria had gone with Clarence to his room in the hotel. As risky as that was, as frightened as she had been, she didn't want to reject him, to cause him any more pain. She envied Lyddy. At least with Chris there was always a house party to attend or a little excursion in the daytime.

"Hell, couple of guys kicking the bucket in the same day ain't nothing for Wrangell," Clarence said. He spoke carelessly, as if he didn't care how his words came out.

"Sylvia Weaver said deaths often come in threes in Wrangell."

Clarence snorted. "That's a superstition all over, not just in Wrangell."

"I suspect that's true." She noticed that the boat was swinging around and she was perplexed, felt a sharp pang of disappointment and uneasiness.

"Are we turning back already?"

"Guess so," Clarence said, looking surprised. "Hey, Steve, are we heading back?"

Though the cabin door was open and Steve was just inside it on the platform behind the wheel, he evidently couldn't hear Clarence with the racket of the engine just below him.

"I'll go see," Clarence said.

Vic was suddenly stiff and cold. In the past few minutes the moon had come up, illuminating the whole channel. The water was silver where the moon shone, a little pale where the light was diffused. Vic stared at the islands and the mountains behind them, silhouetted by the moon, and breathed in the rich sea air.

"Steve's got to be back at nine," Clarence said, squatting down beside her. His voice was resigned.

"What for?" she asked puzzled.

"Didn't ask him. Guess he's got a date."

"This is a strange town. So much goes on at night. In the morning, when I walk down to school, the town looks deserted. Do you know that a lot of the children get up by themselves in the morning, dress and make their own breakfast? Most everyone sleeps late it seems."

"This damn weather makes you dopey," Clarence said.

She couldn't seem to be able to get gay and frivolous with Clarence. There was never any jesting between them. Right now the boat ride called for a song. Yes, they should be singing a song together or talking about light things or even discussing more substantial subjects such as their thoughts about marriage. She felt she could smooth out Clarence's abrasive personality once she got close enough, maybe even married him. If he came home to a cute place, prepared meals, laundered clothes, he would be softer, more gentle. He was so serious and domineering when they were alone together. All he seemed to care about was getting her in bed as soon as possible. She knew now it had been an inexcusable mistake to give in so easily. She blamed herself bitterly.

The troller slipped in around the breakwater and angled over to the far side of the float. The engine slowed, chutting loudly as the boat came alongside another troller. Clarence leaped over to it and secured a line around a guy wire and Steve dropped off a bumper. With the engine stilled, the quiet of the harbor roared in Vic's ears.

"There's some hot coffee in the foc'sle if you care for some," Steve said. "I'll be seeing you folks." And Steve scrambled across over the adjacent troller and disappeared down the float behind the clutter of hulls and masts and trolling poles.

"Mm, sounds good," Clarence said. Without asking Vic or waiting for her, he ducked into the foc'sle.

Uncertainly, she followed after him. There was very little about Clarence that could be called respectful. He didn't seem to care about whether or not she was enjoying herself. This was the first time Victoria had ever been on one of these boats and she hadn't seen the cabin yet. She made her way gingerly down the two steps and looked around. Clarence was hunched over a small two burner oil stove, pouring coffee into two mugs. The cabin was smelly and crowded, with the engine in the middle of the room, but it was rather clean. Then her eye caught the neat blanketed bed forward and her heart pounded against her ribs. She felt something, but couldn't quite identify what it was.

"Here's a cup," Clarence said and sat on the low bench running along the deck against the hull. "Watch out for the engine. You'll get yourself dirty."

She stepped to one side away from the engine and, setting her cup first to one side, began to sit down.

"Wait a minute," Clarence said. "Here, let me take off your coat. I'll put this blanket on the bench and you won't get any stains."

She felt his arms go about her as he approached her from behind. He did not even reach for her coat but placed his hands over her breasts. She felt a sudden anger. She had been tricked. All at once her suspicions poured over. The whole thing was obvious: the quick ride out in the channel, the inexplicable disappearance of Clarence's friend.

"Oh, no you don't," she managed to say.

His hands pressed upon her breasts and she was sick with revulsion.

"Clarence, stop that! I'm going!"

"Turn around," he said. His voice was bitter and hateful and he pushed her up against the bulkhead. Her hip and arm cringed with pain.

"Clarence . . ." The words stuck in her throat. She was so bitter about her own stupidity that she did not resist his embrace. She allowed him to kiss her, to steer her over to the bed without any opposition whatever.

"Suppose your friend comes back?" she asked, though she knew that he wouldn't return.

She felt his hands pulling at buttons, zipping down the side of her slacks. She raised up submissively as he pulled off her sweater and fumbled with the clasp of her bra. She heard his short, hard panting breath and felt his soft and smooth barber hands, his tight body pressed upon hers. She could hear voices out on the float not more than ten feet away. The ceiling was too low for her to bend her knees. She waited for Clarence to be through so that she could go home. She felt like crying when he blurted in her ear that he was ready and asked if she was. But she didn't cry. She didn't care.

When Vic came into the cottage, Lyddy was washing her hair in the kitchen sink.

"Is that you, Vic?" Lyddy called, holding her soapy, wet hair up over her eyes.

"Yeah, it's me."

Lyddy regulated the two taps and rinsed her hair out for the last time.

Whenever she was troubled, she washed her hair. At least it kept her occupied for a while and she needed that now.

Vic went straight into the bedroom, which was strange. In fact, Vic was home early.

Lyddy picked the towel up off the chair behind her and rubbed it briskly through her hair. She would massage it good, she decided. She would rub and rub until her scalp ached. As she worked away at her hair, she noticed that she still wore the doe-skin high heels she had put on purposely for Chris. She bent down to remove them and then decided against it. She fastened the towel around her head and wandered into the living room. On the way, she had to pass the dining room table which was now bare. She'd cleared the silverware and dishes from the table, she'd folded the starched white linen tablecloth into the same creases into which it was ironed and replaced it on the shelf in the linen closet.

Despondently, she plopped down on the same spot in the sofa where she had waited for Chris all evening.

"Hey, Vic!" she called. There was no reply from the bedroom. On occasions like this, Lyddy smoked and she drew a cigarette from the white china holder on the coffee table before her. Her gaze fell on the letter she had started to her mother while she was waiting for Chris. There was nothing else to do. The dinner was cooked, the table set. She had even washed the dishes and pots she's used; she had been in the kitchen wiping down the counters when Clarence came to pick up Vic.

"Hey, Vic," she called. "What are you doing?" She was aware that her voice was husky, almost as if she had been crying or getting over a sore throat.

"I'm going to bed," came Vic's reply from the rear of the house. She sounded as dispirited as Lyddy felt. Something must have gone wrong with her date with Clarence.

"What happened with you tonight, honey?" Lyddy asked, barely raising her voice. She felt an urge to get up and go into the bedroom for Vic was probably in need of consolation but she didn't move.

"I had a swell time," Vic returned sourly.

Lyddy could hear the bedroom closet door open. "How was the boat ride?"

"Oh, that was swell too," Vic said with a hint of irony.

She drifted into the room, wearing her red housecoat, knotting the sash. "Where's Chris?" she asked.

"I've been stood up."

"He hasn't shown up?" She showed no astonishment whatsoever and reached for a cigarette. Like Lyddy, Vic smoked sparingly and she looked like an amateur when she smoked. Lyddy always hoped she didn't look quite as obvious as Vic. Neither one inhaled but they tried to look as if they did.

"Nope," Lyddy said. "The man of my life hasn't shown up." She was impressed by the calm in her voice.

Vic dropped down onto the cushion beside her. "That's a fine howdy do." She shook her head in disgust. "You got stood up and I'm a sucker for a . . ."

"What happened?"

Vic's mouth was pinched. "He's a jerk. That's it. I've been wanting to find the right name for Clarence all evening. He's nothing but a jerk. A pathetic, useless jerk."

"My God, what happened?"

"We're jerks, Lyddy." Her voice had risen. "I want to go home. I want to get out of here. This isn't for me, this town. I'm not cut out for it."

Vic's words struck Lyddy with the force of a hatchet. She knew she had been waiting for such a revelation and yet, now that it had come, she wanted to ignore it.

Lyddy said unhappily, "Well, we can leave by next Monday. We haven't accepted Herb's offer for next term."

Vic rose, agitated. "I'm a sap." She turned to Lyddy. "Didn't Chris tell you or send someone up here to tell you he wasn't coming?"

Lyddy shook her head.

"Then we're both saps. Hey, is there any whiskey left in the bottle?"

"I bought a fresh quart today." Lyddy had learned once she started going out with Chris to keep an ample supply of whiskey in the house. Though Chris on occasions had fetched up a quart or two himself, he generally drank it all before remembering to replenish the stock.

"You want a drink?"

"No," Lyddy said.

"Well, I do."

Lyddy glanced about the room as Vic trotted out. She noticed stains in the carpet that she hadn't detected before, faint finger marks on the light switch by the door, a thin deposit of dust at the base of the ceiling fixture. It was hard to accept that she and Vic were both in the same predicament.

She picked up the letter to her mother and was surprised at its gushy flavor. The letter reminded her of the joyous mood that possessed her while she wrote it. She had written slowly, a glowing description of Chris as he appeared in her mind's eye. Her words had glided along with the movement of her pen. She had written carefully and easily, with no particular audience in mind, without worrying about syntax, just letting the words carry her with their inspiration.

"It's beautiful outside tonight," she had begun, for she had looked out the front door to see if Chris was coming. "There is no overcast—nothing but a star-pierced, moon-loved sky. Chris should be coming up any minute now for dinner." (She remembered pausing, laying down her pen to savor the delicious feeling of anticipation that washed over her.) "There is a glow in my body," the letter continued. "I feel that I want to just sail along with my pen and to concentrate on the sensation. I am so much in love, so steeped in it, drenched. What I am saying must come as a great shock, to have no bearing on what I have written you before but I don't seem to care."

Some time later she had walked down to the road and glanced across the hill at Chris' house. It was dark. She'd returned to the cottage, mystified and disturbed.

Vic came into the living room and sat down on the rocker across from Lyddy. She had evidently drunk her whiskey in the kitchen for she was empty-handed.

She laughed bitterly. "Brother, you should have seen my darling little man operate. We go out on the channel—oh, everything was lovely. Then, not even an hour later, we're back in the harbor and the boat owner has to leave and oh, hell, I'll think I'll have another drink."

Vic left the room with a discouraged shrug. Lyddy sat back, thinking of nothing, trying not to. But the feeling she had suppressed all evening was emerging. In a burst of passion, she tore her letter into tiny pieces.

She burned with the rage she had been able to bank all evening. She was glad it was upon her. She rose, sat down again, determined to give it her utmost attention. She balled up the pieces of letter and stuffed it in her pocket. She felt consoled somehow by her mounting animosity. He was probably down at the bars, probably drunk. The idea of his standing her up was almost unbearable.

This had never happened to her before. If this had happened in San Francisco, she would never have gone out with the man again. But if it did happen in San Francisco, then there would have been some excuse, large as the city was. Maybe car trouble. But here, in this burg, there was no excuse.

When Vic came back, her anger had simply vanished. It was queer but if Chris had happened to drop in at that moment, she would have been able to greet him civilly albeit coldly.

"I'm disgusted," Vic said. "I'm a genuine sap and I hate myself."

"Listen, don't expect any sympathy from me."

"I don't know about you but I know I've just been taken for a ride." Vic sighed. "This was one of the few days it didn't rain and, oh hell!" She paused. "I've hurt Dave," she blurted out suddenly. "I've really hurt that man and he's been so nice to me . . ." Her voice trailed away.

It was rare for her and Vic to be home alone together. They scarcely saw each other lately, hardly ever had a chance for a long intimate chat, both so busy with their dates. Lyddy saw Vic in the hurry of morning, caught glimpses of her at school, and maybe for a few moments at night while they were both preparing to go out.

But tonight, they were alone together and Lyddy was grateful. She wondered how she would have handled Wrangell if she had been alone. Would she take up drinking? She thought of all the drunk women at the dance, in the bars. She remembered the noises that occurred at all hours of the day and night in the hotel. Taking to the bottle seemed like more of a temptation in Wrangell than any other place she had known.

Vic was quiet, staring at her nails. And Lyddy wanted to comfort her, only she felt dead. She felt a deep and sudden craving for the noises of a city, the lights, the great streets and the disorder of traffic, the hundreds of programs on the radio stations, Herb Caen's column in the *Chronicle*, the shows, the department stores. She missed the people who admired her, her friends, even Don Lofton.

"You know, Lyddy," Vic said, staring at her nails, "I've been missing the States lately."

"Well, I'll be darned. I was just thinking of the same thing. The plays and symphonies."

"Market Street," Vic said. "More than anything I miss Market Street."

They were alone together and would be for the rest of the night. They could chat about all the things they missed. Thank God, it wasn't raining. That would have been too much.

Dave couldn't sleep. He was sore and frustrated. He got out of bed and walked around his room, smoking. He had tried to lull himself to sleep by trying all the remedies that worked in the past: hot chocolate with a light sandwich, walking around his room until he was cold. But tonight, none of them worked. He felt starved for love, with a hunger that was vicious and unreasonable. He walked around, dreaming of Victoria Blaissing, dreaming of her in a hundred different ways, as a schoolteacher, as a divorced woman from the States, as a woman who didn't care for him, as a lover.

Each time he got into bed he sweated so profusely that his pajamas clung to his flesh. And besides, the very contact of the sheets, the physical awareness of his outstretched body, alone in his bed set his mind raving. There was no getting away from it. He'd thought a lot of Vic lately, a lot about being in bed with her.

Tonight the hunger was persistent and urgent. Maybe it was because of Leif's and Hank's deaths. Maybe it was because the town was so quiet. There was scarcely any noise down on Main Street, only a car driving by now and then. Occasionally Curly's cab gunned by.

Dave lit his eighth or ninth cigarette. The small noise of scratching a match was almost soothing. The house was dead quiet. His folks were asleep, had gone to bed earlier than usual. Dave wished for a moment that it was raining. At least the rain made a stir. But now, the quiet around Dave was all that he could hear, alive and charged like an electric line humming across an empty field.

He tried turning his thoughts to unfinished dentures and how little time he had to complete them, to tomorrow's patients and their problems, the drills he had broken and needed to replace. He searched through the few novels he kept in the house for the sexy scenes but grew dissatisfied all the more when he realized how the authors had teased him, leaving him to imagine the intimate details. Tonight he wanted the candid, brutal descriptions: the panting, the way the body jerks with uncontrollable joy at the touch of a lover's hand. He wanted to feel in his own body the reflexes and the stimuli, the small noises that signal the approach of the climax, the incoherent motions of the body, the final spasm that jolts through the lovers' limbs with the quenching of the fire in their loins.

Oh, brother, Dave thought, this wasn't getting him anywhere. He dressed and practically ran down the steps to Main Street. He could get what he wanted at Princess'. At this hour, no one would see him enter the place. And once inside the whore house, all the customers were on the same boat. Dave felt excited by his bravado. He pictured the scene. Tall black Princess meeting him at the side door of the building, a gracious smile already fixed on her face even before she recognized her next customer. "Hi ya, Dave. Come in, man! Do come in!" Seeing the dentist in her establishment would produce no look of surprise on her intelligent, hospitable face. That was her business. Princess made her customers feel right at home.

Who would he get? The platinum blonde who was a bit hefty but had nice legs, or the other woman, who was a little older and less showy. On the street she could be any other woman in Wrangell. They'd escort Dave into one of the two tiny bedrooms at the rear of the house which overlooked the harbor. The room would be warm and plain and the bed made, but they wouldn't get under the covers, just do the job on top. He couldn't remember—it had been so long ago—who he paid and when.

Just as he was making the turn around Johnny Bugg's bar into the alley,

Dave caught sight of Red Parker stumbling out of Princess' door. He stood there, paralyzed, and watched Red staggering forward. In the dark alley, Red hesitated as he noticed a man just ahead of him, then ambled forward to greet him. Dave quickly backed away, going across Main Street and ducking into the Johnson's Sweets.

He paused in front of the first magazine stand, picked up an *Esquire* and, pretending to read the page, turned to stare out through the front windows. He spied Red wobbling into Johnny Bugg's bar across the street and felt a sense of relief. He flipped through the magazine pages without seeing its contents, conscious of small talk and fountain noises behind him.

"I've got to wash the windows before I leave," he heard Sally Anne, the half-breed fountain girl, say to someone. In the small dance room in the rear beside the kitchen, a low dreamy number was playing on the jukebox. Some kids were dancing, their feet shuffling along the waxed linoleum.

Then his eyes spotted a magazine cover depicting a half-naked girl with a sultry look. A pulse knocked in his loins as his hunger returned. He forced himself to appear normal and continued to flip through the pages of the magazine he was holding but his eyes kept wandering over to the picture of the full-breasted, scantily-clad girl with the look of abandonment on her face. He glanced around the fountain, then sauntered over to the magazine and read the title: *Jean's Bedevilment.*

The title was catchy and sexy. He'd always scoffed at the lowbrows who read the pulps but now he was only too conscious of a greedy desire to grab the magazine, run to the privacy of his room and devour its contents. He looked up as someone entered the shop. It was Chuck Alder. They exchanged greetings. As Chuck moved off towards the back, Dave snatched Jean from her place and thrust her between the pages of *Esquire*, rolling the two in his hand.

Straightening up, sweating under his arm pits, he went over to the fountain to pay the girl. He waited while Sally Anne finishing scooping up and plunking ice cream into a shaker. Plump, bespectacled Mrs. Regis was perched on one of the red leather stools to his right, apparently waiting for the milk shake. She smiled at the dentist and Dave smiled back.

17

AT FIRST, THE FISHING SEASON WAS A DISAPPOINTMENT. The fishermen who had spent all year getting their boats and gear ready dashed out on opening day and came back with a few dog salmon.

As always, the fever struck Chris all at once. This year was no exception, even with Lyddy in Wrangell. In fact not until opening day did Chris realize that he had a job to do and that it would take him away from Lyddy most of the time. But when the fever came it struck with the same degree of delirium as in previous years. All his thoughts revolved around the fishing season and the cannery. He really didn't have to worry—the cannery made a profit regardless of the size of the catch. The cannery was like the house man in a poker game who rakes off a percentage of the pots, only in this case the fishing boats were the players. No matter who made the largest or smallest catches, who had luck and who didn't, the cannery always came away a winner. Still Chris was struck with the fever.

At first, he experienced it vicariously through Lyddy. Long before the season began, she seemed to pick up the suspended excitement of the town. On most of their walks, they ended up down at the harbor watching the kids fishing for bull heads and tom cod from the docks and the fisherman preparing their boats. The purse-seiners were loading up their aft decks with skiffs, turntables and seine nets, the gill-netters were molding the lead line on the bottom of shackles, the trollers were snapping spoons and hooks to their steel trolling lines.

He taught her how to tell one boat from the other. Trollers had outriggers, long poles fore and aft, fastened upright or angled out for fishing. They fished while moving through the water, trailing lures or baited hooks from trolling lines off the outriggers. A gill-netter had a power-driven roller, usually in the bow, for rolling up the gill nets. The seiner could be distinguished by the seine skiff, a small boat sitting on top of the seine net and the net table in the back, and the power block on the main boom used to haul in the seine net, which was too heavy to lift by hand when loaded with salmon.

"It's incredible," she once said to him. "It's such a picturesque world. And such activity—as if they're coming out of hibernation." She'd laughed. "What is gill-net fishing?"

"Well, they catch the salmon—mostly silvers and kings—by the gills. The gill-netter goes in close to shore, near a river mouth, when the tide's changing. Then he drops one end of the gill-net and then lets out the rest as he moves away. The lead sinkers on the bottom pull the net down to the bottom. The top of the net has cork floats on it to keep it floating so it's called the cork line. It's like throwing up an underwater fence fifteen feet deep and nine hundred feet long. Well, the salmon come swimming into the mesh..."

"Can't they see it? I thought fish had good eyesight?"

"When the tide changes at a river mouth, the sediment comes broiling up from the bottom and dirties the water so much that the net is practically invisible. When a salmon pokes his head in the webbing he instinctively backs away and his gills get caught between the threads. The harder the salmon tugs back, the more entangled he gets. And he can't go forward because the opening in the mesh is too small. Simple, huh?"

"It's unbelievable. I love salmon but I've never thought twice about how it got into the can."

"You're getting the idea now, baby. One of these days we'll go out and catch some ourselves. That's real sport."

During the slack period before the start of the fishing season, Chris made a point of calling on Lyddy every chance he got, knowing that once the run began he wouldn't see much of her until the season was over. He had been in hot water the night he didn't show up for dinner but after he explained to Lyddy how he had fallen asleep on the living room floor because he had stayed up all night and the next day playing poker because he was too happy to sleep, she forgave him.

The boats swarmed in and out of the harbor too restless to lay idle after so long a wait. The fishermen drifted in and out of the bars and the canneries, alert for any rumors of salmon. The weather was cloudy and it rained often which made it easy for the salmon to enter the rivers. But even the short-run coastal streams contained very few fish and those stragglers that were caught were still gleaming silver. They had not yet gone through the changes of body and color which marked their maturity. The first week's catch barely covered the expenses of gas and grub.

The good weather arrived just before the Fourth of July. The land opened, the roads became dry and the days long. Each sunset was more spectacular than the once preceding it, a great release of color that drenched the clouds, the sky and the land. The western sky flamed with violent crimsons, purples, golds and lavenders.

Lyddy stepped outside. The cottage wasn't stuffy but the activity in the outside world drew her: the restless boats puttering in and out of the harbor below, the sun brandishing color on the clouds above the islands.

She had been house cleaning all day. Her hands were gritty from the scouring powder and her arms and shoulder blades ached from washing the kitchen walls. But she was glad that she had washed the kitchen. It gave her something to do. Besides, it needed it, for the oil stove had erupted one night last week and thrown soot all over the place.

She had worked so hard that she could feel her muscles trembling. On top of that a mixed sense of restlessness and loneliness coursed through her. She paused to breathe in the fragrance of the stock that bloomed along the path below the cottage and the honeysuckle that made a horseshoe over the Eaton's side porch. It was incredible the way things grew in Alaska. The weeds, flowers and grass ran riot all over the hill. One had to mow the lawn at least twice a week or else it would get out of hand. People who neglected their lawns had to use a scythe to hack down the tall, flourishing grasses which were much too tough for an ordinary mower once they reached a certain height.

It was the same with the fishing season. The change in the town was incredible. More steamers were running. The town was full of Orientals and Filipinos, high school and college students and other itinerants from the States who flocked into Wrangell to work the season. Every time a new steamer docked, tourists poured into the town, gawking at the totem poles, touring the canneries, buying a few souvenirs from Floyd's Curio Shop before returning to the ship. Seiners and tenders arrived daily from Seattle, each piping a shrill whistle as it rounded the breakwater in Wrangell harbor. A Wrangellite walking down Main Street during the summer greeted the strangers the same way he would greet anyone else, only it wasn't the same. These newcomers would only stay for the season. And there was a different spirit in the town. Everyone was focused on catching fish and making money. The casualness and even friendliness were set aside for the present. Everything else was simply postponed, except for the dance scheduled on the Fourth of July and the smattering of parties that were always going on. All the social organizations—the Elks, the Sportsman and the Redman—had officially closed until the season was over. The stores swarmed with fishermen buying gear and grub, the hotel was full and the bars were doing a land office business.

Every morning the three canneries tooted their whistles using certain signals to tell their crews which time to report to work. The canneries didn't want to be bothered by workers wandering into the office during the morning to find out when work would begin since the canneries never knew from one day to the next when the fish-laden boats would arrive. Once you learned the codes, you could tell by listening to the blasts how each cannery was doing by the earliness or lateness of the report-to-work signals.

It was ten o'clock at night and the sun was still raging in the sky. It would go behind the islands in a short while but the sky would stay bright with the colors of the sunset until about eleven-thirty when it would take on a hazy blue shade. Then at three-thirty, the sun would send out a fine wash of green from the east.

Vic was over at Jean Crawford's making blueberry jam with the berries they'd picked yesterday. Vic was getting along fine now that she had started going out with Dave. So was Lyddy. She was getting along fine with Chris. But once again, after a long day spent almost entirely by herself, Lyddy felt uneasy. She seemed to be suspended in a state which held no promises, only repercussions. Lyddy slapped the dirt off her hands and stood up. She'd take a shower and go down to meet Chris at the cannery. She knew he would be through shortly.

From the stage of the A&N Hall, Matt Fleming watched couples go sliding by him just a few feet below. Another Fourth of July dance. Matt was moody tonight, filled with a dreamy ache of hope and of some wordless knowledge that seemed to be just out of his grasp. He turned his eyes to the piano keyboard. Though he played most of the numbers by ear, he could not help but marvel at the accuracy and nimbleness of his fingers. How is it that they could find the right notes while they moved so swiftly across the board? How does anyone, without even having to think about it, breathe? There was an open door to everything tonight, Matt felt. He wanted to find it, to glance inside.

Because he knew this would be his last Fourth in Wrangell, a feeling of sorrow mingled with joy rose inside him, sweet and pure. It made Matt want to play as he never did before. In his eagerness, he began racing ahead of the drummer. The other players, startled by this sudden burst of energy, struggled to catch up. The tempo became ragged and confused.

He rose when the number ended and approached Earl Lamb, the orchestra leader, who played sax. "I think I'll be going, Earl."

"Sure, Matt. Thanks for helping out this much."

Although it was at first difficult, Matt had learned to accept the courtesy with which people were treating him lately. No one ever asked why or argued with him; they simply let him do as he pleased. He climbed down the steps of the stage and started across the hall. People stopped dancing to say hello to him, compliment him on his piano playing. It was almost as if they felt they had to say a few words. It was getting worse with each new day.

"Thanks," Matt said. He said it again and again as he pushed forward towards the entrance a long way ahead.

"Say, Matt," Holly Dancey said, stopping Matt. "Tell Earl to stir 'em up a bit, play something hot! I've got itchy feet."

"I'll try to," Matt said, not wanting to reveal that he was leaving.

The center of the floor cleared as Earl announced the intermission by running off a familiar arpeggio on his sax and Matt found it easier to walk across to the entrance way.

As Matt moved out of the dance hall he spied Chris and Lydia standing outside on the boardwalk, getting a breath of fresh air.

"Hi, Matt," Chris said and the girl smiled at him.

"Hello, folks," Matt said. He felt guilty all of a sudden and began smacking his lips. "I'm leaving the dance," he said, "I'm a little tired tonight."

"Oh, that's too bad," Lydia said. "You play beautifully."

Matt hesitated, blushing with the compliment. He liked seeing this beautiful girl with the nice young man whom he had known since he was a boy.

The night plummeted down upon Matt as he left the couple and walked around the road, wondering if he had done right. Was he a coward to leave, he asked himself? Did he have to desert the dance just because he felt good? Did he have to be alone to savor his last Fourth of July in Wrangell?

Matt wondered if he felt out of place because he wasn't working as the night watchman at the cannery this year. Two weeks before the season started Matt had told Chris that he didn't think he could work this season. "That's all right, Matt," Chris had said and let it go at that, with the same accepting attitude everyone else was exhibiting, making Matt feel more self-conscious.

Fourth of July was a big holiday in Wrangell and the town had been full of gaiety all day. Firecrackers had started popping all over town the night before and during the day Main Street was packed with hordes of people watching the bicycle races and the sack and foot races for the kids. The day was full of youth and spirit and health and life. As much as Matt had wanted to enjoy himself, there was an ache inside him that would not go away. He was on the threshold between life and death, switching from one to the other as easily as changing sides on a record on a phonograph.

As Matt passed Bea's house on his way down the road to his cabin he began to wish that the end wasn't so slow. He felt too good, too confident, too appreciative of the way he had lived in Wrangell since he was a young man. He wanted more of the precious wisdom that he found in the peace and beauty all around him.

"I feel too good to die," Matt kept repeating aloud to himself as he walked down the dark gravel road towards his cabin.

Behind him, a string of firecrackers exploded. Matt turned, fascinated, as if he had heard a melody cutting through the silence of the night.

"There is one thing about this town that is priceless," Lyddy said to Chris. "And that's the way the people in it can have so much fun. It doesn't matter if things are going good or bad."

"Uh huh," Chris said, holding her rather tight.

"It's contagious. You can see it in the newcomers' faces. They all look like they're having the time of their life."

"They're all swacked," Chris said. He was slightly drunk and was dancing much too fast for the tempo of the music. "Brother, what a dancer, I am," he said as he twirled her round and round.

Lyddy grew dizzy and the couples about her melted into blur, a revolving wall of people all seemingly stuck together.

"You're ahead of the music," she laughed.

"So what? I make my own tempo."

He kept on spinning and she threw herself into the dance with whole-hearted enthusiasm. She closed her eyes and held tight to Chris, feeling his energy, his inordinate enthusiasm.

"You are a wonderful dancer," she said when the music ended. They promenaded about the jammed hall.

"It's been a wonderful day," she said. "Are all the Fourth's the same?"

"Yep. Only difference is sometimes Mayor Slater gives the speech and sometimes Merv Cahill."

They met up with Dave and Vic and decided to go have a drink at the punch bowl.

"Tim Regis sure is in top form tonight," Dave said. Dave looked happy. "He's drunker than a hoot owl and that stuff he's ladling out is pure rot gut."

Afterwards, when Chris and Lyddy were walking up the hill, Lyddy remembered Matt. "Isn't it awful," she said, "about Matt Fleming?"

"He isn't looking good," Chris said.

"And he's supposed to die this year?"

"Not much more time, according to the doctor in the States."

"It frightens me. It's the worst thing!"

"Too bad something like this has to happen to Matt. He's such a nice guy."

"I feel awful thinking of it," she said. "Everyone was so happy tonight and yet there was this one man who . . ."

"Forget about it," Chris said. "There's nothing that can be done."

They stopped outside the cottage. The lights were on inside which meant that Vic, and probably Dave, had arrived before they did. They sat down on the front step.

"I feel tongue-tied," Chris said and rubbed his forehead with his fingers. "I want to talk to you. But I guess I had too much to drink."

She laughed. "First time I've noticed that drinking had any real effect on you."

"You know, sometimes when I'm at the cannery working I get a funny feeling that you won't be in Wrangell when I'm through at the end of the day. I guess I'm tired."

"You're worried about the season too."

He nodded wearily. "It'll be all right once the fish start coming in to spawn. It's not good for the town when there's a poor season. The town changes."

"And you don't want it to."

"No, I don't. It's a good town the way it is. All we need is just a normal catch."

"You know, I look forward all day to the moment you get off too."

"Why don't you come down more often? Three or four times a day."

She laughed. "Each time I do you're so busy that I feel like, well, it's one of those times when I realize what a small town Wrangell is. It's obvious to everyone how we feel about each other, Chris."

"The hell with what they think." He leaned back on the step. "I feel lucky having you, Lyddy. And the wonderful thing about it is that I'm not used to it. I can't seem to feel satisfied just knowing that I have your love." He lit a cigarette and took a deep breath. "That's love, isn't it?"

"It sure is." She smiled and put her hand on his leg.

"Nice hand," he said, covering it with his own. "Nice day, nice night, nice dance, nice girl, nice hand."

"It's been very nice, everything," Lyddy said before he kissed her.

The door behind them opened and Dave looked down upon them. "I know this might not be what you had in mind but Vic's just made a pot of coffee and she's got some butterhorns heating in the oven."

"Sounds all right to me," Chris said and stood up.

There were times when Lyddy felt so happy about her life in Wrangell that she worried about it. It didn't seem natural to be so thrilled. Especially considering the turmoil she was in all the time, trying to decide whether or not to stay. Both she and Vic were putting off making a final decision on teaching for the fall semester. Perhaps the thrill came from her love for Chris. Or from the long hours of emptiness that she waded through before the onrush of happiness seized her. She was alone every day and most of the night and then, at some late, odd hour, she would walk across the hill and down to the other side to the cannery and meet Chris.

She would walk out on the great T-shaped dock, hear the hum of the machinery in the fish house canning the last of the day's catch and the growl of the boats clustered around the cannery's docks. All the people were engrossed in the task of processing salmon.

In a way, she wished that she could be a part of all this. She would like to work in the fish house. She wouldn't care what she did. She felt that packing tins in cardboard cases would be easier than staying in the cottage most of the day waiting for Chris, who was almost too tired to be coherent. She had never expected Chris to be so involved with the cannery or to work so hard.

Lyddy entered the wire gate of the cannery and walked down to the open shed between the warehouse and fish house. She dodged around a lift truck bearing a load of sealed salmon tins, cooled and ready to be packed in cases in the warehouse. At the office, which faced the channel, she looked in through the window set in the door and spied Chris.

"Come in," Chris called, waving his arm.

"Are you busy?" she asked, as she entered. Two men she didn't know stood beside Chris at his desk. The office grew suddenly quiet. She could never get over the fact that Chris was an executive who sat behind a desk and ran a business.

"Be with you in a minute, honey. A tender hit a deadhead out at Baker and twisted its prop. We're trying to figure out who to send after it to tow it in."

Giff came into the office and said hello to Lyddy.

"Figure out who you're going to send out?"

"How about you?" Chris said. "The two other tenders are already on their way in and loaded. We'll get them at the cannery first thing in the morning if they're not stalled. Anyway, they aren't iced and I hate to take a chance on having one of them tow her in."

Giff grimaced. Lyddy had heard from Chris that Giff wasn't having his customary good luck at the beginning of the season. This extra work would put him out a day's fishing.

"O.K." Giff nodded, "I'll take the *Verna* out as soon as she's unloaded."

A man poked his head in the door. "Say, Chris, what label you want put on this last load of humphies?"

"I'll be right out," Chris said.

"I'll go outside on the dock," Lyddy said. "You're awfully busy."

"I'll be through in a little while, honey," Chris said.

Chris brushed past her, with the two men following on his heels. She walked out to the dock. She might have to wait one or two hours, she realized, as she saw a tender unloading salmon and two seiners waiting their turns to unload. They were low in the water which meant they had heavy loads. It was boring waiting for Chris to be through. She felt the eyes of the workers on her, especially the young men from the States, and she began to wish that she wasn't there.

She stood on the dock staring out across the channel, watching the lights exposing of the gill-netters drifting with the tide about the Stikine's mouth.

————

It seemed like hours until Chris was done and could walk with Lyddy up to the cottage. They went by way of the road that climbed up by the city hall, around Cliff Waverly's house, through the tunnel of trees and came out near the cottages. Below them, they could make out the dusky outlines of the buildings on Main Street and beyond, the channel, calm and silent. The harbor was dark and secretive, like an empty stadium.

It was so warm and still outside that she was reluctant to enter the little cottage which would, no doubt, be stuffy.

"I almost hate to go in," Lyddy said. "The nights are out of this world."

"Well, if you want to stay out a while we might as well sit down."

They scarcely spoke. She could hear his breathing and knew that he must be tired. She watched him light a cigarette. He flicked the match down the path.

"How do you feel, Chris, darling?" she asked. "Are you tired? Or are you worried?"

"I'm tired," he said, staring down between his legs at the dirt.

"Well," she smiled, "I'm not tired. Does that make you feel any better?"

"All I know is," he said, "the minute we get inside I want to go to bed with you"

She laughed. "And suppose Vic should come in at that moment?"

He drew on his cigarette. "Well, it was a good thought. I feel perked up already. Let's go down to my house."

"No, let's just stay right here. Outside. I'm enjoying this."

She waited for him to speak.

"Aren't you going to answer me?" she asked.

"Answer you what?"

"Well, if I were alone, I wouldn't be enjoying this. Some people—you're one of them—seem to feel fine whether they're alone or with someone. I'm not that way. If you weren't here beside me, I would be a blank. No, that's not right. I'd be wishing for something."

"What?" he asked, but he didn't sound interested.

"That's it, Chris. I don't know. No one ever really knows . . ."

"I know what I want," he said. He kissed her, caressing her breast. She opened her lips to his, felt his tongue against hers and a flood of desire welled up inside of her.

"Hey," she protested laughing. "We do enough of that in the house. Let's enjoy the night first. I'm lonesome for conversation. All day, I talk with Mrs. Crawford or rather she talks to me about her children and what she's planning to buy from the catalog and how lonesome it is with her husband out fishing most of the time."

Winchester, the Hart's Siberian husky, came snuffling along the path and Chris whistled to it. The dog ran up to him, whimpering with happiness. Chris ran his hands through the dog's thick fur. Winchester rolled over on his back and Chris tickled his stomach, while the dog's hind leg kicked uncontrollably.

"Have you ever had a dog?" Lyddy asked.

"Nope."

"You haven't much of anything."

He turned his attention to her, forgetting about Winchester who got up and ambled back down the path.

"Chris, you are the most easily satisfied person I have ever known," she said. "Right now, I envy you. You fill me with wonder . . ."

"At what?"

"How you are. So confident and happy all the time."

"I'll tell you what it is," he said. "I've made myself that way. I've always believed that I couldn't ask for anything and it's stuck with me. I don't think, though," he added, "that I could have done that anywhere else."

"Than Alaska?"

"Than Wrangell. Now listen," he said, "this is Wrangell. Not Alaska. Have you ever been anywhere else in Alaska besides Wrangell?"

"Just the few hours we spent in Ketchikan while the steamer was docked there."

"Well, Alaska is a big country. And I've been through a lot of it. And to me there's only one place in it and that's Wrangell."

"Why is that, Chris? Aren't the other towns the same?"

"I guess so," he said.

"Well, why Wrangell then?"

"I don't know. I only know that I don't want any other part of Alaska but Wrangell."

"How about the islands out there, the waterways?"

"To me that's part of Wrangell."

"You certainly have a one-track mind."

"You'll have it too someday," Chris said. "Right now," he said, stretching his arms before him, "I feel very happy. Hey, is Vic inside?"

"She might be. Do you know that it's two-thirty in the morning?"

"Let's stay up until daybreak."

"No. Come in for one drink and then you go home. You'll be glad for it in the morning."

"Well, we'll see," he said. They went into the cottage.

————————

Chris liked staying up all night. Sometimes he did it deliberately. He liked how it was so quiet he could hear the splash of a hose in the harbor or the great flap of feathers as an owl winged overhead. As he grew more tired and cold, the silence would become beautiful. He felt that he was alone in the world and the silence belonged to him.

When he left Lyddy's cottage, Chris didn't want to sleep. He was tired but he struggled against it. He wandered down to the harbor. The double-enders looked like crescent moons lying half-submerged in the water. The sight of the brightly-painted boats with their towering masts and poles, nestled next to each other all up and down the floats evoked the poignant and melancholy feeling that he had known ever since he was a boy in Wrangell.

A silver lining of mist ran along the edge of Woronkofski Island across the channel from Wrangell. A thin white line of beach showed beneath the mist, white as snow. Above the mist, the trees poured up the ridge. He felt wonderful. Down below the distant island, a gas-powered boat, no bigger than a speck from this distance, chugged slowly off shore. Chris could see the puffs of white exhaust fumes floating up and mixing with the mist. It was a glorious morning. He heard a bird chirping somewhere nearby, then another.

As he walked back up the hill, heading home so he could shower and change before going to the cannery, he could smell the resinous odor of spruce burning in the wood stove of some early riser. His stomach pinched from hunger and too many cigarettes. It was dawn and he was alone with only the masses of the trees, their tips stained gold with light as they slanted ridgeward. The quiet brought him such a rush of happiness that he was almost dizzy with it.

When he went by the Eaton's, he glanced at the cottage. The trees rose behind it, ponderous and still. A fluffy white cloud sailed overhead. Lyddy was no doubt still asleep. He had left the cottage only a few hours earlier. They had lain side by side on the small sofa in the living room because Vic was asleep in the bed. Once he had even fallen asleep, but always there had been the two of them, close to one another, until the light of dawn crept through the windows and diffused into the room. He remembered the unbelievably soft texture of her skin.

During the season, Chris ate most of his meals in the cannery's mess kitchen. He always tried to be early enough to have his breakfast before the help came in. Consequently, Al Swift, the cook, would generally have coffee made and water boiling in case Chris wanted poached eggs. As Chris climbed up the steps of the green and white building, the smell of perking coffee hit his nostrils. His stomach responded instantly with a lurch of interest. He closed the door gently, because he knew Al hated unnecessary noise in the morning. Al was standing bent over the humming oil stove, just staring at the coffee pot, his white-clad back bathed with the sunlight that came slanting through the front windows.

"Good morning, Al. Got any coffee ready?" Each morning Chris asked the same question whether or not he could smell the coffee.

Al turned around, his eyes full of sleep. He was a loose-lipped man with a big space between his front teeth and curly red hair that was almost kinky. He came up to Wrangell every season to cook for Chris, a man in his fifties who seemed to have no ties. Though he wasn't the best cook in the world, Al liked to feed people, liked to see them eat as long as they didn't make too much noise.

"All ready," Al said. "There's sliced cantaloupe on the table and there's some raspberries still left over in the ice box that Matt brought in yesterday."

"Cantaloupe's all right," Chris said.

The kitchen had just been painted and the pale green and ivory colors looked good. The long narrow mess table ran down the center of the room. Along its sides were low green benches that could seat twenty employees at a time. Another table for four people stood in the corner, covered with a brightly checkered red-and-white tablecloth. This was where Chris always sat. Al had selected the spot in the corner for the table and though Chris disliked it there, because it was too near the hot range, he never suggested moving it.

Chris sat down and glanced at the thick, bone-white china platter piled with slices of cantaloupe. He put away three slices while Al poached three eggs and fried some bacon. The cantaloupe was sweet and refreshing. The room was warm and cheerful with the sun streaming in through the low windows. Al set the bacon and eggs before Chris humming a tune.

"What's that you're humming?" Chris asked, buttering a slice of toast.

"Oh, just a song I heard over the Filipino bunk house the other night."

"They gambling heavy?" Chris inquired.

"They're all broke. Never seen such broke people. They play for dimes and I mean they play for them. They're hard to beat when they're in that shape."

Chris dived into his breakfast. He realized he needed to eat to keep going. He was dead tired and he hadn't even begun his day.

"Want some more toast?" Al asked, warming Chris' cup with more coffee.

"No thanks, Al. That was swell."

The screen door opened and three men came in.

"God damn, you guys are up early," Al protested. "Can't you sleep?"

All the men knew about Al's touchy disposition and practically tiptoed to the table. Chris knew most of these men from the States by name only. They came up for a few weeks and left, seldom, if ever, returning to work two years in a row at the same place.

"Don't get excited, Al," one of them whispered. "Just pour us some of that coffee and we'll eat when you tell us to."

"Pour it yourself," Al said. He gave Chris a disgusted look.

By eight o'clock, Chris was in his office glancing at some wires. He had wired other canneries in Southeastern asking about how they were doing. Most of the answers were what he expected. "Running skeleton crew part-time only, catching nothing but stragglers." "Practically no activity to speak of, very discouraging." A wire from Juneau sounded a little more hopeful: "Getting quite a few humphies but no appreciable catch of reds."

There was a letter on his desk from Malcolm MacLane, the cannery's biggest broker (who sold a large part of the salmon to himself purely for speculation) but Chris left it unopened. He sat in his chair, toying with the cedar letter opener, the facets of a totem carved on its handle. He swiveled around and faced the large bay window that overlooked a part of the dock and the channel.

It was discouraging. Not a boat in yet this morning.

Florence Savard, Chris' secretary, entered the office. She was always at least five or ten minutes late but the cannery suffered no loss because of it. Florence was one of those meticulous women who could do the work of two women which was necessary when the cannery was actually running at top speed. In addition, she possessed a zealous devotion to her work so much so that the few times Chris was forced to hire another girl to help out, Florence seemed offended. She was so wary and protective of the business that she checked over the work (even her own work) at least three times before she was satisfied it was correct. Last year Chris had purchased a new Remington adding machine. The whole season was almost over before Florence was convinced that the new machine was computing the figures correctly and this was only after she went over the daily figures every day by hand. On payroll days, when the office was swamped with other work, Florence stayed until midnight going at a furious pace, double checking each employee's time and rate of pay with the foreman in the fish house and the warehouse. The checks were always masterpieces of neatness and precision. Chris could sign his name to them without any qualms, which was good since he would never dare to question Florence.

She had been with the Ballard Cannery ever since Chris could remember. Once, and Chris winced in shame when he thought about it, the second year that he'd been back in Wrangell after college, he propositioned her. She screamed at him, told him he was a spoiled brat, and then started crying. When he saw how miserable she looked, a homely woman with a long horse's face who would probably live out her life as an old maid, he was embarrassed. But, although they never spoke of the incident again, they became good friends afterwards, went on hikes together. Florence loved tramping about the island, picking berries, going up to Rainbow Falls and having a picnic by the edge of the precipice. Chris actually started considering trying again but then she married Ted Savard.

In the morning when she came in or at noon when she came back to her desk after lunch, Florence looked like she was half-dead. She walked slowly and her eyes behind her glasses were glazed with thought. She always looked to Chris like an old lady shuffling into her bedroom to take an afternoon nap. But once behind her desk, Florence built up a head of steam, working steadily, never stopping, until perspiration dampened her brow as the hours flew by and her desk, cleared of one task, became cluttered with the next.

During the past week, Florence had been practically dragging herself into the office. She abhorred the inactivity in the cannery.

"No boats in yet, I see," she said.

"Nope. Don't see any out on the channel coming in either."

She took off her coat slowly, staring out the window. "You want to see those invoices I made out last night?"

"No. Just put them in the mail," Chris said and lit a cigarette. Actually he didn't have a damn thing to do. He wondered why he came down so early. But he knew that he was following in his father's footsteps, one of the few worthwhile habits he had acquired from his dad. Theodore depended on the success of his cannery to justify his existence. He used to come down to the cannery at five just to make sure that the night watchman was still awake. Though Chris believed he did the best he could to operate the cannery as efficiently as possible, he knew he was no Theodore Ballard. However, the habit of coming down early had stuck with him. Even though the cannery ran well without him, Chris felt guilty the few times he arrived late, felt Theodore's accusing eyes on him clear from Seattle.

Chris left the office and strode across the shed to the fish house. Joe Ball, the machinist, was crouched under the assembly line working a grease pump. Other than that the place was empty. Quiet. It didn't seem right. They should be knocking out tins by the hundreds. He stared at the idle line, at the wash bins where the fresh salmon were separated by species, at the iron chink (so named after the Chinamen of the old days who used to dress the fish by hand, chopping off the heads and tails and removing the guts), at the long belt where the slimers finished the dressing, scraping off the coagulated blood along the back bone and whatever the chink missed, at the filler machine, at the clincher, at the round block retorts at the far end where the salmon were cooked under pressure in the tins. It was dead, waiting for fodder. Like Florence, waiting to be put to work.

"What are you doing?" Chris called to Joe who had hopped out of sight back under the iron chink.

"Sweetening nipples," Joe said, his voice muffled. "Any boats coming in yet?"

"Nothing in sight."

Chris wandered around the rear of the office and went into the radio room to see if the night watchman had received any messages from the tenders and seiners at the fishing grounds. But there was no report of anything coming in. One tender reported that one of the fish traps in Sumner Strait was a quarter full; they were going to wait for the next tide to try and get a decent load.

Chris bit his lips. So far all three canneries in Wrangell were doing about the same. But he wanted to be ahead, to lead the pack. Ballard Cannery should have less breakdowns and better working conditions. His employees should have large checks to cash at the store so everyone in town would know that the fat checks were coming from the Ballard Cannery. All morning Chris listened for the whistles of the other canneries announcing their report-to-work hour and was comforted that none of them sounded. Of the two competitive canneries, the Schnur and State-Pak, Chris was inclined to feel more competitive with the latter because the Schnur was locally-owned while the State-Pak operated under absentee ownership, which meant that most of its money went south with the salmon it canned.

Chris sat down on the stool of the radio room, itching to pick up the microphone and contact all the boats who sold their fish to the Ballard Cannery and tell them to get off their asses. They had waited all year for this moment. Chris stared at the set, flicked the transmitter switch on and off. Every four hours, Florence marched into the radio room, turned on the control panel and waited there fifteen minutes. Most of the boats were equipped with two-way radios and would report their position and movement, as well as the fishing conditions. Before Theodore had purchased the set they never knew what to expect or how to prepare, couldn't advise their boats about where to find the fish or encourage them to stay out and get a better load because the cannery was not hard-pressed for fish that day.

Chris moved out of the radio room and climbed up the outside stairway to the can loft above the fish house. This department was always a source of wonder to Chris, for at one time shipping empty cans to Alaska cost as much as it did to send back the filled ones since freight rates were figured on cubic measurements. But now the empty cans were pressed flat and they used a machine to expand them into cylinders, another to flange the ends and a third to roll on the bottom. Freight expenses were negligible since a case that held 48 full cans could hold 360 empty ones. The bottomless tins were stored in this room, then fed onto carrier belts through an opening in the floor to the filling machine below. Before they quit last night, the girls had filled the reform lines and they were ready to go. The whole room was neat and clean.

Downstairs, in the shed, the place was filling up with Filipinos and some white men, emerging from the mess kitchen, smoking and talking quietly.

"Pretty late today," one of the men said to Chris.

"Yeah," Chris said. He ducked into the office and sat down in his chair. He was used to being in the office with the rumble of machinery jarring the planking, vibrating through the foundation, shaking the desk a little. The whole place was so quiet that he thought he could hear the slight backwash of the channel under the cannery. He checked yesterday's market quotations which came in daily from Western Union and wasn't cheered to see that practically the whole line of salmon had advanced fractions of pennies. Once again he scanned the channel for inbound boats. He would have to work late again tonight. All the boats would be coming in at the same time, staying out for the whole twenty-four hours the law allowed them to keep fresh fish aboard.

Chris shuffled through all the wires on his desk to find Mac's letter. He smiled as he read it.

I hear the season's pretty slow about getting started. That's too bad. I still got sixteen thousand cases of sockeye from last season's catch. And there's a shortage now. With a poor season and the present shortage (let's see, two and two is four, isn't it?) I might make myself an extra ten grand. Not bad for just sitting on my ass (on top of said salmon). This isn't the year for sockeye. Two years from now YOU MARK WHAT I TELL YOU! two years from now, the bottom's going to drop from too much fish.

Be seeing you, Chrissy boy.

P.S. Saw your folks yesterday. Theodore's looking right smart.

Wouldn't surprise me to see him getting out of that wheel chair and walking one of these days. Regards from your mother.

Chris lit another cigarette and stared at Florence through the blue smoke sailing out in her direction. He thought about phoning Lyddy but decided against it. She was probably still asleep.

Once this god damn season was over he would ask her to be his wife. They would live in the big house, have lots of company over and have fun. He would still have Mrs. Fremont come over to clean so Lyddy wouldn't have to work too hard in the house. He wanted her fresh all the time. He didn't want her to be like his mom, worn out at the end of the day. They'd see all the good movies and go to all the square dances. In the fall, he'd take her out to the Stikine flats hunting ducks. They'd go hunting for deer and maybe ride out to the Mainland by themselves, camping for a week or two at a time, hunting for a nice grizzly or black bear to make into a fireplace rug. In the summer, before the season started, they'd go up the Stikine River to Telegraph Creek on one of Jack Jewell's river boats. She'd like the trip. They'd reserve a private stateroom and really have a good time. They wouldn't have any kids for a while. He didn't care much for children. By and by, of course, they would have one or two of them and he hoped they would be boys. He'd name them Chris and Theodore. The oldest would be Theodore. Mom would like that. Dad too.

Chris got up. "Say Florence, do I need a haircut?" Chris could feel his hair straggling down his neck.

"You sure do," Florence said.

Clarence was enjoying his conversation with the young blond stranger when Chris Ballard came into the shop.

"Hi, Clarence," Chris called out. "I see you're busy."

"Yeah, I'm busy, all right," Clarence said, aware of a sulkiness creeping into his disposition.

The stranger who was sitting in the first chair against the wall by the door continued his story. "So this guy keeps telling me that the secret to being a good barber is in the hand. It floored me."

"He's right," Clarence said. He was distracted. He had lost the plane of symmetry in the hair he was clipping. He stopped, dropped the clippers behind him on the shelf and began to comb out the man's hair again.

"Well, I enjoyed myself taking lessons from this guy cause he had a lot on the ball and was sure patient. In fact he lost trade for doing it because he had only one chair and he would let me do the work on the customers while he schooled me. Funny guy, all he preached about was balance of hand—balance this, balance that. Said without it you weren't much of a barber."

"You can't have the jitters and expect to hold the trade," Clarence said, studying his customer's sideburn in the side wall mirror. He could hear Chris talking with Roy Hart and Sam Marcus, watched him pick up a magazine, glance at the cover and flip it open.

That son-of-a-bitch. The lousy, stinking Adonis who gets all the women. Just looking at Chris brought up all the sensations he felt when he encountered Lydia. He would be going along all right, he would feel that he was minding his own business and not bothering anyone, would be almost ready to concede defeat (as unbearable as that was). Then he would see the girl walking down Main Street and the spring would give, all his restlessness would unwind, and his work, his thoughts, his peace would become meaningless and jumbled.

Clarence paid little attention to what the blond stranger was saying. He was hurrying because the shop was filling up. Three waiting and he was only halfway done with the man in the chair, a stranger also.

"You can cut it close," the man indicated as Clarence resumed with his clippers. "There isn't anything to look sharp for in this place."

"You're right," Clarence whispered and laughed.

The man, having gotten Clarence's attention, began to ask the same questions that all newcomers asked about Wrangell. Clarence answered him absentmindedly. Suddenly he knew what he was going to do. He'd slow down, take his time. He'd keep the big shit waiting. He'd take a half hour with each of the customers waiting ahead of Chris. His heart began to throb. He glanced at his wrist watch. If he took his time with these three guys, he would finish up close to twelve. He'd put Chris in the chair, pin the apron around him and then say he was going to run out to get a sandwich. His hands trembled with joy at his plot. He was able to pay attention to the talk around him again. The young blond man had stopped talking about his failure as an apprentice in the barber business and was listening to the men talking near Chris along the rear wall.

"Never saw so many seals," Sam was saying.

"Bastards chewed up half my catch the other afternoon," Roy added. "Although it was pretty small to start with. I wouldn't mind if they chewed on one fish at a time till they finished it. But, no, by God, they do just enough damage so the cannery won't take it, then bite into another one."

"Just goes to show," said Chris, who always maintained that seals were no real scourge, "seals can't catch salmon unless they're gilled in a net."

"Can't you shoot them with a rifle?" asked the stranger. He came over and sat down by Roy.

"By God, you'd be shooting all day. And when you're gill-netting you haven't got the time. Takes all a man can do to pull a shackle in."

"We're using two shackles now even though it's so slow and that's a lot of web over the stern, young man," Sam pointed out.

"I'd sure like to shoot at 'em," the stranger said.

"You couldn't hit 'em. Once they smell a gun around, they duck before you can get a head on them. They're smart as whips." Roy shifted his attention to Chris. "Have you ever noticed the sound the seals make when they duck under the water? They make a ring of bubbles on the water that's damn pretty."

"Who's next?" Clarence asked, flapping his apron.

The young stranger said to Roy, "I'm in no hurry. You want to go next?"

"Well, thank you," Roy said and slid into the chair. He glanced up at the barber. "How are you, Clarence?" he asked.

"O.K." Clarence mumbled. He dawdled away on Roy's head. At the rate he was going it would take three quarters of an hour to cut Roy's shaggy hair. The door opened and another customer entered the shop. Clarence paused to greet the native, an old man with a jutting nose and white hair and shy brown eyes. The native settled down in one of the chairs. Across Main Street, Clarence spied Gwen Olson swinging along in front of the curio shop with Danny running just ahead of her. He waved at his ex-wife and she, as always, stopped and turned and waved at him. This always made Clarence feel good.

"So far I'm only making enough to cover gas and grub," Sam told the blond man. "I'm running like hell all over the place too. But it's the same everywhere. It takes a good days work just to keep expenses paid."

"You're sure using those scissors," Roy commented.

"Your wife won't know you tonight," Clarence said. He was half-way through with Roy's haircut when, glancing up, he saw that Chris was asleep in his chair, his head tilted on his chest, the magazine lying unopened on his lap.

In the crystal-clear mornings, Lyddy liked to stroll along the road. This way she began to see more of the island. In the mornings, the town was fresh and sparkling. Mist lingered along the shore line. Flowers thrived in the yards. People were out, mowing lawns, clipping hedges, picking raspberries. They all said hello to her and she to them.

One morning, shortly after the Fourth of July dance, the front doors of the A&N Hall were open wide. Lyddy peered into the dark cavern of the building. She had never seen it without couples dancing, music blaring and throngs of people standing in the doorway. It took a while for her sun-dazzled eyes to adjust to the dimness. Out of the shadows came Greg Sundberg, the town's undertaker, carrying a push broom.

"Good morning, Ma'am," he said.

"Hello," she responded. She could think of nothing more to say to him. He was wearing a dirty sweatshirt over his protruding belly and he smelled of sweat and rum. Chris told her that Greg and his wife had separated years ago after an argument. Mrs. Sundberg lived by herself in the house they owned on the hill. Greg stayed in the blacksmith shop he used to operate. "Two stubborn people," Chris said. "That's all you can say about the Sundbergs. Both feel the other was wrong, neither will give in and yet they both must regret it for there's never been any talk of a divorce. On holidays, like Christmas and Thanksgiving, Greg is invited to the house for dinner but she never says a word to him the whole time. It's the damnedest thing. They generally have a whole lot of folks up at the same time—to ease the tension, I suppose."

"Well, she's clean and ready for another dance," said Greg, putting the broom into the back of the white panel truck which served as both hearse and ambulance. There wouldn't be another dance until after the season ended, for everyone was too busy.

Once in a while, Vic went walking with Lyddy but she usually had to be back before noon for she had a luncheon date with Dave every day. Most days Vic cooked at the cottage and the three of them ate together. Lyddy was happy for Vic. Dave was a nice, unpretentious man who was more likeable the more she knew him.

Sometimes Lyddy visited Bea Hart who was often alone since Roy was always out fishing. She complained bitterly about the boredom of life in Wrangell and yet she never left the house.

As near as Lyddy could ascertain, Bea was practically alone in her summation of Wrangell. Lyddy discovered this as she became acquainted with the other women in town, with Gwen Olson and Jean Crawford and Babs Bucci. They liked to get together for lunch, which was always sumptuous. A loaf of bread. Cold meats from dinner the night before. Moose patties from breakfast. Hard-boiled eggs. Cheese. Pickles. Jam. Peppers. Mustard. Everyone sat down and made their own sandwiches. These feasts were usually followed with a homemade chocolate cake or blueberry pie.

One night a Coast Guard cutter came to town and Babs, giggling mischievously, herded all of them, including Lyddy, down to Mom's. They danced and drank beer with the sailors. Lyddy enjoyed herself even though it was obvious that Babs, who asked one of the men to escort them all home, had arranged to be dropped off last.

Most afternoons, Lyddy went down to the beach which was just past the graveyard to the south of town. She had bought herself a light-blue, one-piece bathing suit at Mildred's Dress Shop. She loved the water, although it was cold. Flocks of children came, escorted and unescorted. Like everyone else, Lyddy acquired a tan. She found out that Gwen was three months pregnant but it didn't seem to slow her down. She still dashed down the beach and dove into the water. She met Vivian, the waitress at Mom's, who brought her children to the beach. Vi was the best swimmer, staying out in the water longer than anyone. Babs never went in the water. She preferred to stay on the beach, building a fire out of branches that she chopped from the trees along the graveyard and roasting weiners for everyone who came by. Matt Fleming showed up in his white tennis shoes and gave swimming lessons to the kids. In the background, was the channel, silver-sparkling and boat-speckled.

But the days were too long. The women had to go home to make supper and take care of their children. Maybe their husbands would return on one of the fishing boats. Then Lyddy was alone and the hours stretched before her until she would see Chris again.

18

"HEY LYLE," GIFF CALLED DOWN THE HATCH, "bring up that rifle of mine, will you?" Giff went around deck into the galley to pick up his cigarettes from the table. Carl was washing lunch dishes under the hand pump. "How about some nice deer chops tonight?"

"Suits me," Carl said, twisting his head sideways. "You going ashore?"

"Yeah."

Lyle came in with the 270 and Giff eased the bolt back. The cap of a shell slid halfway out of the receiver and the magazine was loaded.

"Well, shit," Giff said, "might as well do something. Help me lower the skiff."

On the aft deck, Clyde, Homer and Mitch were lying belly-down alongside one another, stripped down to their pants. The day was a scorcher.

"By God," Homer grinned, "I'm getting plumb riled up just thinking of that Klootch over there." He had pushed himself up by his hands and was staring at the beach where a native girl was slicing salmon on a table and hanging them up to dry on a curing rack.

"Give me a hand dropping this skiff," Giff said. He knew the half-breed girl, had known her father when he had lived in Wrangell. He had married a native woman and they moved out to this island to set up a fox farm. During their second year the timber wolves had carried off most of the fox pups who were so tame that they were allowed to wander in and out of the coops. A few years later, when they kept all the foxes in their pens, the coops caught fire. Most of the foxes that weren't burned to death had fled terrified into the woods. That ended that business venture. They lived like Eskimos now, curing salmon to eat during the winter.

The men angled the skiff off the net atop the turntable and cast it in the water. Giff scrambled down over the side and set the oars in place.

"Any of you birds want to come along?" The men were staring down at him without interest. They probably wanted him to leave for a while, so they could mope in peace. Probably thinking too of the poor shares to be divided at the end of the season. It was funny, Giff realized, but the men had been more responsive to him lately. They all worked together. Even Clyde, who was usually surly, jumped at his commands. They felt sympathetic towards Giff because the *Verna* wasn't catching any more salmon than any other boat this season.

"Naw, you go ahead," Homer said, blinking his eyes. "I'm too full to move." He slapped his belly. "Just fix it up for me." Homer's gaze swept shoreward, his mouth quivering with mock passion.

"Sure," Giff said. "See you later."

Facing shore, he pushed the skiff slowly ahead. There was plenty of time. They had been lying anchored here since last night. He had donated the few salmon that were in the hold to the family ashore. It wasn't worth the gas to sail all the way to Wrangell with less than half a ton of fish aboard. And if he waited for a good-sized load the first catch would rot.

The water lapped about the hull as he rowed ahead. The girl ran down the beach and helped drag the skiff ashore. She was almost eighteen, a mixture of Norwegian and Tlingit Indian, caramel-skinned and slant-eyed.

"Hi, Giff," she said and resumed her work, splitting the salmon in two with her slim-handled knife. "This is sure nice salmon." Gulls dove down on the water as she scooped up the intestines from the bloody table and tossed them out. She slashed off the head of the next salmon, split it down the back from tail to neck, pinched out the liver and dropped it in a can. With her other hand she yanked out the intestines, scraped off the rest with her knife and then hung up the two sides on the rack.

"Where you going with that gun?" she asked, sharpening the blade against the wood.

"Going to get some fresh meat." He felt some turmoil in his chest and wondered if he should approach her himself. The girl was grateful for the fish and she was developed enough.

"Where's your folks?" Giff asked, sitting down. He'd cool off first and then make the decision.

"They've been up early and now they're taking a nap." She glanced over at the peeling clapboard shack nestled under a horseshoe of spruce near the stream that drained into the inlet. "It's cool in there," she said, lifting the back of her hand to her forehead. "Gosh, it's hot."

It would be a snap. He could ask her to come along with him, show him where the deer were feeding.

He rose, "Want to come along?" There was the right amount of disinterest in his voice.

"Sure," she said with a smile. Her teeth were yellow and bunched in the front of her mouth like a mouse. She wasn't really pretty. He'd known her since she was two. Now her breasts had filled out. She was rather stout for her size and short, coming up to Giff's shoulders.

He followed her around to the back of the house into the dimness of the woods. She ran far ahead of him and pointed to a red squirrel chattering at something across the branches from it. She stared up at the squirrel until Giff's heavy footstep scared it away.

"Look," she said, pointing to some bear tracks that swept by a clump of devil's clubs. "Want to go shooting after bear? Mom likes bear steaks."

"Hell, no. Just deer." The forest was cool and damp. It lay in front of him, a dense mass of trunks, bushes and stillness, a monotonous sea of greenery laying all around him.

As the girl skipped forward, her brown calico skirt and yellow sweater kept catching in the low branches and she had to keep pausing to unhook herself. Lichen covered old stumps and ran around trunks. Gray moss hung from tree to tree. The floor was packed with spruce needles and broken twigs and there was a smell of decay.

Giff heard the gurgling of a stream and almost at once saw it, to their right, falling three feet down a crevice of rock into a deep pool. He paused, his shirt collar soaked with sweat. "Hey" he called. "Let's take ten." Under the shelf of submerged rock he saw a school of trout—red-spotted Dolly Vardens.

"Do you like it here?" Giff asked.

She removed her shoes and dipped her bare feet in the icy cold water.

"Hey, you'll scare the fish away."

"Oh heck," she laughed. "They're used to bears and deer splashing across. They won't be frightened."

Giff waited for the ripples to settle and saw that the fish were still in the same place. "That's the real sign," he said. "Just wait until the salmon start coming upstream. Those Vardens will head up, past the spawning beds, then come back and gorge themselves on the eggs when the salmon are dead."

"I've seen them right in this pool gulping the salmon fry when they start drifting down," she said, staring into the clear, pure water. "I like it here and I don't," she said. "It gets pretty awful sometimes. But when someone comes to visit me from Wrangell I like it here. I know that he must love me to come all the way here just to visit me."

"And who is that?" Giff asked.

She rose without answering and ran behind a mass of ferns, returning with a handful of red huckleberries. She tossed one into the water and in a moment it was gone, in a slurp of water that smoothed out quickly.

"Look at them!" Giff said. "By God, I should have brought a rod along with me."

She tossed the berries here and there. The trout were everywhere, swift as greased lightening. The surface of the water grew turbulent.

"Let's go," he said.

"I think I should go back. There's so much work and I'd be in trouble if Papa should wake up and not find me."

"All right," Giff said. He watched her drop down beside him to put on her shoes. It would be a simple matter to reach over and pull back her dress. She was probably naked underneath. Just pull the dress back over her knees...

While he was still thinking about this, she rose and ran down a tiny avenue between the trees, disappearing in the thick stand of pines.

Giff moved away from the stream and slumped down against a trunk, one leg curled up underneath him. It wasn't any use to try and climb to a ridge where he could command a decent view. The forest was too crowded. Windfalls lay about him, rotting, the branches caved-in, the trunks moss-blanketed.

He was afraid suddenly and gripped his rifle a little tighter. But that was artificial courage so he forced himself to drop it on the ground beside him. He leaned back and closed his eyes.

A blue jay screeched overhead. That was all. There was no other sound. He strained his hearing as he closed his eyes again. As if from a long distance, he heard the sound of the stream and far ahead, the hammering of a woodpecker. He opened his eyes again. Thin shafts of sunlight filtered through the trees not ten feet away. He wasn't scared here. There were no grizzlies on this island; it wasn't the Mainland.

He saw the ears first. Behind a thick cluster of huckleberries, not twenty feet away, the ears flicked and waggled. Must be gnats bothering it, for he knew his presence had not been detected. In a moment the ears disappeared and Giff waited. He heard the thump-thump-thump of loping, syncopated hoofs and then there was silence. The forest crashed in upon him again. He waited ten minutes in a tense savage knot, his body breaking out in a sweat. This was the first time he'd been out alone in the woods since the grizzly got Theodore.

His foot was falling asleep from all the weight pressing on it. It began to tingle. Carefully he stretched out his leg. He was actually shaking when he lifted the rifle to his shoulder and waited for the deer to emerge in the open break in the foliage. It was a doe—he knew because he hadn't seen any velvety horns between its ears—but there was a good possibility that a buck might be following the doe for they banded together most of the year.

Giff crept through the trees and around patches of prickly devils club and reached the top of a knoll that looked down upon a small basin. He sat down again, just below the crest, in a slight depression where the thick trees afforded a blind. His heart was pounding and he was gasping for breath.

The doe sauntered out into the open and Giff froze. The slightest movement would startle her. She turned around and peered in his direction but didn't see him. She began nibbling on the leaves of a huckleberry bush, glanced up, moved over to munch some dogwood, then skunk cabbage. Evidently not very hungry, she settled daintily to the ground.

Giff brought the rifle slowly to his shoulder and was glad the safety was off. At that precise moment, as if a shadow had crossed its path, the doe startled. She turned and faced up the slope, staring straight at Giff. Giff looked into her eyes. The deer was puzzled, not sure what she was seeing. The two were almost in a trance, eyes upon eyes, the deer's curious and large and lovely, Giff's focused and unblinking.

The doe lifted up first her left foreleg, then the other in the same delicate hesitant manner. She appeared confused and unsure. Giff, half-rising, aimed the rifle at a point between her neck and shoulder.

He missed. She went crashing into the undergrowth, her ears tilted back, in two amazing high bounces that carried her far out of sight. The echo of the gun's roar went on and on in the thick gloom of the forest.

Giff sat down stiffly, ejected the shell and slammed the bolt forward. He was tired suddenly. He hadn't had a drop to drink for a week and his distress was mounting daily. He headed back through the woods, knowing that the crew on the *Verna* would jeer at him for returning empty-handed.

Clyde, Homer and Lyle heard the shot as they stood on deck, watching the half-breed girl row the seine skiff towards the *Verna*.

"I go first," Homer said.

"Jesus, you guys got nerve making her row that skiff over here," Lyle said. "Suppose Giff comes back?" His tone was incredulous.

"We'll screw her and then row her ashore right smart," Homer replied. "If Giff shot a buck, it'll take him an hour to gut it and pack it out."

"Hey," Lyle stammered as the girl neared the *Verna*, "I'm going to take that skiff right back and go help Giff lug the deer down."

The girl, rowing with her back to the bow of the wide skiff, banged into the hull as she swung it in alongside the stern. Clyde took the painter while Homer leaned over and helped the girl aboard.

"Hi, fellows," she chirped happily. "Gosh you woke up my folks with all that shouting. What did you want?"

"Oh, we just wanted to talk to you," Homer said, his eyes bulging with lechery. "How about some coffee?"

"Sure. Gee, this is a nice boat."

"I'm going ashore to get Giff," Lyle insisted.

"Suit yourself," Clyde said with indifference.

"But I have to be right back. I want to dress all that salmon before it spoils."

"Hell, that's fresh caught, honey. Come on," Clyde said, taking her by the hand.

Homer put his hand on her breast. "Let's go below. I got a pint stowed away."

"Gee," she said, laughing with excitement. She did not resist as the two men steered her down the hatch.

Lyle swore to himself as he swung his legs over the rail and jumped into the skiff. He stood up to row ashore, hoping that he wouldn't be too late to help Giff. Giff was sure acting different lately.

———

Giff was just emerging from the forest when he saw, out in the channel beyond the bay, the exhaust of a boat heading out towards Sumner Strait. He recognized it as one of the Fish and Wildlife cruisers on patrol. A moment later he saw Lyle, standing in the shade near the edge of the forest.

"You didn't get anything?" Lyle asked. He looked both surprised and disappointed.

"How the hell did you get here?" Giff asked. "I missed one. I saw a doe and missed it." He was bothered by the exhaust smoke.

"That's too bad," Lyle said, smiling sympathetically which annoyed Giff.

The skiff lay beached in front of the cabin. The Norwegian and his wife stood at the slicing table beside it, working on the salmon.

"Where's the girl?" Giff asked.

"She's on the *Verna*. I took the skiff back."

He and Lyle braced themselves fore and aft against the gunwale and pushed it forward a half foot.

"On the *Verna*?" Giff felt a jab of anger. He steadied his voice. "And who the hell told her to take the skiff?" He was mad now. He clenched the gunwale and stared into the boat, his teeth grating together. "What are they doing, raping her?"

"Something like that," Lyle said. He busied himself exerting all of his strength to set the skiff afloat. They clambered aboard and Lyle hastily dropped the oars between the locks.

"They've both got her down below."

"Who?"

"By golly," Lyle said, "there's three of them with that girl now. Mitch was sleeping in his bunk when Clyde and Homer took her down the companion-way."

Giff sat on the stern thwart, checking the sweet onrush of his rage, for he wanted to save it up for when he accosted the men. He stood up and peered past the anchored *Verna*, across the sparkling motionless inlet towards the stream of white exhaust, still visible.

A sudden inspiration seized him.

"Hurry up!" Giff shouted to Lyle. "We're going to follow that bastard."

"Who?"

"That Wildlife boat. They know where the salmon are! The bastards are heading out somewhere right now and I don't want to lose them."

Lyle dug the oar blades into the water, then whooshed them out again, the shafts bending as he applied all his strength to the task.

"What about the girl?" he asked, racing the blades back into the water. The skiff jerked over the surface at a fast clip.

"God damn," Giff muttered, thinking of the time that would be lost returning the girl to shore. This gave him real ammunition. He ought to fire Clyde and Homer, the sons of bitches, the dirty rotten pricks.

The *Verna* loomed up beside them and Giff jumped over the rail, using one hand to steady him. He hoped all the men were below deck so he would have time to execute his plan. He climbed up to the controls and started the diesel.

"Lyle," he shouted below, snapping out the order, "start winching up the anchor."

He lowered himself down the vertical ladder behind the deck house and bumped into Clyde emerging from the companionway.

"What's going on?" Clyde asked, with amiable curiosity.

"We're shoving off. Help Lyle get that anchor aboard."

Clyde frowned with bewilderment. "Jesus, Giff, didn't Lyle tell you?"

"Yeah! Get forward and turn to!"

Mitch came stooping out of the companionway and Giff turned on him. "Where's Carl and Homer?"

"Homer's below," Mitch said. "He's pretty busy."

"He's what?"

"He's long-johning that Klootch."

Giff stuck his head in the companionway and shouted so he could be heard above the clamor of the engine: "God damn you, Homer, come up here."

"Right-ho, skipper," Homer's voice was squeaky.

The girl scrambled up the steps first, wide-eyed and frightened. "Oh, I'm sorry, Mr. Weeks," she said. "I'm sorry," she repeated. The smell of whiskey was strong on her breath.

"God damn, here I am in a hurry to shove off and I don't know what to do with you."

"Oh, gee," she cried. She looked across at the shore longingly, as if she would never set foot on it again. "Oh, I'm sorry. Those men, they . . ."

"Mitch," Giff snarled. The men came skittering around the deck house. "Mitch get this girl aboard the skiff and row her ashore. I'm in a hurry. We'll pick you up tomorrow."

"What?" Mitch asked, confounded.

"You heard me," Giff said. He darted across the rail and was relieved to see the Fish and Wildlife boat still in view. "We're following that tug now!"

All that afternoon, the *Verna*, staying about three miles behind, tailed the Wildlife cruiser. From this distance they could barely see the exhaust fumes, but the boat itself was plainly visible. Giff had calmed down, his anger overridden by his pride at the feat he was undertaking and his self-assurance revitalized by the manner in which he had disposed of the girl with no loss of time.

"Poor Mitch," Giff chuckled.

"What do you mean?" Homer protested, grief-stricken. "Why didn't you let me take her ashore?"

Since he had told them of his plans, the men were elated. The small space of the pilot house was fully occupied, with Lyle and Homer both standing in it staring out the windows. Giff piloted the seiner, keeping her throttled full speed ahead, for they were losing ground with each passing hour.

"I'll bet that son-of-a-gun can go twenty knots if pressed," Lyle said in wonder.

"She's just cruising now," Giff said, his hands sweating around the spokes.

"This takes the cake," Homer giggled. "By God, the mouse is chasing the cat."

"We'll get a load of fish," Giff said, turning to Homer.

The *Verna* was running close off shore while the Wildlife cruiser was in mid-channel, the hull barely visible now as the gap between them lengthened.

"Take the wheel," Giff said to Homer, "and keep your eye on them."

"Do you think they've spotted us?" Clyde asked as Giff strode into the galley.

"I wouldn't be surprised," Giff said. He was completely nonchalant and this pleased him immensely. "Got any fresh coffee, Carl?"

"In just about a minute," Carl said, jumping up and going over to the range. Even Carl was looking up to Giff again, as in the good old days.

They were able to shorten the gap at seven that evening when the Wildlife boat suddenly idled her engines and drifted into a trough. The water flamed with the colors of the sunset.

"They've stopped," Homer announced from the pilot house.

Giff hurried forward and surveyed the craft with his binoculars.

"They're stopping to eat," Homer said. "They've got to stop so's they can all eat together, chummy-like."

"Naw," Giff said. "They're radioing their position and they can't hear above the engine."

"They got plenty of time to pin a fine on someone," Clyde declared. "Uncle Sam's taking care of those boys."

Giff said, "Cut her down to half throttle, Homer. We might even have to pass them if they take too long."

"You think we can get away with it?" Lyle inquired. He had asked this question about once every hour since they had started on the chase. Each time Giff replied, "We're going to sure as hell try."

But this time he was irked and pounced upon the boy. "If you ask that one more time I'm going to brain you. How the hell do I know?"

All through the short night, the *Verna*, running no lights, followed the Wildlife's mast light.

"They're heading to Behm Canal," Giff surmised as he flicked a flashlight on a chart in the darkened galley. "There's lots of streams there all right. Damn, I sure hope there's fish there.

"Why else would they be going there?" Carl asked.

At the first light of dawn, they took the *Verna* out of gear and let the Wildlife boat get away.

"There's four good-sized streams down there and I know them all," Giff said. "We'll wait here, have breakfast and give them a chance to patrol the streams and leave. If they should happen to switch course and catch us near one of those streams, we'll tell them we're heading back to Wrangell to fuel up." Giff yawned. "Lyle, climb up to the bridge and keep a lookout. If there's salmon in those streams, there might be signs of them close to shore."

"Blueblacks!" Lyle shouted. "Christ, look at 'em over there."

Water spilled down into a round flat pool along the shore that was encircled by trees, affording a natural haven for salmon gathering to make the ascent up their parent stream. The fish were milling about in a vast school, whacking the water as they flipped out and jittered on their tails, as if conditioning themselves for the brutal climb upstream.

"Sockeyes, all right," Giff said, stepping out on deck. "Must be a headwater lake up there somewhere." He went forward and opened the pilot house door. "Clyde, shut her down. This looks like it."

The stillness fell like guilt upon the crew of the *Verna* as the diesel was idled. The morning was keen. The water was black along the wooded beach. The sky above the tree tops was violet and apricot. Spots of crimson, like blood, floated on the surface of the channel where it was touched by the rising sun. As they drifted closer to shore, the surface showed blue and brown where the horde of salmon congregated.

"They're massed over there," Homer shouted in glee. "Look at all them jumpers!"

"Keep your shirt on," Giff cautioned. Standing beside the pilot house, he surveyed the stretch of channel forward as far as he could see. No boats were approaching. "We're going to wait until tonight to nab them," he decided. "If we start at evening that should give us plenty of time to see what we're doing."

From the uptop controls, Giff guided the *Verna* around and into a tiny crescent cove and they dropped anchor. "You boys get some shut-eye," Giff ordered. "We'll have to work fast when we start. I don't want to lose that seine in the dark."

In the galley, Giff checked their position on the chart to familiarize himself with the layout of the shore. "Damn," he said to Carl with a scowl, "that's a rocky place. Plenty of depth for the web all right, but we're going to have to be careful, just skim around the edge."

Giff went below to his bunk. He was pooped. He wished now that he hadn't started on this wild goose chase. They'd located salmon, all right. But by God he had kept his nose clean so far this season. He didn't have any fines for illegal fishing. He didn't want to mar his record this year. He was tired of it. It was a God damn strain making the *Verna* the top boat in Wrangell every year.

He rubbed his eyes and squatted on the edge of his bunk. He remembered how frantic he used to get if he had just one bad week. The thrill of pulling into the cannery, scuppers awash with a heavy load, was worth all the chances and the hard work. He must be getting old or chickenshit, he decided.

"I got to hand it to you, Giff," Homer said as he lay on the top bunk stripped to his shorts, his head cushioned by his locked hands. Homer hung his head over the edge and stared down at Giff, who was yanking off his boots. "You sure outsmarted those bastards. Wait'll the guys ashore see us come in with a full load."

"We haven't got them yet," Giff murmured and laid back.

At seven that night they corked their first set. The sun was still high above the ridgeline of the island to the west and the air was hot. Because they were one man short, Carl was in the seine skiff. Homer passed the seine net's hand line down to Carl from the stern. Carl secured it to the skiff and untied the skiff from the *Verna*.

The seine net spilled over the stern into the water while Giff, on the bridge, drove the *Verna* at full speed in a circle. In a few minutes, he had closed off the circle, meeting up with the stationary skiff. Beneath them in the water, the net lay unfurled, a cylinder of mesh. The bottom of the net was weighted with lead, the top made buoyant with cork floats, creating a floating cylinder of mesh. Now they turned on the power roller which pulled on the purse line which ran along the bottom of the net. By pulling this tight, they created a bag of net, like a purse, which held the fish. Carl gathered as much of the cork line as he could on the skiff to tighten the bag in which the salmon were being caught. The men worked furiously, piling the loose seine onto the turntable, glancing over the side for the bubbles that give some clue as to the size of the catch.

The water below began to thrash as the trapped mass of salmon were brought closer and closer to the surface. The gypsy head rumbled as the brailing net was swung into the water. It scooped the fish out of the water like a giant shovel, dumping them down into the hold where they whacked and thumped as they dropped onto their dead companions. When the brail had scooped out most of the fish, Clyde hoisted the load neatly over the boom and Homer released the purse line, sending the remaining fish tumbling into the hold, flipping and slithering over the other bodies.

Once, on the third set, the web snagged on a rock and they had to abandon all the salmon they'd caught while putting the *Verna* in reverse to release the seine without tearing it. But with no other mishaps, the hold was filling up quickly. They worked clear into the darkness, making the last set by pure memory and guess work in the dark. "All right," Giff said, "one last time and we're through."

He had ordered this last set against his own better judgment. He knew he could be stretching a good thing too far. Just before darkness fell, he had scanned the shoreline for the tide was running out. The water level had receded from the beach at least twenty feet. Giff rechecked his chart to determine the closest point where they could drop the web close to shore but still have sufficient depth for the boat. He settled on a hundred yards, which should give him leeway for drift.

The land was cool and sweet. A shaft of crimson streamed out where the sun had set and hovered above them in the sky. Stars lay sprinkled to either side of it, shining softly as they did in summer with no cold or wind to make them waver.

Giff remained on the bridge just long enough to search the canal north and south to see if any boat lights were approaching. They were completely blacked out and it occurred to him that the patrol boats might do the same if they were looking for creek robbers.

When the brailing of the last load was almost done, Giff and Lyle turned to hauling in the slack of the web. Homer was in the hold spreading out the fish by stamping them with his feet. The seine was just about all hauled in when a light shudder ran through the hull of the *Verna*.

"By God," someone gasped, "what was that?"

"We've hit bottom," Homer yelled.

Giff ordered Clyde to release the heavily-loaded brailing net back into the water for fear of overturning the *Verna*. He ran around the railing, pointing his flashlight over the side, and was perplexed for there was water all around them and the boat was perfectly upright.

"I guess we just scraped a rock," Giff said. "Go down to the engine room, Clyde, and see if there's any damage. Lyle, get down in the foc'sle."

A part of the web was still over the side and Carl was still in the skiff, standing on top of the pile of cork line he had pulled in.

"What was that?" he asked.

"We hit something," Giff said. He was puzzled. In the dark it was next to impossible to know just what had happened. It should be deep enough unless the chart was wrong. Somehow he felt that disaster was inevitable, part of the lousy luck he'd been having all season.

"No damage that I can see," Clyde said as he returned on deck.

Lyle rounded the deck house, "No leaks. Everything's ship-shape, skipper."

"Good," Giff said but he felt no relief. "Let's get the web in and haul off."

The men powered up the balance of the seine and hoisted the skiff on deck. Giff climbed up to the uptop controls. The *Verna*'s diesel roared into life and Giff cautiously throttled her forward.

Nothing happened!

He kicked the throttle bar to quarter speed. The low stern lashed out foam but they didn't move.

Sweating, Giff shoved the gear in reverse and throttled her hard.

Nothing. They were stuck on something. The prop was revolving but no power was being generated. The boat hardly shuddered.

"Lyle, get that fathometer from the gear locker and see what depth there is."

The marker had no more than plunked into the water before it stopped.

"Jesus!" Lyle exclaimed in disbelief and all the men gawked over the side.

"Scatter around!" Giff roared. "You want to tip her over?" He hurried down from the bridge and glanced over the side. "We're on a rock," he mumbled. "We must be wedged on a God damn rock." He turned to Clyde, "What time is it?"

Clyde shoved his wrist watch under Giff's flashlight for Giff to read. Just like him, Giff reflected, anger pricking his equilibrium. He's glad this is happening. The bastard's tickled to death.

"One-thirty," Giff read. "That's God damn swell. Now we'll have to wait for low tide to see just what the hell's happened."

The tide reached its lowest point around three-fifteen in the morning, just before daybreak, although shortly before that it became obvious that the *Verna* was straddled on a rock that jutted up out of the water in the shape of a crib. On either side of the crib stood what appeared like a good draft of water.

"We had to drift right over this son of a bitch," Giff snorted as he hoisted himself over the side on a line and jumped down to the rock.

Stooping, he peered at the firmly embedded keel, running his flashlight along the copper bottom aft to the rudder, looking for any splinters and abrasions. He shook his head in disgust. While they were busily loading the hold during the ebbing tide, the boat must have settled into the crib for there was no damage that he could see. Giff stood up and faced Clyde who had climbed down after him. "Hull's scraped some, but nothing serious." He knew the bastard just wanted to see how badly he had wrecked the boat. Being around Clyde at a time like this made Giff's flesh crawl with hatred and shame.

Clyde took the flashlight from Giff and began to inspect the keel himself with a studious look as if he could somehow solve the problem.

"Douse that light!" Giff bellowed, his voice quivering with disgust and anger.

"O.K., O.K. skipper."

"You want to have someone spot us?"

Suddenly Giff was flooded with an attack of dizziness that made his legs buckle. He wobbled over to the hull and leaned against it. Still in a daze, he watched Clyde climb up the side of the hull with the aid of the line. He could hear the water lapping around the crib, the men's voices growing quieter top side as their excitement waned, the plops in the water as Carl tossed garbage over the side, returning to his routine galley work.

For a moment his brain filled with the image of a vicious bear. He could hear his own heavy breathing, feel the ache of his arches in his boots, his wet, slimy hands. He must have stood there at least a full minute leaning against the hull.

"You boys hungry?" he heard Carl call from the galley.

"You ain't just a wolfing," Homer shouted.

He stood there trembling, thinking of a friend of his who died from the fits because he had quit drinking abruptly. But he wasn't getting the fits or D.T.'s. This was a feeling he felt sometimes at night after a long day's drinking when he would trudge up to his room in the hotel and sit on the edge of his bed in a kind of numb stupor. Everything seemed hopeless and insignificant. He would look around at the hotel room, where he would spend the rest of his days, at the wash stand, the two water glasses perched on the glass shelf above it, the white towels hanging from their rods. He would feel the turmoil of whiskey in him and the horror of the grizzly bear, rearing up on its haunches, red-mouthed and claw-thrashing, all mixed in with the hopelessness and the fading memory of a wonderful man. And it all converged upon him until he wished that he had drunk more, that he had not come up to his room when the bar closed but had gone instead to one of the parties where he could get himself stupid drunk.

"Quiet! Quiet, you guys," Homer called out. "I hear something."

"Sounds like a cold engine," Clyde said, as the sound of grinding gears became distinguishable. "Those boys were in a hurry to get started."

"Jesus!" Giff whispered to himself.

"No lights! No smoking up there!" Giff shouted to the men on deck. He grabbed onto the line dangling from above and walked himself up the curving hull. "Quiet!" Giff ordered as he heaved himself on deck.

The sound had grown weaker, as if heading the opposite direction. "I think they're going north," Giff said, more to console himself than anything else.

"They better be," Clyde said. "Look!" He pointed towards the shore.

Faint washes of red stained the sky above the treetops.

The engine retched once, coughed again as it missed. But the sound grew unmistakably nearer.

"That boy's not hitting on all fours," Clyde said, his keen mechanic's ear acute even at a time like this.

The minutes dragged by. The fine blue light of the dawn slipped over the trees and filtered out across the channel. They could see the island clearly now.

And out in the center of the channel, not more than five hundred yards away, they could see the sharp bow of a boat. A stream of exhaust smoke trailed out behind it.

"That's no fishing boat," Clyde said.

"I'll be a son of a bitch," Giff stammered. It was the same Wildlife cruiser that he had tailed all last night. The boat, its cabin windows flashing with the first real rays of the sun, angled straight towards them, moving forward at a tormentingly slow speed, as if amazed at what it had spotted.

19

IN THE PRIME OF THEIR LIVES, the Pacific salmon sweep in from the ocean heading towards the streams where they were born. It is a great migration, a pursuit of procreation and death. Against all odds, despite terrible hardships, they will climb to the places where they were hatched, there to spawn and die. The salmon have no other choice; nature plugs up all the loopholes. So they sweep in, stopping only briefly to feed on the plankton and candlefish rife on the shelves and banks of the Inside Passage. On they come, the reds and dogs, the cohos and kings and humphies, determined to reach their native tributaries.

But there are many obstacles. First they must bypass the fish traps submerged along the shoreline, ranging out to sea into depths of fifty and sixty feet. These traps are constructed of underwater wire fencing, shaped like a funnel at the start but slowly pressing the fish in towards the heart of the trap. Salmon, when encountering an obstacle, will look for an opening rather than turn around, so they swim forward, passing through a slit in the center of the wire wall, and enter the enclosed spiller. There is no escape from it. They will mill about in the spiller, rolling and turning, until a tender pulls alongside and brails them out.

Those that have escaped the traps are plagued by beach seiners, a method of fishing that is so simple that even the women use it. During low tide, the fisherman strings out one end of the net to a buoy placed at the water line, then stretches the web to shore and secures it to a tree or rock. The lead line holds the bottom down while the cork line floats the seine. As the current flows in, the seine bellies out in an arc and the salmon swimming close to shore searching for the outlet of a stream or river get stuck by the gills in the mesh. When the tide recedes again, the fisherman rows out and extracts the salmon from the net and drops them into the skiff.

On they come, the one-way passage of no return. They are driven by an obsession, both Herculean and demonic. As they struggle towards their destinations, their appearances change. They loose their silver sides, develop humps on their backs. Their heads become more elongated and their teeth more needle-like.

There are still more obstacles. Seals twist and curve through the schools of milling fish, nabbing one right out of the middle of the pack. The silver and king salmon are sometimes tempted by a lure dangling off a trolling line or the bright scaly side of a herring, spinning and curling on a hook, and are hoisted up out of the water by a skilled rodsman. Still others are encircled by seine nets and driven up to the surface in a mass as the seine net below and around them is closed into a purse shape, from there to be brailed into the hold of the seiner.

But there is a period of freedom once a week for them, between the hours of 4 P.M. Saturday and 6 P.M. Monday when all fishing is suspended to allow a portion of the salmon to proceed up the streams to spawn, assuring future generations of fish. The salmon who reach the mouths of their native streams and creeks and rivers lounge there for a few days before proceeding. It's as if they are fortifying themselves for the hardships ahead. They turn and roll and splash out of the water, cutting capers, spanking their tails against the surface.

All at once, as though by a prescribed signal, the salmon begin the ascent. They leap over the minor falls of water, thrusting forward and upward, never ceasing. Once they have started on the final stretch of their journey in the fresh-water streams their appetites disappear, their throats begin to narrow and their stomachs shrink, enabling them to overcome the temptation to return to the well-stocked feeding grounds of the straits and ocean. They grow savage with their determination, hurtling themselves at cliffs and ledges, sometimes entering pools and stretches of water so shallow that parts of their bodies are exposed to the open. The female is plump because of the eggs she carries. The male is gaunt. His head flattens, his eyes become sunken, large rakish white teeth appear on both jaws, the upper jaw hooks over the lower. The rocks and falls batter their flesh as they hurtle up and over them. Once gleaming with silver, the once magnificent fish are ugly, their scales scraped off, their fins battered.

Many are flipped out of the streams by natives standing on shore fishing by hand or with nets. Others are swiped out onto the bank by bears, to be gnawed and left for the otter and mink to finish. Others die from bruises and sheer exhaustion. Still others, stuck in shallow waters, are choked out by their companions and die flapping on the banks.

Yet on they go, gallant in their martyrdom, smashed, emaciated, disfigured, with fungus beginning to grow on their red and black and olive bodies. They press on, for as long as it takes them, day after day, until they find the place of their birth. There they rest for a few days, before using their heads and tails to scoop out elongated cavities in the gravel beds in which to deposit the eggs and milt. Not long afterwards, the spawning grounds are awash with floating dead carcasses, some of them borne back down by the descending waters that they had conquered.

The sudden change was amazing. It was at least as good as the 1933 season. Only because it had started late, it was too late for the fishing season of 1936 to become a record-breaker. But that didn't matter because as soon as the salmon arrived, the people were overjoyed. Everyone set to work catching and processing salmon.

During these days the weather was haunting and beautiful. The sun was immense, at all hours, climaxing its swing across the sky with spectacular sunsets, the colors of which hung in the air long after the sun disappeared behind the islands.

Sea gulls and sea pigeons swarmed around the three canneries in a never-ceasing whirl of delirium, screeching as they dove, gorging themselves with the gutted intestines of salmon flung out into the bay from the cannery's dressing rooms. All along the docks men worked furiously under the hot sun, pitching fish from the holds of the boats, loading and unloading freighters, tallying salmon as they were conveyed into the cannery, washing down the seiners and trap-tenders and scows after they had been unloaded.

The newcomers pitched in wholeheartedly. They had come up to make money and now they were working twelve to fifteen hours a day at union wages. But more than that they were beginning to get the feel of the town. At nights after work they went to the crowded bars, to the night picnics, to the many parties, awed by the friendliness and independence of the people of Wrangell.

Wrangell is the second stop in Southeastern for steamers from America. As the steamer rounds Elephant Nose and heads towards the island, it toots its arrival whistle and the tourists flock on deck to view the next locale. They can see small gill-netting boats spread all over the channel around the mouth of the Stikine River, with their nets stretched out over their stern and submerged in the icy depths of the sun-flecked water. One of the fishermen waves at the cluster of passengers on deck. The steamer's wake, rolling through the colored buoys and corks, pitches the fishing boats as they drift with the tide. Others watch Wrangell come into view, a crescent-shaped spread of wooden buildings and houses. As the steamer approaches the dock, they can see many boats of various designs and dimensions, puttering in and out of the harbor and around the piling of the canneries' docks. It is very picturesque, indeed.

The Clinton dock is sprinkled with a good assortment of men, women, children and dogs. Sea gulls sweep overhead, the young white-bellied, the old ones discolored and broader in the chest. The small three-piece band on the steamer strikes up a lively tune. The winch begins to clatter, and as the tourists worm their way through the crowd, the sun beats down upon their backs. The tourists don't mind the heat and confusion. Instead they thrill with anticipation at this chance to view the ancient and wondrous sights of the north. Dust rises on Main Street as a few cars and trucks pass by. The passengers stop at the hotel bar on the corner to refresh themselves with a drink.

They ask the bartender how to find the totem poles, the curio shop, the salmon canneries. A party of four decides to visit the Ballard Cannery and they hoof it up the incline before the Federal Building, admiring the lush triangular patch of lawn that stretches down to Main Street.

The sun flashes on the water to their left. A tender races out to sea, leaving behind a wide glistening wake.

At the north end of town the party of tourists files in through the wire gate that leads down to the mess building. So far they are not much impressed. No totems, nothing very Alaskan. Just some shacks and some middle-class houses about the Federal Building. Although they knew better, they were still disappointed. They are moist from the heat and wish they were back in the bar. They enter the shed uneasily. But in a moment the uneasiness disappears as they realize they are tourists and have a perfect right to inspect the premises for Alaska depends upon their business. They stroll through the great cluttered shed. The mad bustling pace of the cannery begins to affect them and they become more curious.

Long rows of shiny unlabeled tins are cooling in the shed on long metal trays. The tins pop as the temperature of the cooked cans becomes equal with that of the air. A lift truck whines back and forth, bringing steaming tins from the retort pressure cookers in the fish house out to cool. Drays rumble on the dock as longshoremen pull the cases of salmon to a freighter docked at the far end. Inside the fish house, the machinery is humming. The tourists are amazed at the great number of salmon flowing down through the belts. Between twenty and thirty women, aproned and gloved, are scattered here and there among the machines, dressing the salmon and filling the tins that the machines have missed. The tourists head across the shed into the warehouse where they see several groups of men and women hand-packing the cooled, labeled tins in the cases, gluing the covers, stacking the cases all along the walls in tall tiers.

They inspect the open T-shaped dock where the boats are unloading the fresh fish and leave the cannery. They head back down to Main Street, have another drink and go on down the road to Shake's Island to see the totem poles. They are tired and a little bit disappointed. The heat is depressing. They are hoping that the next stop, Petersburg, will be a little wilder.

The steamers brought the mail. Every time a steamer docked, the people of Wrangell flocked to the Federal Building, sometimes arriving before Tim Regis and his staff had finished sorting the mail. People thirsted for news from their friends and relatives in the outside world. Often they tore open the envelopes and read the letters standing there in the building or sitting down outside on the steps.

Chris usually got a letter every week from his sister or Mom. The letters were all about the same, mentioning the weather in Seattle and Theodore's health. This week's letter was from Patty:

Dad is looking much better lately. He doesn't seem to have to rely on his pills as much. The doctor says he is making a remarkable recovery.

We miss you, darling. Aren't you ever going to break down and admit that you're lonely up there all by yourself? Are you still interested in the schoolteacher?

I wish you would come and visit. Can't you get it in your thick skull that Mom and Dad want to see you. Yes, even Dad. He's burning to be able to talk to you about the cannery and so many other things. He won't admit this aloud but he reads your letters over and over again. Try to be a little more specific about what's going on up there, especially at the cannery—Dad lives for those notes. Please, Chris. Please, please, please!

They would never learn, Chris thought, as he trudged back to the cannery. They were the ones that were wrong. Just because Theodore was paralyzed and helpless for the first time in his life, the women had decided to leave Wrangell forever. It was a bad decision. He had argued against it. There was certainly no reason for him to encourage it.

————————

Visiting was unthinkable. He didn't want to see his dad, once a vital and dynamic man, now a fretful and bitter invalid. There was no chance for an alliance between them. Theodore saw to that. He had forced Chris to stick up for himself, to learn his own lessons. He bawled him out whenever he did something wrong, in a loud, bitter voice that cracked with loathing.

As Chris stared out at the channel on his way back to the cannery, reliving those arguments, he realized he didn't even know the color of his dad's eyes. Even though he had struggled to maintain eye contact during those discussions, there was so much inner pandemonium going on between them, that it took all the grit he possessed to maintain a casual, off-handed air that was completely insincere.

As Chris walked to his cannery he passed a few people heading for the Federal Building to collect their mail.

"See you got some mail," they remarked. Their hasty excited voices held the hope that they would be fortunate as well.

————————

Long after Lyddy read her mother's letter, the words kept clinging to her mind. It would be so easy to just go home for a few months, to get her bearings straight, to make up her mind once and for all. Yet she felt a chill of despair.

She walked down to the Federal Building. She decided to return to the cottage before reading Edna's letter. She didn't want to open it and yet she had hurried home, as though to hoard its contents, hoping it would provide her with a vision of San Francisco with its Chinatown and the Opera House, Ransohoffs, Telegraph Hill, the ferries.

But her hopes were dashed when she read the words written in her mother's loose, curving penmanship.

Now you listen, Lydia, you have stayed in Alaska long enough. It's become a joke. Your term teaching in Wrangell is over—it's been five weeks to this date. And I insist that you come back home. What has happened to you? Are you having an affair with this man, Chris?

I must be frank. We are at our wit's end. I know it must all seem romantic and strange up there but what makes you think it will last? There's excitement and romance down here too. Don has been calling me at least once a week to see if you have started back yet. Why aren't you answering his letters?

Lydia, you know you couldn't ask for a better man than Don. He's handsome and has a wonderful future ahead of him. But that's your problem to thrash out. I just want you down here. Your father has been like a changed man since you've been away—he's not himself, Lydia. He's disappointed and misses you. I expect you to be on the first boat south after you receive this letter.

Lyddy folded the letter, following the original creases, and slipped it back in the envelope. Her mood was heavy. Underneath the sharp words, she could hear her mother's desperation and her father's sadness.

And the word "affair" stung. She had been so happy with Chris that their intimacy had never been a source of anxiety. But now she considered it from Edna's point of view as something sordid and furtive and probably doomed to disappointment.

In the bedroom, Vic, who had been asleep most of the day, coughed again. Her cold had gotten worse. She had a rolling cough that was heavy as lead. Vic was not herself lately. She should have been happy being chased by a man like Dave with serious intentions. But Vic was in love with Clarence. She never mentioned his name anymore but it was clear she was miserable.

Lyddy wished that life was as simple for her as it seemed to be for Chris. He never questioned her decision to stay in Wrangell. There was no doubt in his mind about it. He'd even informed her that she wasn't going to teach this fall, that he had other plans for her. Yes, he'd actually asked her to be his wife. They were just waiting for the season to end so he would have time to concentrate on the next phase of his life.

Lyddy stepped outside and sat down on the stoop. She decided to stay home and think instead of going swimming with the other women. Kids played on the road below the yard. Mr. Eaton was trimming the edge of the lawn by the Crawford cottage. He waved to her. He was a thin old man, proud of his neat garden, absolutely satisfied at the prospect of living in Wrangell and tending this garden for the rest of his life.

Like a wheel, her mind spun in the lazy current of air in the hot afternoon. How could she tell Chris she wanted to leave Wrangell? He'd assume there was someone else in the States. He would be unable to conceive of any other reason why someone would leave Wrangell.

Once while he was up at the cottage, he'd picked up an envelope that contained a letter from Don Lofton in San Francisco.

"Has been?"

"Has been."

"Why does he still write?"

"He claims that I'm irresistible."

"Two thousand miles away?"

"Even that."

"Let me read the letter."

"No. This one is private." She tried to keep her voice light so he wouldn't be jealous.

"Do you answer?"

"Of course." She had paused, fascinated by the sight of his wrists as he held the envelope in mid-air as if he were trying to read through it. His wrists were square and large and bony and there were short black hairs that lay on them that were the color of his hair, coal black. In recent weeks looking at the hair on his wrists made her uneasy and she didn't know what to make of it. The uneasiness centered in her belly and was coupled with an image of Chris' hand caressing her naked flesh. She tried to brush it away and couldn't.

The sun struck Lyddy in the face and she felt a pleasurable drowsiness. Somewhere below at one of the docks a pile-driver slammed down in rhythm with the clatter of the winch. Wham! Clat-clat-clat-clat-clat. Wham! Clat-clat-clat-clat-clat.

Lyddy wandered back into the cottage, bored. She was often bored lately. She'd sit in the cannery waiting for Chris for hours. Sometimes she wrote letters to her parents but often she just sat there with nothing to do while Chris kept coming in and out of the office and assuring her that it would not be long before he would be able to leave.

She had checked out three novels from the library in the city hall but somehow, even Steinbeck whose writing she loved, seemed trivial. The town seemed to make everything meaningless, as if it could wipe out the operas and symphonies, the street cars, all of civilization.

She shook her head and went to the pantry where the vacuum cleaner was kept. She yearned to grasp onto something that contained a bit of the materialism of the twentieth century, in the hum of its motor and the magic of its suction. Then she realized she couldn't vacuum, even though the carpet needed it. Vic was asleep and she didn't want to wake her. She didn't want to disturb Vic, didn't want to disturb anything. Let the dust lay, let the heat settle, let the world stop moving.

She should have gone out to the beach. Gwen Olson and Babs Bucci would be there, with all the children. Last week it had started raining while she was at the beach. She had been enjoying herself, staying out in the frigid water for nearly a half hour, swimming back and forth along the shoreline, feeling warm only when she was in motion, listening to the clamor of the children as they played on a raft that Matt had built for them. When she could take the icy water no longer, Lyddy dashed up the beach, shivering, to stand in front of the smoking fire that Babs had built. Babs and some other people were preparing coffee in a coffee can. Nothing fancy. Just coffee from a coffee can poured into paper mugs. But it tasted delicious. Then the clouds that had moved in overhead opened up and rain poured down.

She dressed hastily after a brisk rub down with her towel. Then, as the crowd thinned out on the road back to town, Lyddy decided she wasn't going home. She had heard so much of Rainbow Falls and she suddenly decided to hike up to it. The rain was over and the sky was clearing.

So Lyddy turned around and headed down the road towards the Native Institute. After about a half hour, the impressive oatmeal-colored buildings of the Institute appeared on her left. A group of native girls lounged on the sand beach to her right. The tide was out and as Lyddy picked her way down the beach to ask them how to get to the Falls she could smell the tangy sea odors in the air, the smell of kelp and barnacles just uncovered by the retreating waters. Gulls cried as they swooped down on the tide flats.

"You go right at the edge of the school buildings and there's a trail—it's the only one, you can't miss it. Just follow that."

"Thank you," Lyddy said. She felt sorry for these shy girls who seemed a bit sad, living out here under the school's restrictions during the vacation days. They were probably orphans allowed to go into town just once a week on the school bus to attend a movie and spend a few hours in the Sweets. With school out for the summer, most of the other native children had returned to their homes scattered across Alaska.

As she went back up to the road and along the side of the buildings, she was happy. The sky had cleared. It was bright blue filled with towering white clouds. The ridge that ran along the back of Wrangell Island rose before her, dense with trees. Everything was green and wild. The sunlight coaxed steam from the heavy coarse grass and traced green gold glints along the blade tips. She felt a surge of elation.

Ahead of her the trail vanished into the trees but she was still out in the open and it reminded her of the hikes she used to take back home, from Fairfax to Mt. Tamalpais. She thought about how surprised Chris would be when she told him she hiked up to the Falls by herself. She quickened her pace, looking forward to seeing the Falls. Her shoes were wet and her trouser legs were soaked. But she was not bothered by anything this fine exhilarating afternoon.

"Rainbow Falls is beautiful," Gwen had raved at Lyddy. "We've gone up there hundreds of time, had picnics right on top of the falls. There's a ledge up there that's slippery to get to but there's just enough room for four people . . ."

The moment Lyddy left the clearing and entered the forest, the path narrowed and she slowed down, afraid of slipping on the slick upgrade. The trail was bumpy and often lost in the tangle of underbrush that swept across it. Huge drooping branches hung around her. At first, streaks of sunlight seeped through the dense cover of the trees, but further up the trail, the sunlight could not penetrate the heavy gloom. The thickness and wildness of the forest stunned her. From time to time, huge rain drops plopped onto her head or into the brush around her, startling her. The trail went up and up, over and down ravines, around fallen tree trunks, skirting clumps of devil's club and skunk cabbage, sometimes wandering right through a thick stand of saplings. She wasn't certain why she had come.

She halted before a junction of paths that slanted out in three different directions, then continued on up the more obvious looking main trail that showed a smattering of footprints. A branch tore loose somewhere nearby and Lyddy jerked to a halt, her heart beating wildly. Outside of the rain drops, the sound of the splitting branch had been the first noise she had heard since entering the forest. The silence was oppressive.

She walked on slowly, afraid to look around. She wasn't enjoying the walk anymore. She thought of bears, maybe even wolves, roaming through the trees, perhaps standing watching her just a few yards away. A glob of blackish dung covered half the width of the trail. As she skirted it, she wondered if it was from a deer or a bear. She had never thought about how primitive the island was until she had stepped into the forest. Chris had told her the island was lousy with bears. She looked at the dung again and hurried off. She started thinking about turning back. But she convinced herself to go on a little further. She wanted to see the Falls and she figured she had already been climbing for at least an hour.

She picked up her pace, stumbling at times on the twisting narrow path. At every bend, at every ridge, she expected to see the Falls. But she saw nothing but the endless forest. The trees grew more enormous the higher she went. Lichen thrived on the windfalls and circled the trunks of the upright trees in green bands of fuzz as if staking a claim to the gnarled old relics in anticipation of their inevitable downfall.

She couldn't even hear the rush of water from a stream. Surely a waterfall would have an outlet. She began to worry that she had taken the wrong trail. All of a sudden, she felt very alone. The place was more charged with silence than the town. The huge trees swam about her. It was dark and she was having trouble seeing in the gloom. Maybe it was going to rain again. But she couldn't catch a glimpse of the sky. She wished she had waited and come with Chris. He had promised to bring her the first chance he got.

She glanced up at the great branches drooping with foliage and moved on, anxious to reach her objective. Her ankle twisted in pain as she stumbled over a root sticking up out of the hard earth. No light filtered in. It was all so depressing. The silence was unbelievable. She could barely hear her own footsteps. The silence seemed to swallow them up.

She stopped by a towering hemlock and was aware of a harsh, dry panting in her throat, although she knew she wasn't winded from the climb. And then Lyddy heard footfalls just above her on the trail and the sound of voices. She felt such a wave of relief that she sailed on up the trail, eager to meet people in the midst of this sea of savage nature.

It was Chuck Everett, the bakery owner, and Irma Stolte, the librarian. It wasn't until afterwards that she realized the implications of meeting this pair, both married, in the forest in the middle of the day. At the moment, she was so glad to see them that even though they seemed rather subdued and tentative, she chattered on gaily. They assured her she was close to her destination.

This encouragement helped buoy her flagging confidence and she practically flew up the rest of the path. Atop a long slanting ridge that overlooked a draw thick with blueberry bushes, she came upon Rainbow Falls. The view was ghastly.

At least two hundred feet straight up, a thin gray thread of water descended, falling onto a bed of rocks with a hollow uproar that was muted by the stillness around it. It wasn't so much that the Falls were unimpressive. It was that in the theater-like setting of the gorge, the greenery was much more profound. The vegetation was rampant, vigorous, glossy with green. Even the ledge of rock over which the water dropped to form the Falls was draped with a heavy green canopy. She was appalled by the awful wildness of everything. She fled back down through the dark forest to the road and was grateful that Curly drove by in his cab as she was walking up the road.

"Haven't been up to Rainbow Falls for months," Curly had said, after declining any fare money. "It sure is beautiful up there, though."

The knock on the door made Lyddy's heart jump. She rushed to it, hoping it would be Chris. Sometimes he popped up unexpectedly in the middle of the day even though he was swamped with work at the cannery.

"Hi, Lyddy," Jean Crawford was standing on the stoop, smiling. "I saw you from my kitchen window and I just had to tell you . . ."

"Come in," Lyddy said, interrupting.

"No, Lyddy. I'm right in the middle of getting dinner ready. How's Vic?"

"Oh, she isn't any better. Her cough's worse today."

"That's too bad. Gosh, Mrs. Johnson and Diana are both down with it too. I hope my kids don't get it."

"What's the news?" Lyddy asked. She liked Jean. There was no pretense about her. She never seemed to have time to comb her dark hair or apply make up, what with rearing three youngsters and striving to keep her house in order. Yet Jean was natural and good, overflowing with radiance and sociability. Not once had she cast a disapproving eye on Lyddy because of her affair with Chris. Yet Jean must have noticed Chris' early morning departures from the cottage.

"We're going south as soon as the season is over."

"Oh, how wonderful," Lyddy said. "I bet you're excited."

"I'll say. Dale's been making more money fishing than he expected and we decided last night to go south to see his folks for a month."

"Wonderful," Lyddy said. "Oh, how wonderful." She was suddenly filled with an sense of loss that was keen and sharp and inconsolable.

There was a wail and the sound of running footsteps. Jean turned around and looked down into the yard. "There's a part of my tribe coming up. God, they're dirty."

"How about some Kool Aide, Mom?" one of the twins called out.

"OK! I better hurry," Jean said and went down the path.

Lyddy went back into the cottage. It struck her that people who were honest with themselves, like Jean, who understood the path they had chosen and accepted it, were not troubled with discontent or envy. Babs told Lyddy that Jean had had a crush on Chris years ago before she married Dale Crawford. Jean had admitted this secret to Babs one rainy winter afternoon when Jean was helping Babs dry the dishes after a birthday party for one of Babs' children. That Chris supposedly never paid Jean the least bit of attention surprised Lyddy for Jean was rather pretty, especially when she wore makeup and put her hair up in braids atop her head. But maybe Chris hadn't noticed her because they were so much alike in their sense of well-being. Perhaps Chris needed someone like Lyddy, green from the States, to luxuriate in his own character, to assert his confidence and his delight in Wrangell and the life he had constructed for himself there.

Lyddy went into the bedroom and found Vic awake.

"How are you feeling, honey?"

"Rotten. Christ, what a cold!"

"I should have made broth for you," Lyddy said. "I can open a can."

"Maybe that'll help."

In the kitchen Lyddy opened a can of chicken soup and set it on the stove. She felt annoyed with herself. She wished she had done something useful like making soup for Vic instead of moping around all day. She thought again of Jean's news, her trip to the States. It occurred to Lyddy that Jean was the third woman in as many days who had announced that she was leaving for the south once the season was over.

———

The noise that rose from the hotel bar below was different in the summer time, Clarence reflected, as he lay fully dressed on the bed in his room. For one thing it wasn't as solid. During the winter months, when the inhabitants of Wrangell had more time for uninterrupted drinking, the clamor was sustained, pierced now and then by a woman's shriek or a man's guffaw, and building slowly over the course of the night to a steady roar. During the summer the noise drifted up to his room in spurts as people filed in and out of the bar. Tourists came in and out in waves as the steamers docked, then departed. Fishing crews on seiners and tenders dropped in for a round or two of drinks while their boats were being unloaded at the canneries, shouting and joking because the catch was good at last. Then they'd leave and there would be a few minutes of silence. Clarence would make up his mind to undress and get in bed. Then the noise would flare up again, flooding up from the lobby and up the stairs and through the thin partitions of the rooms on the first floor.

Clarence rose from his bed and wandered about the room, flexing his thin arms, feeling the hard bulk of his muscles. Now that he was up he could hear the rapid, murmuring tum-tum-tum of the cold storage plant's engine, ten feet away across the width of the Clinton dock, right opposite his room. He could get used to machine noise, living by it day and night, hearing it year after year. But the erratic noises of people were something else.

A woman's voice rang out in the still warm air outside. The low rasping voice was unmistakably Indian. It sounded like Violet Lundy. Curious, Clarence stuck his head out of the window.

"You old fart!" It was the Klootch, all right, admonishing some fisherman who had made a pass at her. That's why he hated bars and drinking. This sort of thing happened when you mixed booze and Indian blood and some old tottering fisherman stiff with heat.

"You got nerve, Fred! You don't even buy me one drink and you want to row me across the pond to your stinkin' boat."

"Listen, Violet, I got a bottle aboard."

"Raisin mash! Nuts, cheapskate!"

Clarence pulled his head in. He went over to the low, glass-topped bureau and looked in the mirror. He stared at his eyes, noting the fine crossmarks of 36 years of lines around the corners, at his dull, almost pasty white, complexion, at the widow's peak that was disappearing. It seemed ironic. One guy in a million had a widow's peak, one guy out of a thousand guys with widows peaks lost it, and he was that guy.

"Now, go away, Fred. Beat it. I'm not going with you!"

Clarence curled back his lips and inspected his teeth, relieved to see no nicotine stains. Two months ago Dave Collier had cleaned his teeth and Clarence had been dutifully brushing them twice a day. He wanted his teeth milk-white. He wanted Lydia to notice them, to press her lips to his. He wanted a lot.

He slid out the top bureau drawer and looked at the small felt case which contained the Alaskan black-diamond ring that he had purchased as a present for her. He had been so certain of his conquest, as he had been with Gwen. He was sure from the moment Lydia Prince entered Wrangell that she was meant for him. But things hadn't turned out that way.

He was full of bitterness. Nothing satisfied him. He lived in a torment of emptiness. He woke up depressed every morning and dragged himself to work, nearly sick with hopelessness. He was unable to wrench himself free, to do anything about it. His only hope was that it would smother itself inside him given time, like a forest fire that, having burnt everything in its path, dies for lack of fuel.

He heard Violet's voice again. "Now, listen, you old drunken dope, get your ass out of here. I'm waiting for someone. Understand?"

Clarence surveyed his room, the yellow roses on the faded blue wallpaper, the worn gray carpet, the wash stand, the chair, the table, the bed.

The bar noise rose into his room to harass him, a hellish, wicked stream of people flocking in and out and having a riotous time while their voices roared and dimmed in his pained ears.

When Lyddy showed up at the cannery, she was wearing a blue tweed suit. She scarcely ever wore slacks anymore, Chris had noticed, but always dresses and suits and high heels which must have been uncomfortable for walking on the gravel roads.

As they left the cannery she took her high heels off and tiptoed beside Chris in her stocking feet.

Chris laughed. "Feel better?"

"I'll never forget the first dance. It was the best one, too. But don't you remember afterwards when the people were going home, some of the girls took off their shoes and went home singing. I just thought of it and decided to take my shoes off."

"Might snag your stockings."

Up the hill they walked, as they had done night after night. To Chris, who was tired, the world seemed all the more enchanting for it. It was as if his fatigue let him gather all the beauty of the girl, her voice and sweetness, within him and he drifted in contentment.

"Let's pause," Lyddy said.

Chris sat against the low rock wall which bordered the lower end of the Eaton garden, feeling his limbs ache with tiredness.

"What did you do today?" he asked.

"Oh, I painted the cabinet in the bathroom. It needed it, don't you think?"

"Vic help?"

"She was out."

"Her cold's better then?"

"Much better."

She was so beautiful. There was something outstanding about her that was greater than her physical beauty. Her lovely forehead, her long neck, her small pointed breasts, her legs, the clean fragrance of her body, dazzled him separately. But the combination of them, her being the person who had these attributes, this was even more amazing. The more he knew her, the more his love leaped within him. Sometimes he deliberately put off looking at her because he knew what would happen when he finally did: a small eruption, a feeling rushing at him that was like nothing he had ever known.

It was like the season, he decided. People making money. People working hard, their limbs and backs weary with the endless hours, the gossip and jesting dwindling along the assembly line towards nightfall as they hoarded their strength for the work at hand. The sense of well-being that came from the anticipation of the profit and the pleasure of working outdoors in a land so rich.

Chris stood. "I think I can make it now."

Inside the cottage, Lyddy glanced in the bedroom and saw that Vic was home and asleep. She went into the kitchen and mixed Chris a drink.

"Vic's home."

"Come here."

He gathered her into his arms and held her on his lap on the sofa. His desire swept like fire through his brain. As he kissed her, he felt the softness of her flesh, sensed all the weariness of his body melting away with each kiss, pressing against her more urgently as his desire grew.

She wriggled out of his arms and to her feet. "Now, you're not going to stay late again. You have to get more sleep, Chris. You're worn out and I'm depriving you of it."

"But you're not, baby." Of all the moments he had known with her, these were some of his favorites. Like the moment he lit up a cigarette and enjoyed it for the first time that day simply because he could watch her as he smoked it, see her face and admire the swell of her breasts against the blue tweed coat of her suit.

"Here." She removed the empty glass from his hand. "Let me make you one more drink."

She returned in a moment with the drink, dropped to her knees and stared up at him as if she were going to make portrait of his face. "You've got a good masculine face," she said.

"Rub my neck," he said.

She stood before him and placed her fingers around his neck, moving them in circles.

Chris sat the glass on the carpet between his legs and placed both hands on her breasts.

"Oh, no you don't."

"Say, that's a good angle. You rub my neck while I . . ."

"No, Chris." She backed away. "If you get me warmed up, I won't want you to go."

"All right," he said, standing up. "Makes me feel good. A few kisses and you're like putty in my hands."

"One kiss," she said and smiled but her face was set in stern lines that disturbed Chris for a moment.

At the door they kissed good night and Chris lumbered down the rock-bordered path to the dirt road. A boat whistle pierced the soft still night air. Dogs howled and barked. He lit a cigarette as he walked. As he went by the hospital, he heard an outburst of yelling and cursing. It was probably old lady Chatham, an ancient Indian woman who was sent to the hospital periodically by her husband so she could dry out. They kept her strapped to the bed now because once she had fallen out of the hospital during the delirium of the D.T.'s and broken her arm.

In the harbor the boat whistle rent the night air again with several short impatient toots, as if trying to get someone's attention. The dogs howled again. Then the night was silent, except for the sound of his footsteps scraping along the gravel road. At a moment like this, weary or not, he could feel his existence as it was meant to be felt, as he never could at any other time. The sound of footsteps in the late hours of night with a town asleep around him and only he, Chris Ballard, alone on the roads of Wrangell. He ached for such moments. Just the howl of a dog, the toot of a seiner, the sound of his foot-steps, the sky and the stars and the clean air and the outcome of life unimportant, but clear as old lady Chatham's profanity.

As he picked up the road that led down to his house, his thoughts shifted with his course. He thought of the girl he just left behind. He was beginning to realize that Lydia Prince was no simple ordinary girl. She must really love him to be willing to put up with so much, the lack of time they spent together, the postponement of their plans. He was grateful that the season was almost over.

In the harbor, gas engines sputtered as the gill-netters took off to make their drifts on the changing tide. It was late, after midnight. Lyddy thought of Jean's husband, Dale, who would be taking off with the others. Jean called herself a widow during the fishing season. So did the rest of the women in the town.

"Did I tell you that Virginia Waverly had all the girls over to her house yesterday?" Lyddy asked as they strolled up the hill, lulled by the warmth of the heavy air and the sweet fragrance of night-blooming stock floating up from Cliff Waverly's garden. "She made the most delicious homemade ice cream. All she talked about was Cliff. They seem like the happiest couple on the island."

"So it seems." His voice was strained.

"He's quite a guy. So handsome. Of course, the only time I ever see him is when he's up on a telephone pole mending wires. He looks quite manly high up there, with his black leather boots and his waist loaded down with tools."

"She's fifteen years younger than Cliff but that doesn't seem to make any difference. I think she's jealous of him, though. Old Cliff likes to cat around."

"How can he? She's so adorable." Lyddy was jolted with dismay. "I just don't understand."

Chris chuckled. "Cliff's like Clarence. He goes wild when he gets a few under his belt. Once he got drunk with me and Giff at the hotel bar shooting dice and oh, brother!" Chris shook his head with amusement.

"Oh, brother, what?"

"Believe me, you don't want to hear about it."

"Chris," she said, "how long has Virginia been in Wrangell?" She had been aware as time went along and she heard more of the town gossip, that there were few women in Wrangell with whom Chris hadn't had some kind of an affair.

"Cliff and Virginia came up together from the States years ago when they took over the exchange. It works out well since they can take turns operating the switchboard."

She felt a sense of relief and a touch of dismay at her own suspicions for she despised the thought of jealousy.

Chris yawned. "I'll be glad when Monday comes around."

"I'll bet," she said. On Mondays the boats were out fishing and the cannery shut down, processing Monday's catch on Tuesday. It was supposed to be a day of leisure for Chris but he usually spent it taking her out. Last Monday they had hiked to Pat's Creek and caught some trout in the headwater wake from atop an old flimsy skiff. The week before they rode across the channel to Woronkofski Island on an outboard-driven skiff with Dave and Vic. They had found a secluded beach, eaten a picnic lunch and swam in the channel. "Let's do nothing this Monday. No going out. Let's just loaf."

"I've already made arrangements for us to go fishing. You're going to get the thrill of your life hooking into a coho."

"No, Chris, I'd rather not. We get back so late. I'd rather we just stayed home. You need the rest."

He stopped on the road to tie his shoelace. "What did you do today?"

"You didn't answer me. Let's not go anywhere, please, Chris."

"Honey, I've made arrangements with Tim Regis to take us out on his cabin cruiser to Point Beauclaire to do some trolling."

She felt resentful even though she was grateful that he was trying to please her. Not that she cared much for the fishing—she didn't consider herself the outdoor type—but the ride on the boat sounded like fun.

"What did you do today?"

"Oh, just about everything." There were times when their conversation was so banal they might have been already married. She knew Chris was tired. And lately he had seemed concerned about her, asking the same question every night, as if he realized how lonely she was. "In the morning, Vic and I did a lot of housework. Then Dave came up for lunch and afterwards Vic and I took a walk around to the beach and laid in the sun."

"Everything all right?" He was looking not at her but down the road.

"It was fun." Without considering, she added, "The Crawfords are going south in September."

"Are they?" He didn't sound interested.

"Yes. Jean's sure excited about it."

"I only wish there was more to keep you occupied."

"But I am occupied. I'm enjoying myself."

She released his arm as they approached the cottage. His whole world was there in Wrangell. It ended at Elephant Nose. There was an abyss to the south, a vast remoteness to the north, but in the center he had peace and freedom all wrapped up in independence. Nothing was lacking in his life.

Other people talked happily about going to the States for a vacation. It was their reward, their dream. Even if they did think of Wrangell as home, they looked forward to going shopping, seeing the shows, watching the people and buildings and activity. Lyddy was beginning to suspect that Chris didn't even believe the States existed. It aggravated her, though she couldn't show it.

In his room, Chris struggled between wakefulness and sleep. Lyddy had been behaving strangely. There was a hint of tragedy about everything she did, even the way she handed him a drink of whiskey. She wasn't herself. She was acting, forcing everything, putting on a facade and he didn't want that from her. He didn't know what to make of it. But he suspected it had something to do with her offhand remark about the States. She was probably homesick. She wanted to go to the States and she couldn't understand his lack of interest.

He remembered his last year at the university and the dive where he used to hang out with Louise. She was a blonde with a cat's sharp but undecipherable eyes. She was well-built, with plenty of beef around the rump and a solid chest, but she had little sex drive. He thought they were well-suited since they were both partial to drinking and adverse to studying.

But he had made an ass out of himself with her. She took money from him sometimes and he pretended not to notice. She often stood him up. She loved bars and drinking—she would drink sidecars all night until she was plastered, scarcely able to mumble but never unsteady on her feet.

He felt disgusted at the memory of his obsession for her. In his room in the hotel she would strip and sink down on the covers, drunk and distant. She didn't even bother to pretend. She was simply willing and accommodating. At first, when she was trying to make an impression on him, she had gone through the motions of ecstasy but she didn't bother after the first few times. He could never get enough of her because she never gave him anything. After a while his only mania was to smash into her, to make her cry out that she was his, that she adored him, but she just lay beneath him, indifferent.

One night two men with white carnations in their lapels joined them in the booth at the bar. They talked and talked to her while Chris tried to figure out the chatter, the giddy and jumpy quality of their speech. Louise told him later they were stoned on reefers. Eventually she dropped out of college and became a prostitute. She didn't see anything wrong with it. She could put on an act as well as anyone. "Hell, it's a job," she told Chris, her voice bland. "I don't like some of the bitches who work there but I get along all right with the old lady. She isn't bad if you smile at the customers and dust the furniture when you ain't busy."

By the glow of his cigarette ember, Chris located the ash tray beside the bed on the night stand and put it out. He wondered what had happened to Louise and why he was thinking about her now.

———

"Chris, I've been thinking a lot about life lately," Lyddy said. It was late, after one, and she and Chris were alone in the living room of the cottage. She had been waiting all day to tell him her latest thoughts. "And it struck me as a novelty. Awful, isn't it? That thinking about life is something new to me. What sort of character does that make me?"

"Beautiful."

"I've never thought much of philosophy before. . . ."

"You're still beautiful. I like that dress—thin and soft."

"Chris, please." She frowned at him. "Generally, the only time people discuss philosophy is at a small party or gathering. They never think of it when they're alone. At least, I never did. It seems to me that people think only of their woes or bad luck or good times but very little of life itself. And it's so complex, so rich, so intriguing. Why, the subject is so big. There's so much to think about."

"I never think about it. In fact I've never talked about it with anyone."

"You must have!" She hesitated and shook her head. "I've got to hand it to you, Chris. You've probably never thought about philosophy as I have. I mean your life revolves around you, doesn't it, Chris?"

"Maybe that's it. Yeah, maybe that's the way I've always felt."

She shook her head again and smiled. A sense of pathos clutched her, almost draining away the enthusiasm with which she had begun.

"Now get comfortable and let me tell you what I've been thinking."

"Shoot, baby, I'm all ears." He sank lower into the corner of the sofa, his eyes brimming with amusement.

"Are you making fun of me?"

"No, by God!" he said but his mock seriousness disappeared under a burst of laughter.

"I'll keep it to myself. It wouldn't make any difference to you what my philosophy is or what I'm trying to feel about my life. You feel confident that you'll change me so that I'm exactly like you, don't you?" She was angry and it made her even angrier that she couldn't convey it with the tone of her voice.

"What makes you say that, honey?"

"I know it. You think you can easily convert me to your ways, even your way of thinking."

"My God, Lyddy!" he said.

271

There was silence between them. Lyddy was suddenly aware of how late it was. Her eyelids were heavy. She tried to change the mood.

"Chris, I don't want to disappoint you. But there are some things that worry me. I don't want you to expect too much of me. Don't put so much confidence in me. So far it's been easy, having a drink together, exchanging a few words, loving . . ."

"Yes, sir, it's been loving," he said and angled over to kiss her.

"No, Chris, no!" she said, but she let him kiss her.

She let him kiss her again and again. She couldn't resist him. She wanted him, a man with a vision, haughty and strong. Ever since the first dance at the A&N hall, she had cataloged Chris as confident, unrestrained, domineering. This made her want to tackle him, tone him down and flatten him out, for at that time, fresh up from the States, Chris was the kind of man she wanted to put in his place.

But it hadn't happened that way. Instead she was succumbing, to his attitudes and his desires. Her head rang as she felt his hands on her legs, lifting her dress. He whispered to her about going in to the bedroom. They were hurried and breathless for fear Vic might return at any moment, aching with yearning and their love for each other.

Afterwards, she made two drinks and they sat in the living room. Chris was tired, scarcely able to hold his eyes open, looking at his drink and poking at the ice cubes with his fingers.

Far away, she could hear the growl of a boat in the harbor. She could picture the boat chugging across to its berth, the grind of its motor as it reversed, the fadeout of its mast light. She missed the sounds of the city, an automobile going by, a street car grinding away on its tracks, the hum of a community. Up here there was no hum, nothing but silence.

"You can go, Chris," she said after a while. "I know you're dead tired."

"No, we'll have a few drinks together."

"You know, I don't understand," she said, getting up. "Under these same circumstances, most anyone else would be grateful for the chance to leave."

"Sit down," he said. "I'm not leaving."

"I've got you where I want you," she said, returning with two more drinks. "I'm going to tell you about my philosophy. It's wonderful to let your mind wander."

"Baby, I love you. I'll tell you what's going on in my mind right now. I was thinking of the other women I've slept with." He slipped his drink. "The sensations were never like this. Before, it was an annoying lustful craving that had to be satisfied. Afterwards, it was how soon can I dump this dame and go to my house and sleep. Yes, that's the way it was. I was after only one thing."

"But with me it's different," she said mockingly. "Oh, Mr. Ballard, I bet you said that to all of them."

"Oh, no," he said. She was sure he lied. She was convinced all men had only this one line.

"With you it is different. I sleep with you and there isn't the rotten feeling afterwards. I sleep with you, hoping I can increase my showing of love . . ."

"You're so good at it," she teased.

"You're not following me. There isn't any pretense. It's not all leading up to a conquest." He looked abstracted, as if he were searching for the words from somewhere deep inside. "There is only a feeling I want to bring over, to express. It's not just a good time with you, there's no end in sight. It's going to be like this . . ."

She jumped up and said she would be right back. She didn't want Chris to finish his sentence. She swept into the lavatory and switched on the light. Her head was beating fiercely. The drink had been strong. Coupled with her fatigue, it was making her feel tipsy. The bathroom mirror showed her drawn white face and blue eyes that appeared sad and confused. She stared into them for a least half a minute, unable to recall whether she had been here just a few minutes ago applying makeup. No, she watched her lips form the word. No, I don't want to hear him talk about marriage. I don't. I don't.

When she returned to the living room, Chris was standing up, smoking.

"Feel better?" he asked with a smile.

She smiled and kissed his cheek. "I'll see you tomorrow," she said.

"Yeah, I better be going."

"If I thought it was proper I'd walk you to your house. I really feel like doing it."

"Come on," he said.

"Oh, it wouldn't be right. Anyway, it's too close to daybreak."

"Suit yourself, honey." He headed out the door without kissing her.

She watched him go down the path and turn onto the road that would lead him across the hill. She was very tired. The thought of bed was heavenly.

She closed the door and savored the sound of the latch clicking. She even felt a momentary impulse to press her body against the frame, a gesture she had watched performed by thousands of love-smitten heroines in the movies.

As she went into the bedroom, she realized that Vic wasn't home yet. She smiled at the thought that the schoolteachers were giving the men of Wrangell the time of their lives. She got into bed feeling unbelievably smug, for no reason whatsoever.

"All right," Dave said, "we'll forget about us for a while."

"I think it's the best thing," Vic agreed. Pain spurted into her heart as the finality of the decision hit her.

Dave didn't even touch her as they sat side by side on the wicker sofa in his reception room. If this was her last date with Clarence, he'd be trying to seduce her for the last time. But Dave hadn't tried to kiss her tonight, not once since the moment they had started out on a stroll around the island, almost as if he had been alerted by some inward suspicion.

"I feel terrible about the whole thing. But I think you must understand."

There was silence and Vic realized Dave was badly hurt but fighting to maintain an outward appearance of calm.

"It'll work out," he said. There was a rattle of distraction in his voice and at once the image of Clarence burst into her mind. Doubtless Dave was thinking of him too.

"Don't worry so, Vic," Dave said. "Everything works out."

"I'm sure it will. I'm just going to lay low, give myself time to think."

"I won't have to do that," Dave confided. "My mind's made up. I know you're the woman I want."

She stirred in her seat. "You don't have to walk me up the hill."

"Why not?" he said. "I'd feel terrible if I didn't."

"All right, Dave. We'll go up it together."

"The good old hill," Dave said, and he smiled as he opened the door for her to pass through before him.

They said scarcely anything all the way up to the cottage. It was done and finished and she was depressed. In the sultry heat of the night, dogs barked fitfully, birds chirped, some already fully awake. A cat wailed from behind a nearby house. It was as though the noises of the animals and birds were a prelude to a shift in the weather, or to some change that was approaching, for everything seemed restless.

20

LYDDY STOOD UNDER THE OPEN PORCH of the hospital waiting for Vic, who was visiting Henry Rushworth, the Episcopal minister. He had fallen off the church roof early one morning and shattered his hip in three places. Apparently he had gone up there early in the morning, hoping to make some repairs before anyone was awake to see him. As he inched up the steep roof, his foot slipped on the slick shingles and he rolled off the eaves, hitting the earth below on his side. He wasn't discovered until eight o'clock, when Gwen Olson, who was walking down the road on her way to Main Street, heard faint moans coming from behind the enormous hydrangea bush that bordered the church lawn. The town was stunned by the accident, especially when word leaked out that despite a long and delicate operation Mr. Rushworth might never be able to walk normally again.

The breeze darted about at random, teasing her nostrils, playing on her nerves, bringing with it a sense of wild and growing things. Lyddy looked out at the channel, stretching away to Elephant Nose. She had seen it day after day for more than three months now. Usually it was swathed in rain and mist, but during the last few weeks, with the sun shining every day, a myriad of blinding reflections gleamed across its surface.

Vic came out and they descended the steps. "Golly, he's in bad shape," she said. "He's in a lot of pain."

Below, trollers and gill-netters seiners and skiffs growled and chutted and whined about the island's three canneries, just like bees docking about honey-combs. With all the boats out fishing, the harbor was almost empty, except for a few old relics moored here and there. The water glimmered with purple and crimson as the sun sank in the west.

Lyddy was restless. She felt she was reaching a climax of some sort, moving steadily towards it, like her hike up to Rainbow Falls. Everything was part of it, the Reverend's accident, the endless days of boredom, her love for Chris, the pull towards home and the fear of making the wrong decision, of making a mistake.

"Let's go to the show," Vic said. She had been avoiding serious conversations since she had decided to drop both her suitors, Dave and Clarence. Her face was sour with restraint for she wasn't the type to suppress the impulses of her heart so easily. For amusement, they had been playing cards, spending most of their time at the cottage. The question of the future loomed over them at the card table, at the sink, in bed, like a dangling, tempting bait but they avoided it. The summer was almost over and they would have to decide soon.

"Let's stay home and play cards," Lyddy said.

"Sure."

Vic went into the cottage and Lyddy lingered outside. The sweet odor of honeysuckle filled the air, ruffled occasionally by the breeze. Lyddy felt it was up to her to define her relationship to this land, the desolation and terror sandwiched between the peace and beauty. She could choose. But she was mortally uncertain and afraid to make the choice. Her eyelids grew heavy with weariness.

"Hey, you coming in?" Vic called from deep in the house.

Lyddy didn't answer. She was thinking of the first time in bed with Chris, in the float house after the party. A storm was raging outside. The small oil stove in the kitchen spread warmth through the small rooms of the float house. The dismal feeling of emptiness that came with the storms in Wrangell over-came her and she succumbed to the comfort Chris provided, responding to his every wish. Gradually the dreariness and emptiness were obliterated from her consciousness by the warm, real contact of their bodies. Lyddy brought herself back to the present, chiding herself for dwelling on these memories. Every time that she saw Chris, her body flushed with weakness. She wanted him again. A freighter appeared off the Nose, rounding itself towards Wrangell, probably to take on salmon. Lyddy watched it with fascination. Something simple like this, the slow progress of an arriving boat could catch the attention of a part of her mind that had been dormant in the States. In Wrangell, she perceived the most simple things in totally new ways.

She sat down on the step, clasping her hands. She felt as if she had entered another era, as if she had never really been alive, and wasn't even now. The past had been drained away and the present required a patience that would take all eternity to acquire. The stillness wafted up the hill, bringing with it an overwhelming sensation of loss and despair. She rose quickly, nettled, closed the door behind her and started down along the path. She'd go see Chris and maybe convince him to take her to Mom's to dance.

At the bottom of the path, she paused and looked back up at the cottage. She realized she had totally forgotten about Vic but she felt too tired to climb back up. She despised herself for her thoughtlessness but told herself that Vic would understand. They were both feeling the same depression.

A fine thin blue film of dusk began soaking into the red embers in the sky. She was suddenly anxious. It was too early to go see Chris. He had phoned during the afternoon and said that since the catch was heavy, he'd be working late.

She started slowly across the hill. A rind of moon, unbelievably luminous, appeared behind the ridge. Trees and grass glowed silvery and green-black in the dim night. From the harbor below, she could hear the gurgle of a running hose; some fisherman had neglected to turn it off after supplying his boat with fresh water.

Her fright increased as she entered the tunnel of tall hemlock trees that lined the road. Chris had warned her to avoid this part of the road unless she carried a flashlight. Black bears were apt to roam there at night, searching for the raspberries that grew on the bushes off the road.

Yet Lyddy made no effort to move any quicker. She seemed to be moving slowly as if in a dream. She felt dead inside, resigned, as if her senses were so knotted up she could no longer respond to danger.

She heard footsteps crunching up the hill. A hundred yards ahead the road made a jog around Cliff Waverly's house and the footsteps were approaching the turning. She didn't want to meet anyone tonight, didn't want to say hello or make polite talk, so she stopped and stood quietly by the trees. The footsteps grew louder now that her's had stopped.

She thought of the numbness that had crept up on her during the past weeks and which she had not challenged. Vaguely and with a kind of dread, she knew what was wrong. There was a flaw between Chris and her. Small, yes, but it was there and would eventually tear them apart.

The footsteps had turned the corner and were heading towards the tunnel of trees. Lyddy, realizing she would feel ridiculous if she were caught trying to hide, moving out from the shadows. It was Danny Olson, she saw, with a sense of relief.

"Hello, Danny," she said. "What are you doing out so late?"

"Oh, hello, Miss Prince. I was helping my dad take inventory at the store but I got tired so I decided to walk home."

"But why this road?" Danny had been one of her students. She knew he was Gwen's boy by her first marriage with Clarence. It always surprised Lyddy to think of Clarence married, and to such a sweet girl as Gwen. He didn't seem the type. He was too sullen, too wounded, consumed by a bottomless rage that could be set off by the slightest provocation.

"Heck," the boy said, "this road's just as good as any of them." He looked at her with disbelief as if her question was incredibly stupid.

"Aren't you afraid of bears?" she asked.

"Shucks, no. They're scaredy cats. We had three black bears munching on our raspberry bushes the other morning. Heck, I went outside and took a snapshot of 'em and they got scared and high tailed it into the brush."

From one of the trees lining the road came the sound of a bird twittering in its sleep. Danny wheeled about, curious. In the stillness and quiet of the warm night, Lyddy could imagine the tiny creature huddled in deep sleep in the heart of the tree. The bird twittered again.

"That's an English sparrow," he said.

Danny waited, tense, listening. As the moon climbed above the trees, she could see his face better. He looked like his father, the same pale face and widow's peak, only his forehead and jaw were broader and more pronounced. His face was alight with intelligence and confidence.

The boy whistled.

"What are you doing that for?" she asked.

"Sh-h," he said. His face was rapt and eager; his body radiated excitement. He stood stock still, his face angled in the direction of the tree. Then from the tree nearest them, she heard the sleepy puzzled chirp of a bird.

Instantly, the boy whistled back.

The bird answered.

Lyddy gasped in wonder.

Danny whistled again, louder. This time, his whistle elicited a response, a perplexed chirp from a tree on the other side of the road. Then another one. And another. Four birds chirped in unison.

Clumsily, Lyddy whistled through her lips, along with the boy, a lilting joy pouring through her veins. The splash of water from the hose in the harbor wafted up to them, a counterpoint to the magic of the sleepy birds chirping in the dark tunnel of trees. All the birds in the trees were now awake, some chirping heartily, others emitting drowsy twitters.

"I like birds," Danny said, turning to address her. "I was out one day shooting BBs with Harry Bucci when I saw a pheasant with its wing busted. I just put my gun down and walked straight up to it. The bird was scared and tried to flutter away but I reached down and picked him up and took him home with me. Mom and Pop were sure surprised but Pop brought up some feed from the store and I took care of him and fixed up a coop out of an old box and took care of him until his wing was better. Then I let him go." He paused to listen to chorus of chirps all around them. "Well, I better be going. Otherwise Pop might beat me home in the pickup and start worrying what happened to me."

He marched away, his head held high, through the chorus of bird song that he had created. Lyddy watched him go, a pang of loss in her heart. She continued on down the road, savoring the sensation of having witnessed something magical.

Beat as he was, from spending fifteen to sixteen hours a day on his feet working, Clarence paced around the small area of his room, past the wash basin and the crumpled towel on the rack, past the window covered with a shade, past the splotch of gray rain-soaked plaster on the wall, pausing at the side of the bed to punch a tight fist upon his upturned palm, then off again. lightheaded and keyed up. The clamor from the bar was ebbing a little towards the end of the season for the fishermen were tired and overworked although they still came to the hotel bar to have a few snorts to celebrate the close of a profitable year.

Clarence could visualize the half-numb, half-jubilant crews tramping over from the canneries and entering the noisy, music-filled bar, slapping the backs of friends, bragging about the size of their catch. They would push up through the crowds, order drinks, calling out over the shoulders of the men sitting at the bar stools. Couples jammed the small space of the dance floor. Buster Fountain bobbed and weaved through the crowd, tray in hand, replenishing orders. The two rooms almost rocked on their foundation of piling, a rumble of sound that carried up to the first floor and into the rooms.

For the last four years, Clarence had thought about moving out of the hotel. He could rent a cabin or, like Steve, live on a boat in the harbor. It was quiet in the harbor. But he knew that no matter how much he hated the racket, it would be even worse to live away from it. At least at the hotel, he bumped into people in the hallway—he might meet a woman or listen to an old fossil rattle on about his life in Alaska.

Glancing in the mirror, he realized he was sweating. The oval glass caught the crease down his forehead, the shiny veneer of sweat on his temples. He rubbed a finger across one of them, gazing at the oily sheen with a frown. He moved to the wash basin and scrubbed his face in a thick angry lather of soap, muffling the roar downstairs with the towel in his ears.

Tonight the unflagging hum was unbearable. It jarred his nerves and made his heart ache. Without really knowing what he wanted, Clarence combed his hair and went downstairs. He found himself standing at the bar with a beer in his hand before he realized where he was and what he was doing.

He drank the beer slowly. He was aware of Violet watching him from the adjoining stool. Aware of the crowd around the drink-littered bar. Aware of the group bunched around a table by the front window where Buster Fountain and some other man where shooting horses for drinks, of the people dancing in the other room, of the commotion. He loathed the sight of people drinking and making assholes of themselves at bars.

"What's the matter Clarence? You sore about something?"

He looked over at Violet. Her lips were thick with some cheap lipstick that she kept moist, out of habit, with her restless tongue. "I don't feel good, Violet. I'm tired." The beer was cold and it went down hard and sharp. He drank half of it and rose to leave.

"How about a drink, Clarence?" Her black eyes almost smoked with entreaty though the tone of her voice was bland.

"Sure, Violet. Hey, Max!" Clarence beckoned to the bartender, tossing a half dollar on the bar. "Give Violet what she wants."

"Leaving?"

"Yeah. I need a walk."

"Wanna meet me later?"

"No, not tonight, Violet."

Outside, it was hot. Not sultry like in the States, but a rich warmth that washed in off the channel and the islands with a kind of purity to it that made a man, no matter what was eating him, pause a moment to notice. Across the street a dog sniffed along the front of the building which housed the offices for Jack Jewell's shipping business. The air was full of noises: the chut-chut-chut of a gas boat and the swish-swish-swish of the air-cooled engine in a large seine skiff. Somewhere back of the hotel a bilge pump droned on. Close to shore Clarence spied the mast light of a large fishing boat as it made its way in the direction of the Ballard Cannery. And off to the right of the Canadian dock, clear out the channel below the mouth of the Stikine River, he could see the flickering lights of the gill-netters.

"They can have it," Clarence muttered of the fishermen and lumbered slowly across the dirt road. A group of teenagers came spilling out of the front door of the Johnson's Sweets up the block. Their jabbering, fervent voices carried down the length of Main Street with startling clarity. They were making plans for a wiener roast at the beach.

With a qualm of shyness, Clarence ducked out of sight in the alley between the shipping office and the Olson's grocery store. He followed the narrow, dirt path behind the business establishments of Main Street and then, feeling quite foolish, started up the hill.

As he realized he was heading towards the cottage where Lydia Prince lived, he felt a bolt of panic that made sweat break out along his spine. He knew he was butting his head against a stone wall yet he made no effort to alter his course.

Wild joy seized Clarence as he crossed the center of the hill. He found it next to impossible to breathe. Her image was lodged in his brain like pieces of jagged metal. She was tearing him apart, leaving him floundering. He wanted to stampede her, to victimize her.

There was a thousand to one chance he would run into her by accident. But he could picture the encounter so clearly: a man and a woman alone at the top of the hill, overlooking Wrangell and the channel, separate yet united in their appreciation of the Alaskan night. He would speak in a low wistful voice, expose the sadness in his soul, stun her with his sophistication...

He shrugged his head. He knew she didn't care for him. The thought, though shocking, was not novel anymore. Yet it was still hard to believe. He had fallen for her, from the moment he first saw her, like any sixteen year old kid might do. And once having fallen in love, he was lonelier than he had ever been in the months and years that followed his divorce from Gwen. He was angry at her for disrupting his routine. The smooth, calm Alaskan life he had created for himself shattered. He grew restless and avaricious, like he had been back in the States, searching, lost, greedy, playing dirty.

Clarence had succeeded in Wrangell, even at the terrible cost of divorcing Gwen, of ridding himself of the feelings of revulsion brought on by too much contact with people. In the solitary life he created, he found security and simplicity. Now it was gone, all because of Lydia Prince. It was unbearable, seeing her practically every day, yet exchanging only polite greetings. His restlessness and dissatisfaction were alive and growing and he felt he must act at once to smash them. Until he had her wholly to himself, he would not be free from the greed and the loneliness.

He found it impossible to believe that some other son of a bitch was taking her away from him. It couldn't be true that she didn't care for him. She belonged to him, flesh and blood, heart and soul.

Sweat rolled from his forehead and down his eyes as he hurried up the hill. It was like being caught in a net, like a salmon that pokes his head into the web of a gill-net and can't push ahead anymore, backs away from the obstacle only to discover that his gills are entangled in the mesh.

Clarence stopped near the summit of the hill, on the last road. With a kind of dread, he goaded himself to continue towards Guy Eaton's place. The fir trees on the sloping lawn blocked the view of Lydia's cottage. The heavy fragrance of stock and honeysuckle assailed his nostrils, along with the smell of freshly-mown grass. Below, a diesel engine growled as a boat splashed out of the harbor, the engine notching down to a purr as it moved farther away. A dog barked near by and it brought him to his senses.

He stood directly below Guy Eaton's property. His eye ran up the rock-bordered path, making out the outline of the last cottage at the top. The windows were dark. He guessed she was down at the cannery, like she was every night.

The dog barked again. A dish splattered to the floor in one of the nearest cottages and he heard the faint high shrill of a woman's voice. Out in the channel the pattern of lights was dissolving and reforming in long streamers as the fishing boats began heading in now that the tide was played out. The night sky was blue, tingling with stars, frosted by the radiance of the moon. Clarence felt like crying because he needed her so. His love for her seemed to build every day. It was an obsession that grew more violent as he stood before the house in which she lived, ate, slept, took a bath. After all his experiences with Gwen he knew so much more about how to make a marriage work. He knew he could be a good husband.

He drifted aimlessly across the hill towards the hospital and turned down the dirt road. A car came purring up the hill in second, its headlights sweeping up and illuminating the tall wild grass on either side of the road, picking out fences, trees, houses, wash on the lines. The car stopped by a tree lamp and Clarence noticed that it was Jon Olson's red pick up. He had parked it opposite his house.

"I beat you, Pop," Clarence heard a boy shout and then he saw Danny come down the front porch steps and run over to his stepfather who was slowly extracting himself from the pickup. "Let me help you, Pop. I wanna carry some of the groceries."

Gwen tripped down the steps—she was three or four months pregnant now—and kissed her husband on the cheek and withdrew one of the paper bags from his grasp. They went into the house.

Clarence plodded by, self-conscious, hoping that Gwen hadn't seen him. He was grateful that Gwen had found a good man to marry and Danny seemed to like Jon, too. A feeling of remorse tugged at his belly and he decided to go back to his room.

As he picked up the main road that curved around the island, he saw Steve Svenson coming up from the harbor. He was holding an enormous king salmon, its guts slit, its forked tail dragging the ground.

"Hi, Steve. Where the hell you going with that?" Clarence hadn't seen Steve in a long time.

"I'm taking this to Babs," Steve said. He smiled and hoisted the magnificent specimen high into the air.

"How much does the damn thing weigh?"

"Fifty-one pounds, bare."

"How the hell is she going to eat it?"

"Oh, you know Babs. Three kids and her old man. She'll take care of it."

They started out along the road. Clarence was aware of how much he had missed his friend during the summer. Steve's face was glowing from the effects of a whole summer of wind and sea and sun. "You sure are quiet for a guy who knows all the latest," Steve observed. He sounded apologetic, almost as if he were intruding, which hurt Clarence's feelings.

"Ah shit," Clarence said. "There was so much racket at the hotel I couldn't sleep."

"Well, come on down to Babs'. She'll fix up some hot cocoa or something." He spoke with such compassion that Clarence felt even worse.

"Nah. Hey, what you doing here this late? Lots of boats in tonight. Mitch might be home."

"Guess what? Last I heard, the *Verna* was stranded out in Sumner Strait with a stern bearing shot. Should be a couple days before they get it fixed."

"No kidding?"

"Yeah, Giff's sure having a bad time this year. He had to pay that huge fine when he got caught by the Wildlife cruiser. Lots of boats are way ahead of him."

"I'm glad, the son of a bitch."

They trudged on around the familiar road, passing no one. In a couple of hours the drunks would be staggering out of the bars, the couples going home to bed, the kids returning from the wiener roast. For a brief moment, Clarence felt a curious alienation from all happiness and fun. Everyone else had someplace to go except for him.

"What's wrong, Clarence?" Steve's voice was concerned.

"She's in this town, Steve, right here and I feel like I'm a million miles away." Bitterness washed through him. "She doesn't know I exist. She's nice, says hello, even waves to me sometimes when she walks by the shop. But what the hell? She's ga ga about Chris."

"Give it up, Clarence. It's hopeless."

He was furious at Steve's bland reply. "I can't stand the way some guys have all the talk, the personality boys, getting the choicest, always getting the best parts, leaving the tailings for the other guys."

"You had Gwen, remember," Steve said.

"Steve, forget about Gwen."

"Anything you say, Clarence."

"Guys like Chris," he muttered, "with the dough and the looks, they get all the women."

Steve said abruptly, "You think you've got troubles. Think about me. I have it worse than you. I want to marry a woman with three kids who's married to a lazy no-good-for-nothing bastard of a husband."

"We both are nuts." Clarence felt a little better. This was why he liked Steve. Steve was cool and accepting and had two loves: his boat, which gave him freedom and a livelihood, and Babs. And Babs loved Steve too even though she wouldn't divorce Mitch. She was just that way. She stuck it out.

"Well, here we are," Steve said "Come on in." They had reached the sagging front porch of the Bucci home, a shack at the edge of the native section.

"No, Steve. It's pretty late and I'm tired."

"I hate to see you in such a mess. Forget her, Clarence."

"How do you manage in there?" He suddenly didn't want Steve to go. "Don't the kids hear you?"

"The couch squeaks a little but what the hell? She don't seem to mind."

"You'll have clear sailing for a while, anyway."

"I've got to catch the next tide," Steve said.

"Well, give my regards."

Clarence lumbered on down the road between the shacks. The disorder of the native section appalled him. The roofs were patched and warped, the flues sagged, the fronts of the houses were unpainted and the porches rickety. There were no front yards or flowers. Near the end, spaced several yards from the nearest house, was a one room shack that looked as if it had never been painted. Looking at this privy of a dwelling, Clarence wondered if people actually lived in it, although he knew they did.

Right across the road, Clarence could look through the open front door of a wind-battered shack sheathed with peeling yellow clapboards and a dull red shingled roof. The room inside was lit by a kerosene lamp that stood on the floor in one corner. The floor was littered with newspapers, chips of wood, an axe and a broken-toothed saw with a split handle. There was a pile of chopped logs behind the pot-bellied stove and a shabby green studio couch against the far wall. An old Indian man lay sprawled on the couch. He faced the ceiling and his right hand hung limply over the couch, touching the floor. He seemed dead.

Clarence moved towards the door, his heart thumping against his ribs. He heard footsteps approaching, on the main road that curved past the entrance to the native section. He paused, his foot on the step, and wheeled about in a motion of terror and guilt.

"Hello," the girl said. "Is something wrong?"

It was Lydia.

Clarence was bowled over, simply knocked off guard.

"Hello," he said to her. His voice was a whisper.

The girl was serious. "Is the man sick?" she asked, looking at the man on the couch who had not moved.

"Aw heck, I was just wondering that myself." The words had come out and were gone before he realized that he had managed to speak after all.

"What a dreadful place!" she said with a shudder as she stepped into the room.

He stared at her in wonder as she went by. She was so beautiful with her auburn hair swept back around the sides of her head exposing her small ears. Her blue eyes were fixed, staring. Clarence forced himself to approach the man on the bed and poked him in the ribs. The man wore flannel long johns and a faded pair of woolen trousers held in place by a single suspender over his shoulder. There was no response and he shrank back in terror.

He prodded the man again, aware of a sour, distasteful odor coming from the prostrate form. The man's eyes flashed open. They closed and opened again, like a doll's eyes. They were dull and glazed and showed no surprise or irritation about the invasion of his house by two strangers. He looked at Clarence and then at the girl. He didn't say a word.

"He's all right," Clarence said. He was sickened by the man suddenly.

"Are you sure?" she asked.

"Hey," Clarence said. "You all right? Need anything?"

The man's hand which had been lying on the floor fluttered up and dropped on to his waist. His eyes closed again.

"That's the way some of these old fogey's are," Clarence said. He stepped back to indicate that it was time to depart. Lydia seemed reluctant to leave.

"He's all right." Clarence assured her. He was regaining his poise and thinking of inviting her for a walk. They could go out to the beach below the picnic grounds and sit on the sand.

"Isn't there anyone else in the house?" she asked.

"Probably all out fishing," he mumbled. His voice was once more a whisper, subdued by awe and petulance. They stood outside, indecisive and awkward now that the business which had brought them together was over.

"Well," she said, "it's a nice night. I was just going to Bea's." She appeared impatient. "There seems nothing else that can be done."

Clarence stood dumbfounded. He wanted, with all his heart, to ask if he might join her. They moved off the path and on to the main road.

"How's everything?" he managed to say.

"Well, to be truthful" she laughed, "I can't say for sure. I may be leaving." She paused, as though she had said something that shouldn't have been said.

"What?"

"Oh, it's not definite," she said. "Well, I'll be seeing you, Clarence. I want to get to Bea's before she goes to bed."

She was gone. He could see the straight form of her back moving down the center of the road. He stood watching her until the road turned and she disappeared.

Chris lit another cigarette as he waited for Lyddy. He was too weary to bend forward and drop the match in the ash tray on his desk, so he pitched it aside to the waste basket. As he expected, it missed.

His limbs ached with weariness, his eyes smarted. He felt grimy. His swollen, sweaty feet itched to be free of their bondage.

Outside the crews were returning from the post office, some of them drifting up to the front of the office door and chatting, others reading mail. A lift truck rumbled in the corridor. Lyddy should have been back already since she had been one of the first to leave the cannery. Maybe Tim was slow getting the mail out. Or there was a big crowd.

He inhaled slowly, almost tired of smoking. He was looking forward to the end of the season. Only four more days. He slipped open the lower drawer and filled a paper cup of whiskey discreetly, below the eye level of the desk. He bent down and gulped it.

Most of the workers were back already. He wished George, the foreman, would get the crews started on the assembly belt. He hated to have a minute lost, what with a seiner and a trap tender yet to run.

He moved out on the dock.

"He sure looks lovesick," said a girl in the group near the fish house.

There was laughter.

"Oh, go on," Chris protested.

"Bet he's already married," another girl said. Her words were sharp with excitement at addressing her boss so brashly.

There was more laughter.

"Tell us, Chris, are you married? Have you sneaked off and married the pretty school teacher?"

The girls giggled and the men shifted forward to get in on the fun.

"No truth in it, is there, Chris?" asked George.

"No," Chris said with a laugh. "There's no truth to it!"

He went off to the north end of the dock, past the bow of the freighter loading salmon. All day they had been kidding him about Lyddy. It was almost as if they were reading his mind, for he had decided to marry Lyddy as soon after the close of the season as he could get away. It was too bad about Rushworth. They'd have to go to Petersburg or Ketchikan if they wanted to have the ceremony performed in the Episcopalian church.

All at once the Reverend Rushworth's accident irritated Chris. He didn't want to get married away from home. But he would. He would invite the whole town to sail over to Petersburg in an armada.

He was relieved to hear the machinery in the fish house starting up and the cries of his employees shouting to each other as they resumed work. Longshoremen rolled the drays loaded with salmon to the side of the freighter near where Chris stood.

Lyddy had been behaving very strangely. She was unresponsive, sort of cool and yet nervous too, dissatisfied about something. She barely let him kiss her, just a quick peck when they met and when they said good-bye.

She had showed up today much earlier than he expected. He had been in the fish house, having ordered the exhausted crews to take a twenty minute break for sandwiches and coffee that he furnished from the mess gallery. He was with them, squatting down in one of the larger groups with the workers and they were all cracking wisecracks at him, really razzing Chris, when Lyddy appeared at the open door. She stood there, rather stiff, almost as if she were petrified. He rose, full of welcome, and she stuttered. She seemed shocked that all was still, that all eyes were turned on her.

They moved out on the dock and into the office, Chris not knowing what to say. Surely she recognized the fact that he had left a group of people behind. She must have noticed the coffee and sandwiches he had left on the floor.

"Hi, baby. It's good to see you," he had said.

"Hello, Chris, I'm really sorry, sorry," she repeated, "that I busted in . . ."

"What? Hell, I'm tickled. You're a shot in the arm."

She opened her bag as if searching for something.

George entered the office. "Chris, the crew wants to knock off for a half hour and go get their mail. Tim's sent word around that he's just sorted the mail off the freighter and he's only going to keep the post office open for thirty minutes as he's got a bad cold."

"Sure," Chris said, shaking his head in dismay at the thought of more time lost.

The instant George closed the door, Lyddy said, "I think I'll go see if I have any mail."

"Stay a while, Lyddy." She surprised him. "There's never much mail on a freighter. Just a bag or two."

She snapped her bag shut and walked to the door.

"Heck," he said, "there'll be a mob at first and you'll only have to wait."

"You've got so much to do and I'm in your way." It was obvious she wanted to leave.

"O.K." he said and let it go at that.

"I'll be right back."

But she wasn't. It was over an hour and there was no sign of her. Chris left the cannery and headed over to the Federal Building. The building was dark, deserted with only the telegraph office lights burning dimly inside. He didn't bother to go up the steps and investigate. Instead he trudged down the slope of the hill and went into the hotel bar.

Lyddy heard the whir of bicycle tires behind her on the road. She stepped to one side and watched Judge Slater whiz by on his bicycle. He nodded his head and smiled and went on without breaking his rhythm.

She stepped back onto the road, slowing down that she realized she was far ahead of Clarence. For a moment she had been seized with the absurd idea that the rider on the bicycle would be Clarence. In fact, once she had left him, she hadn't felt at ease. Thank, God, he hadn't followed her. That was one thing, she realized that Clarence never actually did: no physical attempts, no embarrassing overtures, just that hounded expression on his lean, tragic face. The poor man was almost frightening.

The road along the harbor was deserted and she felt apprehensive. There was scarcely a sound or soul out tonight, which was strange, for Wrangell, as a rule, was lively at night. Lyddy had passed only a family of natives.

Her thoughts slowed with her steps. She was anxious to reach Bea's and yet she could think of no reason to hurry. She remembered one warm afternoon when she and Chris had gone out to Woronkofski Island on the *Verna*. They had dropped anchor close off shore and Chris had gone in swimming, by himself because it had been her time of the month. Later, they were cruising near the shoreline and watching the tree-studded shore from the bridge, when Chris spotted a black bear sucking seaweed by an outcropping of rock on the shore. He handed her his 30-06 rifle and told her to take a shot. She didn't want to disappoint him so she had taken it meekly, asking if it kicked like the shotgun while she hesitated, in mortal fear about fitting it her shoulder.

She plodded on, aware of the warmth in the air, the strip of stars above the road. She stared at them, these stars that would be there, when she—and Chris—were gone.

Lyddy looked back over shoulder, but the road was empty behind her. She had been certain that Clarence would tag along behind her after she left him at the junction by the native section. Just last week Vic had told her about the night after the first dance when Clarence came barging into the hotel room drunk and demanded that she sleep with him. Vic wasn't quite clear as to what had happened though the whole thing sounded pretty sordid. Vic was distraught when she spoke about the incident yet Lyddy couldn't seem to react to it. She felt as if she were numb, her senses and feelings wrapped in cotton. Nothing outside of her own thoughts bothered her.

She remembered a few moments she and Chris had spent sitting on the dock in the harbor just before they took off to go seal hunting. They had walked across town, over the wooden bridge and down the stairway to the float which was lined with a clutter of boats. It was warm and still in the harbor. They sat down on the low rail of the float, their feet stretched out. She recalled the moment vividly, feeling the isolation of the town, the hushed quiet of the air. It was the beginning of summer. They could see the green trees on the ridge and the oil-stained waters and feel the mystery of all that was past and yet to be, two people loving each other with a love that contained all of that afternoon in the harbor filled with indolent boats and lazing birds.

Her footsteps scrunched along the dirt road. Most of her dates with Chris were spent outdoors. That's what he enjoyed doing. She enjoyed it too but not the same way he did. He seemed to soak it up, every minute of it and sometimes she resented it. She felt he took her for granted, like a bowl of fruit, a delicacy to be picked up whenever he wanted. It was odd and uncomfortable, a sensation she had never experienced before, this sense of competition for Chris' attention. She thought about him waiting for her at the cannery. He would undoubtedly be sore because she had jilted him. There wouldn't be any fruit to select at random tonight.

The steady hum of the power plant's generator got louder as Lyddy approached the Hart's house. She remembered the fishing trip on Tim Regis' boat. Mrs. Regis, who was supposed to join them, wasn't on the boat when Chris and Lyddy came aboard.

"I'm afraid my wife wasn't up to it today," Tim had explained briefly. With that, he ducked forward and started the motor of his small white cabin cruiser.

"She's probably on a drunk," Chris said as he and Lyddy sat out in the open on the broad railing astern.

"Drunk?" The word seemed ugly on that beautiful summer morning. Lyddy knew Mrs. Regis from her work assisting her husband in the post office. Not only had she gotten him the position, but it was well known that without her help he would never have made a go of it.

They had been rather quiet as they sailed out the channel to the pass, through the pass and beyond towards Sumner Strait. Lyddy stood on the deck, savoring the sight of the sea and the islands, feeling the wind on her cheeks and she was overcome by wonder. All this could be hers forever, along with this tall man standing so close beside her.

"You'll love it!" Chris said. "When you get one of those babies on a line, you've got something. You'll be fighting them, baby."

The wind whipped his fluffy silky hair which always looked uncombed. Chris never used hair oil, never applied face lotion or powder after he shaved. She thought of Don Lofton, how fastidious and well-groomed he was. Even his car was perfect, never a speck of dirt and the seat covers glistened. She wondered why Chris didn't own a boat. Tim was obviously proud of his. She supposed there was nothing that Chris wanted, except clothes and a roof over his head.

Toward mid-morning, Lyddy made a pot of coffee on the Bunsen burner in the cabin. She and Chris drank theirs outside, sitting on the stern.

"Whew!" she said, "that stove was hot. I could scarcely stand it in there."

"Bunsen's are worthless on a boat. Tim must have bought everything that he could lay his hands on when he decided to be an outdoorsman."

The coffee was the worst she had ever tasted, strong and bitter. She had let it percolate too long.

She watched the wake thrown out by the propeller, greenish, crested with foam. With stubborn pride, she forced the coffee down.

"You make coffee like the Indians," Chris said. He set his mug down, still half full. "Heap big wallop."

The thickly-forested islands rolled away on either side of them. The sea was smooth and tinkling, the sky bereft of clouds. They stopped at the landing at Point Baker long enough to gas up and ask where the kings were running. It was another couple of hours before they arrived at their destination. Lyddy made sandwiches and Chris spelled Tim at the wheel.

When they arrived at Point Beauclaire, Lyddy was amazed by the sight. She had never seen anything like it, not even during the trip on the steamer up the Inside Passage from Seattle. The islands looked like a flotilla of sailing vessels in a harbor, they were so small and grouped so tightly. The sparse trees on them looked like the sails of old-fashioned schooners. The sight reminded Lyddy of the moment sitting on the float, of all the moments out of time that had seemed to be waiting for her and Chris to experience them together.

"Point Beauclaire," Chris said. He laughed. "By God, I was seasick here once. On Dad's yacht. It was my first cruise. I'll never forget that ride. I was so green my hair stood out on end. Me and the galley sink stayed glued together, me over it, going up and down, up and down . . ." He pantomimed the motion, cupping his mouth with his hand.

"Stop!" she said with a laugh. "Let's not spoil the scenery."

A host of trollers were patrolling the area, crawling back and forth along the narrow curving waterways, like spiders, with their outstretched poles and dangling lines. Lyddy felt a squeamish feeling in her stomach. She had never fished before, in fact, she had never once had a desire to go fishing. She had never even gone skiing, though Don Lofton had invited her over and over again. She just wasn't the outdoor type.

Tim stepped out of the cabin door grasping a black leather case in each hand. Lyddy studied his face which was interesting for its contrasts. His weak chin and small mouth were balanced by the up-sweeping range of cheek bones, his tiny nose and beady eyes were dwarfed by his high forehead capped with a thick thatch of black hair. Aside from his fondness for drinking and detestation of clerical work, Lyddy had heard that Tim was an avid reader and wrote a little. His most cherished role in Wrangell, of course, was playing chief bartender at all the A&N dances.

"There's your poles, folks," Tim said, placing the two cases against the bulkhead. "Let's see who can catch the biggest."

"No, I'm not going to fish," Lyddy said. "You two men fish. I prefer to watch."

"This is for you, my dear," Tim said, glancing at Chris with an amused crinkle in his eyes. "I'm the flunkey of this trip. And I'm enjoying it." Tim skipped forward, retreating inside behind the wheel.

"This isn't like a sportsman's boat," Chris said, unfastening the cases and removing the sections of bamboo, "which would have outrigging and anchored swivel chairs and cockpits, but this'll do." He fitted the rods together, sticking them in their slots, and inserted the reels. "We'll just stand and brace ourselves against the stern." His whole body was tense with haste as he strung out the lines and attached sinkers and leaders. He peeled off a whole herring from the frozen cold storage package between his feet. Using his knife, he sliced down each side of the bone and removed the fillets, basting them on the hooks, scale side out so it looked like a real fish. As he worked he leaned against the railing, happy and entranced.

"O.K., I'll try it," she said, more to herself than to Chris.

She was happy the fish weren't biting as Tim steered the boat through a back waterway, passing and being passed by trollers which appeared rather stately as they circled the area slowly, in their regalia of out-hanging poles and varicolored fathom markers on the lines extending far beyond into the strait.

Suddenly Chris' pole nearly leaped out of his hands. He hung onto it and it curved almost in two over the stern. Chris shouted back for Tim to slow the engine down.

"By God, look out there Lyddy! See him?"

At that moment her rod pulled in her hands. She felt the muscles in her arms and back wrench and tighten in response to the yank on the line. Her pole eased over like Chris', only not as far.

"Play her out!" he shouted, returning at once in full concentration to his own struggle. His reel screamed for an instant before he braked it, then screamed again.

She could feel Tim watching behind her as she held the bent, quivering pole. He remained in the background, no doubt amused for it was obvious she was trembling more than her pole. On the next furious tug her body slammed up against the bulkhead and she hit her shin. The pain was intense. Her hair blew into her eyes and her fingers were clumsy as she played with the intricate, awkward reel. She was grateful that Chris was too busy with his own pole to notice her ineptitude. All she could do was hold on, the bursting pressure on the line knotting her muscles. Ahead, a supple silver body careened out of the water in a twisting lunge of agony, splashing broadside.

"You've got a nice one, Lyddy," Chris cried. "Just hold him steady. He's tiring."

"Tiring?" She was aghast at the intensity with which the salmon fought, diving deep as the line would permit, then lunging out again as if in a fit of rage and disbelief. She clung on grimly. She reared back on the pole as Chris was doing. She strained her mind out to the end of the line, feeling the agony of the thrashing, wriggling body, diving and racing under the waves in an effort to escape, only to be pulled back short once more, its gills yawning. Then, suddenly, she became scared. She didn't know what to do. She wanted to be rid of it, but she was too conscious of Chris' own hectic struggle to disturb him. Her arms were at the breaking point.

"Tim!" Chris called over his shoulder, his reel squeaking as he pumped on it. "Get the gaff, will you? I'm getting this baby in."

While the two men were engaged on the far side, landing Chris' salmon, Lyddy let her pole slip out of her grasp on the next yank. She watched the slim black shaft disappear into the water and from the corner of her eye, as though she had known that Chris would be watching her, she saw Chris turning to her.

He stared at her with astonishment. His jaw hung open. Incredulity glazed his eyes and twisted his forehead. Still holding onto his pole, he asked, with obvious anger, "What happened? Why didn't you call me?" There was a trace of hatred in his voice that stunned Lyddy into silence.

"Your line's slackening, Chris!" Tim blurted out. "Wheel him in before he gets away." Chris shifted his attention away from Lyddy. For a moment he just held onto the pole, seemingly unable to readjust. Then he returned to the task of angling his fish alongside the boat. It was an enormous silver-plated king. It flapped on the deck as Tim knelt down and extracted the hook from its upper jaw.

"I just couldn't hold on," she said matter-of-factly to Chris. She was not going to offer any further explanation.

Chris still looked puzzled. He couldn't seem to believe that she had actually dropped the pole. In his bewilderment, Chris offered her his rod, encouraging her to try again, but Lyddy declined. She would no longer pretend. They were both angry by the time they decided to call it quits and have some dinner. Lyddy tried to mollify Chris by fixing the best meal she could with the canned goods on hand. The dinner of hot beans and boiled eggs and tamales did seem to ease the tension a little for Chris became his old self again as they sailed towards Wrangell.

"Heck, you'll get the knack of it. You won't let 'em go next time."

She didn't want to talk about fishing. "Chris, whatever became of your father's yacht?"

"Why?" he asked, inhaling on his cigarette.

"I'm just curious."

"I sold it to a guy in Juneau."

"But why? Couldn't you have made use of it?"

"Hell, what would I do with that chrome-plated old thing? It was top heavy. For all Dad's brilliance, he never had a navigator's license. He had no sense of balance, no sense of proportion. Look at the cannery! A huge warehouse which comes in handy once in a blue moon and the fish house is just barely big enough to squeeze in four retorts." Chris flicked his cigarette overboard.

She was afraid that he had stopped. It was rare that he talked about his family.

"By God, you ought to have been on that first cruise. Mom and Theodore were the only ones enjoying it. Me and sis and the rest of the party were down below . . ."

"Do you miss them, Chris?"

"Sure. Listen," he said, cupping her face in his hands, "you're going to be the best dang fisherwoman in this town. You're going to land 'em in style, baby."

It was like Chris to assume that she would enjoy the same things he did. But she was sure she would never fish again. At least not for salmon. Chris would have to go out by himself.

She would never forget the way Chris was out on the cruiser. He was ebullient, confident, bent on impressing Lyddy with his ease in the outdoors. He told her a hunting story about shooting a bull elk. She realized that she wouldn't have him back after the fishing season ended. It wasn't like the States where a man went on a weekend duck shoot once or twice during an entire season. Up here it was constant, the fishing, the hunting, the boat rides. No one sat around the dinner table at night discussing new trends, describing the latest play or symphony performance or rhapsodizing about a new restaurant. No, it would be fishing, hunting and what else? The usual gossip of friends and neighbors? But Chris seldom if ever spoke for or against or even about anyone. Still she would have the children and housekeeping, plenty to keep her occupied, plenty to bridge the gap.

Yet Lyddy resented the one-sidedness. She thought of her life in the States, before she met Chris, when she was aware of her charms, outwitting poor Don Lofton, accepting as her due the longing glances of strangers at dances or in streetcars or passing by her on the sidewalk. The memory was precious and disturbing. By removing herself from San Francisco, she had withdrawn her wares from display but in some subtle way that only increased their appeal. It was inconceivable that she had lost all her ability to charm in so short a period.

Bea Hart's low-hanging fence gate was unhinged. Lyddy stopped. All the lights were on in Bea's house and she could hear treble voices inside. It was obvious a party was in progress. Lyddy nearly turned back. But then she pushed aside the low gate and moved into the yard, thinking still of Chris' reaction on the fishing trip, how he had been so disappointed in her. As she raised her hand to knock on the door, she realized she was disappointed too.

Bea was surprised that she was having such a good time. She was elated and the glow of the company warmed her spirits. Especially after Lyddy arrived.

"My, you look striking, Lyddy," Bea had said, greeting the girl at the door. "What a stunning hairdo!"

"Hello, Bea. I hope I'm not intruding." Lyddy glanced through the foyer at the women sitting about the living room, with knitting needles and crochet hooks and embroidery hoops suspended in their laps as they waited for her entrance.

"Why no, Lyddy. We're just having a plain old sewing bee."

"Hi, Lyddy!" came a chorus of voices as she entered the room.

"Widows in confab," Jean Crawford said. "Yakety, yakety, yak."

Bea suggested they have a snack and while the women were sitting about the card table, Diana Johnson began saying how awful it was that Mr. Rushworth had broken his hip. Bea, carrying in the second pot of coffee, remembered a similar accident from the previous year.

"Jean," Bea said, to the dark-haired girl sitting beside Lyddy, "do you remember, last summer when Judge Slater's wife broke her leg?"

Jean broke out laughing.

"Well, what's so funny?" Virginia Waverly asked. She seldom came over to Bea's. Usually she stayed home, with her housework, her garden, the switchboard and her husband to keep her occupied. Tonight she had been peeved with almost everything, often interjecting sarcastic comments or doubting what was said. Once she interrupted a cute little story that Bea was telling with a joke of her own.

Bea turned to Virgina.

"It was the way the Judge reacted when his wife broke her leg," Bea said.

"Oh, that old fart!" Virginia said with scorn. She rose and headed out the door towards the lavatory. But before she disappeared, Virginia added over her shoulder, "Imagine! The Judge of Wrangell not wanting a pesty phone in his home!"

The girls were stunned. This wasn't the Virginia they knew, the cheerful girl at the switchboard, who always found time to chat with them between phone connections.

"Is there anything the matter with Virginia?" Lyddy asked. She seemed upset by the way Virginia was acting.

"Oh, she's probably just tired," Jean said. "She's been working at the switchboard practically the whole time lately. Cliff's been so busy with repairs that he hasn't spelled her much."

"What happened?" Diana inquired, dressing the side of her cake with fresh raspberry jam. "Anything about the Judge is always good for a laugh."

"Just a minute," Bea said. She went into the bedroom and found Virginia jabbing a burgundy lipstick on her lips. Her movements were tense and furious. A profuse amount of powder and a tinge of rouge lightened her face but her sharp, jet-black eyebrows stood out in sharp relief.

"Anything I can do for you, Virginia?"

"No, I guess I'm just a cow tonight."

"Anything wrong? How's Cliff?"

"What do you mean?" Virginia turned, anger in her eyes.

"Virginia . . ."

"Don't Virginia me. You know as well as all those bitches in there what the matter is . . ." She swung aside to face the mirror. "Thinks he can get away with it, does he! Well, he's free to do as he pleases!"

Bea moved towards Virginia. "Don't talk like that, Virginia. If there's anything wrong I certainly know nothing about it."

"We're not married, Bea."

"What?"

"Oh, skip it."

"You're not what?"

Virginia smiled. "Well, I feel better." She had changed moods so fast that Bea could hardly believe the transformation. As Virginia replaced her things in her lizard handbag, she was once more the impeccable, charming Virginia Waverly. "Skip it, honey. I'm a little blue tonight."

When Bea and Virginia returned to the table, Diana repeated her request. "I want to hear about Judge Slater." Her voice was urgent, reminding Bea of how young she was. Unlike her sister Gwen, Diana lived in a world of dreams that would someday crumble, especially under the onslaught of her fiancé, Curly Weeks.

"You tell her, Jean," Bea said. She had been thrown off track and wanted a moment's peace.

"No, you should, Bea," Jean responded. "After all, you were the one who saw everything."

Bea sliced and placed a tiny rectangle of cake on her plate, even though she knew she wouldn't touch it. She was feeling strange suddenly, as though on the verge of a crisis. She glanced at Virginia but the girl was intent on her cake, wielding her fork with her left hand. Was her defiant statement true? Bea could hardly believe it. It was all so exciting that it left her spent. She wanted to find out for sure. Already she was formulating a plan. Lyddy's arrival had been fortuitous. She could suggest that Lyddy phone Chris and tell him to come over after work.

"Jean, you tell the girls," Bea said. She was nearly hysterical and wanted to weep. She pushed back her chair and rushed into her bedroom but when she got there no tears would come.

If Cliff wasn't at home at this hour to answer the call on the switchboard, if instead, Lizzie Cahill was the operator, then Bea would know that what Virginia said was true. She remembered Roy telling her about running into Cliff and Doreen Barnard in the sweet shop one rainy afternoon this spring. "By God, they were talking like two thieves," Roy had said. Bea wondered why she wanted to hurt Virginia. Was it because Virginia was always so full of vitality and satisfaction? Because Cliff was big and handsome and undoubtedly wonderful in bed? Virginia always hinted at his prowess as she chatted with the women while working at the switchboard, waiting to make contact on calls.

". . . so all of a sudden," Jean was saying as Bea re-entered the living room, "up comes the Judge, cool as ever and asks Bea if he can use the phone."

"I said, 'Why, certainly, Judge,'" said Bea, taking up the story, "and then without further explanation, he rings up Doc Little. Doc wasn't home and he calmly asked—you, I think, Virginia—where he could locate Curly and all that time, I'm wondering why does he want Doc Little. So I went running down the path to Judge Slater's house and the front door was wide open and there was Mrs. Slater laying there in the hallway, at the bottom of the stairs, crying and moaning with her leg bent. She asked me to run up to her room and get the bottle on her night stand. I flew up the stairs and went into the first room I saw, only it was Judge Slater's room. He had a huge collection of guns in a wall cabinet..."

"Does the Judge hunt?" Diana asked mystified.

"No. And that wasn't all. I found a stack of lewd pictures on a table and a tall glass with whiskey in it . . ."

"Come on, Sherlock," Virginia said. "Hurry up with it!"

"Well, I ran down the hall into the other bedroom and what do you think I was sent for?"

"A bottle of hootch," Jean couldn't resist giving it away.

"That seemed to help Mrs. Slater get more comfortable until Doc Little arrived. He called for the ambulance and they took her to the hospital."

The silence that followed rattled Bea. Somehow she had muffed the story. She hadn't conveyed the humor of the situation, how ridiculous it was for the Judge to ask for permission to use the phone as though it were just a routine call. Nor did she get across the incongruity of the gun cabinet and the snapshots of naked men and women in grotesque positions. Nor Mrs. Slater, consuming nearly half the wine in the bottle while lying in pain at the bottom of the stairs.

Lyddy rose to her feet and Bea felt panicked.

"I'm going to have to rush off Bea. Chris will be wondering what happened to me."

Virginia stood also and Bea saw her plan going to pieces.

"I'll drive you back home. I'm tired."

"No," Bea said but her voice was soft as though it came from the other room. "Please stay. Why don't you call up Chris and have him come out and pick you up?"

"Curly can bring him over," Diana said to Lyddy. "He's due to come after me in a short while."

"Oh, heck, let the girl leave if she wants to," Virginia said. "Come on, honey, I'll take you."

"What's the matter, honey? You look glum," Virginia said. She seemed nervous. Her print dress had furled back over her knees as she twisted her head and body to the side to maneuver the gearshift of the old pickup truck.

"Virginia, how long have you been in Wrangell?"

"Eleven years, honey." She struggled with the gearshift, which was locked in reverse and yanked it free, grinding a gear in the process. "Damn this old crate. You've got to pull this God damn clutch out half way and then push it all the way to the floor before you can get the thing to go." She grappled with the stick, trying to shove it into low. "I came up to Wrangell with Cliff. He was down south buying some discarded equipment from Bell." She smiled. "I still remember one of the pieces—a pole digger."

"And you met him and came up?"

"Yep."

The pickup bumped along the main road. It was an ancient GMC used by Cliff for hauling his line equipment.

"Do you like it here, Lyddy?"

"Well, it's obvious, isn't it?"

"Sure, you couldn't pick a better man. Chris is all right."

"How was he? Before I came up?"

"Simple. Very simple. Lived by himself in that big house. Went with a girl for a while, whole town talking about it and suddenly it's all over. He goes out with another, whole town jabbering again, and again it goes for naught." Despite her agitation, Virginia drove rather carefully and slowly. "I'll never forget a clam bake we had down the road. Chris got drunk and went in swimming. It was cold and it was dark and he just disappeared. He was pretty drunk before he went in the water. We were scared silly when he didn't come back. Before you know it the clam bake was off and the men got in their cars and rushed back to the harbor to get a boat to go after him. Well," Virginia started to chuckle, "their boats pull out, two seiners and a cabin cruiser, and who do you think was piloting the seiner when they got to the spot where he was supposed to have drowned? Chris Ballard!"

"Oh no," Lyddy said.

"Yep. Giff was on the seiner and everyone thought he had one of the deckhands in the wheel house. But Chris had gotten around to the harbor and told Giff to keep mum. That's the way he is. Why that man will play poker for two days straight. He'll go out on a skiff and not come back for a day. Heck, there was that time at the Redman folk dance . . ." Virginia's voice lagged. "No, I better let that go."

"What happened?"

"Oh, he just made a sap of himself."

"Dancing?"

"Uh huh." Virginia's cautious agreement let Lyddy know she was covering up. "He was wild that night. He gets that way, gets a streak of wildness in him. He doesn't mean any harm, but he does hurt people's feelings sometimes. You want me to take you to the cannery?"

"No, I was just faking. Would you mind driving me home, Virginia?"

21

Chris was coming out of the hotel bar late in the afternoon when he saw Lyddy coming out of the steamship office on the Clinton dock. They both started as if the coincidental meeting caught them at a disadvantage.

This was the first time Chris had seen Lyddy since the night before when she had failed to return to the cannery. She stood there outside the steamship office, calm and composed, waiting for him to approach her. It must have been closing time for Ted Sanard came out with his briefcase in his hand and tried the door to see if the lock was fastened properly. Lyddy said goodnight to him in a pleasant voice. Ted waved a greeting at Chris and crossed the street.

Chris and Lyddy were no more than twenty feet apart, the width of the Clinton dock. In the split second before Chris headed across the street to meet her, he felt an intense pang of the same sense of discomfort he had felt throughout the day.

He had woken that morning, hungrier than usual, feeling stiff and dried-up from overwork, voracious smoking and lack of sleep. He trudged across the hill, not even glancing up at the cottage when he went by the Eaton place. The first whiff of coffee sent his stomach into a spasm that was both harsh and ecstatic. He pushed into the mess-kitchen. The sunlight glared off the red-and-white checked tablecloth on his table. A spiral of flies were buzzing frantically as they bumped head-on against the windows. A pot of coffee was bubbling on the great, empty range of the oil stove. Al Swift, the cook, was poised before the row of windows with a fly swatter in hand. He stood there as one would before an enigmatic painting in an art gallery, staring at it with puzzlement and concentration. Swat! Al brought the pink paddle down with a deft twist of his wrist. A fly dropped to the floor.

"Good morning. This getting up is getting you down too, huh?"

"Everybody working already?"

"Hell, man, where you been? It's past seven o'clock."

Chris ate his breakfast in silence. He poured some catsup over his eggs and dipped pieces of buttered toast in the gleaming yellow yolks with his fork. When he was finished he pushed his plate away, lit a cigarette and sat back, one foot propped up on the edge of his chair.

Swat!

The room was hot. Chris rubbed out his cigarette on the saucer.

Swat!

He felt alone this morning. Worse than that, he felt wounded.

Swat!

"Missed that one," Al commented.

Chris rose and went out the door. He waited a moment for the screen door to swing back and close. BWHANT. The sun stung his eyes.

Everyone was working. He looked into the fish house through the open sliding doors, at the women clad in beige rubber aprons and the Filipinos who wore elaborate gloves to protect their hands from calluses. They were removing the shining tins from the roller belt and stacking them in the trays. All the motion and commotion of a well-run cannery.

He lit another cigarette. Joe came up and said something about the iron chink needing a sleeve in one of the rollers. Chris nodded and Joe hurried off to take care of it. Chris inhaled and wondered what he was doing there. Everything was going fine without him.

Florence said, "Hello, Chris," as he entered the office. He sat in his chair for at least an hour, staring out the window at the sea gulls and the wisps of mist in the distance, before he decided that this was the one day in this season that he wasn't going to spend at the cannery.

He left the cannery and walked down to the hotel bar. During the whole time he was there, he tried not to think about Lyddy. His mind seemed too dull to figure out what was wrong.

She looked as calm as could be standing there in front of the steamship office. Chris looked down at her, his hands in his pockets. Her composure riled him.

"Like to go for a walk?" he said.

"Yes, I'd love to." She spoke in the same cheerful, polite voice she had used with Ted.

"How are you?" It must be obvious that he was disturbed. Since her disappearance last night, they were like total strangers.

"Chris," she said, with a preoccupied air, "do you mind if we walk up to the Federal Building?"

"More mail? Is Lochinvar still writing?"

She nodded and suppressed a little smile. She was altogether too cheerful.

"What's the rush?" he asked as they cut across the street and marched up the slope of the hill. The warmth of the sun came pouring over the bank of lawn on their right. The sun cast a bright stripe of light across the gray masonry of the Federal Building.

Lyddy didn't answer him but tripped up the two flights of cement stairs and went into the building. He waited outside. It suddenly occurred to him that she hadn't gone to get her mail last night. There was a complication setting in, a bad one, and he didn't want to think about it. There was too much at stake.

She was taking an awfully long time. He watched for her through the plate glass door. A few people came out and greeted Chris, the outswinging glass glinting in the sun. And then he saw her and she him as she pushed on the door. He dropped his eyes before her gaze, feeling suddenly as if he had done something wrong.

"Sorry to keep you waiting, Chris." She said it with a condescending concern that was almost more than he could bear.

"I see you're loaded."

"Yes." She held up the letters with a cluck of satisfaction. "Two from my parents, one for Vic and two from Lochinvar."

They went down the steps to the road. She paused abruptly, before he was aware of it, and he had to backtrack to where she had stopped, her gaze riveted out on the channel. She was using the envelopes as a shade to protect her eyes. Her breasts strained against the white fabric of her blouse. She could have been standing there by herself for all she paid attention to him.

"Like to go to the old cannery?"

"Aren't you supposed to be at work?"

"I said would you like to go to the old cannery?"

"No." She was watching a troller near shore. "It's much too long of a walk and it's late. Let's walk down to the dock."

He was peeved. This was the first time she had ever refused him. He felt a peculiar giddiness which he attributed to uncertainty. It wasn't pleasant. At the bottom of the slope, before the cold storage plant, they turned onto the Canadian dock which swung out in a slow arc to the rectangular warehouse on the end.

"Season's just about over," he said. "By God, that's going to be a relief."

"I should think so." She sounded sympathetic.

He ran his hand over the rail. He looked across at Jack Jewell's two river boats with their bands of copper paint just above the water line and their yellow-and-red trimmed deck houses perched above the shallow, flat-bottomed hulls. They were lying abreast of the float in the harbor, getting ready for another trip up the Stikine River to Telegraph Creek. "Say, before it freezes up north, let's take a trip up the Stikine on one of Jack's river boats."

He was silent waiting for her to say something. Somehow he didn't want to look at her. Below on the beach two boys were leaping amongst the rocks, pressing their bodies against them and shooting over their heads with cocked fingers. PA-TA-KOU! PA-TA-KOU!

"The best time in Wrangell is when everything is quiet," Chris said. "Just plain loafing and tinkering around. Heck, there are parties and dances galore, hunting . . ." He heard himself rattling on and on. He knew he was in some sort of a jam and it seemed the only way out was to try and divert her attention. They walked around in front of the warehouse and immediately were cut off from the view of Wrangell. Lyddy sat down on a cleat in the center of the dock and opened one of the letters.

She hadn't been listening to him, he realized. What was ailing her? Had he done something?

He lit a cigarette and waited. "Any bad news?" He wondered if his tone was as casual as he wanted it to be.

"No," she said. "Just the usual." She resumed reading her letters while he stood above her. The channel lay glinting in the bright glare of the sun. A low, gray Canadian river boat shaped like an old slipper with its heel pressed flat, was cutting across it from the mouth of the river. The sun touched the girl's hair, creating a halo of rich copper. Christ, she was beautiful.

"Hey," he complained, "hurry up."

"In a moment." Her eyes continued their slow survey of the blue pages.

"What's Don Lochinvar got to say?"

"Misses me, misses me, misses me . . ."

"You're nuts today." He said it because he felt that it was about time that he said it.

She stood, evidently unaffected, and looked out at the channel, her back turned to Chris. There was a flock of gulls circling the water a good distance away and her gaze fixed on them for at least a full minute.

"I like to watch the sea gulls. Their landing is pure art."

A young, white-bellied gull swooped past, his head jerking from side to side, the sun glinting off the back of his dove-gray wings. He came down low, skimming over the water and suddenly settled on a spot, that one bit of a spot on the railing that was just his size. He settled down, wings flapping, before he folded them back gracefully against his sides.

She tired of the birds and turned her attention to the river boats in the harbor. "I'd like to take a ride on one of those boats someday. I think it would be fun."

"Hell, I was just talking about that."

"Were you? I wasn't aware."

Her iciness was painful.

"Lyddy, do you like it here?"

"I think we'd better go, Chris."

"Hell, let me talk to you."

"I must go. It's getting late."

Losing his patience he steered the girl against the closed door of the warehouse.

"No, Chris, I must go."

"What's the matter, baby?"

She hesitated.

His hands grasped her wrists; he could feel the small pulse beating next to her watchband. At this spot on the dock, high above the water and shielded from Wrangell by the towering tin side of the warehouse, it was as though they were away from everything.

"Chris," she sighed heavily, "I'm leaving Wrangell."

He felt like he had been plunged into the farthest depths of icy cold black water.

"I've got to get back to the cottage. We're leaving tomorrow night on the *North Star* and there's lots to be done . . ."

Then it was as if he were rocketing up towards the surface. His first physical achievement was to drop her hands and back away a few steps. He felt at ease all of a sudden. He was pleased to see her eyes crinkle up in a passion of despair. He hunted for a cigarette and found the package empty. He crumpled the package and threw it over the dock. He emitted a hollow laugh. "You can't mean that, Lyddy. I mean . . ." He sketched a gesture of impossibility with his hands.

"Chris, listen . . . Oh, I can't explain it."

"It's Don, isn't it?"

"You know it isn't. It's just that I'm not sure of all this, Chris. You must try to understand. I'm not blaming you. It's just that I'm not sure I'm prepared to make my home in Alaska."

"But after all that's happened between us?" He detested himself for the desperation that crept into his voice. "We don't have to live here, Lyddy. I love you. That's all that counts to me. We'll be happy together, Lyddy."

She was shaking her head. "I wouldn't do you any good . . ." One of the letters in her hand tumbled to the planking and she stooped to pick it up. "This is one aspect of me you know nothing about, Chris. Nothing you can say will change me. I'm leaving." She wheeled aside and walked past Chris. When he sat down on the dock cleat, she continued on around the warehouse and disappeared.

Chris picked up a card and discarded a ten of diamonds.

"Hey, Dave," he said, "did ya hear the latest?" He wasn't a bit surprised that Roy Hart picked up the ten.

"No," Dave said, studying his cards with deliberation. He toyed a moment with the discarded queen of hearts that Earl had culled from his hand, thought better of it and reached over to the gin-rummy deck.

"Well, the schoolteachers are leaving." Chris' voice was full of contempt. He thought about forcing a laugh just to see how Dave would react. He was sure he would get a big kick out of it.

Dave was peering at the cards crammed into his large hand. A heavy crease appeared down the center of his forehead. "Check me out," he called over to Johnny Bugg.

Dave rose.

"Hey," Roy protested, "ain't you going to finish the hand?"

Dave showed no sign of having heard. He fixed his eyes on Chris across the table. "So they're leaving Wrangell?"

Chris nodded his head up and down.

"When?"

"Tomorrow night."

"On the *North Star*," Dave recollected. He strode across the oil-soaked floor to cash in his chips.

Chris gathered up his chips too and Matt Fleming, who had been sitting to his left, said, "Maybe I can get some of your lucky cards, Chris."

"Hell, boy," Chris exclaimed, standing, "I carry my luck with me."

Matt looked up at Chris and said, "Hate to see you quit though."

It was so unexpected and hit so solidly, this bit of solicitousness, that Chris glanced down again at Matt. "Why you old son of a gun," he said, touching Matt on the shoulder. Matt sure looked like hell. His cheeks seemed hollower than usual and his eye sockets more cavernous. "Thanks, Matt," Chris added.

Matt slid over onto Chris' chair, a trifle flustered by the concern in Chris' voice.

"Come on, let's deal a new hand," someone said. "This hand's all wrecked now."

Chris decided to leave his chips with Matt, who was down to almost nothing.

"Matt, we'll split, if you win."

"You don't have to, Chris."

"We'll split, Matt. O.K?"

"If you say so, Chris."

Outside, Dave said to Chris, "Sure stuffy in there."

Chris said, "It's funny but I haven't had a drink since she told me. What the hell does that prove?"

"You weren't kidding?" Dave asked.

"By God, hasn't Vic told you?"

Dave pursed his lips. "No," he said. He was angry and Chris, seeing this, wanted to pacify him.

"Maybe it's for the best, Dave."

"She could at least have told me," Dave muttered.

"I can't figure it," Chris said as they walked up Main Street. "Everything looked so rosy and suddenly they decide to leave."

"I wonder if Herb Weaver knows about it?" Dave asked. "He was counting on them to teach this fall."

"By God, don't worry about Herb," Chris said. "He's still out at Point

Baker fishing, none the wiser."

"Let's have a cup of coffee," Dave suggested as they approached Mom's restaurant. On looking in, they saw the place was jammed so they went across to Connell's.

Neither Chris or Dave visited the Connell restaurant often. People came to the small dingy place for an occasional cup of coffee or a beer just to be sociable and spread the business around. Adjoining Floyd's Curio Shop, the Connell restaurant contained only six battered, wobbly stools. The place was always cheerless and dimly lit. It was run by the groggy Mrs. Connell who drank by herself now that her husband was gone. It was amazing that she found the money to keep going.

Cliff Waverly was sitting by himself on the far stool, a bottle of beer and a glass set before him. The passageway behind the counter led through a drawn beige drape to the Connell residence in the rear. The wall facing the customers was partitioned into racks that contained an assortment of cigarettes and peanuts, candies and punch boards. A Silex range and a frying plate stood on a stand by the front window. Mrs. Connell sat next to it, looking haggard. Helen Connell came out through the drape as the bell jingled.

"What'll it be, gents?" she asked, smiling at the two men.

"Coffee for me," Dave said.

"Give me a beer," Chris said, eyeing Cliff. It wasn't right to see Cliff out this late.

Even before Cliff's head bobbed around to face Chris, Chris could tell that Cliff was drunk. Generally he liked Cliff, because Cliff kept pretty much to himself and was usually a lot of fun at parties and dances. But Cliff was belligerent when drunk.

"Hi," Cliff said in his low mellow voice, which sounded rich, often unctuously refined, over the telephone. Cliff's head dropped a notch, apparently from the effort it took to speak.

"What the hell you doing? Getting drunk?"

"A man's got to drink sometime," Mrs. Connell said, rising from her chair and wagging her head at the two men to signal them to leave Cliff alone.

Helen deposited the beer and coffee on the counter.

Chris let his gaze linger on Helen, hoping to let her see the appreciation in his eyes. She was primped up, wearing a necklace and make-up. The vivid colors of the rouge and lipstick brought a stark beauty to her features.

"How's the coffee?" Helen asked Dave.

"Just fine," Dave said.

"What's ailing you?" Chris asked Cliff.

"Give me another beer," Cliff said to Helen, sliding his half-filled bottle to the edge of the counter.

"You haven't finished it all yet," she said.

"I want another bottle."

Helen hesitated, surveying Cliff with a disturbed frown, then produced a fresh bottle from the refrigerator and jerked off the cap.

Cliff snickered, as he tipped the spout of his bottle inside the tilted rim of his glass. "This is a hamburger joint. You know, by God, I don't think I ever ate a hamburger here."

"No you haven't," Mrs. Connell said.

"Well, by God, I want one."

"Suits me," Mrs. Connell said.

Cliff jerked his head towards Chris, as a drunk does, just his neck pivoting while his body remained stationary, facing forward.

"You remember the time I had the booth outside Floyd's Curio Shop? Naw, you wouldn't remember, hell that must have been ten years ago."

"Sure I remember it," Chris said. "That was a good idea."

"Yeah, but for those God damn Indian's pissing in it."

Dave was laughing though, like Chris, he had heard the story several times.

"So I wired the damn walls and sprinkled salt on it and soaked the floor, best God damn conductor there is, salt water. By God, the next Indian who pissed in that booth . . ."

Dave was laughing so hard that Cliff paused to appreciate the reception of his story. "You're God damn right he felt a jolt. That was one-hundred-ten D.C.'s I had those wires connected to."

Dave laughed so hard he began to choke. He lurched off his stool and buckled up. Chris didn't even turn around to watch him. Mrs. Connell was standing over the range with a spatula in hand, eyeing the glob of meat sizzling in a pool of oil. Helen was suppressing a laugh; her lips were pressed tightly together.

Doreen Barnard drifted by the shop, then came back and pushed open the door.

"What the hell took you so long?" Cliff shouted. Doreen had grown plump since her husband died. She had a heart-shaped face that was wearing remarkably well for her forty odd years and her eyes, gray and well-lashed, were large and striking.

"Cliff, you better go home," Doreen began. She glanced uneasily at Chris and Dave and said hello to the two men.

"Sit down," Cliff said, motioning to the stool between him and Chris. When Doreen shook her head, Cliff seized her by the arm.

"You better go home," Doreen said. She gave Chris a look which conveyed her disgust over Cliff's behavior and a plea for help.

Chris turned away. Doreen sat down gingerly beside Cliff. "Give us another beer," Cliff said to Helen.

Doreen shook her head at Helen.

"All right, by God, I'll have another one then," Cliff said.

Doreen leaned over and whispered something in Cliff's ear and he whispered back. The son of a bitch wasn't as drunk as he seemed to be.

"Look at that guy, will you," Chris said derisively to Dave.

Dave kicked Chris' leg.

"How's everything?" Chris said to Helen. "How's Lyle? See much of him any more?"

"As a matter of fact he was in earlier tonight," Helen said. Her gaze was clear and direct.

Chris felt let down. "Good boy, that Lyle."

Chris was aware of Dave's foot again. "Come on, Chris, finish your drink and let's clear out."

"Okay, Dave," Chris said. He watched Helen retreat to the corner by the refrigerator. She was skinny and pert. Brother, if people only knew how much she could drink without the slightest dent in her poise. He didn't know why he ever went out with Helen. Once he thought it was because of the way she smoked. She smoked beautifully, in rapture almost, her manner delicate and aristocratic. There was no slouch in her fingers while she held a cigarette. In fact, when he thought about it, Helen had little or no slouch in anything. There was a kind of confidence in her that always irked Chris because he couldn't figure it out. Even when they broke up, after everyone had been certain, probably even Helen herself, that they would be married, she showed no sign of rancor or disappointment. He remembered how soft she was, almost as if she had no bones. Only her thin lips were hard, and her small breasts.

"Let's go," Dave said again when Chris drained his glass.

"Thanks, men," Helen said as Chris and Dave slid off their stools.

Outside Dave sad, "Chris, sometimes you can be downright miserable."

"Ah shit, Cliff's a jerk when he drinks."

"The guy's drunk," Dave said wearily. After a bit, he added, "He's nuts too, that Cliff. You couldn't ask for a better woman than Virginia."

"That's what I mean," Chris said.

"Well, don't take it out on him. He'll get his."

"Dave, you love Vic, don't you?"

"I think I do, Chris. But then it's about time I fell in love with someone."

"Hell, you're young, Dave. You'll always be young."

"That's what you think. I've been having a little pain in my back lately. I never had that before."

"What you ought to do is close up the place and go on a three months toot."

"You seem to be taking it all right. Interested in everybody else's welfare all of a sudden."

"I feel philanthropic. Hey, is that all right?"

"I guess so. Chris, you're crazy to let her go without a fight. She loves you. Anybody can see that."

"Listen, are you going to do anything?"

"I would, if Vic loved me."

"Say, you know we haven't been out like this since by God, since . . ."

"You said it," Dave interrupted, "since they came up."

"Well, now they're going down . . ."

"It won't be the same, Chris."

"Oh yes, it will. It'll be the same all right. Say Helen looks ripe again." He glanced in the window. "I think I'll go in and ask her."

"Chris," Dave pleaded, "please be sensible . . ."

"Damn certain I'll ask her. And say, there's Fanny. I've been hankering to get into her pants."

"You haven't given her a thought. You haven't given anybody a thought."

Chuck Alder came running diagonally across the street and Chris and Dave stopped talking for Chuck was heading their way.

"Hey, Dave, I'm glad I found you. Curly's been in a fist fight and knocked some Indian's front teeth out. The old boy's mouth is bleeding pretty bad . . ."

"Where is he?" Dave asked.

"In jail. He-he-he!" Chuck giggled. "The guy thinks he got a raw deal, what with Curly knocking his teeth out and me tossing him in the clink."

"Want to tag along, Chris?" Dave asked.

"I'll see you later, Dave," Chris said. "It's late. I think I'll go hit the sack."

Dave mumbled something indistinguishable. "Chris, for Christ sakes!"

"I'll see you, Dave."

He walked off, though he knew his friend was still looking at him. He strode on, the sounds of his heels clacking up from the boardwalk in front of the old Russian's shoe shop, heading down the road.

In the past he would have been delighted to go down to the jail house and see the Indian behind the bars, yak with Chuck in his little cubicle of an office, sitting on an army cot or one of the folding chairs. He would have derived some sort of satisfaction from Chuck's amusement—Chuck was always entertained by his drunks and petty noisemakers. But lately Wrangell had been a blur, as if he hadn't been in it.

Chris stopped by one of the cabins along the edge of the harbor. He heard voices, singing voices, coming from somewhere in the harbor. He listened intently for a while. It sounded like a bunch of teenagers out on skiffs, singing. He let the joy of their happy, carefree voices soak into his soul. Jesus, he decided, I'll just go down the harbor and row out on the channel. It's a nice night for it.

Violet's mother was finally asleep. Violet glanced once again at the clock on the cluttered table in the house and saw that it was ten past twelve.

Knowing her mother, she remained rooted to her chair. She dared not even cross her legs for she knew it was the first few minutes that determined her mother's sleeping pattern for the whole night. For a moment she felt a rush of feverish anxiety. She really wanted to leave the house. In the quiet, she could heard the mice scrambling around in the ceiling and the rats thumping as they jumped down from the toilet seat to the floor of the back porch. Every night they came up from the harbor, skittering along the pilings and slipping up through the toilet hole that hovered over the water's edge. Their squealing as they ran across the porch terrified her. They frolicked on the shag rug spread out on the cold bare floor of the porch, sliding on it as it slipped under the momentum of their dashing feet. All about the room was evidence of their depredations—holes in the walls and bite marks on the furniture.

Violet could tell her mother was completely asleep by the dead quiet that lay over the lump in the bed against the wall. She got up, concentrating on keeping her steps noiseless as she tiptoed across the blue linoleum floor. Because the front door had a loose hinge, she went out through the kitchen.

Behind the house she stood still, looking at the gray-yellow adobe hovel where her Granny lived. The front door was ajar. It was the only means of ventilation Granny had for all the shutters had been nailed shut. She could see the flickering candlelight inside. She felt a curious mixture of suffocation and revulsion when she thought of her grandmother. She hated Granny, her poor vision and her helplessness. She was a crazy old thing, ninety-two years old and set in her ways. She slept all day and stayed up all night.

She was far down the road before she realized that, since her mother had started smoking salmon at the Tupman's two days ago, no one had visited Granny. It was true Granny could always complain, bang her stick against the wall, her signal that she wanted something. But Granny was proud and would starve to death before she'd ask for food.

Violet hurried through the native section and walked across the bridge and down the stairway to the float. No one was around. The float made an elbow just away from the shrimp cannery piling and she stood on the square turning, waiting for Victor. She was not surprised that Victor wasn't already there to ferry her across the harbor in his skiff to the other float where he moored his troller. She had seen him late this afternoon, wobbling across the bridge and looking very drunk. It was always strange to see Victor drunk and today it had really surprised her because he was supposed to be out fishing. She hadn't dared to run out and meet him. It was a standing rule between them that whenever Victor was in the harbor, he would pick her up sometime after midnight at the float, here by the shrimp cannery, providing, of course, that her husband was out of town.

She hoped that he would still be drunk. She liked Victor when he was drunk, the more drunk the better. He cried when he was drunk and he seemed wonderfully handsome with his small, weather-beaten eyes dripping with tears. He would talk about his dead wife and children, all of them burned to death in a fire in his home in France, and she would be so moved by his tales of woe that it would make her want to cry too.

She must have been waiting a half hour before she realized that something must be wrong. Maybe Victor was so drunk he had forgotten about her. She put two fingers to her mouth and let loose a low, short whistle. She waited a couple of minutes but she could hear no oars banging into oarlocks across the way. She whistled again and still there was no sound of anyone preparing a skiff to come after her.

She strode up the float and spied a skiff moored to the railing behind a troller. She untied the painter and shoved the skiff out in the water. She sat down in the center thwart but quickly jumped up for the seat was wet with dew. Adopting the characteristic pose of the native fisherman, she swung one leg forward over the thwart and rowed across standing up. For some reason, she felt determined to see Victor. It would be nice to snuggle up with him. She hoped he hadn't drunk all the whiskey aboard his boat.

It was when she was nearing the float across the way that she saw a man sitting on a skiff with his hands limp on the gunnel. She grew frightened and veered off.

The swish of the approaching skiff stirred Chris. The creaking roll of the oars stilled for a moment, the skiff sliding from its own momentum. He saw Violet, braking her starboard oar and swerving, heading the skiff up to the far end of the float as though she had been frightened by the sight of him sitting alone and so still in a skiff in the harbor.

Ever since he came down to the harbor and made a half-hearted attempt to generate some enthusiasm by rowing out into the channel, Chris had been thinking of Tom Hart. He felt that he understood Tom better tonight than he ever had when the kid was alive. The only time that Tom ever really looked up at Chris was when the kid was choked up with something. And tonight, for the first time that he could recall, Chris felt the same way. Even his father's accident hadn't affected him this way.

Tom had hidden the pain in his ears from his parents his whole life, holding himself aloof from everyone, even his mother. Tom would be all choked up with feelings like a barrel bursting at the seams. Then when he and Chris would start working on an outboard motor spread out all over the porch of the float house, Tom would start to talk about what was bothering him. "My ears have been hurting me a lot lately. It's getting worse, I guess. And that damn engine knocking all the time in the cabin doesn't help." "Why don't you go to a doctor, Tom?" Chris had pleaded. "Tell your parents! You're crazy to keep it to yourself." But instead of voicing what was in him—the anger, dismay, confusion—the kid would clam up, choking with the problem, unable to find release for it. Except when Tom was out in the woods, hunting, fishing or cruising in his double-ender by himself. There he found release. At least Chris hoped so.

Chris was stone sober, sitting in the center thwart of this skiff which he had borrowed without knowing whose it was. He had been sitting in it for at least an hour, thinking of Tom who was dead, thinking of Red Parker, who was turning into such a wino, thinking of Giff's wife, Viola, who had left town on the Princess Elizabeth and was never seen or heard of again. The lives of the people he knew seemed to unfold before him as though they were going to vanish in just a brief while and he was rushing over the names and faces for one last look before they were gone.

Occasionally a soft wave sneaked through the mouth of the harbor and rolled under the skiff. Occasionally the skiff rubbed up against the hull of the seiner along which it lay idle. The thump scraped against his consciousness like some familiar sound that he couldn't place. The sky was filled with a million bright stars, blinking so far away and yet strangely near in a mystery that Chris felt he could comprehend in his despair. Often on the dark roads of Wrangell, with the star-filled sky above him and his blood tingling from his walk about the island, he felt at one with the sky, as if his thoughts, the upsurge of joy in his life could raise him to such a height.

But today he had been kicked in the ass. And kicked squarely in the ass. By a gal from the States.

Chris poked an oar against the hull of the seiner and pushed out into the harbor, rowing slowly, not turning to face forward to see where he was going. He knew the harbor so well that he didn't need to. He slipped along by the edge of the breakwater wall. The red light on its tip blinked steadily and surely, a red bit of light that touched the night and the water with warning. He rowed lengthwise across the harbor, not shoving out into the channel as he had planned to do. Where were the skiffs full of singing kids?

He bent forward and pulled hard on the oars. He was stone sober. This thought kept recurring in all its implausibility. Funny, when Lyddy told him she was leaving, his first impulse was to go get drunk. In fact he'd headed straight for Johnny Bugg's bar, only to bypass the bar entirely and get into a seven-card gin rummy game instead.

He was beginning to feel warmed by his efforts. He pulled the big seine skiff harder. He would pull and pull until his grief was pulled out of him. The skiff bucked across the water with each vicious stroke. He sped across, panting fiercely, and, misjudging the distance, rammed the skiff's nose up on the ramp of the aeroplane float and nearly tipped it over.

He tied the skiff to the float and headed up the stairway to the dock. He went round the front of the hotel and strode up Main Street to Johnny Bugg's bar. Still he had no desire to drink He stood outside, aimless and exhausted, his body racked from lack of sleep, his eyes burning.

Matt Fleming came out of the bar and dashed across to his bicycle, which was sprawled out on the road.

"Why, hello, again, Chris." Matt inspected the spokes and frame and seemed satisfied no damage had been done. "Somebody must have pushed it off its rest," Matt said.

"Say, how'd you come out in the game?"

"I lost," Matt said.

"Hell, you let those sharks beat you?" Chris kidded. All the while he was aware of how bizarre the scene was. There was no sense in him having this conversation with a cancer-ridden old man in front of Johnny Bugg's bar at two o'clock at night.

"They're good," Matt said of the gin rummy competition. "Do you know that Earl memorizes every card that falls? How does he do it? And how can you beat a person like that?"

Chris yawned. "Care for a cup of coffee before you ride out?" This old man knew what it was to live alone, forever, with no respite, alone morning, noon and night. After a while, time slowed down until at night the events of the afternoon seemed so far away they might have happened ages ago. Tonight Chris could feel the weight, the slow progression of all his nights alone. His eyes burned and he rubbed them, only to have them smart the more.

rid of the phlegm that had been suffocating him since he had laid down to sleep. The howl of the wind drowned out the rattle of his coughing and Matt, momentarily relieved, hoped that Chris hadn't heard him in the other room. Chris was sleeping on a mattress that Matt had dragged in from the wood shed and placed on the floor in the narrow kitchen. Matt felt a new assault of coughing well up inside of him and began again, pressing a towel to his mouth. Although he couldn't see in the dark, he knew he was spitting up blood. He tried turning over on his stomach which sometimes eased the pain. The wind pounded overhead, ripping into the trees. His lungs and stomach were rotting away. He had only a few months left. There would come a time when he would not be able to move from this bed. He would die on this bed. The wind was so strong it seemed like it could wrench off the roof, smash in the walls. Matt began coughing again, a harsh cough, as harsh as the wind, wanting to rip up everything in its path.

The heavy slap of water against the hull woke Giff. Inside the cramped forward hold of the *Verna*, it sounded like a monster was ripping sheets off the hull. Clothing and bits of gear tore loose from their mooring. A piece of metal—a belt-buckle—clanged against the steel brace of Clyde's bunk. Homer peered over the edge of his bunk at Giff in the lower berth.

"Hey, Giff," Homer said, "you awake?"

"Yeah," Giff said. He had known this was coming. Ever since they had replaced the burnt out stern bearing at Baker, which cost them four days of probably the best fishing of the season, he had known that something else was going to happen.

In a moment he swiveled out of his bunk and called to Homer, Clyde, Mitch and Carl.

"Come on," Giff roared, "get off your asses! This boat's about to sink!"

Giff held his back jammed against the bulkhead while he drove his legs into his trousers. He was filled with disgust. The hold was stuffed full with beautiful, high-priced salmon, the deck was awash with salmon, and now this God damn storm. The ribs and the planks of the seiner groaned under the onslaught of the water. It was overloaded and battling to remain afloat. Giff thought of Harvey's boat last year.

A mixture of guilt and shame coursed through Giff as he slipped on his shoes. He shouldn't have allowed the crew's greediness to influence him. It wasn't his year. Everything he did turned out wrong. After they had filled the hold to capacity he should have made them stop but instead he allowed them to brail the fish onto the open deck.

The boat lay on its side, struggling to right itself, when the men scampered up the companionway to the aft deck. They started throwing the fish, which had slithered in a heap against the port railing, over the side.

Lyle was in the pilot house, both hands on the wheel, when Giff came in from the starboard side.

"Keep her there," Giff said, noting the throttle set to quarter speed. He dashed out to help the men toss the salmon.

It was dark. The wind lashed across the deck, the waves tilted the floundering seiner, keeping the men off balance. A wave crashed over the railing, followed immediately by another, sluicing the entire deck with a torrent of water. The seiner hung poised on one side. The men crawled across the tilted deck, sliding and slipping, and held onto the opposite rail to try and stabilize the craft. Slowly the *Verna* righted somewhat but she refused to budge more than a few points from her giddy angle.

"Come on! Come on!" Giff rasped.

Homer and Clyde pushed off the hatch cover. Giff was bitter. It was the best season in years and he wasn't even in the running. He stared numbly at the black waves, tipped with phosphorescent foam, that besieged the boat. In a fit of rage, he began to pitch the fish over the side. He slipped and slithered in the slimy, salmon-packed hold and water splashed over him but he knew that at least the boat was saved.

"Just seven miles more and we would have made it," Clyde shouted, his body in a whirl of motion as he flicked the fish out of the hold and into the air.

Giff stomped up the starboard deck, holding onto the rail. They were coming through the pass and in the distance, just barely visible in the first glimmer of daylight, lay Wrangell. As soon as they got into town, he was heading straight for the hotel bar.

22

By mid-afternoon the cottage had been stripped. The luggage and trunk were packed and shipped off in Curly's cab to the steamship office down at the Clinton dock. The southbound steamer was due to arrive from Petersburg at seven o'clock and depart for the States at nine thirty.

The girls sat in the living room, Vic on the sofa and Lyddy on the rocker in the corner. Vic could think of nothing to say and kept her eyes fixed on her nails that were chipped from all the scouring. With all of their belongings gone, the cottage was dead. It had lost all its meaning. Lyddy sat in the rocker as though in a coma. The chair was absolutely still.

Vic felt a aching sensation of shame. They were letting down Herb Weaver who was still out fishing with his family in their troller at Point Baker. The principal had assumed the girls would remain in Wrangell to work the fall semester. They were cowards to slip away like this. She thought of Dave, too, whom she had treated so badly.

Vic rose and glanced out the front door window. She felt even more agitated by Lyddy's absolute stillness. Lyddy might have been a statue set down on the rocker momentarily before being placed in a permanent niche in the room. She wanted to shake her.

The clouds overhead were dark and sinking low. The trees on the hill were very still, unnaturally so, after the furious storm of the early morning. She sat down again, glancing in Lyddy's direction. Her friend hadn't stirred. She sat there, perfectly balanced on the precarious axis of the curved rockers, her hands clasping the arms, her eyes fixed on a spot on the wall across the room.

"Well, it's over," Vic said.

Lyddy did not reply.

"What do you expect?" Vic asked, flustered and angered by Lyddy's withdrawal. "What do you want him to be doing? Wishing you a Bon Voyage with a basket of fruit and champagne?"

Lyddy dropped her head and the rocker swayed a little with the motion. "I wish the steamer would hurry and come."

"Say, where are we going to eat tonight?"

"Are you hungry?" Lyddy's voice was toneless, which galled Victoria.

"Well," she said, "I was thinking by the time seven o'clock rolls around that we would be."

Lyddy eased back in her poised position, apparently dismissing Vic.

Vic remembered her first few weeks in Wrangell, with Dave coming to meet her each day at noon, wading up the school steps through the stream of children, getting caught in the maelstrom, trying to skirt the kids who bounced off him in various directions. She'd walk down to meet him and they'd go down the hill to Mom's for lunch. There was a lovely freedom to those meetings. Dave showered her with attention during the time allotted to him and although his attention was sometimes stiff and sometimes chafing, she was nonetheless rejuvenated by it. Often, after lunch they'd stroll about the road, go clear down to the native section and come around to the school by the path across the center of the hill. When it rained and they walked together under her umbrella, they were closer than at any other time, even when Dave was kissing her. The rain lashed by the wind, spattered on the canopy of the tilted umbrella. They picked their way carefully around the dirty puddles and car tracks. Dave's tall, vital presence radiated warmth. Vic wondered in utter disgust why she had ended her relationship with him. Clarence Wick came to her mind but she wiped his image out of her mind as she had been able to do lately.

———————

"I'm going to phone Chris," Lyddy said.

"Well, isn't that nice of Miss Prince!" Vic's voice was sarcastic.

"What's come over you?"

"Lyddy, you and me have got this all wrong. We did everything wrong. We should have postponed all this weeks ago."

"Well, it's too late now, Vic."

"I wish we had never made these plans in the first place."

"It was your idea!"

"You were the one that got the tickets!"

Lyddy stomped out of the room and went into the kitchen. Instead of throbbing with rage she felt more at ease than at any other time since they had agreed to leave. She recognized the need for this quarrel with Vic. It released some of the tension that had been building between them. The strain had been more than she had ever counted on. The physical activity was hard enough, packing all their things and cleaning the cottage. Her back was sore from mopping and waxing the floors. But she hadn't realized how leaving would affect her emotionally. Every minute she prepared to go, she was severing all of her relationships and the routine into which she had settled in Wrangell. She picked up the telephone which was set into the wall next to the pantry.

"Virginia," Lyddy said to the operator, "would you connect me with the cannery?"

"Sure can, kid. How ya doing?"

"Vic and I are leaving on the *North Star* tonight." It occurred to Lyddy suddenly that except for Chris and Ted Savard, the steamship ticket man, and their landlords, the Eatons, no one else knew of their leaving. "We've decided to go south, Virginia."

"No kidding. My gosh, nothing wrong is there?"

"No, it's just—well, we decided that it would be best for a while, at least." She tried to sound assured through her throat was tight. "I don't think Wrangell has seen the last of us."

"I should hope not!" Virginia exclaimed.

"Would you connect me with the cannery?"

Virginia had no sooner tripped the three short buzzes which signaled the Ballard Cannery than someone snatched up the receiver at the other end. "Ballard Cannery," said a breathless voice. Lyddy recognized the voice of Florence Savard, Chris' secretary.

"Hello, Florence. This is Lydia Prince . . ."

"Hi, Lyddy. How's everything? Say, do you know where Chris is? The cannery's been running on one leg ever since he left here yesterday. So much has happened that needs his attention."

"No," Lyddy said. "No, I don't know where he is, Florence."

"What a goof I am," Florence said. "You probably called looking for him. Ted told me you were leaving . . ." Her voice had dropped from hysterical panic to sympathetic pity.

"If Chris comes in, will you have him call me?" Lyddy said. She hung up in a daze. She had never felt so insecure. She had expected Chris to come up to see her so that they could discuss their plans for the future. She wasn't planning to leave forever. She just wanted to go south to visit her parents and reorient her mind. She wanted to be positive she knew what she was doing. She couldn't continue living in Wrangell on courage and hope and misgiving. His disappearance was baffling. It didn't seem like him. She felt suddenly that she didn't know him at all.

Lyddy whirled the crank again.

"Give me Chris' house, Virginia."

"Giving you the run around, huh, honey?" Virginia said. "I'm getting the same treatment here from my old man. Cliff's been gone since this morning. You haven't seen him by chance?"

"No," Lyddy said.

There was no answer at Chris' house. She phoned Dave's office and his nurse said that Dave had taken the afternoon off and was down at Johnny Bugg's bar. As far as she knew, Chris was not with him.

Lyddy wandered back into the living room. She was tempted to phone the bar—she had to talk to Chris before she left—but she wanted a few minutes to compose herself.

"I'm sorry, Lyddy," Vic said, getting to her feet. She came over and touched Lyddy's arm. "I shouldn't have jumped on you like that. I'm a rat. A pure bubonic rat."

"You mean I'm a stinker," Lyddy said.

"Can't locate him, huh?"

"No."

"Why don't you phone the bars? That's the most logical place."

"I don't know, Vic. I don't want to."

"Go ahead. See him. Tell him it's only for a while. You just need a break."

"All right."

Lyddy turned and hurried into the kitchen. She felt a weakness in her knees as if she were about to hear Chris' voice for the first time in months. She asked Virginia to connect her to the bar and asked for Dave.

"No, he's not here, Lyddy," Dave said. His voice was subdued and muffled by the commotion of the bar.

"Do you know where he might be, Dave?"

"Did you try the cannery?"

"Yes."

"Maybe he's home."

"I tried there."

They lapsed into silence. They both knew that there was more to be said. Dave ended it. "Try again, Lyddy. I'll see you."

"Bye, Dave."

She went into the bedroom and put her arms on the cold glass-top of the bureau and lowered her head into her hands. She wanted to cry but she didn't give in.

I'm going to search for him, she decided. I'm going to find him.

Virginia Waverly smoldered as her hands flew about the switchboard.

"Number please?" "Number please?"

"You give," said a guttural voice, "Mrs Jamieson's house. You give me."

"That line is busy." Virginia abruptly unhooked the line.

"Number please."

"604, Virginia." That was the number of the Schnur Cannery.

"Hello, Mrs. Schnur," said Virginia. "How are you, dearie?" "Fine, Virginia. You're working late today."

"Gotta keep at 'em," she chirped. "Here's your party."

"Number please?" "Number please?"

"Hi. Virginia."

"George!" she said. "What you want, baby?"

"Give me the hotel bar."

"You won't find Chris there."

"Then forget it."

"I'll give you a buzz if I get anything on him, George."

Her eyes were dazed by the red flickering lights which sprang up all over the board during this time of the day. Her arms from the shoulders down were numb from the effort involved in jabbing all the plugs into the jacks in the complex jumble of cords crisscrossed before her. Virginia worked steadily, automatically, with a certain rhythm which made the job easier.

"Number please?"

"Hi, Virginia." She recognized Fanny's voice.

"Hi, honey! What you know?"

"Nothing much, Virginia."

"You sound dead, baby. Come on, pep up."

"What for?" Fanny asked. "I have nothing to look forward to but selling tickets at the show at nights."

"Honey, that's the wrong attitude."

"And you never help, Virginia, hopped up as you are. I wish I had one iota of your energy."

"Hell, you say," Virginia chirped, without enthusiasm, wanting to be rid of Fanny.

"Give me the laundry, Virginia." There was a brief pause. "209," Fanny added, knowing Virginia's disdain for callers who didn't use the correct number for the four hundred odd subscribers in the exchange. "I might as well bitch at Robby. He shrunk that blue crepe dress of mine. I look terrible in it now. Little fat-legged Fanny with the round knee caps."

"Send your clothes to Petersburg. Robby's no dry cleaner. He admits that himself."

Virginia rang the laundry, cutting off Fanny quickly.

"Number, please?"

"Virginia, Virginia," said a breathless voice, "ring the fire alarm. I see smoke in the native section."

"What, again? Those God damn ignorant natives!" Virginia swung around in her chair and reached over to the alarm box just below the window sill. She executed the signal for a fire in the native section: two short toots. She waited a full count of sixty seconds while the board, as she expected, went wild with flashing red lights, then pressed the push button twice again. Each time that she did so the fire siren, which was rigged on a stanchion above her roof, let loose a screech loud enough to convey the message to the town below.

"Where's the fire?" The first call came through.

"Native section." You big dumb loco, Virginia fumed.

The next plug. "Where's the fire, Virginia?"

"Two short toots," Virginia said, straining to keep control. "That's the native section." The damn numbskulls. What was the use of having codes if no one paid any attention to them?

And where was Cliff, she wondered. He hadn't showed up at the house as he usually did at noon to relieve her so she could make lunch.

"Native section," she informed the next caller.

She hadn't had anything to eat all day, since she had been working the switchboard alone since the morning. And Cliff hadn't even called in. Virginia glanced at her wristwatch. Four o'clock.

"Number please?"

"Hi, Virginia. Another fire, I hear?"

"Hello honey," It was Diana Johnson. "What you want, baby? I'm kinda busy."

"Gwen's house, please," Diana said.

Damn you, Virginia thought. That's 202, that's 202. She clenched her teeth as she yanked out the dead lines from the board, clearing a path before her in which to work.

She plugged in 608 where a light had been burning for quite a while.

"Virginia, this is Helen."

"Hi, honey. What do you want, baby?"

"Virginia . . ." Helen sounded hesitant and embarrassed.

"Yes, honey." She disconnected two more lines and held the next cord ready for 130. Impatient, she plugged it in anyway.

"One minute," she advised the 130 number while she waited for Helen to make up her mind.

"Is there anyone listening?" Helen asked cautiously.

"Oh, wait," Virginia said and contacted 130. "Number please?"

"345 please."

"Sure, Sid. How's every little thing? Say, have you heard . . . Oops, I can't tell you that one now. It's a cutie, though. Call me back later!"

She connected Sid's number and remembered Helen Connell.

"Now what is it, Helen?" Virginia said in her attentive voice.

"Virginia, your husband is passed out, or very near to it. He's in here, on a stool, and he looks pretty bad."

Virginia howled with glee. "Well, slap the big lug between two buns and serve him up as a Waverly sandwich!" Virginia's laughter, though loud was hollow, and both she and Helen knew it.

"What shall I do, Virginia? I'm stuck. If it was anyone else, I'd call Chuck Alder."

"I'm stranded here," Virginia said. "My relief won't be here until five and I can't contact anyone now with this fire going on." Virginia paused a moment to consider. "Is there anyone else there?"

Helen paused a moment before she replied. "Uh, no," she said. Virginia knew she was lying but she didn't press it.

"All right, I'll send someone down there to pick him up as soon as I can."

She worked the switchboard for another hour, the rage coiling in her so that her words squeaked out in a reedy staccato to her subscribers. He'd been with Doreen all day, she knew. She worked furiously, keeping the board clean, cracking jokes and laughing with her customers.

At a quarter to five, just before her relief arrived, the board went dead. Her whole body sagged in the chair. She tapped out a cigarette from the package on top of the board and lit it. She felt the nerves flickering in her hands, the blood humming in her veins. Halfway through the cigarette she stamped it out on the floor, feeling as though she were coming out of a trance. In the interval between the board going dead and the time she snuffed out the cigarette, she suddenly knew what she was going to do.

She plugged in to the steamship dock ticket office. "Hello, Ted, how are you?"

"Just fine," Ted Savard said.

"Ted, book me a passage on the *North Star* tonight."

"Just one, Virginia?" He sounded matter-of-fact.

"Yes."

"And to where, Virginia?"

"Seattle."

"Do you want a private stateroom with shower?"

"Yes."

"Uh, huh. When will you pick up the ticket?"

"I'll pick it up tonight just before I board the steamer."

"I'll have it here for you, Virginia. The steamer will be in until nine thirty, taking on frozen fish." His deliberate monotone was becoming more exaggerated as he tried to conceal his excitement. Virginia feared he would start spreading the news of her departure around before the steamer left Wrangell.

"And Ted," Virginia said, "I'd appreciate it if you'd keep this quiet."

"Certainly, Virginia," he said with a tight, little squeak.

Virginia leaned back in the stiff unwieldy chair. Well, it was all over. This was her last day, perhaps her last shift.

She looked around at the narrow, bare room in which she had spent so much of her life in Wrangell. It contained only an oil stove, an ancient blue leather armchair, an end table displaying a triangular ash tray and a few copies of old and new directories, and the upright board itself in the center against the wall. Her vision blurred as tears came to her eyes, a delayed emotional response to the decision she had made so impulsively.

This room off the back of the house, on the porch, separate from their living quarters. She wanted it that way, a world independent of everything else, her housework, her garden, even Wrangell itself. Friends who dropped by to call on her while she was on duty were subtly discouraged. Virginia had made it clear to young Lizzie Cahill, the relief operator, that she must come around from the rear to enter the office and that Virginia and Cliff were never to be disturbed while they were off duty. If anything important did come up that required their immediate attention, she was to ring them on the private house phone, one short ring, two long.

Virginia had grown into the job gradually, over the years since the moment when she had sailed up from Seattle with Cliff, not knowing a thing about switchboards and transformers and magnet-generators. She worked at it, this hunk of wood and steel, priding herself on her efficiency and the board began to become an obsession with her. She hated it and yet her life would be empty without it. Perched on the chair before the network of numbers, she was energized. She became transformed, her words pouring out smoothly without thinking, in her fever to keep up with the lights. In the heat of the rush hour, she stayed several steps ahead of her clientele, often answering their questions before the words were out of their mouths, after knocking them off balance, severing their line of thought, cold and unprepared as they were, by the rapid tempo of the excitement that she brought to her job.

When she worked, she had her fingers on the pulse of Wrangell. All the voices of Wrangell had passed through this room, the Indians and the whites, the teenagers and the old folks, all the tears and gossip and plans. Although she was isolated in this small room, she knew more about what was going on in town than anyone else. Often Virginia could tell by the caller's voice, what they were thinking, what state of pressure they were in, whether the call was urgent or social or trivial. Virginia heard Lizzie coming up the back steps, singing to herself. At that precise moment, with the sound of the door opening and Lizzie's footsteps, she came up with the ultimate piece of her plan.

"Busy today?" Lizzie asked, as she did every day, depositing a book (never a magazine) on the edge of the board and removing her scarf from her ash blond hair. She was a young thin girl of seventeen who seemed dull and overly responsible to Virginia. Still, there was no dilly-dallying going on while Lizzie was operating the board. She never encouraged the boys who called her up, trying to get her to talk. Lizzie worked slowly and carefully and Virginia was glad to have her.

Virginia removed the headpiece and placed it on the table. "They knocked me daffy, today. It's quiet now."

Lizzie took over the chair and fitted the ear piece to her ear.

"Number, please?" she began.

Virginia stretched her arms, enjoyed the sensation of standing on her feet and walked to the door. The sight of the destruction in her garden, the giant marigolds flung to the ground in a litter of yellow, orange and green, barely bothered her. She had plenty to do. First she would eat. Then she would prepare the proper welcome for Cliff. He was going to be quite surprised.

The hotel bar was quiet, except for some low ragged conversation. Lyddy felt lonely. Giff sat across from her in the booth, drunk and morose. A ring of tufted hair circled his bald spot. His shoulders were littered with dandruff. Violet Lundy sitting beside him kept peeking at Lyddy with her black cagey eyes. Her tongue darted out to moisten her lipstick-smeared lips.

"I wish you'd go away, Violet," Giff said. He pushed against her shoulder.

"What's the matter with you?" she asked huskily, without anger.

Giff drew his wallet from an inside pocket in his woolen plaid jacket, surveyed its contents for a moment and clumsily thumbed out a five dollar bill.

"Hey, Max!" Giff shouted, leaning sideways out of the open booth, "Hey, Max!"

"Please," Lyddy asked, "can you tell me where Chris is? I thought you said you knew where he might be."

"By God, I did," Giff mumbled. He grimaced in deep recollection as if he found it hard to follow his own thoughts.

Lyddy felt self-conscious. She wished she hadn't sat down. She felt Giff was stalling her, enjoying the predicament she was in. She caught Violet peeking at her again.

"Give us a round," Giff said to Max, as the bartender appeared from the room in front.

Max looked at Lyddy. He waited. He looked tall and elegant as he stood there in his white apron, white shirt. His hands at his sides were rosy in hue, his nails were manicured and his tie was a pure sword of blue.

"I don't care for anything," Lyddy said, realizing Max was waiting for her to order.

"Go 'head, give her a drink," Giff insisted, gesturing halfheartedly with his hand.

"All right," she said. "I'll have a martini."

Max gave her a surprised look, held it for a moment, and left. He returned shortly with a tray of drinks. Lyddy tasted the martini, ate the olive and then took several quick sips, wanted suddenly to be like the others in the bar. Usually the place was gay and lively but tonight it was deathly cold and quiet. Somewhere a cat meowed. Ice tinkled in glasses. A floorboard groaned as someone crossed the room.

Violet hung her arm over Giff's shoulder. He took the hand and jerked it over his head. "Now listen, Violet, that's enough!"

Giff slouched out of the booth to make room for her to leave. When she didn't move, Giff gestured at her. "Come on," he said.

"What's wrong?" she asked. "You don't like my company?"

Giff reached out to take her by the arm. She evaded his grasp and his hand sailed on and knocked her drink against the wall. She came scrambling out of the booth with a screech as the drink splashed all over.

"That's one way of getting 'em out," Giff said to Lyddy.

"You're cute!" Violet said. She did not look back as she headed towards a stool at the bar.

"Say, Max," Giff called, "give us a towel here."

Giff settled down when the table had been wiped and stared at Lyddy. "I'm going to tell you something," Giff said. Then he seemed to change his mind. "You know," he smiled, "I started the whole thing. I introduced you to Chris right here in this bar."

Lyddy kept her eyes lowered. She knew the three women in the side booth across the room were watching her, knew she was making a fool of herself hoping to get information from this man but she couldn't leave. This was the first place Chris would come to, wherever he might be now. She had given up thinking that Giff knew where Chris was.

"I've known Chris since he was a baby," Giff mumbled. "I remember him when he was a terror at school here. Then," his face became haggard for an instant, "there was a blank, as you know."

"I know what?" she asked.

"Let's have another drink."

She finished her martini and ordered another. She began to feel warmer and her mind, taut and apprehensive, was relaxing a little. Her heart leaped up each time the front door swished open in the other room but Chris never came in. The place was slowly filling up. She heard laughter, sharp as glass, coming sporadically from the bar behind her.

The place grew darker. It felt like rain. She shifted her weight on the hard bench of the booth. She looked around at the gray dirty walls, the yellow and gray booths, the people in them. Most of them were not talking, just sipping on their drinks in silence.

"You know, my dear," Giff said suddenly. This caught Lyddy's attention. "We are laced with bad qualities—selfishness, hate, rottenness. Very little good."

She declined another drink as Max appeared again at the table.

Giff was quiet until Max returned with his whiskey and water chaser.

"I guess you think I'm pretty stupid," Giff said.

"I can't seem to be able to think of anything at the moment," she confessed. She heard the front door open. It was all she could do to make herself sit still.

Giff leaned out and stared down the length of the two rooms. "It's not Chris."

"I didn't think it would be," she said. After a while, she said. "What do you want to tell me, Giff?"

"You go on living," Giff said. "There's a thousand days, a hundred thousand hours." He paused. "Theodore sent me upriver to this little piece of land to set up camp for him and his party from the States—friends of Theodore's. He wanted to make an impression. It was nice up there on the mainland. Big spruce planted all around the cabin and the willows spreading down thick to the lake. Snow-capped mountains all around. And the weather was cold and blustery, just fine for a duck shoot. I had plenty to keep me busy . . ."

His voice became clear and strong once he found the thread of the story. "I hacked a trail with a machete right down through the brush and willows to the lake. I packed my three-seventy-eight Winchester all the time I was working. That's grizzly country and I wasn't taking any chances. I climbed up a spruce once and spotted two moose, a cow and bull, gorging themselves on water grass in one of the sloughs about a half mile south. I had an urge to stalk 'em down and kill the bull but I didn't want to fire a gun if I could help it. There were mallards and teals and geese browsing on the flats and Theodore sent me up to get things ready, not to scare them away."

He broke off. "By gosh, Lydia, why don't you go look for Chris if it's so important?"

"He'll come here," she said. "I know he'll end up here."

"He'll never hold a candle to Theodore. No, siree," Giff mumbled and downed his whiskey straight.

A fisherman in hip boots inserted a coin in the nickelodeon and swaggered across to the booth.

"Like a dance?" he said. "Dance floor's empty."

"No, thank you," Lyddy said. She had never seen the man before and his hard face repulsed her.

"Come on, kid, plenty of room out here."

"I'd rather not," Lyddy said, fixing her gaze on her empty glass.

"All right, all right," Giff said to the fisherman, who still lingered by the girl.

"Just not my luck," the fisherman sighed and strutted off across the room.

"Go on," Lyddy said. "Where was this place?"

"About thirty miles up the Stikine River."

"So close," she said.

"The first thing Theodore said to me when the party arrived at the camp was about the trail I'd built. 'Giff,' Theodore said, 'you're a wizard. That's a Godsend, huh, fellows?' You should've seen those men from the States. They had just barely unpacked the skiff and carried their stuff to the campsite before they wanted to go hunting. Well, they had a few drinks and went down to the lake packing their shiny guns and game bags, all fit to kill. I stayed behind as I wanted to have a big dinner ready for them, knowing they'd get all the ducks and geese they wanted without my help. Well, you should've heard the shooting? By God, they were having a time!"

"The next morning I woke up early and cooked a big breakfast. I roasted some of those ducks in the dutch oven outside the cabin and they went for them, along with eggs and fried potatoes. Theodore and the men helped me with cleaning up and I went with them this time down to the lake. It wasn't really a lake, just a long shallow swampy stretch of rain water, filled with lilies, wild rice and reeds. We shot ducks and geese, shot 'em all morning long. Finally, I said, 'Come on, we got enough birds. Let's go back to camp and get our rifles. I saw some moose about a week ago in a slough just south of here.' Theodore told me to go get lunch ready and they'd be along shortly. Those men were wild with the shooting. You never saw so many birds. Some of the men were using the canoe that Theodore had towed up with them. They were paddling through the tall reeds, scaring up the birds. You could see the ducks and geese flying in all directions, almost bumping into each other as they tried to get away. By God, that morning you could've hit 'em with an oar."

Giff paused, staring into his empty glass. Lyddy was barely conscious any more of the sounds in the bar.

"Well, I went back to the camp with a load of birds and started a fire for lunch. The men must have gone around the other side of the lake because I couldn't hear any more shooting. The silence was a relief. Then, about a half hour later I heard a shot—one blast from a twelve gauge shotgun barrel. I ran without thinking towards the trail. I started so fast I forgot to pick up my three-seventy-eight Winchester. But the sound wasn't far off and as I ran I began to get puzzled. Why the hell am I so jittery, I thought. Boys probably just coming back and firing a shot to let me know, maybe a signal to give 'em a hand with the birds. Lydia, I didn't have the slightest idea there might be a bear around. Well, I tore down the trail and right away saw Theodore stuck between the branches of a willow. He was wedged into that tree. His head was hanging down and I could see the top of it, and then I realized it wasn't there. I was seeing his scalp hanging down the side of his head. The string of birds

Theodore was carrying—about thirty of 'em—were lying on the trail. I could hear the other men coming up the trail, talking and laughing. 'Is that you, Giff,' Theodore spoke, without lifting his head. 'Yeah, Theodore, it's me,' I said. 'I'm all right now,' he said. I guess he thought at first that the bear had come back to maul him some more. That's why, up until then, he was quiet. Bears will do that. Knock you flat and walk away and then if you move, they'll come back and maul you some more."

"I didn't like the way Theodore talked. His words came out all broken, like something was in the way of his tongue. Well, I carefully lifted his head up to see what was wrong and just then the other men topped the small rise and saw him too. Right away they dropped their birds off their backs and scrambled over to the willow. When they got a good look of Theodore's face they all turned around. Every damn one of those men turned around. Bowley, he's a president of an oil company back east, just vomited. Andy finally turned around and looked at Theodore with his mouth open and couldn't say a thing. 'Get him to a doctor,' someone said. I hurried back to camp for the hatchet and chopped Theodore free from the willow. We couldn't move him otherwise, he was wedged in so tight. It was then that I saw the gashes across his belly, his intestines hanging out."

Lyddy gasped.

"I'm sorry," Giff said. "The man from Hollywood, by God, I can't remember his name, wanted me to wash Theodore's face as soon as we got back to camp. 'All right,' I said, but I couldn't stand it any longer. I walked away. We had him lying on the bare ground, no blankets and him half naked. It was cold, too. But I couldn't wash his face. I couldn't do anything. By God, I cried. Finally I staggered back to where Theodore lay and looked at him. He wasn't conscious. And he wasn't bleeding much, which was strange. Andy said to me, 'Giff, don't wash him. He might start to bleed.' 'What about infection?' the Hollywood man said. 'Gangrene might set in.' 'Isn't there any medicine here?' Louie Sipola said. Well, there wasn't any medicine and the men were staying far away, about fifteen feet away. They weren't even looking at Theodore, just at me. They couldn't bear to look at Theodore. I was the only one doing anything for him. I got some blankets and covered him. His head I didn't cover. His right eye was gone and part of his nose. His mouth was tore open with all his front teeth gone. That's why he talked so brokenly. When I was putting the blanket over his stomach I noticed that his right side was caved in. The bear had crushed his ribs with one swipe."

"Well, we finally pulled ourselves together and made a crude stretcher out of willow branches and blankets and carried Theodore to the flat-bottomed skiff. People will tell you that Theodore told us how to pilot the boat downriver, but that's a lie. I piloted the skiff down. Theodore never blacked out. The whole time down he was talking to me. He was very brave and at times a little delirious, shouting to me to watch out for a sandbar or a bad current or a deadhead. But he was lying on the planking and couldn't see where we were heading."

Giff wagged his head. "No one knows what happened exactly. The grizzly was either on the trail or beside it. Everybody has his own story about it. I'm sure Theodore didn't see the grizzly. He had about twenty five or thirty fat birds strung over his back. When he came near the grizzly his head must have been down, certainly not aware of any danger. The grizzly just reared up, cocked his paw, and swiped off Theodore's scalp, shocking Theodore but not knocking him unconscious, for he fired a shot. He must have missed for I never saw any trace of blood on the trail. The bear swiped again, tearing off Theodore's eye and part of his nose and breaking his mouth. Theodore must have been paralyzed by the attack. The bear grabbed Theodore, dug his claws across Theodore's belly and hit him a lick in the ribs and then tossed Theodore in the branches of the willow and stalked off."

"It's hard to believe that he ever lived through that. We took him to Doc Little, then down to Ketchikan for better medical treatment. Fortunately the mail boat was in Wrangell and we took Theodore down to the dock, with the whole town already there, hearing about the accident. Well, we took Theodore off the ambulance on a wheel stretcher and set him on the dock. The tide was high and there was no way of getting Theodore up the narrow gangplank. Everybody was just stunned, couldn't move, couldn't figure out a way to get this man on the boat. Well, I got mad and yelled to the winch driver to swing the boom over. I grabbed the ropes and hooked them onto the ring bolts on a pallet and rolled the stretcher on, all by myself with everyone just frozen around me. Holding the wheels of the stretcher I signaled to the winch driver and he jerked Theodore and me up and over. Why I couldn't even get help from the sailors. I had to yell to the skipper for some help before we could get Theodore settled on board."

"Verna and Patty and Chris came aboard. That was a trip, a real trip. By this time Theodore realized how seriously he was hurt. He was paralyzed, couldn't lift his arms, and he wanted no one around. Not even me. We had to transfer Theodore by plane from Ketchikan to Seattle after a few days. Everybody was sure he was going to die. In fact, in Seattle I went and bought a suit of clothes just in case he did die. But Theodore didn't die. The cold weather must have saved him, that's how I figure it. He didn't lose a pint of blood. It just coagulated in the cold."

"The rest of the party . . ."

Just then the phone in back of the bar rang with two long strident clangs.

"That damn phone sounds like an alarm clock," Giff grumbled.

Lyddy sat stiff. Giff held his glass, which was empty, in his big hand and stared at it.

Max came to the booth and said that the telephone call was for Lydia Prince.

At a quarter to five when Cliff staggered up the side steps under the honeysuckle and into his house, Virginia had everything ready. First she had a bite to eat. Then she packed her suitcase and concealed it behind some clothes hanging in the closet. Then she took down Cliff's 300 Savage rifle and loaded it from the box of shells Cliff kept in his bureau drawer. She chuckled softly to herself as she jammed the cartridges into the grooved magazine and struggled to get the lever-action to shut. When it was done, she was filled with a delicious sense of satisfaction.

Lizzie Cahill buzzed the house phone once and Virginia hurried down and unlocked the back porch door so the girl could come in and use the bathroom, the only time Lizzie was allowed to enter the house. Once Lizzie was back in the switchboard room and the door was locked, Virginia hurried back to the bedroom, brought the rifle downstairs and stood it carefully behind the kitchen door. She poured herself a glass of water and paced about the living room, waiting for Cliff. Every now and then she yanked aside the drapes and glanced into the rain-soaked garden. The tension set her nerves sparkling, made her jumpy with excitement.

When she heard his heavy, scuffling tread on the steps, her heart leaped. The front door swung open. He stood there, glassy-eyed, swaying slightly. The first thing she noticed was the smear of lipstick on the collar of his green shirt. She was glad for this proof of his infidelity for otherwise there was no sign of anything wrong with him except for drunkenness.

"Hello, darling!" she called out.

Cliff made a feeble effort to straighten up. He shook his head stupidly.

"My God, you are drunk," she said.

Cliff moaned and lurched forward.

"Shut the door, darling."

In doing so, he nearly lost his balance and swayed against the wall.

"Where were you?"

He stared at her, glassy-eyed.

"Doreen. You were with Doreen?"

"No I wasn't."

333

"You were!"

He swung his head from side to side, his jaw gawking.

"All right, darling," she said. "All right, baby. We'll fix you up. You're in bad shape, baby darling." She took his arm and led him up the steps and into the bedroom. He flopped down on the bed and she pulled off his trousers, his jacket and shirt. She moistened a wash cloth in the bathroom and bathed his face tenderly and fondled his hair.

Lizzie went home at seven o'clock and Virginia replaced her at the switchboard. She worked in a gay frivolous mood until nine o'clock at which time she heard the steamer's thirty minute warning whistle. She disconnected the board completely and went into the bedroom and woke Cliff.

"Get up darling," she said, flipping back the covers.

"Hi, see," he mumbled in his mellow bass voice.

"Get up and wash. I'll make some strong black coffee." She wanted him awake so he would know, for just that fraction of a second, that she was going to kill him, the bastard, the rotten son of a bitch.

Downstairs Cliff washed himself noisily and came out of the bathroom in his BVD's daubing his face with a towel.

"Mm, smells good," he said. "Oh, brother what a hangover."

"What smells so good?" she asked as she stood just behind the kitchen door within arm's reach of the rifle.

"Ain't you making coffee?" He lowered the towel to his side and stared at her puzzled.

"I said what the hell smells, you son of a bitch?"

"Listen, honey, save it till tomorrow."

She darted behind the door and came out with the rifle pointed at him. He ducked and was toppling backwards before the gun roared.

Virginia was terrified. The pool of blood by Cliff's head sickened her. She couldn't believe it. But the blood was certainly proof that her aim was accurate which surprised her.

In bewilderment she put the rifle back behind the kitchen door. She ran past Cliff's body and glanced out the window in the front door to see if anyone had been passing by when she fired the shot. She could see nothing but the rain falling in the darkening night. She fled up to the bedroom, took her suitcase from inside the closet, slipped into her coat and ran out of the house, forgetting to shut the door.

Dave pulled the two girls aside. "Let's stand over here," he said, leading them away from the cluster of people who had come down to watch the steamer depart. They walked around to the front of the dock and stood with their backs against the warehouse. The flood light illuminated the elegance of the steamer's top decks; the lower decks were below the height of the dock because of the low tide.

Vic's glasses were spotted with rain and Dave didn't understand how she could see through them. She was wearing her high heels and she seemed uncomfortable in them. Unlike the low sturdy pumps Vic had bought for the Wrangell roads, the high heels gave her an enticing and prim air.

"I suppose we might as well go aboard," Lyddy said dispiritedly.

"We still have time. He might show up."

"No he won't," Lyddy said.

The winch rattled forward. The longshoremen moving the frozen cases of fish from the cold storage plant were shouting and laughing, obviously all of them drunk, but getting the work done. The steamer would not be delayed because of them, thought Dave, with some chagrin for he had been hoping for some delay. Where in the hell was Chris?

He'd gone up to the cottage late this afternoon in a last desperate attempt at reconciliation. Vic had been by herself, evidently drinking. She kept her face half turned away as they exchanged greetings. Still she looked lovely in her green jersey dress. The alcohol seemed to bring a flush of color to her face that he had never seen before.

"I'm so glad you came," Vic said. "Lyddy's out looking for Chris. Oh, Dave, it's all wrong. We're wrong to be going."

"That's the way things happen," he said.

"Would you like a drink?" she'd asked, her face averted so he couldn't smell her breath.

"Well, all right." Dave lit a cigarette and sank down in the sofa. He heard Vic moving around in the kitchen, opening cupboards, looking for something. He got up and peered out the window and thought of all his lonely nights alone in Wrangell and how nice it would be if Victoria Blaissing were his wife, to fill those empty nights with her warmth and love. Dave dumped the long crumbling ash of his cigarette in the ash tray on the coffee table and sat down as Vic came into the room holding two glasses.

"I've searched all over," she said, "but there's nothing left in the house to mix it with."

"Water will do."

She sat down beside Dave and gulped her drink nervously. He felt detached and yet he was aware of the blighting of his hopes that would settle down once she left town. Vic rose and looked out the window. They were quiet, the rain dribbling softly on the windows.

"There it is," Vic said.

Dave stood beside her at the window. The *North Star*, studded with lights, was sweeping around Elephant Nose, heading straight for Wrangell.

"In a few hours, we'll be on our way to the States," Vic muttered.

"It's hard to believe," Dave said.

"Care for another drink?"

He was surprised to notice that he had drained his glass. "All right." She tripped out of the room in her high heels. The clack of the heels as she crossed between the carpets of the living room and dining room aroused Dave's attention. She had nice legs, he realized. She had a nice body.

"Dave," Vic said, coming back into the room. "Please try to understand. I have to give Lyddy credit for making a decision and sticking to it."

"Sure," Dave said. "But what about you? Do you have to do what she says?"

From deep in the channel, he heard the first heavy groan of the steamer's whistle. A dog down below the cottage howled in response.

"Listen, Dave," Vic said, "we came up together. It has to be that way."

"How do I stand?"

"Do you really mean it? I mean are you sure you want to know?"

"I'm asking." He felt rather sardonic. He wasn't behaving at all as he thought he would when he had trekked up the hill in the rain, wondering what was the best way to approach Vic, what to say to her.

"I'll tell you what," Vic said. "I'll write to you. I'll tell you in my first letter."

"I want to know now."

"I can't tell you. I'm all muddled and I don't want to hurt you."

"You won't hurt me. Why didn't you let me know you were leaving? At least Lyddy told Chris."

She stood up and he stared at the swell of her large breasts against the sensuous material of her dress.

"Come here and stop being so elusive."

Vic sat down again and Dave put his arm about her shoulder, his hand on her breast.

After he kissed her, he said, "O.K. I'll wait to hear what the verdict is."

"Say, do that again," she said. "I've been cold all day. Chilled."

He kissed her again. "When will Lyddy be home?"

"I'm expecting her any time. I phoned her a while ago at the hotel bar and she said she would be up shortly."

"Phone her again. See if she's left. Tell her you'll meet her down there."

"But why? She's all alone down there with Giff Weeks."

"Phone the hotel bar and tell Lyddy we'll pick her up there. There's no need for her to come all the way back up here."

"May I ask why?"

"Because I want to go to bed with you just once before you leave."

She drew back and grew taut in his arms. Then she laughed. "What in the world has come over you?"

"Hurry up and call her."

"But Dave, it's just not . . ."

"Call her, darling."

After Vic phoned Lyddy at the bar she disappeared into the bathroom. Dave stood at the window, watching the rain drenching the hill. He opened the door and breathed in the lush sweet fragrance of the rain-soaked air. The street lights were on down on Main Street. He could hear the noise of the boat crews as they removed the hatch cover preparing to unload and load freight. A car came grinding up the hill, headlights cutting into the streamers of rain and jumping up as the car hit a bump.

Dave shut the door, then locked it and wandered into the bare, neat kitchen. He poured himself a stiff drink from the pint bottle on the sink. Then he rinsed the glass and sat down in a chair at the kitchen table. He found it difficult to contain the excitement in him. He could hear water running from the bathroom tap. The idea he was alone in a house with a woman who evidently now cared enough for him to sleep with him was almost too much.

He went into the bedroom, took off his shoes and sat down on the edge of the double bed, staring at the freshly vacuumed rug, the bare vanities, the matching nightstands with their white doilies and the pleated shades of the lamps. The room looked as if it had never been lived in. Just for hell of it, he went back to the kitchen and returned with an ash tray and set his cigarettes and matches on the stand.

Vic entered the room and laughed.

"What's so funny?"

"Your shoes," she laughed. "You took your shoes off."

"I'm ready to go. No delay." He wanted to maintain the right note of intrepidness. He flung back the covers of the bed and started to undress.

"Come on," he said, when he had his shirt off. He finished undressing while she kicked off her shoes and shifted around to unfasten the garters on her stockings.

"I'm sorry there's no sheets," she said. "Guy Eaton doesn't provide sheets and we packed ours."

"This is good enough," Dave said. He lit a cigarette. The smoke as he drew it into his lungs filled him with pleasure. "By God, I feel good," he said.

337

"You should."

"Take everything off."

"Yes, sir!" She laughed.

He watched her undressing. First she pulled the dress over her head, then the slip and brassiere—he liked the way her arms flexed behind her back while she unfastened the clips—then the panties. When she stood for a moment naked before him, he said, "You do that beautifully."

She slipped into bed and cuddled up to him. He could feel her breasts, the soft flesh of her belly, her arms twined around him. For a moment she was cold, then she melted into warmth.

He said, "Do you know that you have a cute little frown on your mouth when you unhook the clips of your bra?"

"Dave, darling," she said, "you have an eye for detail."

"I like your figure."

"I like yours, only I didn't see enough of it. You jumped into bed so fast after you undressed."

"By God, it's cold out there."

"It's nice here. I wish we could be like this forever."

"You mean it, Vic?"

"Do you want it that way, Dave?"

He sighed with exasperation. "Listen, you know the answer to that already!"

He allowed the richness of her body to flow through him. His hands caressed her breasts, marveling at their fullness. The he moved down to her belly, feeling her soft fine hairs while he kissed her breasts. He said, snuggling down under the cover, "Throw the covers over our heads. I want to die down here in suffocation."

She grew amazingly warm and lithe. Every little jerk of passion that her body gave was a small victory to Dave.

"How long are you going to keep this up?" she asked after a while and rumpled his hair.

"The book says to get them at the right pitch."

"I'm there."

Without disturbing the covers, he climbed on top of her.

"There's nothing left but us," she said huskily and her eyelids trembled. He caught a glimpse of her face, taut with passion, before he rushed on in his own motion of love.

Afterwards, they lay in dreamy silence for a while but Vic grew restless, worried about Lyddy waiting for them. They dressed in haste and Dave called Curly's cab which brought them down to the dock to meet Lyddy. Now they

Afterwards

23

OLD MAN HOBBS WAS IN FINE VOICE Saturday night. He stood in front of the three piece orchestra, facing the dancers. Old Man Hobbs was a taciturn, parsimonious old-timer, half-crippled by frost bite, who lived off the rent of a number of shacks that he owned. He cooked his own meals, washed his own clothes. Few people knew anything about him and those who did, didn't care to know more. But he was the focal point of the Saturday night dances at the Redman Club. For a modest sum, the entertainment committee could hire him to call the dances. He would stand there at the front of the musicians stand, face contorted, neck swelling, vocal cords stretching as he pushed his voice to carry over the noise of two hundred people, not to mention the fiddle, drums and accordion. And what's more, there was bite to his commands. He roused people to get up and dance.

Forward, center and the sides divide,
Swing in the center and swing on the sides.
The same two couples forward and back.

Giff and Buster turned in the blind alley between the union hall and the butcher shop and trudged up the flight of wooden stairs behind a line of people carrying platters muffled in cloth and bowls of salads and sandwiches and pie tins. The two men paused in the open door of the entrance. The long hall used for the Redman dances spanned the length of the second story of the union building. The front room was the dance floor, covered with waxed black-and-white linoleum; the musicians performed on an elevated platform just before the partition. The banquet room in the rear contained long tables and an enclosed kitchen where the refreshments were received and sorted for the tables and where, from a Dutch door, punch was being served.

Now circle there as nifty as can be
And shoot that pretty girl home to me.

Most of the dancers on the floor were finding it difficult to follow the commands.

The couples in the worst fix tangled themselves up in patterns of their own design, getting far more fun out of this than if they were doing it right.

The faster you go, the better you feel . . .

"Going to be some dance," Buster said, handing the bag of bottles he was carrying to Gene Schnur, the doorman.

Meet your sweetie with a great big smile . . .

"Come on," Buster said to Giff, "let's get rid of these coats before Old Man Hobbs loses his voice."

The two men entered the large cloak room and found Chuck Everett unbuttoning his overcoat.

"By God, I got lost in the shuffle somewhere," Chuck said. "I was the first to come in here and now I'm last to get this God damn thing off."

Giff and Buster wriggled out of their coats.

"Any you boys want a snort?" Chuck said, folding his coat into a cubby hole.

"Why not?" Buster asked.

Chuck dug into his coat. He pulled out a pint of V.O. and patted the bottle tenderly. "Such color, such fine rich mellow texture," he murmured. He took a swig, then passed the bottle to Buster who helped himself and passed it to Giff. Just then several other men entered the room.

"Hey, what's going on?" asked Dale Crawford.

"By God, get away!" Chuck protested with a grin. "No drinks for them," he said to Giff.

"Why the cheap son-of-a-bitch," said Merv Cahill. He took the bottle away from Giff who hadn't yet imbibed and, tilting his head back, poured some down his throat.

"Look at that bastard drink, will you!" Buster said.

"By God, give me that," said Chuck, taking it away from Merv. "I'm going to tie one on tonight. I was at the bakery until nine o'clock tonight making all the bread I need for tomorrow and Monday too. I've made up my mind that a fellow has to throw a good one, every six months or so."

"What about two weeks ago at the masquerade ball? You were pretty soused that night," Merv pointed out.

"Hell, that was nothing," Chuck said.

A new group of men pushed into the room.

"What the hell is this?" Homer Bray demanded, bullying his way into the huddle of men. "Oh, no, I thought so. Give me that vile stuff!"

"By God," Chuck said, watching Homer down the stuff, "I bought that for a life saver."

"Selfish bastard!" Tim Regis said with a scowl, jerking the bottle away from Homer.

"Hey, save some for me and Doc," Dale bawled out.

Doc Little's shoulders drooped. "I just can't get in the mood tonight," he said.

"Why you son-of-a-bitch," Tim responded, "you drank up most of my

Manhattans earlier tonight."

"Yes, I know," Doc said. "But it hasn't done me any good." He eyed Dale with the bottle. "By the way, let me wet my throat, just a lick."

"Oh, gosh, Doc, it's all gone!"

"Then let's go where they have the stuff in barrels," Dale sang out.

Most of the men from the cloak room dispersed to find their partners. The next dance was just starting. Giff, Dale, Doc Little and Merv remained on the side line, watching the couples on the floor, swinging and twirling and tripping around the room to the *Heel and Toe Polka.*

"Some affair," Dale said. "By God, I think I'll get the wife and give it a whirl."

"My wife'll shoot me if she sees me here with you riff-raffs," Merv said and took off down the side of the hall.

Giff turned to Doc. "You going to dance?"

"I was going to ask you the same questions."

"I'd rather have a drink."

"You took the words right out of my mouth, Giff. By the way," Doc said as they threaded their way through the couples, "I'd like to see you come over to the office for a check-up one of these days. Not often, say, every five years or so."

"By God", Giff chuckled, "I think you're getting in the mood, Doc."

Gwen Olson sat next to her mother-in-law on the sidelines. "You know," she said, "Danny's at such a cute age right now. He's constantly bringing home all kinds of animals, some dead, some alive. He caught a toad the other day and cried when I told him to toss the ugly thing out. Finally I gave in and told him he could keep it in the house providing that he put it in a box. Ugh! What a horrible-looking creature!" Gwen shuddered. "He takes it out and holds it upside down and strokes its stomach. I hope this next one is another boy," she went on, smoothing down the fold of her Chinese spring maternity smock with one hand. "Jon won't say but I think he wants a boy too."

"Was Jon tired tonight?" his mother asked.

"Oh, you know Jon," Gwen said. "He hates dances. He'd rather stay home and watch Danny."

She wondered where Dave Collier was. She ached to dance. She wiggled around in her seat, watching Lyle Hobson, who was drunk and making a fool of himself trying to keep up with the rest of the quadrille. The onlookers roared as Lyle nearly fell after executing a swing, saved only by the capable force exerted by his partner, stout, giggling Babs Bucci.

Gwen felt overjoyed. She couldn't wait to get out there. Even with her girdle, she was much larger with this, her third pregnancy, and she worried that maybe no one would ask her to dance.

Fanny Regis and Helen Connell and Alice Hobson sat on folding chairs, a circumstance brought about by the inadequacy of the seating space which irritated Fanny. After the usual exchange of felicitations, they watched the dance floor for the better part of a minute, then Alice asked Fanny if she had heard from Alan.

"I've received a few letters from him," Fanny said. She realized with unhappiness that the two girls, who were best friends, would focus all their attention on her because of the obvious—and to them, painful—fact that she was by herself.

"What did Alan have to say?" Helen asked.

"Oh, the usual things. He's got a job selling sporting goods for an outfit down in Washington."

"He's a go-getter, that Alan is," Alice said, tilting her head and rolling her eyes. Fanny realized suddenly that Alice was pretty tipsy. "He sure is missed at Olson's."

"Do you miss him?" Helen asked.

"I certainly do," Fanny said, because she felt that Helen honestly wanted to know. For a moment there was a bond of sympathy between them but she knew it was fragile, forged out of a few words, and could snap the next moment.

"How long do you think he'll stay away?" Alice asked.

"It generally takes about three months before we pull together," Fanny said. "This time it's taking a little longer." It was six months, almost to the day.

"Gee, you two make such a nice couple It's a shame. Who's the stubborn one?"

"I guess we both are."

"It must get pretty lonesome for you at times."

"I manage to keep myself occupied."

Cliff Waverly came up to the girls and held out both his hands to Alice. "That punch is a hard thing to drink," he said. "And it's a hard thing to keep away from."

"It sure is hard," Alice said with a scream of delight at her pun. She jumped up and went off with Cliff.

Helen waited a moment before she said, "Alice is slightly inebriated—to put it mildly. She's just about blown her cork since Virginia left town. You know she's always had a crush on Cliff. She doesn't care whether he has two ears or not."

"Cliff doesn't seem bothered by the loss." Virginia's hasty shot had struck Cliff's left ear, blasting it completely off his head. Now he had only a hole for the ear canal on that side.

"I guess he was glad to come out of it alive."

"I miss Virginia," Fanny said. "The town doesn't seem right without her."

"Nor without Alan. You should tell him to come back. He worships you, Fanny."

I've written to him. I told him he should come back or I'd go down, but he keeps stalling. It's not like him," Fanny said.

A Swedish waltz was just beginning and the Yorgensens were doing their usual solo. Olaf Yorgensen's face was beet-red, his expression tense with concentration. He took his dancing as seriously as he took his boat-building. His wife, Eva, had the same serious proud air about her. She revolved around, moved by the music and elevated by the powerful thrust of her husband's hands, following the proscribed sequence of steps, a stance and a leap, over and over, until the waltz ended and the crowd clapped in appreciation and politeness.

"What about you, Helen?" Fanny inquired. "Aren't you ever going to make up your mind?"

"Lyle's asked me to marry him," Helen said quietly. "Isn't it funny? Lyle wants to marry me and Alice is planning to marry Cliff."

"Well, brother and sister have married at the same time before."

"In this case it just doesn't seem right," Helen said.

Fanny wondered if Helen was still hoping that Chris would turn to her for comfort now that the schoolteacher had jilted him. Maybe she should have a cup of coffee in the Connell restaurant some afternoon and get to know Helen better.

Old Man Hobbs' voice rang out as harsh as a loon.

You promenade with your corner pivot,
you prom-en-ade.

Giff looked up. He wasn't sure whether the dance was just beginning or coming to a close. It must have been the end for the couples on the floor were regrouping in sets of four for a new dance.

Come on, come on, folks
Swing 'em high, swing 'em low.

"He certainly has a knack for calling dances," Sylvia Weaver remarked.

She sat next to Giff, near the edge of the musician's stand.

Giff nodded in agreement. The back of his mind was blank as he sat there trying to remember what had motivated him into coming to the dance. Even his vision seemed blurry. He stood up on wobbly legs, intending to leave and was promptly struck by a whirling couple and knocked back into the chair.

"Dangerous out there," Sylvia said.

He struggled to regain his concentration. This was it, the high point of life in the winter months, the Redman folk dance, held every other Saturday night up until the edge of the summer. It was a damn good place to spend an evening, restricted chiefly to members and their friends, no natives allowed, with refreshments served at midnight.

"Do you good," Buster Fountain had said. "Come on. Go upstairs and change into a suit."

Giff had considered it carefully. The winter stretched before him, empty and bleak. His ass ached from sitting on the hard bar stool for so many hours. The only exercise he got was trekking to the lavatory and back. He agreed to go if Buster provided the provisions, for everyone had to bring something to the dance since the club charged no admission. He went upstairs to change into a suit, then went back down to the bar and waited until Buster was ready to leave for the dance.

Pass right through and you roam
Split your corners and head for home.

Giff struggled to his feet again and headed towards the banquet room. He figured if he kept moving it would appear that he was doing something.

"Where are you going?" Giff heard a man behind him ask and whirled around to see Chris.

"To get some punch," Giff said. "You just come in?"

"Yeah. Things look pretty lively."

"You said it."

The music came to a resounding finish and Old Man Hobbs' voice boomed out in the sudden silence. "All right folks, this next one is going to be a schottische." Though still commanding, his voice quavered slightly, raising ripples of laughter about the hall. To dispel any concerns, Old Man Hobbs extracted his handkerchief from his pocket, coughed into it and started out again in a fine, clear timbre. "Now, let's all get off our asses."

Laughter filled the hall while couples milled out onto the dance floor and the schottische began. With drinks in hand Giff and Chris stood outside the circle of dancers, who bobbed and twirled and laughed gaily. Gwen Olson went by with Dave, as light on her feet as ever, despite her increasing bulk. A few of the older Norwegians were showing off with intricate steps brought over from the Old Country. Helen Connell made her way through the cluster of men around them and greeted Chris.

"You're late," she said. Giff noticed that she was looking at Chris with the same expression of tenderness and concern that Lyddy used to wear.

"Yeah," said Chris. "What's new?"

"Well, if you want to know the latest, Alice and Cliff are going to announce their engagement tonight."

"By God, no!" Chris exclaimed. Just then the happy couple appeared before them, twirling and hopping with the other dancers. Cliff was jabbering away and Alice was laughing.

As a new number started, Chris asked Helen for a dance.

"I'd rather not," she said.

"Why not?"

"I don't know. I'd rather have a drink."

"Is Lyle here?" Chris asked.

"Yes."

Chris turned to Giff. "You through with your drink?"

"No."

"Well, baby," Chris said to Helen, "you'll have to get it on your own. God have mercy on you. There's some awful hounds around the punch bowl."

"Why can't you get it for me?"

"I still got plenty."

"Oh, never mind."

"Quite a gal, that Helen," Chris said to Giff after Helen left.

"She can drink me under the table anytime," Giff replied.

"On second thought," Chris said, "I think I'll get the lady that drink."

Left by himself, Giff lumbered over to his chair by the front of the musician's stand.

"I saved your seat," Sylvia told him patting the seat of the chair next to her.

"Do I look that bad?" Giff asked.

"You look tired," Sylvia said. "I wish you'd come up and see us sometime, Giff."

"Heck, I haven't visited anyone in years."

"You've lost track of us," Sylvia said. "I bet you don't even know what my children look like."

"I probably see them on the street. No, I guess I wouldn't."

"You know you used to be quite a dancer in your day."

Giff laughed self-consciously. "I should ask you for a dance."

"What the heck is there to stop you?"

"No, Sylvia, I might be a fool but I won't."

"Listen, at least I can talk to you. My darling husband is over at the punch bowl and has forgotten I exist."

"Want me to get him for you?"

"Heavens no. Let him have his fun. He's been sick since he lost Lydia and Victoria. He's one teacher short and the one he did find keeps getting sick all the time. She says she can't stand the wet climate."

Dale came up and asked Sylvia for a dance.

"As I live and breathe," she exclaimed, "I'd be glad to."

"Heck, you're the best dancer on the floor," Dale said, leading her off.

Giff turned his attention to the musicians. He watched Mitch fiddling his violin, his hair plastered across the side of his head for he only combed his hair when he performed at the dances. He saw Buster dancing with Mona Sarber. He waved and smiled at them and they executed some fancy footwork to catch his attention. Giff lit a cigarette. After a few hours in the suit, he felt like he was suffocating. He realized that it was the suit he had bought to wear to Theodore's funeral.

Giff rose and concentrated on proceeding out of the building as steadily and inconspicuously as possible. He climbed down the outside stairway and followed the alley to Main Street. He sensed the sweet fragrance of the night air, felt the drizzling rain against his face and was comforted by the sudden joyful recollection that he had stocked his bureau drawer with two fifths of Canadian Club early that morning.

After Roy left for the dance, Bea went out on the back porch for a breath of fresh air. The house was too warm. With all the windows shut, the heat was stifling. Winchester emerged from his barrel, stretching and yawning. She patted him on the flank as the dog plopped down beside her on the porch.

Ever since Lyddy left, a fever had been mounting. Bea started to believe that she would be leaving soon as well. Her conviction was fueled by a furious impatience. First she had to convince Roy and she waited, in excruciating agony, for just the right moment to come along so she could broach the topic.

She wondered if she should have gone to the dance. Roy was hurt and offended that she wouldn't go. His patience with her was almost tragic. Maybe when they were coming home afterwards in Curly's cab, with Roy feeling high from the punch and the good time, Bea could have introduced the topic and, awash in good feelings, Roy would have consented. "Sure Bea, why not. Let's go to Vermont. Do us both good." The words spun in her brain, the promise for which she lived in an agony of anticipation.

But she had refused to go to the dance. She wanted to take no chances. Suppose she had a dizzy spell and fainted on the floor, right there in front of everyone?

Beyond the porch, the rain drizzled down. It had been raining for ten days in a row. Everything was wet and soggy. She took a breath of the night air and sighed. Like a candle flame dancing in a gust of wind, her mind flickered with images of the people at the dance. She could picture them, happy, frolicking, composed and self-assured, with sound bodies and clear voices.

She felt pity for herself welling up, warm waves of it. Tears sprang into her eyes. Here she was childless, sick and unable to please Roy. The thought of all the happy women in Wrangell irked Bea suddenly. She felt a vicious, choking hatred for them all. She envied and at the same time was jealous of Lyddy. Lyddy was smart, nobody's fool. She had left. The ones who didn't leave were the ones raised in Alaska. They stuck with it, contented. Their acceptance was a source of wonder, even shock to Bea. Since she was so miserable in Wrangell, she couldn't conceive of any woman wanting to live in these conditions.

Bea leaned her body against the dry side of the porch rail. She could almost smell the States. Lyddy was there. She would win out. Sooner or later, Chris would sail down to her, settle in the States as his folks had done, come up just for the fishing season.

Suppose she couldn't get Roy to agree? What would it be like to live out the rest of her life, to die in Wrangell?

She turned to go into the house. Winchester lifted up his head, his tail spanking the planks of the porch.

"Come in," she said to him, holding the door open.

"Is that you, Roy?"

Roy stopped in his tracks and glanced up at the woman who stood on the porch of a two-story frame house along the side of the road. "Why, yes. Hello, Doreen. How are you?"

"Fine. Couldn't sleep. Thought I'd take a walk," she said, coming down the steps.

"It's not a good night for a walk," Roy commented.

She certainly didn't look like she was dressed for a walk. She wore a pretty dress and sandals. Her face was carefully made up, as if she were planning to go out. In the drizzling light, her eyes had a stony glitter that was mysterious.

"Isn't it late for you to be coming into town?" she asked.

"I thought I'd go to the Redman dance. I'm a member and the least I can do is attend the affair."

"Certainly. How is Bea?" She winced as her sandal-clad foot touched the wet ground. "Gee, it really is a rotten night. Would you like to come in for a drink before going to the dance?"

"Well," Roy said stalling, feeling disturbed for some reason, "I don't see why not, Doreen."

Inside the house, Roy stood while Doreen fixed the drinks. "Bea hasn't been herself lately," he said. "She isn't functioning like she should."

"Is she ill?"

"That's what I want to find out. I can't get her to go to Doc Little. I think she's deficient in something. Perhaps even anemic. She just wants to stay home—read a book or sew or listen to the radio. I was hoping that she'd go to the dance, but she wouldn't come."

"Maybe that's her way of being content," Doreen smiled. "She likes the fireside and all that stuff."

"Yes, I'm beginning to think so." He accepted the drink, which was straight, and was struck by the size and value of the ring on Doreen's finger. It contained three large diamonds and must have cost almost a thousand dollars. "That's a beautiful ring," he said with admiration.

"It sure is," Doreen said and flicked her hand before Roy for a moment. She sat down on the horsehair sofa and it came over Roy all at once that his meeting with Doreen wasn't accidental. Warmth flooded him and he trembled. He wasn't at all prepared for this. It could turn out to be his first affair with another woman in years. Not since Bea was in her eighth month while carrying Tom. The notion was tantalizing and Roy's heart raced.

"Take a load off your feet," Doreen said. She wasn't at all nervous. Neither was he. He sat down beside Doreen. Everything pointed to it. It was as if fate had swept him up and guided him along the road so he would be there in front of Doreen's front porch just when she needed someone. She must have been lonely now that Cliff was courting Alice. She must have known about the Redman dance, known that someone would go by on his way to it. Roy just happened to be the one. He was more intrigued by the odds than the actual event. He could go for it. With her heart-shaped face and long-lashed gray eyes, Doreen was quite attractive. He wondered what had happened between her and Cliff.

Roy savored the thought for a moment, then emptied his glass and picked up his hat. "Thanks Doreen. I'll be seeing you."

He was proud of his self-control as he strode down Main Street. Yes, sir, that Doreen was quite a lady. She wouldn't be bad, and God knows he could stand a little.

He went up the steps of the Union Hall building, two steps at a time, whistling, and plunged into the noise and hilarity of the Redman dance.

Chris jerked his head, awakened by footsteps coming down the planks that joined the float house with the road. Heavy footsteps mingled with loud talk and laughter. It was Holly Dancey and friends barging into the house. They must be on their way home from a party and decided to drop in on Chris as a last-minute prank.

"Hey, Chris, wake up," he heard Holly shout. But he was not in the mood for further merrymaking. He remained silent, sprawled across the bed, hoping they would leave when he didn't respond.

This strategy worked but after they left, he couldn't get back to sleep. He found some crackers in the cupboard and slathered them with Mrs. Fremont's quince jelly. The sweet penetrating flavor of the jelly couldn't hide the staleness of the crackers. Chris turned up the oil stove. He could hear the rain drumming down on the roof of the float house. He stared out the kitchen window which faced the rear of the harbor, but he could see nothing but a lamp burning on the bridge across the way. The oil stove rumbled as a gust of wind drove down the flue.

He shouldn't have drunk so much at the dance. It was always worse when he drank. He hadn't felt like going up to the big house on the hill after the dance. It was too cavernous and cold. Instead he had wandered down to the float house and pulled open the door. As always, just before he switched on the light, he had an absurd expectation that he would find Lyddy standing in the room.

Lately he often found himself imagining that she was nearby, watching him. It made him self-conscious about his actions, as if he were an outside observer of his own life. It made him aware of his loneliness. Sometimes to escape it, he went to the bars. He could find friendship and laughter and conversation there.

The float house suddenly seemed too small and constraining. He got dressed and left. He strode up onto the road, turned right, away from the town and followed the road around the harbor. The wind slammed the rain into his face, pushed against his legs, jerked at his hat, pulled at his trousers. He rounded the power plant, went past Bea's house on the corner, and strode on down the dark road by the channel. He was out of the town now, alone in the night.

Chris stopped on the road below Matt's cabin. It was there that he had spent the night prior to Lyddy's departure. In the morning he'd heard voices coming from the picnic grounds, a party of Indians on a wiener roast, and he'd gotten drunk with them, squatting before the fire. They all laughed as they got a dog drunk on beer, the dog lapping it up greedily, then falling asleep before the fire. Towards noon, at the height of the fracas, Chris embraced one of the girls and felt the men about him grow tense. He dropped her and lurched out of the lean-to. He angled down around the beach until he came to the break-water wall, which kept the tide from creeping into the graveyard. He sprawled out against it. Even though it was overcast, kids were on the beach, kids whose fathers were out fishing and whose mothers worked in the canneries. He watched them construct frail, flimsy rafts from fallen tree limbs. He laughed with them as the rafts shredded apart in the water. He felt himself fighting to keep from falling asleep. The constant wail of glee surrounding the children stung against his brain, like one pain trying desperately to besiege another. Some of the kids, weary of the water, dashed up on the sand and talked to him. The whole afternoon his brain felt heavy, as if a great force was pressing on.

The rain and the steamers' whistle woke him up hours later. One long, one short. The hoarse blasts rent the dark air. He could see the light-studded steamer moving slowly towards the dock. He stood on his feet, weak and hungry and confused. The beach was deserted. She was going south on the steamer. The thought drifted through his weary mind. Hell with her. She could do what she wanted. The rain drove him to shelter inside the lean-to, which was deserted. From the embers, he poked up the fire and sat huddled beside it, cold and miserable. He sat there until the steamer left Wrangell and then walked home.

24

DAVE WASHED UP IN HIS OFFICE and went down the steps to Main Street. He hated going into his apartment these days. Ever since suffering a mild stroke a month earlier, his father was driving him crazy with his constant demands, like a kid begging to be entertained constantly. There was only so much he could handle. At least once a night, his father would call out and Dave would go into his room and set the bedpan in place, then empty it in the bathroom. Every morning before he started work, he gave his father a massage, moving his hands over his father's dry, tight flesh until he had massaged out a little of the irritation and stiffness that set in every night. His mother

"Right! Hey, Mom, give me another beer."

"She didn't hear you."

"I know it. I just like to hear myself yell once in a while. So as I was saying, I've decided to stop brushing off the sentiment. I want to feel it. Anguish is the thing. Moping is the thing. Try it sometime."

"Let me tell you something, Chris, as a friend . . . "

"Go right ahead."

"Stop chain smoking. Let's clear out of here."

"No. Let me finish eating." Chris turned to his plate and drove his knife into his T-bone.

"Now that that's over with," Dave said, "let's talk about the weather."

"OK. That's the closest to snow yet," Chris said, craning his neck around to glance out the sleet-streaked front windows.

"Do you think this winter will be another bad one?"

"Oh, I don't know."

Dave smiled and folded his arms on the counter before his half-finished plate. "Seriously, I hope this winter isn't like the last one. You know I'm beginning to feel the winters more. There's too much of it, for too long a period,"

"You hate winters?"

"Not exactly. Only this one in particular."

"You going to Sarber's party?"

"No, I'm not," Dave said, lighting a cigarette. "I just don't see it anymore," Dave added, sending a spiral of smoke into the air. "Parties, dances, getting drunk, shooting off a lot of words . . ."

Chris poured the rest of the beer from his bottle into his slanted glass. "We could go play some gin rummy."

"No. You go to the party."

"Hell, it makes no difference."

Dave wriggled off the stool. "I've got a good sexy book at home. Irma recommended it to me. In fact, she brought it with her when she came for an appointment."

"Hell, if you're hard up," Chris said with a wave of his hand, "I can fix you up with the real stuff."

"That, as well," Dave said, "doesn't interest me."

"Hey, Mom, slow down will you?" Chris called as she went hurrying by again.

"Be a good boy and pay for my dinner, Chris," Dave said.

"Well, Jesus, wait a minute . . . "

"No, you finish your beer. I'll be seeing you."

"OK. Dave. Mark out the hot scenes in the book. I'm getting a little rusty on the intellectual side."

Chris rounded the power plant. His feet were numb from tramping around the island in the freezing cold. He stopped to light a cigarette. The orange, stucco building hummed like some self-sustaining organism. On an impulse, Chris decided to go in, thaw himself out and talk with Pete Jaggard, the power plant's superintendent. But even as he started back around the structure, he stopped. He knew what to expect from Pete. A glowing account of his most recent trip in the woods, the deer Pete killed, the birds Pete shot. Pete didn't consider any other immediate subject worthy of discussion.

Chris paused. His cigarette had gone dead and he shifted so his back was towards the slight wind and lit it again. His eyes ran across the road towards the Hart's home. He thought of going in and saying hello to them but he knew he wouldn't. He used to think a lot about what went on in there. When he was out walking through the slush on the roads, he would glance at the neat green-and-white house, picturing Roy and Bea in there together, hibernating together during all the months of cold and sleet and rain. He thought with envy about Roy's life, coming home to Bea after a day spent hanging out with the boys on Main Street or cold and tired from a three-day moose hunt or a trip to the flats after bagging a mess of white geese. Roy had it made. He earned enough money fishing during the summer to live on during the winter, with a beautiful little woman for a wife and friends over to stir things up a little. He wondered how Bea looked at night, perhaps after brushing out her dark hair, with only her strand of pearls around her neck in the double bed between the warm cotton sheets. Hell, he thought. Hell. Hell. Hell.

As Chris started back, he ran into the Hart's dog, Winchester, returning from some jaunt about the island. Chris pulled his fingers out of his pockets and patted the dog's smooth fur, but Winchester seemed impatient and Chris let him go by.

He skirted a puddle glazed with ice and followed the road around the harbor, conscious of the buildings on either side of him, their lights and their noises crackling against his solitariness. He wondered what to do to take up the time before Sarber's party began. It was no use being there before eleven. He had three hours to kill at least.

He tried to think back to last winter. Was he as conscious then of time as he was now? Was it so important to occupy himself all the while so he wouldn't feel the pressure of time passing? He thought about going to play poker. There'd be a game going at Red's. But if he started now, he'd end up staying until the next afternoon and leave feeling like he had been knocked over by a threshing machine.

Chris walked past his float house without glancing down the bank at it and crossed the small wooden bridge over the small stream spilling into the harbor from a spring. He stopped, stunned by a thought, right by the old assembly hall. Myron and Anna Johnson passed him, each carrying bags of groceries in their arms. They stopped after receiving no response to their greeting. He must have been in a daze.

"Hello, folks," Chris said and watched them continue on their way.

It wasn't only Bea and Roy whose lives he envied. It was all the married couples, the happily married couples. Not the unhappy couples, though in truth it was their difficulties that consoled him. This winter he was doing more walking than he had ever done. He was staying up all hours playing poker, sometimes eating breakfast at five in the afternoon. He liked his life that way, constantly in upheaval. Getting in a routine would make him stagnant.

His feet couldn't seem to thaw out no matter how quickly he walked. He stopped to thrash his arms around his chest and stamp his feet. He was undecided whether to go in ~ town or return to the float house, mix himself a drink and play the radio for a while before going up to Sarber's party.

If Lyddy were here, he'd know what to do. Her name burned in his mind. She'd written a short, sweet two-page letter and written it in haste evidently for the handwriting was almost illegible. She had arrived home, the trip down was stormy, Vic got quite seasick. That was the extent of the letter. Arrived home, stormy trip, seasick. Nothing else that amounted to anything.

Chris moved ahead, deciding to go into town, and rounded the corner by Marie's green and white grocery. The road, filled with puddles, bumps, cartracks was so familiar, filled with memories.

He'd been so infuriated by the paltry letter that he had never answered it. She never wrote again. That was over two months ago.

Chris stopped as he heard a woman's voice call out behind him. The shout came from the native section. He turned around and saw a woman running towards him, beckoning frantically with her hand.

"Hey, mister," the woman called. When she got up close, she recognized him. "Oh, it's you, Chris. Thank God, I found someone. Could you come over and give me a hand?"

It was Betty Marcus. She and her husband were some of the more prominent natives in town, reserved, determined families that took advantage of the opportunities the white man brought with him to Alaska. They lived on the hill in the same area as the Regises, the Littles and the Schnurs. Sam Marcus operated a fishing boat that was as well-equipped and successful as the best outfits in Southeastern. Betty was short, with the characteristic jutted nose, the round flat face and the small eyes of the native women. She was clad in galoshes, a white slicker and a shawl of black wool. She pulled a cigarette out of her pocket and lit it before leading him back into the native section.

"What's happened?" Chris asked.

"Granny's dead," she said with anger. "I came down to visit Mrs. Jefferson and found her. The only person around was John and he was drunk. What a mess!" she went on. I sent him off to round up the family. They're all in town playing bingo. It looks like she's been dead quite some time." As she spoke she prefaced each sentence with a hasty, scornful puff on her cigarette, a trait which reminded Chris of an actress he had seen in a movie.

They went along the dirt path beside the Jefferson shack and came to Granny's adobe house in the rear.

"She died right in the center of the room," Betty commented, leading the way into the jumbled, dank hovel.

"Did you notify Greg?" Chris asked.

"I told John to."

Granny was lying on the floor on her back. Her mouth was open, exposing black gums. Her white hair was spread about the dirty wooden floor and one hand still clutched onto a cane that she must have been using at the time she collapsed. The room was icy cold.

"Help me put her in bed, Chris," Betty said. Her voice was as cold and concise as if she were referring to a sack of potatoes which had fallen from its pile.

As Chris picked up the body by the legs he felt a soft, lukewarm substance drop on his wrist. He glanced down and saw, to his disgust, excrement of the purest apricot coloring. He nearly let go of the tiny, weightless body. As he angled his end of the body over to the bed in one corner of the room, the waste-matter slipped and fell on his other hand. With an old newspaper he found on the floor he tried to wipe the stuff off his hands.

"I got some on me too," Betty said. "Still warm, isn't it? And I'll bet she's been dead two days now."

"By God, doesn't anyone come in here?" Chris said. He glanced about the dishevelled room. The table was loaded with plates and empty cans and bottles. There were cobwebs everywhere and dirt on the floor. Chris looked around at Granny's possessions: an old buckskin jacket, some shabby dolls, a cradleboard, a few longhouse rattles made out of turtle shells and a rack of medicines, purges and toxins that Doc Sebannon must have sold her. Chris sensed a tremendous desolation in the dark room.

"Those darn people should be ashamed of themselves. Neglecting her the way they did. I'm going to tell them off when I see them," Betty said. "Do you know Granny was ninety-two years old? Poor woman! She was so feeble, she had to depend on her children. Her children!" Betty repeated. "I think she froze to death, that's what. She got so cold in here she must have had a stroke or a heart attack."

Footsteps sounded on the dirt path outside. Greg Sundberg and John Roosevelt came into the house, each holding one end of the wicker basket used for transporting bodies. They were followed by Mrs. Jefferson and her daughter, Flora, who was married to John Roosevelt. Evidently they had been unable to locate Violet which was odd since she was usually easy to find. Greg went to work immediately, setting the basket on the floor parallel to the bed and unbuckling the leather straps about the lid. The natives congregated about the table, shouting blame at each other and showing no interest whatsoever in the dark corner.

Greg asked Chris to help him lift the body into the basket and he found himself unable to warn the undertaker about his experience a few moments ago. This time he had to remove the stuff from one of his shoes as well as his hands.

"No!" Betty was shouting at John. She was so angry she flung her cigarette out the open door.

"Listen, we're going to buy the one-hundred dollar casket, so forget it," John said in his bland voice.

"I hate all of you! You haven't been in here to tend to Granny in days. I bet her fuel tank is empty!" Betty stammered.

John ignored her accusation. "What's the difference anyway between a hundred-dollar casket and hundred-and-sixty-dollar casket?"

"There's plenty of difference," Betty protested.

"Stop arguing," Flora said softly. "Let's give her the hundred-sixty dollar funeral."

"Sure," snickered her husband, "but who's going to pay for it?"

"The native association will give you a hundred," Betty snapped.

"And the other sixty?" John asked. He was wearing a gray pin-striped suit and his face was smooth and coppery and young.

"John, you're rotten, you're just plain rotten." Betty's eyes flashed with rage.

"We'll get the money somehow," said Mrs. Jefferson. She began to cry.

"Tell me," John asked his mother-in-law patiently, "how are you going to get sixty dollars more?"

"We'll scrape it up somehow," Flora suggested.

"That's the least you can do for your grandmother," said Betty. "She deserves that much."

Mrs. Jefferson, who appeared stymied by the event, edged over to Greg, who was kneeling on the floor and buckling the leather straps across the lid of the wicker basket. She knelt down beside Greg, a bulbous woman with square crude legs encased in cotton stockings. "We come in morning with dress."

"O.K." Greg mumbled, struggling to his feet, his jowls mottled with red.

"Yes," Flora said, "we'll get Granny's dress ready tonight and we'll be over early to change her."

Greg turned to Chris, his eyes apologetic. "Would you give me a hand getting this into the wagon?"

Outside it was warmer. A milky shimmer of light infused the dark air.

"By God, I think it's going to snow," Greg said, lugging the front end of the basket down the path.

Chris helped him slide the wicker basket into the panel truck and closed the two half-doors. "I might as well ride into town with you," he said, going around to the front seat.

The wagon lumbered forward. "Ain't they the damnedest people you ever saw?" Greg asked, shaking his head with amazement. "They ought to live on an island by themselves. They'd be better off. We certainly ain't doing 'em no good. Look at that drunken punk John—all dressed up and ready to go on a binge and he can't see where they're going to raise money for a hundred-sixty dollar burial." Greg gripped the steering wheel firmly. It vibrated in his hands as the truck wobbled along the wet uneven road. "And their names! They pick the grandest names—Jefferson, Roosevelt—when they give up their own. It's a shame the way the government keeps giving them handouts."

"Say, where can I wash up?" Chris said.

"There's no water at the morgue. I generally go to the fire hall after I'm through to wash up."

"How the hell do you wash the bodies?" Chris asked.

"Talcum powder," Greg said, wheezing. "Plenty of talcum powder."

"You ought to wash 'em up, for Christ's sake," Chris said.

"If they're real dirty, I wash 'em," Greg said. "I generally scrape the fingernails. That's what people notice first—dirty fingernails. But you'd be surprised—a dead person looks clean."

"Drop me off at the fire hall. I can't stand this stuff on my hands."

"Sure," Greg said.

He pulled up in the double driveway before the fire hall on Main Street and Chris got out. As Chris went inside the cold gray asphalt building, his heels clacked loudly on the cement floor, making him feel as if he were intruding. In the rear of the building, he washed his hands, wiping them dry with his handkerchief. Since leaving Granny's place he had felt a great weight descending upon him. It pressed on his muscles and his mind.

Chris wandered through the side door into the jail house. The three cells were vacant, Chuck's little office was deserted. He sat down on the cot on which Chuck cat-napped between patrols or slept whenever he had a particularly bad customer behind bars for the night. Chris switched on the radio and stretched back on the cot. He felt cold. He felt dead. He wished he was drunk or asleep or out with someone.

This was his most miserable night yet. As always, when he was least on guard, he felt the girl tearing him slowly to pieces once more. It was as if all his senses were being shredded and each separate nerve was pierced by a burning needle of pain. Instead of running away from it, he decided to surrender to the feelings. He would allow the memories to return, the way she walked, the way she looked, the way her lips felt when she kissed him.

He couldn't believe he felt so bad. The whole world was laughing and dancing, making plans and going somewhere and he was lying on a cot in the jail house with a woolen blanket rumpled under his head. Could there be anything worse? Feeling dead while still alive? He wondered why he was taking it so hard. Was it because he was thirty and his sister was unmarried and his mother would never be happy again? Was it because he never had a brother and Tom Hart was like a younger brother to him and Tom had committed suicide with Chris' own gun? Was it because he was alienated from the only family left?

He lit a cigarette and let the soft music from the radio swirl about him. He drew on his cigarette deeply, then slowly exhaled. He stared at the gray-white plaster ceiling. What was she doing? He imagined her taking a bath, with her hair piled up on top of her head, soaping her body. Maybe she was thinking of Alaska. It must seem like a dream by now, the islands, the town itself, him. Would she be pensive as she soaped her body, going over and over the same spot, lost in thought? Perhaps she wasn't pensive as she bathed. Maybe she was in a hurry to scrub herself so she would be on time for her date with Don. This thought came as a blow and he recoiled from it, sucking hard on his cigarette. The vision of her setting off on a date stabbed into his guts. He crushed the cigarette between thumb and forefinger, wincing from the heat of the coals of the lighted end.

He submerged himself again in the daydream. She was in the bathtub, she was thinking of him, missing him. There were tears in her eyes and a catch in her throat. He opened a gate into his body so he could experience the melancholy of her mood, make it one with his. He held it to his heart for a long moment, longer than he held a breath of air in his chest when he dove under water and swam about, fighting to stay under.

The radio brought him up. The music was gone, replaced by a heavy angry blur of static. He reached out his hand and switched it off.

He lay back. The walls of the office closed in on him, engulfing his vision and his mood. He wanted to just drift off to sleep. Chuck would wake him up when he came him. Then he could go to the party, get drunk and get up in the morning and go hunting. Maybe he could convince Dave to go along. Just before Chris dropped off to sleep, he thought of the dead native woman and he felt a surge of compassion for her that filled him with remorse. He should have given Mrs. Jefferson the money for the funeral, he thought, remembering his temptation to butt in on the argument between Betty Marucs and John Roosevelt and settle it with his own donation. But that wouldn't have been wise, he knew. You couldn't buy dignity, not in Wrangell.

"He-he-he," Chuck was laughing, sitting on the folding chair next to the cot. He nudged Chris again. "You wanting in?" Chuck's eyes were crinkled in delight.

"Hi, Chuck. Guess I fell asleep." Chris eased his legs over the side of the cot and sat up, running his hand through his hair. There was a spotted dog leaning against Chuck's legs. "What you got there?"

"About once a week lately I've been getting a patient," Chuck said. "One-way patients." Chuck bent down and fondled the head of the mongrel. Chris stood up and lit a cigarette.

"Distemper?"

"Yep. Crippled up to his neck." Chuck caressed the dog again. "I tried everything with this one. Enemas. Pills. Diet. Well," Chuck said, slapping his knees and picking up the dog, "the sooner we get it over with the better." He carried the dog down the aisle to the last cell and settled him down on the cement floor where the dog could see the 22 rifle standing against the wall. Chuck came back and poured some milk in a soup bowl and set the bowl within reach of the dog. He returned and sat on the center of the cot. Chris sat down in the chair.

"Heard old Granny died tonight," Chuck said, lighting a cigarette.

Chris nodded. "I helped Greg bring her in."

"Haven't seen her in months. Been up to the flats?" Chuck asked.

"Not yet," Chris said. "I'm just now getting through with all the detail work at the cannery."

"Geese aren't in yet to speak of but there's plenty of ducks. Got me a bag full Wednesday."

Chris tipped his chair back against the wall, listening to the sheriff. Chuck talked effortlessly, almost as if for his own amusement. He didn't care if people listened as he spun out stories about a long-ago grizzly-hunting expedition or the latest disturbances in Wrangell or the treatment for worms he was using on a friend's dog. While he sat listening to Chuck ramble on, as he had done a thousand times before, Chris began to thaw. The feeling of deadness started to dissolve. It occurred to him suddenly that this was a very important occasion, that Chuck's presence brought back together the scattered pieces of the pattern of his life in Wrangell. He looked at Chuck with a new respect. Despite his small size and delicate features, Chuck was a brave and unassuming man. There wasn't a trace of discontent in him. He was happily married, had two kids, loved animals and went about his thankless job, as the only peace officer in Wrangell, with a confident, quiet air. He handled the disorderly drunks, both natives and whites alike, as fairly and graciously as possible under the circumstances unless they gave him trouble. He never carried a revolver.

"I caught Doreen down at the harbor tonight, drunker than a skunk." Chuck was saying, "She's sure sore at everyone lately."

"Since Cliff became engaged," Chris said with a laugh.

"Heck, she might have had him herself," said Chuck, "if she wasn't so scared that Virginia would come back and shoot her too. He-he-he, did I tell you she kept asking me if I could issue an all-points bulletin that would prevent Virginia from booking passage on any boat coming into Wrangell?" Even with his eyes half closed as he looked back on the encounter, Chuck's face still glowed with delight.

Chris watched Chuck with affection. The sheriff was so damn easy to get along with. Of course, as everyone in town knew, in a clinch he was something else. A natural boxer, cool and adroit with his fists, he made every punch count. Facing an obstreperous drunk, he'd stop them in their tracks with a blow to the mid-section before he'd haul them off to jail to sober up.

"By God, I received a letter from a party in Chicago the other day wanting me to guide them on a grizzly hunt," Chuck said. "They have all the provisions, yacht, camping equipment, all they want is a guide who'll be sure to track down bear."

"You going to take it?" Chris asked.

Chuck's eyes were sparkling in sheer joy. "Yep. I had the wife answer the letter. It's a little late but I told 'em I would. I enjoy it, watching those city boys get a grizzly. You see them strain out there. I get an even bigger kick out of watching their wives."

"You haven't got a snort around here, have you, Chuck?" Chris asked.

"Say, this is a respectful jail house," Chuck laughed and left the office to visit the dog in the cell. This was his usual routine when putting down terminally ill animals. He would let the dog lap up the milk, get used to the sight of the gun and then, when the animal was relaxed and at ease, Chuck would send a well-aimed slug through the dog's head.

Chuck returned, handed Chris an unbroken pint. "I found this under one of the mattresses." He laughed and settled down on the cot, lighting another cigarette.

He laughed and settled down on the cot, lighting another cigarette. Chris took a pull on the bottle and capped it again, watching Chuck as he inhaled deeply and finally ground the stub into the wood floor with his heel. The sheriff let out a sigh.

"Might as well get the thing over with," Chuck said, standing up. He took the bottle of milk from under the counter. His face was grave for Chuck hated what he was about to do. He hated being the one everyone came to when their pets needed to be killed.

Chris followed Chuck back along the corridor to the last cell. The door was partly open. Chuck knelt down, poured more milk in the bowl and picked up the rifle. He balanced the rifle in the palm of his hand while the dog watched him, then nudged the bowl against the dog's mouth. He closed the door and inserted the rifle through the bars, resting it on a cross-bar. The dog continued to watch Chuck with its listless eyes. Chuck waited for the dog to tire, automatically releasing the safety catch without glancing down at the rifle. The moment came. Chuck nodded his head as the animal bent its attention to the milk. The shot rang out, sudden and vicious.

"Well, that was clean," Chuck said and lumbered back to the office. He sat down again and lit a cigarette.

"You want me to dump him?" Chris said.

"No. I'll do it. I'm going out pretty soon anyway."

"That's a helluva job," Chris said.

"Somebody's got to do it, and I feel better that I do it."

Chris shook his head in admiration. He took another sip from the bottle and set it under the counter. "I'm going up to Sarber's party. Might as well get going."

"He-he-he, that woman and her parties," Chuck said laughing.

Bea heard Roy's voice outside and went into the kitchen to heat up a pot of stew on the hot plate of the oil stove. As she was measuring the coffee for the percolator, she looked out the window and saw the snow. It was the first snow to fall on the town itself, although the mountain peaks of the surrounding islands and those across the Back Channel and Wrangell Mountain itself over on the mainland were all capped with white. The sight caught at her heart. Snow! The first snow! Without anticipating anything Bea opened the back door and stepped out to see it better, to smell it, to see the sparkles at the heart of the snow. The whole island was already covered with it. It was so beautiful.

She could still hear Roy out in front of the house, talking to another man. It was impossible to make out what they were saying. Roy was late again for supper. The pattern of their life together was starting to unravel. In the past, if he came home at the appointed time for supper and found Bea lying on the sofa, with dinner not even started, he would be furious. Now he seemed not to care. Oh, how important that was to her. Roy's consistency! His demands! Even his anger!

Bea was sick with bitterness. She had nearly fainted again earlier. Maybe she had. It had happened so quickly, she wasn't sure. Not three hours ago she had gone out to the porch to see if Winchester had returned from his wanderings around the island (Roy would never permit the dog to be chained). The cold air had been sharp against her legs and arms. The frosted puddles in the yard gleamed with gray iridescence in the light cast by the misted moon as it appeared from behind the range of mountains to the east. Winchester wasn't in his wine barrel (which Roy always claimed was warmer than any home-built doghouse) nor under the porch. She had looked across the front of the yard, towards the power plant, and then she had seen him. Her body went stiff. Her hand came up, as if from a long distance away, and clutched at her throat. She felt the cold smooth contact of her pearls around her neck.

He was lighting a cigarette as he stood, quite still and tall on the road. Her heart pounded. She knew at first sight that it was Chris Ballard but for a moment, in a flood of self-pity and hope, she thought it was Tom. She fought free from the clutches of fantasy and watched the man, fascinated. His hands were cupped as he lit a cigarette. The glow of the match illuminated his face, which was unshaven and gaunt. Bea watched him for a long time, as if she were gazing at a lover. He looked forlorn. She wanted to call out to him, "Don't try to be sufficient onto yourself, Chris. Don't try it." But she bit back the words, thinking of her own discovery of the futility of trying to find completion through another.

Just as she opened her mouth to call out to him, Chris started back along the road towards town. She watched as Chris stopped to pet Winchester. Maybe she could catch him if she went out the front door. She hurried through the living room. She was sure a cup of coffee and a nice long talk would do him good. It would be nice for her too, with Roy away so much, playing cards, tinkering with his boat, drinking more and more.

But as she swung open the door, she was struck by a bolt of dizziness. She leaned against the door jamb, too weak to collect her strength. She wondered if she were going crazy and the terror of the thought made her sob. Then she felt her mind flicker, a succession of darks and lights, and the awful weakness poured through her veins.

When she raised her head, Chris was gone and Winchester was not in sight. Roy had trained him never to enter the house by the front door so he had probably gone around to the back and was snuggled in his barrel on the porch, waiting for her to let him in. The icy sting of the air numbed her and she closed the door and sat down, then stretched herself on the sofa, glad that the stew was cooked and she wouldn't have to get up till Roy came home.

The voices were laughing, laughing. She went back into the kitchen to see about the coffee. The peculator was bubbling and she slid the pot off the hot plates. What on earth are they talking about out there? She headed into the living room to open the door and invite them in. They must be frozen standing for so long in the snow.

At the door, Bea stopped, with her hand on the knob, hearing the voices distinctly.

Roy was saying, "That's the goddamnedest sight in town. It tickles me. Take tonight. Dave came into Johnny's to play gin rummy, but he couldn't follow a hand, so he just got up and left the table. And Chris—Chris has it really bad."

"He-he-he!" Bea recognized the sheriff's laugh.

"By God, Chris is crazy!" Roy said in an outraged voice. "Anytime I'd take that crap . . ."

Bea fled away from the voices and found herself in the center of the kitchen so blind with rage that she took the coffee pot off the range and dumped the contents into the sink. The red-hot handle of the coffee pot singed her hand and she dropped it. It went clattering over the grounds and against the sink wall. She waved her hand back and forth in the air to cool it, saying, "If they ask for something to drink, I'll give them cold water." But in a moment she regretted her rash action and promptly refilled the pot and set it back on the stove. She wanted to serve them hot coffee. She'd even put brandy in Roy's cup. Strangely the thought of pleasing Roy was almost more than she could bear. She wished frantically that the men would come in.

25

G IFF AND BUSTER ARRIVED EARLY ENOUGH to watch Mona Sarber make the punch for her party. They hopped up and sat on the drain board next to the sink, alongside Holly Dancey and her husband, Moose, who were resting their feet on partly-opened cupboard drawers. Sally and Evelyn sat on the laps of their husbands on the two small chairs in the room. Mona stood before the table, poring over the ingredients. She wore a plain black dress printed with slender lavender leaves. Her arms were bare and her long bony fingers grasped a fifth of whiskey which she was pouring into the huge cut-glass bowl on the table.

"Now for a successful blow-out, folks, you use a quart of whiskey to one can of juice. I like orange or grapefruit . . . "

"By God, Mona, that's a little stiff, ain't it?" said Moose.

"What you want to do? Kill us all?" Sally asked, rubbing her hands together in anticipation.

"After you dump in, say, ten or twelve quarts, then you top it off with a cup of lemon juice—so—and a bottle of grape juice—so—to sort of cut the taste." Mona sampled the punch and seemed satisfied by it. "Then, if you're smart, you sit back—or stand in a corner—and watch the fun."

Giff sampled the punch, along with the rest of the crowd. Mona was right. It tasted more like grape juice than anything else.

After helping himself to a fresh cup, Giff drifted out of the kitchen into the living room. As usual it was stripped bare of furniture for dancing. He watched the couples and groups entering the house. Within an hour the party was at a fever pitch, with people exclaiming over the wonderful punch and dancing wildly. Every once in a while someone quietly passed out.

"Sally's just been laid out on Sarber's bed," someone said, roaring with laughter.

"That makes four out, doesn't it?"

As the evening progressed, the chairs and sofas (which had found their way back into the room) filled with couples, entwined together, unmindful of the others. For some reason, Giff felt great. He wasn't affected by the punch, which had been thoroughly spiked and robbed of its grape juice flavor. He began dancing when the floor cleared enough to allow him some space. The use of long-dormant muscles was stimulating.

"Take it easy, you big lug," Evelyn groaned as Giff twirled her about.

"Come on, get in time," Giff said. He took a firm hold of her waist and executed a series of swift, close twirls.

"I don't feel so good alla' sudden," Evelyn said.

She tumbled forward, soft and limp in Giff's arms as though she had been pushed from behind, and slid down his chest to the floor in a beautiful, graceful heap, falling on her side, with one arm extended to cushion the contact of her head on the floor. Giff laughed despite his annoyance.

"There goes the fifth one," someone said from a corner.

"Give me a hand, will you, Chris?"

Chris was sitting on a straight chair by the phonograph looking bored. He was acting as the DJ, hadn't danced all night. He rose to help Giff carry Evelyn into the bedroom.

"Should be more beds in the house," Giff observed as they deposited Evelyn crosswise alongside the other four women.

"By God," Chris said with a smile, "that's mighty powerful stuff Sarber concocted."

"Doesn't seem to have affected you."

"That's what you think," Chris said. He pulled Evelyn's dress down to her knees to cover her fleshy thighs. "Might as well lay them out proper." He turned and went back into the living room.

Giff decided to leave. He wondered where Buster was. He should get him straightened out and to bed. Buster's wife's was due back in Wrangell first thing in the morning. She was coming in from Petersburg on the mail boat.

"You see Buster anywhere?" Giff asked Holly.

"Sarber found him and Doreen in the woodshed. Both out cold."

Giff stepped outside. He decided not to go into the woodshed. Buster was liable to wake up with his fists flying if roused from a drunken sleep. Giff pulled the brim of his hat down snug over his head as he stood in Miss Sarber's sloping front yard. The snow fell thick and light as he jogged down the hill. He'd had a lot to drink but hardly felt it. Sometimes that happened. He could drink all day and never even get peppy. Other times, a bottle of beer in the morning knocked the daylights out of him.

The school yard was blanketed with snow. Down below, he could see the white-covered rooftops of Main Street and the dark expanse of the channel. The snow crunched under his feet, the only sound disturbing the silence of the small sleeping town. It seemed absurd that he was awake and completely sober at such a late hour. Generally by this time he was in a stupor of drunkenness, steeped in the pleasure of sentiment. Though his head might pound and his vision blur, he enjoyed the dreams in which he spent nine-tenths of his life ashore, the dreams he saw as he lifted the glass to his lip, holding it still for a moment after the swallow, then returning the glass to the bar mechanically

moving around. Giff had hated Clarence ever since the night of the crap game. It was a grudging hatred and Giff nursed it privately, with no desire to express it openly. He never spoke of it to anyone and when someone else criticized Clarence around him he felt grieved as if he was the only one who had a right to hate Clarence.

Giff made a lot of noise thumping over to the bureau again, hoping it bothered Clarence. As Giff helped himself to another swig from the bottle, he decided to take it back over to the bed. His feet were chilled from trekking over the cold floor to get to the bureau. He placed the bottle and glass next to the bed where he could reach them by stretching out his hand. Then he closed his eyes again.

———————

Clarence pulled up the shade. It had snowed heavily all night. He glanced at his alarm clock. It was only five o'clock. That God damn Violet had woken him from a sound sleep. Still he hadn't meant to hit her as hard as he did. She must be out cold in the hallway. He hadn't heard a peep from her since she went down against the wall. She had probably fallen asleep, melting from unconsciousness into a drunk-stupefied sleep. Somebody would be getting up soon, see her lying in the hallway and shake her awake. Hopefully, she'd think twice before bothering him again.

Clarence got back into bed. His routine was disrupted. He wondered whether to get up and intercept the alarm clock's ringing at six. It was Sunday and he could sleep longer and still get in all the exercise he wanted.

He heard Giff moving around next door. He was drinking, he could tell, from the way he went thumping across to the bureau where he kept his bottle. He knew the old fart inside and out. Giff was probably laughing at him as he drank. Sneering, despising, hating Clarence as everyone in Wrangell seemed to hate him. He was just that sort of person. People loved to hate him, tear him apart in their minds and conversations.

Clarence's face twisted as he tried to accommodate his back along the uneven stretch of the thin mattress. He kept his ears open for fresh sounds in Giff's room. Must be plastered by now, since he wasn't tramping to the bureau any longer. He had probably taken the bottle to bed with him and would finish it off there. Clarence couldn't figure out why the stuff hadn't killed Giff yet. It seemed so unfair that someone like Giff should have the capacity to drink as much alcohol as he wanted while others, like Clarence, were poisoned if they just sniffed the fumes.

Giff coughed. It was a rich slaggy blast of a rattle. Giff's feet thumped on the floor and he strode across to the wash basin and spat. The faucet hissed loose and the air in the pipes screeched and groaned.

Knock, knock, knock! "Clarence! Clarence!" He heard Violet's husky voice at his door.

Oh, Jesus, she had gotten up. He decided to pretend he was asleep. Maybe Giff would kick her out.

Knock, knock, knock! "Let me in, Clarence!"

Clarence held his breath, staring up at the shadows above him. It was terribly dark inside in his room. Then he heard Violet's footsteps shuffling off down the hallway. She would try Snake, the Indian janitor. He would probably be getting up soon to turn up the furnace and sweep out the bar and make a pot of coffee in the kitchen for the early risers.

The pre-dawn quiet had a different quality than usual with the heavy snow on the streets. It almost muffled the ticking of the clock. Clarence flicked on the reading lamp above his head. His eyes started at the sudden outpouring of light. He pulled the overhead shade so it curved under the glaring bulb. The light cast a square pattern on the ceiling and he lay staring at it.

Hell, he might as well get up. He was feeling terrific since he had started exercising again. It felt good to get up early and go to bed early, dead-tired. It was the nights in Wrangell that were dangerous. He didn't feel lonely in the mornings.

A fresh outburst of coughing came from Giff's room. Clarence stiffened in bed. He was beside himself with fright until the attack subsided, until Giff had stalked over to the wash basin again and discharged the phlegm torn loose in his throat by the violent hacking. He didn't want to have to go in there to see if Giff was all right. He was afraid of Giff. Giff was the one man he tried to stay away from. He had just realized that Giff was a crazy son-of-a-bitch. Clarence thought with horror of that night he wanted to have it out with him in the bar. Giff might have killed him. He had nothing to lose.

The quiet was shattered by the sound of a dog barking wildly. It came from the hill and Clarence listened, fascinated by the dog's frenzy. The barks were like the sounds of a fine-tuned drum, rolling forth.

What a miserable way to start the day. He had been planning to start the day by rowing out in Steve's skiff. What was it Merv Cahill said yesterday in the shop? "Clarence, I don't know what's gotten into you lately, but, by God, stay that way." They had been alone in the shop and Clarence had been trying to keep a steady conversation going. The newspaper editor was usually aloof and Clarence felt a glow of triumph. He didn't even resent it when Merv left none of the change in Clarence's hand after he paid for his haircut.

Clarence had a goal. And in order to achieve it he needed to wait on customers with consideration and combine exacting work with wholehearted interest in what they had to say. He had adopted this goal shortly after Lydia Prince left town. No, that wasn't quite right. For about ten days, he hadn't been able to do anything. He felt like he had died. Then one night after work he went into the hotel bar, wanting to get drunk, anything to get rid of the despondency which dogged him. It was cold and raining outside and though the bar was warm and noisy and merry, it jarred with his depression. Max was surprised when Clarence ordered another right after tossing down the first bourbon. Chris was down at the far end of the bar, shaking dice boxes with Buster.

"Shoot you for a case of V.O., Buster," Chris said.

It was for a party at Merv Cahill's, Clarence discovered. He watched Chris and Buster pound the boxes and shout at the dice and yell "horses." Clarence was tempted to edge over a few stools to view the outcome. Already the whiskey was softening his resolution to remain aloof.

He sent the next shot of whiskey down his throat. It was then, before he had time to order the third drink, that he saw Jon Olson, sitting with another man, who was wearing a suit, probably a salesman of some sort peddling his wares on a tour through Southeastern. Jon hardly ever came into the bar now that he was married to Gwen. Clarence noted with elation that Jon looked old for his age, sapped and strained.

"No! No more!" Clarence said, waving Max away as the bartender approached to ask if he wanted another drink. He got up and walked out of the bar into the rain and walked in it until he was good and soaked. While he walked he knew with glorious clarity where he stood and what he must do. Lydia was gone. Gwen was still in Wrangell. He would take himself in hand. He would become a new man. He would win her back. He never stopped to consider the rashness of his plan, given that Gwen was now in her sixth month of pregnancy.

Buying the alarm clock was the first tangible thing Clarence had done following the night of the revelation. It reminded him of the clock they kept on the nightstand in the house on the hill when he was married to Gwen. Bringing the clock into the room was almost like bringing in another person. At times, because the room was so small, the ticking of the clock would become overpowering. Then he would leave the room or put the clock in the closet under his soiled laundry and close the door. Even then he could still hear it, beating away steadily. He tried not to let it get on his nerves. He wasn't used to it yet.

Just then the alarm clock rang, seeming to jar through the whole hotel. Clarence jumped out of bed and silenced it. He was lighthearted as he thought of having breakfast at Mom's with only the cook there to wait on him.

Afterwards he would go for a walk and finish the novel he was reading.

––––––––––

Chris was just getting home from Sarber's party when he heard a Ford grinding and spitting as it made its way up the hill in second gear. He stopped halfway up the porch steps and waited to see who was coming up the hill in so much haste. Even before Red Parker pulled up with a shuddering screech, he knew whose car it was. And even before Red slid out of the front seat and came stumbling around the front of the Model-A, he knew what Red wanted. Chris had to laugh despite the lateness of the hour. Or was it the earliness of the morning? He figured it was around seven o'clock. He had been too drunk to leave the dying party until he heard the mail boat's whistle. Then he suddenly decided he had done enough boozing for one night.

Even before Red asked, Chris was declining, "No, I'm not going, you crazy son-of-a-bitch."

Red laughed. Despite the snow and the cold, his upper lip was beaded with sweat. "Hell, you can't miss out on this. It's a big game. Jack and Buster . . . "

"Buster's there?" The last he heard Buster was out cold in Sarber's woodshed.

"You know Buster. He likes to play when he's loaded. Jack's lit too. It's a wide open game."

"What the hell do you need me for?" But Chris knew and couldn't resist the thrill of pleasure that came with the knowledge. Jack and Buster wanted some action. Both of them were hot and impatient with the other boys who held their cards, holding close and being patient, waiting for them to make a slip due to their drunkenness. So they sent Red out to track down Chris who would liven up the game. Sure he'd show them some action. Besides, Chris knew that all the men yearned to beat him at cards or dice.

"All right, you crazy son-of-a-bitch. I'm going to wash up first."

Chris ran upstairs to change his clothes. He was glad. Even at this hour the prospect of poker could revive his flagging spirits for he loved the game. He was already visualizing the opposition, his heart throbbing as he pulled a bluff, waiting for the other guy across the table with a better hand to decide.

Chris put on a fresh shirt, slipped into his heavy woolen plaid jacket and went outside.

Red lit a cigarette, wobbling a little as he steered himself around to the driver's seat. Chris was glad he had never started drinking wine. It had a debilitating effect.

The car shuddered forward as the rear wheels spun in the snow and caught onto the gravel. "We have to pick up Mitch," Red said, chuckling. "He went

they all tramp up to his house and have Victor cook up a big spaghetti dinner. No one rose from the table. Red passed the bottle which Chris had refused. Chris got up to leave but Jack, the heaviest winner, upped the ante to five dollars a game, so Chris sat down again. He poured himself a cup of coffee in the kitchen and decided to teach the son-of-a-bitch a lesson. He remembered vaguely that he had planned to go hunting today, perhaps coax Dave into going along with him. He felt that he had let his friend down. Remorse stewed in his guts. His neck ached and his ribs felt scorched with the drink and the smoke.

Towards evening, he got up again and said, "For Christ's sake, let's cut this God damn game. Anybody want to go down to Mom's for a steak?"

Again no one rose, though several men stared at him with blurred eyes, as if they were hoping that Chris would lead them out forcibly.

"Ha!" said Jack, elbowing Buster, "that young man can't stand the gaff."

"If you see my wife anywhere," Buster said, "tell her I'm here playing poker and losing my ass."

But Chris hadn't seen Mrs. Fountain, hadn't seen anyone but Max until he ran into Dale and his daughter. He noticed how hard Dale was working to include him in the conversation, as they walked up the hill. He felt unwanted again, certain that Dale would rather talk with his daughter or stroll in companionable silence rather than make conversation with Chris.

"Say," Dale whispered to Chris, "did you get a load of that new native girl in town?"

Chris shook his head. "No," Chris said, "I guess I haven't."

"I just saw her for a minute in the Sweets. The place was buzzing with excitement, guys after her already. She came in on the mail boat this morning."

Dale opened the cottage door and Chris smelled the sweet fragrance of cooking food. "Boy, that smells good," he said by way of greeting to Jean, who approached them wiping her hands on a towel.

"Why, hello. It's meat loaf and I've baked a pie." She smiled at Chris. She was all dressed up to leave the house as soon as dinner was over.

"You two go inside," Jean said as she directed them through the kitchen. "I still have to find the twins. They disappeared in the last half hour."

"Maybe they're over at the Sackett's," Dale said.

"I'll phone them," Jean said.

Chris sat down in the living room and Dale mixed two drinks in the kitchen.

"Still working on your boat?" Chris asked.

"Up to my neck. I yanked the motor out and I'm giving it the works.

Valves ground, new rings, bore job. By God, I bought me a new Johnson while we were in the states. It's a honey. I can idle her down to trolling speed and has she got zip when you want to let up and go."

"I'd like to take a ride out with you," Chris said.

Jean came to the door. "Dale, they're not at the Sackett's. They might be over the hill in their fort. Would you go out and call them? Dinner's ready."

"Sure, excuse me, Chris."

"Go ahead, Dale."

With Dale gone, he was acutely conscious of Jean's movements in the kitchen. He followed the pattern of noises, from the running sink to the icebox to the stove. At any moment, he expected Jean to pop in and he tried to think of something to say to her. She had been his sister's best friend until she married Dale, right after she graduated from high school, and he always felt awkward around her.

He stared at the plain Monterey furniture, realizing that this cottage, except for its slight variation in floor plan, was almost identical to that on the top of the hill in which Lyddy had lived. "I'm not sure, Chris," she had said. "I'm not sure." He hoped that anger would overwhelm him as it did whenever he thought back to that warm afternoon on the Clinton dock. Once or twice lately he had even considered going down to San Francisco, although he was unsure of what to do once he got there.

He heard Jean humming, opening the oven door, setting plates on the kitchen table. He wished Dale would come back. The reality of his time with Lyddy was fading. He could call it back in his mind by looking at snapshots or walking into the float house. But it seemed very distant. Meanwhile he lived his days as if in a fog.

"We're going to eat in the kitchen. I hope you don't mind," Jean said, appearing in the living room. "I hate to be late for the show."

"That's O.K by me," Chris said.

Footsteps clattered up the steps to the door and the twins burst into the room with their father right behind them.

"I was not shot," Bobby was saying to Jimmy.

"Yes you were. Danny shot you first—I saw him."

"Listen, you kids, run into the bathroom and wash up."

"Dale," Jean said, "will you wash them tonight? They take forever."

"Oh, all right," Dale said.

A steady babble of voices came from the bathroom, which was in the center of the house, like the pivot of a merry-go-round. Chris listened, curious. He heard Dale break out laughing heartily at something that was being said or done. Then his voice grew stern.

"No Bobby, I told you how to use the soap. You don't scrape it off with your fingers," he shouted. A few minutes later, the twins appeared in the living room.

"Hi, Chris," they said.

"Hi, boys, what have you been doing?"

"I was Roy Rogers today and he doesn't ever get killed, does he?" Bobby asked, frowning at Jimmy.

"You were dead. Harry and me saw Danny hiding behind the tree. You came by and he stood up and jabbed his gun in your ribs."

"I shot him first! I pulled quicker!"

"All right, you wild Indians, dinner's ready," Jean yelled from the kitchen.

At the table Dale sliced the meat loaf and Jean spooned portions of string beans and mashed potatoes on the children's plates. Then as Dale placed a slice of meat loaf on each of their plates, Jean cut the slices for them. Yvonne pushed her food around with her fork while the boys gobbled theirs down.

"Now you eat," Dale said to the girl.

"What are you going to see tonight at the show?" Bobby asked.

"Fred Astaire and Ginger Rogers."

"Are they cowboys?" Bobby asked.

"No, they dance."

"Any cops in the picture?" Jimmy asked.

"I don't think so," Dale said.

"Now children eat your dinner and stop talking," Jean said. She glanced across the table at the girl. "At least drink your milk, Yvonne," she said, with despair.

"All right, Mommy."

The little girl sat back in her chair, her big solemn eyes looking directly at Chris. He felt as though he were paralyzed. Even though he had known this family for years, he couldn't think of anything to say to them. He ran into them all the time at dances and parties but they seemed different in the down-to-earth atmosphere of their home. Then he recalled that they had only recently returned from a vacation in the States, but before he could ask how the trip was, Dale spoke.

"Yvonne's our food problem. So help me, I don't know how she stays together." He scowled at her and held a glass of milk to her lips. Yvonne allowed one swallow to go past her throat then waited, stonily, with upturned eyes, for her father to remove the glass.

"This is sure good," Chris commented. "Never thought meat loaf could taste like this."

"Babs Bucci gave me the recipe for it. It's got just about everything in it:

tomato sauce, onion, parsley, egg." Jean reached over and wiped the crescent-stain of milk from Yvonne's upper lip.

They were just finishing the pie with ice cream, when there was a knock on the kitchen door. Dale opened it and Joyce Hall came in. Chris was surprised to see that the seventeen-year-old girl was babysitting. Joyce was a pert little blonde who was popular with the boys.

"She's early," Jean whispered with a sigh. "Time to get the children into their night clothes."

"Say," Dale said to Chris as they got up from the table, "do you want to go to the show with us?" Chris was about to respond when Dale said, "Oh, I forgot, you saw the picture already."

"Yeah," Chris said, sliding his hand over Jimmy's head.

Joyce sat on the sofa and flipped through a magazine while Chris sat across from her and smoked a cigarette. He wanted to leave but couldn't without saying goodnight to Jean and Dale.

The front door opened and Buck Harrington and his wife came into the living room. "Where are the Crawfords?" Buck asked Chris.

Dale and Jean came in. "Hi folks. We're all ready." Jean turned to Joyce. "Will you wash the dishes again tonight? And if you'd like, there's ice cream in the ice box."

Chris followed the foursome outside. Buck was babbling on about the barber shop he planned to open in the empty space where the Olsons used to sell their large appliances. He was waiting for a barber chair which was being sent up on the *North Star*.

"You know I just don't feel right about it. But Doc says I got to be indoors or . . . "

"Now stop it, Buck," his wife interposed. "He's been in a stew ever since Doc suggested the idea."

"Well, you know I haven't had any real practice in years except for the few times I've cut Clarence's hair in his shop or when I cut hair for our kids . . . "

"And all the kids in the neighborhood," his wife reminded him. "At no charge."

"I just wish it didn't look like I was horning in on Clarence's business."

"By God," Dale said, "the town needs two barbers. Why should one guy have all the play? Clarence needs some competition."

At the first crossing on the road below the group of cottages, they separated. "Come again," Jean said to Chris.

He watched the two couples go down the hill as he walked across it. He came to his house and sat down on the top step of the porch, his feet in the crunchy snow on the lower, unprotected steps. He looked out across the snow-covered hill. Gwen had her wash strung up under her porch. The bay was smooth, black as paint. He smelled the resinous odor of burning spruce logs. Then he rose and went upstairs to take a bath.

26

HUGE BANKS OF WHITE CUMULUS CLOUDS were drifting south. The breeze coming down Main Street rubbed along the edges of his face and pulled at his hair. Chris was just coming out of Mom's after having breakfast when he saw Mitch standing outside the Johnson's sweet shop.

"Storm last night should brighten things up," Chris said. "The deer will be down low enough so you won't have to kill yourself packing them out."

"We should take off early in the morning and get a few," Mitch said. "My locker's as empty as the inside of a skeleton's belly."

For a moment, as a cloud passed across the sun, they stood in shade. Then the sun came out again but it wasn't warm.

"Like a drink?" Mitch asked.

"Let's go down to the float house. We can have one there. I haven't been in the place for a couple of months."

"Not since those schoolteachers left town, huh?" Mitch pulled at his cigarette. "Damn, everything's dead today. Not even a crap game."

"I wanted to see Dave a minute," Chris said. "If you care to wait, we'll go have that drink."

"Sure, Chris. Sun feels good."

Chris pushed open the door and climbed the stairs and walked into Dave's reception room. A bar of sunlight slashed across from the curtained window to the feet of two native women sitting in wicker chairs. Except for the faded picture of the glacier on the wall, the square room was dim and bare. A girl stood before the window facing Main Street and when the door closed she turned and saw Chris.

"Hello, Chris," she said in a low and bored voice.

"Hi, Fanny."

The door to the dentist's room opened just a crack and Dave's nurse poked her head through it. Her face wrinkled into a hesitant expression and her eyebrows almost touched one another. "Did you have an appointment, Chris?"

"Oh no," Chris said. "I'm here to see Dave."

Dave's face appeared in the opening above the nurse's head. "Come in, Chris," he said.

Chris stepped into the warm room.

"I hope I'm not butting in," Chris said glancing at the dentist chair. A girl with straight black hair sat facing the front window.

"She's just had novocaine," said Dave. He looked taller in his white smock. "I'm giving her a minute's rest and I need one myself."

Chris pulled out a package of cigarettes. The girl shifted against the arm of the chair and spit into the bowl. Chris saw that it was Vivian, the waitress at Mom's. She waved a hand at him and he waved back. The pretty vivacious girl who was so popular with the fishermen in the harbor looked out of place in the chair.

"Give me one of those cigarettes," Dave said. He looked tired.

"Lots of guts in that girl," Dave whispered as he and Chris went over to the corner of the room away from the dentist chair. "She's ready to cry but she's taking it like a trooper."

"Is it serious?"

"She'll be lucky to have more than the four front lowers left after today."

"It's a God damn crime," Chris said to his friend.

"No calcium or iron in the water. And there's not enough sun for Vitamin D requirements. You think they'd spend a few dollars and buy some vitamin pills. I've preached to them until I've grown disgusted, but it's no use." Dave took a deep drag off the cigarette. "She's twenty-three. I might save one or two of them but she's definitely going to need false teeth and I'm not good at fitting them."

"Jesus!" Chris said and pulled on his cigarette.

"What brings you up here?" Dave's eyes glinted with curiosity. "Going to ask me to go South with you again?"

"I'm not going South, Dave. And I mean it."

"Sure!" Dave laughed.

"Hell, Dave let's go together. It'll do us some good."

Dave gave a sigh that could have gone further but Dave checked it before it was half way out.

"You're working your ass off. You haven't taken a decent day off since—hell, I can't remember when."

"Well," Dave confessed, "I could do with a rest. But I've got so many patients waiting for appointments—bridges, temporary fillings, all sorts of work."

"Oh brother," Chris laughed.

"I thought you had to wait for MacLane to come and get that salmon you've got stored for him in your warehouse," Dave said.

"Mac's probably on a two month toot and has forgotten all about it. Anyway we won't be gone that long. All I want to do is go down there and see what the hell the score is."

Dave threw his cigarette onto the floor and mashed it out with his foot. "I'll think about it," he said. He went back across the room and began mopping Vivian's gums with cotton.

Chris said, "I'll see you later, Dave." He knew Dave wouldn't go. Dave was too conscientious to leave the people of Wrangell without a dentist.

Dave mumbled something as Chris went into the reception room. Fanny was reading a magazine and he went out of the room without waiting for her to look up.

Two fisherman clad in bright wool jackets stood before the movie house studying the posters. Mitch was nowhere on Main Street.

Chris decided to go to the float house. He hadn't been there in two months. It seemed like forever. It might be forever unless he went down to San Francisco and straightened her out. As Chris walked past Buck's new barber shop, he saw Mitch emerging, a fist full of bills poking out from his hand and a grin stretching across his face. He joined Chris and the two sauntered over toward the float house.

They went across the bridge and through the native section. Chris led the way single file down the plank to the porch of the float house. The incoming tide had floated the house up a few feet and the skiff tied to the railing rubbed against the side. A buzz saw in Yorgensen's boat yard screeched through a board and a cat meowed from somewhere on the roof. Inside, the three small rooms were as shining and neat as if they had just this morning been cleaned.

"Your housekeeper sure keeps the place up," Mitch said, plopping down on the couch. He began counting the money he'd won in the crap game. "You'd think Mrs. Fremont was getting it ready for someone to move in."

Chris made some drinks and, after handing Mitch a glass, sat down on the arm chair by the radio. He played with the dial but then shut it off. The reception was never as good in a house as on a boat.

"God damn!" Mitch exclaimed in wonder, after he'd counted the money. "I won eleven hundred and thirty six dollars. In nothing flat, too! And me with only forty bucks in my pocket." He paused a moment and sipped his drink. "Chris," he said, leaning forward, his legs spread, "I'd like to buy the float house back from you."

Chris finished his drink which tasted flat. He thought of the times he had spent with Lyddy in the float house. She liked the snug little place with its kitchen, living room and bedroom.

"Yeah, I'm serious, Chris. I'd like to buy this house back. I'll give you a profit." Chris had purchased the house from Babs and Mitch eight years ago. He bought it for two reasons. It was a good place to bring a date and he liked to be able to have someplace of his own to go when he got in a row with his father.

"I'll give you eleven hundred for it," Mitch said. He went into the kitchen and poured himself another drink. "That's four hundred more than you paid for it but you've done a lot of repairs."

When the Bucci's lived there, there was always a party going on. Mitch was out of town a lot that year, working in the gold mine at Juneau. People came to enjoy the cakes and roasts and spaghetti Babs prepared and the card games and dances in the small living room. It was Chris' first year in Wrangell after graduating from college. He really enjoyed himself at the float house, especially when Babs selected him from the rest of the male crowd, allowing him to sleep with her whenever they found the opportunity.

"Well, what do you say, Chris?"

"Eight hundred is fine," said Chris. He got up and went into the kitchen and poured water into his drink. He had no use for it anymore, he thought, staring through the window at Shakes Island. And it would be nice for Babs and the kids to have a decent place after the years they'd spent living in a shack.

Mitch was so nervous he gulped down his drink in one swallow. He coughed and banged on his chest with his hands. When he recovered he began counting out the money.

"If you think you can hold onto the money until we get the title papers transferred, keep it and pay me then."

The float house seemed warm suddenly. Chris opened the kitchen door to let some air in. The incoming tide rippled under the old seine skiff that bobbed and banged against the side of the porch.

27

THE CRASHING RAIN AGAINST THE WINDOWS of the hospital woke Gwen Olson. She lay in the narrow bed in the dark room, wishing daybreak would come. It seemed like ages since the baby had been born although it was probably only a few hours.

Gwen clenched her teeth, fighting off a growing cramp. The cramp turned into a powerful hand that twisted her insides into a small ball and Gwen prayed that it would leave her. As the sensation ebbed, Gwen thought of her daughter.

The baby was premature, like her second child with Clarence. Only this time she had been more careful. When she was pregnant by Clarence she had walked carefree and happy around the island to the beach in her sixth month and swum out in the icy water of the back channel until she was exhausted. She had barely made it to shore when the labor pains came. This time she had been at home. Matt Fleming had just left after giving Danny a piano lesson and Jon had fallen asleep on the couch. Forgetting her condition, Gwen tried to pull Jon up to a sitting position while he was still heavy with slumber. As the pain struck her, she gave a little shriek. Fortunately Diana, who was in the kitchen making a pot of cocoa, hadn't heard her.

Jon woke, groggy and sullen.

"Would you like some cocoa?" Gwen asked. "Diana's making some."

They had the cocoa in the kitchen and Gwen was glad that Jon drank his quickly, even though it was burning hot. The pain was coming in regular waves and she wanted to lie down in bed. She could barely undress herself and finally crawled into bed without taking off her slip. For hours, it seemed, she simply endured the pain, but after a while it came so frequently and so sharply that she began moaning out loud without even realizing it. The door opened and Diana stood in the doorway with the hall light burning behind her. She had been staying with her sister since their parents had left for Arizona in the hope that a drier climate would improve Myron's health.

"Gwen," she said in a whisper. "Gwen, you're not having labor pains, are you?"

"I think I am. I think you better phone for Doc Little . . . " Just then, a cramp seized her and the pain was so pure and so long that she cried out. Jon woke.

"Gwen," he muttered.

"But, Gwen," Diana exploded, "you're only eight months along."

Gwen shrugged her shoulders. "Maybe I made a mistake," she said, holding her breath as a pain streaked through her and disappeared. "You know how bad I am with dates and figures."

Diana dashed into the hallway and turned the crank on the telephone vehemently.

"Gwen, what is it? Not already?"

Jon asked the question with a low groggy voice as if he had gone through this ordeal a hundred times, although this would be his first child.

"Yes, Jon. I'm afraid so. Anyway, I'm not taking any chances this time. Diana's calling Doc Little right now. I think I'd better wash up." Gwen struggled into a sitting position and put her feet on the floor. Another cramp hit her. "Oh!" she cried and bent forward, rocking with the pain.

Jon's fingers gripped her arms. "Don't be afraid, my darling."

Gwen kissed Jon. "Jon, I'm not afraid. The pain is just so terrible I can't keep from crying."

"Doc can't come over," Diana stammered as she came in. "He's delivering Mrs. Forbes' baby. Miss Sarber said to come over to the hospital."

"Call the bar for Curly's cab," Gwen said.

"I did," said Diana with a sigh of disgust. "Curly's not at the bar—as I expected."

"Curly's busy on a night like this," Jon commented in his mild voice.

"I think I can walk to the hospital," Gwen said. "It's only a short ways."

"Oh, Gwen, don't be silly," Diana said, biting her nails.

"What are we going to do?" asked Jon. "You know the pickup is in the shop for repairs."

Diana said, "I'll run down to Main Street and flag Curly."

Gwen got up, moving slowly and stiffening with pain from time to time. She began to put on her clothes, praying that Diana would find Curly soon, for the pain was intense.

"Maybe we should try to walk there," Jon said. "Diana might not find Curly so easy."

"She can find Curly if anyone can," Gwen breathed. "After all she's been going with him for three years."

Once she was dressed, she lay down on the bed again and passed into a trance of pain. She heard Jon muttering in the background. She didn't know how much time passed by but it seemed like the entire night had gone by before Curly arrived in his cab. She had given birth to her second child in Curly's cab. But this time they made it to the hospital. She told Doc Little she could walk, but on the way to the elevator, she was gripped by a pain so fierce that it bent her over. Doc braced her with his pudgy hands and sent for a wheel chair.

The wind lashed the rain against the front windows of the hospital. Down below a car sloshed through the mud on the road and disappeared. For the first time, Gwen could distinguish the quick eager sound of the streams that ran down behind the hospital from the roar of the rain water in the drain pipes. She heard a baby wail downstairs. It grew frantic and loud. Then a door slammed, muffling the cry.

It must be Mrs. Forbes' child. She knew it couldn't be her daughter. Her baby had been born premature and was under an oxygen tent. Her sister and her husband and his parents had reassured her, telling her over and over again that her daughter was healthy and strong, a respectable five pounds and one ounce. But so far she had not seen her and would not be permitted to see her until she was strong enough to be able to get out of bed and go down to the nursery where they kept the premature babies in the incubators. Incubator. The word frightened her. It was like a little glass coffin enshrouding the baby. Her second baby, a boy, had stayed in the incubator for two weeks before he died.

Poor Clarence. He was a total wreck during those two weeks. He stayed at the hospital most of the time; the barber shop on Main Street was closed. A smear of stubble formed on his chin and nicotine stained his fingers. She had never seen him like that. Always before he took such care of his appearance. He didn't seem to notice her or how she was feeling. He was crazed, restless. After Gwen was strong enough to come home, Clarence wanted to burn the baby's clothes even though she told him they could try again as soon as she was well enough. Finally she agreed and let him burn them. After that, nothing went right. Suddenly Clarence wanted a divorce. She gave it to him, of course, taking custody of Danny and going to the States to stay with her aunt until the divorce papers were made final.

Clarence. It was odd to think that he was only a few rooms away down the hall. Diana had told her that he had fallen off the bridge near the shrimp cannery during the night and come in for stitches. Gwen hoped he was all right. She still loved Clarence and always would. He was a remarkable human being, separate from all the rest. Yes. Even from Jon. She married Jon because he provided security and stability and never once got jealous when she went to the dances without him. Jon would rather stay home with Danny after a hard day's work at the store. Every Sunday morning they went trout fishing at Virginia Lake in his outboard-driven skiff. Gwen loved the swift boat ride across the back channel and the fishing on the lake even more than he did. She loved the outdoors and fishing and hunting. For a thrill, she would go into Johnny Bugg's bar on Main Street, pretending she was looking for Curly, and watch the men playing cards on the two tables by the huge silver oil stove. The room would be hushed with only the sound of the blower in the stove and the clicking of the chips. At the bar, she would hear the small constant hubbub of afternoon talk going on between the customers and the bartender.

Clarence didn't like any of that. He hated cards played in any manner or form. He wouldn't even play gin rummy at home with her. He was restless all during their four years of marriage as if he couldn't adjust to the fact that he was tied down. She knew him well enough so that she knew he was just as restless after the divorce and that he longed for her body and home-cooking and the boy, Danny.

One night at the end of the summer, she saw Clarence from her darkened bedroom window. He was climbing up the path of the hill in the direction of her house. It was a sharp, cold, moonlit night and the collar of his overcoat was buttoned tightly around his neck. He moved slowly as though thinking and not caring about the cold and the brilliant moonlight falling in his path and on the town and channel below. Gwen stood by the window, quivering and hushed, a cold thrill brushing over her flesh. She felt a stab of warmth as she remembered the soft and gentle hands of the barber. Watching him climb the path, his body slanting forward a little, she sensed his restlessness. Gwen shivered. The sight haunted her, the sight of the man in the moonlight walking in a pool of loneliness. She wanted to rush down the stairs and onto the porch and call him in. But he went on by, disappearing behind the line of trees which marked the path. And just then, Danny burst in the door with a story about meeting Miss Prince and making the sleeping birds sing for her.

Gwen felt sorry for Clarence. She knew he was probably pining over the schoolteacher. She had seen him at the A&N dances, sitting with his friend Steve in one of the folding chairs strung along the wall. Clarence would be watching Lyddy and Chris as they circled the floor, his face white with anger. Steve would be trying to cheer him up by laughing and joking. Clarence loved Lyddy and he would have done anything to have her but she was all wrapped up in Chris and Gwen was glad. If Clarence married Lyddy, he would worship her in the beginning, as he had with Gwen, but later he would grow restless and aloof, become miserable and resentful. Gwen wished Clarence had been more fair about their marriage, that he hadn't worshipped her so much in the beginning, that he had made friends with some of the men of the town, by playing cards or going fishing or even getting drunk once in a while.

Gwen heard Doc Little going down the hall. She recognized the busy quick shuffle of his feet. Two nurses followed him, their rubber-soled shoes squeaking over the linoleum floor. Then she heard the staircase creaking with the familiar rhythm of her husband's steps. Gwen realized that Jon was coming to see her before going down to open the store. Suddenly, she was very happy. She brushed back her hair and straightened the covers of the bed. The hospital was quiet except for Jon's footsteps coming up the stairs. There was a dull gray light shining in the window and the rain had stopped. Jon reached the landing and turned towards his wife's room. Suddenly, she knew that the baby girl born last night was going to be all right. She just knew it. Tears came into her eyes as she thought about how happy Jon would be with a child of his own.

28

MATT PICKED UP THE AXE which was leaning against the shed. Back here under the trees, it was always cool. He was miles away from town. Except for the faint noise of kids playing on the beach below, it was quiet. The breeze shook rain from the branches of spruce and hemlock. He could hear the water drops spattering on the earth around him.

Matt set a tree stump on the block, spat into his hands and heaved the axe with all his strength. The stump split apart and both halves tumbled to the ground. Matt stooped and set another piece of the stump on the block. A crow flapped off a branch of the Jack pine by the cabin.

As Matt swung the axe with vigor, his blood warmed. He chopped steadily for a half hour, realizing as he worked that he was overdoing it, but the rhythm of his body and the ease with which the wood split beneath his blows made him heave the axe all the harder. Time and energy slipped by in a warm glow of sweat and rhythm. The singing wind stirred his soul as if he were playing a new piece on his piano.

All of a sudden he was winded. He gasped for air and dropped the axe as an attack of dizziness struck. The cabin looked like it was miles away as he wobbled towards it. He should have known better. He chastised himself for working so hard without any breakfast. He didn't eat in the mornings any more because the pain in his stomach was so bad that he threw up whatever he ate. But it was close to noon and he should be able to keep something down now. He took the huckleberry pie he'd baked the night before out of the cooler on the porch and sat down at the kitchen table.

After finishing several slices of pie, Matt felt lazy and tired. He could barely stay awake. He stood at the front window and watched the four boys playing on the beach. The two taller boys were jumping off an old beat-up seine skiff anchored in the shallow water and swimming towards shore. Matt got goose bumps just thinking about the sharp bite of the icy water. The wind was creating white caps on the channel.

Matt stretched on the narrow cot against the wall and tried to sleep. Lately his health puzzled him. There were times when he couldn't hold anything down for two and three days at a time. But his lungs were fine. He hadn't had a serious coughing attack for over two weeks. In fact, sometimes his lungs felt so good, he wondered if the TB was gone.

"Rest," the doctors at the sanitorium in Seattle had told him. "Get plenty of rest." But he couldn't, not with all the clamor coming from the beach. He got up and looked out the window. The kids were still splashing around in the water. Out across the flashing silvery back of the channel, just rounding Elephant Nose Point, he saw the American steamer, *North Star*, heading towards Wrangell.

Against his better judgment, Matt decided to go down to the beach and talk to the children. He thought of the beach as his front yard and he enjoyed visiting with his guests. He put on his old tennis shoes and hiked down from his cabin to the beach, crossing the road and picking up the trail which skirted the edge of the graveyard.

When he got down closer to the shore, he couldn't resist the impulse to go swimming; the water looked so glorious as the sun flashed off its silver scales. He removed his duck trousers and sweater and laid them across the logs that made up the breakwater wall, then strode down the sandy incline and splashed into the icy water. He came up with a gasp and flapped his arms and legs until circulation started, then swam towards the skiff where the children were playing.

The water felt so good he changed his mind and headed away from the shore. He was a good swimmer and the water around him seemed to sense this, barely making any sound as he moved forward with rhythmical strokes. When he was warm and used to the temperature of the water, he turned over on his back and floated. He could see the square, ugly house belonging to Judge Slater near the water's edge and behind it the Harts' home, encircled by its white picket fence. The trees swept up from the shore to the ridge behind Matt's cabin. He saw a cloud brush across the tips of the trees. A battalion of Canadian geese swerved around it, heading north, probably towards the flats at the mouth of the Stikine River. Matt enjoyed floating so much he stayed out there until his limbs were stiff with cold, then turned over and headed for shore.

The boys were certainly having fun with the skiff, screaming and splashing in the water. Gwen's boy, Danny, was there, and Mitch's kid, Harry, and the Crawford twins. Of all the children in Wrangell, Matt liked Danny the best. Perhaps it was because of Gwen. Matt had taught Gwen to swim when she was a youngster and this past summer Matt had begun showing Danny the basics. Gwen had always been a cheerful girl. The only time he had seen her sad was after the sudden and heartbreaking divorce from Clarence. Danny was four years old then and Gwen seemed to have centered all her love on the boy afterwards. She treated him as an equal and Danny was intelligent enough to realize and appreciate this. The first time Danny heard Matt play the piano, he told his mother that he wanted to play the piano too. Gwen arranged for Matt to give him lessons. Danny turned out to be a natural, although, like many musically gifted children, he disliked practicing scales; he wanted to compose and play music that was somewhat above his level of aptitude.

As he got closer to the shore, Matt realized he didn't want to speak to the kids at the moment, so he swam around the fringes of land that jutted from the shore. The beach on this side was rocky and he was glad that he had kept his tennis shoes on. His wet shoes wheezed and whooshed as he headed up the incline between the rocks. He cut through the trees and came to the edge of the graveyard.

Bea Hart was placing a potted plant on Tom's grave. Roy stood next to her. He seemed restless, shifting from one foot to the other, looking off through a break in the trees at the kids playing on the beach.

Matt had dug Tom's grave. At the time the search party found Tom's body, Greg Sundberg was swamped with funeral preparations for two native women who had died in the space of three days so he asked Matt to dig the grave for him. It was a bright, sunny afternoon and the snow was melting, as Matt shouldered a pick and shovel from the graveyard toolshed and crunched across to the designated plot. A party of natives were singing a tuneless rendition of *Sweet Adeline* in the picnic grounds at the edge of the graveyard. They sang the song as a deep rhythmical chant that jarred against the familiar melody. The work was slow and Matt's keen ears cringed at the discordance of their singing. He began to hum the tune himself, to drown out their version, and quickly developed a rhythm which he applied to his work with the pick and shovel. There was so much moisture in the soil that he had to go to the toolshed to locate an empty can with which to bail out the water. The sun was brilliant and sharp; its warmth evoked spirals of smoke from the melting ice in the small graveyard. Matt worked carefully, hacking through the muck and tangled roots, wanting to do a good neat job. When he was nearly through, two drunken natives from the picnic grounds ambled over and stood above the grave.

"That's as good a hole as I've ever seen," said Campus with a drunken nod. They stood gawking, looking down into the grave, where Matt stood ankle deep in water as he shoveled the dirt out and onto the ground above.

"For poor Tom," the other added.

A woman squealed with laughter in the lean-to in the picnic grounds.

"Yes, poor Tom," Matt said, standing in the hole and bailing out the last of the water. He stuck up his mud-covered hand and Campus pulled him out. Matt's body was shaking from the physical exertion and his blistered hands throbbed with pain.

"Wasn't it a shame the way he died"?

"Suicide, sure," the other native said.

Matt ran his eye along the gaping hole. "I don't know if it's large enough," he said.

"Hell, I'm about a foot shorter than Tom," Campus said. He stretched down on his back alongside the grave.

"Sure, it's big enough," he said, raising his head and noticing the distance from the end of his feet to the grave.

"You shouldn't have done that," Matt said. "You've got yourself all dirty."

"How do I look?" Campus pasted a beatific smile upon his lips and crossed his chest with his arms. Out of the corner of his eye Matt saw his wife heading across the graveyard.

"Now what the hell's wrong with you, you crazy bastard!" she screamed as she reached them. "You're filthy!"

Campus rose and slunk off with his wife towards the picnic grounds.

"That bitch," the other native murmured and ambled after the pair.

Matt put the tools away in the shed and trudged out on the dirt road. It was a beautiful day and yet the thought of death tainted his pleasure. The channel rubbed along the shore without a ripple of sound. The sun glinted off the islands, like a sword of light, knighting them one at a time, as his eyes moved from one to the other. On a bright day like this after a storm, the land dried out in a great waft of smoke and mist.

As Matt climbed up the path to his cabin, he saw a familiar figure on the road below. It was Chris Ballard, tall and stopped, his face dark and serious. Chris disappeared across the shoulder of the road and went through the trees into the graveyard. He reappeared again where the trees thinned and Matt could see him standing beside Tom's grave. Westward across the channel, Matt could see Two Tree Island, where Tom Hart had died. Above the island, the sky was a fine dusky red. The channel suddenly drew the color into its bosom, the islands picked it up, the sky became softly suffused with it. Matt stood outside his cabin and watched the painted islands and channel and beach. The whole land was ablaze with the color as though the heavens suffered from a bleeding wound. The ache in his muscles slipped away, the blisters on his hands stopped throbbing and a strange peace settled over the land, a peace so wistful that Matt's strained breathing jarred against his ear drums.

The first thing he saw when he went into his cabin was his battered old upright. The piano stood by the window against the wall. The dull worn keys and the music on the rack pulled Matt to the stool. He began playing all the pieces that he knew by memory. A breeze poured through the open window, rubbing against his eyes and blinding him with emotion. It was as if he had been walking through his life on one level and suddenly he was on a higher plane and a new and mysterious and glorious world was awaiting him. Tears rolled down Matt's face as he played without pause. He played Chopin,

Brahms and Gershwin, whom he loved even more than Tchaikovsky. As he played, the rose tint faded from the sky. Matt threw his heart into the music of *Rhapsody in Blue* and the genius of Gershwin filled the cabin and warmed Matt's soul.

Somehow the rapture of that moment had been mixed up with Tom's death ever since. Matt strode out from the trees along the edge of the graveyard and walked over to the grave where Roy and Bea were standing.

"Hello, folks," Matt said.

"Hello, Matt," Roy said, his voice dark and serious.

Bea just nodded. Her eyes were wet and rimmed with red and her face pallid and tight. There was an awkward silence. Matt was uneasy in his bathing suit. He wished he had remained concealed in the trees until the Harts had departed. With a murmured farewell, he moved off towards the beach where the children were playing.

"Oh, there's Matt," one of the boys cried.

They splashed out from the water and swarmed around him.

"Gosh, you're a good swimmer, Mr. Fleming," said Bobby Crawford. His blue eyes sparkled.

"Row us out on the channel, Matt!" Harry cried.

"We want to see the steamer tied at the dock from the skiff," Danny said.

"You boys brought the skiff here," Matt said. "You should row it back where you found it."

"Fred Racht said we can have it," Harry said with pride.

"What's wrong with it?" Matt asked, knowing Fred wouldn't voluntarily part with any of his meager possessions.

"He got himself a new skiff and he said we could have this one."

Matt waded out to the skiff. It was warped and the paint was peeling. Matt noticed there was a bailing can astern. It looked as if it was needed for there were a few inches of water in the bottom.

"All right," Matt said. "I'll row you boys out on the channel to see the steamer. But I'm going to ask Fred if it's true about him giving you the skiff."

"Yowie!" the boys yelled. They splashed out in the water and crawled over the side of the skiff, almost tipping it over.

"Now Danny, you take the can and bail this water out and I want the rest of you to be still. A skiff is no place to play when you're out in deep water."

Matt fitted the oars in the oarlocks and pulled on them with a slow steady rhythm. Everything that Matt did, from picking berries to riding his bicycle, he did with rhythm. Sometimes he became so entranced by the rhythm of his work that he lost consciousness of his surroundings.

They were quite a ways off from the beach when he became aware that the kids were making a terrible rumpus. There was as much water in the bottom of the boat as there was when they started out. He swung around and reprimanded Danny who was standing with his feet spread on either side of the forward gunwale, attempting to balance himself.

"Get down from there, Danny, and bail this water out!" Matt shouted.

The three boys facing Matt were cupping their hands in the water and sloshing each other.

"Now you stop that, you hear, or I'll row the skiff back to the beach and make you walk around the island!"

The boys settled down but their laughing and shouting continued, making it difficult for Matt to concentrate on his rowing.

Matt rowed straight out into the channel. He liked the pull on the oars, the rhythm he created, the swish of the skiff each time he swung the oar blades out of the water. He was complimenting himself on the good steady stroke he had developed when Danny shouted out, "There's the steamer!"

Matt decided to rest for a moment. He slid the oars in across his knees. The beautiful white steamer was tied along the Clinton dock, the forward boom moving the cargo over the side. Matt could see all of the town, spread out in a crescent above Main Street and framed by trees. He was surprised to see how far out they were.

"Danny's not bailing!" shouted Bobby.

"Oh, you bail yourself," Danny shouted. The bailing can flew over Matt's head and Harry jumped up to catch it. The can flew over his outstretched hands and Harry nearly went over the bow reaching for it.

"Harry, sit down! You want to tip the boat over?"

"Row for the can! Quick! Before it sinks!" Harry shouted back.

Matt dug the oars into the water and propelled the skiff towards the can that was bobbing in the water, tilted to one side.

"There! I got it!" Harry shouted with triumph.

Matt pulled in the oars, crossed them and looked back at Danny with a scowl. "Now what's wrong with you, Danny? That's no way to act aboard a skiff."

Danny reached up and caught the can thrown back at him by Harry.

Matt was flabbergasted. "I'll dive in and swim for shore and leave you wild kids alone out here if you keep that up!"

"If you're tired, I can row," Danny said with good nature.

Matt wished he had never agreed to take the boys for a ride.

"Hey, the water's getting deep in here," Jimmy Crawford squealed. "If you don't want to bail, let me do it."

Danny replied, "I'm the bailer on this tub. Matt said so!" He stooped over the thwart, filled the can with water and spilled it over the side.

For the first time since he'd been aboard the skiff, Matt realized that this wasn't just an ordinary leak. He peered down between his bare legs. The water was actually three inches above his ankles.

Matt scrambled forward over the thwart, took the can from Danny and began bailing as fast as he could.

"I can bail the water all right," Danny said, offended.

Harry came jumping over the thwart, rocking the skiff, and yanked at Matt's free arm. "Let me bail, Mr. Fleming. I'm stronger than Danny."

Matt didn't even notice the boy pulling at his arm. He was totally absorbed by the rhythm of his motions as he bent over, dipped the can in the water and emptied it over the side. After a long while he straightened up, winded and worried, and glanced at the kids. The boys were screaming and shouting with excitement about their predicament.

Matt stood up and shouted, "I want you boys to be quiet now. This is serious!"

Matt's lungs seared with pain as he fought for air. He found it difficult to get sufficient oxygen. His habit of concentrating on one thing at a time had precluded his paying attention to his breathing. As he strangled for air, he saw the steamer cutting across the channel astern of the skiff. He waved desperately but in vain. The steamer's stern turned towards them as the ship headed towards Petersburg.

Matt scrambled back to the amidship thwart to row towards the beach. He pulled on the oars until his muscles refused to go on any further and he slumped over the oars in a state of exhaustion. He knew that he was doing a poor job, running the blades too deep or missing the water entirely. He fell backwards twice, scraping his elbows. What hurt more than anything was the fact he had no rhythm and he couldn't seem to develop one. His muscles wouldn't respond to the messages from his brain. He felt like he would never be able to recover enough strength to put the oars in position. They twisted in his hands, slipping sideways with the water and sticking there, halting the skiff's progress rather than pushing it forward.

He stopped again for air. The Crawford twins were quiet but Danny and Harry were still arguing about who could do the better job of bailing.

Matt looked up, with sweat dripping in his eyes, and saw the beach shimmering in the distance across the flashing back of the channel. It seemed so far away. He sighed with exhaustion, then ran his gaze along the shoreline towards the harbor. He'd been rowing in the wrong direction! The harbor was closer to them than the beach! Matt swore. It amazed him because he hadn't sworn for such a long time that it sounded foreign to him.

"Why didn't you kids tell me the harbor was closer?"

Matt sat down, turned the skiff around and began rowing again, as steady as he could in his state of panic, making a little better time. He noticed that all of the kids were quiet now. He didn't think they were really afraid. This was new and strange to them and they were curious.

A wave of happiness swamped him and he began to cough. Out of habit he reached for his handkerchief, embarrassed that the boys might see blood on his lips. At that moment, Danny came to his side, said, "I'm afraid the water's coming in much faster than we can bail."

Matt coughed again. A long overdue attack seemed to be boiling in his lungs. The phlegm and blood rattled in his throat and he spat over the side. He eyes grew misty as his head hung over the gunwale, waiting for relief.

"Bail faster, Danny," Matt said, wiping his mouth with his wet, bloody handkerchief.

"Sure, Mr. Fleming."

"Bobby, you stand up and wave towards shore!"

Matt set the oars in position, glanced back over his shoulder at the harbor, and began to row again, knowing that only a miracle would save them. The water in the skiff was so deep it wasn't even sloshing. The kids sat crouched with their feet on the thwarts, holding on to the side, and watching Matt with wide eyes.

29

FROM DOWNSTAIRS IN THE HOSPITAL a baby's cry droned and scratched. It felt sandpaper on his nerves. Clarence turned over on his back and stretched out on the narrow bed. He knew it couldn't be Gwen's baby. Miss Sarber told him that the premature baby was in an incubator.

He felt rotten. It wasn't just physical. His flesh crawled with disgust when he thought of how he had behaved. He must have knocked himself out when he fell. When he woke up, the tide was coming in and lapping around him, nibbling at his clothes. He had screamed in horror, thinking it was pulling him under. If he'd used his head, he would have realized that it was just the tide coming in. He could have crawled up the beach and climbed up the mud bank in back of the native section without anyone knowing what had happened. Instead he screamed. And Chris came to his rescue, along with Olaf

Yorgensen. They had taken him to the hospital.

He expected to leave soon. Aside from a few stitches on his head, he had suffered little damage. His left side was still sore and his nose and forehead stung a little but it wasn't enough to keep him in the hospital.

He heard Miss Sarber's energetic footsteps clicking along the hallway outside. It must be four o'clock since that was when Miss Sarber relieved the regular nurse. With a sense of relief, Clarence waited for her to come in.

Sarber was always willing to work the night shift whenever the hospital was full. She had been on duty when Chris and Yorgensen dragged his drunken carcass into the hospital last night.

"Hold still," Miss Sarber had told Clarence as she applied an ice pack to his bleeding nose. "You want to bleed to death?"

He was still drunk as he lay sprawled out on the operating table while Doc Little bent over his head wielding a razor. "Yeow!" Clarence had yelled. "You're shaving more than hair off, Doc."

"Pretty busy tonight, aren't you, Doc?" Miss Sarber's voice was remote as she spoke to the doctor.

"Gwen's going to have another premature baby shortly," Doc said. The razor scratched across Clarence's scalp. Doc spoke casually, as if unaware that Clarence had once been married to Gwen. Clarence had been in the bar last night, having his usual nightcap, when Diana burst in looking for Curly, practically hysterical because Gwen was in labor.

In the past months Clarence had watched Gwen from the barber shop window whenever she'd come tripping past on Main Street. For some reason, he felt nauseated the first time he noticed the bulge in her belly. The nausea intensified as the months rolled by and as Gwen grew so large that she looked like she was waddling down Main Street.

"Now for heaven's sake, Clarence, lie down," Miss Sarber said. "Your nose is still bleeding and Doc's trying to work on you."

"Sure. Sure, honey. Anything you say," Clarence replied. It was hard to speak since she was pressing an ice pack against his mouth.

Fragmented memories of their life together. That's all he had left of the four years he spent married to Gwen. He hated hunting and fishing. That's how he knew Gwen loved him dearly for she would rather go after trout and ducks than anything else. He knew she was disappointed that he disliked boating and the outdoors. But she must have made up her mind that she was married and that meant settling down and staying home. She really played ball with him. She stayed in there pitching until it was no longer any use. The best thing he had given her was the big house at the top of the hill. Gwen loved that house and never tired of admiring the view of the channel stretching out to Elephant Nose Point. That and Danny.

"Ouch!" Clarence shouted.

"Clarence, hold still!" Miss Sarber said.

"Hell, that ain't a love tap he's giving me with that needle."

Her fingers pressed the ice pack down firmly over his nose and mouth. "Pshaw, you're so drunk you can't feel it."

If Clarence could get down off the operating table and look out the window, he'd be able to see the house, painted gray and white with red sashes. The small square lawn was bordered with rocks and planted with mountain ash. Hemlock, cedar and spruce trees ran back from the bedroom window into the muskeg. Many a time he and Gwen had seen black bears munching on the raspberry bushes and deer nibbling at the lettuce sprigs in the garden. Once, in the frosty light of a winter morning, they saw a wolf by the mountain ash, a magnificent silver-gray creature that pricked its ears towards the house, exhaling puffs of smoke from its gaping mouth.

"All right," Doc Little said, "I'm through. Just keep that ice pack on his forehead for a while longer and try and get that swelling down. But he's all right and can go home."

Clarence remembered climbing up the hill on the dirt road after working in the shop all day. He remembered how lovely it was in the winter with a southeaster knifing down across the channel and the trees behind the house swaying, stirring Clarence's blood with an ineffable thrill that was intensified by the prospect of a warm house and dinner and Gwen and the youngster, Danny. After Danny began to walk they adopted Taku, brother of the Hart's dog, Winchester. He remembered climbing up the hill in the summer with the sun flashing off the channel, saying hello to the neighbors, watching Taku straining at the leash hooked onto the shed. Danny was usually out in the yard absorbed in some project (at that time he had a mania for digging holes with an army shovel that Clarence had found in the wood shed). Gwen would see him coming and pop out of the house by the kitchen door, clad in some freshly-ironed cotton dress. The sun would illuminate the mountain ash, the lawn, the trees in back of the house. The sun would fall on Gwen, making her appear like an angel. She'd be waving her hand, almost kissing him with her bright, happy smile. Then Gwen would release Taku and the dog and Danny would come tearing down the hill to greet him.

He remembered the afternoon Curly's cab came shooting out of the hospital driveway just after Gwen had unleashed Taku from the shed. Clarence stood frozen on the side of the path while the cab sped forward towards the crossing and Taku came dashing down the hill towards him. He saw the God damn wild kid, Curly, sitting with a slouched ease in the driver's seat as he prepared to make the turn on two wheels. Then he heard the sudden scrunching of the tires on the road and one paralyzing yelp.

Gwen and Danny rushed down the hill, Gwen ahead of the boy. She stumbled in her frantic pace, fell and slid down the gravel path. Clarence was numb. He didn't know what to do. Taku was right in front of him, lying squashed in the center of the road, his bloody intestines flowing out in a small stream of smoke. Gwen got up, her dress dirty, her knee caps bleeding, and ran the rest of the way down the hill, bawling when she fell into his arms.

"All right," Sarber said, "one more application on your head with this ice pack."

"Hell, I'm all right."

"Now you lie back and take it easy. You're not as well as you think."

"For Christ's sake, I'm all right, I told you."

"Clarence," Sarber said, as she plunked the ice pack on his forehead, "there are four expectant mothers in the place. And I mean they're all groaning and about to deliver."

"What the hell you want me to do about it?" Clarence asked.

"And Sally and Evelyn chose this moment for their annual drying out and Shirley is having a beautiful case of the D.T.'s. They all came in this afternoon."

"I'm getting out of here. That's enough with that God damn ice pack."

"And what the hospital needs is a man patient to help balance things up. I'll fix you up with a nice room topside."

So he'd stayed for the night. Sarber practically undressed him and put him to bed. He knew he wasn't really that bad. He'd taken worse beatings when he was boxing in the gym in Detroit. But he felt too groggy to navigate his way back to his room.

Clarence slept fitfully, what with all the commotion in the hospital. Sarber came into his room once and threw a blanket over him. She announced that Gwen had just given birth to a baby girl that was normal and healthy but they weren't going to take any chances and had placed her in the incubator downstairs. For some reason, he spent a lot of time thinking about Danny.

Miss Sarber entered the room, her rubber-soled footsteps squeaking.

"Hi, Clarence. I'm having a sandwich and a glass of milk brought up in a minute. Something went haywire with the stove and you'd better have the sandwich. God knows if the stove will be fixed in time for supper."

"You don't think I'm going to stay here for another night?"

"You don't need to go," she said, straightening Clarence's pillow and tucking in the loose ends of the covers. She cranked up the bed, dumped the contents of the ash tray into the paper bag pinned to the side of the bed, and pulled up the half-drawn shade.

"Say," Clarence protested, "sit down, will you? I'm getting tired watching you." He tried to keep his voice level and normal. "How's Gwen's baby getting along? She's on this floor, isn't she?"

Sarber's long face split into a smile and she slumped down with a sigh into the chair by Clarence's bed.

"I'm pooped," she said. "Worked till three in the morning. I haven't even gone into the nursery yet to see the baby. She's still in the incubator, though."

"How's Gwen?" he asked, nervous.

"Fine. She's your neighbor—the first room off the hall down front."

"Why do you do it?" asked Clarence, knowing Miss Sarber had already worked for eight hours at Olson's.

"They're shorthanded and I can help." Miss Sarber cocked her ear. "That baby's sure putting up a fuss," she said. "I'll have to go down and see what the matter is."

When she left, he tossed the covers to one side and slipped out of bed. He was surprised to find that he was weak and unsteady. He put on the fresh clothes that someone must have brought up from the hotel last night.

"Where are you going?"

Steve Svenson stood in the doorway, as solid as the frame itself. Sometimes Steve reminded Clarence of a bull elk, with his dumb, curious eyes and that air of being alert and ready to spring into action.

"I just heard about you being in here. You sure went haywire last night. I came right up. Is it serious?"

Clarence touched his nose and winced. "Nah. Got a cigarette?"

"You bet." Steve dug into his pockets.

Clarence lit the cigarette. He felt good, as if his friend had given him a warm hearty slap on the back. He pulled on the cigarette meditatively. "Gwen, had a baby girl this morning."

"I know. Babs told me. In fact, she told me you were up here. She's all excited," Steve's face tightened with dismay. "Mitch bought back Chris' float house yesterday. The lucky bastard won the money from some drunken fishermen in a crap game."

Outside in the hallway, Clarence's heart pounded like a piston against his ribs. "Steve, would you mind waiting for me downstairs? I want to see Gwen a minute."

"Sure," Steve said.

When Steve turned off the hallway and headed down the stairs, Clarence realized that he was nervous. His teeth chattered. He took a few steps down the corridor and stopped before the half-open door of Gwen's room. All the while they had been separated he had believed that all he had to do if he ever wanted her back was to ask. From where he stood, he could see the corner of the bed and the silhouette of her legs and feet, swathed in a blanket. It seemed very intimate somehow.

"Is that you, Doctor?" Gwen called out.

Clarence stood dead still. What should he do? He knew Gwen. He probably knew her better than her husband. Sometimes this thought gave him a secret thrill, as if he still had access to her body. Sometimes he felt like he was cheating on Jon Olson. But at the moment he just felt sick.

Clarence turned, tiptoed as quickly as he could away from Gwen's room and went downstairs. He was glad that the baby was still bawling and requiring attention.

"I'll have to check out at the office," Clarence said to Steve who was in the waiting room.

Outside the wind revived Clarence's senses considerably. Westward across the channel, he could see the steamer, a small smoking speck, heading north between Woronkofski and Two Tree Island. The islands looked magnificent in the winter sunlight.

"How you feel?" Steve asked as they picked up the path that led down to Main Street.

It was a beautiful day and it felt good to be out of the hospital and he said so to Steve. Great hunks of cloud moved south in a steady procession like floats in a parade. The whole side of the hill and the roofs on Main Street would blaze with sunlight for a moment, and then, as a cloud lumbered by, the hill and houses and harbor would melt into shadow until the cloud passed. Down below, just outside the line of the harbor, a skiff loaded down with people was going as slow as hell. It looked like it was half submerged.

Steve stopped, his nautical eye caught by the lumbering craft. "God damn," he mumbled and shaded his eyes with his hand. "That skiff ain't setting just right."

"Probably overloaded," Clarence said with a shrug.

Steve took another look. "It's listing. But most of those kids are sitting to port."

"Kids? God damn, Steve, you got good eyes."

They took the short cut across the ball park by the school. For a brief moment, Clarence imagined Lydia popping out and greeting him. He rarely thought of her anymore. Her presence had stirred up all the restlessness and emptiness inside of him. With her gone, he could fall back into his routine with a new goal in mind—the revival of his marriage.

On Main Street, in front of the Johnson's Sweets, the two men stopped.

"Like a coke?" Clarence asked his friend.

"I tell you, Clarence, I don't like the looks of that skiff out there. I think I'll take a walk down to the dock and have a better look."

"O.K. Steve. I'll be here."

The sweet shop door swung open and Diana came out. He heard the sound of shuffling feet, the chatter of kids and jitterbug music before the spring-controlled door slammed shut with a bang.

"Hello, Clarence." Diana looked serious. "I heard about you falling off the bridge last night. How do you feel?"

"Except for a few stitches under my hat I feel as good as new. Can I get you a coke?"

He had never liked Diana. Even though she was younger than Gwen by five years, she was always telling her sister how to run her life. Luckily, Gwen never paid any attention to Diana or else he'd have brained her for sure. Gwen never argued when Diana reprimanded her for some escapade, like going swimming in January with Vivian while all the fishermen popped out of their musty foc'sles and stared goggle-eyed at the happy girls, shivering in their bathing suits.

"I've had three cokes all ready," Diana said. "Clarence, would you do me a favor?" She seemed nervous.

"Sure, if I can."

"Curly's in Johnny Bugg's." She nodded at the drab frame building across the street. "He's drunk and I know he's acting up. Would you go in there and sort of talk him into coming out?"

"That doesn't sound too hard to do."

"You know Curly when he gets to drinking pretty heavily. He doesn't listen to reason."

"I can manage Curly."

"I'll drive his cab up in front of the bar and you can steer him out. Then I'll help you get him in the car and we'll take him to his room."

Clarence and Diana crossed the street, and Diana went on down towards the cab which was parked by the hotel bar. She kept her head up and shoulders straight, walking with a sexy, swaying motion of her legs as if for the benefit of her admirers.

Clarence was amazed and happy that she had asked him to do her a favor. He tried hard to be liked by everyone in town. Even when he was the only barber, he had given good haircuts and shaves when he could have done as he pleased. But except for the store owners and the Federal and City Hall workers, Clarence was an outcast, especially to the rough Main Street crowd. And it was simply because he didn't act like them. They didn't take care of themselves. They drank too much. They were too busy having a good time to take care of the essentials. Parties all the time. It was fine to go to a party or dance once in a while, have a few drinks, have some fun. But every night! Curly was a good example of their mentality. Here he was getting drunk, neglecting his job and fiancee.

Clarence waited until Diana reached the cab. He wanted to be sure that the car was parked in front of the bar before he made any effort to haul out Curly. The wind blew up Main Street as he stood outside the door of Johnny Bugg's bar. There was a kind of sweet power in it that made him inhale again and again as if he could not get enough of it to satisfy him.

The cab came lurching along Main Street, the engine revving. Diana, an inexperienced driver, must have had the throttle wide open while her foot rode the clutch.

Inside the bar, Clarence searched for Curly among the afternoon crowd of fishermen and Klootches and some white women. The bar smelled of old beer and sweat and wet wool. Cuspidors stood on the oil-soaked floors ringed with yellowish splotches of wet and dried spit. Most of the fishermen were playing gin rummy or three-handed pinochle or standing around the tables and watching the players. The huge oil stove dividing the bar and the card room hummed with a steady roar and threw off a cloud of heat that no one seemed to notice.

Clarence spied Curly sitting in one of the small side booths in the card room. Curly was slouched against a Klootch, one hand clutching a glass, jabbering to Greg Sundberg who was sitting across the table from them. Curly was rubbing his hand along the girl's leg. He had pushed her dress clear to her buttocks, exposing her black slip and pink panties.

"Hello, Curly," Clarence said.

Curly was drunk. His hair stood out in crazy curls all over his head. His eyes stared at Clarence with dull, glassy wonder. His normally ruddy face was pale and milk white.

"What you want?" Curly's voice was itching for an argument. "My sweet little fiancee send you in here to drag me out?"

Clarence's cheeks burned. "That's right, Curly. And I think it would be a good idea if you left."

The bar door swung open with such force that everyone in the room looked around. Steve came rushing through the crowded room and stopped in front of Clarence.

"Well, well," Curly said with a snicker. "Reinforcements!"

"Clarence," Steve said, with an agitation that was unusual, "Come quick! That skiff out in the channel looks like it's in trouble."

As Clarence and Steve rushed out of the bar, Curly said with contempt, "Well, if that ain't like the chicken son-of-a-bitch! Running out."

Clarence flapped his hands at Diana who was sitting in the cab outside the bar to indicate that he was unsuccessful and took off after Steve who was already halfway down the block.

"God damn it, Steve, this better be good," he said. "You just made me look really bad. What the hell's going on?"

"I'm not sure, Clarence. Maybe the kids are just playing on the skiff. But I thought if there was trouble we could both row out after them in my skiff. It's tied at the float."

The two men went around the corner of the hotel and hurried out along the Clinton dock, past the warehouse.

The skiff was in trouble. In fact, no one on board was rowing. All the kids were standing. Danny! Clarence's heart stopped beating. Yes, the boy on the bow looked like his son!

From the dock he could barely see their faces and he couldn't hear anything because the wind was blowing south across the channel between them and the skiff. But he could tell by the way they were facing shore with their hands cupping the sides of their mouths that they were screaming for help.

"By Jesus!" Steve shouted. "The boat's sinking! Let's get out there!"

They ran back the full length of the Clinton dock, cut down along the side of the hotel and ran out onto the float where Steve's skiff was tied. Clarence untied the painter and jumped into the bow. Steve banged the oars into the oarlocks. The piling of the dock cut off their view of the channel. As they rowed out, the first faint cries of the children on board the distressed craft became audible.

As they got closer, Clarence saw Matt Fleming on board, clad in his familiar red bathing suit. One of the boys was bailing water as fast as he could but the craft was now almost submerged. He could see only the top of it. Danny was standing forward, his eyes trained on the skiff as it rowed across towards them.

"Hurry, Steve!"

Clarence scrambled over a thwart and took one of the oars from Steve's hand. The two men fought wildly with the oars for a while in a effort to row in unison.

"I can do better by myself, Clarence."

Clarence relinquished the oar and scrambled out of the way. He turned his agitated eyes out across the channel to the skiff again. It was gone. For a moment he thought that he might have been looking in the wrong direction. He swept his eyes back and forth across the water. There was no sign of it.

The skiff had disappeared. An awful quiet pervaded the channel.

"Oh, my God!" Clarence cried. "Hurry Steve! The skiff's sunk."

Steve's big body bent over the oars. They flashed back and forth with such force that it seemed surely either the oars or his back would break. Yet the boat still seemed to be standing still.

"This isn't happening," Clarence gasped. Maybe it wasn't his son.

His eyes picked up a tiny splash off starboard. An arm was coming up out of the water and spanking down on it. Could Danny swim? Clarence couldn't remember. It must be Danny.

The lone figure in the water was raising an arm out of the water and letting it drop, raising and dropping, doing it so slowly that it seemed it would stop at any moment.

Steve propelled the skiff towards the figure.

It was Matt Fleming, swimming. Clarence's heart dove into his belly. Matt was holding someone at his side with one arm. It was Harry, Mitch's kid. Harry was trying to help Matt by pushing his free arm sideways against the water.

Clarence reached over and caught Harry's arm and lifted him over the side. Steve pulled Matt on board.

Clarence scanned the channel around them. Except for a few whitecaps, there was no sign of anything else.

"I can't see anything," Steve said in a wild voice.

Clarence grabbed Matt's shoulder. He saw the blood on his lips, the tears in his eyes.

"I could only save one," Matt gasped.

"Was Danny aboard?" Clarence said. "Danny, my son?"

Matt nodded.

30

THE ONLY SOUND IN THE HOUSE was the fast tick-tick-tick-tick of the clock in the kitchen. Chris shook a cigarette out of the pack of Lucky's on the kitchen table before him and stuck one it between his teeth without bothering to light it. He didn't want to go to Mom's for dinner this evening, didn't want to hear any more talk about the afternoon tragedy. He'd gone up the hill to his house to have a bite to eat, but when he opened the cupboard door and saw a quart of whiskey, he decided he'd rather have a drink. He sat there with the cigarette dangling from his lips and poured himself another stiff drink, then went into the living room, his feet moving noiselessly over the carpet.

The sharp glare of the moon through the front window annoyed Chris. He walked to the open blinds and looked out through the slats. He saw the school building across the way, the grass growing along the slush-lined road, two dogs wrestling and yipping in Sally's yard.

He started to shut the blinds, then left them half open. He lit the cigarette in his mouth and sat down in the arm chair. He was tired. Upset, more than anything. He felt like he wanted to vomit but he couldn't. He had spent all afternoon, until the sun dipped from sight and they couldn't see what they were doing, dragging for the kids on the channel. It was useless. Even before they set out, they knew it was hopeless. The water outside the harbor was too deep and the tide was ebbing out so fast, the harbor buoy was tipped westward almost to the surface of the water by the force of the outgoing tide.

Chris was tending the tackle. It was his job to yell aft towards the pilot house to tell the men on the bridge to kick the boat out of gear every time the dragging tackle caught on a bunch of sea grass. Then he would pull it up as fast as he could, feeling the weight of the load as it moved up from the bottom, up through the space of the unseen and mysterious fathoms. It would take at least ten minutes, until the drag hooks would pop up against the hull so that he could clean the drag and drop it back in. Every once in a while it got stuck against something heavy and solid and then he was certain he had one of the Crawford twins or Danny Olson (hopefully hooked by the trunk of the bathing suit, although he knew it was more likely the hooks were embedded in flesh). He'd pull up the wet line with his eyes trained on the green surface of the water, hoping that he wouldn't see the body of one of the boys dangling limp from the end of the line, although that was the only reason they were doing this. But every time, it was just another bunch of grass in the tackle.

He was glad they hadn't been successful. Dragging for a body that had drowned just didn't seem right. He thought they should let it go, drifting along the bottom of the channel, as if it belonged in the water, staying deep until the fishes had gotten most of it, rising to the surface later and floating along with the tides to a quiet place of its own, hundreds of miles away.

Chris reached for the bottle of whiskey which he had set on the coffee table. It was so quiet he could hear the clock ticking in the kitchen. He sipped his drink slowly.

He could see the hospital through the window and he thought of Gwen. Poor girl. She would be heartbroken. He felt sorry for Jon who would have to tell her the news as soon as she was strong enough.

Clarence had acted pretty wild, out there in one of the boats, pulling on a dragging line himself. He was probably still out there in Steve's troller. Chris figured he'd be doing the same thing if it was his son who had drowned.

Chris jerked up at the sound of footsteps coming up the steps and across the porch. The knock on the door tore through the house like a convulsion.

It was Mrs. Fremont, standing on the porch with a tray covered with a towel in her hands. "Hello, Mr. Ballard," she said, her expression sweet and her tone serious. "I know what an awful day it's been, but you must eat."

"Hello, Mrs. Fremont," said Chris, taking the tray from her. He led her into the living room which showed no evidence of having been cleaned on Thursday. It was littered with whiskey bottles, overflowing ash trays, disarranged furniture and piles of magazines on the floor.

"My goodness, Mr. Ballard, you are careless!"

Mrs. Fremont was the only person in Wrangell who called Chris by his last name. It made him self-conscious. Yet he loved the old lady, who lived a few houses down the hill from him. Her hair was white but she was as slim and straight as Lyddy. She wore a faded cotton sweater over a gray starched dress, cotton stockings on her thin legs and white shoes which were damp from the slush on the path.

Chris set the tray on the coffee table in front of the arm chair. The whiskey bottle seemed as out of place as a calendar portrait of a naked girl in the room. Mrs. Fremont didn't seem to notice it.

"I cooked you a big bowl of chili," she said. "I know how much you like it."

"You shouldn't have done it," Chris said, peeking under the white towel. There were crackers and a slice of butter on a dish, too. Leave it to Mrs. Fremont to think of everything. She kept an eye on him. Sometimes she came by on Sunday afternoons, after services at church, to see if he wanted anything. Or nights after supper she'd bring up an apple pie. Chris felt grateful for these attentions. She fitted into his life, filling the lonely corners and crevices left when his family left Wrangell.

"Eat it right away, Mr. Ballard, while it's hot."

Chris started eating. The aroma of the hot chili filled his nostrils. He was suddenly ravenous. Yet he ate slowly, dipping the buttered cracker in the sauce and letting it soak awhile, before bringing it to his mouth.

"Wasn't it awful?" Mrs. Fremont said. "I feel so sorry for Gwen and Jean."

"Yeah."

"There is so little one can do. Poor Gwen. And Clarence. Clarence was right there when it happened." She paused, sucked in her cheeks and said, "I do hope they can at least find the boys. It would be better, don't you think, Mr. Ballard?"

"Yeah," he said, although he didn't agree.

"At least then their mothers will have . . . "

She burst into tears and covered her face with her hands. Chris stopped eating. The tragedy had touched her heart, as it had all over town, squeezing out compassion like whiskey in the process of distillation, powerful, clear, pure.

"There is so little one can do," Mrs. Fremont moaned. "I want so much to help." She fought back the tears.

There was little anyone could do. Death was final. One night Matt had played that *None but the Lonely Heart* on the piano at his cabin for Chris and Lyddy. Chris felt that Matt played it just as Tchaikovsky wanted it played. For Chris, it wasn't about a broken heart or the loss of a friendship. It was a remembrance of a funeral, the emptiness, the sense of desolation, the loud crashing void and the stillness, all there in the music.

"I'll make a pot of coffee for you, Mr. Ballard," Mrs. Fremont said, wiping her nose with her handkerchief and heading towards the kitchen door. She stopped by the fireplace and ran her forefinger over the mantel with a back-to-business air. "Dust!" she exclaimed, her voice sharp and fussy. "And I cleaned this house thoroughly only this Thursday. I should come up more often, Mr. Ballard."

"You work hard enough as it is."

"Sometimes, Mr. Ballard, you're a stubborn man. You pay me more than I get at the hotel and I work there six days of the week and you want me up here only twice a week."

"How about that coffee?"

Without further comment, Mrs. Fremont went into the kitchen, her soles squeaking on the linoleum.

Chris concentrated on the chili. It was wonderful chili, with a lot of fat red beans and chunky bits of moose meat.

"So you like chili," Lyddy had said. "I'll have to learn how to cook it."

"Ask Mrs. Fremont."

"Your housekeeper?"

"Yeah."

"I'll call her up the minute I get home."

"You ain't going home just yet."

"Chris, what do you mean?" She laughed up at him, her sharp teeth glistening in the sun reflecting off the sand of the beach.

"Come here."

"Cave man!"

"Then I'll come over there."

"I'll run."

She ran off in that curious way women run, with short awkward steps, flapping her hands. He caught up with her at the turn in the beach, by the trees, and pulled her down to the sand.

"This is a better place," he said with a laugh. "No one can see us from here."

"I want to go home and call up Mrs. Fremont and find out how she makes chili."

"That's a helluva thing to think about right now."

He kissed her. He kissed her again. All along her baby-soft cheek and down her neck. His lips couldn't seem to get enough. His mouth slid down the opening of her blouse until it rubbed against her bra. She held him close and they lay together on the sand for a long time as if they were kids shocked by the wonderful things their bodies could do and feel.

"Chris, let's go. You'll be wanting to do it right here if you keep it up."

""All right, let's."

"Chris, don't be silly. Let's go home where there's privacy and a nice bed with no sand and rocks and people watching."

They'd gone up the hill to her cottage. That was the second time they had slept together. Lyddy wasn't half as good as Fanny but she would learn. Yeah. She had a lot of possibilities.

Chris pushed the plate away and lit a cigarette.

What a thing to think about at a time like this. Sex. Death and sex. An afternoon in bed with Lyddy and three boys drowning in the cold waters of the channel.

Mrs. Fremont emerged from the kitchen entrance pulling a yellow piece of paper out of the pocket in her sweater.

"Oh, I completely forgot to give you this telegram, Mr. Ballard. Vernon brought it home with him from the Federal Building."

Chris accepted the wire. It was from Ketchikan, from Malcolm MacLane, the cannery's largest salmon broker.

JUST ARRIVED KETCHIKAN. COME DOWN SEE ME. URGENT. CAN'T LEAVE HERE AS HAVE BIG DEAL COOKING WITH A LOVELY PIG. ALSO, TWO DRUNK SCREWBALL INDIANS IN JAIL WANT TO SELL SEINER. LOOKS GOOD FROM WHAT I HEAR.
                                                MAC.

———————

Chris felt as if a trap door had opened somewhere inside him, and a flood of relief and excitement poured into him. God damn it, he would go to Ketchikan. It would do him good to leave town.

He heard a Ford grinding around the bend below, spitting and whizzing up the incline with the throttle wide open. It must be Red Parker's car. He could distinguish the sound of that souped-up contraption from any other car. Red ran the car like hell but he was a good driver, even when drunk. Red had been a racer in the States until booze and age made him unfit for the competitive grind.

The Ford sloshed to a stop in front of the house. A door slammed and Chris heard footsteps shuffling and lurching, shuffling and lurching, up the stairs and across the porch.

Mrs. Fremont headed towards the door.

"I'll get the door, Mr. Ballard."

"No. I'll go." Chris went to the door, not wanting the old lady to see Red, wondering what the hell Red wanted. There surely wouldn't be a poker game tonight.

Red stood on the porch swaying. Chris had never seen him so drunk.

Mrs. Fremont stepped back with a sniff. The air was moist with the sour smell of sherry.

"Well," Mrs. Fremont said, turning to Chris and fidgeting with the buttons on her sweater, "the water's boiling and all you have to do is pour it in the drip." She paused as though having trouble breathing. "Good night, Mr. Ballard. I'll be up again Tuesday."

Red staggered to one side as Mrs. Fremont marched down the steps and out into the yard. The moon glowed on the dirty slush of the snow.

"Jesus, Red, you're a sight. What do you want? Not poker, for Christ's sake."

Red couldn't seem to talk. His small eyes were sunk deep into their sockets. His lips were the color of ashes and beads of sweat stood out on his upper lip. He waved a hand at Chris and rocked back and forth, struggling to stay upright.

"Come in," Chris said. "Take a load off your feet."

Out of the corner of his eye Chris could see a woman sitting in the front seat of Red's car. Her head was resting against the side door window; it looked like she was sleeping.

Red stepped in with a lurch. Chris wondered how he had managed to drive.

Theodore Roosevelt mustache, wore a serious expression as he stood beside his bride who was an inch taller than him.

"Holly, I'm going to call up Curly and tell him to take you and Red home."

Holly put the photo down and looked at him, her amber eyes hurt. "Now, Chrissy darling, I'm drunk. I'm weeping for all that's happened today. Chrissy boy, I love you. I came up here so's the two of us can screw and feel sorry for ourselves and weep over what's happened today." She tossed her hair to one side to get it out of her eyes. "You can't kick me out for that?"

"Oh, yes, I can, Holly. Some other time."

Holly sank back down on to the sofa. Then she stretched out flat on her back along the three cushions. "It's a big house. Don't you go crazy living in it alone?" She opened her eyes, which were always remarkably clear and limpid. "Come here," she said, waving an arm at Chris. "I want to hug you. I want you to know I love you, Chrissy honey."

Chris went over to the door, stopped, and looked back at the big woman lying on the sofa. Holly never had children of her own. He had heard rumors that her husband, Moose, had contracted gonorrhea at one time and was sterile because of it. Holly treated the midget, with a kind of maternal love. And she gave every kid in town a present at Christmas. Looking at her lying there, with her eyes closed, he knew she was in as much pain as if the three kids who had died had been her own.

Chris went down the hallway to the telephone to call Curly. When he went back into the living room, Holly was standing up, trying to peel off her dress. She was crouched over, with the dress half over her head. She seemed to be in a jam.

"God damn this dress," she mumbled, pulling on it in a effort to wriggle it over her head. "I knew Sally's dress wasn't my size." She yanked wildly, stamping one foot, "Knew it the minute I put it on this morning."

Chris wrapped his arms around Holly's shoulders. "Hey there, hold everything." He tugged the dress down to its original position,

"Oh, Jesus Christ, I'm sad."

"Yes, Holly."

"I heard you calling Curly. I just wanted to make you laugh. If I wanted to I could have taken the dress off, easy."

"Sure Holly, maybe some other time."

She examined herself in the oval mirror on the wall. "I'm a wreck."

Chris picked up his drink and handed it to Holly. He wondered what was taking Curly. When he wasn't in a hurry, he would no sooner hang up the receiver and the kid was at his front door.

"Remember when Danny sneaked into Hansen's barn and rode that cow onto Main Street?" Holly said, holding the drink and staring into it. "I busted a blood vessel I laughed so hard."

"Yeah. Danny was quite a kid."

"I feel so sorry for Mrs. Crawford. Two darling boys gone, like that." Holly snapped her fingers, glanced at herself in the mirror again and ran her fingers through her hair. "I'm going out of town for a few days. Sally and Evelyn are in the hospital and I can't take too much of Al by himself. He's always after me, completely falls apart when I send him away."

Curly was blowing the horn outside. Toot! Toot!

Chris jumped up from the chair, looked out the window and saw the cab. He wished Curly had come up to the front door.

"Help me drag Red out," Chris said.

Chris grabbed Red under the shoulders and Holly pulled on his legs and together they got him out the door and stuffed into the back seat of the cab.

"Sorry to be late," Curly said gruffly. "Had to take Jon Olson to the hospital. Now there's a sight for you. He was the last man to leave the harbor."

Chris handed Curly a dollar bill and told him to take Holly and Red home.

"He can take Red home," Holly exclaimed with dignity and authority. "But Curly-locks, you're taking me to the hotel bar."

In the cold night air Chris watched the tail lights of the cab vanish down the road. He could hear the Chevy engine purring across and down the hill. He stood there in the slush waiting for the sound of the engine to dim and vanish as it turned into Main Street. He stood there, waiting for something else but he couldn't figure out what. Then he heard the scream. It was a wail of despair that froze his blood. He turned and stared at the hospital fifty yards up the hill, at the squares of lighted windows, but he didn't hear Gwen Olson scream a second time.

31

THE NOISE FROM THE HOTEL BAR filtered through the thin walls and into his room. Clarence let it swirl around him. Alone now that Steve had left, he let the laughter and the shouts and music wash over him.

He lay on his bed, staring up at the gray ceiling, hearing the rain and sleet slashing against the window. Both of his children were dead now. One had died in an incubator at the hospital, the other in the cold waters of the channel.

Danny was dead and a stranger, for he hadn't known the boy very well. Danny would be alive if Fred Racht hadn't given the boys his leaky old skiff. He should go down and thrash the living daylights out of the son-of-a-bitch. But what good would that do? The bastard probably felt like Santa Claus when he gave the boys his skiff.

Now Danny was lying at the bottom of the channel along with the Crawford boys. Clarence tossed on his side, aware of a heavy pain in his chest. His heart ached with the loss of his boy who had been lost to him twice, once in the divorce and now in death.

Gwen would understand his grief. He remembered how she cried the few times he spanked Danny. She showed Danny so much attention that when Clarence came home at nights from a day's work, he couldn't think of anything to do with the boy that would increase his pleasure. Danny loved to play with his toys in the kitchen while Gwen washed the supper dishes. About the time she was through, it was bedtime. By then Clarence would be settled in the wicker chair in the living room, drowsy and relaxed, disinclined to help with the bedtime ritual which consisted of Gwen catching Danny, undressing him as he wriggled, helping him wash and don his nightclothes, and then reading him a story (Danny was enraptured with the tale of Biting Josephine, a steam shovel). In the living room Clarence would read the *Wrangell Sentinel* and eavesdrop as Gwen played with Danny in his bed ("All right, one more jump off the bed but then you have to get into it!").

The last year, right before the divorce, he began to enjoy the kid. It came upon him slowly. Danny was able to talk fluently and he never tired of asking Clarence questions. When Clarence talked about his day at the shop, Danny was all ears, breaking in now and then with a question. Buying the dog, Taku, was the icing on the cake. After that, Danny's eyes were full of worship every time he saw his dad. Clarence, feeling both proud and thrilled, began to spend more time with Danny, showing him how to box when the boy came in with his face cut and bruised after tussles with other kids.

His muscles were hurting from pulling on the drag line. He wished that he were dead. It was the first time in his life that he thought of death as a relief. He thrashed about in bed, his mouth flat and bitter from smoking too many cigarettes, his body craving release from the inner fire that was consuming him.

Suddenly he heard a commotion in the hall outside his room. He recognized Shirley Parker's voice. She was drunk and loud. Just yesterday she had been in the hospital recovering from the D.T.'s.

"Get your fucking hands off me!" she bellowed.

"She's getting tough," a man said with a laugh.

"Look at me, baby," said another voice. "Ain't I a sight for sore eyes? You haven't forgotten me?"

"Yeah," said another man. "I was with Johnny. Your husband was working and you wouldn't let me in the apartment because you wanted to be alone with Johnny."

Clarence rolled over. Shirley always got into trouble when she was drunk. Here she was about to get raped by those guys out there, then she'd start screaming and protesting and before the night was over the sheriff would be locking them up.

The knock on Clarence's door hit him like a punch in the stomach. He stormed over to the door and opened it wide.

"Hi ya, honey!" Shirley said. As usual, her lips were pulled back in a wide grin. She smiled when she was happy, when she was bored, when she was angry, when she was scared.

"What do you want, Shirley? God damn it, leave me alone!"

"These lugs are after me!" Shirley said, flapping her hand in the direction of the four burly men who stood behind her in the corridor.

"Who's the runt?" the man nearest Shirley asked. "Not your hubby?" He roared with a great burst of laughter.

Clarence eyed them with contempt. Four fishermen, probably docked for the night in the harbor, drunk and on the make for anything wearing a skirt, ready to fight any man that stepped in their way.

"Let me come in," Shirley said. "These guys irk me."

Clarence said bitterly, "Beat it, Shirley!"

"Oh, come now, you ain't yellow!" Shirley was offended.

"Yeah," a man countered," you ain't chicken-shit, hubby-dubby?"

Suddenly Clarence grew insane with fury. He found himself striking out coolly and accurately, as if this was just what he needed. His fists made fast, straight jabs against the blur of faces. In the scuffle, a fist crashed against his shoulder, another against his chest. His body hit the door frame and he struck back, not even thinking of the fresh stitches under the bandages on his head. He hit again and again, lashing wildly at the men.

When a blow struck the side of his face, Clarence realized that he was no match for the four men. With one of his lightning quick moves, he ducked under their arms and raced off down the hallway and around the corner. He took the stairs down to the lobby two at a time and went into the bar. It was crowded and thick with smoke and noise. Clarence went outside to get a breath of fresh air.

The rain and sleet beat down on his bare head. He moved across the street in a daze, thinking he would go into the Johnson's Sweets and have a cup of coffee. A few people passed him as he walked along the street and stared at him with wonder.

"Hey, Clarence, you'd better get out of the rain," a man said. "That bandage on your head is getting soaked."

He didn't even see who was talking to him. He moved along slowly, his body trembling from the cold and the fight with the men.

Chuck Alder, clad in slickers and boots, stopped him right in front of Olson's grocery store.

"You'd better get under shelter," he said. "You'll get pneumonia in this weather."

Clarence walked past Chuck. They were so friendly all of a sudden. But he had to lose a kid before they showed any signs of concern. Danny is dead, lying there under the water, and they tell me I'll get pneumonia if I don't get under shelter.

As Clarence approached the sweet shop, a black and white bulldog came running towards him and attacked his hand. He jerked away instinctively. But the dog's teeth had sunk deep into his flesh and it held on with a ferocious grip. The surprise and terror and pain of the dog's action angered him. He aimed a solid blow at the dog's head with his free hand. The dog fell on its side with a yelp. Clarence was so beside himself with rage that he kicked the dog in the chest, kicking it repeatedly until the screaming dog lay quiet. Without even realizing what he was doing, Clarence pulled from his pocket a razor-sharp pocket knife that he kept honed on his strap in the shop and, holding the dog's head up by one ear, sliced through the dog's neck. He threw the bleeding mass out into the street and stared at it.

He heard footsteps come running up behind him. "Hey, Clarence," Chuck said, "you know it's against the law to kill a dog."

"Yeah," said Clarence, waving his bleeding hand in front of the sheriff, "and it's against the law for a dog to bite a man."

The occupants of the sweet shop came tumbling out into the street. A cluster of people stood around the headless dog. Clarence took off down the street.

He found himself going up the hill. He heard the familiar sound of the streams, swollen with the rain, tumbling down the hill. The wind whipped across the island, splashing the rain and sleet against the trees and houses and road.

In front of the hospital, he stopped. It was dark and lonely. He pushed open the door and walked across the dim lobby. He found the stairs leading to the second floor. It was warm inside and quiet. He headed along the corridor towards Gwen's room. The door was closed which was strange. She must be bad. He knocked lightly. There was no answer.

He clicked open the door and went over to the bed. By the dim light that came in the window, he could see that Gwen was sleeping soundly. Her face was white and pale and peaceful. Doc Little must have given her a sedative.

Clarence pulled up a chair and sat down, fumbling in his shirt pocket for a cigarette. He put one in his mouth and groped in his pockets for matches. He struck a match against the package but it was so wet that the matchhead dissolved in the contact. Then he noticed the back of his hand. It was covered with blood and already swelling. He could see the gashes left by the dog's teeth. He cursed.

After a while he rose and left the room. On his way down the stairs, Miss Sarber spied him as she crossed the corridor below.

"Why, Clarence . . . " she began, then stopped as she took in his wretched appearance. She didn't even ask him why he had come to the hospital, though she must have realized.

"Your hand's bleeding," she said matter-of-factly. "Come in here and let me bandage it."

32

A SEAL POPPED ITS HEAD OUT of the placid silver-gray water. Dave jammed the last shell into the chamber, slammed the lever shut and offered the gun to Roy. "Here, Roy, you take it. It's the last one." He didn't want Roy to see what a poor shot he was for he knew how Roy sneered at green horns.

"No, go ahead," said Roy with the confident tone of experience. "I've shot so many of them it doesn't matter to me."

Dave watched the seal weave its head from side to side, its stiff black whiskers protruding just above the surface of the water. It was so close to shore that he could hear it snorting. Dave aimed. The seal's snout flickered in the sights. Dave's moist finger squeezed on the trigger and fired. The plop missed the seal by a yard.

"High," Roy said with his critical eye. "You're still shooting high."

"But I aimed the damned thing low. It shoots high," said Dave. It made him mad that he always came up with excuses when he was around Roy.

Roy laughed tolerantly. He took the rifle and peered through the sights with a trained eye. "I'll take it up the range one of these days," he said, "and see what I can do with it."

Roy handed back the gun. "What do you say we start back?" he said, glancing off across the motionless channel. "Southbound steamer should be rounding in about now," he remarked.

"Chris is going out on it," Dave said. He hated to leave just yet, only there wasn't any reason to remain any longer. Usually being on the shore brought him solace. When Dave felt that he would explode if he had to look into another patient's mouth, he would send the patients home, have a stiff drink, grab his 270 Savage, walk down to the beach and shoot a couple of boxes of shells at ravens, gulls and sometimes a seal if one happened to be close to shore. Sometimes it worked to relieve his tension and sometimes it didn't. Today he was deriving no pleasure from the shooting or the beach.

"Where's Chris going?" Roy asked.

"Ketchikan."

Roy snorted. "I thought he'd be going down to San Francisco. That man sure has a case on that schoolteacher, hasn't he?" His voice oozed with contempt. "Hell, there's lots of girls in this town who'd probably make him a better wife. Why, if a girl ever did that to me—left me flat—I'd forget her fast."

Dave kept his head down, watching to make sure he didn't step into any of the puddles of water in the path.

"You're quiet, Dave. What's the matter?"

"Just tired, I guess."

Roy tossed his head. "Victoria Blaissing? That's her last name, isn't it?" His tone was full of contempt.

Dave nodded reluctantly. "Chris and me are both in the same boat."

"Rot," Roy muttered. "Why, Dave, you can't be serious about that girl. You saw how she fell all over herself for the barber?"

The tide was coming in like a cat. The air hummed with the strange, sad noises the water made as it lapped against the sand: swa-a-ash, swa-a-ash. A raven flew overhead, its wings straining and whacking the air. Dave aimed the 270 Savage rifle at the raven and pulled the trigger. There was no sound; the bird continued flying in the direction of Matt's cabin.

"Got him!" Roy said with a laugh. Then he added, "You do need a wife, if anyone in this town does. You work hard, cooped up in that room all day, and you need more diversion at night than just a good night's sleep." Roy chuckled, enjoying himself in the role of advice-giver. "You're healthy and you're getting on in years."

425

"Forty-two," Dave said. There were times when he hated Roy Hart, pure and simple. In fact the only thing in Roy's favor was that he was married to Bea. Bea was an example of what Dave wanted in a wife, a woman whose beauty and charm would fill his nights with companionship and pleasure.

"Vic was a nice girl," Dave said in a mild voice. "My only mistake was that I stood aside while Clarence . . . "

"You did right. Sometimes it pays to stand aside. You see the girl's character. Why, hell," Roy's voice was offhanded and certain, "it was as plain as day that Clarence was pulling down Victoria's pants regularly."

Dave stopped, his lip quivering. "Listen, Roy, that is an unfounded accusation." Although he was furious, his words came out smoothly, as if he were inclined to agree with Roy.

"Now don't look so peeved," Roy said with good nature. "I'm just stating the facts."

Dave shook his head. Maybe Vic had allowed Clarence some liberties. She certainly hadn't been easy with Dave. He hadn't heard from her for some time—she had stopped writing about the same time Lyddy stopped writing to Chris—but her last letter seemed hopeful. She said that both she and Lyddy were missing Wrangell, talked about it all the time and thinking of returning. Herb Weaver had written them twice telling them he was dissatisfied with the current schoolteachers and asking them to come back for the second semester. The big obstacles were Lyddy's mother who had hysterics every time Lyddy mentioned the subject and Lyddy's own indecision. Vic was doing everything she could to persuade Lyddy to return.

"You know what I think of you, Dave," Roy said, puffing out his chest. "You're one of my best friends. I'll tell you something. You should marry a girl much younger than you. There's a few in town: Joyce Hall, Lizzie Cahill. I married Bea when she was 17. Right before the wolves could spoil her with attention. She was a knockout in those years."

Dave thought she was still a knockout.

"Anyway, I made a private study of her after we were married. I got to know her from every angle that I could find: emotion, temper, likes and dislikes, habits. I discovered the best times to tell her what I wanted her to do. I learned to be quiet and patient. I taught Bea everything that she knows today."

They climbed over a downed tree trunk that stretched across the trail.

"It fell early this morning," Roy said. "I heard it crash down from my bedroom. No reason for it really—the wind was blowing light."

For a moment Dave was stabbed with weariness. It seemed poignant, the death of this tree, that had been growing in the same place for perhaps a thousand mornings, and suddenly one morning, for no apparent reason, toppled over and died.

Ahead of them on the side of the hill, he could see smoke coming from Matt's chimney. It would be a relief to get to the cabin. Dave had run into Chris this afternoon as he was heading towards the beach. Chris was just returning from the ticket office and decided to tag along. When they arrived at the road below Matt's cabin, Chris said that while Dave was firing his rifle he'd go up and see the old boy. Matt was taking it pretty hard. He couldn't get the notion out of this head that he was to blame for the three boys drowning.

Looking back at the channel, Dave could see the steamer swinging around Elephant's Nose. "There's the *North Star*," he said.

Roy was so absorbed in his story he didn't even look up. "I made Bea see things my way from the start. I practically taught her how to cook. I took her to places where I wanted to go and not where she suggested. It got so I'd ask her where she'd like to go and she'd say she wanted to go anywhere that I wanted to." Roy chuckled with delight at the outcome of his experiment.

He could have been talking about breaking in a colt, Dave thought, with revulsion. Roy always talked about his married life with Bea as if it were a business and he was just passing along the secrets of his success.

"Yes, sir, marry them young, train them yourself. Don't be mushy with them. Learn when to put the pressure on and when not to. Make as if you take the little girl for granted and then when she starts getting sulky, take her out and show her a good time."

Roy stopped and laced his shoestring. "Naturally," Roy said as he straightened up, "there are lots of different opinions about what makes a marriage work. I'm just telling you what worked for me. And you've got to admit Bea and I are a lot happier than most couples."

Dave noticed an underlying air of defensiveness in Roy's speech. Somehow he felt that Roy wasn't talking about the present. He was describing a golden era that was gone. He was boasting about the early stages of his marriage, the tender and passionate years before the edge of irritation and staleness set in. Dave had watched this deterioration in his parents' marriage and then saw it transform into a vague appreciation for each other when they realized that they had only themselves for comfort and companionship. Yes, in the early years Bea was young and healthy and green and probably worshipped Roy. But since Tom's death, three years ago, Dave knew there was something wrong with her. She seemed to be eroding, something was crumbling inside of her. The strange thing was that no one, especially not Roy, seemed to notice it. There was a twinge of hunger in Roy's voice as he spoke, as if he hadn't been satisfied lately with the way Bea was behaving.

Dave hadn't seen Bea out for a long time. She still had a temporary filling in her mouth that he had put in during the summer. It must have worn off by now but Bea hadn't come in to have it replaced. She didn't go to the dances anymore either. And Roy was doing all the shopping lately. Once Roy came up for an appointment with his arms loaded with groceries. He explained why, his face coloring a little, "The missus doesn't see why I can't do the shopping when I'm already out. She must be getting lazy—doesn't care too much for the long walk around the road."

"It's like raising a child," Roy said. "You have to set firm guidelines at first. Then when they know you're the boss, you can let them have a little bit of freedom. Bea didn't understand that. She thought I was being too harsh on Tom. She went behind my back and tried to soften him up, told him I'd eventually give him permission to go off on his own. She was wrong. The boy was too young, too green, too stubborn to be out on his own."

With a sense of relief, Dave stepped onto the main road. He looked up the side of the hill to Matt's cabin tucked between the trees. Today the cabin looked tiny and isolated from the rest of the world, like an emblem of Matt Fleming's guilt.

"Chris is probably at a loss for words by now with Matt," Dave said. "Want to come up?"

Roy glanced at his wristwatch. "I'd like to but Bea's just about got supper on the table." Roy chuckled. "When I'm not in town we have supper early so we can have a snack about ten."

Dave watched Roy move off along the dirt road. Roy was getting chubby. It made Dave feel a little better although he knew that Roy had only started gaining weight after Bea made him promise to give up guiding tourists through the forests of the Mainland looking for wild mountain sheep and grizzlies. Now when he wasn't fishing or hunting, Roy spent his time sitting around at Johnny Bugg's playing cards. He played cards the same way he kept up his gill-netting boat, neat and perfect.

From the cabin a blast of music suddenly spilled into the air. Chris must have convinced Matt to play a record on his phonograph. The music was strange and loud, filled with horns and kettle drums and a cymbal. Though Dave didn't care for longhaired music, he knew how much it meant to Matt.

The cabin door opened and Chris emerged. He hurried down the hill, along the footpath.

"Hi, Dave. I was watching for you out of the window. Dave, that man's in bad shape. Worst I've ever seen him. It's serious."

"Are his lungs giving him trouble?"

Chris nodded. "His lungs and the kids. I'm trying to get him to listen to his records. You know what music does to him."

"What the hell is that?"

"Hell if I know. I put on the first record I grabbed without looking at the title."

"Shall I come up? After a session with Roy I feel like I have the gift for gab."

Out in the channel the steamer's whistle brayed: one long blast, one short. Down the road at Roy's house, Winchester joined in with a long howl.

"There's my ship," Chris said. "Listen, I think it would be better if you didn't come up. I've got him mellowed a little and if he saw you he'd only start in again."

"Well," Dave said, "I'd like to have a drink with you before you board the steamer."

"I'll see you later at the hotel bar. I'm all packed. All I have to do is pick up my suitcase."

"The ship will be tied up a couple of hours at least. See you before she sails."

He watched his friend enter the cabin and close the door. Chris surprised Dave at times. He was really softhearted. He acted like he didn't gave a damn about anything, yet here he was, trying to cheer up the old bachelor who used to work for him as the night watchman at the cannery during the fishing season.

Dave rounded the power plant. The oil truck sloshed by and stopped down the road at the Hunt's to fill up their oil tank perched outside the house on a wooden horse stand. The tide was still coming in. All along the lip of the harbor, the sand was spotted with the usual debris: tin cans, broken chunks of boats, lichen-covered logs and old skiffs. To his right were the better homes, frame houses set back among lawns and shrubs and trees. To the left, on the harbor side, were shacks and cabins, standing on pilings, all crowded together.

Along the way, Dave greeted the people he met. He probably knew the thousand inhabitants of Wrangell as well as anyone in town, since he was the only dentist. Just the other day, Princess, the Negro woman who ran the whore house, was slouched in the dentist chair. Dave was having a difficult time fitting a tiny gold filling into one of her teeth. At one point, the filling slithered out of his fingers and fell on her large breast. Dave grabbed for it before it could fall to the floor. She raised her head with a smile.

"Why, Mista Collier," she said, and her broad shoulders shook with mirth, "you ain't getting fresh with me?"

"I was grabbing for the filling," he said.

"You got it before it touched the floor. You's quick as a cat," she said.

"Now don't get any funny ideas with me," Dave said. "What I should do is

429

make that hole larger in your tooth so that I can work properly."

"Oh, go on, Mista Collier!" Her hearty laugh filled the little office.

Yes, Dave knew the whole town pretty well. At one time or another, they all came to his office and sat in his chair while he peered into their gaping mouths.

That was how he started dating Vic again, after she stopped seeing Clarence. One of her teeth was causing a lot of pain and she had come in for an appointment. Dave asked her to have lunch with him the following day. After that they used to meet for lunch every day. They'd go to Mom's or Vic would fix lunch for them at the cottage. After Vic left, it took him weeks to get used to eating alone again.

Dave trudged on. He could see the channel through a break in the houses. It was silver-gray, long and round and flat, with that lifeless feeling common before or after a storm. Dave could sniff a storm brewing, getting ready to show that winter was still with Alaska.

Dave glanced sideways at Chris' float house nestled on its bed of logs. Babs Bucci was standing on the front porch which was littered with boxes and furniture. "Come down for a cup of coffee, Dave."

He stood on the road, unbelieving. "What's going on?" he asked.

"We're moving in. Chris sold us the place back," she said. Her voice lilted with happiness.

"No thanks. Some other time when you're all straightened up."

Dave was stunned by the news. He never thought Chris would sell the float house. Maybe rent it, but never sell it. Dave remembered all the good times they had there, good parties and good talks. He remembered hanging out there with Tom Hart and Chris. One of them was always around. They used it for storing their guns and tackle, outboard motors and camping equipment. There was always a skiff or two tied to the railing of the porch. Whenever he came by he would find Tom tinkering with a stubborn Johnson outboard on the porch or Chris packing for a fishing trip. The summer before Tom died, they practically lived in it. Despite the difference in their ages, Tom and Chris were best friends. Chris really liked Tom, his restlessness, his excess energy, the way he blurted out his words.

Tom never got along too well with his father. In fact, Dave imagined that was part of the reason Tom and Chris got along so well. They both had dominating fathers and they both were both stubborn and had a hard time taking orders. Tom bought himself a double-ender troller with money that he made longshoring and working at the cannery. He was planning to start fishing on his own the next summer but Roy insisted that his son should be helping him. When Tom died, Chris was heartbroken. For a long time all he did was talk about Tom. It irritated Dave. There was no fun going out in the woods any-more, Chris once remarked. And Dave had been hurt. He felt insignificant because there was nothing he could do to ease the suffering in Chris. Dave just couldn't measure up to Tom. Dave worked in a warm, clean office. Tom was a pure Alaskan, a fisherman, a hunter. He was wild and prodigious for his age and he was only a kid when he died.

Vivian's father, John, a shrunken old man, was waiting on Main Street in front of Dave's apartment house. The native's short hair was black as tar; it stood out against his parched gray face like a wig.

"Hello, John." As Dave expected, he was drunk, almost in a stupor. The whiskey fumes on his breath were so foul that Dave took a step backwards.

"Dave, Vi's bleeding pretty bad. She bleed all last night."

"Why in heavens' name didn't you let me know this morning?" Dave said, trembling with rage.

"I didn't think it bad. Everybody bleed when they get teeth pulled out."

"I'll be right out."

Dave took the flight of stairs three at a time, located his satchel in his bed-room and headed down the hall toward the door. He caught a brief glimpse of his father, sitting in the living room reading a paper. His mother was probably in the kitchen, preparing dinner. They seemed resigned to spending their remaining years in Wrangell. Yet they both hated winters in Alaska and com-plained about the weather constantly. He wished that they would go south where it was warm and dry and they could end their days in comfort. Their bitterness made him uneasy. They had lived in Wrangell for fifty years and now they weren't sure if they had done the right thing with their lives.

In the office he washed his hands, stuffed cotton and medicine in the satchel and hastened down the stairs. Outside, he swung ahead of the native and crossed the street. Puffing from the sudden exertion, the native caught up with the dentist and tried desperately to keep in step with Dave's long strides.

"Has Vivian been rinsing her mouth in salt water?" Dave asked.

"Yep. Regular all the time. Just like you said."

"Have you been helping her?"

"Jeannette most time," he said, referring to his seven-year-old grand-daughter.

Dave and the native went up the hill on the road that ran diagonally across it. They came to a row of flimsy wooden shacks and their feet rumbled over the first boardwalk that led to a rickety unpainted porch. Inside, the shack was musty and sloppy. Unwashed dishes stood on the wooden sink, the table was loaded with lunch things. There was a whiskey bottle on the floor and the faded blue linoleum was smeared with dirt. Usually it was one of the cleanest native houses in Wrangell. But with Vivian in bed, it was a mess.

Dave went into the bedroom which contained only an old iron cot that sagged in the middle under the girl's weight and a torn leather chair. The hole in the chair was usually concealed beneath a blanket but it had slipped off and no one had bothered to put it back on. The walls were covered with mustard-colored wallpaper and a naked light bulb hung by a cord from the ceiling. On the floor next to the bed was a tin can full of blood. Vivian's three children, stood by the bed, their eyes dark with fear. Jeannette, the oldest, was holding her four-year-old brother on her hip.

Vivian looked so weak and frail that it shocked Dave. She could barely nod her head. Dave pushed open the window, bent over the girl and examined her gums.

"Get me a glass of warm water," he said to the old man.

In a moment he mixed a solution, which he squirted into her mouth and let her rinse out. He sent her father out for ice. He asked Jeannette to clean the front room. From his satchel, he produced tightly rolled stems of cotton. He held them above the can, poured an anesthetic over them and stuck them into the girl's mouth.

"Now bite down," Dave said.

Vivian clamped her jaw shut. Her dark eyes were getting bright and eventually she closed them.

A half hour went by, during which Dave changed the rolls and smoked two cigarettes in silence. The old man returned, carrying a chunk of ice wrapped in an old newspaper, an ice pick and a bag.

"Break the ice into small pieces and put it in the bag," Dave said.

He extracted the bloody cotton rolls and swabbed the girl's gums with a solution of gentian violet. He couldn't remember whether he had told Vivian to apply cold compresses to her face. Evidently not, for there was none of the stuff in the house.

The old man stood dumbly in the bedroom doorway. "How is she?" he asked.

"Bring the bag here," Dave roared, taking out his irritation on him.

He placed the ice pack over her cheek. "Now I don't want you to worry. Just rest," he told her. "Take a couple of aspirin every few hours. When I have your impressions, I'll make you a bridge that will be something special. It will look just as good as your own teeth." He knew he was lying because he wasn't good at making bridges but he wanted to say something encouraging.

Outside, he felt lousy. He went down the hill to Johnny Bugg's bar and had a drink. The place was almost deserted. Most everyone was probably down at the dock where the steamer was moored. A few fishermen were playing cards in the other room. Two couples from the ship were sipping drinks at the bar. The tourists never flocked into Johnny Bugg's like they did into the hotel bar. It looked too old-fashioned and shabby from the outside. Dave walked around the bar to the telephone and turned the crank.

"Mix me another drink, Johnny," he called out to the bartender as he waited for the operator to connect him with Chris.

"Guess he's not home," Cliff said after trying Chris' line. "You want me to ring again?"

"No. He must still be out at Matt's," Dave said.

"That man shouldn't feel so bad," Cliff said. "Hell, it wasn't his fault. Someone ought to wring Fred Racht's neck for giving those kids that rotten skiff of his."

Dave could think of nothing else to say and hung up abruptly. He finished his drink in two gulps, then strode outside. He was beginning to think it was a mistake to send his patients home. Maybe he should have stuck it out. He was feeling worse than he did before he left the office.

He went past his apartment and headed down Main Street toward the docks. Passengers and town people were strolling back and forth along the Clinton dock. The hotel bar was packed. Dave crossed over to the Canadian dock where there was comparative peace. He stood on the edge of the dock. The sun was concealed behind the clouds and the sky was soaked with a creamy hue. There seemed to be a lassitude in the air which covered everything, the mountains and the islands, the air and water.

He could hear the steamer's winch cranking away over at the Clinton dock. A seiner moved by, the light from the mast leaving a quicksilver wake in the dark waters of the channel. As Dave stood there, the creamy color in the sky dissolved into night. A wind tugged at his clothes. It was stirring down from the north, brushing against the channel, bringing with it a few rain drops which spattered against his forehead.

He stood there at the edge of Wrangell, the place of his birth and the only place he had ever lived except for the years he spent in Los Angeles going to college. He thought of Roy's allegations about Vic and Clarence. The suspicion, which had been like a worm in the back of his mind, began to gnaw at his heart.

The rain was coming down heavier, in fat drops. He remembered that he was supposed to meet Chris. He wheeled around and headed towards the hotel bar.

33

THE HOTEL BAR WAS CROWDED WITH TOURISTS. There was a man over by the window telling a joke about a Klootch from Klawock but the noise in the room muffled most of his words. Shirley Parker was out on the dance floor dancing with stranger after stranger while her husband was out on the dock working, supervising the longshoremen.

Chris looked about him and said to Dave, "It's taking that ship a hell of a long time to get started. She should have sounded her thirty minute whistle long before now."

"Buster doesn't mind," Dave said, gesturing at the hotel owner who was mixing a tray of drinks behind the bar. "He appreciates the business."

From somewhere in back of him, Chris heard Doc Sebannon's voice. "They're loading a big shipment of frozen halibut. The steamer's due to sail about one o'clock."

"It's just after midnight," Dave said to Chris.

Chris wheeled around on his stool and stared at Doc Sebannon who wore a gray sweat shirt, covered with stains, which was tight across his bulging belly. "You wanna drink, Doc?" Chris asked with sarcasm.

"I got nice pickled herring I just fixed," Doc replied.

"Pickled herring, huh?"

"I fixed myself."

Chris hated herring. He always thought of them as parasites, since they hung around the cannery's cull chute in a broiling mass during fishing season, stuffing themselves on the bloody intestines of the gutted salmon flowing into the bay.

"Max," Chris called to the swamped bartender. "Give Doc a glass of water." Chris stared with open disgust at Doc. "I want three jars of the stuff."

"For water?" Doc asked incredulous.

Dave laughed, then blushed self-consciously. "I never know what the hell you'll be doing next, Chris. Haven't you any decency?"

"Show you my heart is in the right place, I'll buy him a genuine brown bomber." Chris called out to the bartender, "Max, one brown bomber for Doc Sebannon."

"Thank you," Doc said, wetting his lips in anticipation of the rum and coke.

"For three bottles of your choicest pickled herring," Chris said, licking his lips in pretended anticipation.

"You bet," Doc said. For some reason, Chris got a cynical pleasure out of watching Doc operate. Doc was the best moocher of Wrangell. Whenever anyone (usually a lonely bachelor or deserted squaw) was too far gone in sickness to be tended by anyone else, Doc stayed by the patient's side until the very end. Then he would take as payment any of the belongings of the deceased that might have any value. The sweat shirt he wore had belonged to old man Halvord who died a lonely, hungry death from stomach cancer.

"Did you hear about Clarence?" Max asked when he brought over the drink.

"Heard he killed a dog last night," Chris said.

"Yeah, and cut off its head." Max shook his head and went back to work.

"What's the matter?" Dave asked Giff who was sitting beside him in the bar.

"Did you ever see so many tourists?" Giff muttered with disgust.

"Christmas holidays," Dave said with a chuckle. "Hell, you can't expect to shoot dice in here every night."

Chris noticed Babs and Mitch Bucci dancing on the packed dance floor. They were both so relieved and jubilant about Matt rescuing Harry that they had come to the hotel bar to celebrate but they seemed to be spending most of their time arguing with each other.

"Dave," Chris said, "do me a favor, will you?"

"Certainly, Chris, you lucky bastard. If I wasn't so busy I'd go with you to Ketchikan."

"Dave, go see Matt in a day or two. He's sick. I don't like the way he's taking it."

"Sure, Chris. Just like the old codger to be so hurt."

"Hurt? Hell, he's dying."

Doc Sebannon nudged Chris in the ribs, his drink finished, hoping to get him to buy him another. "When are your father and mother coming up?"

"Listen, Doc, move off, will you?" In the crowded bar, the sour, fishy smell emanating from Doc's clothes was revolting.

Giff leaned across the bar to get Chris' attention. "Hey, did you know Theodore had a pilot's license?" he asked.

"Your mother and Pat should be coming up soon," Doc Sebannon observed from behind Chris.

Chris wheeled around, angry. "Beat it Doc. Mooch somewhere else."

"You were in school the year Theodore bet that I'd catch more salmon than anyone else in Southeastern. I worked my ass off that season. And Theodore won the bet," Giff said, in a drunken trance. "Couldn't let Theodore down."

A long shuddering blast came from the steamer's whistle at the dock.

"Hey, there she goes," yipped a tourist in the other room.

Chris got down from his stool, feeling suddenly excited and happy.

"Hey," Giff complained, "I didn't get a chance to tell you about how Theodore saved my life. If he hadn't fired that warning shot, the grizzly would have ripped my head off." For a moment, there were tears in Giff's eyes. Chris noticed this with a spasm of remorse.

"See you later, Giff," he said.

Chris and Dave moved out on the dock. The longshoremen were working in the rain, moving the crates of frozen fish from the cold storage plant to the ship tied at the other end. Chris caught a glimpse of Fanny Sundberg, clad in a green coat and galoshes, heading towards the steamer with her parents.

"Well, I'll be," Chris said. "Fanny's going aboard too."

"She's going back to Alan. Another reunion." Dave was amused. "She told me all about it in the office the other morning."

Outside they stood alongside the warehouse, under the awning and out of the rain. The steamer looked massive, taking up most of the dock. The last trickle of passengers were climbing up the gangway. The longshoremen were wheeling out the railway express shipment which Red and Charlie were loading upon the flats. The winch cranked and rattled away, hoisting the trunks and suitcases over the side and into the hole. Fanny stood at the rail, staring down at her folks on the dock. The lights from the steamer and on the dock cut up the rain into confetti.

Suddenly, as always when he left on the steamer, Chris wanted to hurry up and get started on the adventure. He wanted to be roaming through the luxurious interior of the ship on thick rich carpets, lost in a maze of staterooms and passageways, mixing with friendly new people, meeting the steward, getting to know the night chef at first hand, bumping into a new girl, perhaps some lovely, soft-fleshed girl from Boston or a drawling lush girl from Texas.

Dave edged closer to Chris. The people who had come down to watch the steamer were squeezing in out of the rain and it was getting crowded.

"It'll be good to see Mac again," Chris said. "That beefy Scot is a shot in the arm."

"Why didn't he come to Wrangell?"

"You know how Mac is when he gets loose from his wife." Chris chuckled. "Mac was probably heading for Wrangell but got sidetracked by some pressing business—in the form of a dame."

The rain lashed down, beating a vicious staccato on the warehouse roof. The rain blended with the late hour and the channel and the moored steamer. It was a rather mournful rain.

powering.

"Good morning, darling," she said, matter of factly, closing the door behind her. "How about taking me to breakfast?"

"Sure. Be with you in a sec," Chris said, finding it difficult to enunciate his words. She must have poured a bottle of some kind of heavenly-smelling perfume over her. Chris found it difficult to concentrate on what he was doing. He finished shaving quickly, sloshed some after-shave lotion on his face and a little powder to remove the bright, morning glare. He looked pretty good, he decided. He hadn't had a haircut for quite some time and he thought his sideburns looked heavy and romantic. Putting on his sports jacket, he said,

"Sleep good last night? I slept wonderful. Like a lamb!"

Fanny didn't respond but that was like her. She sat on the rumpled lower berth, studying her polished nails. Her diamond wedding and engagement rings sparkled as they caught the morning light coming through the porthole. Her body was stiff, her expression enigmatic.

"Well," Chris said, "let's go."

Fanny sighed. "Chris, have you got a drink?"

"Sure," Chris said. He opened the cabinet door above the wash basin and removed the pint bottle he had opened last night. As he poured a drink for Fanny, he analyzed the situation. This was rich. Fanny wanting a drink! And so early in the morning too. Chris handed her the drink, feeling ridiculously lucky for Fanny drank only on rare occasions. Something must be bothering her.

"This is not like you," he said.

Fanny sipped at the whiskey and water. "I'm going back to Alan. I need this when I think about how hopeless it is."

"You're starting early. Seattle's a long way from here."

"I've got to start fortifying myself now." She swallowed her drink in small measured sips as if she were taking medicine. She wasn't a real drinker, nor, for that matter, did she seem to enjoy its effects. One drink had the same effect on her as five—she was either elated or totally unaffected.

Fanny was strange. Chris could never tell what sort of mood she would be in when he made a date with her. Sometimes she was passionate, accepting his advances with recklessness; sometimes she was aloof and distant. She would just sit back on the sofa, listless and depressed, or play the piano or talk about Alan. Chris would get so angry he'd announce that he was going down to the bar to get drunk or play poker. Then she'd chastise him for being impatient and put on some music and ask him to dance and he'd stay, pleased that she didn't want him to go.

Chris stood above Fanny waiting for her to decide about breakfast. He hoped the whiskey would excite her. He never knew though. It might shut her up like a clam and she wouldn't want to do anything, not even eat. But after one drink, she suggested going down to the dining room. After they had eaten, they went out on the deck and stood watching the islands, swathed in fog, drifting by on either side. Chris lit a cigarette and inhaled deeply. The air was moist and refreshing, filled with the odor of sea.

"Wonderful morning," Chris said. Mist clung above the water along the shore, long delicate streaks of vapor dissolving as the sun rose higher. Beyond the low, dark, forest-sheathed hills, mountains jutted up, tipped with bright snow, catching the flash of the sun. Above the sun, painted clouds the color of a ripe peach slowly split in half. The snow-capped peaks in the distance were tinged with the soft orange color.

Chris and Fanny stood a long time in silence. A Negro mess attendant smoked a cigar, sitting on the rail. The wake of the steamer produced a broad white trail, with scores of sea gulls sailing above it.

Chris said, "Some day I'm going to take this trip just to see the view. We take it too much for granted. The only time I realize I'm traveling through some of the best scenery in the world is when I open a porthole to toss out an empty bottle of whiskey."

Fanny didn't stir. She had scarcely spoken to him. Chris wasn't worried. They still had about two more hours on board and the steamer would dock in Ketchikan for three or four hours. He'd get her up to his room in the hotel.

"Shall we have a drink?"

"Might as well."

The went into the bar which was filled with people playing cards, reading magazines and sipping drinks. The noise level was low. It was still early morning and people were waking up, snapping out of the drug of the night's sleep. The bar was filled with leather upholstered chairs and bright-colored round tables. As they threaded their way through the narrow aisles towards a vacant table near the back, Chris noticed how men eyed Fanny who looked attractive and voluptuous in her bright suit. It made him feel good. As they approached the vacant table, Chris spied the sad-looking man and his companion sitting just beyond them. They were nursing cokes and their faces were swollen and heavy as if they hadn't had a good night's sleep.

"Hello there!" Bruce called out.

"Where you going?" the other man asked. "Come on over here."

Chris and Fanny went over to their table.

"How are you folks? Say, excuse me," the man said, getting up and gazing with intent interest at Fanny. "I don't think I've had the pleasure. This is Bruce." he said, indicating the sad-looking man, "and I'm Norman Block."

Chris finished the introductions and they sat down at the table. Bruce wore a clean, light-gray serge suit. He looked like he lived in a world of tragedy. He poked his straw around in his drink, his whole expression one of pathos.

"Sleep well?" Norman asked cheerfully. "Not me! I got sick. Awfully sick. That damn storm we hit last night made me feel awful . . . "

"Oh, hell," Chris scoffed. "The steamer only rolled a little."

"And to top that off," Norman went on, glancing at Bruce, "this seagoing salt here had the gall to talk with the nurse aboard this tub about Russia! In our stateroom! Russia! All they talked about was Russia this, Russia that. And in my condition! It was bad enough that they were in the stateroom, I didn't mind that so much while I was in my berth, but they just went on and on about Russia. And then he wanted me to leave the stateroom! He had called the nurse in the first place only because I was so sick. But then when the nurse was in the room they began to talk about Russia and plumb forgot about me. He offered her a drink and they talked and got chummy and then he wanted me," Norman stared ruefully at Bruce, "he wanted me to leave the room."

"Oh, go on," Bruce said. "I was only thinking of your own good. All I said was take a walk around the deck, do you good."

"In my condition? I was seasick. They had no mercy. Then to top it off, they made me move up to the top berth because there was no room for both of them to sit down except on the lower berth. Damn, do you think he even helped me get up there?"

Chris and Fanny were laughing.

Bruce smiled with self-satisfaction. "She was an unusual woman," he said, and then his face grew sad again.

Norman looked at Fanny. "How'd you like a drink in our stateroom?"

Chris got up and said, "Sure, let's go."

They strolled down the starboard passageway, past door after door of staterooms. In the carpeted, compact enclosure, the sound of the engines and the movement of the steamer were barely discernible. Once inside the room, Norman mixed them drinks. Bruce sat down with a heavy sigh.

Chris stared at Bruce. "What are you so sad about?"

Bruce fumbled in his pockets for a cigarette.

"I don't want to talk about it," he said, tears springing into his eyes.

"Sorry," Chris said with an apologetic smile.

"Don't mind him," Norman said, handing Chris a drink. Then winking at Chris, he said very soberly, very softly, "Bruce just lost his wife. About a month ago."

"Oh, how dreadful!" Fanny said, "I'm awfully sorry."

Somehow after catching Norman's wink, Chris knew that all was not as it seemed to be. There was a general uneasy silence in the room.

Norman laughed. "Now listen, folks, we don't aim to spoil this little gathering with sad news. Bruce and I took this trip to forget about it. We've traveled all through Alaska, going from town to town, having a lot of fun." He gave a searching glance to his friend. "But it hasn't helped much."

"Let's forget about it," Bruce said.

"If you don't mind," Fanny asked. "How did it happen?"

Bruce stared at Fanny, his eyes slipping down from her face and roaming for a moment over her bulging breasts.

Norman said, "A car wreck."

"Oh, how dreadful!"

She was with Bruce's partner," Norman added.

"My partner!" Bruce said with bitterness. "The bastard!"

There was a pause. Chris visualized an overturned car with perhaps one of the back wheels still spinning and stretched out on the road beside it, mangled and bloody, the bodies of a man and a woman.

Chris gulped his drink and said quickly, "Well, we'll see you two later. You're coming into Ketchikan, aren't you?"

"Sure," Norman said.

Bruce looked up at Fanny. "Do you have to go? I don't remember when I have enjoyed myself more." His eyes roamed over her breasts again. "You're very nice. I like you."

"So do I," Chris said with a laugh, taking Fanny by the arm. Turning to her he suggested, "Shall we go? We'll be in Ketchikan shortly and there's packing to be done." They agreed to meet Bruce and Norman later at the Stedman hotel for a drink in the bar.

Fanny accompanied Chris to his stateroom. Chris unlocked the door and waited for her to go in before him. He was fairly certain she was in the right mood although she appeared more detached than ever. He hoped she hadn't fallen for Bruce's bereaved act.

"Care for a drink?" he asked, thinking that drinking had played a prominent part in his actions over the past few days.

"Oh, all right," Fanny said.

Chris poured whiskey in two water glasses. Fanny sat down. There was silence for a moment. Then she asked, "Did you hear about how Alan's doing?"

Chris handed Fanny the drink and sat down beside her. He didn't feel like talking about her husband.

"Listen, let's forget about Alan. After all, we're having a nice trip and what's the use of spoiling it talking about Alan."

Fanny's face flushed with irritation though not a muscle in her body stirred. "Have you heard about how he's doing?" she repeated.

"No," Chris replied.

"He has a route in Washington selling sporting goods for one of the better outfits down there."

"Is he doing well?"

Fanny thought awhile. "Yes, only he's got himself into some trouble."

"Well," Chris laughed, "don't look so worried about it. I thought you and him were through."

"We'll never be through. We always fight and can't seem to get along but we're never through."

"If that's the way it is, don't go back."

"As simple as that!" she said with a sneer. "But I couldn't expect you to understand. It's . . . " she paused, searching for the words, "it's like there's something that's always pulling us back to each other again, even when we quarrel and run away from one another for months on end."

Chris fretted with exasperation. "Listen, Fanny . . . "

"I don't know what it is," she mumbled to herself. "I have no real reason to go down there. But I want to see Alan so much. I really love him and yet I know after a few months I'll be wanting to get away from him again. It's awful."

There was silence. Chris rose and added some water to his whiskey.

"Listen, let's forget about it." He slipped his hand in hers, but she drew it away.

"I'm never sure of myself," Fanny said. "I can never tell at the end of the day if it's been a good day or a bad one. I'm so confused. I can't figure out at any moment if I'm happy. A lot of people know that, even though they may not have much else. But not me. I never seem to know. And that is one thing that I want so much—to know whether I'm happy or not." She paused for a moment studying the chip in her nail. "Like now. I'm going to live in the States. I'm returning to Alan. Mom and Dad convinced me that it was the right thing to do. They thought we should be together for the holidays. But I'm just doing it because they seem so sure it's the right thing to do. I have no desire one way or the other."

"It seems to me," Chris said, "that if you don't know what you want, then . . . "

She interrupted as if Chris wasn't speaking. "I detest Wrangell, yet I detest everything else. I detest the States. Only I can't overlook the fact that when I'm away from Wrangell, I miss it."

445

Chris tried to side with her and at the same time calm her. "Why don't you relax? If you're constantly trying to understand yourself, you never will. Here," he said, putting his arms round her, "let me kiss you . . . "

She stiffened. "Oh Chris, for heaven's sake, cut it out." She frowned and sipped her drink. "Why don't you grow up?"

Chris got up, nettled by her reaction. "Listen, you're always talking. You never listen. Why don't you shut up for a minute? Why don't you just let things happen instead of always trying to analyze everything? I should think living in Wrangell all these years would at least have taught you that." He was suddenly tired. "Why don't you leave? Yeah! Get out! Go out on deck and find someone who is old enough to appreciate you." He felt mean and bitter.

"All right, Chris." Fanny said with no expression on her face or in her voice. She placed her drink on the floor, buttoned her jacket and left the room.

34

LYDDY STOOD BY THE PORTHOLE in the stateroom, peering across the narrow channel at the islands slipping by the steamer. She stood still, caught in a web of sentiment, both wistful and happy. She was scared too. Scared of returning to Wrangell. Scared of seeing Chris. Scared of what he might have been doing with himself in the past months. She should have written him but she hadn't even wired him that they were coming up.

Behind her, Vic was taking an after-dinner nap in the lower berth. The trip so far had been dull. There were no passengers from Wrangell, which seemed strange. She remembered all the times she and Chris had walked down to the docks to watch the steamer arrive. It seemed there was always someone returning home and a group of friends and relatives gathered to greet them.

The steamer shuddered as it labored up the channel. Hour after hour went by as it moved forward, pushing the water in small waves from its hull, trailing a white wake which stretched behind into the distance. The islands drifted by on either side, all kinds of islands from large to small and of every shape. Lyddy saw an island that looked like a birthday cake and a group of small islands resembling private schooners wrapped in a mist and lying at anchor.

Lyddy hadn't realized how much she missed Alaska, the constant presence of sky and water and islands, the open space. She remembered walking at night on the dirt roads of Wrangell under the stars. She remembered the presence of the channel, the way the fishing boats moved across its surface and the mystery that lay in the utter quiet. It had taken six months in the States before she realized how happy she had been in Wrangell and accepted Mr. Weaver's offer to come back and teach during the spring term.

The evening star flashed out, dazzling in the pale blue of the night sky, which was slowly darkening. The islands and the mountains in the distance were disappearing into the gloom of night. Outside the stateroom an elderly couple strolled past along the deck. Most of the other passengers were in the lounge where the nightly bingo game was going on.

Lyddy heard a groan behind her and knew Vic was awakening from her after-dinner nap. She did not move but stood by the porthole and watched the Alaskan sky.

"Hot in here," Vic said. "They must have the heat turned on full blast." As usual, Vic was having a hard time making the transition from sleep to waking. She twisted restlessly in the berth.

"What's so fascinating out there?" she asked.

"Nothing really," said Lyddy.

"Well, come on," Vic sighed. "Lie down. You've been standing there for an hour."

"I've been standing here trying to figure it out," Lyddy said. "I'm glad to be going back." She turned around and faced her friend. "Don't you feel the difference already?"

"Not yet." Vic stood up to unbutton her dress and wiggled out of it. "Man, that feels better." She switched on the light wedged in the upper right hand corner of the berth and lay back, clad in her slip.

Lyddy, sitting down at the front of the berth, was conscious of the steamer's shudder as it turned left at one of the many bends in the channel.

"Gosh, I'm nervous as a jay bird," Lyddy explained. "I'm so darn happy and excited."

"Yeah, it's fine," Vic said. Although she didn't show it, Lyddy knew she was excited too. "It will be great to see all the people in the town again: Bea, Roy, Mr. and Mrs. Weaver, Gwen . . ."

"I wonder if Gwen's had her baby yet," Lyddy interrupted.

"And Clarence and the Crawfords and Chris . . ."

"I wonder if Matt's still alive," Lyddy mused.

"And Chris," Vic said again.

"Chris." Lyddy spoke the name with a soft smile. "Chris is such a wonderful person. And I treated him awful."

"Oh, it was good for him."

"I'll know better this time," Lyddy said. She pursed her lips. "At least, I think I will."

"Don't worry, honey, he'll be waiting." Vic's voice grew reminiscent. "Remember the dances, the way everybody got so terrifically drunk?" She giggled. "And the way they dressed just any old way so long as they were clean and comfortable?"

"And the way they would walk in a circle around the floor when the music stopped?"

Vic clasped her hands under her head. "I loved the hospitality, more than anything. The way they all wanted you up to their house for something or other. They just couldn't seem to understand that we had to get up early and go to work the next day—they kept insisting we play cards until two and three in the morning."

"I haven't noticed anyone from Wrangell on the ship."

"Neither have I. Oh, well, Wrangell's a small world."

"A pinpoint on the face of the map, as my dad always says. You need a magnifying glass to locate the dang place." Lyddy laughed thinking of her father searching for Wrangell in the encyclopedia at home.

"You know, Lyddy, I've thought about Clarence a great deal. I never could really figure that man out but I liked him. I think I could have fallen in love with him. Only he was in love with you. The only reason Clarence ever bothered to go out with me was to make you jealous." Vic laughed.

Lyddy interrupted. "Clarence is twisted. He doesn't know what he wants."

"He wanted you, Lyddy. At the dances I used to see this glint in his eyes— a wild look—while you were dancing with Chris."

"He wasn't my type. He was shorter than I am and older too. I can't understand what Gwen saw in him. Or why he divorced her. He was lucky to have her."

"He's a nice person, honey. He's just got a heck of an inferiority complex." She paused. "Are you really serious about staying in Wrangell? Making it your home? It wasn't all rosy, you know."

"Yes, I know." Lyddy smiled. "But I intend to stay."

Vic sighed. "You know, every time I think about the darn place, I just can't believe that we were ever there. But I remember so many things. Like the way the town flocks down to the docks each time a boat pulls in. The beautiful islands in the distance and the fishing boats. So much happening all the time— parties and picnics and dances. And we were happy and independent, remember, Lyddy? I hated to leave it. I was having such a good time, despite the way Clarence treated me. But you were so insistent on leaving . . ."

"I was wrong, Vic."

"Brother, when your mind's made up, it's made up. And just when Dave and I were getting friendly with one another."

"I was wrong. I just couldn't accept that I could stay there and be happy living in Wrangell."

"With Chris."

"Yes, with Chris."

Vic kicked off her shoes, raised her head and admired her toes. "He was crazy about you. He loved you more than anything, even his old cannery. If anyone loved me the way he loved you, I wouldn't walk away."

"Not everyone likes Wrangell," Lyddy said. "Remember Bea? She hated it. She hated the rain. We left Wrangell in the rain, remember?"

When it rains, it rains pennies from heaven, Vic sang.

Lyddy walked back to the porthole and looked out. There was a half moon rising over the dark islands and mountains. She watched it spill a path of silver across the water towards the steamer.

Two boys clad in sailor suits and pea jackets strode past, gazing back at a young woman who had her hand tucked in a man's arm.

The steamer turned hard right, sending a shudder of strain through the small stateroom. Lyddy's mind seemed to turn like a wheel with it. She thought of her parents back in San Francisco. Her father had been so patient throughout the weeks of indecision and worry.

Lyddy could always count on her father for support. He had encouraged her to go to college even though her mother dismissed it as a waste of time. Her older sisters had never even considered it; they were each married and had two children apiece. John had encouraged her to go to Wrangell, Alaska the first time when Vic told her about the teaching position. And he advised her to return when he saw how restless she was back in the States.

Not so Edna. Edna considered Alaska an uncivilized country and nothing Lyddy said would change her mind about it. She was still complaining bitterly about Lydia's folly when they took the two girls to the station to catch the train for Seattle.

Five minutes before the train departed, John Prince, with a brave smile, drew a thick envelope from his inside coat pocket and handed it to his daughter. "Have a wonderful trip," he said. "And don't forget to write."

At the last moment, Edna began to cry. "I think you're making a big mistake."

Lyddy thought of those parting words often, especially because she had not told Chris she was coming up, even though she had plenty of opportunities. She could have sent a wire or a letter from Seattle before catching the steamer for Wrangell. She said she wanted to surprise him but she knew that she was afraid. Afraid his feelings had changed. Afraid he didn't love her anymore. Perhaps he was in love with someone else? Maybe he was even married?

But all along she was sure there would be someone from Wrangell on the steamer and she could get the news about Chris ahead of time and still surprise him. It frightened her, not knowing the situation into which she was sailing. There was so much involved and she wanted more time.

Lyddy grew light-hearted with an idea. She sat down on the bulkhead and opened her suitcase. The envelope her father had given her was tucked into the side pocket. It contained 25 crisp twenty dollar bills. Five hundred dollars.

"This money's giving me a juicy idea," she said, fanning the bills. She was trying to sound brave and offhanded. "We have plenty of time to get to Wrangell. The term doesn't start until after the Christmas holidays. What do you think about spending a few days in Ketchikan? We could see the sights..." she thought out the rest of the sentence before she spoke, savoring its contents, "and maybe we could send a little wire to Chris and Dave telling them that we're in Ketchikan and . . ." her voice trailed as she saw Vic lift her head, "perhaps they'll join us in Ketchikan for a Christmas holiday."

"I'd like to, honey, but you know I'm broke."

Lyddy scarcely heard her. "It will be a kind of shock-absorber. A chance to get acquainted again without everyone in Wrangell watching." She looked down at her crossed legs and settled her skirt over the tip of her knee. "If Chris has gotten himself another girl . . ." She stopped, rose to her feet. "I like the idea. What did you say?"

"I said I was broke."

"You can pay me back, dopey," she said, knowing that she had to make the offer so Vic wouldn't feel obligated even though she knew Vic would never pay her back, which was just fine.

"I thought you had ants in your pants to see Chris?"

"We've waited this long. And anyway, I think the idea is wonderful. We'll get a chance to see Ketchikan and maybe . . ." she toyed in her mind with her next word, "maybe he'll come down on the plane that flies back and forth every day."

"Maybe Dave will come with him!" Vic said with excitement. "OK, honey, that suits me!"

"Let's go out. Take a walk around the deck."

"Not again. That's all we've been doing all day since we got aboard this tub. Ring for the steward. I need a cool drink!"

Lyddy got up and stood before the mirror above the sink. She ran a brush through her hair, replaced some loose bobby pins and powdered her face.

"So long," she said, as she rang for the steward. "And don't get any wrong ideas with the steward!"

"That old goat!" Vic protested.

Lyddy laughed and opened the door.

In the passageway, she met the steward. "Excuse me, but when do we get to Ketchikan?"

He deliberated a moment before making an answer. She could sense by the irritation in his eyes that he must have answered this question one hundred times since the steamer left Seattle in the morning.

"Day after tomorrow," the steward said politely. "I believe we are scheduled to arrive at five o'clock in the afternoon."

"Thank you," Lyddy said, setting off down the hall. She heard the steward knock on the door behind her. A man down the end of the passageway was coming out of a stateroom door. She stopped, struck with amazement. For a moment she could have sworn it was Chris. Another man came out of the stateroom and the two of them headed down the aisle towards her. The first man was tall and had coal-black hair. Something about the strained look on his tan face reminded her of Chris.

A chill ran up her legs. She couldn't keep her eyes off him as he approached. She knew almost at once that it wasn't Chris. The resemblance was slight. But the man had noticed her staring and he slowed down as she walked by.

Lyddy lowered her eyes and hurried past the two men down the small incline of the passageway between the staterooms. She was moving so fast that she bumped into a jabbering covey of middle-aged women. Excusing herself, she went out on the port deck.

Outside, she stopped and filled her lungs with the cold air. But the damage had been done. The two men followed her out on to the deck, walked past her and stood looking over the rail. She headed past them. The men followed her.

Oh damn, she thought. It isn't really his fault. She should explain that it was all a mistake.

She stopped amidship and hung over the rail, peering across the channel at the groups of islands lying low and dreamy and mysterious in the moonlight.

She wondered what Chris was doing tonight. Was he down at the hotel bar or playing cards at Red's? Maybe there was a dance and he was going over to Bea's to have a few drinks with Dave and Roy before heading for the A&N hall. There was probably snow on the ground at Christmas. There would be parties everywhere.

She heard two sets of footsteps clicking to a halt not far away. For a moment she'd forgotten about them. The tall man was gazing at her sideways, his lips creased in a knowing smile as he sized up his prospects which appeared good. She could feel the electricity in the air.

Lyddy took a deep breath, conscious of her heart thumping swiftly. Still she allowed herself to enjoy the rich cold air of the sea. She gazed at the half moon, still rising over the luminous clouds that hung low above the outline of the mountains.

"Nice night," the tall man said. His voice surprised her because it was soft and smooth and calm, concealing the excitement she knew that he felt.

"Lovely night, just like you," the other man said. He was a husky blond. His crude remark made the tall man wince; he flashed his friend a warning glance.

Lyddy leaned over the rail, noticing the silvery trail the moonlight made in the black waters. The two men moved closer.

"All alone?" the tall man asked.

"Yes," she said. "I'm alone and I'm sorry that I stared at you in the passageway a moment ago. I thought you were somebody I knew."

"My misfortune," he said.

"Yes, I'm afraid it is."

Lyddy moved away from the rail but the men followed, right on her heels. She strolled forward along the moon-drenched deck, past the portholes of staterooms and empty deck chairs with folded blankets lying on them. She went up to the edge of the bridge, under the pilot house. Below on the fore-deck, the moonlight played on the hawsers and cleats and two automobiles lashed on either side of the tarpaulin-covered hatch. As she stood there, sensing the tremendous power of the steamer knifing its way up the channel, Lyddy saw a man standing alone at the extreme tip of the bow peering out at the channel.

"First time up?" this from the tall man again.

She sighed and decided to say nothing.

"Well?" he asked again, firmly.

She turned towards him. He had large eyes set wide apart and a wide forehead.

"No," she said. "This is my second time up."

"Where are you going?"

"Wrangell."

"We're from Petersburg. Damn our luck." He moved closer. "We're going home for the Christmas holidays."

"We go to Washington College," added his friend.

"Oh, college boys," she said with a smile. "I went to Cal."

They started talking enthusiastically about football, dances and rowing. Meanwhile she watched the lonely-looking man on the bow out of the corner of her eye. It was a beautiful night. Only a few stars shone in the moon-drenched sky. Lyddy decided she had had enough of the two Petersburg men.

"Oh, there's my father!" she exclaimed as if she had just seen the man at the bow. She walked away from them, climbed gingerly down the steep ladder, crossed the forward deck and came up to within a few yards from the man. He was a small man, thin and bony. His clothes were shabby and fit loosely as if he'd lost weight or was wearing a heavier man's clothes.

"Hello, ma'am," he said with a friendly smile.

"This seems to be the nicest place on the ship. I hope I'm not intruding."

"No, ma'am," he said.

He was awkward and shy in her presence. She thought he probably hadn't spoken to a woman in ages. No doubt, he had come up here to be alone with his thoughts. Something about his loneliness captured her fancy.

She put her hands on the great steel bow and looked ahead at the winding channel, mysterious in moonlight and shadows.

"It's wonderful up here," Lyddy said, filling her lungs with the cool night air. The man was quiet and she liked that. He kept his distance. All about them there was beauty—the channel, the islands, the stars, the silence and the moonlight. In the west, a fluffy peach-colored cloud lay in the dark abyss of a mountain gorge like a dog curled up in sleep. Suddenly, long spears of gold appeared in the western sky, piercing the darkness.

"Looks like the northern lights, but it's just the sun setting, kind of late," the man said. Lyddy could picture the sun, somewhere west, across the ocean, sinking at last behind the darkening horizon and sending up the shafts of flames that reached into the Canadian sky.

"Where are you bound for?" she asked.

"Oh," the man said, and he smiled self consciously, "I'm just wandering. Probably stop off at Ketchikan, or maybe Wrangell, and see some friends. I've got to be in Juneau on March tenth and then, well, maybe I'll go to Skagway. You see, I'm just hoofing it." He coughed and added, "And you?"

"This is my second time up. I teach school in Wrangell."

The man was quiet for a moment. She knew he was thinking about the time he spent in Wrangell and what he liked most about it.

"Wrangell's a good town," he said. "I once spent a few weeks there in the fall of the year. Went bird hunting every day on the Stikine flats—you know where that is, at the mouth of the river. I may even do that again next year, after I take care of some business in Juneau. You should see the white geese around November. The flats look like they're covered with snow." He went on talking, shifting topics from Alaskan wildlife to the time he worked in the gold mine in Juneau. Every now and then he'd cough and wipe his mouth with the palm of his hand.

At length he grew silent. Turning to look at him, Lyddy gasped. His thin pale face had turned a dull, ashy color. He clutched the bow of the ship with both hands, his knees sagged under his weight and he was tense as if in great pain.

"What is it?" Lyddy asked, frightened.

"Nothing to get alarmed at, ma'am." He coughed again. "It'll go away."

She watched him struggle to regain his composure. He stood with his head down, his hands clenched tight on the bow.

"Got hurt real bad . . . two years ago . . . in Juneau." He spoke in spurts, struggling to get his words out. "Doctor, can't figure it out. Broke my leg, cracked four ribs, ruined my kidneys, cracked my elbow." Slowly he seemed to recover. He lifted his right arm and waved it back and forth. She imagined she could hear the bones and ligaments within his joints cracking like dry twigs. "That's why I have to be in Juneau on March tenth—to see what I can collect from the insurance. After that, well, I ain't fit to do anything. I'll travel a little and loaf. Got me a small pension coming every month. I wasn't one to go spending my money when I earned it."

In one paragraph, he had told her his whole life. She was struck by the sadness of his story, and also the twinge of pride she heard in his voice when he spoke of the injuries he suffered in the gold mine and the compensation he received from it.

"Is there anything I can do to help? Call the nurse?"

"No thank you, ma'am. Well, it's been very pleasant talking to you. I guess I'll go back to my room and fill myself with another mess of pills that don't seem to do any good."

The man left. Lyddy turned to look at the sky. The spears of orange had dissolved. She stood there for a long time, listening to the hiss of the high steel bow cutting through the water. The few bright stars in the sky seemed remote. Like fireflies, their sputtering blue flame illuminated only their own secluded worlds. She heard a woman speaking on the deck behind her. Some bingo players had come out on the deck for a breath of fresh air. "Wasn't that one for the books? The luck of the Irish. The last game—the sixteen dollar jackpot at that! And I won it."

"Say, it's cold out here," a man said. "Let's go in and have a drink on that sixteen dollars."

Laughing, the couple disappeared.

Lyddy felt cold but she didn't want to go back inside. Her excitement about sailing to Alaska was too much to confine in the space of a narrow stateroom. Ever since they had left Seattle, she felt a pure joy surging through her body. There had been many men in her life, dates and infatuations and proposals, but Chris was the first man that meant anything to her. He had shaken her, had made her open her eyes to the simple things about her. They had slept together three times, and it was that more than anything else that scared her. Afterwards when she saw him on the streets of Wrangell, she felt guilty. She wanted to do it again and again. Perhaps that was it? She liked sleeping with Chris.

She wondered what it was that worried her about Chris. What was it that had caused her to destroy letter after letter that she had written to him? There was something she did that irritated and bothered Chris, something that made him uneasy. Looking back over all the incidents, she realized it was when she talked about Wrangell, about the beauty she saw in Alaska. He would get stiff, a little reserved, almost gruff. It seemed like he considered her remarks an intrusion. He loved Alaska, he talked about its strong points all the time, so why did it make him uncomfortable when she did the same? Perhaps because he had lived there so long, he thought her enthusiasm was shallow, the effusions of a tourist. Perhaps her love for it took away something from him. Chris was a little spoiled. He'd been living by himself for so long, that he found it difficult to share. She'd have to go slow, let him think he was overcoming her reluctance, coaxing her into loving the place he loved.

When she returned to the stateroom, Vic was asleep.

35

C HRIS MOVED OUT ON DECK and stood before the rail. Most of the passengers were already outside. He scarcely noticed them. So far the trip had been terrible.

They were in Tongass Narrows, passing the unkempt outskirts of Ketchikan. He could see the canneries on Marine Way, the white and green houses scattered across the low hill and the curving stretch of piling supporting the houses and business establishments along the shore. It looked a lot like Wrangell, only there was more of everything.

The engines slowed and the steamer began angling towards the distant docks. They passed fishing boats at anchor and tied to floats and the tenders of huge freighters taking on fuel at the oil tanker. A beautiful white yacht, graceful and luxurious in comparison to the drab commercial boats, lay at anchor off the Forbes Air Transport shed.

"How long have we got in Ketchikan?" Chris heard a woman ask.

"Four hours," her companion replied.

"Lovely, isn't it? Did you ever see so many fishing boats?"

"Very picturesque."

The steamer moved its bow towards the heart of Ketchikan. Chris began to feel a little better. It was a beautiful day. He inspected the Ketchikan canneries as they went by—the green-roofed and triangular building of the Johnson Salmon Packing Company and the King Fish Packers building with its name in large black letters on the side.

A cloud of mist clung to the tip of Deer Mountain, which loomed enormous above the town with its sweep of snow. It was suddenly colder as if the steamer had entered a cold air current, though the sun was still shining.

The large fishing fleet came into view, clustered together in two basins, the boats four and five abreast, with their masts and trolling poles standing up against the sky in a shower of russet points.

The steamer edged its flank alongside the dock. The engines rumbled into reverse to break the forward momentum. The ship maneuvered slowly into place with the water gushing from the prop and swishing between the hull and the piling of the large American Steamship dock.

When the gangway was let down and the passengers started spilling down it, Chris saw Fanny was among the first to leave. Bruce and Norman were directly behind her. When they reached the dock, they spread out and walked beside her, one on each side. Well, what do you know, he muttered, slightly offended. The hell with them.

Keeping a discreet distance behind Fanny and her companions, Chris moved with the crowd across the street. He turned left at the Imperial Hotel and strode past curio shops, bars and a restaurant, before crossing over to the Stedman Hotel just as Fanny and the two men disappeared inside.

In the lobby he signed the register and looked about self-consciously to see if he knew anyone. There were a few people sitting in the chairs. Soft music from the bar leaked in through the door in the back of the lobby.

"Is Malcolm MacLane registered here?" Chris asked the desk clerk.

"Yes, sir!" the clerk said emphatically, as though Mac's name was unforgettable.

"I don't imagine he's in his room."

"He hasn't been around all day, sir," the clerk said discreetly.

On an impulse Chris went over to the entrance of the hotel bar, thinking that Mac might be in there, although he was hoping he wasn't since Fanny was in the bar. Mac wasn't in the bar. Norman and Bruce were standing on either side of Fanny, who was talking away, probably telling them all about her problems and the trouble that Alan was in, the story she never got a chance to tell Chris.

Chris wheeled around and went up the stairs to his room. He should have whacked Fanny once or twice in the stateroom. He shouldn't have tried to be so nice to her. That was all wrong. She liked to be bullied. She liked it when he was rough, when he pushed her around. That was what got Fanny excited. She would try to fight back and at some point during the conflict, her small husky arms which had been pushing him back would wrap around his back with a grip so fierce she might have been drowning. She would groan and cry out with ecstasy when he pinched her. After that, there was no satisfying the flames that raged in her body. In fact when he would leave, drained of all desire for further love-making, he was aware that Fanny was still smoldering. He could never quench those fires once he stirred them up and this made him feel contemptible in her eyes.

The Stedman was a nice hotel. He liked his room which was clean with a pink bedspread and gray carpet. He threw his luggage on the stand before the iron-posted bed. He pulled up the shade and stared at the narrow street which was crowded with people. He saw people he recognized from the steamer going into the curio shop. Cars lumbered by, slowing at the corner.

The room looked out on the Narrows. He could see clouds hugging the mountains on the horizon and the round brilliant gold sun, blazing out of the royal blue of the wintery sky. Suddenly he wished he was back in Wrangell. It reminded him of one time when he had come up on the Canadian steamer during the summer holidays. When he reached Ketchikan, there was a raging sunset that struck the same peaks he was looking at now, sending up a huge crimson flare. The sight inspired such a desire to be back to Wrangell that he hopped on a late plane at Forbes Air Transport and beat the steamer by eleven hours. Dad was sore about that. It nearly spoiled his whole summer in Wrangell. He remembered his dad's comments. "You had your steamship tickets purchased so why in hell did you have to fly up from Ketchikan? What did it cost you?" And then when Chris told him, he said, "Sure, we've got a lot of money to throw around." That was when his dad was only worth about forty thousand.

Chris poured himself a drink, laid out his shaving equipment and hung up his clothes. The sound of automobiles moving on the street below was strange and exciting. Out in the Narrows two fishing boats tooted their whistles, hailing one another.

He locked the door behind him and went out, roaming through the winding streets of Ketchikan, going into bars and restaurants, searching for Mac. He enjoyed moseying along and wasn't upset that he couldn't find Mac. A few people recognized him and stopped to chat.

The Foc'sle bar was one of his last stops. He pushed open the door and stopped. Through the open door, Chris saw Malcolm MacLane straddling a stool at the bar. For a moment he hesitated, not sure why. But when he saw that Mac had spotted him, he went in.

"Well, for the sake of Mary," Mac cried out. "Look what the wind blew in!"

"Hi, Mac. You're an elusive old bastard, you know that. What the hell do you want with me in Ketchikan?"

"Bartender, a royal drink for my compatriot in business."

The woman sitting on the stool beside Mac seemed familiar. She had thick black hair that fluffed out around the nape of her neck and sharp dark eyes. Her eyelashes were so thick and pointed they looked false. Her nose was aquiline and she had a large full mouth. She was wearing a black crepe dress with an oval neckline and looked about forty years old.

"Hiya, big boy," she said with a smile. "Any friend of Mac's is a friend of mine."

"What's your name? I think I've seen you somewhere before."

"Hey, quit horning in," Mac protested, grabbing the woman's hands. "I found her right here in this bar. Don't you get any wrong ideas."

"Where you from?" the woman asked Chris as he sat down beside her.

"Wrangell. You didn't tell me your name."

She frowned at him. "You're probably getting me mixed up with my sister, Cora. She and her husband used to fish up there."

"That's right, Cora!" Chris exclaimed, recalling a woman from a couple of years back. She and her husband brought their catch to his cannery. "Your sis is quite a gal," he said. "She almost killed my checker one year when she thought he gave her a wrong tally."

"Hey," Mac protested, pulling the woman around. "Now listen, Selma, you're with me and not that rich good-looking cheese from Wrangell."

They all laughed. This was a little better, Chris thought. He knew a few girls in the town and he'd call them up later. One of them should be available.

Mac was absorbed with the woman. They had drinks three deep on the bar. Mac was pulling on the woman's hand, trying to get her to put it between his legs, but she politely refrained. The bar was empty except for them which seemed weird for a bar in Alaska. The wall behind the bar was paneled in brown walnut and dotted with tiny glass portholes which served as frames for portraits of boats of all types. On top of a tender hung a portrait of a morose, brown-skinned Indian with a long heavy nose and black hair swept back over his neck with a feather held at the side of his head by a flamingo band.

Mac and Selma were engaged in a low and apparently personal conversation. Chris ordered another drink, then realized he'd better slow down a little if he wanted to enjoy his stay in Ketchikan. As always when he drank consistently, his stomach ached with hunger.

"Hey, Mac," Chris said, trying to divert his attention.

"Don't bother me, Chrissy boy."

Suddenly Chris felt sorry he had come down. He should have known better. Mac hadn't come to Alaska for business. He was on a spree. He had sent Chris that wire on the spur of a drunken moment, thinking nothing of it.

"Bartender, you're new here," the woman said suddenly. "What's your name?"

"Tommy." He was young, with a pink flush on his smooth, pointed face.

"Well, she said, smiling gaily, "let me mix my next drink, will you?"

"Sure," he said. "Name the stuff and I'll put it on the bar for you."

As she asked for the bottles, Chris rose and went to the jukebox and inserted a quarter in the slot. He was amazed to notice that he'd selected moody, romantic pieces. He lit a cigarette and inhaled deeply, savoring the music and the melancholy mood of the empty bar. Standing by the jukebox he watched Mac who was completely absorbed with the woman. One beefy paw clutched Selma's waist, the other held his glass. He was watching her mixing drinks, never once turning to notice what had happened to Chris.

A glass splintered on the ground.

"What do you call that?" the bartender asked the woman.

"It's my own discovery and I haven't selected a name for it."

"Let me taste it," Mac said. "I'm good at coming up with names."

"No! Don't give me a name for it. It's my own discovery and when the right name comes to my mind, I'll name it myself." She turned around to look for Chris. "What's the matter, honey? You look sad. Come on over and try my creation."

Chris tasted the concoction and didn't like it. He'd been drinking whiskey straight. This was sweet and dark and it turned his stomach. However, the woman was nice and friendly and he drained his glass before any of the others did.

"It's good," said the young kid tending bar.

"You better scrape up that glass I dropped," she said.

"Give me some more of that," the bartender said. The shyness in his voice was dissolving.

"Clean up the mess first," she insisted.

As the bartender picked up the shattered pieces of glass, Selma turned to Mac, "I'm getting hungry. We haven't had breakfast. Or have you forgotten?"

"Hell with it. I'm dieting."

She turned to Chris. "Will you take me to lunch?" she asked.

"Sure," Chris said. "I'm starved. How about you, Mac?"

"No one's going out of here till I say so," Mac said. His normally jovial voice was suddenly hard and contemptuous. Chris decided to humor him.

The woman seemed to feel the same way. She patted Mac on the cheek and rubbed his groin with her other hand. Mac rubbed his lips against her neck. The jukebox went silent and Chris debated about whether to load it again.

"I cut my finger." The bartender said, standing up and grinning. "God, that glass is sharp."

"Hurry and put some iodine on it," she said.

"Naw," Mac said with authority. "Piss on it. That'll cure it."

Chris realized that Mac must be pretty boozed up. He never grew vulgar until the stuff had practically made him unintelligible.

The woman ignored the remark. She tossed her head up and looked at Chris. "You look glum. Anything wrong?"

He liked her. She seemed intelligent.

"I liked your drink," he lied. "Would you mix me another?"

"I don't think so, honey. That's fifty percent cordial. No good for the stomach. Makes you sick."

"Are you married?" he asked foolishly.

"Widow," she said. "He died last summer. Damn fool never would learn to swim. Drowned after getting tangled up in his anchor chain."

"Sorry to hear that."

"It isn't that bad. He deserved it."

Mac was fumbling with the woman's hand.

"Take it easy, Mac," she said.

"Shit with you!" Mac bellowed. She allowed him to put her hand where he wanted it.

Chris was alone again. He went back to the jukebox and selected some more songs and thought about what he would do when he got back to Wrangell. He'd take off by himself, go on a two-week hunting trip. He'd outboard up the shallow sloughs and camp along the sandbars under the willow trees and fish and hunt. Maybe, if he felt like it, he'd tramp in deeper, get himself a nice grizzly and send the fur to some friends in the States. Anything to offset the drain of life in the bars.

Chris said, "You know I once killed two seals on a sandbar with a single shot with a thirty-thirty." No one heard him. The woman and Mac were whispering to each other and the bartender was standing at the other end of the bar sucking his bleeding finger.

Chris got off the stool. "I'm going to have something to eat," he said.

For the first time that morning, Mac looked directly at Chris. "Hold on a minute," he said. It sounded like, and it was, an order. Mac was the cannery's biggest buyer. So he waited until Mac downed his drink.

Mac was potbellied and short, his feet hung six inches from the rail, and his speckled gray-yellow eyes were bloodshot and full of lust. When he came to Wrangell on business he hardly ever showed up at the cannery. He took on any woman—whores, natives and white women—who came his way. Money bought that. Mac bought his fun.

"Fill 'em up," Mac said to the bartender.

"I really don't care for another," Chris said. His mind was blurring into a fog. The drink the woman had concocted was making him sick. He felt like his flesh was pulsing and the small hairs on his body rose, stiff and uncomfortable. He felt like he did the time he got seasick while on his dad's yacht off Point Beauclaire.

"Mac, you're hurting me," the woman whimpered.

"That's rich!" Mac started laughing. "Me, hurting you." He kept on laughing to himself. Selma twisted away and offered Chris one of her drinks to distract Mac's attention.

"Here, have one," she pleaded.

Suddenly Chris remembered something Mac had mentioned in his wire.

"Say, what's the deal with those two Indians?" he asked.

"They got drunk in here a couple nights ago," Selma said quickly. "They were rowdy and got slapped in jail. They should be out by now."

"They wanted to sell me their seiner," Mac said, wiping away his tears of laughter. "They're broke and want to raise some money so they won't feel disgraced when they get home."

"Got their names?" Chris asked.

"They didn't give any," Selma said.

"Well, if they're still in jail, I'll find them."

Chris didn't really give a damn about the natives in jail. He didn't need a seiner. It was probably an old wreck anyway. He wished Mac would come to the point about why he had asked Chris to come to Ketchikan. There was that large shipment of salmon in the warehouse, over 20,000 cases, and Chris was anxious for Mac to remove it.

Hoping to get Mac on the subject, he spoke casually, "I think I'll go see those boys. Maybe get the boat for a song."

"Have another drink. Hell, the longer they're in the cooler the less they'll take."

"Mac, what about that shipment of salmon? You don't expect to keep it in Wrangell until next season, do you?"

"Don't worry about it." Mac's voice was flat and uninterested. "I've got a freighter chartered and due to be in Wrangell tomorrow night to pick it up."

"What? Jesus, Mac, why don't you let me know about these things?" He was enraged and didn't give a damn what Mac thought about it. "You know I have to be at the cannery when they load that salmon."

Mac brushed the whole matter aside. "Well, if you'll only hold onto your shirt, I'll let you in on a little secret. We're leaving today."

"Mac, you're a crazy old fool! How the hell do you expect to get there?" Though he secretly wanted to return to Wrangell he felt slighted about being told he was going to return immediately. "I came down here to spend a few days in Ketchikan."

"Call the airlines," he said to Chris. "We'll fly up." Mac shifted his gaze to the woman. "Maybe you'd like to come up with us?" he asked Selma.

Chris asked the bartender, "Have you a phone here?"

"You bet. It's under the bar."

"Would you call the airlines and see if there's a plane leaving for Wrangell?"

While the bartender was placing the call, Chris turned back to Mac.

"Why don't we take the mail boat?" Chris said. "It leaves at two thirty."

"I'd rather fly up," Mac said. "The mail boat is worse than a cattle boat."

The bartender cradled the transmitter across the hook. "Sorry, last plane left an hour ago."

"Winter schedule," Selma added.

"Well," Mac said happily, "we'll take the mail boat. A nice long sleep aboard would do me good."

"You won't sleep on the mail boat," Chris said. "They don't supply shuttle passengers with beds."

"They have seats, don't they?" Mac said. "I can sleep in a chair better than on a Simmons mattress."

Chris was sore. He felt let down. He had been so excited about spending a few days in Ketchikan. The trip had seemed to promise some kind of adventure or excitement. He sat down at the bar. "Whiskey and water, please," he said to the bartender.

He decided to drink straight through until they left. He wouldn't move from the Foc'sle. God damn it, he'd play Mac's game his way. But around one o'clock, he remembered the Indians in the jail and decided to check on them.

"Where you going, honey?" Selma asked.

"Merry Christmas, baby." He wove his way around her to Mac. "You know where the mail boat docks?" Mac's eyes were half-closed. "No, I guess you don't. Well, you go . . ." He paused, trying to breathe away the queasy feeling in his guts. Then he wagged his head at the bartender. "You tell him how to get to the mail boat."

"I'll find it, Chrissy boy. Don't worry about me."

Chris moved to the door. "Two thirty," he muttered, not knowing why, for he knew no one would hear him.

He lumbered across the street and bumped into an old man who tipped his hat at Chris. "You better watch your step, young man," he said.

The air was still and sharp, spiced with an odor of burning spruce logs, a sweet clean smell. He inhaled thirstily. He lurched into a young couple. The man had a small fir tree angled over his shoulder and he growled at Chris, "Take it easy, brother!"

"Who the hell you think you are?"

He debated about slugging it out with him but by the time he decided, the man was gone.

At a corner, Chris turned and moved up the street. He struggled against the dim haze of the whiskey. He had to fight to move ahead in a straight line. He was concentrating so intently that he was aware of nothing else until an old Indian woman with a wrinkled face the color of a walnut came into his line of vision. She wobbled towards Chris, dragging one leg, and passed him. Aleut. Chris remembered a story about how the midwives of the Aleut tribe dislocated the leg of newborn baby girls so the men of the tribe would recognize the women of their tribe, no matter how scattered they became.

The Ketchikan Federal Building rose before him, gleaming white and new. There was an elevator in the building, which was something for Southeastern Alaska. Above the roof, Chris watched the mist slide down the side of Deer Mountain. It looked like it would snow for Christmas. He thought of the rain in Wrangell and how the snow capped the surrounding mountains and he wished it would snow in town so he could slide down Wrangell hill.

Chris climbed the Federal Building steps, shaking his head to try to clear it. People moved by him, jabbering and clutching Christmas cards. His head was ringing and he was trying to remember why in the hell he was going to see the natives. The jail was on the sixth floor. When the elevator made its swift smooth lurch upward, his legs buckled at the joints. He reached for a cigarette, then decided against it.

The jailer led Chris down the aisle between the neat white cells. They were cleaner than the inside of any galley.

"They're pretty quiet now," he said, referring to the natives. "At first they couldn't understand what was going on. It's their first time in jail—at least we can't find any records to prove otherwise—and they can't believe they have to stay locked up."

Numbly, Chris recognized the two natives. They had sold salmon to his cannery on and off during the past years while fishing near the Wrangell vicinity. They told Chris they were broke, and "very, very hungry." They glared at the jailer as if he was responsible for their incarceration.

"You can go now," the jailer said. "Just behave yourselves."

The two natives sat in the lower berth, unbelieving. "Hear, that, Mr. Ballard? We didn't do any harm to anyone. There was a fat man in the bar and he teased us all the time about how he wanted to buy our seiner, *Lily of Klawock.*"

They seemed hesitant to leave. One said, "Only the fat man he kid us and we got a little mad."

"I think he told the bartender to call the police."

"We weren't going to hurt him. He buy us drinks and we friendly and police come in. Jesus, they slapped handcuffs around our hands and off they take us in car."

The natives might have been lying but the fat man in the bar sounded a lot like Mac. Mac was contemptuous at times, and growing more so each time Chris saw him. He'd watched Mac change over the years from a jovial, easy-to-please business man into a sneering bully who treated everyone around him with scorn.

Chris took the two natives out to eat lunch at a small dingy restaurant shaped like a diner car. They shoveled down steak and french fries with plenty of catsup and bread. Chris played with his ham and eggs. He drank the coffee but he couldn't eat. He was feeling better but the idea of food repelled him.

They marched down to the Thomas Basin, where their seiner lay moored along the float. Most of the boats were low-lying trollers and gill-netters; the seiners looked massive alongside them.

"She looks terrible," Chris said as they went on board. "Don't you fellows know how to paint?"

He loved seiners, the square stern, the proud sweeping snout of a bow and the cocky pilot house. He liked the enormous skiff lashed atop the cradle aft, the confusion of purse nets, tubs, hawsers, the narrow well deck abaft and the old tire bumpers hanging over the sides cushioning the hull's roll against the float.

"Been working her hard all summer and fall. Didn't have no time to paint." The native gazed at the boat with a smile of sweet content as if it had been faithful throughout.

"Well, I should try her out, before I give an offer," Chris said, acting dubious though he couldn't imagine why. The two men looked remarkably alike. They had square compact faces with rounded features and short black hair.

"Say," Chris asked, "are you fellows brothers?"

"Yep! He's George and I'm George Jr."

"Ah, for Christ sakes."

"Try her out," George Jr. said, with confidence. "Here, I'll start her up."

"No, never mind. I'm in a hurry to go somewhere. Say, do you really have to sell the boat?"

They looked very downcast at this.

"Well, I'll give you fifteen hundred dollars for it."

"But we paid more . . ."

"Fifteen hundred!"

They exchanged quick sly glances, then long uncertain glances. Finally they just stared at one another blankly.

"Fifteen hundred," Chris repeated. He felt rotten all of a sudden. His advantage in this situation was unfair. He had been lambasting Mac in his mind but he was acting like Mac really. Money was like that. It made a man smug, superior.

"I want two thousand," George said abruptly. He seemed to feel out of place saying this and stared intently at the rigging of the boat. The back of his head was tinted with silver and there was a sprinkling of dandruff along his shoulders.

Chris squinted his eyes. "For this piece of junk?" He wheeled around and climbed off the seiner.

The two brothers froze for a moment in fear. Then they ran to the rail, begging him to come back.

"All right," Chris said. "Take it up to Wrangell. You know where the Ballard Cannery is. I'll pay you tomorrow in the afternoon."

"Why don't you try her out?" George Jr. suggested.

"Got any coffee aboard?"

"Sure," George said.

"How about whiskey?"

"Used to. But I don't know now."

George Jr. said with a sheepish smile, "I have half bottle saved for occasion such as this."

The two brothers disappeared into the galley. Chris sat down on the hatch cover and rubbed his hand over the rough surface of the planking, thinking for a moment of all the gleaming salmon the hole had carried for the Indians. The seiner scarcely moved in the placid water of the basin. The harbor delighted

Chris with its myriad of boats and the trolling poles and masts striking up into the sky. It gave him the same thrill he got when he was snug in bed as a child with a storm raging against his bedroom window. It seemed so peaceful.

He rose and wobbled over to the rail and stared at the dark green water between the seiner and the hull of the adjacent boat. A film of oil spread forward with the tide. He sat down and looked around, at the mountain above, the trees, kids fishing from a float, two boys jumping about in a skiff while another attempted to row across the basin. A gas boat chugged in, slowed its engine, spat-spat, spat-oo. He felt the sense of sweet sadness and utter contentment in the harbor. There was joy and eternity in the air, in the boats lying clustered four and five deep, in the small noises of the water sucking against the float, in the murmuring drowsiness in the land of Alaska.

Chris could hear the Indians jabbering in the galley. They were probably both tickled and frightened. Tickled about getting so much money in one lump. Frightened by the consequences of returning home without a boat. It meant they would have to look for jobs, work for someone else. He felt uneasy again about his part in this transaction. He wondered whether to loan them some money, with the boat as collateral, until the next fishing season came around.

Chris lit a cigarette. The smoke curled into his nose, singing his nostrils and making his eyes sting. He flicked the cigarette over the side.

The two Indians emerged on deck with a half empty quart. Chris took a swallow.

"Don't you have any glasses aboard?" he asked.

"Sure. Only we never use 'em for whiskey. I go get it."

"No, never mind."

George Jr. said, "Hate to lose boat. We had lots of fun on her. You should've seen this boat this November. Thirteen deer strung up—all bucks, two five pointers." He grabbed the bottle from his brother and shoved the neck into his mouth. His throat clucked as he swallowed the fiery whiskey down.

"If we able to buy boat someday," George said seriously, "would you want to sell?"

"When I have this tub in shape you'll never have enough money to buy it."

"We save sometime when we home no place to go."

George Jr. suddenly grasped this fact. "No fish and hunt no more?" he asked, bewildered.

George persevered. "We go in skiff." He peered at the large seine skiff aft. "Can we have skiff, at least?"

"How the hell you gonna get it to Klawock?"

"Skiff got outboard. We sail it up."

"I'll think about it," Chris said.

"Where we get money for boat?" George Jr. said suddenly.

"In Wrangell. We'll have the papers transferred there. You have your registration and ownership papers?"

"Oh, sure. Want me to get?"

"No. Just don't lose them." Chris dug out his wallet. "How's the fuel? Got enough to take you to Wrangell?"

They watched his wallet with hungry eyes. "Plenty of fuel, no grub."

Chris peeled off two twenty dollar bills. "Now give me that bottle and go buy yourselves plenty of grub."

The two Indians climbed over the rail and disappeared up the float. Chris realized he'd have to hurry if he wanted to pack and get on the mail boat. He looked around and was relieved to see the mail boat, a top-heavy, weather-beaten, reconverted tuna clipper, chugging noisily past towards the mouth of the basin. It had probably just fueled up and was heading towards the dock. The whining screech of the saws in the nearby sawmill grated against his ear drums. Further down the basin, he saw the *North Star* heading south on its way to Seattle. It felt like he had been in Ketchikan for a lot longer than four hours.

Chris pulled on the bottle. The whiskey burned in his stomach. He tossed the bottle over the side. He felt lousy. He sat down on the hatch cover. His blood was warm though the air was chilly against his damp face. He wondered if he was getting a fever. He lit another cigarette and inhaled deeply. The smoke numbed his insides and he swam in a haze of utter loneliness. He felt bitter and forlorn and wished he were near the woman in the Foc'sle. She was friendly and nice.

He was conscious of people walking up and down the float, staring at him as they passed the seiner. Finally he rose and went to his hotel and packed. Even though he knew many people in Ketchikan, he felt like a stranger.

36

L YDDY AND VIC ARRIVED AT THE DOCK where the mail boat was moored in a cab.

"We made it," Vic said with a sigh. "I thought you were never going to get out of that jewelry store."

"The jeweler took so long to engrave it," Lyddy replied.

The cab driver carried their luggage to the edge of the gangway, which was only a narrow two-by-two plank with two loose pieces of line suspended on either side of it. It slanted down from the dock to the well deck of the mail boat at a steep angle.

"Thank you," Lyddy said to the cab driver as she paid the fare.

"You didn't tip him, did you?" Vic hissed. "He could have at least carried the luggage down to the boat."

"Just wait a minute, ladies," a native boy shouted from the mail boat. "I'll be up for your luggage as soon as we get through here."

Lyddy stood on the dock with at the top of the gangway watching the crew members battened down the hatch cover in the center of the foredeck. The mail boat was about sixty feet in length, old and weather-beaten. Its peeling hull rubbed against the pilings of the dock. The deck house rose up square and two-storied at the back of the long bare forward deck. It made the boat look unbalanced, as if the heavy weight aft would tip the high bow up.

White gull droppings lay splattered over the planking of the dock. The Tongass Narrows strait was busy. All types of boats puttered back and forth sending low sweeping swells rolling under the keel of the mail boat. Deer Mountain was completely hooded by clouds but the sky above the island across the strait to the west was blue-green and clear.

Except for a few longshoremen who were waiting at the cleats to unmoor the mail boat, and a young boy and girl who were playing hopscotch twenty feet away, the long winding dock was deserted. The boy and girl were using fish hooks as keys to toss in the chalked squares. Lyddy admired the deftness with which they scooped up the fish hooks as they hopped towards home.

"Can you remember playing hopscotch?" she asked Vic. "I can. We lived at the top of Twenty Third Street—what a hill!—and there was one house in the neighborhood that had a flat driveway into the garage and we kids used to fight for that spot."

"I never played it with fish hooks," Vic said with a shrug.

Below on the mail boat, the galley door opened and a white-clad cook stepped out on deck. In one hand he held a baby seal and in the other a nursing bottle filled with milk. He gently laid the seal on the deck and pushed the nipple in the seal's mouth.

"Well, I'll be!" Vic said. "What kind of a tub is this?"

One of the windows in the pilot house slammed open and a gray-haired man yelled down, "How many times do I have to tell you to keep that seal off the deck when we're tied up in port! We've had enough trouble this afternoon, or have you forgotten already, spud?"

The chef, holding his hat against his head with his hand, peered up at the pilot house. His face was thin and rather childish. With a shrug, he picked up the seal and went back into the galley.

"The seal was cute," Lyddy said. "Did you see how he went for that bottle?"

"That man's mean," Vic said, pouting in the direction of the pilot house. "What harm was the seal doing?"

They stood waiting for the native boy to take their luggage down to the boat. The delay made Vic irritable. She hadn't wanted to take the mail boat in the first place.

"This is not going to be easy," she said, peering at the narrow, steep plank that connected the boat with the dock. "What a tub compared to the steamer! We should have waited a few days and taken a northbound steamer to Wrangell."

"Let's don't go into that again," Lyddy said. She was anxious to leave Ketchikan. It had been flat. From the first hour they arrived, Lyddy had been sorry that she suggested stopping over. As soon as they made arrangements for a room at the Imperial Hotel they had gone to the Western Union office and wired Chris that they were in Ketchikan and would he please tell Dave as well. That was all. No hint for either Dave or Chris to come down, no hint how long they would stay in Ketchikan. The Western Union clerk told them that the wire should be delivered the next morning as he believed that the Western Union office in Wrangell closed at six. They expected a reply the next day but when they checked, at ten and again at eleven, there was nothing. A nervous anxiety seized Lyddy.

"What if Chris went south for the holidays?" Vic had said.

Lyddy, for some reason, didn't feel that Chris had gone south to visit his folks. She was convinced that Chris was in Wrangell but that something had changed since they had left. She felt too worried to eat lunch. She watched Vic nibble at her lunch and knew that Vic, who usually had a healthy appetite, was upset too. She didn't believe Chris was out of town either.

"Let's wire Dave!" Vic suggested.

They put off wiring Dave and went for a long walk back of the town. A stream meandered down from the encircling mountains and they took snapshots of one another below a wooden bridge against a background of gray rocks and rushing waters. At twelve thirty they went back to the Western Union office. There was still no reply. Lyddy became totally upset. She wanted to get out of Ketchikan. It was dull and meaningless. She felt imprisoned in it, as far away from Wrangell as if she were in San Francisco.

"I'm so damn sorry that I ever suggested stopping here," she said to Vic. There was an air transport service out of Ketchikan and they telephoned for a reservation but the last plane had already left for the day. The friendly clerk at the hotel suggested the mail boat. Lyddy decided at the last minute that she had to get Chris a Christmas present and they had spent the last hour at a jeweler's so she could have it engraved.

Now she was impatient to be on her way. Ketchikan was much larger than Wrangell. It reminded her a little of the States with all its shops and sawmills and hustle and bustle. Many of the townspeople were walking around with Douglas firs hoisted over their shoulders. They had chopped them down in the nearby woods for their Christmas trees. This sight only made her more anxious to return to Wrangell.

The native boy ran up the narrow plank of the gangway and on to the dock. He was about seventeen with curly black hair and soft large eyes spaced wide apart in a smooth, narrow face. His nose was straight and very delicate, as was his mouth.

"I'm sorry you had to wait so long, ladies," he said, glancing sideways at the pilot house. "Mr Johnson, the skipper, is mad that we're so late getting started."

"Well," Vic protested, "I hope he doesn't think it's our fault!"

The native boy laughed as he picked up the luggage. Despite his small size and youth, he handled the three pieces of luggage easily.

"All right!" the skipper shouted from the pilot house, "Let's get that plank on deck!"

The diesel engines of the old mail boat split the air with a shattering roar. The native boy hurried down the gangway with the luggage. He dropped the luggage, then wheeled about and came back to assist the girls as they made their way down the perilous gangway.

"Ugh!" Vic said, as her feet touched deck.

"I have to help stow the gangway away," the boy said. "Then I'll show you where you go."

They moved out of the way and waited while the native boy and two other crew members secured the gangway along the rail. The longshoremen removed the lines from the cleats. The mail boat backed off from the dock, growling noisily, and swung its nose up channel.

"This way," said the native boy, leading them along the open forward deck to a horn-shaped aperture that rose above the foc'sle. "You're supposed to be down in the passenger quarters by now," he said. "Skipper likes to see the deck clear when we shove off."

Vic stared down the steep companionway. "Down there?" she asked, incredulous.

"It's not very comfortable but it's the best we can do."

"Thank you," Lyddy said. A faint film of smoke rose through the companionway and she hated to leave the fresh air on deck. Sea gulls by the hundreds swooped and glided about the mail boat, emitting piercing, pleading shrieks. The mail boat was just passing the outskirts of Ketchikan. The endless piling that lined the shore was left behind and there were only a few houses scattered on the hill. The blue-green sky seemed unreal against the gray clouds suspended over Deer Mountain.

"Look at those stairs," Vic hissed, pointing to the almost vertical ladder with its closely spaced rungs. "Reminds me of a slave ship with all the Negroes chained like sardines below."

"I'll go first," Lyddy said, sternly. She was suddenly peeved with Vic's resentful attitude as though it had been all her fault.

"It's OK," Vic said. She grabbed the rail and made her way down. Lyddy followed, clutching her traveling bag and purse, feeling the slight roll of the boat. She let out a sigh when her feet touched the deck. They were in a dank, smokey, dimly lit room that curved into the stem of the boat. There were two low benches along the sides of the foc'sle occupied by a number of people who had been watching their entrance intently.

"There's room over here," said a middle-aged woman, who was sitting on a blanket near the center of one of the benches. She smiled at them as they came over. The clattering of the engines came through the bulkhead with a steady throbbing persistence.

"I'm Mrs. Ruth Ogilvie," the lady said. She was a rather prim-looking woman, middle-aged, wearing a jet-black hat with a gossamer wisp of veil on top. She was holding a boy of about seven in his lap. Most of the passengers seemed to be drifting off. A short, pot-bellied man, his legs thrown wide apart, was already asleep directly across from them.

Lyddy sat down beside Vic and leaned forward to face Mrs. Ogilvie. "How long does it take to get to Wrangell?"

"Oh, about twelve to fourteen hours."

Vic moaned. "In this tub?"

"I like this boat," the boy protested.

"Now, Craig, you better lie down and get some sleep. It's going to be a long trip and you're tired."

Vic whispered in Mrs. Ogilvie's ear, "Where's the rest room? My God, are we going to be holed up in here the whole trip?"

"You have to go up on deck for that. It's one of the doors just before the galley."

"Oh God," Vic moaned. "Did you hear that, Lyddy?"

Lyddy was excited and restless. "I like it, Vic. At least, we're on our way."

"Sure, honey. Say," Vic asked Mrs. Ogilvie, "what about food?"

"That's one thing they have aboard. Plenty of good food."

"Wonderful," Vic said. "I'm starving already." She shifted back to Lyddy. "It's not so bad. Smokey and noisy but heck, we're Alaskans now." She laughed. "Look at him!" She nodded at the sleeping man. "He's comfortable as a bug in clover."

The fat man certainly looked like the most comfortable person in the room. His head had slid down upon the shoulder of the man beside him who didn't seem to know what to do, whether to push the head away or to wake him up or to forget about it.

"What's the matter, honey? Don't look so scared."

"But Vic, he didn't answer our wire."

"He's giving you a hard time, honey. He's making you hang for what you did."

"I'm a rat. A bonafide goon."

"When he sees you, he'll change his mind. Wear that print dress you bought in San Francisco when we get off this rat trap."

"How in the world am I going to change into it? I don't even know where our luggage is!"

"Ask the skipper!" Vic said with a laugh. She seemed to be feeling good. "I can't wait to see Dave. It's wonderful to be going back."

Lyddy's mind wandered. A terrible doubt assailed her. It was strange to be overwhelmed with joy and frightened at the same time. She couldn't imagine waiting twelve more hours. She wondered what was going on with Chris. Had he fallen for someone else? Mentally she reviewed all the different girls she could remember in Wrangell who might have attracted Chris. Diana Johnson was engaged to Curly, Helen Connell was dating Lyle Hobson. Then there were all the cute girls who graduated from high school this past summer—six of them—but they were too young for Chris. And Fanny, well, Fanny was married. She felt a stab of relief as she proclaimed them all unfit for Chris.

"I wonder if we'll miss the convenience of the States?" Vic was saying.

"I couldn't help overhearing some of your conservation," Mrs. Ogilvie said to Vic. She had been busy rolling up a blanket to serve as a pillow for her little boy, but now that he was settled down she began an amicable conversation with Vic.

Lyddy scarcely listened. She studied the various passengers, who seemed a motley bunch. She thought maybe they were workers, headed for the sawmill or the gold mine in Juneau. Perhaps they were fishermen or cannery help out of a job. There was a big difference between them and the passengers on the steamship.

Restless, she rose to her feet and said to Vic, "I think I'll go up on deck for some fresh air."

"You have to go already?" Vic teased her. "No control, huh?"

Lyddy whispered in Vic's ear, "You can go fly a kite!" "While you're at it, your hair needs combing."

Lyddy had to stoop to go out on the deck. The air was refreshing and she tossed back her head and filled her lungs. The open, slanting deck was deserted except for the chef who sat on a stool before the deck house peeling potatoes. Lyddy caught a glimpse of the skipper staring out of the pilot house windows. She felt self-conscious under his stare and went over by the chef.

The chef kept his eyes on his paring knife as he peeled the potatoes over a pan. In his haste he was doing a poor job of it. A spud slipped out of his hand and into the pan of peelings between his legs. He felt around in the pile of slippery potato skins, couldn't find it and reached for a new potato in the sack beside him.

Across the channel, she could see the beautiful islands of Southeastern, lush with thick stands of trees, slipping by.

"You certainly have a lot of potatoes to peel," Lyddy said.

"I'm used to it," he said, twisting in his chair.

"Where's the seal?" Lyddy asked, glancing about the deck for the animal.

"He's in the galley." The chef nodded his head towards the pilot house. "Skipper doesn't like to see him on deck unless he's sleeping in the bunk that I fixed up outside the galley." The chef thawed quickly, though he was very shy. He giggled as he talked. He had small round blue eyes and large ears that stuck out like flaps on the side of his head. Lyddy scarcely paid any attention to what he was saying. He was so nervous he strung his words together without pause and she could understand very little of what he said.

The open deck left her restless. She thought of going into the galley to see the seal. Instead she stood looking over the rail, thinking about Chris. She was really scared. And worried. She and Vic would look pretty silly returning to Wrangell if Chris and Dave were not interested. Clarence would hound her, pleading with his sad eyes. She couldn't believe that Chris had changed. But then why didn't he answer her wire? Maybe he was out hunting. That was something he did a lot in the fall. She thought about how surprised he would be if he returned from a hunting trip and found her back in Wrangell.

Lyddy felt so good and relieved that she turned to the chef. "Do you trust the seal all by itself in the galley?" she asked.

"Oh, he's a destructive cuss at times," he said, twitching his head from side to side. "But there's someone in there getting a cup of coffee. He isn't feeling so well. Drunk. So drunk I figured it would be wiser for me to let him drink his coffee alone while I peeled the spuds out here." He giggled wildly. Lyddy forced a smile. She was beginning to feel a liking for the cook. Actually it was more pity than anything else. He was such a shy, wiggly little fellow. He reminded her of the thin sick man on the bow of the steamer. They were almost two of a kind, only the man on the steamer was serious and quiet. She knew there must be so many similar men in the world: timid, confused...and lonely.

"I'm going to train Uno—I named him after a candy bar." the chef was saying. His eyes were sparkling with excitement."Yes, I'm going to train him. Like they do at circuses." Lyddy half-listened as he revealed his plans. He had gone to the trouble of ordering a seal training pamphlet through a catalog. "He minds me even now. He isn't housebroken yet but it's very hard to house-break a seal on a boat. When we get to Sitka, I'm going to fix me a sandbox and I'll train him in that. Seals are very intelligent, you know. Uno is very lovable. Do you know he went overboard just this noon at the oil dock in Ketchikan? That's why we were late getting started. I almost had a fit! Marsh—he's the chief engineer—threw Uno over the side! Oh, that man, how he's tormented me! I think he's jealous of my seal. Uno was minding his own business and Marsh tossed him over the side. The native boy, Mike, told me so. Luckily Uno didn't swim out far. It surprised everyone on board. He waited for me to pick him up. Mr. Johnson was a hard one to convince but he told the men to lower the lifeboat and I rowed after Uno." The cook looked with approval at a freshly-skinned potato. "By God, Uno waited for me. He's going to make a nice pet."

"Yes," Lyddy said, stepping back to the rail, "he did look very intelligent." She moved a few steps away, along the narrow side of the deck house. She was tempted to go into the galley for a cup of coffee. But she was disconcerted by the prospect of encountering a drunken man. She stood outside the closed galley door, uncertain about whether to chance it. She leaned against the rail, sensing the vibration of the chugging engines, and stared at the swells sweeping back from the hull, a ruffled series of waves that washed across the green strait towards the shore. The sky was overcast.

She hoped it would snow for the holidays. Christmas would be cozy and wonderful in Wrangell. She couldn't wait to give Chris his present. Lyddy had purchased an expensive wristwatch for Chris because she remembered he didn't have one. For all his money, there were so many things that he went without. A car, a watch, clothes—he had few smart clothes. "Well, honey, I just never needed a watch or a car in Wrangell," he had told her once when she asked. "You don't walk yourself to death to get anywhere and there's no appointments to keep." He had seemed self-conscious about it, as though she might consider him a hick, but Lyddy understood. She was worried that he wouldn't understand what she meant by giving him a watch. She had it engraved with the date and her love, for to her dates were exciting. When she was a little girl her father had given her a gold lapel watch for her birthday and he had inscribed the date on it. With each new year the watch grew more and more precious. She treasured the watch because it represented the passage of time. She scarcely ever wore it for fear of it breaking or becoming lost. For a moment, thinking of her father, she smiled.

She was standing outside the galley door which was closed. Suddenly she heard the tinkle of silverware and the thud of a plate being placed on a table.

"Now, what the hell are you looking at?" she heard a man ask. Her heart constricted. She waited tense, quivering. She moved a step closer to the door, conscious of her heart pounding in her chest.

There was an awful quiet inside the closed galley. Against the background of the boat's chugging engine, she heard the shuffle of feet and a clank as if a lid was placed on a pot.

It was Chris' voice, she knew.

She put her hand on the door handle and twisted the knob until the latch clicked. She grew frightened as the door opened.

Chris didn't notice her. His back was to her. He was facing the enormous iron stove. Tucked under his right arm was the baby seal. He seemed to be waiting for the pot of coffee on the range to boil. With his free hand, Chris lifted the lid of the coffee pot, having a hard time holding himself steady. He juggled the seal under his arm and inspected the level of coffee in the pot. His hair was uncombed and tousled. He was dressed in tan gabardine slacks and a rumpled light blue sports jacket. The seal seemed as fascinated as Chris with the coffee pot on the range. Both of them gave it their undivided attention.

"Chris!" she called out, her voice trembling.

When Chris turned around, she saw at once that he was very drunk. For a moment she was seized with panic and disappointment. "Chris, how are you? Oh, Chris . . ."

He stood watching her with a dazed look in his dark eyes. Then he bent over and deposited the seal on the floor. It flopped over on its side and looked at Chris inquisitively. "Now you run off," he mumbled, apparently more interested in the seal than in her.

Her mouth closed. He isn't glad to see me, she thought, terrified.

With one step he reached her and pulled her into his arms. His arms crushed her and she gasped. He kissed her. Immediately she felt a dizziness so intense she had to open her eyes. She felt rapture flowing through her body at the reality of having Chris again in her arms. Her joy was overshadowed somewhat by the piercing odor of whiskey on his breath and his inability to keep his balance.

He pushed her back. "Christ no!" he mumbled. "Am I that plastered? Is it really you, for Christ's sake?"

"Yes," she said. "Yes."

"Where did you come from?" He rubbed his fingers against his eyes. "For Christ's sake, Lyddy! It's Lyddy! Where did you come from?"

"Darling, Vic and I are on our way back to Wrangell."

"Is that true?" He seemed dissatisfied with her answer. "For Christ's sake, it can't be. I thought you were dead."

"I've been horrible, Chris. I'm sorry. Oh, Chris! It's good to see you, to speak to you."

Out of the corner of her eye she spied the seal flopping up against Chris' leg. Chris staggered off to one side. The seal wiggled up onto his feet.

"Cute, ain't he?" said Chris scooping up the seal. He leaned back against the table. The seal lay happily in his arms, apparently fond of Chris—or the odor of whiskey emanating from his mouth.

Lyddy felt bewildered and on edge. These weren't the right circumstances, the ones she had imagined. She felt helpless and out of place.

"I think the poor devil is hungry," Chris muttered, rocking on his feet, continuing to gaze at the seal.

"Really?" she said with feigned interest although she was so furious she couldn't think straight. Why did Chris have to be so under the weather at this moment?

Chris belched. "Look at him. I feel sorry for the cuss. All he wants is someone to cuddle with. Yeah!" He laughed and belched again. "I'm maternal as all hell."

She didn't know what to make of this. She had seen Chris drunk before but never so far gone.

She played along. "You make a good father."

Chris set the seal down and laughed uproariously at this. His laughter was so loud that it made her self-conscious. He stopped and motioned with his hand for her to come to him. He flopped down in one of the galley chairs and she stood above him. Roughly, he pulled her into his lap. His hand groped for her breast as he kissed her. She was afraid someone would enter the galley and she tried to break away. His strength was amazing.

Breathlessly, she pulled away from his lips. "Chris," she said. "Chris, I love you."

He kissed her again. She felt his hand leave her breast and slip down across her belly and down her leg.

"Not here," she said. "The cook or someone might come in."

"God damn!" he mumbled, his lips against her neck. "God damn, Lyddy. I can't believe it!"

"Have you missed me?" she asked, then wished that she hadn't. She felt it was her fault that Chris was in this condition. She wanted to cry suddenly.

"Yeah, I missed you," he said roughly. "Sure, I missed you."

His arms crushed her as if he wanted to hurt her. She was pleased to know that he had missed her, that he was as lonesome for her as she had been for him.

At length he loosened his grip and stared at her. "Pretty as ever," he said. His eyes were dazed; he could barely focus them. "This is no place to be the way I feel. We should be in a room. I'm hungry for you, baby."

"I'm hungry for you, Chris. Oh, Chris, will you ever forgive me?" Her tremendous joy soared into a thrill beyond anything she had ever known. Chris loved her, she knew. He was drunk because of her. She kissed his cheek and laughed at the crimson smear her lipstick left. "Oh, Chris," she said, "I'm so happy to see you. I love you, Chris. Oh, Chris, I'm in love with you so much. Hold me tight, darling."

He didn't respond. He looked down at the seal, which was angled on one of its flippers and watching them.

"What have you been doing? What's happened to you since you've been away?" he mumbled.

She didn't know what to say. She fumbled for something light. "Well, for one thing, I've acquired a ravenous taste for ice cream . . ."

He looked confused. "What else?" he asked.

"Well, I had one of my molars pulled out . . ."

Chris kissed her again.

"Chris," she said, "I was lost without you. I can't believe I ever left you."

He clutched her tight. She was suddenly aware of a foul odor in the room. It was surprising that any odor could overpower the whiskey smell emanating from Chris but this odor did. She stiffened in his arms.

"Jesus!" Chris said. "That damn little seal!" he mumbled.

On the floor beside the seal was a smear of grayish-blue substance that she realized was excrement.

"Just like a baby," Chris said, wagging his finger at the seal. He pushed Lyddy off his lap and got up and went over to the corner of the galley where he picked up a galvanized bucket with a rope attached to it. On his way back across the room, he dropped the pail and it clattered on the floor. Swearing, he bent over, grabbed the bucket again and wobbled towards the door.

"What are you going to do?" she asked.

"Get some water. Wash that stuff off."

"Why don't you call for some help? After all, it isn't your seal." But she could see that Chris was determined to go outside. Perhaps he needed the air. He hesitated in the doorway, as if uncertain what to do. Then he coiled the end of the rope around his wrist a few times, staring into the pail in a sort of daze.

He looked up and faced her. "Lyddy," he mumbled, his eyes glazed with alcohol. "I'm sorry to be in this mess."

"Oh, Chris, forget it!" she said. "We have plenty of time to be together."

He lurched outside. The door slammed behind him. Lyddy sat down in the chair, thrilled. Her body throbbed in a dream of bliss. The sight of the seal slithering through the mess it had made didn't even bother her. She barely noticed when the chef entered the galley from the opposite door. She heard him talking to the seal.

"Well," he said, in a scolding tone, "so you've done it again. I knew I shouldn't have left you in here. If the skipper sees this . . ." He stopped, apparently noticing Lyddy for the first time.

"Oh," he said with a self-conscious giggle, "is that why Mr. Ballard stepped out on deck? To get some water to wash it off?"

She heard herself say, "Yes."

"Why, heck, ma'am, there's plenty of water in the pump here. I'll go stop him."

She laughed. "He's probably got it by now. I think he needs the fresh air more than anything."

"Well, I hope he hurries back with it before the skipper sees this mess."

Her heart was settling now that Chris was out of the galley. She sat in the chair, examining the row of coffee mugs hanging by hooks from the from the open china cabinets behind the enormous stove. As she looked about, she sensed the slight steady roll of the mail boat. The boat was groaning and creaking which seemed strange for the water was comparatively smooth. The chef put the seal in a large pan under the hand pump, preparing to wash him off. The throb in her body was quieting. Acting as if she were giving her complete attention to what the cook was saying, she was slowly folding within herself, savoring the exquisite sense of contentment. She was quenching a long aching thirst.

There was a splash of water outside the galley door.

"Well!" the chef commented, "he's finally got that bucket in the water."

Instinctively, she prepared for Chris' entrance. Everything was going to be all right. Chris loved her. He was drunk because of her. "I'm sorry to be in this mess," he had said, and she flushed as the words hammered against her heart. The separation had done them both good. It had eliminated the barriers between them. They were going to be happy together. Suddenly, she felt slighted because Chris hadn't said that he loved her or asked her to marry him.

She calmed down when she realized she was rushing things. She was so excited she couldn't bear to let events settle in their own time. She wanted to gulp him down. There was so much she wanted to talk to him about. She wanted to give him his Christmas present immediately.

The galley door remained closed. She watched the seal, who was lying quietly in the basin while the cook scrubbed him clean. She thought of Vic, probably asleep by this time. She would certainly be surprised to find out that Chris was on the same boat. It explained why he didn't answer the wire. But what was he doing in Ketchikan? She wished they had run into him while they were there.

She wondered what was taking Chris so long. The smell in the galley was giving her a headache. He was probably trying to clear his head with the fresh air. But she wanted to see him, at once. She wanted to tell him all about how she had missed him. In San Francisco, every time she saw couples on the streets or in restaurants, she had felt miserable. This meeting was too good to be true. She was really lucky.

She felt so overjoyed that she decided to pay attention to the cook. He was drying the seal with a towel and scolding him as he did so. The animal assumed an air of humbleness as if he were actually responding to his master's rebuffs.

The smell on the floor was growing stronger. Suddenly she felt acutely out of place in the galley. Chris must be feeling pretty bad to stay out so long. She rose to leave.

"I think I'll go out and see how he's coming along."

The chef's eyes clouded with despair, as if this were a blow to his ego. "Tell him to hurry with the bucket," he said. "I really should clean this up before it stains the deck."

She opened the galley door and looked outside. The deck was deserted. The air was raw and charged with a deep foreboding gray. Chris was nowhere in sight. Perhaps he had gotten sick and gone into the restroom.

She poked her head back into the galley. "I think you better go ahead and clean the mess the best way you can," she said. "Mr. Ballard and the bucket are not around."

The chef giggled at this. Lyddy closed the door before he could say a word. On an impulse, she circled the deck house, but the port side was empty too. In the windows of the pilot house, she could see the skipper and the native boy staring at her. She decided to go below. Maybe Chris was down there.

She climbed down the steep narrow companionway and stood, looking around at the passengers in the dim, smokey room. The fat man was still sleeping soundly, his head resting on the shoulder of the man next to him. But Chris wasn't there.

"Lyddy, what are you looking for?" Vic asked.

Mrs. Ogilvie's boy was awake and Vic had him sitting on her lap. He was a little towhead, with a direct gaze that was unblinking.

Lyddy said, "Vic, you'll never guess what just happened! Chris is on board!."

"Chris!" Vic exclaimed. "No, that's impossible."

Lyddy smiled. "He's really here. I met him above."

"I don't believe it!"

"It's true. He was in the galley. He was making himself some coffee and I opened the door . . . No, I heard him first . . ."

"I'm so happy for you, honey. What a wonderful coincidence. No wonder we didn't get an answer to our wire."

"Chris was in Ketchikan the same time we were."

"That's so remarkable. How in the world could we have missed him? Say, is there any chance that Dave is with him?" She paused, looking at Lyddy brightly, then shrugged her shoulders. "No, don't answer me, I can see that he isn't. Where is Chris?"

Lyddy hesitated. "He's up on deck. I just wanted to tell you."

Across the room the fat sweating man groaned in his sleep and brushed his lips against the neck of the man beside him. There was a vulgar quality to his unconscious gesture. Shuddering with distaste, the man beside him pushed the fat man's head away. The fat man opened his eyes.

"What time is it?" His voice was loud and demanding.

"Three fifteen," said the man beside him.

"Morning or afternoon?"

"Afternoon. You only slept a couple hours." The man's voice was belligerent.

"Well," Vic said at length, "what are you doing here? Don't stand there. Go back to Chris."

Lyddy flushed. Mrs. Ogilvie and her son were all eyes and ears. She bent down and whispered in Vic's ear. "He's drunk—very drunk—but he's wonderful. Oh, Vic, I'm so happy to see him. He loves me! I think. I mean, well, it's all so wonderful."

"I'm thrilled for you, baby," Vic whispered. "Now go on up there and get him sober and bring him down when he feels up to the descent."

Lyddy hummed to herself as she ascended the ladder. The muscles in her legs were beginning to ache from the unfamiliar exercise. On deck the cold raw wind smacked her face, reminding her of the heady sensation of a cold dip in the ocean. She inhaled deeply, wondering how the passengers below could stand being confined in the foul-smelling noisy room. The world was green and gray now. She felt this had all happened to her before, the dull deep greens and the grays, the chugging clatter of the engines, the strain in her legs, the heady tonic of the wind. She remembered going for a ferry ride on a Sunday afternoon with her dad when she was a little girl. Somehow she had gotten lost on the crowded upper deck of the ferry and wandered around looking for her dad. Then she hurtled forward, as if through the wrong end of a whirlpool, through the spirals of years, and came twirling out to the surface, here on the mail boat with the waves swishing against the hull, the engine clattering, the exhaust fumes spewing from the funnel, the skipper behind the pilot house window, and a tall man who was simple and nice and the most wonderful man in the world.

She stood by the rail, her eyes searching the empty deck. Her flesh was cold and her teeth began to chatter. She opened the galley door and hurried inside. The stove's fan was making a whirring noise. Walking into the clean, snug galley was like putting on a jacket of heat.

"Hello," she said to the chef. "It's cold out on deck."

Several pots and pans were on the wide range of the stove and the chef was stooped before the oven door basting a large browning chuck roast. The pungent odor of peeled onions and sizzling meat filled the room.

"Mm!" she commented. "Do you mind if I wash my hands?"

The chef shut the oven door. "No ma'am, go right ahead." He reached under the table and pulled out the seal. "I guess you're dry enough, Uno," he said, rubbing the animal's sides. He opened the door and put him out on the deck. "Now you go under your box and sleep!" the chef ordered. He closed the door. "That's one thing I can count on Uno to do," he said. "But I wanted him dry before I put him outside. I never heard of a seal catching cold but I don't want to take any chances with Uno."

The chef picked up a wooden spoon, turned to the range and grew busy with the many pots. Lyddy was having a difficult time with the hand pump on the side of the sink. It took one hand to pump the lever and she couldn't catch enough water in her other hand to wash the grit off both. The chef noticed her distress and came over to help her.

"Well, I couldn't find Mr. Ballard," she said, drying her hands on the

481

towel he offered her. It looked like it was made from a flour sack. "It must be wonderful to be the cook on a boat on these cold days," she said.

"Oh, sure," he said with a blush. "But I don't generally cook for a living in the winter. I have a cabin in the mountains where I go each fall and trap." He was giggling as he revealed his pattern of life. "After a summer of cooking, I like being in the outdoors. Last time out, I got twelve wolf skins and a load of mink pelts. But this summer I had pains on my right side—felt like it might be appendicitis—and I didn't want to chance the mountains." He turned back to the range while Lyddy curled up into a chair. "So you couldn't find Mr. Ballard? I worked on one of Mr. Ballard's tenders for two seasons straight. Been on this mail boat almost a year now." From the wooden icebox in the far corner of the room the chef produced a large leg of lamb and slapped it on the sideboard.

Then she noticed the bucket, with the line on the handle, standing beside the ice box.

"Oh," she said, "so you found the bucket."

"No, this isn't the galley bucket," he said, honing a knife against the sharp edge of a cleaver. "I had to go aft and get this one from the rack that the men store their swab buckets in." With the same nervous haste with which he had peeled the potatoes, the chef hacked the fat off the leg of lamb with the knife. "Late dinner tonight. Fishing Uno out of the water after lunch today in Ketchikan set me behind."

"Would you do me a favor?" Lyddy asked.

"Sure, ma'am."

"I'm rather worried about Mr. Ballard. He really isn't feeling well. I think he might be in the restroom. And I was wondering—would you peek in and see how he's getting along?"

The chef giggled with amusement as he opened the oven door and slid in the lamb. "Well, ma'am, I'm pretty busy," he said, going over to the sink, gathering up the scraps and tossing them into the garbage can. "I did take a quick look around the deck for the bucket. But I never thought of going into the restroom." He swabbed the drain board clean. "Sure, ma'am, I'll go see how he's coming along for you."

While the cook was gone, a deck hand entered the galley, tipped his hat at Lyddy in surprise and poured coffee into a mug. "Skipper's tea time," he said with a smile and left.

The smells coming from the bubbling pots on the range and the sizzling roasts in the oven were tantalizing. She was so hungry all of a sudden she felt weak. She had eaten very little of her lunch in her worry about Chris.

The galley door opened and the cook came back in.

"Well, he's not in the restroom, ma'am" he said. "Guess he went below to the passenger quarters. You know," he went on quickly as he busied himself at the pump rinsing dishes, "another reason I didn't go trapping this winter was on account of Uno. A friend of mine in Sitka gave him to me in October when I was still debating whether to chance trapping with my side. But the seal settled it. I decided I wouldn't go. And it's a funny thing, but my side hasn't bothered me since. Only if I was in the mountains, frozen in for five months, I'd probably be having trouble with it. Trapping in the winter is no time to get sick. I once caught pneumonia and I laid in my cabin for five days without food or help. I still don't know how I lived through it."

The native boy came into the galley.

"Hello," he said to Lyddy with a smile. He turned to the chef. "I'm hungry," he said. "Anything ready yet?"

The chef shrugged. "I'm going to be late tonight. Why don't you make yourself a sandwich?" He pointed his finger at the ceiling. "Is the skipper still mad about the seal today?"

"He's cooling off, I think."

The boy made a thick peanut butter sandwich. Lyddy grew even hungrier as her eyes transferred the message of food to her stomach.

"Do you know Mr. Ballard?" she asked the boy.

The boy's mouth was full with the sandwich. He gulped it down, "You mean the man who was up here awhile ago?"

"Yes. Would you see if you could locate him for me?"

"Sure, ma'am. I'll go right now."

"Mike's a nice boy," the chef said. "He's a hard worker and he loves boats. He's the skipper's right hand man—he has him at the wheel more than any other hand on board. I guess he trusts Mike more. Mike has a natural knack for boats. He knows the mail boat like he does his own hand."

"He seems very nice," Lyddy said.

"Would you like a cup of coffee, ma'am? Excuse me for not asking sooner."

"Yes, thank you."

The chef filled a mug. The coffee was very black and steaming. It made her hungrier.

"Sugar and cream is over there," the chef pointed.

"Thank you, but I never use either." The coffee was wonderful. She loved the galley suddenly. She loved the mail boat, its compact size, clattering engines and groans.

The chef gossiped amiably. "Mike's only sixteen. He should be going to school. He was going to the Native Institute and doing good but his father drowned and he had to go to work to support his mother. Plus he has three younger sisters . . ."

The galley door opened and Mike poked his head in. "I couldn't find him in the foc'sle, ma'am, and he's nowhere forward. I'd look around a little more but the skipper wants me."

"Thank you," Lyddy said. "Oh," she called after him, "could he be up in the pilot house with the captain?"

"Not unless he went up there since I came down."

"Would you tell him to come down if he's there. Tell him Lyddy is looking for him—he'll understand."

"Sure, ma'am."

In a little while the native boy returned. "I just thought I'd tell you that he wasn't topside. I have to get right back. Johnson doesn't like me to be running around while I'm on duty."

"It's funny how many places there are where a man can be on a boat this size," the chef said. "Uno got into the engine room once. How he went down that companionway to the engine room I'll never know, unless someone ditched him there on purpose. But I searched and searched for him and if it wasn't for Mike, who found him in a tool locker, greasy and . . ."

Lyddy rose. "Would you see if he's down there now?" she asked.

"Well." His eyes flickered to the pots and pans on the range. "Sure, I'll go, ma'am. Be right back. I'll bet he's down there trying to figure out what makes these old engines hold together. You know, I'm used to their racket, but the passengers sure don't like it. Their ears hum for days afterwards they tell me."

She sipped the hot coffee with a spoon. She thought about returning to the foc'sle. No doubt, she was making a nuisance of herself. The skipper was probably furious at the sight of the chef popping out on deck when he was supposed to be preparing dinner. What could have happened to Chris?

She went out on deck. Snowflakes were tumbling lightly in the air. She felt one touch the side of her neck and it thrilled her. She was filled with glee. There would be snow for Christmas. She anticipated the pleasure of walking in it, hearing her footsteps crunch. She had only seen snow in Yosemite National Park on vacations with her parents. Now she would see it covering her future home town. The scattered bits of snow flashed and tossed in the dirty-brown air. It was much colder now.

"Storm might be coming up," the chef said as he emerged from around the deck house.

"Was Mr. Ballard in the engine room?"

The chef sniffed the troubled air. "No, ma'am. And the engineer said he hasn't been below at any time since we pulled out. Gosh, it's cold out here. Come inside, ma'am."

Lyddy saw Vic step out from the companionway. Vic hurried down the slanting, snow-speckled deck. "God, it's cold up here," she said with a shiver. "Say, honey, you look a little under the weather. What's the matter? Chris giving you the run around?"

"We just can't seem to find him anywhere."

"If he's as drunk as you say, maybe he's passed out somewhere." Vic sniffed the air, "God, I'm starved. What's that?"

"It's in there," Lyddy nodded to the galley. "Two roasts . . ."

"Smells heavenly. Let's beg."

"It's not ready yet. Would you like a cup of coffee?"

"Sure, anything. I'm starved."

They went in and sat down.

"Would you pour us one more cup of coffee?" Lyddy asked the chef.

"Where's the seal?" Vic asked, looking about.

"He's sleeping in his bunk, ma'am." the chef said with a giggle. "He must have been tired. I checked on him when I went out and he's sleeping like a baby."

"He's really cute," Vic said.

The chef began to chatter again. This time it angered Lyddy, put her on edge. He certainly had an endless torrent of words for someone who seemed so shy and timid. It dawned on her that he was actually pompous and fussy. He was like a silkworm, that wraps itself in its own secretion of silk threads, only the chef withdrew from the world about him in his own secretion of words. She stopped listening to him.

"I wonder where Chris is?" she asked.

"He might have gone aft behind the deck house somewhere," the chef said, his voice bubbling with amusement at the evident embarrassment it was causing her.

"We haven't looked back there, have we?" Lyddy said.

"Well, I did take a quick glance around when I went for the bucket . . ." The chef paused, then answered the message that was in Lyddy's eyes. "I really shouldn't go out on deck again. Johnson's probably furious with me for being so late getting supper ready. He'll blame it all on the seal if he sees me outside. He'll probably make me toss him overboard or else give him away . . ."

"Oh, that's all right," Lyddy sighed.

"Mm, this coffee hits the spot," Vic said, drinking her coffee with pleasure. "How long have you been aboard?" she asked the chef.

"Almost a year now." His face was twisted, as if he was listening to an internal debate, trying to decide whether to respond to Lyddy's request or to go on about his duties.

The door opened. The native boy looked in. "Got supper ready yet?" he asked the chef. "Johnson's getting wild topside."

"Tell him in about an hour. I'm sorry for the delay."

The native boy flashed a grin at Lyddy. "Find Mr. Ballard, yet?"

Lyddy turned her most winning smile upon the boy. "No, we haven't." She nodded at the chef. "He thinks he might be somewhere in the back."

"Take a look aft, Mike. He might be curled up on a tub." While Mike was gone the chef glanced with relief at the girls. "That's where I would go if I was in his shoes," he chirped. "The deck house will protect him from the wind."

The native boy was back in no time at all. The boat was only about sixty feet long and the upper deck was easily covered in a few minutes. His face was troubled and there was an edge of puzzlement in his voice. "He's not aft." he said. "I searched everywhere possible . . ." His mouth remained open as if he wanted to say more and didn't know what to say.

"What's the matter with you?" Lyddy said sharply. She was surprised at her own harshness. Annoyed at herself, she said, "Well, please find him! And don't tell me the skipper will bawl you out for doing what a passenger on his boat asks you to do."

"I'll try the engine room," Mike said.

"I've looked there already," the chef said.

The boy's eyes flickered with distress. "You did?" He made no further comment, but wheeled about slowly, seemingly in great thought.

"Was he in the passenger quarters when you came up?" Lyddy asked Vic.

"If he was, I didn't see him."

"Want me to try there again?" Mike asked.

"No it isn't necessary. I just can't imagine where he could have hidden himself. Is there a small room or compartment below that a person could go to?"

"I'll search the boat from stem to stern," the native boy said with determination and disappeared through the door.

"He's playing hide and seek," Vic said in a cheerful tone. "He's going to make you come looking for him."

"You'd be surprised," the chef murmured, "at the places a person can hide on a boat like this."

The chugging clatter of the engines grew loud and absorbing as silence fell upon the galley. Lyddy could sense her whole body recoiling from the jarring racket.

The native boy appeared in the doorway. "I can't find Mr. Ballard anywhere."

There was a moment of puzzled silence. "That's funny," Lyddy said.

The chef stood unmoving by the stove, his work forgotten. One of the pots was bubbling furiously against a tight lid and drops of water sputtered and sizzled on the hot range. All at once, Lyddy felt suffocated by the heat of the room.

"He must be somewhere on the boat!" she said with a patient smile. "Please search again." She turned to Vic. "It's so hot in here," she remarked. "Let's go outside."

The chef, dropping his work, moved quickly before them. "I'll go below to the foc'sle," he said to Mike.

Mike ran aft.

Lyddy and Vic went outside. It was very cold. Gray. The sky was filled with low swollen clouds. A scattering of snowflakes flashed in the air, describing curlicues before perishing in the water. Lyddy shivered. The swishing waves soared away from them, cold and green and ominous, like the back of a huge snake.

"Where the hell can that big ape be?" Vic asked after a long silence. Her brow creased as she searched her friend's face. "Was Chris glad to see you, honey?"

"Yes! He was very drunk but he was glad to see me." A doubt began to form in her mind, the same doubt she had when Chris hadn't wired her and she had boarded the mail boat anxiously wondering what sort of reunion they would have.

They waited. Lyddy recalled the way Chris' arms circled her back and tightened. Her back ached a little from the rough embrace. Chris was surprisingly strong. Chris was surprising. There were so many things about him she didn't know. She wanted to find out everything about his life. Well, there was plenty of time for them to do that.

The native boy came loping around the deck house. "I'm sorry," he said, catching his breath, "but that man's hard to find. I searched the gear room, crew quarters, I even went into the hole."

The chef emerged from the companionway. As he hurried across the deck towards them, he kept his eyes on the windows of the pilot house.

"Take a look at the skipper!" he said. "No, on second thought, you better not. Looks like he's ready to blow a fuse."

"He shouted at me," Mike said, holding his head high, "but I thought it would be better to do what the ladies wanted."

The chef looked up at the pilot house again, definitely worried.

"Well," Vic said, "did you find Mr. Ballard?"

"I've searched everywhere I could," the chef said apologetically. "I'll go down to the engine room again. Maybe the engineer was lying to me. Marsh is mean like that sometimes. He once hid my seal from me . . ."

Lyddy said, "Hurry, please."

"That big goon!" Vic grumbled.

"I can't understand it," Lyddy said. "But he was drunk. Oh, God," she smiled, "wait until you see him. He smelled, well, he smelled awful."

The pilot house door opened and the skipper and the native boy came down the ladder. The skipper had a florid, mottled face. He was barrel-shaped, muscular and very tough-looking. Gray bushy eyebrows clung like bird's nests to his forehead. Right now, they were lowered conveying irritation and impatience.

"Mike here tells me Mr. Ballard can't be found anywhere."

"Yes, that's right," Lyddy said. She felt embarrassed although she didn't know why. Perhaps Chris was trying to avoid her.

The pot-bellied little man who had been sleeping below emerged from the aperture above the foc'sle. He waddled down the deck towards them.

The skipper sighed, then said with a growl, "Well, only one thing to be done." He turned towards the native boy. "Tell all hands to search fore and aft." He looked at Lyddy with displeasure. "The crew will be hopping in a minute."

"Thank you," Lyddy said. "We'll be waiting in the galley." The fat man followed them inside the warmth of the galley.

"What's all the rumpus about?" he asked.

Lyddy ignored him. His jowls were puffed with sleep. His left cheek still bore creases from where it had leaned against his neighbor in the foc'sle. His eyes were glassy with alcohol. The man yawned, removed a mug from the row suspended on hooks above the stove and poured himself a cup of coffee.

"What's happened?" he repeated.

"We can't seem to find someone." Vic's voice was annoyed.

"Who?" The man was bossy as he thawed into wakefulness.

"Chris Ballard. Do you know him?"

"Sure, I know Chris." He slurped a mouthful of the hot coffee. "I'm Malcolm MacLane. Came aboard with Chris. We're going to Wrangell together."

"Oh," Lyddy commented.

"You can't find the stiff, huh?" He bent his lips and slurped.

"He seems to have disappeared," Lyddy said. "He was just here in the galley—not over half an hour ago. Then he stepped outside and that's the last anyone's seen of him."

The fat man chuckled. "Chris was drunker 'n a skunk when he came aboard. I told him to go below with me and sleep it off. But he wanted a cup of coffee first."

"Have you seen him on board since then?" Lyddy asked, flushing from the heat in the room and the man's candid stare.

"Took my own advice. I've been asleep. What's the matter?" He was suddenly gruff. "Is he really lost or are you kidding me?"

"No, we're serious. He's disappeared. Like you say, he wasn't feeling well and I'm afraid he's gotten sick and we can't seem to find him."

"Look in the restroom," he said with a knowing air. "I'll bet he's in there sicker 'n a dog."

The skipper and Mike came into the galley. The chef slunk in behind them, his face ghastly pale. The change in his appearance shocked Lyddy. He was as white as his uniform and he stood over in the corner of the room, as far away from the others as possible.

"Well," the skipper announced, "I've had my men search the boat and there is no sign of the man."

"By God!" the fat man bellowed.

"What could have happened to him?" Lyddy asked.

"He couldn't vanish in thin air!" Vic protested.

"Maybe he fell overboard," the native boy suggested.

Silence fell over the galley.

"Oh no!" Lyddy said weakly. Her stomach lurched.

"It's the most likely possibility," the skipper confirmed. "I've already given orders to bring the boat around. We're going back over our same course to see if we can find him."

Lyddy gasped. Sweat broke out on her back and her lower lip trembled. "You've got to find him," she begged. Her voice trembled a little. She could barely comprehend what he was saying. She felt numb and a little faint. She grabbed at the back of the chair for support. The room was very hot.

"Open the door, Mike, and let the lady get a little fresh air."

Lyddy slumped into a chair, conscious that several of the passengers were clustered about the galley door.

"My God," she heard someone say, "how can a man fall overboard on a calm day like this?"

"Don't worry, honey," Vic mumbled.

Lyddy was trembling violently. She knew it was from the effort of holding back the choking anguish within her body. She wanted to cry.

"Are you absolutely certain he fell overboard?" MacLane questioned the skipper.

From the corner of the room, she heard the chef's shrill voice. "It's the only explanation. He's not on the boat. We've searched everywhere for him."

The passengers were shoving into the galley. "Who drowned?" someone said.

"A man's overboard," another cried.

"Now I don't want any hysterical yelling aboard this boat," the skipper ordered. "It's not the first time a man went overboard." The skipper turned to the native boy. "Mike, go topside and take the wheel from Herman. Hand Herman the glasses. Keep your eyes opened. And full speed ahead over the same course."

The captain came over and stood in front of Lyddy. She tried to stay calm. She felt strangely aloof from her own experience. It was as if there was one part of her which was reacting to the reality of the situation and another part that sat in a dark corner, repeating over and over again that Chris wasn't dead. Wasn't dead.

"Now lady, pull yourself together!" the skipper said. "You've go to tell me a few things." He paused.

From the darkened corner of her mind, she watched herself respond to the captain's words.

"Now lady, I need all the information you can give me. How long has it been since you missed him?"

"Well, I don't know exactly."

"Did you notice the shoreline by chance? Any landmarks?"

"I was inside when he went out," she said.

"How long has it been?" he asked again. His voice was steady and business-like.

Lyddy cleared her throat. "Well, when I went down into the foc'sle to look for him—that was about fifteen minutes after he left the kitchen—it was three fifteen."

"Well, that's a help. A big help." He pulled out a pocket watch and noted the time. Then, quickly, he wheeled about, facing the passengers clustered in the galley. "I want all of you people to get into position along the deck. Look for a man swimming." He glanced down at Lyddy's bowed head.

"Miss," he asked, "could Mr. Ballard swim?"

"Yes."

"All right. He'll be swimming. Let's all go on deck and see if we can spot him. Chances are he'll be swimming towards the east shore as we were a mite closer to it."

Lyddy felt a ray of hope with this new image of Chris, striking out through the cold water. She had gone swimming with him on many occasions.

He was a good swimmer with a long, powerful stroke. A few times they had raced each other and though she had always darted ahead in the beginning, he always caught up, using his steady and powerful breast stroke.

"Come on," Vic said to Lyddy. "let's go outside. Let's get some fresh air. The big ape will probably be waiting for us down the line, floating on his back without a sober care in the world."

Lyddy stood on her feet, scarcely seeing, scarcely able to move her legs. With Vic's assistance she wobbled out on deck. The cold moist air stunned, rather than revived her. The numbness she felt began to spread. Her eye drifted along the east shoreline, picking out nothing in particular. She stared vacantly, and sensed, rather than saw, the blur of land loom closer upon them as the boat plowed in nearer to shore.

"Keep your eyes peeled!" she heard the skipper shouting at the passengers and crew members who lined the rail.

"We can't miss him," Vic said. "Look, there's even a man on the bridge with binoculars."

With slow, painful effort, Lyddy forced herself to open her eyes. She noticed the gray sky above the nearby island. With a start she saw the thin film of darkness creeping into the gray and knew with horror that in a matter of minutes night would fall.

"Vic, it will be dark soon!" she cried. "Vic, he's drowned! He's died that awful death!"

"Lyddy," Vic blurted out, "get control of yourself. We'll find him. I'll bet by now he's on the shore."

"No. It was too far. I know Chris swims, Vic. But he's slow. It was too far. Can't you see? Even from here, it's too far."

The skipper approached the girls. "No sign of him yet." He shook his head in emphasis. "We're doing all we can, lady. Right about here should be the spot where he went overboard." The skipper called out to the man on the bridge. "Hey, Herman, tell Mike to kick her down half speed and patrol this area."

A small boy began shouting. It sounded like the boy who was in the passenger quarters. He was jumping up and down beside his mother and shouting, "Look I see him. There's the man overboard. There he is! I see him! I see the man!"

The skipper leaned over the rail and peered in the direction the boy was pointing. Close to shore, a dark elongated object lay almost still, drifting in the gray-green waters of the strait. "No movement," the skipper said. He stared a moment longer. "Probably a deadhead." He shouted up to the bridge, "Are you looking at the object, Herman?"

"It's a log, skipper," the man on the bridge announced.

The skipper turned to Lyddy. She saw the blur of his ugly face and the cruelty in his lips and she didn't know what to make of it. She wanted to hate him suddenly.

"Mike tells me Mr. Ballard was drunk. Is that right?"

"He was drunk as a lord," said MacLane approaching the group by the galley.

"And he stepped outside to get some air," Vic said.

"No," Lyddy muttered. "It was the seal. The seal had dirtied the galley floor and Chris picked up the bucket with the line . . ." She hesitated, having trouble remembering the exact sequence of events. "He picked up the bucket and went out on deck to get some water to wash it off. The splash!" Lyddy recalled, aloud. "I heard the splash!" She tore away from the group and went searching for the chef. "Come here, please," she shouted. The chef slunk down the deck towards them, his face stunned and pale.

"You heard the splash," Lyddy asked him.

"Yes, that's right. We both heard it."

The skipper said, "I see. Well, where is the bucket?"

"I can't find it," the chef said. "I've looked everywhere."

The skipper stood quietly in thought for a moment. "Well, if he went out on deck to fill the bucket with water, he probably went over to the lowest point on the boat, which is right here off the galley door. That's why we didn't see him from the pilot house."

Lyddy felt herself falling apart, felt her mind collapsing.

"We were moving about seven knots and, given his condition, he probably wasn't prepared for the jolt when the bucket hit the water." The skipper was attempting to reenact the scene.

"He had looped the line about his wrist, I think," Lyddy whispered, remembering how Chris stood there at the door, hesitating, coiling the rope around his wrist. I'm sorry to be in this mess, Lyddy. "Yes," she said, "he coiled the line around his wrist, I remember."

She pushed herself away from the group and moved out on the deck. She felt the realization of what had happened tear through her again. It felt like a fire raging through her. Then she heard what was in the back of her mind all the time.

"Sure," MacLane said, "with the line around his wrist the bucket pulled him down like an anchor. He didn't have a chance."

She knew she was never going to see Chris again. She knew that he had disappeared forever. She burst out crying and slumped down in the center of the deck on the hatch cover.

"We might have missed him," Vic mumbled kneeling before her.

It was beginning to get dark. Flakes of snow were falling on the deck. The passengers were standing around, letting the snow fall on their shoulders and heads. Their voices were hushed.

Somewhere behind her she heard the skipper's voice boom out. "Herman, take the wheel and tell Mike to report this over the wireless to the Coast Guard in Ketchikan."

Lyddy saw the chef standing by himself close to the deck house. He held the seal in his arms. He looked hurt and scared.

She thought back upon her encounter with Chris, what she now knew were her last moments with him. She remembered the dazed look in his eyes, the shock of disappointment she felt when she saw how drunk he was, then the thrill of joy when he kissed her. She remembered his last words: "Lyddy, I'm sorry to be in this mess." She remembered her response: "We have plenty of time to be together."

A cold mist seemed to rise from the sea. She turned away from its cold presence. She knew he was lost, that he had always been lost to her. She began to cry. There was nothing to stop her. She cried for everything.

About the Author

During World War II, Leftare P. Delis was stationed on the Bendora Coast Guard Cutter out of Wrangell, Alaska, where he began writing his novel. While in Wrangell, he married his wife, Irene, and they had their first son, Peter. After the war, Delis moved his family to Bakersfield, California where he began farming and he and his wife had a daughter, Pamela, and another son, Dean. Delis continued writing the book in winter months when farm work was slow, but he never found the time to publish it. More than four decades later, his eldest son found the handwritten manuscript tucked away in a filing cabinet in his father's office. He was so intrigued by the story, he wanted the rest of the world to be able to enjoy *The Inside Passage* as well.